Henry Adams
& *the* Need to Know

In Memory of
Charles Vandersee, 1938–2003

Massachusetts Historical Society Studies in American History and Culture

1. *American Unitarianism, 1805–1865*, ed. Conrad Edick Wright (1989)
2. *Massachusetts and the New Nation,* ed. Conrad Edick Wright (1992)
3. *Puritanism: Transatlantic Perspectives on a Seventeenth-Century Anglo-American Faith,* ed. Francis J. Bremer (1993)
4. *Entrepreneurs: The Boston Business Community, 1700–1850,* ed. Conrad Edick Wright and Katheryn P. Viens (1997)
5. *Transient and Permanent: The Transcendentalist Movement and Its Contexts,* ed. Charles Capper and Conrad Edick Wright (1999)
6. *John Adams and the Founding of the Republic,* ed. Richard Alan Ryerson (2001)
7. *Faces of Community: Immigrant Massachusetts, 1860–2000,* ed. Reed Ueda and Conrad Edick Wright (2003)
8. *Henry Adams and the Need to Know,* ed. William Merrill Decker and Earl N. Harbert (2005)

Henry Adams & *the* Need *to* Know

Edited by William Merrill Decker & Earl N. Harbert

Published by the
Massachusetts Historical Society
Boston, 2005

Distributed by the
University of Virginia Press, Charlottesville

Massachusetts Historical Society
Studies in American History and Culture, No. 8

Designed by Ondine Le Blanc

Library of Congress Cataloging-in-Publication Data
Henry Adams and the need to know / edited by William Merrill Decker and Earl N. Harbert.
p. cm. — (Massachusetts Historical Society studies in American history and culture ; no. 8)
Includes bibliographical references and index.
ISBN 0-934909-87-3
1. Adams, Henry, 1838-1918. 2. Adams, Henry, 1838-1918—Criticism and interpretation. 3. Historians—United States—Biography. 4. United States—Historiography. 5. Historiography—United States. 6. United States—Intellectual life. 7. United States—Politics and government. I. Decker, William Merrill. II. Harbert, Earl N., 1934- III. Series.
E175.5.A2H455 2005
973'.072'02—dc22

Contents

Preface

WILLIAM MERRILL DECKER &
EARL N. HARBERT

THE TITLE OF THIS VOLUME, *Henry Adams and the Need to Know,* originated as the name of a conference hosted by the Massachusetts Historical Society in May 2001. Then and now it admits of several meanings.

Need to know refers, first, to the omnivorous intellect of Henry Adams, whose relentless inquiry and massive erudition made him a legend in his own time. But it refers as well to our need to know Adams, privileged legatee and prolific author, who speaks to a need to clarify the role of critical intelligence in our own time. The title reflects our need to know the relation of present to past, the historical depth of the passing moment, the relevance of old ideals to a volatile contemporary world. It refers to our need to know the world as something other than ourselves, as Adams increasingly sought to do in his career as an ambitious traveler. Not least, it refers to a life of the mind that knows delight to be essential to its perseverance. For Adams, pleasures of mind derived from many sources—art, literature, music, the play of wit, the alternately droll and grotesque spectacle of human affairs—and such interests do much to balance his more somber intellectual engagements. Much of what Henry Adams tells us is indeed somber. Few of his contemporaries so unerringly discerned the growing disparity between technological power and the human capacity to apply that power to something other than acquisitive and destructive ends. Few observers so exactly perceived the degree to which power threatens the civilization it would serve. For us as for Adams, there are no ready answers to the question of how mass society can rise to the level of enlightened self-government or how an informed intelligentsia may speak to the recurrent crisis at hand. For Adams as for his successors, however, the relation of mind to a world remade by explosive human intervention must largely determine the destiny of civil life.

Intellectually aggressive, fascinated by a broad range of human activity, uniquely positioned to observe the intimate workings of political power, Henry Brooks Adams (1838–1918) led a life that elucidates thresholds and documents change. Descendent of two presidents and the son of a man who might well have made a third, Adams was born into the lap of opportunity and his biography had every reason to proceed as a tale foreordained. As narrated in *The Education of Henry Adams,* expectations of a legal or journalistic career culminating in high public office were checked by numerous developments: the Civil War, the consolidation of party politics, the rise of corporations, the advent of new technologies, the globalization of finance capitalism. Behind such events, harbingers of the increased magnitude of human activity and the obsolescence of traditional ways of knowing the world, Adams detected "an unknown energy which played with all his generation as a cat plays with mice," and it became his object to study this energy as it shaped his course and that of his generation.[1] Yet it is possible to imagine someone of Adams's circumstances, able but lacking his singular gifts, clinging to the old ways and living the life of the Boston Brahmin in defiance of the world's transformation. Why did he so assiduously chronicle change and why did he respond with such eager engagement to historical forces that threatened his standing? Naturally, he wished to extend the influence of the house of Adams and looked warily upon the obscure politicians and new industrialists who assumed the lead in post–Civil War America. Still, his early public policy commitments (currency and civil service reform) and his long-term philosophical inquiries were not principally driven by the need to defend status. It is not Adams the reactionary who chiefly compels our attention. Even what he felt to be the lamentable disappearance of his family from national office receives in his work fairly objective treatment as a lesson in American demography.

Something more than an advantage of birth, and something higher than a need to conserve status, must account for the fact that Adams defines America's coming of age more comprehensively than does any other author of his or subsequent generations. Indeed, he may be said to define two comings of age. In the nine-volume *History of the United States during the Administrations of Thomas Jefferson and James Madison* Adams identifies the events and theorizes the developments that forged the United States as a functioning federal entity and placed it on a competent footing on the international stage. And in the *Education,* he traces the later emergence of the United States as a dominant world power, imposing its system beyond its borders, succeeding at the probable expense of its Enlightenment ideals. In the *Education* as well as in the *History,* the novels, and *Mont Saint Michel and Chartres,* Adams explores other transitions less obviously concerned with a strictly political sphere: changes in the lives of women; evolutions in popular intellect, in religious susceptibilities, and in a people's dream life. While interested in the ideas that constitute our national intellectual history, he is also attentive to the ways in which ordinary people live out those ideas. His angle of vision remains that of a male, upper-class New Englander, and his perspective is never free of a certain reflex condescension. Yet his conception is broad and tells the story of a national community that rises on merit and stagnates or falters owing to deficiencies that cut across lines of region and class.

His capacity to think beyond conventional expectations of social class and historical moment is unusual if not unprecedented among New England intellectuals. In Adams this capacity awakened early and promptly took on a life of its own. The *Education* depicts antebellum Boston as slow to recognize the signal changes brought by the nineteenth century, and while Adams presents his youthful self as an average specimen of a time and place, he nevertheless creates the portrait of a mind precociously cognizant of aspects that did not connect. In the differences between grandfathers J. Q. Adams and Peter Chardon Brooks, between Quincy and Boston, between Mount Vernon and State Streets, the boy surmises that life is multiple against any effort to unite it in a single conception. The childhood chapters argue in fact that conscious selfhood begins in the negotiation and repression of contraries. Henry's anticipation of problematic issues inheres in memorable anecdotes: J. Q. Adams's silent enforcement of the maternal edict that the boy attend school; Charles Francis Adams's injunction that the young man exempt George Washington from that sum of all wickedness that is the Slave South. Political initiation comes early to Henry Adams and with it the sensation of being outside as well as inside the circle of power. The family disposition to quarrel with the conservative regional elite and to find its true calling in an international sphere conditioned him to prefer a wide horizon and to recognize the provincial character of his—or anyone's—origin. As the *Education* relates, and as a close reading of his letters confirms, formative experiences as a traveler, within and beyond the United States, inclined Adams to seek alternative and antithetical worlds. His life of peregrination begins with the youth's erotic response to a southern landscape that he was obliged to loath. The Boston origin and Harvard education persist in the form of personal standards by which he judges the world, but early and late he exercises the liberty of subjecting those standards to suspicion, skepticism, and satire.

Through a combination of circumstance and preference, then, Adams was to find himself perpetually between worlds, an experience that could only enhance his powers of alienated discernment. Undeniably, individual peculiarities that he possessed both means and occasion to indulge strengthened his resolve to escape origins. His cosmopolitanism was promoted by his youthful circulation among powerful figures as bizarrely varied as Algernon Charles Swinburne and Giuseppe Garibaldi; it was fostered by his intimate association with the personalities of exceptional and conflicted individuals, most notably Clarence King, John Hay, Marian (Clover) Hooper Adams, and Elizabeth Sherman Cameron. Henry Adams matured as a man of wide acquaintance, temperamentally as well as intellectually equipped to theorize an era of rapid and accelerating change. Paradox dominates every attempt to catch him in thumbnail description: a New Englander who lived most of his adult life in the "southern" city of Washington, a compulsive observer of current events who sought the long view of the historical archive, a private citizen who chose to dwell among men and women of high public profile, a secular Unitarian of Puritan sentiment attracted to the popular art of medieval Catholic Europe, a sociable host who lived much of his life under seal of bereavement and solitude.

The *Education* deals at length with contradictory susceptibilities and in so doing builds upon an established theme in his writings: the individual's tendency to internalize the indescribable and often unreckoned conflicts of a society undergoing change. We see the fissured and multiple self in Adams's political biographies, *Life of Albert Gallatin* and *John Randolph,* in the central characters of the novels *Democracy* and *Esther,* in the unpredictability, flawed decision making, but also the creative resource of the principals in the *History*; in the ambivalence of Pierre Abélard in *Mont Saint Michel and Chartres*; and in the sixty-year epistolary record that Adams generated as a prolific, politically astute, self-analytical letter writer. Narrating the life of one who endeavored to understand and adjust to his times, the *Education* takes the exceptional case of Henry Adams and makes it illustrative of a general rule: no preparation that fails to allow for change in what are always the already obsolete models of the world—with which the mind must in any case conjure—can equip the thinker to react to that world with success. Even as he establishes that rule Adams also insists on this corollary: not to see the world as in some qualified sense unitary threatens both individual and collective survival. No writer of Adams's generation was better acquainted with the dangers of fragmentation: the twenty-year hiatus at the heart of the *Education* speaks volumes on that theme, as does the narrative of his sister Louisa's death, which attentive readers recognize as a surrogate account of Marian Adams's suicide. For Adams, not to understand the self as the site of involuntary upheaval in one's culture is a particularly grave danger. Against that peril, and against the self-destructive tendencies of civilization as a whole, Adams enlists the self in its conscious multiplicity as the instrument of knowing the life of a people and an era. He proposes that the need to know and make known alone can provide human experience with coherent shape against the forces of disintegration. The inquiring mind that speaks in the *Education* can hardly repose in a static family identity or class formation however much it bears an indelible stamp. This mind recognizes that it must look for an audience in an international community of scholar-inquirers and it is that community that has answered Adams's appeal—with and without approbation, much as he expected.

In the end, Adams's life experiences favored an ideological commitment to open inquiry, a commitment that within certain limits transcends region, class, and nationality. The mind at work on his page exhibits the play of intellect that has always drawn readers to Adams's text: an active, ironic, emotive intelligence that confronts contradiction and evinces a readiness to sacrifice sacred doctrine (and Adams certainly had a sense of the sacred) at the altar of free inquiry. Such open-mindedness rescued him—most of the time—from the bigotry into which heritage and passion might send him and developed in him a capacity for habitual reconsideration. A need to know commits the inquirer to a life of provisional unities, and Adams exhibits a heroic willingness to defer closure. Such a life has the effect of unsettling privilege and affirming the doctrine that ideas and people alike must be judged on their merits. The need to know without restriction is profoundly democratic, and while Adams entertains deep suspicion of the capacity of mass societies to govern themselves, he exemplifies habits of mind that resist instituted privilege and concentration of power.

The conference of May 2001 celebrated the many aspects of Henry Adams: scion, partisan, scholar, traveler, observer, author of a rich and eclectic body of work. Attendees and viewers of the C-SPAN tapes stand witness to the fact that Adams continues to inspire energetic discussion and controversy and that his writings serve as the occasion for good fellowship as well as the focus of unresolved issues. The conference celebrated the publication of *Improvement of the World,* the final installment in Edward Chalfant's massive three-volume biography, so questions of how best to represent the life of Henry Adams were very much in the air. Formal discussion and informal exchange were productively intergenerational and interdisciplinary; to converse in such company on the subject of Henry Adams in the building that houses many of his papers and books was to take part in a supremely privileged moment. To remember the conference now, however, is to see it at a liminal moment. The events of September 11, 2001, a little less than four months later—two of the highjacked airliners departing from Logan International only a few miles away—would usher in a phase of experience with which we must struggle for a very long time. The conference acquires, in retrospect, a dimension of pre-9-11 serenity, and yet the works of the man our conference honored, while they have much to say on the subject of intellectual fellowship and the equanimity of enlightened contemplation, theorize above all thresholds and unpredictable irruptions of force. With its weird compounding of power and paranoia, the eerie description of the New York City skyline in the final chapter ("Nunc Age") of the *Education* prefigures catastrophe general if not specific. Again, the urgency with which Adams continues to speak does not always provide cause for cheer.

THE CONTRIBUTORS TO THIS VOLUME were entirely at liberty in choosing the theme and emphasis of their essays. There were no expectations that they would share assumptions or agree in their conclusions and no insistence that they uniformly valorize their subject. By the evidence of the essays, Adams's work appeals to a wide spectrum of historical and literary inquiry and claims a place in multiple scholarly contexts. One of the great opportunities presented by the conference and by this publication has been the encouragement of scholars to explore highly significant but often overlooked details of Adams's relationships with people and ideas. Rather than restate old themes, the essays in this volume break new ground and, together with the forthcoming publication of *The Education of Henry Adams,* newly edited by Edward Chalfant, represent significant reconsiderations of Adams's work.

The sequence begins with Paul Bové's "Henry Adams and the American System." This essay, reflecting changes in the world since the conference, considers post–9-11 global ambitions of U.S. foreign policy in view of the tensions between republican principle and imperial design that Adams identified at the time of the Spanish-American War. Taking as his occasion a contemporary reference, Bové examines the Adams family heritage in analyzing Henry's cautious and principled stance toward the prospect of an imperial America. Adams's relationship to a family history that also imparted to him a philosophical and political heritage is the subject of Richard Samuelson's "Henry Adams's Need to Know John Adams," which probes what Henry looked upon as the intellectual and temperamental integrity of his Revolutionary-era ancestor. As Samuelson demonstrates, in his recurrent assessment of his family's public achievement Henry consistently esteems his great-grandfather's grasp of republican constitutionalism as well as the cosmic and comic frailty of the human being that makes such constitutionalism necessary. Ormond Seavey's "Henry Adams and Henry Cabot Lodge—Student and Teacher: A Complicated Interaction" examines the two Bostonians as men who, in more and less explicit dialogue with one another, define themselves with reference to family and to New England history in ways that enforce Lodge's narrow association with regional interest and party politics and Adams's transcendence of the same. With a view to the international context of Adams's politics, Leslie Butler, in "Investigating the 'Great American Mystery': Theory and Style in Adams's Political Reform Moment," studies Adams's reform movement activities as an expression of a liberal doctrine informed by Alexis de Tocqueville and John Stuart Mill—yet destined to fail given the fluid nature of U.S. political coalition-making. Crosbie Smith and Ian Higginson approach the young Adams's ideological orientations from a different and complementary perspective. In "'No Traces of a Beginning, No Prospect of an End': Henry Adams, Charles Lyell, and the Politics of Uniformity," they explore the links between Adams's interest in Charles Lyell and the espousal of a view of democracy that, setting the corruptions of politics aside, favors a long-term uplift of a minimally differentiated populace.

The three subsequent essays address Adams's fascination with the human subject. In "Massachusetts to Virginia: Knowing Henry Adams's John Randolph," Richard Androne considers what is in many ways Adams's puzzling decision to write the biography of the mercurial Virginian and demonstrates the degree to which Adams's profound fascination with mental instability, transgressive behavior, and public morality emerge in his text. In "Henry Adams and John Singer Sargent: Public Histories, Private Lives," Barry Maine similarly puzzles over Adams's fascination with the works of a painter for whom he entertained such qualified opinions. A fellow portraitist, Sargent rehearses much of what Adams felt to be a fragmenting of the self that must simultaneously support a public and private life. In "Mr. Secrets," Joanne Jacobson sets Adams's preoccupation with the public self and its private disorders in the larger context of American autobiographical narrative. Addressing the acknowledged need to know Adams as a major participant in the genre of life-writing, she identifies the *Education* as a signal and healthy retreat from the "exemplary voice" of Enlightenment self-narrative.

Another trio of essays examines Henry Adams as an author whose work is informed by travel. In "Henry Adams: Travel as Episteme," Pierre Lagayette explores Adams's migratory habit as a way of knowing the world at a time when the parameters of time, space, and subjectivity were changing. This essay at once addresses Adams's vocation as tourist and his abiding concern with epistemologies of self and world. In "Henry Adams's Unwritten American Travels," Charles Vandersee laments the fact that Adams, a globe trotter who also happened to be one of his era's most authoritative North American travelers, never produced a volume devoted to his native land, but then proceeds to suggest by the light of passages culled from his epistolary record how this text might read. In "'I measured Her As They Did with Pigs': Henry Adams as Other," John Orr considers one of the most interesting of Adams's travel phases, his journey to the South Seas, and how these voyages, as evidenced in the letters and *Memoirs of Arii Taimai,* measure the extent to which Adams did and did not transcend the male Euro-American subjectivity that he brought to the task of knowing the South Seas and Arii Taimai.

The three essays that conclude the sequence emphasize in different ways the fluidity of Adams's models of knowing and the openness within closure of Adams's thought. In "From True Woman to New Woman," Cindy Weinstein addresses Adams's need to know the world of male activity from a woman's perspective, his need to know what women want, and his need to construct a woman (Madeleine, Esther, the Virgin of Chartres) who explains the world's fragmentation but can also propose some principle of restorable coherence. In "A Martyr to the Disease of Omniscience," William Merrill Decker examines the intellectual protagonist in Adams's various narratives and the tendency of that protagonist to inquire at intellectual, spiritual, and even bodily peril. The essay ends by considering Henry Adams as an inquirer who put his own reputation on the line in writing *A Letter to American Teachers of History,* his last word on the "disease" of intellection. We end with "Henry Adams, U.S. Grant, and Evolution: Practicing History in the Age of Darwin," an essay in which J. C. Levenson reconsiders Adams's intellectual debt to Darwin. Levenson finds in that relationship evidence to support a view of Adams as a mobile, subtle, and open thinker, one for whom the multiplicity of Darwin's theories encourages an expectation of surprise, possibility, and saving adjustment in the world of human events.

The essays in the volume represent ways of thinking *with* as well as *about* Henry Adams. They reopen settled topics and reframe truisms. They look in detail at less-studied works and themes in Adams's writing. They demonstrate the ways in which the prophet of gloom can help us identify our own resourcefulness, resistance, and capacity for life. Together they substantiate R. P. Blackmur's famous claim that "Henry Adams is a mountain to be mined on all flanks for pure samples of human imagination without loss of size or value."[2] Each essay affirms, in one way or another, that to study Adams is to discover his continuing and astonishing relevance.

NOTES

1. Henry Adams, *Novels, Mont Saint Michel, The Education,* ed. Ernest Samuels and Jayne N. Samuels (New York, 1983), 809.
2. R. P. Blackmur, *Henry Adams,* ed. Veronica A. Makowsky (New York, 1980), 3.

Acknowledgements

The editors wish to thank the Massachusetts Historical Society, William M. Fowler, Jr., Director, for hosting "Henry Adams and the Need to Know" and for supporting the publication of this volume. Conrad E. Wright, Ford Editor of Publications, and Celeste Walker, Associate Editor of the Adams Papers, were at the center of efforts to organize the conference, and Jean Powers, Editorial Assistant, coordinated arrangements and communicated with participants in the weeks leading up to the event. A number of colleagues not included in this volume greatly contributed to the success of the conference by presenting or responding to papers: Henry Adams, Richard Adams, Edward Chalfant, Donald Fleming, Eugenia Kaledin, Cynthia Mills, George Monteiro, Samuele Pardini, Linda Smith Rhoads, William Stowe, and Henry Wasser. In preparing this volume for publication, we are deeply indebted to Ondine Le Blanc, Associate Editor, and Melissa Pino, Editorial Assistant, who assumed the formidable task of copyediting a manuscript comprising the work of authors from various academic disciplines.

We dedicate this volume to the memory of our friend and colleague, Charles Vandersee, who died suddenly on January 2, 2003. No one who worked closely with Chuck will ever forget the generosity and reliability of his counsel. The essay by which he is herein represented does much to convey the charm, originality, elasticity, and insight that he brought to his life and scholarship.

Henry Adams & the American System

PAUL A. BOVÉ

THE TERM "AMERICAN SYSTEM" has had a long history in the United States and the historical political debate over the term's meaning is almost as long. Intellectuals contest the exact starting date for the American System.[1] Some locate it after the War of 1812, the second war of independence the United States fought against Great Britain.[2] Others choose the American Civil War and its industrial aftermath, while yet others place it in the 1890s when the United States defeated Spain in a brief war and took its first colonies by conquest, including Cuba, Porto Rico, and the Philippines. Intellectuals debate the origin of the American System because many believe that the historical circumstances of its emergence define its nature and our understanding of it—and by "our" I mean not only Americans' understanding but that of intellectuals and others around the world with an interest in the workings of the global hegemon.[3]

There are good reasons supporting the claims for each of these three starting points. Cultural critics normally want to place the origins farther back in time, finding the sources of Americanism in Puritan resistance to English orthodoxy and so on. Bernard Bailyn and Sacvan Bercovitch join Perry Miller as the outstanding and valuable exponents of this line of inquiry. While political theorists, especially those involved with political philosophy, necessarily interest themselves in the Founders' ideas and the institutions they constituted, for the most part more economically oriented historical scholars find the American System's global emergence in its later economic and state transformations. These scholars often take the

Civil War or the Spanish-American War as the transformative event that puts the United States dominantly on the world stage.

By keeping in mind the work of Henry Adams, I hope to illuminate the continuity of the American System. If time allowed, we could follow Adams from the War of 1812 to the period between the Spanish-American War of 1898 and the onset of the European war in July 1914. Henry Adams was, of course, the great-grandson and grandson of two American presidents. His great-grandfather John Adams was one of the most influential and powerful leaders of the U.S. revolution, and his continuing importance to U.S. history and cultural self-understanding recently received new evidence in the best-selling book on his life by David McCullough. Henry Adams also authored a volume entitled *The Education of Henry Adams*, which the Modern Library editors voted the most important nonfictional work of English prose; in this book, Adams invented a new genre of literature, the education, and fit it to American and global realities.

Adams also wrote a nine-volume historical study entitled *The History of the United States during the Administrations of Thomas Jefferson and James Madison*. Covering only sixteen years in American history, from Jefferson's inauguration in 1801 to Madison's departure from office in 1817, Adams demonstrated how American national identity emerged during the War of 1812. He showed how the conflicting founding ideologies of Jeffersonianism and Hamiltonianism not only contrasted but also supplemented each other as responses to political, natural, and economic forces. Most important, he explained how U.S. citizenship and national institutions created a republican form of government that, paradoxically, influenced their own supersession in the emergence of a U.S. imperial order later in the same century. Following the death by suicide of his wife, Clover, Henry Adams withdrew from public life. Living what he called a posthumous existence, he never again published under his own name nor took part in any public office. Nonetheless, as his life went on and his friends came to occupy high positions, Adams gained intellectual influence as well as a prime position from which to observe the United States in the world. (I refer here specifically to Adams's friendships with Theodore Roosevelt who became president and with John Hay, his closest friend, who, as secretary of state, elaborated the U.S. "Open Door" policy, first regarding China, and then as part of an effort to liberalize global trade for U.S. industry.) Adams always wrote history from the point of view not of his own time but of what he could best understand about the emerging future ascertainable dominant forces seemed likely to produce. Even though the *History of the United States* appeared before the United States entered openly on its overseas imperial adventures, Adams wrote it understanding that the Civil War and its aftermath not only had changed the internal institutional arrangements of the United States—making the Constitution of 1787 itself irrelevant—but that they had made the United States already the world's dominant power, a fact of which American intellectuals and political elites were not aware even as they struggled with its developing consequences. Adams's technical decision always to write history as if from the future makes special demands upon his readers and it licenses those who follow to do the same—thereby compounding the difficulties for readers.

In the September 1999 issue of *Foreign Affairs*, Richard Haass, who serves Colin Powell as director of policy planning for the U.S. State Department, published an essay entitled "What To Do with American Primacy."[4] At first, this document appeared to be one of many urging a specific policy on a U.S. state still somewhat uncertain of how to proceed after the Cold War. Now that Haass occupies an important planning position in the government, his arguments take on a new interest as part of a larger effort by Anglo-American state intellectuals to legitimate empire as a means of preserving order and assuring a peaceful and prosperous future. In recent years, as globalization theory has developed, many intellectuals have asserted that new technologies and expanded trade have eroded the system of nation-state autonomy as established in Europe by the Treaty of Westphalia signed in Münster on October 24, 1648. Not until the middle of the 1990s, however, did U.S. intellectuals begin publicly to voice an imperial policy as part of what during Clinton's administration officials came to call "nation building." Of course, we all remember very well how the United States, sometimes with United Nations' authority and at other times with only the backing of NATO or less formal groups of nations, intervened militarily within other sovereign nations such as the former Yugoslavia, ending in the bombing of Belgrade that included the bombing of China's embassy. In Beijing, in the summer of 2000, I laid out an analysis of how the United States made strategic use of human rights as part of the processes for spreading neo-liberal political and economic regimes throughout the world. The Clinton government did not propose, to the best of my knowledge, anything like this imperialist theory that revises long-standing notions of state sovereignty. In fact, this theory does not yet seem to be declared U.S. policy even though it is voiced in high places by important intellectuals and, not surprisingly, in alliance with

British neo-imperialists who seem to feel that the United States finally can be convinced to take up the British civilizing mission.

Henry Adams puts us in a position to see more clearly some of what is happening in these processes, to understand their historical depth in the U.S. polity, to weigh their chances of success for U.S. power, and to measure alternative possibilities. Above all, Adams illuminates how imitative, how unoriginal, and how traditional thinkers such as Haass really are. Of course, the fact that his ideas are old thoughts, as William James would call them, makes them more rather than less forceful or interesting for those trying to theorize America. Knowing the genealogy of these old thoughts lets us grasp them more easily and while placing them in the history of the United States lets us learn how to deal with them.

If we study Henry Adams's writings and career, we will engage with every aspect of U.S. modernization and expansion from before the Civil War through the first decades of the twentieth century. In this case, his political intellectual involvement in the crises in Cuba after 1880, intensified by the U.S. role in Cuba's liberation from Spanish colonialism and aggravated by his relations with Theodore Roosevelt and John Hay, forces our attention back to the U.S. solution to its Cuban problem. This in turn draws our attention to the thinking underlying Haass's theory of limited sovereignty within a larger vision of U.S. imperialism.

Haass begins with the assumption that the United States faces a problem new in its history and requiring a new policy. The new policy goes under a familiar name: imperialism. Haass reckons the United States so dominates the world stage that no configuration of other powers can balance it. He calls this situation a "surplus of power" and asserts that it poses dangerous problems for the U.S. state: "The fundamental question that continues to confront American foreign policy is what to do with a surplus of power and the many and considerable advantages this surplus confers on the United States." As a political thinker, Haass is a realist tinged with the idealism of Woodrow Wilson. He is an internationalist who desires the rule of law to control natural conflicts between states. He understands power's fluidity and realizes that the surplus of power cannot go on for long because in globalization other centers of power will develop: "U.S. advantages are not permanent. . . . [T]he U.S. position relative to others is eroding. The reality is that other countries and non-state actors (be they Osama Bin Laden, Amnesty International, the International Criminal Court, or George Soros and one of his hedge funds) are accumulating ever more significant amounts of power in one or more forms." What, then, is the United States to do in its world-leading role while it has this temporary opportunity to make use of its surplus power? The answer Haass proposes is simple, idealistic, and ambitious. The United States, he argues, must recognize that the emerging world will inevitably be multipolar and that it should not waste resources in a futile effort to prevent this. The United States, rather, should use its power to assure that the new multipolar world is not an order of competing and hostile states. (That would be something like what the British confronted in the nineteenth century; the failures of that balance of power strategy appeared for all to see in 1914.) Haass writes that

> Multipolarity can reflect a world . . . in which a number of states, each possessing significant power, work together in common pursuits. . . . As much as possible, the U.S. objective should be to persuade other centers of political, economic and military power to see it as their self-interest to support constructive notions of how international society should be organized and operated. The proper goal for American foreign policy, then, is to encourage the emergence of a multipolarity characterized by cooperation and concert rather than competition and conflict. In such a world, order would not be limited to non-belligerence based on a balance of power (or fear of escalation) but rather on something much more broad, reflecting agreement on both global purposes and the means to accomplish them.[5]

This is an exceptionally lucid statement of the American System in foreign affairs. It restates a long-standing wish for what we call the Pax Americana, the American peace. Only a very small minority of Americans think this policy represents a coercive strategy of unfair impingement on the world. Rather, the majority of Americans see it as an example of U.S. leadership based on a right that comes with the success and power that America's advanced modernization provides. The idea is very familiar; it embodies a long-standing U.S. ideologeme that underlay even the Cold War containment of the USSR.

At its heart, Haass's policy relies on an idea of international relations that denies the theoretical and ideal equality of nation-states while relegating to the United States and a few other allied powers the right to determine which nation-states retain sovereign control of their internal affairs. In order to produce the Pax Americana—"a world premised on peaceful relations, non-proliferation, respect for human rights and economic openness"—the world must accept that certain states shall not have sovereign rights. On what basis can Haass make this claim? Intellectuals believe globalization has weakened the nation-state itself while admitting that some states remain more powerful and essential to the global order than others do. Haass extends and revamps this general idea, understanding that, for now, the U.S. hegemon polices the world order guiding it toward a set of goals requiring international powers to deny "rogue states" sovereign rights.

> But over the past half century, and especially over the past decade, the idea that sovereignty should not be absolute has gained strength. Instead, sovereignty is increasingly judged as conditional, linked to how a government treats its own citizens. When a government is unable or unwilling to safeguard its citizens—when the inherent contract between the government and the governed is violated—the leadership forfeits its normal rights. It then falls upon the international community to act—be it diplomatically, with sanctions, with aid, or with military force—under the banner of humanitarian intervention. The obvious challenge is to gain broader recognition of this modified view of sovereignty and with it acceptance of (if not support for) humanitarian intervention.[6]

Haass's thinking belongs to the tradition of social contract theory extended to the international arena. Haass implicitly follows Hobbes, hoping to make state agents understand that accepting the American System would best serve their interests. Haass asserts that national sovereignty derives from a government meeting its contractual obligations to its people and that a government's failure to meet these obligations threatens not only local turmoil but, in a globalized era of international relations, world peace itself. In other words, rather than attempt to balance power among nations, the United States would bring the world into a jurisprudential set of assumptions about and relations of power, open markets in trade, and representative democracy in politics, to assure that a balance of power would be unnecessary. The U.S. hegemonic role would yield to a concert of powers agreeably and contractually meeting their own self-interest in a shared order taken to be the best of all possible worlds. Limiting the sovereignty of illegal states in theory justifies their rearrangement in fact. (In the aftermath of the September 11 attacks, the assistant secretary of defense radicalized this imperial theory by asserting that the

United States would "destroy states" if necessary in an effort to smooth the globe.) Psychologically, of course, Hobbesianism assumes that humans act from self-interest and rarely from transcendent interests, although Haass would presumably claim that the American elites' foreign policy goals have a utopian dimension. The state of nature brings conflict; a surplus of power provides a once and only chance to erase the possibility for the foreseeable future by establishing a universal system in which all members of the species accept a common ontological definition and permanent arrest within a well-policed if beneficent regime.

Haass erroneously believes that his policy recommendations are an original solution to a new problem. For Henry Adams, Haass is merely a familiar type and his policy is something we have seen before. Adams understood that the United States had become the world's dominant power by 1863, at a time when Great Britain's decline was not clearly understood. Adams saw American superiority not merely in military power, although in 1863 the United States had the largest, most technologically advanced army in the world as it destroyed the rebellious and treasonous slave power, the American Confederacy. Nor had U.S. economic power, calculated in terms of primary material production—coal, steel, rails—yet exceeded Britain's. Adams, of course, noticed that the United States would soon exceed the empire in its economic and military potential, but, more important, he understood that the British system, based on empire and controlled markets, could not rival the American System in its ability to innovate, accumulate, dominate, and modernize. Adams had his own troubled and often critical relation to these features of the American System, but he knew their force to be irresistible, poorly understood, potentially dangerous, but nonetheless more advanced and modern than any previous system. In effect, the United States made outmoded all preceding sets of relations and the imbalance of power proved it. A surplus of power is the constant American state.

As Cuba struggled to gain its independence from Spain, Adams, acting out of a commitment to democratic values of self-determination and a family tie to the Monroe doctrine, which his grandfather John Quincy Adams had authored when he was secretary of state, worked to support the Cuban rebellion against Spain. He celebrated the U.S. defeat of Spain in the Caribbean and he came to understand the geopolitical necessity for U.S. control of all access routes to the mouth of the Mississippi River, which the Civil War had revealed to be a military vulnerability. Like many other Americans, though, Adams resisted U.S. expansion into the

Pacific, especially into the Philippines, which the United States took from Spain in 1898 and in which it fought a several years long counter-insurgency war to suppress Filipino aspirations to freedom and self-determination. During this period of U.S. expansion beyond its continental borders, a multifaceted anti-imperialism movement developed in the United States reflecting varying and complex sets of motives. Indeed, not all anti-imperial motives were pure or benevolent. Racist reluctance to absorb, colonize, or take responsibility for populations largely of African descent played an important role in the U.S. decision not to retain Cuba and in the general and still effective refusal to allow Cuba then or Porto Rico now the possibility of becoming, like Alaska and Hawaii, separate sovereign states in the U.S. federation. Henry Adams stood among those intellectuals who strongly opposed American colonization but who also accepted the seeming historical necessity of U.S. global prominence. For Adams, the issue was not American power but American intelligence—especially the dearth of intelligence among both the people and the leading elites. American power had to be taken for granted as it appeared everywhere he looked, especially in comparison to crumbling European empires and exhausted but dangerous European paradigms for social formation and foreign relations. The best Adams could say for American intellectuals was that they lagged American power and innovation. Very few American intellectuals appear in Adams's work as capable of the anticipatory intelligence political leaders would need to direct such powerful and novel forces as the United States embodied. American intelligence lags American force—this is an Adams truism that typifies the peculiar danger the United States poses to the world and to itself and its own residual originary democratic ideals. For Adams, these dangers appear in what he believed was the stupidity of American policy in the Philippines. Adams held two complementary positions on U.S. overseas expansion: first, it was inevitable but should never take the form of colonization; second, it posed a profound risk to American democracy unless American power were intelligently directed to minimize damage to democratic institutions at home and sovereign aspirations in modernizing parts of the world.

In a letter of November 2, 1901, Adams advises John Hay, the secretary of state, to change U.S. policy, to withdraw from the colonial war underway to subjugate the Filipino people, and to arrange what Adams refers to as the Cuban solution: "I should like to see the government declare its avowed Cuban policy for the Philippines, even at the cost of inconsistency. Anything to escape British ruts!"[7] This letter, Adams tells Hay, is his own report on the state of the union, a mockery of the report officially issued each year to Congress by the president—in 1901, of course, by the avid imperialist Theodore Roosevelt. The letter is a report to the secretary of state of his best friend's view of the world and of the U.S. place and proper policy within it. The largest part of the letter criticizes the British for the murderous stupidity of their colonial policy, especially as Joseph Chamberlain, attempting to retain control of South Africa, rejected the principles upon which the Treaty of Paris, signed in 1783, made the United States an independent nation. Adams insists to Hay that America's success in two wars of independence and two treaties of peace had established in principle the illegality of British attempts to hold colonies against their will: "We [the Adams family leaders] thoroughly believed that British constitutional law was settled forever on that point, and that England was bound never again to restrain a free colony by force from adopting whatever government it chose."[8] Adams's letter makes its case clearly if indirectly. The United States should not adopt the British model of colonization, not only because it is not in the U.S. interest but also because it violates the founding principle of the U.S. revolution—namely, the right of people to self-determination. Colonization is precisely what the American System makes outmoded. In a letter written on November 3, 1901, to his brother Brooks Adams, Henry takes note that in their moment, as the British and European systems are collapsing, the American System struggles to control its new dominance. Adams warns that war, like colonization, cannot be the American mode. Rather he insists that history teaches and American democracy demands that struggles have an intellectual side, that they be understood as a conflict of "processes." The merits of different processes should test themselves not by violence but "on economical principles."[9] Adams does not mean a conflict of national economies—although there is no doubt that America would win such a conflict. Rather, he means that the employment of power conceived as process should be measured in terms belonging to economy, no matter in which venue that power inheres. On this line of thinking, the United States should hold no colonies: "Violence is always a waste. The road of a true policy is always that of least resistance, but it is sometimes that of no resistance at all. In other words, every country held and administered by force is a danger, and therefore uneconomical."[10] Richard Haass, like Adams, worries that the United States could overextend and waste itself, hurrying its downfall as a global power. Each of them clearly believes it is in the best interest of the United States to make arrangements that will allow the given U.S. advantages and principles to spread across the globe. There are, however, substantial differences between the two, especially on the issues of sovereignty and democracy and the qualifications of America to lead.

In urging Hay, Adams refers to the "Platt Amendment," which is a precedent for Haass's theory of limited sovereignty.[11] Article 3 of the amendment makes this quite clear: "That the government of Cuba consents that the United States may exercise the right to intervene for the preservation of Cuban independence, the maintenance of a government adequate for the protection of life, property, and individual liberty, and for discharging the obligations with respect to Cuba imposed by the treaty of Paris on the United States, now to be assumed and undertaken by the government of Cuba."[12] Haass and Elihu Root assert the U.S. right to limit national sovereignty on the same Hobbesian contractual model and make clear that governments not as modernized and responsible as the American can be removed to assure not only peace but the expansion of the American System, which, as we have already seen, is both an extension of the Hobbesian thesis on natural conflict and a visionary effort to overcome it.

Adams always and everywhere insists, by contrast, on the essential fact of national sovereignty. The origin of the United States lies in forcing the constitutional recognition that the British model has no legitimacy. In essence, he warns Hay in 1901 that the U.S. exercise in the Philippines is an example of how the British have the United States by the tail and are trying to wag the much larger dog. The Adams family struggled politically against British domination and ideas, and Adams warns Hay that the United States must not follow British values, theories, or interests in its foreign policy: "my life and my father's and my grandfather's and my great-grandfather's and my great great-grand uncle's lives have been passed in trying to prevent America from obeying English stupidity." It is not merely that Britain would colonize while U.S. expansion rests upon a more indirect process of economic, cultural, and ideological transformation. It is, rather, that Britain's and Europe's colonial system rested upon murder: "Europe has always said: Buy or Fight! So the Irish, the Boers, and the Chinese are likely to remain unassimilated. We Americans ought to invent a new method. The old one creates, nourishes and preserves more dangers than it eliminates."[13] Criminal stupidity had its economic doctrine. Adams's insistence on judging economically invites us to consider him a liberal or libertarian except that Adams anticipates this reading and corrects it. To his brother Brooks he writes, "This, you will say, is pure Manchester Doctrine! Not quite. Manchester was a superfoetation on English force; only so far as its markets were natural was the doctrine candid."[14] Setting aside for the moment Adams's increasing dissatisfaction with socialism, this comment is important for it suggests that he wanted to find a non-liberal solution for the American System in world trade. Not only does this sharply contrast with Haass and his commitment to Hayekian neo-liberalism, it marks once more both Adams's distance from the Hobbesian position and his own commitments to democracy and self-determination. Brooks Adams was a stridently racist and imperialist voice in American society whose own libertarian commitments forced him to an intolerable conclusion. As Henry wrote to his brother Brooks: "You may properly object that the economical law leads to the extermination of the hostile elements, as we exterminated the Indians and England is exterminating the Boers. Again arises the question of process. Does it pay for England to exterminate? Is it feasible to exterminate the Chinese?"[15] The English model, the European capitalist logic, has a murderous stupidity about it, an inefficiency that, as it were, embodies the Hobbesian position from which Haass sets out and which, he hopes, American power can overcome. Adams always assumed that European practices and the ideas upon which they rested should be irrelevant to America except as lessons because, if adopted, they threatened to destroy America's principles, its democracy, and hence its difference from the Old World. The specific danger always is that Americans can be misled into being British, which means, for Adams, adopting an out-of-date murderous stupidity for their own. What worried Adams was always the specific question, does American have enough intelligence to overthrow the weight of inherited stupidity?

His researches mostly led him to conclude that the answer to this question was no. In 1901, he judged the United States to have a surplus of power confronting the question how best to use it. Anticipatory intelligence alone prevents errors that power obscures: "Our enormous resources, of course, tempt us to waste . . . and it will need all of our intelligence to check it."[16] It should be clear how Haass's judgment that at this moment the United States faces an unprecedented situation is not true; the limited sovereignty argument is itself, as the Platt Amendment shows, a repetition of an old U.S. practice based on complex interests. In important ways, Haass is closer to the British model Adams warns against because Haass's theory rests upon a global acceptance of a Hayekian neo-liberalism that echoes the Manchester School of the nineteenth century. It is a commonplace in the history of ideas to place Hayek and the Austrian School in the Ricardian genealogy of the Manchester School.[17] Equally important,

Haass assigns Hobbesian barbarism to non-American others in the world system whereas Adams worries that the dearth of American intelligence, even as the United States is the dominant power, creates waste, which, in this set of documents, means war and violence. The absence of intelligence is a mark of the Hobbesian state of nature and not its alternative. Haass has no skepticism about the U.S. agenda, no modesty about U.S. intellect. Specifically, Haass has no worry that by directing the United States to adopt an imperial foreign policy he runs the risk of making America British.

Related to Haass's thinking on limited sovereignty and the new imperialism stands the work of an important English state intellectual named Robert Cooper. Cooper's writings reflect quite an old but mainstream position within what Edward W. Said has called Orientalism, although Cooper has nicely updated the policy rhetoric:

> The challenge to the postmodern world is to get used to the idea of double standards. Among ourselves, we operate on the basis of laws and open cooperative security. But when dealing with more old-fashioned kinds of states outside the postmodern continent of Europe, we need to revert to the rougher methods of an earlier era—force, pre-emptive attack, deception, whatever is necessary to deal with those who still live in the nineteenth century world of every state for itself. Among ourselves, we keep the law but when we are operating in the jungle, we must also use the laws of the jungle. In the prolonged period of peace in Europe, there has been a temptation to neglect our defences, both physical and psychological. This represents one of the great dangers of the postmodern state.[18]

Cooper generalizes the policy that justified the NATO bombing of Serbia and, in part, buttresses U.S. actions against terrorism.[19] For Adams and others who think like him, getting used to double-standards is rather a horrible and undesirable idea. Surely, it implies reversing or troubling the results of national liberation struggles carried out during the Cold War, as long as the emergent nations' governments trouble the Anglo-American vision of global order. No doubt, this new imperialism finds easy justification in countries where governments neglect or abuse basic human rights because such neglect facilitates the domestic politics necessary to form the political consensus within especially the American representative political system that Cooper and Haass's policies require. That consensus, once formed, quickly acquires near-permanent status because it combines the comforting psychological elements of stability and beneficence.

Haass has one particular worry about the ability of the United States to conduct successfully the neo-imperial policy he recommends. Indeed, he insists that his policy's necessity rests upon this weakness: "American society and domestic politics will hasten the fading of American primacy. Tocqueville's judgment that democracy is ill-suited for the conduct of foreign policy goes double for world leadership." Cognate with the formation of a neo-imperial policy goes a manipulation of U.S. democracy so that the Pax Americana can emerge while the surplus of power still exists. Of course, only the elite that credit this policy as intelligent and necessary can rule—all other components of a democratic polity implicitly lack legitimacy. How then does such an elite govern? Only by turning the American mind into consensus by operating all the necessary media of power to produce a majority willing to support such imperial ambitions. How this is done is relatively clear. Why it can be effective is not.

Adams's endless meditations on why intelligence constantly lags force should trouble intellectuals concerned both to challenge consensus formation and to educate so that intellect remains capable both of skeptical critique and of imagining alternatives to the anodyne old thoughts newly dressed as fantastic answers to often-unreal dilemmas. Adams is no Hobbes. Violence in the state of nature is not the principle danger in modern society, especially dominant American society. Throughout his minor writings especially, Adams chooses to represent the actual danger in two different ways: first, phenomenally, reporting as if it were on pure impression; second, analytically, laying out the nature of the American System and its inadequacies. Each of these two comes to require the other: the first gives anyone who can see, even for a moment, a sense of the unreality or surreality of it all, while the second helps explain how the first can persist in time despite all the evidence mind can perceive that the future is at risk. For example, writing to Elizabeth Cameron on July 5, 1905, from Paris, not long after the death of John Hay left him with no adequate interlocutor, Adams reports on how he spent the Fourth of July evening in France: "Armenonville was packed with Americans last night, not one of whom I ever saw. I sit outside under the window, and wonder whether I invented them, and whether they would all vanish if I said the word. You are all too ridiculous for me to take seriously."[20] Four days later, he once again writes to Elizabeth Cameron from Paris, this time reporting the results of his weekend alone, trying to understand the Americans he sees. In the middle of this letter, he explains the geopolitical ambitions of the American System as a plan to dominate, first, the North Atlantic world, from France to Russia, and then to "run our system through Asia" so that, in fifty years, the center of the system would be in China, "the coal-fields of Shanhsi." Now, however, Adams realizes finally that the system cannot be made to work. Anticipating the crisis of the 1914 European war and the concomitant social upheavals, he concludes that the American System was wrong on two counts. First, it will not last: "the machine won't much outlast me [he was then sixty-seven years old]. We are near the theoretical end. . . . I see more and more clearly that . . . nothing whatever stands longer between us and the actual dissipation of our energies." At this point, he drives home his conclusion, a truth he had long meditated and still worth considering. The dangerous American System must fail for an important and inescapable reason that is essentially contradictory to the nature of the rapid, flexible, innovative system itself. "We have not the mental power to run such a complicated and vast machine. Our mind is chaos, and the most chaotic is the optimist. Since I was a boy in 1850, I have seen a weird show, such as the universe since eternity perhaps never saw before."[21]

When Henry Adams described his friend Theodore Roosevelt as "pure act," and so essentially American, he offered no simple personal commentary but a reflection on the American capital system that defines its central and dangerous contradiction.[22] On the one hand, the surplus of power results from forces acting always in advance of those who try to understand or guide them, while on the other hand, those same forces produce a population of consumers and elites predominantly unreal in their ignorant dance within the world these forces compel into being. So accustomed by innovation and speed to the kaleidoscopic phenomenality in which they live, Americans necessarily have no chance to direct the forces that privilege them. Oddly, if there is intelligence in America, it exists in two disparate places: in the forces that themselves drive their own direction and in the extremely rare critical historical mind, which, as Adams shows in the *Education*, does not turn away from the abyss, from the difficult and seemingly timeless problems that American invention and American intellectuals purposefully disregard. In the July 9 letter to Elizabeth Cameron, Adams links American stupidity and boredom not only to the unreality of appearance and thoughtlessness but to the end of the system. Eventually, the energy will dissipate and the system will crash, but tragically because the crisis will be enormously destructive, unanticipated, a surprise to minds defined by the chaos their limits seem merely to reflect.

While Haass is a political realist, Adams's word for him would be "optimist," and this makes Haass's mind the most dangerously chaotic of all. While it concedes that America's power surplus will decline, it concedes nothing of its certainty about the value and persistence of the American System. Failure can come from only two sources: poor execution by the American state of an imperial foreign policy or recalcitrance and resistance by the others on the world stage. Of course, if properly carried out, for Haass, American power and planning could achieve its end, the Pax Americana.

Adams sat in Paris during 1905 watching the American System in its social and geopolitical forms. The more he watched, the more often he recorded his sensibility's disorder, the pain this combination of thoughtlessness and power caused him. His ability to differentiate day from night, waking from sleep, weakens as everywhere he looks he finds images essentially alike in their iterative ephemerality. Indeed, dreaming gives him no respite and seeing the world as dream image causes him nothing but near despair: "This constant narrowing of the horizon all round us is at times unendurable. . . . I suppose they were real;—but often I wonder if it is not my dream. . . . The thing has become frankly visionary—pure abstraction,—and I take it so. One day is no more serious than another. One person seems to be the exact equivalent of the next. . . . I don't understand myself as I did, and I seem to be getting seniler every day, especially in America. . . . As America I am downright loony."[23]

These letters are, of course, highly contrived pieces of writing and these tropes are familiar. Nonetheless, they are letters recording responses to the American System of a kind that have value for understanding it and its limits. Adams can put a question to Haass: "Why can you not see the repetition of stupidity in your plan?" Alternatively, Adams could put a question to the American electorate: "Why can you not overcome your inability to see especially when all the world presents you with the images you need to understand?"

A great deal of work needs to be done to answer these questions publicly, in ways that can be heard and acquire legitimate force to counter the surplus of power defining an American System that demands the right to run unguided. American writing contains scarce but strong resources for doing some of this work because Americans have been confronting this set of realities longer and more immediately than anyone else has. Yet, that is exactly the problem. These resources have their assigned place in the kaleidoscope of the American System and they remain, at least for now, infinitely too weak to resist their assignment or to inspire skepticism or curiosity about the American System. We can end by referring back to Adams, the author of the major American book on education, and say that the American System aims to prevent anyone from being a pupil who can learn to study its effects and its realities.

NOTES

1. Ideologues assert that the "American System" has a history as long as that of the United States itself, finding it in the earliest constitutional debates over the U.S. form of government. See, for example, Eyler Coates, Sr., "The Parliamentary vs. the American System," The Jeffersonian Perspective, http://www.geocities.com/CapitolHill/7970/jefpco20.htm. (accessed Sept. 21, 2004).
2. See, for example, the "American System" entry in *The Reader's Companion to American History*, ed. Eric Foner and John Garraty (Boston, 1991), http://college.hmco.com/history/readerscomp/rcah/html/ah_003600_americansyst.htm (accessed Sept. 21, 2004).
3. The term "American System" resonates in teaching, research, and general discussion. For one example, see "American System," U.S. History.com, http://www.u-s-history.com/pages/h278.html (accessed Sept. 21, 2004).
4. Richard Haass, "What To Do with American Primacy," *Foreign Affairs* 78(1999):37–49.
5. Haass, "American Primacy," 38.
6. Haass, "American Primacy," 40–41.
7. Henry Adams to John Hay, Nov. 2, 1901, in *The Letters of Henry Adams*, ed. J. C. Levenson et al. (Cambridge, Mass., 1982–1988), 5:304.
8. HA to John Hay, Nov. 2, 1901, in *Letters,* 5:302
9. HA to Brooks Adams, Nov. 3, 1901, in *Letters,* 5:306.
10. HA to Brooks Adams, Nov. 3, 1901, in *Letters,* 5:306.
11. The *Internet Modern History Sourcebook* summarizes the Platt Amendment and its context in this way: "The United States occupied Cuba for five years after 1898. In 1901 Secretary of War Elihu Root drafted a set of articles (later known as the Platt Amendment) as guidelines for future United States-Cuban relations. Despite considerable Cuban resistance, they became a part of the 1902 Cuban Constitution. In following years the United States used the amendment several times to send troops to maintain or place friendly governments in power and to protect investments. The amendment was abrogated in 1934." Paul Halsall, comp., *Internet Modern History Sourcebook* (New York, 1998), http://www.fordham.edu/halsall/mod/1901platt.html (accessed Sept. 21, 2004).

    The *Sourcebook* is a collection of public domain and copy-permitted texts for introductory level classes in modern European and World history. Unless otherwise indicated the specific electronic form of the document is copyrighted. Permission is granted for electronic copying, distribution in print form for educational purposes and personal use. If you do reduplicate the document, indicate the source. No permission is granted for commercial use of the *Sourcebook*. © Paul Halsall, July 1998. http://www.fordham.edu/halsall/mod/modsbook.html.
12. *Internet Modern History Sourcebook*.
13. HA to Brooks Adams, Nov. 3, 1901, in *Letters*, 5:306.
14. "The general term 'Manchester School' has been used to refer to radical liberalism/libertarianism in economic policy: laissez-faire, free trade, government withdrawal from the

economy, and an optimistic stress on the 'harmonious' effects of free enterprise capitalism. As a result, the school's nature is largely 'political' rather than purely 'economic.' Its arguments are not necessarily couched in any particular economic theory." From "Manchester School," The History of Economic Thought Website, ed. Gonçalo L. Fonseca and Leanne J. Ussher, http://cepa.newschool.edu/het/schools/manchester.htm (accessed Sept. 21, 2004).

15. HA to Brooks Adams, Nov. 3, 1901, in *Letters,* 5:307.
16. HA to Brooks Adams, Nov. 3, 1901, in *Letters,* 5:307.
17. See, for example, "Manchester School," The History of Economic Thought Website.
18. Robert Cooper, "The New Liberal Imperialism," *Observer Worldview*, Apr. 7, 2002, http://www.observer.co.uk/worldview/story/0,11581,680095,00.html (accessed Sept. 21, 2004).
19. Jürgen Habermas defended the bombing of Belgrade in exactly these terms. In *Die Zeit*, Habermas published a long article entitled "Bestiality and Humanity—A War on the Borderline between Law and Morality." For a convenient summary that reveals how Habermas's justification of bombing Belgrade as a pre-modern other to the emerging world order of democracies parallels Cooper and Haass's thinking, see Ulrich Rippert, "Bestiality, Humanity and Servility: How Jürgen Habermas Defends the Balkan War," World Socialist Web Site, http://www.wsws.org/articles/1999/jun1999/habe-j05.shtml (accessed Sept. 21, 2004).
20. HA to Elizabeth Cameron, July 5, 1905, in *Letters,* 5:685.
21. HA to Elizabeth Cameron, July 5, 1905, in *Letters,* 5:688.
22. Henry Adams, *The Education of Henry Adams* (New York, 1999), 349.
23. HA to Elizabeth Cameron, June 26, July 2, July 16, 1905, in *Letters,* 5:678, 682–683, 692.

Henry Adams's Debt to John Adams

RICHARD A. SAMUELSON

IN 1909 HENRY ADAMS READ his brother Brooks's manuscript biography of their grandfather John Quincy Aams. Brooks thought John Quincy was the model American statesman and citizen, but Henry disagreed, favoring their great-grandfather John Adams. After reading nearly three hundred pages of his brother's hagiography of John Quincy, Henry lost his temper: "I have turned myself inside out like an india-rubber ball to make a case for everybody, and especially for J.Q.A. whose case is the weakest of the lot, at least for me to defend, because I am most interested in profiting by the defense. The result is what you see. All I ask is to be civil. I will not be as big a brute as J.Q.A. was, but I am ready to go all lengths for his father."[1] Why did Henry want "to go all lengths" for John Adams?

An exploration of Henry Adams's thoughts about John Adams is long overdue. Although scholars, notably Earl Harbert, have studied Henry Adams's intellectual relationship with his ancestors in general, they have not paid sufficient attention to how Adams discriminated among his various ancestors and their ideas.[2] By paying close attention to Adams's thoughts about, and intellectual and political debts to John Adams, this essay will shed new light on Adams's career. The first half of the essay deepens our understanding of Adams's relationship with the American republic and in so doing enriches our understanding of Adams's goals. The second half explores the relationship of both Henry and John Adams to other important political and religious thinkers, notably Alexis de Tocqueville and Blaise Pascal, and in the process it shows the true origin and extent of Henry's political pessimism.

One can understand why previous scholars have failed to appreciate the importance of John Adams to Henry Adams. Henry's admiration for his great-grandfather comes through indirectly in his writings. In his *History of the United States during the Administrations of Thomas Jefferson and James Madison*, despite the obvious need to discuss his great-grandfather in the first part of the story, Adams manages to avoid actually using his name for several chapters. As Donald Hall has noted, that is "a neat trick were it not for the magic of euphemism." Adams's effort to hide the relationship between the first President Adams and the *History*'s author failed miserably, as Hall has pointed out: "Not mentioning the name of your great-grandfather—who was President . . . is roughly like hiring a blimp to fly overhead with John Adams Was My Great-Grandfather stenciled on its side in letters thirty feet high."[3] Whatever the effect of such indirection, it does make it difficult to conduct a close study of what Henry Adams saw in his great-grandfather.

Henry Adams hardly lacked opportunities to write about his ancestors, but he turned them down on principle. That may have been why he chose to write about Jefferson's and Madison's presidencies in the first place. They took place during the sixteen years between the American Revolution and the end of the Civil War during which he would have to write the least about his own family. In 1880, Justin Winsor asked Adams to contribute to the Revolutionary-era section of the *Memorial History of Boston*. Adams wrote him, "I know of but two statesmen produced by Boston at the Revolution. One was Sam Adams, the other John Adams. As for Hancock, Josiah Quincy, Otis, and the others they either amounted to little, or died before the war."[4] For that reason, Adams would not contribute to Winsor's book. "Your request is in substance that I should write a laudation of two members of my own family, twenty pages long. I can't do it. I never write about such subjects when I can help it, because, if I admire them, it may be family prejudice, and if I criticize their failings, my criticism as coming from me, jars on the readers' sense of propriety."[5] Part of the reason why Henry Adams said so little about John Adams is that Henry did not wish to be the judge in his own case.

Despite this reluctance to marshal his thoughts about John Adams, we can nonetheless discover them in the scattered references and allusions that Adams made to his great-grandfather throughout his life. More generally, we can see John Adams's shadow looming over Henry Adams's lifelong intellectual journey. Henry admired his great-grandfather, though not without reservations. Commenting on relations with South America in 1895,

Henry wrote Brooks, "I quite decline to defend [Secretary of State Richard] Olney's manners . . . or my own or yours, or those of your grandfather, who wrote the Monroe doctrine, or of your great-grandfather who helped to write the Declaration of Independence, or of your great-uncle Sam, who must have been really rude to Governor Hutchinson and others."[6] Politics was a rough business, and often led to actions and statements that were bad form. At the same time, Adams thought his great-grandfather leavened his bluntness with humor and a love of life that his son John Quincy never shared. Writing to one of his nieces about his grandfather, Henry commented, "I do not think the old gentleman a subject of compassion. His father was worth two of him, and really suffered and enjoyed greatly."[7]

To begin on the most superficial level, Adams enjoyed his great-grandfather's sense of humor. Henry Adams was proud of his character as an ironist and an amusing writer and conversationalist. His campaign to be the "alligator" of the Hasty Pudding Club at Harvard set the tone for his lifelong zest for irreverent satire. He clearly enjoyed joking about his great-grandfather. In one of the more memorable commentaries on the difference between John Adams and Thomas Jefferson, Henry considered what kind of humor a writer would need to employ to describe them. "With regard to T. Jefferson," Henry wrote John Hay, "who, between ourselves is a character of comedy. John Adams is a droll figure, and good for Sheridan's school, but T.J. is a case for Beaumarchais; he needs the lightest of touches."[8] John Adams could laugh at himself and often did. He was an earthy character, a man who had the charming habit of comparing the manure piles he saw in his travels around America and Europe.[9]

Henry Adams never understood why so few people saw his great-grandfather's lighter side. He was pleased to find that the historian John Franklin Jameson agreed with him on this score. While some stereotyped John Adams as an austere neo-Puritan, Jameson knew better: "You are the only person I've ever heard speak of John Adams as a letter-writer and humorist. If he had lived in Pennsylvania or Virginia, he would have been classic. I never fail to laugh at the droll likeness of himself at the bottom of p. 88 of the Boston Patriot Correspondence. No one else, unless perhaps Franklin, could have done it."[10] In American humor, comparison to Franklin was high praise indeed.

Henry's enjoyment of his ancestor's sense of humor reflected a deeper political and moral sentiment that he shared with his great-grandfather. John Adams's sense of humor grew from his appreciation of human frailty and of human limits. Next to their Creator, humans cut a comic figure, and for that reason John Adams was content, with Erasmus, to laugh at human folly, including his own.[11] Henry Adams also laughed at his own vanity and at human vanity in general. Like John Adams he enjoyed poking fun at those who had a greater faith in human reason than he. He wrote his brother Charles in 1910, "I know I'm a damn fool, and my folly ends in the logical and mathematical demonstration that the human race is going to end just when I do;—which ought to suit the metaphysicians."[12] An appreciation for man's imperfection underlay the moralist streak in the writings of both Henry and John Adams. Because they understood that human beings lacked any great capacity to progress socially, they concluded that the proper sphere to judge men was individual and moral. Because John Adams and his great-grandson acknowledged that men were weak, they judged human greatness as a matter of overcoming that weakness rather than as contributions to the general progress of human society. Since they held such similar understandings of human nature, Henry studied John Adams closely. Page citations like the one we noted to John Adams's letter to the *Boston Patriot* seldom come to a casual reader.[13]

Like his ancestor, Henry Adams thought helping one's fellow men was a worthy endeavor, but not one that excused dishonesty or vice. Precisely because man's capacity for progress was so limited, they concluded that the pursuit of progress did not excuse lies, deceit, or corruption. It was not man's failed attempts to "be just and good" that amused them, but rather man's vain efforts in pursuit of other, worldly goods. Quests for fame, glory, and riches, however natural, were vain. All of us end in the same dust out of which we were created.[14]

Human weakness and frailty were as central to John Adams's politics as they were to his humor. He believed in political liberty not because he was an optimist of the Jeffersonian sort, confident that men would behave themselves should government cease to interfere with their lives, but rather because he did not trust the men who would staff the government any more than he trusted anyone else. Power was tempting: "it is weakness rather than wickedness, which renders men unfit to be trusted with unlimited power."[15] John Adams believed that neither individuals nor the institutions they created deserved unlimited power; the elaborate scheme of checks and balances enshrined in the American regime was fundamental to the American experiment. Checks and balances were the means of turning human weakness against itself, securing liberty thereby. To ensure liberty, "power must be opposed to power, and interest to interest."[16] Checks and balances worked because one could count on most men to be self-interested most of the time. Human weakness worked in predictable ways.

Henry Adams absorbed his great-grandfather's political point of view at a young age. His political education began in the 1850s when his father, Charles Francis Adams, impressed him into service as a copyist and proofreader of John Adams's *Works*. The lessons he learned there stayed with him, or at the very least he remembered enough to return to John Adams's writings when his own political career began in earnest. After serving as his father's secretary during the Civil War, Henry returned to the United States ambitious to begin his own career in politics. That effort began with John Adams. In the first paragraph of his first major piece of reform writing, Adams quoted the State Constitution of Massachusetts, which his great-grandfather had drafted ninety years before: "That among the precautions absolutely necessary for the maintenance of a free government is a frequent recurrence to the fundamental principles of the Constitution."[17] The reference was reflexive: by citing his great-grandfather, Henry practiced the principle that John Adams taught.

As Charles Vandersee has noted, Adams quoted his great-grandfather several times in these early political essays. In his essay on "Civil Service Reform,"Adams quoted the Massachusetts Constitution's statement of the principle of separation of powers:

> In the government of this Commonwealth, the legislative department shall never exercise the executive and judicial powers, or either of them; the executive shall never exercise the legislative and judicial powers, or either of them; the judicial shall never exercise the legislative and executive powers, or either of them: *to the end that it may be a government of law and not of men.*[18]

Elsewhere in the same essay, he quoted another of John Adams's comments on the separation of powers. This second passage comes from John Adams's great treatise on constitutions, the *Defence of the Constitutions*: "If the executive power, or any considerable part of it, is left in the hands either of an aristocratical or a democratical assembly, it will corrupt the legislature as necessarily as rust corrupts iron, or as arsenic poisons the human body; and when the legislature is corrupted the people are undone." Henry Adams then commented that "This principle, laid down by an American writer upon government before the Constitution was framed, received a striking illustration in the result of that revolution which threw the executive patronage into the hands of the legislature."[19] In other words, Henry Adams applied John Adams's political writings to the problems of his own day.[20]

Young Henry Adams, like his ancestor, saw in checks and balances the key to liberal constitutionalism. He feared that the constitutional architecture his great-grandfather had helped to create was no longer suited to the exigencies of the day. Changes had occurred in American society that had to be addressed, and some rot had seeped into American institutions that had to be removed in order for the American republic to continue into the future. It is, after all, quite possible that people call a government a "republic" long after it had ceased to be one. Hence young Henry Adams undertook a close study of politics to learn about both the necessary and the possible in the political world in general and his own political world in particular. Adams gave close attention to civil service reform because he thought that the republic needed to create a class of disinterested public servants to restore the constitutional organs that the spoils system had eviscerated. Hence he wrote, "laying aside, therefore, the usual arguments in favor of civil-service reform,—arguments drawn from finance or from administrative convenience, this essay will attempt to show that the soundness and vigor, nay, even the purpose of the reform movement, must depend upon its recurrence to the fundamental principles of the Constitution."[21]

To his chagrin, Adams soon concluded that human weakness could not be so easily or so well managed as his great-grandfather had hoped. As early as 1870 he feared that historians would find that "the most interesting experiment that has ever been made in the laboratory of political science . . . only demonstrates the impossibility of success through its means."[22] After making some efforts in politics through the 1870s, he concluded that that indeed had been the case. John Adams's faith in the ability of constitutions to secure liberty under law for an extended period of time had been misplaced. Henry reinforced this idea in *The Education of Henry Adams*, when he wrote about the fight of the early 1890s against the creation of government-big business cartels: "he thought it probably his last chance of standing up for his eighteenth-century principles, strict construction, limited powers, George Washington, John Adams, and the rest."[23] Henry concluded that the political science in which John Adams had placed his hopes for political improvement had failed. Over time, human nature found ways to join what America's constitutional masters had tried to keep apart.

Although he concluded that John Adams's constitutional system had ceased to function, Henry still cherished his great-grandfather's memory and tried to serve his legacy. Why did he do so? It may be that Henry simply thought that John Adams had led an honorable life; failure to solve an insoluble problem is not necessarily a sign of weakness or of misplaced idealism. But there may have been more to it than that. What did Henry Adams think remained useful in John Adams's politics if not his constitutional architecture and his political science? Perhaps Henry sought to learn from his great-grandfather's experience in the art of practical politics. John Adams had been not only a political scientist but also a practical politician as well. As Peter Shaw has noted, Henry Adams remained engaged in American politics until very late in his life, but behind the scenes.[24] Adams helped organize the Cuban resistance to Spain in the 1890s, even making his house a meeting place for Cuban exiles and agitators and their friends. He also wrote the 1896 Senate Report on Cuban Independence for Sen. Don Cameron. Similarly, he did his duty as Secretary of State John Hay's closest informal advisor. When Adams was in Washington, every day he and Hay would walk for an hour discussing the world. In the *Education*, Adams crowned Hay with the pinnacle of republican achievement:

> In his eight years of office he had solved nearly every old problem of American statesmanship, and had left little or nothing to annoy his successor. He had brought the great Atlantic powers into a working system, and even Russia seemed about to be dragged into a combine of intelligent equilibrium based on an intelligent allotment of activities. For the first time in fifteen hundred years a true Roman pax was in sight, and would, if it succeeded, owe its virtues to him.[25]

As Hay's Svengali, Henry Adams could claim a share of the credit. By hanging around the center of power in America, Henry Adams did his duty as a son and as a citizen.

Though the domestic dreams of constitutional progress had been dashed, Henry Adams still found the principled foundation of John Adams's politics useful in foreign policy. Fortunately for the historical record, Adams did not stay in Washington throughout Hay's tenure as secretary of state; hence we can read the advice Adams gave Hay in his letters of the period. Discussing British actions in South Africa led Adams to consult his American first principles:

> The proclamation of a state of war, or of siege, in Cape Colony, assimilates the situation exactly with that of 1776. Personally

> I was not alive in 1776, I own with sorrow, and therefore am not a gallows-bird; but I had some relations by blood who were. It is not two hundred years, or six generations, since these relations of mine undertook to teach the English how to manage a colony, and we thought we had succeeded at the cost of two wars, and two hundred years of preaching. We thought it was acknowledged that we were right, and that G. Washington was not a felon. We thoroughly believed that British constitutional law was settled forever on that point, and that England was bound never again to restrain a free colony by force from adopting what government it chose. To this understanding the United States supposed themselves to be a party, tacitly admitted by the Treaty of 1783, definitively recognizing our success, primarily by force, and subsequently of right. On this understanding, three of my presumably respected blood-relations have been representatives of their country in London, and I humbly believe that there would have been a shindy if any British government had treated them, either in fact or in law, as felons.[26]

The right of a people to establish, alter, or abolish its government was as central to Henry Adams's politics in 1901 as it had been to his great-grandfather and his cohort in 1776. While advising the secretary of state, Adams made sure that the nation did not forget it.

Like John Adams, Henry believed that the American nation was built on the principled belief in the right of all people to self-determination and self-government, but he also thought the nation's responsibility to ensure that right stopped at the water's edge. John Adams was hardly an isolationist; he understood the need for the Union to fight to secure its place in the world. Hence he oversaw a quasi-war with France during his presidency. At the same time, he did not believe that the Americans should export republicanism. For that reason, he believed in observing strict neutrality with regard to the French Revolution. His great-grandson also thought that the republic's independence demanded that it be willing to fight when insulted by foreign nations, but that it ought not actively to engage in nation building. Doing so would make it a colonial power, in violation of the principle that justified American independence itself. That was why Adams supported the Cubans, providing political and rhetorical assistance to them in the 1890s, and why he was furious with the McKinley administration for holding on to both Cuba and the Philippines after the Spanish-American War.

Up to the end of his life, Henry Adams upheld the principle of neutrality in a world of nation-states. On March 3, 1916, he wrote from his home on Lafayette Square, in Washington, D.C., "I look across the Square into the White House windows, and wonder how John Adams felt, and whether I shall still be looking, a hundred years hence, or whether neutrals will at last be kicked into being Germans or Russians or Japs or something new. How we do squirm and squeal and cling to our pathetic old visions of peace and green fields!"[27] With the Germans practicing unlimited submarine warfare and the Franco-Anglo alliance seeking to buy more and more goods from the Americans, Adams thought it was the early 1800s all over again. The nation had to defend itself, but Adams nonetheless clung to the principle of neutrality: perhaps the nation could somehow ride out the war, or at least emerge from it with its principles intact.

In the 1790s, John Adams's America had faced the same problem that his great-grandson's America faced in World War I: asserting the rights of self-government and the policy of neutrality in a world at war. Upholding the right to national independence in the abstract was rather different from either being able to sustain it in practice or to defend it on principle. Unlike his great-grandson, John Adams believed that he could do so. That may be the ultimate reason why Henry cherished John Adams's memory. Henry stressed two of his great-grandfather's political principles. The first was the need to have principles that brought a regime together, and therefore the need to recur to them even as one tried to update the political system. And the second were those principles themselves. A political man could not function without principles, but not all principles were created equal. The American nation was fortunate to have begun with the principles of 1776. "No man whose mind will not work on its own independent pivot," Henry Adams wrote Henry Cabot Lodge in 1878, "can escape being drawn into the whirl-pool of party prejudices. Unless you can find some basis of faith in general principles, some theory of the progress of civilization which is outside and above all temporary questions of policy, you must infallibly think and act under the control of the man or men whose thought, in the times you deal with, coincides most nearly with your prejudices."[28] Without some higher principle to guide one through life, Adams feared, one would simply be guided by passions and prejudices. The family patriarch had been fortunate not to have faced the profound existential crisis that his great-grandson faced; his "need to know" had been quenched in a much more satisfying fashion than had that of his loyal descendant. Nonetheless, Henry Adams clung to his ancestral principles even while he feared they had degenerated into mere prejudices.

Given the number of years separating Henry Adams from his great-grandfather, and given the profound difference in religious belief, it is striking that Henry not only claimed to respect and cherish John Adams's memory, but that he also in some sense embodied his very spirit as well. On the centennial of John Adams's last full day as president, March 3, 1901, Adams wrote Elizabeth Cameron, "I look over to the White House wondering what my old friend Thomas Jefferson would say. It is just a hundred years since he turned my harmless ancestor into the street at midnight, and I think he must wish he hadn't, for there is mighty little left of him; whereas my venerable ancestor has at least me."[29] By 1901, Henry had concluded that Jeffersonian politics was dead in fact, though perhaps not in name. On the other hand, he still gave vitality to his ancestor's politics.[30]

Henry Adams's claim to be his great-grandfather's faithful political disciple in 1901 is both strange and striking, and perhaps an exploration of what the younger Adams meant by that claim will shed further light on the relationship between the two men. In 1901 Henry Adams was hard at work on *Mont Saint Michel and Chartres*, a book reveling in, if not glorifying, the medieval world. His great-grandfather had had few kind words for that era, and even fewer for its church. Even though he deserted the Calvinism of his ancestors, John Adams was proud to have been a child of New England Puritanism. It was the Reformation, he thought, that had made the American Revolution possible. As he wrote in his "Dissertation on Canon and Feudal Law" in 1765, "Liberty, and with her, knowledge, and virtue too, seem to have deserted the earth; and one age of darkness, succeeded another, till God, in his benign providence, raised up the champions, who began and conducted the *reformation*."[31] The Reformation led to the rise of Puritanism in England, which in turn led to the settlement of the New World by his ancestors, and ultimately led these ancestors to bring with them the seed of liberty that would bear fruit in 1776. Henry Adams was well aware of this; indeed part of what drew him to the Gothic was its distinctiveness from the American world his ancestors had done so much to create.[32] And yet he considered himself John Adams's loyal legatee.

How did Henry Adams reconcile his love of the Gothic with his devotion to John Adams's memory and his principles? To answer that question, perhaps we should consider other men with whom he identified himself, as we might find they all fit together into a pattern in Henry Adams's thought. Two thinkers stand out in particular, Alexis de Tocqueville and Blaise Pascal. In the 1860s as he prepared for his career, Adams turned to Tocqueville. "I have learned to think De Tocqueville my model," he wrote his brother Charles, "and I study his life and works as the Gospel of my private religion."[33] Several years later, he wrote of getting "as near positive satisfaction as St Francis, or Pascal or I could reach."[34] The link between John Adams and Tocqueville is not difficult to discern. Both believed in political science. The *Defence of the Constitutions* was a work in political science, and Tocqueville maintained that "a new political science is needed for a world itself quite new."[35] In his younger days, Henry Adams thought of the American republic in terms of its foundation in political science. As previously noted, he called the United States "the most interesting experiment that has ever been made in the laboratory of political science." That Tocquevillian strain of Henry Adams's devotion to John Adams lasted through the first part of his career, perhaps through his writing of the *History* in the 1880s. One can read the *History* as a lab report in political science. Unfortunately, that report concluded that the experiment had failed and that success was not possible through the chosen means.

While establishing the link between John Adams and Tocqueville is relatively easy, the connection between John Adams and Pascal may be a bit more obscure. Tocqueville himself may provide the link. Tocqueville kept Montesquieu, Rousseau, and Pascal constantly in mind as he wrote.[36] Henry Adams seems to have moved from the political science of Montesquieu and John Adams through Rousseau's effort to build a new philosophic synthesis to overcome the failings that he had seen in most Enlightenment thought, to the stark dichotomy between faith and reason in Pascal. The *Education* begins with Rousseau. In its preface, Adams wrote that "Jean Jacques was a very great educator in the manner of the eighteenth century."[37] By "educator," Adams meant what the political scientists his great-grandfather read called a "legislator." Tocqueville wrote that "it is not force alone, but rather good laws, which make a new government secure. After the battle comes the lawgiver. The one destroys; the other builds up."[38]

Like Tocqueville and Rousseau, Henry Adams set out to legislate in the highest sense, to create a new foundation for his civilization. "The American statesman or philosopher who would enter upon this great debate [about how to update the republic]," Henry Adams wrote in one of his early political essays, "must make his appeal, not to the public opinion of a day or of a nation, however large or intelligent, but to the minds of the few persons who, in every age and in all countries, attach their chief interest to the working out of the great problems of human society under all their varied conditions."[39] Adams agreed with Shelley that poets were the true legislators of the world, and he set out to be his nation's poet.[40] Frustrated by politics, he turned to literature to perform his public rites.[41] In 1879 he wrote that "America is increasing so rapidly, and her future is so vast, that one man may reasonably devote his life to the effort at impressing a moral on the national mind, which is now almost a void."[42] But as the *Education* demonstrates, the only lesson he learned was that human intelligence was not capable of that kind of education or legislation.

In Pascal, Henry Adams found a thinker who had a much more profound sense of the limits of human intelligence than did Rousseau. Pascal was a ray of hope in an age of dogmatic skepticism. Not long after publishing the *History*, Adams wrote in despair, "if only I still knew a God to pray to."[43] Despite his efforts, Adams never managed to find such a God. Henry James joked with him in 1914, "You see I still, in the presence of life (or what you deny to be such) have reactions—as many as possible."[44] Arational stimulus-response and cause-effect were all that Adams's reason found in his godless universe. If there is no God, what else can exist, he reasoned. One sees this conclusion in the discussion of Pascal in *Mont Saint Michel and Chartres*, which Adams completed in 1905. There, Adams dwelled upon the wager. Amid the philosophy of his age, "Pascal wearily replied that it was not God he doubted, but logic."[45] In Pascal, Adams found, "the French language rose, perhaps for the last time, to the grand style of the twelfth century. . . . It belongs; to a century of faith and simplicity; not to the mathematical certainties of Descartes and Leibniz and Newton." Pascal "forced himself to disbelieve in himself rather than admit a doubt of God."[46] Adams saw in Pascal someone who realized that even the most reasonable man would be lost without turning to faith.

Henry Adams knew that John Adams, like Pascal, bristled at the modern thinkers who denied that reason only gained traction when grounded upon faith. The family patriarch reflected this belief in his letter to Jefferson on Christmas day, 1813. "Philosophy which is the result of Reason, is the first, the original Revelation of The Creator to his Creature, Man."[47] For John Adams, reason was not the gift of nature, but of God. As he wrote Jefferson elsewhere, "I hold there can be no philosophy without religion."[48] In other words, reason discerned its own limits, demonstrating the point at which it was helpless; one had to turn to a higher standard to discern the path of right conduct. John Adams wrote to his son John Quincy in 1816 that "Mosquitos are not competent to dogmatize. . . . Philosophy and theology must submit to the Decalogue and the Sermon on the Mount, and trust the Ruler with his skies."[49]

The reasoned submission to the most basic ethical teachings of the Bible was at the heart of John Adams's moral calculus, and hence at the heart of his politics. John Adams's enlightened Puritanism had a great deal in common with Pascal's mystical Jansenism, as the student of both men knew. Both John Adams and Pascal believed that many Enlightenment thinkers, or their seventeenth-century precursors, placed excessive faith in reason. Neither man thought naked reason could provide ethical guidance. As Pascal wrote, "Man without faith can know neither true good nor justice."[50] The New England republican and the French mathematician both rejected the strain of modern thought that culminated with Jefferson or perhaps with Jeffersonianism. Ernst Cassirer, the great intellectual historian of the Enlightenment, has noted that "Pascal had come to the conclusion which he never tired of stressing, that philosophy as such, that reason left to its own resources and deprived of the support of revelation, must necessarily end in skepticism."[51] In other words, for the Enlightenment project to succeed, at least as it was understood by most of the *philosophes*, it had to get past Pascal's challenge to Descartes. Hence, Cassirer writes, "French philosophy of the Enlightenment recurs to Pascal's Thoughts again and again as if it were impelled from within, and that it repeatedly tests its critical strength on this work."[52]

Henry Adams learned from his ancestor's critique of the dominant strain of Enlightenment thought, and he used it to analyze Jefferson's brand of republicanism. In the *History*, Adams silently quotes his great-grandfather for support. Early in the work, Adams points to the materialism of the Jeffersonian American project: "under our democratic stimulants . . . every man is potentially an athlete in body and an Aristotle in mind."[53] Such improvement was good, but, Adams wonders, was it good in the highest sense? "To this doctrine the New Englander replied, 'what will you do for moral progress?'" Democracy had no ready answer; it had neither religion nor higher law by which to judge moral progress. That was the crucible upon which the republic broke. In such a republic, law, in its true sense, could not exist. Rather than fail to seek moral progress, and, what was worse, to forget what moral progress was, "give us rather the worst despotism of Europe," New England says, "there our souls at least may have a chance of salvation!"[54] Adams here alludes to the "Discourses on Davila," John Adams's 1790 response to the French Revolution:

> Is there a possibility that the government of nations may fall into the hands of men who teach the most disconsolate of all creeds, that men are but fireflies, and that this *all* is without a father? Is this the way to make man, as man, an object of respect? Or is it to make murder itself as indifferent as shooting a plover. . . . [Rather than that] *give us again the gods of the Greeks; give us again the more intelligible as well as more comfortable systems of Athanasius and Calvin; nay, give us again our popes and hierarchies, Benedictines and Jesuits, with all their superstition and fanaticism, impostures and tyranny.*[55]

John Adams emphasized his disagreement with the atheist and materialist strand of modern political thought most clearly in a letter he wrote shortly after losing the presidency:

> We in this age are more unfortunate in one respect than the ancient gentiles. Among them the philosophers were divided into numerous sects—the followers of Socrates of Plato of Pythagoras & of Zeno as well as of Epicurus. All the former had a mixture of good morals, manly virtues & true opinions among their errors & all of them served to counter & counteract the poisonous pestilential & most fatal doctrine of Epicurus. . . . But our modern philosophers are all the low groveling disciples of Epicurus.[56]

If his great-grandson did not actually know that letter, he certainly knew and shared the spirit that motivated it. Traditionally, Epicureans were materialists and atheists. John Adams believed that, regardless of what they actually said, or perhaps even believed, the vast majority of modern thinkers were in fact disciples of Epicurus—materialists in fact and practice, if not in profession.[57] Henry Adams shared with Pascal and his own great-grandfather an aversion to that school of thought, however tempted to believe its truth he might be. That destined him to remain in the intellectual and moral, and perhaps even theological and political, quandary from which John Adams had escaped.

In other words, Henry Adams regarded his great-grandfather as a great man not only for his political accomplishments but also for building a reasoned foundation that did not degenerate into materialism and atheism.[58] Paradoxically, then, the younger Adams's retreat into the medieval world was an act of *loyalty* to John Adams. John Adams had understood what most of the modern thinkers had been up to, and he disagreed with much of their philosophy profoundly, but he agreed with their desire to tame religious fanaticism. For that reason, he sought to work with them, even as he tried to curb their excesses. As he wrote Jefferson,

> Checks and balances, Jefferson, however much you and your party may have ridiculed them, are our only security, for the progress of the mind, as well as the security of the body. Every species of these Christians would persecute Deists, as soon as either Sect would persecute another, if it had unchecked and unbalanced power. Nay, the Deists would persecute Christians, and Atheists would persecute Deists, with as unrelenting cruelty, as any Christians would persecute them or one another.[59]

From John Adams's perspective, Jefferson and his fellow modern Epicureans were no less religious fanatics than were the Christians they excoriated. Like the Christians, the *philosophes* dogmatized, presuming to know more than men could know. It was a classic case of hubris and self-deception disguised as philanthropy.[60]

Recognizing this tendency in his teammates in the fight for true religious liberty, John Adams had hoped that by a combination of writings in political science and actions in politics, he could help more people to understand the limits of human reason. Adams placed considerable hopes on America's constitutional architecture. As he wrote at the conclusion of the *Defence*, "the best republics will be virtuous, and have been so; but we may hazard a conjecture, that the virtues have been the effect of the well ordered constitution, rather than the cause. And, perhaps, it would be impossible to prove that a republic cannot exist even among highwaymen, by setting one rogue to watch another; and the knaves themselves may in time be made honest men by the struggle."[61] Though possible in theory, it was no easy task to get rogues to watch over each other. Constitutional architecture needed two supports: statesmanship and mores. The republic needed statesmen who knew how to lead and adapt the regime to changing circumstances, and it needed a certain character in the people.

Henry Adams found that America lacked such statesmen in his own day. Part of the problem was that the nation's mores had changed so greatly since the founding of the republic. Contemporary democracy had little room for republicanism. People living in the American democracy enjoyed a certain degree of liberty, a far greater degree than had most regimes in most periods of history. Yet the American democracy lacked the high sense of purpose that had built the old republic. John Adams's fondest hope had not come to fruition. The vast majority of Americans, like the vast majority of human beings through the ages, continued to revere various false gods, spiritual and material.

John Adams's hope, which he himself admitted faced long odds, was that large numbers of people could be moved to a firmer foundation of both reason and faith, but that had not happened. Both John and Henry Adams agreed that the American Revolutionary project had been the culmination of centuries of development that had taken philosophy out of the Academy and brought it emphatically into the political world. In practice, Henry found, the project could not function on any other foundation than upon an expanded faith in reason that turned into the quest for a universal state or anti-state. The project could only become popular enough to work when the otherworldly Christian hope was brought down from the heavens and focused instead on creating a worldly utopia. Henry Adams made this conclusion clear in the *History*. The founders had been "political philanthropists," deploying reason to overcome war and tyranny.[62] As Adams showed in the *History*, however, Jefferson's grand ambition failed. Jefferson was an aristocratic republican who spoke like a democrat. He wanted to use the rhetoric of democracy and of the truths men "hold" to be self-evident to manage the American regime. In practice, however, the people took over for themselves. When Jefferson took office, "the reign of politics showed no sign of ending," yet it was.[63] In practice, as Tocqueville found, American society moved according to the desires of the people, without consulting the prudent direction of statesmen. An American politician served the people not by cultivating what was best in them, but rather by helping them fulfil the common wants of men. Epicureanism was the only public philosophy available to an American statesman.[64]

Given the options, Henry Adams concluded that the only way to sustain his ancestor's moral priorities was to disengage from politics. John Adams had hoped that the active political life in the American republic would be a moral life. "I would define liberty as the power to do as we would be done by," he wrote. "The definition of liberty to be the power of doing whatever the laws permit, meaning the civil laws, does not appear to me to be satisfactory."[65] In a good regime, the laws were secure, but they were also of a character that disposed men to right conduct. Henry Adams found that laws of that character could not be sustained over the long term—degradation was inevitable. Given that reality, an Adams could serve, and indeed should, but he should do so only informally and on his own terms. It was his task to advise, to teach, and to write, but not to hold office. Whatever he did, he would do from behind a veil. For that reason, he ceased to publish for the public. As he worked on his *History*, Adams still had some faith in mass enlightenment. "I am writing for a continent of a hundred million people fifty years hence," he wrote.[66] By the time he published *Mount Saint Michel and Chartres* privately in 1904, he contented himself with a select readership.[67]

By retreating intellectually to the medieval world, Adams escaped to a place and time in which many more people understood that retreat from politics than they did in his own. Reason still had a place, even though it denied that reason could remake the world. Moreover, Adams studied the era in an attempt to discover where the wrong turn had happened. Perhaps in the past he could discover a new path forward. Unfortunately, he only found a partial answer. Adams thought the wrong turn occurred decisively with Aquinas's effort to achieve a Summa, as *Mont Saint Michel and Chartres* made clear. "To students of architecture," Adams wrote, "the quality that rouses most surprise in Thomism is its astonishingly scientific method. The Franciscans and the Jesuits call it Pantheism, but science too is Pantheism, or has till very recently been wholly Pantheistic."[68] He made the point more clearly in his marginal notes on his books in medieval philosophy. In Charles Jourdain's *Philosophie de St. Thomas d'Aquin*, he wrote beneath the line (which he underlined) "selon saint Thomas, l'élément générateur l'individualité": "Is not this materialism? . . . In fine, is scholastics, a form of matter?"[69] In the middle of two pages of finely written comments that he inserted at the end of B. Harreau's *De la Philosophie Scholastique*, he wrote, "Is not this the doctrine of Spinoza."[70] In other words, Aquinas's great synthesis paved the road for the victory of the Epicureanism that John Adams loathed and to which Henry Adams wished he could find an alternative.

As he read and reflected upon the past, Adams found one possible alternative, aestheticism. Pascal had opened this door with both his strong attack on reason and his mystical, semimonastic practice. We can see this idea most clearly in Adams's discussion of the Virgin in *Mont Saint Michel and Chartres*. Medieval Christian devotion to the Virgin showed the joy that men could find in devotion to irrationalities. They redeemed life from boredom and diverted man from sensing his own irredeemable weakness. Furthermore, the Virgin was not irrational in the sense that reason simply could not say anything about her. John Adams held that reason had discernable limits and that men needed to embrace certain beliefs that were suprarational—not in contradiction of reason but beyond it—in order to function. Reason could never decide whether it was more reasonable to think that the universe had a creator or that it was self-existing. Pascal had said much the same thing. The Virgin exceeded these reasonable limits; she was irrational in the anarchic sense, reveling in "arbitrary acts of mercy."[71] Adams pointed out that "our age calls it false taste, and no doubt our age is right;—every age is right by its own standards as long as its standards amuse it."[72] That was what drew Adams to the cult of the Virgin: it was fun. Throughout his tour of the medieval world, Adams dwelled upon the joy of the Gothic, taking to task those who thought it dour. It was a great diversion, and diversion was man's only salvation from confronting the utter pointlessness of his existence. In his *Pensées*, Pascal argued that a great source of human activity was man's reluctance of man to confront his wretchedness without God. "What people want," Pascal wrote, "is not the easy peaceful life that allows us to think of our unhappy condition, . . . but the agitation that takes our mind off it and diverts us."[73] Pascal had an out; he believed that man could find joy, even in stillness, with God. Adams lacked that option. Hence he turned to aesthetics for amusement.

However drawn to aestheticism Adams was, he never quite trusted raw aesthetics, any more than he trusted naked reason. Interestingly, Adams thought through the problem partly by recurring to his ancestors. Aesthetics was a sentimental attachment, and Adams never trusted sentiment unassisted by reason. Commenting on Brooks's characterization of their grandfather, Henry noted, "You say that J.Q.A.'s *double* was not, as I thought, a Puritan with the usual puritanic self-confidence, but a sentimentalist. . . . I am the more inclined to admit the truth of this theory because I have always felt in myself the sentimental weakness, and have always avoided responsibility in consequence. The likelihood is great that I inherited some share of the old man's nature because I loathe it so heartily."[74] Henry Adams did not trust the sentimental and romantic streak he shared with his grandfather. That element of John Quincy Adams's character had, as his grandson Henry read it, led the sixth president to place too much faith in his powers.[75] He thought he could legislate in the highest sense, transforming the world with his power of will. He was mistaken. In fact, his belief in his own powers was a form of escapism, blocking his own quest for self-knowledge and for knowledge of the world around him. It fed his vices, his selfishness, and his ill temper, turning him into the "brute" that his grandson denounced. Henry may have turned to his great-grandfather and Pascal for support here. Like John Adams's puritan republicanism, Pascal's Jansenism was emphatically antischolastic; both men found the idea that the tension between reason and faith could be overcome not just incorrect but dangerous. Both tried to balance the two. They embraced the terrain between reason and faith; it was the stuff of life. These two thinkers, with whom Adams readily identified in the early 1900s, pulled him away from pure sentiment: blind devotion to art was by its very nature divorced from any sense of justice, and so was divorced from that which was highest in the Adams legacy.

Adams's distrust of sentiment and of play as an end in itself came to a head in his discussion of Jews in *Mont Saint Michel and Chartres*. Of the Virgin, Adams noted, along with her mercy, "she had many of the failings and prejudices of her humanity. In spite of her own origin, she disliked Jews, and rarely neglected a chance to maltreat them."[76] However amusing was the worship of the Virgin, Adams also realized that it was not adequate because it was not just. His reaction against Mary's injustice led him back to his ancestors: "Mary's treatment of respectable and law-abiding people who had no favors to ask, and were reasonably confident of getting to heaven by the regular judgment, without expense, rankled so deeply that three hundred years later the puritan reformers were not satisfied with abolishing her, but sought to abolish the women altogether as the cause of all evil in heaven and on earth. The puritans abandoned the New Testament and the Virgin in order to go back to the beginning."[77]

When Adams mentioned the Puritans abandoning the New Testament and going "back to the beginning," he probably had John Adams in mind as well. John Adams's religion had more to do with law than belief and sentiment. Richard B. Morris has pointed out that Adams "captured much of the Hebraic spirit that animated the founding Puritans. . . . Adams would later take up the cudgels against Voltaire for his scurrilous attacks upon the Jews."[78] If or when he read his great-grandfather's denunciation of Epicureanism, Henry Adams would have noticed that John Adams spoke of "the ancient gentiles." The ancient Jews had superior morals to even the Stoics and the Academics. In a striking passage, John Adams declared:

> [France and England are] the two nations, to whom mankind are under more obligations for the progress of science and civilization than to any others, except the Hebrews. . . . I excepted

> the Hebrews, for in spite of Bolingbroke and Voltaire, I will insist that the Hebrews have done more to civilize men than any other nation. If I were an atheist, and believed in blind eternal fate, I should still believe that fate had ordained the Jews to be the most essential instrument for civilizing the nations. If I were an atheist of the other sect, who believed or pretend to believe that all is ordered by chance, I should believe that chance had ordered the Jews to preserve and to propagate to all mankind the doctrine of a supreme intelligent, wise, almighty sovereign of the universe, which I believe to be the great essential principle of all morality, and consequently of all civilization.[79]

Elsewhere, he wrote a friend, "I believe you will agree with me that it is not worth our while to exchange the Cosmogony of Moses for any other that has appeared ancient or modern."[80] As a firm Unitarian, John Adams believed that Jesus was a great man but he was not God, and John Adams did not dwell upon Jesus in his writings. He dwelled instead upon Moses as the great lawgiver. John Adams held that love was not the solution to the world's problems; it was the source of many of them. The desire to be loved, he thought, was the principle cause of war, murder, and strife in human life. His great-grandson reached a similar conclusion. He found that the spirit of love, which was tied to the spirit of the Virgin, was dialectically tied to hate in the human heart. Hence the Virgin hated her own people because they refused to worship her lovingly. She may have been a god to medieval man, but she was not God. "Whatever the heretic or mystic tried to persuade himself, God could not be Love. God was Justice, Order, Unity, Perfection; he could not be human and imperfect, nor could the Son or the Holy Ghost be other than the Father."[81]

By his own admission, Adams's alienation from America was related to his respect for the Hebraic elements of John Adams's politics. As J. C. Levenson has noted, Adams saw that he shared something with the Jews. At times, that could take an ugly turn. From Warsaw in 1901, he wrote, "The Jews and I are the only curious antiquities in it." This identification had a self-hating character to it. Adams continued, "My only merit as a curio is antiquity, but the Jew is also a curiosity. He makes me creep."[82] Yet Adams also found something that was at least symbolically Judaic in the Adams project. He made that quite clear in the second paragraph of his *Education*:

> Had he been born in Jerusalem under the shadow of the Temple and circumcised in the Synagogue by his uncle the high priest, under the name of Israel Cohen, he would scarcely have been more distinctly branded, and not much more handicapped in the races of the coming century.[83]

The reference to the ancient Temple in Jerusalem was Adams's way of saying that the American republic no longer had an official place for an Adams and what the Adams family stood for. The God of justice, order, unity, and law had been pushed aside, at least rhetorically.

John Adams's politics, which Henry regarded as the only moral foundation for an American politician to take, no longer functioned in Henry Adams's America. Henry Adams failed by his own standard because he never managed to educate himself so as to make himself the useful citizen that he had hoped to be. That he confessed in the end to an ignorance of which he was almost certain was small consolation.[84] He "needed to know" something, anything, in order to do his duty as an Adams. In the end, he found that the only truth he learned was one that he could share with but few, and teach to still fewer. Finding all that a moral man could do was be honest, pay his debts, avoid hurting others as much as possible, and try to help others when he could, Adams gave up on the active life. Such old truths hardly made for a successful political program in the twentieth century. When he saw he could help the Cubans and his friend Hay, he did so, but he did not go out of his way to find causes to support. When Hay suggested that Adams become American minister to Great Britain in 1898, Adams turned it down. Though it would have continued the family line of service, he wanted no such public role.[85]

In the end, Adams linked his failure to live up to his ancestor's standard to a failure of knowledge. An engaged political life would have required a more thorough knowledge of political means and ends than man could attain. Even among the brightest and best trained, man's capacities for reason and virtue were simply too limited to lead or to "legislate" for his fellow men. An active political life demanded moral compromises that simply were not justifiable. That was why, according to the *Education*, holding office broke his friend Hay, despite his achievements.[86] In his last surviving letter, Adams tried to make this the final lesson for his students: "The function of continuing to sit on the stile and of practicing that genial smile is, after all, a branch and even a meritorious branch of high art. I recommend it now to all who approach me and I judge from their expression that it bores them, as much as it always bored me."[87] At the end of a lifetime seeking to know what a good man should do with his life, he concluded that the best a man could do was to help his fellow men through the world with good humor, easing their burdens as best he could. A good man did his duties as a father, son, brother, neighbor, and citizen, negotiating between his obligations to himself and to others. The last great Adams met his maker, laughing with his great-grandfather at the grand folly of human ambition.

NOTES

1. Henry Adams to Brooks Adams, Feb. 18, 1909, Adams Family Papers, Massachusetts Historical Society. This is Henry's lengthy critique of his brother's manuscript biography of John Quincy Adams (Brooks Adams, "John Quincy Adams" [typescript], Massachusetts Historical Society). The editors of the *Letters of Henry Adams* printed the covering letter Adams sent with the critique, but the 82 pages of direct commentary remain unpublished. For the purpose of clarity, I will note the page in HA's comments from which I am quoting and the page of BA's manuscript upon which HA is commenting: HA to BA, Commentary, p. 67, ref. to p. 289 of "JQA."

   Earlier in his comments, Henry criticized his brother's effort to play up the importance of the Quincy bloodline. Henry reminded his brother John Adams's mother, Susanna Boylston, came from a prominent family: "I take it that the Boylston marriage was, next to the Quincy, the most aristocratic claim the Adamses ever had to rank. Also, from them I imagine John inherited his abilities. Why not insert a sketch of the Boylstons?" HA to BA, Commentary, p. 1, ref. to p. 5 of "JQA." For another example of Brooks emphasizing the Quincy line, see pp. 16–17. Brooks says that "In temperament . . . John Adams remained through his life a New England farmer." "John Quincy Adams" (typescript), 17. By contrast, he notes that "Abigail Adams, on the contrary, inherited from a long line of ancestors that temperament which has stamped its imprint on the religion and literature of New England from the days of Winthrop to those of Emerson. A temperament at once practical and emotional, reserved but intensely affectionate, and capable of self-devotion which shrinks not from the sacrifice of life itself." "John Quincy Adams" (typescript), 18. Writing to his brother Charles in 1812, HA gave an amusing commentary upon his brother's obsession with breeding: "my own theory for Boylston influence is that you and I have the Boylston strain three times repeated. John Adams had it but once. Which accounts for you and us others being three times as damned a fool as John Adams—which seems hard." HA to Charles Francis Adams, Jr., Dec. 21, 1912, in *The Letters of Henry Adams*, ed. J. C. Levenson et al. (Cambridge, Mass., 1982–1988), 6:574. In addition to John Adams's mother, the Boylston "strain" came to Henry and his brothers from Abigail Adams (John Adams's wife) and Abigail Brooks Adams (their own mother). On Brooks Adams, see Arthur Berignause, *Brooks Adams* (New York, 1955).
2. Earl Harbert, *The Force So Much Closer Home: Henry Adams and the Adams Family* (New York, 1977).
3. Donald Hall, "Henry Adams' *History*," *Sewanee Review* 95(1987):523.
4. HA to Justin Winsor, Nov. 25, 1880, in *Letters*, 2:412.
5. HA to Winsor, Nov. 25, 1880, in *Letters*, 2:412.
6. HA to Brooks Adams, Dec. 27, 1895, in *Letters*, 4:351.

7. HA to Mabel Hooper, Jan. 28, 1896, in *Letters*, 4:364.
8. HA to John Hay, Sept. 3, 1882, in *Letters*, 2:468.
9. Page Smith points this out in *John Adams* (Garden City, N.Y., 1962). See, for example, 2:702. Smith may use a phrase like the above somewhere, but the writer has been unable to locate it.
10. HA to John Franklin Jameson, Feb. 2, 1907, in *Letters*, 6:45. The editors note the reference: "In some of my jocular moments I have compared myself to an animal I have seen take hold of the end of a cord with his teeth and be drawn slowly up by pullies, through a storm of squibs, crackers, and rockets, . . . and never let go, till his four feet were safely landed on the floor."
11. John Adams praised Erasmus in his letter to Thomas Jefferson, Dec. 3, 1813, in *Adams-Jefferson Letters*, ed. Lester J. Cappon (Chapel Hill, 1959), 403 (cited hereafter as *AJL*).
12. HA to Charles Francis Adams, Jr., Oct. 10, 1910, in *Letters*, 6:376.
13. When reading Brooks's biography of John Quincy Adams, Henry came across the passage "on turning over the pages of any family record of a hundred years ago, it is astonishing to find how little really steady good health the women and children enjoyed," on p. 172. He responded, "My dear Brooks, you know better than I do that you can *not*, and really *should* not, in cold blood, write, 'on turning over . . . it is astonishing.' Any one [turning over or not turning over your phrase] is or will be astonished." HA to BA, Commentary, p. 31. (The bracketed phrase belongs to HA.) In all likelihood, Henry was recycling John Adams's comment in *Novanglus*, "The man who is capable of writing, in cold blood, that our interest lies in an absolute subjection to parliament. . . ." *Papers of John Adams*, ed. Robert J. Taylor et al. (Cambridge, Mass., 1977–), 2:335.
14. John Adams wrote that the essence of morality was "to be just and good." John Adams to Thomas Jefferson, Dec. 12, 1816, in *AJL*, 499.
15. John Adams, *Defence of the Constitutions of Government of the United States of America* (cited hereafter as *Defence*), in *Works of John Adams*, ed. Charles Francis Adams (Boston, 1851–1856), 4:406.
16. Adams, *Defence*, 4:557.
17. Henry Adams, "Civil-Service Reform," *North American Review* 109(1869):443. The passage quoted from the "Massachusetts Constitution of 1780" can be found in Adams, *Works*, 4:227.
18. HA, "Civil Service Reform," 443. He is quoting the text of the Massachusetts Constitution, which the people of the state had ratified in 1780. According to Charles Francis Adams, John Adams's draft was slightly different. Before submitting the constitution to the people, the convention combined two of Adams's statements: "The judicial department of the state ought to be separate from, and independent of, the legislative and executive" and "In the government of the Commonwealth of Massachusetts, the legislative, executive, and judicial power shall be placed in separate departments, to the end that it might be a government of laws, and not of men." Adams, *Works*, 4:230. The italics, significantly, are Henry Adams's. "Government of laws, not of men" was John Adams's definition of a "republic." See John Adams, "Thoughts on Government," *Works*, 4:193–200.
19. HA, "Civil Service Reform," 449.
20. HA quotes from volume 1 of John Adams's *Defence*, 4:290. Charles Vandersee noted this in his dissertation, "The Political Attitudes of Henry Adams" (Ph.D. diss., University of California—Los Angles, 1964), 55.
21. HA, "Civil Service Reform," 443.
22. Henry Adams, "The Session," *NAR* 111(1870):29–30.
23. Henry Adams, *The Education of Henry Adams* (Boston, 1961), 335.

24. Peter Shaw, "The Success of Henry Adams," *Yale Review* 59, no. 3 (1969):71–78.
25. HA, *Education*, 503.
26. HA to John Hay, Nov. 2, 1901, in *Letters*, 5:302–303.
27. HA to Elizabeth Cameron, Mar. 1–3, 1916, in *Letters*, 6:724.
28. HA to Henry Cabot Lodge, Feb. 1, 1878, in *Letters*, 2:333.
29. HA to Elizabeth Cameron, Mar. 3, 1901, in *Letters*, 5:212. This is exactly 15 years to the day before Adams's 1916 letter reflecting on "how John Adams felt" as he looked across the square into the White House.
30. By highlighting himself as John Adams's only surviving political heir, Henry excluded his brothers. Hence he was not making a comment about Jefferson having had no sons.
31. John Adams, "Dissertation on the Canon and Feudal Law," in *Papers of John Adams*, 1:113.
32. "The gothic is singular in this; one seems easily at home in the Renaissance; one is not too strange in the Byzantine; as for the Roman, it is ourselves; and we could walk blindfolded though every chink and cranny of the Greek mind; all these styles seem modern when we come close to them; but the gothic gets away." Henry Adams, *Mont Saint Michel and Chartres* (New York, 1986), 87 (cited hereafter as *MSMC*).
33. HA to Charles Francis Adams, Jr., May 1, 1863, in *Letters*, 1:350.
34. HA to Elizabeth Cameron, May 13, 1905, in *Letters*, 5:660. At the end of his life, John Adams kept Pascal's work among the books on his bedstand. David McCullough, *John Adams* (New York, 2001), 636.
35. Alexis de Tocqueville, *Democracy in America*, ed. J. P. Mayer, trans. George Lawrence (New York, 1969), 12. Tocqueville singled out Massachusetts's government for praise on p. 249, n. 2.
36. Tocqueville wrote Louis de Kergolay on Nov. 12, 1836, that "There are three men with whom I live a little every day; they are Pascal, Montesquieu, and Rousseau." Quoted in the introduction to *Democracy in America*, ed. and trans. Harvey Mansfield and Delba Winthrop (Chicago, 2000), xxx.
37. HA, *Education*, xxiii.
38. Tocqueville, *Democracy in America* (Mayer edition), xiii–xiv.
39. HA, "The Session," 62.
40. Douglass Adair has pointed out that Francis Bacon expressed a similar sentiment, according philosophers an even higher place in the scale of fame and merit than the founders of empire. They bestowed "true character of the Divine presence, as coming without tumult and noise." Douglass Adair, *Fame and the Founding Fathers: Essays by Douglass Adair*, ed. Trevor Colbourn (New York, 1974), 14–17.
41. Adams wrote to Charles Milnes Gaskell, "I hob-nob with the leaders of both parties, and am very contented under my cloak of historian. I am satisfied that literature offers higher prizes than politics, and I am willing to look on at my friends who differ with me on that point of theory." HA to Gaskell, Apr. 14, 1877, in *Letters*, 2:303.
42. HA to Hugh Blair Grigsby, Sept. 1, 1879, in *Letters*, 2:371.
43. HA to Elizabeth Cameron, Nov. 12, 1891, in *Letters*, 3:560.
44. Quoted by Robert Mane, *Henry Adams on the Road to Chartres* (Cambridge, Mass., 1971), 240.
45. HA, *MSMC*, 304.
46. HA, *MSMC*, 304.
47. John Adams to Thomas Jefferson, Dec. 25, 1813, in *AJL*, 412. From that statement Adams continued, "When this Revelation is clear and certain, by Intuition or necessary Induction, no subsequent Revelation supported by Prophecies or Miracles can supercede

it. Philosophy is not only the love of Wisdom, but the Science of the Universe and its Cause. There is, there was and there will be but one Master of Philosophy in the Universe. Portions of it, in different degrees are revealed to Creatures. Philosophy looks with an impartial Eye on all terrestrial religions. I have examined all . . . and the result is that the Bible is the best book in the World. It contains more of my little Philosophy than all the Libraries I have seen."

48. John Adams to Thomas Jefferson, July 15, 1813, in *AJL*, 358.
49. John Adams to John Quincy Adams, Nov. 13, 1816, Adams Papers Microfilm, reel no. 434.
50. Blaise Pascal, *Pensées*, trans. A. J. Krailsheimer (New York, 1966), 74. (*Pensée* 148, according to the order of Pascal's copy.)
51. Ernst Cassirer, *The Philosophy of the Enlightenment*, trans. Fritz Koelln and James Pettigrove (Princeton, 1951), 8.
52. Cassirer, *Philosophy of the Enlightenment*, 144. Interestingly, when John Adams pushed Jefferson on the question of whether man can achieve any certainty with reason alone, Jefferson responded by inverting Descartes, "I feel: therefore I exist." Thomas Jefferson to John Adams, Aug. 15, 1820, in *AJL*, 567.
53. Henry Adams, *The History of the United States during the Administrations of Thomas Jefferson and James Madison*, ed. Earl Harbert (New York, 1986), 1:122.
54. HA, *History*, 1:122.
55. John Adams, "Discourses on Davila," in *Works*, 6:281. Italics in original. Rather than extend the quotation from John Adams, Henry turned to the Gospel for comment: "Even should the new experiment succeed in a worldly sense, what was a man profited if he gained the whole world, and lost his own soul?" *History*, 1:123. See Matthew 16:26.
56. John Adams to John Rogers, Feb. 6, 1801, Adams Papers Microfilm, reel no. 118.
57. Jefferson admitted he was an Epicurean. See Thomas Jefferson to William Short, Oct. 31, 1819, *Jefferson: Writings*, ed. Merrill Peterson (New York, 1984), 1430–1433. "I too am an Epicurian," he wrote.
58. That may be the source of Henry's comment on Karl Marx's *Kapital*: "I never struck a book which taught me so much, and with which I disagreed so radically in conclusion." In Ernest Samuels, *Henry Adams: The Major Phase* (Cambridge, Mass., 1964), 139
59. John Adams to Thomas Jefferson, June 25, 1813, in *AJL*, 334. John Adams wrote Charles Francis Adams in 1816, "my dear boys! You have a vast field of inquiry before you. You all belong to the family of the Socratics. Be cool, be cautious, be reserved in your researches. But be not afraid to read. . . . Let the truth be your object." John Adams to Charles Francis Adams, Aug. 28, 1816, Adams Papers Microfilm, reel no. 433.
60. "Power always sincerely, conscientiously, de tres bon Foi [in very good faith], believes itself right. Power always thinks it has a great soul, and vast views, beyond the comprehension of the weak; and that it is doing God service, when it is violating all his laws." John Adams to Thomas Jefferson, Feb. 2, 1816, in *AJL*, 462.
61. Adams, *Defence*, 6:219.
62. HA, *History*, 1:131.
63. HA, *History*, 1:1020.
64. For more on this idea, see my dissertation, "The Adams Family and the American Experiment" (Ph.D. diss., University of Virginia, 2000), especially chapter 5.
65. John Adams to J. H. Tiffany, Mar. 31, 1819, in *Works*, 10:377.
66. HA to Charles Milnes Gaskell, Feb. 3, 1884, in *Letters*, 2:535.
67. "My idea is that the world outside,—the so-called modern world,—can only pervert and degrade the conceptions of the primitive instinct of art and feeling, and that our only

chance is to accept the limited number of survivors,—the one-in-a-thousand of born artists and poets,—and to intensify the energy of feeling within that radiant center. In other words, I am a creature of our poor old calvinistic, St Augustinian fathers." HA to Albert Cook, Aug. 6, 1810, in *Letters*, 6:357.

68. HA, *MSMC*, 353.
69. Henry Adams, marginalia in Charles Jourdain, *Philosophie de St. Thomas d'Aquin* (Paris, 1858), 1:275, copy in the Henry Adams Library, Massachusetts Historical Society. The underlining begins at "l'élément." The books I have consulted to read HA's marginalia are all in the possession of the Massachusetts Historical Society.
70. HA, notes in B. Harreau, *De la Philosophie Scholastique* (Paris, 1850).
71. HA, *MSMC*, 233.
72. HA, *MSMC*, 233.
73. Pascal, *Pensées*, 68. Pascal devoted an entire section of the thoughts that he organized in what later became the *Pensées* to this theme. In the *Education*, Adams wrote, "For thousands of years in history, he found that Force had been felt as occult attraction—love of God and lust for power in a future life. After 1500, when this attraction began to decline, philosophers fell back on some *vis a tergo*—instinct of danger from behind, like Darwin's survival of the fittest; and one of the greatest minds, between Descartes and Newton—Pascal—saw the master-motor of man in *ennui*, which was also scientific: 'I have often said that all the troubles of man come from his not knowing how to sit still'" (427). See Pascal, *Pensées*, 67.
74. HA to Brooks Adams, Commentary, p. 75, ref. to p. 429 of "JQA." Interestingly, science too was ultimately sentimental: "For himself he knew, that, in spite of all the Englishmen that ever lived, he would be forced to enter supersensual chaos if he meant to find out what became of British science—or indeed of any other science." HA, *Education*, 451.
75. For a discussion of this aspect of John Quincy Adams's career, see my "Adams Family and the American Experiment," especially chapter 3, "The American Ambition of John Quincy Adams."
76. HA, *MSMC*, 250. J. C. Levenson pointed to this passages in his "The Etiology of Israel Adams: The Onset, Waning, and Relevance of Henry Adams's Antisemitism," *New Literary History* 25(1994):593.
77. HA, *MSMC*, 248, 261. A few pages earlier, Adams quoted Gaston Paris condemning the irrationality of the cult of the Virgin: "Our own English ancestors, known as Puritans, held the same opinion, and excluded her from their society four hundred years earlier, for the same reasons which affected M. Gaston Paris. These reasons were just, and showed the respectability of the citizens who held them. In no well-regulated community, under a proper system of police, could the Virgin feel at home" (244).
78. Richard Morris, *Seven Who Shaped Our Destiny: The Founding Fathers as Revolutionaries* (New York, 1973), 80.
79. John Adams, *Works*, 9:609. Interestingly, Voltaire was among the *philosophes* who criticized Pascal the most and among those who criticized Jews the most. Jefferson took up the same strain of "enlightened" thought. When Jefferson denounced Judaism with Voltaire's fervor, John Adams tried to change his opinion. See Richard Samuelson, "What Adams Saw over Jefferson's Wall," *Commentary* 104, no. 2 (1997):52–54.
80. John Adams to Benjamin Waterhouse, Feb. 5, 1818, in *Statesman and Friend: Correspondence of John Adams with Benjamin Waterhouse*, ed. Worthington C. Ford (Boston, 1927), 140. Interestingly, in his conversion experience Pascal had found the "'God of Abraham, God of Isaac, God of Jacob' not of philosophers and scholars." *Pensées*, 309.
81. HA, *MSMC*, 248.

82. HA to Elizabeth Cameron, Aug. 10–18, 1901, in *Letters*, 5:276. Levenson quotes this passage in "The Etiology of Israel Adams," 592. The timing of the rise of Henry Adams's anti-Jewish rhetoric is itself suggestive. Levenson shows that Adams was sympathetic to the Jews' plight up to around 1890. If Adams deserted the Adamsian republican project just as he finished the *History*, and if he interpreted that project as I suggest, then the anti-Judaism may somehow have been related to Adams's frustration with his chosen life's work.
83. HA, *Education*, 3.
84. He wrote his brother Charles, "Yes! I'm a dam fool! I never denied it. The older I grow, the more conscious I become of it." HA to Charles Francis Adams, Jr., Nov. 8, 1910, in *Letters*, 6:382. This belief echoed John Adams: "Oh delightful Ignorance! When I arrive at a certainty that I am Ignorant, and that I always must be ignorant, while I live I am happy." John Adams to Thomas Jefferson, May 12, 1820, in *AJL*, 565.
85. Samuels, *The Major Phase*, 192.
86. HA, *Education*, 502–505.
87. HA to William Roscoe Thayer, Mar. 15, 1918, in *Letters*, 6:792. This is the last extant letter according to the editors of his letters. It is possible that he wrote others after this one.

Henry Adams & Henry Cabot Lodge—Teacher & Student

A Complicated Interaction

ORMOND SEAVEY

THE READER OF *The Education of Henry Adams* might conclude that Henry Adams's destiny as a historian of the United States was determined in 1850 when his father Charles Francis Adams enlisted his assistance in proofreading the volumes of John Adams's *Works* that the father was editing.[1] But in fact the young Adams would shift his directions several times before settling in to compose the *History of the United States during the Administrations of Thomas Jefferson and James Madison* in 1879. He had in effect been in the foreign service during the Civil War, followed by a period in Washington as a lobbyist and political operator from 1868 to 1870. The record of his own letters and his published work during that Washington interlude and his father's reactions in his journal indicate that he was eager to work in Washington as an independent lobbyist for various causes. This was not the more straightforward political work of serving in public office and winning elections that earlier Adams family members had done. In a letter late in 1869 to his good friend Charles Milnes Gaskell, he wrote, "I am actually winding myself up in a coil of political intrigue and getting myself the reputation of a regular conspirator."[2] Adams's glee at engaging in conspiracy represents a departure from the lugubrious unrelenting long-term campaigning John Adams or John Quincy Adams had undertaken for political causes important to them.

His father viewed the 1868 move to Washington in a distinctly dubious light and two years later encouraged him to return to Massachusetts to join the Harvard faculty as a teacher of medieval history. Henry Adams's response to President Eliot that he knew nothing about medieval history might appear to be merely Brahmin self-deprecation except that it appears to have been largely true at the point when Adams said it. But one of the incentives for Adams to leave Washington was the opportunity, coupled with the assistant professorship of history, to edit the *North American Review*, which had long been virtually an adjunct publication of Harvard College. Adams had ambitions of converting this venerable but rather creaky review into the mouthpiece for the Independent position.[3]

Regardless of his lack of formal preparation to teach medieval history, Adams quickly worked up the subject so well that a large class of Harvard seniors enrolled in his course. Ever a quick study and by then able to read German historiography without strain, he managed to keep himself just ahead of his students. No doubt the most noteworthy member of that class was Henry Cabot Lodge. Lodge's academic record had been less than sterling before this point, but he excelled in medieval history as taught by Professor Adams, though a good performance in one course would not itself erase a generally indifferent college record, and he graduated "not far above the middle of the class."[4]

Lodge's enrollment in Adams's course began a history of interaction between the two extending from 1870 to 1915. After completing Adams's course, Lodge graduated with the class of 1871, married, and set off for a prolonged European honeymoon. His period of leisure seems to have prompted Lodge to wonder what he might do with his life, and he wrote to Adams from Paris to ask whether he had any possible future as a historian. One of the challenges of reconstructing the relations between the two men is that Adams kept none of Lodge's letters, while the dutiful and admiring student preserved all of his teacher's letters. We know that Lodge wrote to Adams from Paris because Adams's response mentions the date of the letter, sent not long after the Lodges had paused in Paris for the birth of their first child.[5] Adams wrote back at length his own assessment of the opportunities available currently in that branch of literature that deals with history:

> The question is whether the historico-literary line is practically worth following; not whether it will amuse or improve you. Can you make it *pay*? either in money, reputation, or any other solid value.
>
> Now if you will think for a moment of the most respectable and respected products of our town of Boston, I think you will see at once that this profession does pay. No one has done

> better and won more in any business or pursuit, than has been acquired by men like Prescott, Motley, Frank Parkman, Bancroft, and so on in historical writing; none of them of extraordinary gifts, or who would have been likely to do very much in the world if they had chosen differently. What they did, can be done by others.
>
> Further, there is a great opening here at this time. Boston is running dry of literary authorities. Anyone who has the ability can enthrone himself here as a species of literary lion with ease, for there is no rival to contest the throne. With it, comes social dignity, European reputation, and a foreign mission to close.[6]

Adams's assessment of the historico-literary scene in antebellum Boston delivers the sort of brusque unsentimental judgment that is characteristic of him. Figures like William Hickling Prescott, John Lothrop Motley, Francis Parkman, and George Bancroft—not to speak of other members of the American intellectual establishment—are mentioned as merely the best that Boston had had to offer before the war. He then enjoins Lodge to read deeply in German historiography, a body of historians led by figures like Leopold von Ranke and Theodor Mommsen but extending very considerably to others whose names represented at the time the most significant historical work being done, the sort of reading to which he himself had been driven by the necessity of preparing his Harvard courses. This first letter to Lodge is avuncular and affectionate; he sees Lodge as a potential protégé.

Indeed the generally received account of the Adams-Lodge relationship has been that Adams was the gracious mentor and friend, Lodge the grateful and dutiful student who spun off into politics. John A. Garraty's 1953 biography of Lodge, which remains the standard treatment, says of Lodge's experience in Adams's undergraduate history course, "he 'took the highest marks' in the course and made of Adams a lifelong friend. Adams on his part saw in Lodge the makings of a first-class historian."[7] Edward Chalfant, in *Better in Darkness: A Biography of Henry Adams: His Second Life, 1862–1891*, has characterized Lodge as Adams's protégé whom Adams destined for the Senate, where he would try to enact in law Adams's political leanings.[8] The reasons for this perception of the Adams-Lodge relationship are readily apparent: the two remained on easy sociable terms for years, often traveling to Europe with each other; after Lodge went to Congress in 1887 he frequented the Adams home on Lafayette Square; at the point when Adams left Harvard for Washington to research the Gallatin *Life and Letters*, the prelude to the great *History*, he left Lodge as his successor on the Harvard history faculty—or perhaps more accurately as one of his successors, together with Ernest Young and Ephraim Emerton.[9]

But the real nature of the relationship between Adams and Lodge is much more complicated. Not long after Lodge returned to Harvard for graduate work, Adams took him on as the assistant editor of the *North American Review*, so the younger man was getting intimate coaching on writing and editing from Adams. Years later, in his partial autobiography *Early Memories*, Lodge wrote of his excitement when Adams asked him to assist with the *North American Review*.[10] Serving as Adams's assistant editor also entailed association with Adams's designs in the early 1870s of using the *North American* as the standard-bearer for a somewhat forgotten political movement constituted by people who called themselves Independents. The Independents were nearly all Republicans in terms of their recent party affiliation, but they found the excesses of the Grant administration repugnant, wished to restrain the hoggish disposition of post-war capitalists like Jim Fisk and Jay Gould, and saw no compelling need to continue the Reconstruction program. For a while Lodge entered the Independent movement with considerable enthusiasm. When Sen. Carl Schurz issued an invitation for prominent Independents to meet in 1876 at a hotel in New York, it was Henry Cabot Lodge who handled the details of organization.

After completing his dissertation on family law among the Anglo-Saxons, Lodge turned to American history for his next large scholarly project. This would be a full-scale biography of his great-grandfather George Cabot. This historical project suggested itself naturally to him through his contacts with the Adamses, including Brooks Adams, who had graduated from Harvard shortly before he did, and Charles Francis Adams, Sr. No family name in the 1870s carried so much distinction in Massachusetts politics—indeed in national politics—as that of Adams. Lodge visited the Adams family compound in Quincy and marveled at the historical resonances. Lodge's own father had been a highly successful merchant, expanding a family fortune already substantial by antebellum Boston standards, but John Ellerton Lodge had not been a public man like the Adamses. However, the name by which Lodge was known by his intimates—Cabot—was enough to remind him that he did have some claim to a distinguished family ancestry. He was the great-grandson of George Cabot, a man whose name, at present and even by 1876, has been largely forgotten. Recognizing the link between family associations and success in Massachusetts politics, Lodge set out to write a *Life and Letters of George Cabot* in order to rescue his great-grandfather's name from oblivion, as he somewhat plaintively expressed it in his preface.[11]

George Cabot presented Lodge with several challenges. First of all, Cabot's native disposition toward concealment of his own political activities probably caused him to destroy the sort of personal materials so readily available among the papers of many colonial and early republican figures. Also, although George Cabot represented Massachusetts in the U.S. Senate in the 1790s, he resigned before completing his six-year term and returned to Brookline, Massachusetts. Between 1795 and 1814, Cabot's real political function was to serve as a senior consultant to figures who, like Alexander Hamilton and Timothy Pickering, were more directly embroiled in the political process. Thus, though Cabot was perhaps the central figure in what might be described as the first political machine in early national Massachusetts, a loose-knit group known as the Essex Junto, his own significance, though genuine, was relatively amorphous. That faction of the Federalist Party was in continual tension with John Adams, who was their senior in age and more moderate. The Essex Junto was strongly in favor of an outright war with France during the Adams administration, in part because of its interest in maintaining close commercial ties with Britain, with which France was already at war. The final problem with lifting Cabot from obscurity was that Cabot's final public service was as the president of the Hartford Convention in late 1814, an episode in Massachusetts and New England history that proved to be not only futile but also rather risibly ill-timed. Despite these biographical difficulties, George Cabot's deeply felt conservatism was a political perspective increasingly congenial to the young Henry Cabot Lodge.

Lodge and Adams's collaboration on the *North American Review* had made it clear to Adams that the two did not view contemporary politics in the same light. Though they shared an interest in civil service reform and both voted for the Democrat Samuel J. Tilden in the 1876 election, they took different political directions beyond that limited area of convergence.

After a few years of teaching medieval history, Henry Adams turned to teaching early American history.[12] By 1876 the political differences between Adams and Lodge were sufficiently clear to Adams that he made President Eliot an unusual offer: "I wish to establish a rival course to my own in United States History. Of the general propriety of creating rival courses in such a subject, I presume there can be no doubt. . . . I propose that Mr Lodge should have a course in U. S. history coterminous with mine. His views being federalist and conservative, have as good a right to expression in the college as mine which tend to democracy and radicalism. The clash of opinions can hardly fail to stimulate inquiry among the students."[13] It should be mentioned that Adams's sense of radicalism borrowed some of its meaning from the English context with which he had become familiar in the 1860s, where Disraeli could be considered both a Radical and a Conservative. By the standards of such Boston radicals as Elizabeth Peabody or Lydia Maria Child, Henry Adams was no radical at all, though in contrast with the Harvard faculty of the 1870s he might well have felt radical.

The Henry Adams of 1876 no longer felt the interest in engaging in the minutiae of contemporary political broils that the Henry Adams of 1870 had felt. Though he and Charles Francis Adams, Jr., had assembled a scathing critique of the Hayes candidacy and published it in the *North American*, Henry Adams's own letters from the same period display indifference to the outcome of the vote. He intended to vote for Tilden but had little expectation that his candidate would be elected.[14] A certain fatalism about election results seems to have been a family trait.[15] Lodge on the other hand spent the 1870s growing increasingly involved in Massachusetts and national politics. One of the important first steps he took toward a political career was the project of writing the *Life and Letters of George Cabot*. At the same time that he was at work on the Cabot book, Henry Adams was taking an interest in the diplomatic history of the first Adams administration. Adams and Lodge at this point shared their findings as they explored the papers of Timothy Pickering, whom John Adams inherited as secretary of state from the Washington administration, unaware that Pickering had his own foreign policy agenda quite independent of the senior Adams's own ideas but closely tied to the schemes of Alexander Hamilton. In a September 4, 1876, letter, Adams thanks Lodge for extracts the younger man had copied from the Pickering papers. The letter is revealing in several ways about the relations between the two. Adams begins with a mention of the galleys of the *Essays on Anglo-Saxon Law*, which would be published the following month. He then thanks Lodge for pointing out what he had found in the Pickering papers:

> I have read all Timothy's diplomatic papers lately. What a man to deal with tête-montés Frenchmen! Washington certainly felt

> the absurd incongruity of this, and Adams still more so. The surly contempt, varied by ingenuity of insult, with which he treated the insanely sensitive Frenchman of that day, is entertaining to see. But I am wholly of my great-grandfather's opinion as to his fitness for his post. There could hardly have been a worse selection for it. . . .[16]
>
> Console yourself about politics. You are indeed the one who has the best right to complain, for you had the most trouble in forming that rope of sand, the independent party. I cannot help laughing to think how, after all our labor and after we had by main force created a party for Schurz to lead, he himself, without a word or a single effort to keep his party together, kicked us over in his haste to jump back to the Republicans. If he had taken the least pains to hold his friends together, I feel sure we could have spoken with effect. I, for one, would have been glad to join in any combined action, whichever way the majority decided. And in that case, Schurz's voice would not now be isolated and shrill.[17]

At this point it is clear that Adams considers Lodge to be a valuable junior colleague, someone with whom he can share his pungent assessments of early national history. Adams also assumes that Lodge shares his detached and somewhat cynical view of the Independent movement and its erstwhile leader Schurz. Adams sees himself and Lodge as safely free of the entanglements of current electoral politics—a freedom Adams finds wholly gratifying.

But in fact Lodge did not share Adams's sentiments. He felt no disdain for Timothy Pickering, and he was acutely aware that his own most prominent public act thus far in his twenty-six years had been his work as the organizer of Schurz's Independent meeting earlier that year in New York, so the shipwreck of the Independent movement had left him awkwardly adrift. Adams's observations to him could hardly have offered any consolation.

One measure of the growing disparity between the views of Adams and Lodge appears in their attitudes toward that Federalist icon Alexander Hamilton. In the July 1876 *North American Review*, Lodge reviewed John Torrey Morse, Jr.'s two-volume *Life of Alexander Hamilton*. No complete biography of Hamilton had yet been written, though many of the details of his life could be readily assembled from published sources. Morse had undertaken this sort of assemblage. Having lately acquired his own credentials as a historian, Lodge is mildly disdainful of Morse's casual scholarship, though the two men were cousins. A typical *North American* review ran just a few pages; Lodge's review essay runs thirty-two pages and considers more material than Morse had dealt with. Lodge's review is a wholly admiring portrait of Hamilton as "Orator, Writer, Soldier, Jurist, Financier," in the words of the Boston monument to Hamilton.[18] The classically educated Lodge indulges in an extended use of the figure of *praeteritio*:

> Mr. Morse has passed lightly over Hamilton's military career, and in doing so has acted wisely. The Revolutionary period is the most picturesque part of our history. Every actor in it is known, and every battle-field familiar. To describe Hamilton's mission to Gates, his conduct at Monmouth, his reception of d'Estaing, is not necessary. Nor need his biographer quote the vigorous yet pathetic description of the flight of Arnold and the execution of André, for this has become classic. Still less is it needful to detail the attack at Yorktown. Americans know well how Hamilton led his countrymen across the abattis and captured in nine minutes one of the British redoubts, whose fellow occupied our French allies half an hour.[19]

Morse's neglect of Hamilton's military career affords Lodge the opportunity to fill out the picture with his own brushwork. The Hamilton who appears in Lodge's review is a starkly flat character, somewhat as if Lodge were writing for an audience of younger age than the readers of the *North American*. Lodge had small taste for the sort of subtlety that would be Adams's preferred domain all his life, and in fact a significant share of Lodge's later writing would be expressly addressed to children. Complexities and complications largely disappear from the Hamilton picture: "To analyze Hamilton's character is the simplest part of such an undertaking. His was not a complex nature, and like many great men, especially those of strongly masculine qualities, the mental lines are clear, direct, and easily followed."[20] Masculine natures are apparently always straightforward. Lodge's objection to Morse's volumes is that Morse is insufficiently critical of Hamilton, but Lodge's own portrait includes only a single major objection, to Hamilton's retaliation against John Adams in the 1800 election. Overall, Lodge sees Hamilton in quite idealized terms. Reading Lodge's essay on its way to press, Henry Adams comments,

> You do not of course expect me to acquiesce entirely in your view of A. H. I can hardly explain the reasons of my own *kind* of aversion to him. That it is inherited is no explanation, for I inherit feelings of a very different sort towards Jefferson, Pickering, Jackson, and the legion of other life-long enemies whom my contentious precursors made. I dislike Hamilton because I always feel the adventurer in him. The very cause of your admiration is the cause of my distrust; he was equally ready to support a system he utterly disbelieved in as one he liked. From the first to the last words he wrote, I read always the same Napoleonic kind of adventuredom, nor do I know any more curious and startling illustration of this than the conclusion of that strange paper explaining his motives for accepting Burr's challenge. I *abhor*, says he, the practice of dueling, but "the ability to be in future useful in those crises of our public affairs which seem likely to happen, would probably be inseparable from a conformity with prejudice in this particular." What would you or I say if our great-grandfathers had left us those words as a deathbed legacy? I think we should not have so high a moral standard as I thank those gentlemen for leaving us. And I confess I think those words alone justify all John Adams's distrust of Hamilton. Future political crises all through Hamilton's life were always in his mind about to make him commander-in-chief, and his first and last written words show the same innate theory of life.[21]

For Henry Adams, Alexander Hamilton must be understood as a text, a text that reveals an irresponsible adventurer. Hamilton's role in the John Adams administration had been to second-guess, subvert, and undercut the president's program. Adams even tries to enlist the memory of George Cabot, certainly no sort of adventurer, against Cabot's longtime party leader. Aware that Lodge appears to be at variance with his own views, Adams's tone is blandishing, hopeful that his student can be led away from the snares of a dubious ideological position. The allusion to their respective great-grandfathers suggests that Adams was aware of Lodge's plan to write about George Cabot. And Lodge's journal for the early part of 1876, even before his Anglo-Saxon dissertation was finished, indicates he had begun collecting material about George Cabot.[22] In March he had talked with

James Hamilton, one of Alexander Hamilton's sons, who had offered a glowing characterization of George Cabot.[23]

The Independent position that Lodge had shared with Adams was becoming increasingly uncomfortable for the younger man. For one thing, as a political phenomenon the Independent movement collapsed in 1876 when most of its Republican adherents fell in line with Hayes. For Adams, positioning himself outside of the existing political parties merely fit into a family past that included John Adams's estrangement from the mainstream Federalists in 1800, John Quincy Adams's vote for Jefferson's embargo in 1807, and Charles Francis Adams's candidacy for vice president in 1848 on the Free Soil ticket. Sure that their political principles were right, the Adamses needed no party allegiances. Lodge was beginning to see that such a stance spelled political helplessness in the post-war era. His reading about Alexander Hamilton provided him with an example of a committed political partisan. George Cabot would serve as another exemplar of unrelenting partisanship. Though the young Lodge seems in some part of his mind to have continued to regard his future as that of a historian and man of letters, his involvement with Henry Adams had introduced him to Massachusetts and national politics, albeit at first as a genteel dabbler.

As one examines the young Lodge, it is clear that if not for his contact with Adams Lodge's path probably would not have culminated in political life. In the 1870s Lodge struggled to define his political and family identity. For several years after his graduation from Harvard College, he seems to have been discovering what his own nature might be. After a January 1876 meeting with Charles Francis and Brooks Adams in which the three men discussed revivifying the *North American Review* or seeking some other mode of publishing their views on a weekly or monthly basis, Lodge noted this lesson from the inconclusive discussion in his journal: "Moral[:] stick to one thing—Be a literary man & not a dabbler in politics & a theater for periodical literature for wielding a journal-power. No work as result of all this."[24] Certainly Lodge would end up thoroughly immersed in politics, but even at this point more commitment to politics than to letters struck him as a mistake. Henry Adams never floundered about wondering what he should be. His own sense of identity was to a considerable extent acquired with his surname and was continually reinforced by family ties. As a political man, Henry Adams was disposed to operate behind the scenes, as he had done in London working for his father or in Washington from 1868 to 1870 lobbying for reform. The Lodge Adams encountered as a student, both as an undergraduate and even later as his assistant editor, graduate student, and fellow political plotter, had yet to develop the self-control necessary to accommodate an ego given every possible ounce of inflation by a considerable fortune and a mother who idolized him. A more critical eye reading the admiring biography of his boyhood friend Bishop William Lawrence or the biographical sketch for the Massachusetts Historical Society by his cousin and longtime collaborator John Torrey Morse, Jr., reveals a young man who might be deemed to have been bumptious and arrogant.[25] For his part, Adams had had since early childhood the sort of self-control Lodge spent his twenties in acquiring. Though Lodge could anticipate a fortune quite substantial by Boston standards, his prospective wealth did not itself distinguish him from a considerable number of young Harvard graduates approximately his own age. While working with Adams, Lodge came to wish for something of the distinction his teacher and mentor enjoyed as a birthright.

Lodge's claim to some share of the distinction Henry Adams enjoyed would be asserted through the biography of George Cabot. The precise point where this emulation began to take the form of a writing project cannot be identified. It is not clear that Henry Adams and Lodge had been aware of the nature of the acrimonious relations between their great-grandfathers when they began to collaborate. Certainly Lodge saw a volume devoted to Cabot as one of the literary responsibilities of descendants of prominent Federalists: he was familiar with John C. Hamilton's biography of his father and Edmund Quincy's life of Josiah Quincy. Charles Francis Adams had performed this service in editing the *Works* of John Adams, and in his Quincy retirement he was editing the mammoth diary of John Quincy Adams, eventually in an edition of twelve volumes. Lodge's own diary records his reading of the latter diary, drawing appropriate lessons from it about diligence.[26]

Henry Adams had the opportunity to observe the development of Lodge's book. It is not a book that treats John Adams kindly. Though Lodge concludes that John Adams's policy of negotiating peace with the French in 1799–1800 was ultimately sound, he characterizes the execution of that policy as blundering, evasive, and weak.[27] Henry Adams did not detect in his student's writing the sort of ironic detachment from its materials that he saw as necessary to the successful historian. To be sure, such detachment is easier to maintain in relation to Anglo-Saxon land law than to one's own family, but Adams expected it nonetheless, as the reader of Adams's *History of the United States* can observe wherever John or

John Quincy Adams appears. So the fault with Lodge's approach was not its negative view of an Adams but its too positive view of Cabot. Lodge's preface acknowledges his indebtedness "to my friend, Professor HENRY ADAMS, for many suggestions and for much valuable aid."[28] Apparently Adams even read the book in manuscript. In a letter to Lodge he warns, "I don't know but what my late marginal notes are becoming offensively personal. If so, rub 'em out."[29] Adams's lapse into Yankee dialect ("I don't know but what ...") reveals his own self-consciousness about his criticisms of the younger man. Earlier in the same letter, Adams twits Lodge about a passage in Latin apparently discussed in a missing letter: "As for the Latin, how was I to know what it meant? A much better translation would be: 'What a shame it would be to regret an Essex Junto head'!"

Shortly after Lodge's book was published in 1877, Adams tossed off a quick note to Lodge in which he mentioned that his review had "gone to Godkin to be published next week. It is ingeniously calculated to make everyone, yourself included, furious with indignation. But I think it will excite interest in the book and sell the edition."[30] The combination of information in these three sentences reflects the conflicted relation Henry Adams had with everything: he had already arranged an early book review with his old friend E. L. Godkin, the editor of the *Nation*; the review was calculated to enrage Lodge; the review would spur sales of a book both men must have realized would be a struggle to sell. The tone of the letter is jovial, as if Adams is going to have a little fun with his student and friend. But in fact Adams's review makes a frontal assault on Lodge, his book, and his ancestor. The review coincided with what might be seen as a career change for Adams. He resigned his faculty position at Harvard and made plans to relocate as an independent scholar in Washington.[31]

The culmination of George Cabot's career was his service as president of the Hartford Convention. Lodge devotes three chapters, totaling 153 pages, to the Hartford Convention. Writing scarcely more than a decade after the end of the Civil War, he frames the discussion of the convention by the assertion that the germ of secession had grown from the heritage of Thomas Jefferson, who "grasped the terrible weapon of States' rights, and sought to coerce the national government by the doctrine of nullification, by threats of secession, and by the imminence of civil war."[32] Lodge adds a footnote to point the lesson, calling the reader's attention to the Kentucky Resolutions of 1798 drafted by Jefferson and mentioning "the fact that Virginia troops were ready to seize in 1801, as they did in 1861, the arsenals of the United States."[33] Rebellion against the national government, Lodge implies, derives from the tradition of Jefferson.

In his review, Adams set out to offer in the *Nation* the appropriate context in which the *Life and Letters of George Cabot* should be seen. He locates it among historical treatments of Federalism written from a spirit of frankly partisan admiration. He compliments Lodge for candor about his bias in the biography. Adams's own summary characterization of George Cabot the man, presumably derived from Lodge's book, is edged with irony:

> George Cabot is now principally remembered as the head of the Essex Junto and the president of the Hartford Convention. Next to Hamilton, and side by side with Rufus King, he was revered in his time as the oracle of Federalism. His public life was of little importance. Natural indolence and dislike of the rough personal collisions of politics led him to resign his seat in the Senate in 1796 after only five years' service, and decline a seat in the Cabinet in 1798, but he was not the less a party leader: his friends came to him for advice, and whenever it was possible, they pushed him into responsible positions in spite of his obstinate resistance.[34]

In other words, George Cabot was not really the equivalent to John Adams that Lodge would have liked him to be. He was for most of his life a private citizen corresponding actively with like-minded figures who were themselves more actively involved in the political arena, unlike the first Adams, who had persisted in political offices until finally defeated by Jefferson in 1800. John Adams and George Cabot presented two alternative models of political engagement, the politician and the advisor to politicians. Henry Adams underlines the limits to Cabot that Lodge had unwittingly revealed:

> He was Federalist to the core. He hated two things with all the vehemence of which his indolent and liberal nature was capable, and these two antipathies were democracy and France. He held the firm conviction that democracy must, in the end, overthrow society and itself, and that from the ruins a conservative government must arise. Like Hamilton and Fisher Ames, he believed that a 'crisis' was inevitable, but the difference between him and his more ardent friends was that while they al-

> ways thought the crisis at hand, he passed his time in convincing them that the fated moment had not yet arrived.[35]

Lodge's biography of Cabot is conspicuously lacking in tension or excitement, but Adams found in it the makings of a suppressed drama. Since the time of John Quincy Adams it had been a fixed belief in the Adams family that the Hartford Convention had convened to discuss or arrange for the possibility of secession from the Union. What Lodge wished to frame as a responsible conservative movement to contain hot-headed young Federalists is framed quite differently in Adams's review, which gives no hint that his reading is a family peculiarity. Referring to the convention in the *Nation*, Adams asserts, "This episode, one of the most dramatic in our history, is as yet little familiar to the public, and indeed the subject has never been one of those on which New England is fond of talking."[36] Adams then proceeds to quote letters between Timothy Pickering and George Cabot in which they discussed the advisability of New England secession. Lodge's effort had been to demonstrate that his ancestor had gone to Hartford with the motive of moderating the extremist impulses of the Massachusetts Federalists who were pushing for secession or some other intransigent gesture that would have been unacceptable to other regions of the country. Adams reads Lodge's text as

> making it an easy task to settle the longstanding controversy in regards to the purposes of that body [the Hartford Convention], and to see why it might be looked upon as a conservative and patriotic measure by Mr. [Harrison Gray] Otis, and by Pickering and his friends [among whom Cabot was a leading figure] as merely a stepping-stone to their long-expected "crisis." How startlingly close the Union was to this "crisis" Mr. Lodge's book proves; and if the collapse of the plot of 1804, in the blood of Hamilton and the flight of Burr, was theatrical, the crash of the conspiracy of 1814, under the news of the peace of Ghent and the battle of New Orleans, was the final and culminating situation in this great historical drama.[37]

For Adams, the Hartford Convention was a conspiracy. He invites the *Nation* reader of 1877 to draw a parallel between the Hartford Convention and the defeated secessionists in what was commonly called in the North the War of the Rebellion. For Adams there was suppressed drama in the final public act of George Cabot's life, and there is offstage an implied hero in this drama: the principal negotiator of the Peace of Ghent, which suddenly collapsed the hidden schemes at Hartford—John Quincy Adams. In New England, the War of 1812 had never been popular, hence the clamor for resistance culminating in the Hartford Convention, but the Peace of Ghent had resolved the war in so advantageous a way that the resistance to the war collapsed at once. Lodge's text, in one of its conspicuous editorial silences, after including a series of letters from Pickering in which he considers the consequences of the imminent and inevitable British capture of New Orleans and the loss of the trans-Appalachian states, concludes the chapters on the Hartford Convention noncommittally with a pathetic bleat from Christopher Gore, a Federalist senator from Massachusetts, mentioning that peace had been concluded.[38] George Cabot engaged in no further political activity in the ensuing years, and the remaining pages of the final chapter are turned over to miscellaneous anecdotage.

It is noteworthy that Henry Adams nowhere voices what we might see as the most significant defect of the *Life and Letters of George Cabot*: Lodge's failure to note that its protagonist was a casualty of political forces that extinguished voices like his before their physical death. Rather, Adams takes Cabot nearly as seriously as Lodge does and is determined to impale the old Federalist on the very shaft Lodge had raised. A more devastating review it would be hard to imagine. Yet there is no indication that Adams's *Nation* review led to any disruption of the cordiality between Lodge and Adams. The two men continued to correspond, and to an extent Adams's departure from Harvard left Lodge as his designated successor in the teaching of American history. The Adamses spent their summers in Beverly, Massachusetts, not far from the Lodge country place at Nahant. It is quite possible that social visits between the two families continued. The harshness of Adams's assault on Lodge's book reveals how little this cordiality meant. Certainly at this point areas of political and ultimately personal difference that the two had personally discussed and exchanged letters about were now in published circulation. It would be a lame explanation to state that the two men had agreed to disagree, because for each the issues were too important for mere mutual toleration. Adams would go on to write an immense and still largely definitive historical treatment of American history between the end of the John Adams administration and the conclusion of the War of 1812, and most of Lodge's historical work concerned this same period. The fuller explanation of how this association of mutual provocation played out over the forty-five years the two knew each other is a much longer story.

Adams was in fact so engaged with the issues Lodge had raised in the *Life and Letters of George Cabot* that he set out at once to publish his family's perspective on the events leading to the Hartford Convention. His own awareness of the Adams family papers, formed first when he assisted his father in the edition of John Adams's *Works*, had informed him of the existence of a very long unpublished letter John Quincy Adams had written in early 1829 in response to a public *Appeal to the Citizens of the United States* dated November 24, 1828, signed by a number of old Federalists and descendants of old Federalists. The second President Adams had recently been defeated in his attempt at reelection and was acutely aware of the number of conservatives who had failed to support his candidacy actively, even in his home region. The *Appeal* had culminated a published exchange originated by opponents of John Quincy Adams who aimed to discredit him based on his willingness in 1807 to collude with Thomas Jefferson. After his old Federalist adversaries had published their last assault on him, John Quincy Adams undertook to answer them definitively, as he felt, but he left his angry letter unpublished in the Adams family archive.

The published dialogue that John Quincy Adams's letter concluded had begun with William Giles of Virginia, a Jackson supporter, who wished to show that Thomas Jefferson, then recently dead, had had reservations about the John Quincy Adams administration. In the last months of 1877, Henry Adams set out to present his grandfather's vindication of himself and his charges against the Federalists of the first decades of the century.

During that year, Adams was also at work on a life and letters of Albert Gallatin, and his research led him to contact the president of the Virginia Historical Society, Hugh Blair Grigsby, to inquire for materials related to Gallatin's time spent in Virginia and also to see about purchasing volumes of the *Richmond Enquirer* "say to 1830";[39] the Richmond paper could not have said much of anything about Gallatin, but it had been the place where Giles launched his first assault on John Quincy Adams. Henry Adams was looking for all the relevant preliminaries to his great-grandfather's denunciation of the Essex Junto and the Hartford Convention. Working rapidly, he had a volume modestly titled *Documents Relating to New-England Federalism* ready for publication by December.[40]

The centerpiece of the collection is John Quincy Adams's *Reply to the Appeal of the Massachusetts Federalists*, constituting 222 of the book's 425 pages. Henry Adams's preface begins by stating, "This book has no controversial purpose. Under the ashes of half a century the fires of personal and party passion still glow in these pages; but only curious students of history care any longer to stir them."[41] Indeed, Adams goes on to cite Lodge's life of Cabot as representing "the moment when party-spirit begins to yield to the broader spirit of impartial investigation"—implying that there could no longer be any objection to the revelation that Lodge's ancestor had been a party to a conspiracy against his native country. The pose of the impartial historian thus authorizes Adams to expose his protegé's great-grandfather as little different from the Southern rebels of the recent war. One of the oddities of the collection Adams assembled is that it begins with retrospective opinions from 1827 to 1829 concerning the final stages of New England Federalism that had occurred between 1804 and 1815. He includes documents contemporaneous with New England Federalism in what is designated as an appendix, consisting of 95 pages. There is something distinctly modernist about this structure, in which the rival interpretations precede the material being interpreted. It resembles Vladimir Nabokov's *Pale Fire*, supposedly a scholarly edition with textual notes in which the text is subordinated to the notes.

The first document Adams collects is Virginia governor William Giles's publication of an excerpted letter he had received from Thomas Jefferson that was critical of John Quincy Adams's presidency, in response to Giles's previous letter complaining of the usurpation of states' rights by the federal government. As Henry Adams indicates in a footnote, Giles had omitted Jefferson's introductory indication that this letter was not intended for publication.[42] A year later—less than a month before the 1828 elections—a supporter of John Quincy Adams, apparently suspecting that Giles's version of the late president's views had distorted them, inquired with Jefferson's grandson and literary executor if Jefferson's papers included a letter that vindicated Adams's conduct as a senator in the period during Jefferson's presidency. Discovering that such a letter did exist, the Adams supporter had Jefferson's more positive, earlier letter published, describing Adams's report to President Jefferson "that certain citizens of the Eastern States (I think he named Massachusetts particularly) were in negotiation with agents of the British government, the object of which was [that they withdraw from the war with the British and] without formally declaring their separation from the Union of the States, they should withdraw all aid and obedience to them."[43] Giles in turn published his own reading of this other Jefferson letter, alleging that the old Virginia statesman had apparently been confused about time sequences and too distracted to tell the story clearly. At this point in the controversy, President Adams sought to offer his own anonymous clarification of the events Jefferson's letter had described—that he had visited Jefferson in 1808 to inform him of his awareness of a conspiracy among New England Federalists to secede from the Union. In doing so, he indicated that his concurrence with the Embargo of 1807 had been motivated by nationalist feeling, in contrast to the purely sectional loyalties of his erstwhile Federalist allies in Massachusetts.[44] Adams's vindication of himself appeared in print on October 21, 1828, obviously just before the presidential election date. Giles quickly followed with a reiteration that the incumbent president was not a genuine Jeffersonian.

After the election of 1828, in which Adams had lost to Giles's candidate Andrew Jackson, but while Adams remained in office, a group of old Federalists and descendants of Federalists pursued Adams with the complaint that he had traduced them. Adams refused to answer publicly while still in office. He indicated that the evidence he had about a Federalist conspiracy was not of the sort that could be proved in a law court, but the thirteen signatories to the *Appeal* insisted that he bring forth what evidence he had on the grounds that their reputations or the reputations of their fathers had been attacked. (Among the signatories to the *Appeal* is George Cabot's son Henry Cabot, Lodge's grandfather and namesake.) "We insist," they wrote, according to John Quincy Adams's paraphrase, "upon it that you shall give us matter of indictment against you for a false, scandalous, and infamous libel; for you have told us that you cannot prove the fact in open court, and so we mean to intimidate you by our numbers, wealth, and power. Come, sir, give us the names of your Federal leaders, and all your evidence charging them with treason."[45] The old Federalist signatories claimed that Adams's refusal to make his case against them was merely legal hair-splitting to conceal the absence of evidence.

Returned by the voters in 1829 to his home in Quincy, John Quincy Adams wrote his massive response to his Federalist adversaries, filled with the sort of ironic invective that had become a sort of family specialty since his father's time. In it he characterizes the writers of the Federalist letter as the pathetic remains of the Essex Junto, an ideological position that by 1829 looked wholly out of step with both its own past and the direction of national developments since.[46] He also builds the case for the genuineness of his evidence by pointing to specific sources, in particular to letters from John Henry, a freelance political operator who had come to New England as a British spy in the first decade of the century. On the eve of the War of 1812, the Madison administration had gained access to Henry's correspondence with the governor-general of Canada and published it, to the general discomfiture of New England Federalists. In his use of these documents, John Quincy Adams notes the certainty with which Henry had written: in 1809, for example, Henry had stated that Federalist leaders in Massachusetts were considering a New England convention aimed at erecting "*a separate government for their common defense and common interest.*"[47] Adams therefore wonders how Henry could make this kind of assertion without consulting genuine Federalist sources.

At least one New England Federalist leader, Josiah Quincy, entertained quite different notions of John Henry's activity at the time, as recorded in his son's biography of him:

> From the year 1809 to 1812, there had been residing in these States a man, John Henry by name. He had married a lady of good family in Philadelphia, and with her and two children came to Boston, ostensibly for health and amusement, bringing letters of introduction to many families in the place—among others to mine. He was received with the attention due to the respectability of the letters he brought; and regarded as a man passing idly through the world, seeking and entitled to no special interest or confidence. He flitted about New England,—sometimes at Windsor, and sometimes at Burlington, in Vermont,—but chiefly resided in Boston. . . . During all this time, as it afterwards appeared, he was a spy, authorized by Sir James Craig, Governor of the British Province in North America, to travel in the Eastern States, to gain and communicate such knowledge as he could of the state of affairs and of the opinions of men, with authority also, if he found any parties or persons of leading influence in those States willing to enter into any political connection with the British government, to receive and communicate such disposition to him, for which purposes he received credentials of his authority in this respect, which he was at liberty to produce. For these services he was paid, and was to receive such pecuniary aid as he might require. After having been three years in this agency, having collected nothing but what every newspaper in the country could communicate, having done nothing, and not having, or pretending to have, found a single individual in the United States, of any section or party, disposed to have any political connection with

> Great Britain, to whom he could exhibit his secret credentials, he laid before the British government exorbitant claims for services, which they instantly rejected.[48]

Quincy appears appalled at both the breach of etiquette of Henry passing himself off as a gentleman of independent means and the effrontery of his seeking compensation from the British government for achieving nothing.

John Quincy Adams's argument with the Federalist remnant, a group that by an ironic coincidence he designates as the "Confederates," is based in large part on the concurrence between John Henry's letters and various events occurring in the years from 1804 to 1812. That Timothy Pickering in particular and various other New England Federalists seriously contemplated the breakup of the United States in the first two decades of the nineteenth century is apparent, as Henry Adams had pointed out in his *Nation* review of Lodge's biography of Cabot. In his magisterial biography of Harrison Gray Otis, Samuel Eliot Morison has pointed out that the resistance to American union is evidenced in the writings of Pickering, Fisher Ames, Uriah Tracy, and Roger Griswold, all of them New England representatives to Congress, around 1804.[49] John Quincy Adams's contention in his *Reply* is that the idea of New England secession persisted in the political air breathed by the New England Federalists and reached its culmination at the Hartford Convention. Indeed the decision of that convention to conduct its business in secret left it open to speculation about what really was considered there.

John Quincy and Henry Adams aside, the prevailing view of the Hartford Convention has been that it served to defuse populist Federalist irritation at the Union and the War of 1812.[50] In the view of this majority position, the lethargic George Cabot probably did try to contain the impulses of New England sectionalism. Josiah Quincy, not himself selected to attend the convention, expressed pungently to a friend what the result of the convention would be: "'I can tell you exactly,' was his reply. 'Can you indeed?' exclaimed the other. 'Pray tell me what it will be?' 'A GREAT PAMPHLET!'"[51] Quincy anticipated nothing from the Hartford Convention but another Federalist gesture.

John Quincy Adams, who had left the Federalists in 1808 and was viewed by them thereafter as a renegade, was convinced that the Hartford Convention represented the culmination of New England secessionist impulses, which could be traced back over ten years before its 1814 meeting.

In his *Reply*, he contends, in fact, that the Federalists' *Appeal* was intentionally timed to curry favor with the incoming Jackson administration, "at the very moment when the favor of the successor to his [Adams's] situation might best be propitiated by a rancorous and unrelenting persecution of him."[52]

Having written the *Reply*, Adams thought better of publishing his irritated reaction to the political behavior of the old Federalists, perhaps anticipating that his political career might not be over and that an attack on Massachusetts's conservatives would alienate his natural constituency. This explanation for the older Adams's choice to suppress the letter is what Henry Adams offers as an explanation for its suppression—probably as good an explanation as one could find. Certainly John Quincy Adams had not changed his mind, or he would have destroyed the letter. Irascible and willing to offend as he always was, he was capable of occasional outbreaks of political prudence. So the manuscript was set aside, joining the mass of Adams family papers where his grandson could locate it in 1877.

Together with John Quincy Adams's indictment of the Essex Junto for what in 1877 would look like a plot to engineer secession, Henry Adams included in his appendix the testimonies from Junto leaders to display their openness to the idea of secession. In January 1804, Timothy Pickering wrote to George Cabot lamenting the festering effects of the Jefferson administration even in New England:

> Apostasy and original depravity are the qualifications for official honors and emoluments, while men of sterling worth are displaced and held up to popular contempt and scorn. And shall we sit still, until this system shall universally triumph? until even in the Eastern States the principles of genuine Federalism shall be overwhelmed?. . . The principles of our Revolution point to the remedy,—a separation. That this can be accomplished, and without spilling one drop of blood, I have little doubt. One thing I know, that the rapid progress of innovation, of corruption, of oppression, forces the idea upon many a reflecting mind. . . . The people of the East cannot reconcile their habits, views, and interests with those of the South and West. . . . I do not believe in the practicability of a long-continued union. . . . But *when* and *how* is a separation to be effected? If, as many think, Federalism (by which I mean the solid principles of government applied to a federate republic,—

> principles which are founded in justice, in sound morals, and religion, and whose object is the security of life, liberty, and property, against popular delusion, injustice, and tyranny),—if, I say, Federalism is crumbling away in New England, there is no time to be lost, lest it should be overwhelmed, and become unable to attempt its own relief. Its last refuge is New England; and immediate exertion, perhaps, its only hope. It must begin in Massachusetts.[53]

In the climate of opinion of 1877 this letter would certainly look seditious, though Henry Adams saw in it nothing more objectionable than a querulous and ineffectual sectionalism.

Adams took the text of the letter from Lodge's *Cabot*, where he also found—and then chose to reprint—Cabot's reply. In the latter, Cabot does not indicate any enthusiasm for Pickering's insistence on immediate New England secession, but he does concur to a certain extent:

> All the evils you describe and many more are to be apprehended; but I greatly fear that a separation would be no remedy, *because the source of them is in the political theories of our country and in ourselves*. A separation at some point not very remote may probably take place. The first impression of it is even now favorably received by many; but I cannot flatter myself with the expectation of essential good to proceed from it, while we retain maxims and principles which all experience, and, *I may add, reason too*, pronounce to be impracticable and absurd. Even in New England, where there is among the body of the people more wisdom and virtue than in any other part of the United States, we are full of errors, which no reasoning could eradicate, if there were a Lycurgus in every village. *We are democratic altogether;* and I hold democracy, in its natural operation, to be the *government of the worst*.[54]

This passage reveals the complacent provincial conservatism that was in fact George Cabot's prevailing note. Adams had also quoted it in his *Nation* review of Lodge's biography. It is the note of despair.

John Quincy Adams was evidently convinced that virtually the only New Englanders who believed in the persistence of the Union were people whose surname was Adams. Implicit in his *Reply* is the effect on New England Federalism of the news of the Treaty of Ghent ending the War of 1812. The upshot of the Treaty of Ghent was the final collapse of New England Federalism, so the Hartford Convention had been the last convulsive throb of the dying conservative party. Henry Adams's motives for accepting a Federalist conspiracy can, I think, be distinguished from those of his grandfather. John Quincy credits a Federalist conspiracy based on the evidence he assembles and evidently also as a corollary to his belief in the fallen nature of man. Of the Federalist accusers, he contends,

> These are my accusers,—the relics, the mouldering relics, of the Essex Junto. That among them should appear the name of Franklin Dexter would have surprised me, could any thing in political vicissitude, at my time of life, surprise. Well might he withhold his signature from a defense of the Hartford Convention, for the vindication of his father's fame. I hope he will forgive me the infectious rudeness of my answer to his remark that he has seen no proof, and shall not readily believe, that any portion of his father's political course is to be attributed to the influence of my confidential conversations with him in 1809. Be it so.[55]

Henry Adams for his part had always been a believer in the existence of conspiracies, largely because he had been engaged in conspiratorial behavior for most of his adult life. In the winter of 1860–1861, while ostensibly acting as his father the congressman's secretary, he was busy submitting anonymous newspaper articles to the *Boston Advertiser* in support of his father's political position and also in opposition to Sen. Charles Sumner's more intractable stance.[56] Later, while serving as his father's secretary in the American mission to London, he followed the same practice, this time for the *New York Times*. In fact Henry Adams's newspaper contributions assisted in defusing the first problem that Charles Francis Adams faced in London, the *Trent* affair.[57] (A Union gunboat had boarded the British packet *Trent* in November 1861 and apprehended two prospective Confederate diplomats, creating a diplomatic confrontation between the United States and Great Britain which Charles Francis Adams had to deal with shortly after arriving in London.) In his first extended period in Washington, he had become a political commentator with an important coterie audience and excellent contacts among influential people. Even his teaching career had been a sort of successful private conspiracy—he had made the world believe he was a qualified medievalist. In the years when Adams and Lodge collaborated at the *North American Review*, Adams had been working behind the political scene to advance his own agenda, albeit without conspicuous success. Taking a cue from his own maneuvering, Adams read the letters of the New England Federalists indicating an interest or expectation of New England secession as conspiratorial. When Adams would go on to write his *History of the United States*, the Federalist conspiracy would become a continual leitmotif.

Just as Adams had reviewed Lodge's *Cabot* in the *Nation*, Lodge used the same forum to review *Documents Relating to New-England Federalism* only a few days after the book was published. The review quickly tries to disarm Adams's historical assertions by displacing the volume from the realm of history to the realm of dramatic literature.

> A collection of historical documents can rarely be called dramatic, but this term may be very fitly applied to the contents of the volume whose title we give below. In the political drama which is here unfolded the various personages tell severally their own stories in their own language, state their own opinions, and reveal their own characters, while the editor preserves as scrupulous an impersonality as the most finished playwright.[58]

Lodge's metaphor suggests that Henry Adams, the editor, is more a dramatist, a presenter of vivid fictions, than he is a historian. Lodge describes the volume as the record of a quarrel between John Quincy Adams and some supporters of Andrew Jackson that led to an intemperate exchange with some Massachusetts conservatives, culminating in John Quincy Adams writing a long, angry, historically dubious description of New England Federalism.

> There are many other interesting features in this collection of papers besides those of purely historical value. From a literary point of view, the main document, Mr. Adams's "Reply," is a remarkable composition. There is no noticeable richness in Mr. Adams's ordinary style, but when he launches out into invective the wealth of his vocabulary, the vigor of his sarcasm, the savage ferocity of his direct assaults, combine to make this paper an almost unequalled piece of political controversial writing, worthy to rank with the best efforts in this branch of literature. It reveals also, in a striking manner, some salient traits of the writer's character. His inability to judge character coolly and

> justly by casting off prejudice, his strong sense of right which led him to act correctly in essentials, and his want of tact which led to his failure in details, and to many of the bitter hostilities which always environed him, are all conspicuous here. Hardly less so is the strange habit of forming a clear, sharply-defined theory, and then forcing men and facts to fit it by an absolute rejection of the endless modifications of human character and motives.[59]

Embedded in Lodge's review is a discussion of the Hartford Convention, about which Lodge states, "opinions must always differ."[60] After that stipulation Lodge proceeds to set forth the basic thesis about the convention that he had laid out in *George Cabot*. As to whether there existed a conspiracy among the leadership of the Massachusetts Federalists in favor of secession, Lodge notes that during the period of the Embargo of 1807 secession was so common a subject of discussion in New England that issues of conspiracy could hardly apply. As to whether the provokers of John Quincy Adams were innocent of any thought of secession, Lodge is forced to be more circumspect:

> With the state of facts disclosed in these papers, it is difficult to reconcile the general denial just quoted from the "appeal" of the Boston Federalists. The signers of this appeal were all men of honor, integrity, and high position in the community, which makes still more insoluble the difference between their statement and the facts displayed in this volume. This contradiction is, however, susceptible of explanation in large measure. Some of the signers were too young to have been in the party councils from 1804 to 1814, and none of them, with the exception possibly of Mr. Otis, occupied such a position as would have admitted them to the carefully-kept secrets of 1804.[61]

In other words, Adams's *Documents* undercut the denials of complicity in plans for disunion that the Federalist defenders had made. In particular, Lodge's own grandfather would have been too young to have contributed to the discussions of secession at the same level with Pickering or George Cabot. Lodge concludes by noting that, however hostile John Quincy Adams had been toward the old Federalists, his tone in relation to his Southern antagonists was contemptuous beyond ordinary hostility. Lodge's review is respectful toward Henry Adams but quietly demurring.

In keeping with their curious minuet of overt courtesy disguising underlying antagonism, Adams wrote to Lodge commending him for the review. "I have just read your notice of N. E. Federalism and congratulate you on the judicial elevation you are attaining. The notice is really excellent and leaves nothing to be desired."[62] Despite his subtle defiance of his old teacher, Lodge had already written to alert him about the review the day after it had appeared, prompting Adams to note in reply that he had already written:

> I will only add that as I kept myself out of the book so far as possible, I think it just as well that I should keep out of the notices. I have even had the binding altered so as to take my name off the back where it was put, contrary to my express order, in imitation, I suppose, of your volume. As there is nothing of mine in it but the preface and the index, it is ridiculous to put my name on the back like an author's.[63]

The idea that either Adams or Lodge had kept themselves out of their books appears truly ridiculous. Lodge was calling as much attention to himself with *George Cabot* as he possibly could, and Henry Adams in reply had found a way of showcasing his grandfather's most vivid piece of writing. The gesture of having his name not appear on the spine of *Documents* is best understood as another instance of Adams playing peekaboo with his readers. Even in the *Education*, as Edward Chalfant has recently pointed out, Adams sought to delete the author's name from the title page.[64] Peekaboo is a game whose aim is not anonymity or genuine concealment, but rather a more intense sort of discovery or self-revelation.

After reading an unfavorable but prominent review of the Cabot biography, Adams wrote to Lodge to offer some general advice:

> Your danger is a very simple one, and no one can hurt you but yourself. It is that of adopting the view of one side of a question. No one whose mind will not work on its own independent pivot, can escape being drawn into the whirl-pool of party prejudices. Unless you can find some basis of faith in general principles, some theory of the progress of civilization which is outside and above all temporary questions of policy, you must infallibly think and act under the control of the man or men whose thought, in the times you deal with, coincides most nearly with your prejudices. This is the fault with almost

> every English historian. Very few of them have scientific minds, and still fewer have honestly tried to keep themselves clear of personal feeling.[65]

In effect, Adams admonishes Lodge to avoid the route of party politics and take the sort of independent course that three generations of Adamses before him had followed. As Adams frames it, it is a heuristic, methodological choice between party prejudice and "science."

It is unclear whether Adams at this point had any hope that his former student would escape being drawn into the whirlpool of party prejudice. In fact, Adams himself had provided the occasions for Lodge's baptism in the waters of party politics by dispatching him from Cambridge to Washington in 1875 and 1876 to advance the cause of the Independents. By 1877 Lodge was moving toward a political career of his own, one characterized by the principle of absolute adherence to political party, though at the point when Adams admonishes him he was still an active adherent of that anomalous position of the 1870s called Independence. Writing in January 1876 under the signature "LIBERAL," Lodge had placed a letter to the editor in the *New York Tribune* contending for the existence of a grassroots movement in support of Charles Francis Adams, based on the support Adams had received at a Republican Party convention in Worcester, Massachusetts.[66]

The tensions that existed between Adams and Lodge from 1876 to 1880 are detectable only in their public writing. Adams's letters to Lodge continued to maintain the rather overbearing cordiality that had been Adams's characteristic note with such figures as his brother Charles, people whom he worked with but whose limitations he had measured.

To both Adams and Lodge, the issues about which they differed—party loyalty, the relative precedence of Boston and Massachusetts in the nation, the wisdom of the Essex Junto branch of the Federalist Party—mattered enough that they wrote thousands of published pages on those questions. Lodge evidently could not let the *Documents* be the last published chapter of the exchange, so he turned to another Essex Junto figure for an occasion to express his views about the rightness of the Federalist cause even in the aftermath of Jefferson's election. Though relations between John Adams and George Cabot had soured by the early years of Adams's presidency, Cabot never figured as the major adversary to Adams, even among the high Federalists of the Essex Junto. The distinction of being John Adams's most despised adversary from his home state certainly fell to Timothy Pickering, foreign minister both to Adams and simultaneously to Alexander Hamilton while owing allegiance only to Hamilton. Pickering went on after the election of 1800 to represent Massachusetts in the Senate from 1803 to 1811, serving at first alongside John Quincy Adams. The relations between the two Massachusetts senators were poisoned by the younger Adams's awareness of Pickering's betrayal of his father and Pickering's sense of injured merit for being cashiered in 1800.[67] Lodge contributed to the *Atlantic* in 1878 an admiring essay on Timothy Pickering, who by then had nearly as much need of rescue from oblivion as George Cabot. His portrait cites the recent publication of *Documents Relating to New-England Federalism* with its extensive correspondence to and from Pickering as the pretext for the essay.[68] Lodge implies that Adams's *Documents* now permits a more accurate portrait of Pickering.

Near the beginning of the essay Lodge plunges into one of those set pieces of adulation of the forefathers that gladdened the hearts of nineteenth-century New Englanders:

> Timothy Pickering was a true descendant of the Puritans. He was a fit representative in the eighteenth century of the race which colonized New England in the seventeenth. His ancestors were numbered among those men who had wrung a livelihood from the rocky soil of Massachusetts and the wild seas of the North Atlantic. Surrounded by hardships, in conflict with man and nature, combating earth, air, and the savage with the same grim determination, crushing out domestic dissension with relentless severity, and stubbornly resisting foreign interference, the Puritans in America founded and built up a strong, well-ordered state. Here was worked out to the end the Puritan theory of government; here, and only here, Puritan Englishmen, for a century and a half, kept their race unmixed and their blood pure. The passage of years, the advance of civilization, modified and softened the character of the New England people, but their most marked qualities, moral and mental, remained unchanged.[69]

Lodge's representation of the Puritans lacks one notable feature of the historical Puritans: the belief in Puritanism as a creed. That Puritans actually believed something is omitted from this and many other late-nineteenth-century treatments of them. What persists once that belief is leached away is a habit of mind that Lodge commemorates in the Pickering essay. It is sharply drawn and stark, depicted in terms of combat, severity, purity of race and blood, and congenital conservatism. The Pickering essay marks an important development in Lodge's efforts to find his political bearings as a New England conservative of a very old school. The kind of conservative into which Lodge was evolving required an affirmation of the negative dimensions of the position embraced. Thus the article is not a cover-up of Pickering's deficiencies, and Lodge's Pickering does not differ greatly from Henry Adams's Pickering. Both versions sabotaged the John Adams administration from a politically maladroit ideological position. Lodge, however, salutes Pickering for helping to lead the Federalists in their long retreat into New England isolation. Even though Lodge can present Pickering as a dogged and dedicated public man, the gallant and cerebral qualities one could single out in a Hamilton are absent here.

Lodge's Pickering is not an attractive figure, so it was distinctly defiant for Lodge to publish a defense of the Adams family's most inveterate opponent, one who hated John Quincy Adams so fiercely for his apostasy from Federalism that while in his seventies in 1828 he campaigned in print for Andrew Jackson. Pickering's persistence in advocating a foreign policy different from the president's appears in Lodge's rendition as Pickering's allegiance to the real head of the Federalist party, Alexander Hamilton. Lodge tries to argue as well that Pickering was not merely the tool of Hamilton while serving as a cabinet officer, but he offers no instance of Pickering diverging from Hamilton; rather, the article shows that Pickering took the lead in the cabinet to secure Hamilton's preeminence among officers in the army mustered against France. The essay displays Lodge in the process of shifting from his former allegiance to the Independent position toward a commitment to the unwavering ideological party position that Pickering himself represented. Lodge's Pickering emerges as quarrelsome, dogmatic, narrow, physically unappealing, and guilty of sabotaging the Federalist party to get back at John Adams. It is nonetheless a sort of tribute.

The Lodge family had long been socially close to the historian George Bancroft. Bancroft had lived across the street in Boston when Henry Cabot Lodge was born.[70] After *George Cabot* appeared, Bancroft wrote to Lodge commending him for offering a better defense of the Adamses than they had done at the time for themselves.[71] Bancroft's sense of irony was evidently lost on Lodge, who later sent the Pickering article to him. Bancroft, the old Jacksonian Democrat, wrote back to thank young Lodge for sending the article but observes that he considers Pickering's conduct close to treasonable and that Pickering's state papers as secretary of state do not compare with Jefferson's. "You men of the future must write history with the impartiality of Thucydides, or the calm delineation of the war of antagonistic elements which distinguishes Ranke."[72] The dean of American historians invokes the greatest ancient historian and the leading historian of his own century as guides for the promising but misguided young man.

Understandably miffed to receive a rebuff from the old historian, young Lodge immediately replied with a defense of his characterization of Pickering, arguing that Pickering's disposition toward accommodation with the British was a holdover of colonial attitudes into the early national period. Lodge is forced to display a characteristically conservative defensiveness: "If Pickering's attitude towards England and her Envoys be branded as treasonable what shall be said of Jefferson's conduct to [the French ambassador] Genet—which coming from a member of the administration was far worse not only per se but from the position Jefferson held."[73] Lodge includes Madison more vaguely in his sideswipe at Jefferson: "It seems to me that these manifestations of subserviency to foreign powers are due to the fact that although we were politically independent the minds of many leaders were still in a colonial condition. On this account I should be slow to believe that either Jefferson or Pickering behaved treasonably." Lodge goes on to regret that Bancroft saw the article as an apology for Pickering, asserting, "I am far from being an unqualified admirer of Pickering or his manners or his policy though I am one of some traits of his character. My intention was to make a careful study of what seemed to me an interesting character historically & individually." In other words, what some might read as a supposed defense of Pickering is in fact primarily a study of a certain character type:

> I cannot help regarding Pickering as a typical representative of the race from which he sprung. I have a profound admiration for the Puritan too great to be expressed in a letter but I believe them to have been in pursuit of the freedom of worshipping God in their own way alone & not to have aimed at the freedom of the human kind. They aided the cause of freedom more powerfully but I think they sought only their own freedom in their own way & were quite ready & in my opinion very often right in coercing other people.

Lodge's response to Bancroft reveals the confident young conservative defending himself against criticism by the old liberal. In embracing Pickering as a Puritan, Lodge appears to be adapting Bancroft's own modification of the Puritan past in his *History of the United States,* in which the Puritans are the originators of American democracy.

In fact, Bancroft is silent about one of Lodge's central points—that the high Federalist Pickering was nonetheless a democrat, a believer in popular sovereignty. "Pickering's aversion to aristocracy in the ordinary sense of the word," Lodge wrote, "and his hatred of shams and false pretenses, carried him far in devotion to the *nil admirari* principle."[74] Pickering in that regard supplants Lodge's own great-grandfather in pointing Lodge in the direction of political office in circumstances where conservatism could be combined with democracy.

Concluding his response to Bancroft, Lodge differentiates between Jefferson and Pickering in terms of literary style. He acknowledges the elegance of Jefferson's state papers but insists that Pickering's had a quality always lacking in Jefferson's:

> vigor. In short Pickering to my mind was a man of the most reckless courage while Jefferson was conspicuously timid & cautious. I think I do justice to Jefferson. I certainly mean to. I admire his abilities. I regard him as the most consummate party leader of modern times but I think as a statesman he was a failure, as all our history seems to me to show. Dexterous & possessed of marvelous tact he appears to me insincere & I am not ready to admit that the principles of which he was the apostle & which he did more than anyone else to stamp upon our nation were sound.[75]

Lodge's assertive conservatism addressed to the surviving avatar of Jeffersonian liberalism appears more strident as printed here than it may have appeared to the seventy-seven-year-old historian, who was by then so frail that he had had to dictate most of his letter to Lodge and might well have found it impossible to read Lodge's difficult handwriting. In any case, Lodge's papers do not include a response from Bancroft to the letter.

It was a natural gesture for Lodge to seek Bancroft's approval despite what he might have anticipated in the old liberal's response. After all, Bancroft was by this time a sort of national institution. He had begun publishing his weighty *History of the United States* in 1834, before the birth of either Henry Adams or Lodge, and continued to compose or revise his volumes although he never advanced in time to the point where the United States as a political entity existed. Henry Adams's dealings with

Bancroft were rather different. Bancroft recognized Adams as a substantial historian, one who was beyond exhorting to emulate Thucydides or von Ranke. For his part, Adams's references to Bancroft in his correspondence are somewhat superior; he saw the older historian as an eminent compiler, but the kind of history Adams would write represented several steps beyond Bancroft. Writing to Lodge after the 1876 Harvard commencement at which Lodge had received his doctoral degree, Adams, who had skipped the ceremony, as he was prone to do for nearly all ceremonies that could be avoided, remarks, "I would have liked to see G. B. He is an entertaining man, and is the great authority on American history, at least for facts."[76] The last four words reveal the limitation to Adams's appreciation of Bancroft. Already Adams had criticized what he saw as Bancroft's defective scholarship about Capt. John Smith in his own 1867 *North American* article about Smith and Pocahontas.

Boston and Cambridge in the first half of the 1870s made Henry Adams feel uncomfortable and out of place, and he had married Clover Hooper, another person who never adjusted readily to Boston expectations. By contrast, Henry Cabot Lodge was completely at home in his combined habitats of Boston, Cambridge, and Nahant. He had completed two advanced degrees from Harvard simultaneously, and he had developed a taste for political life that seemed to dovetail neatly with his work at Harvard and at the *North American Review*. He was moving away from the Independent position and toward the sort of political regularity that was a prerequisite to advancement in Massachusetts politics. Lodge is the sort of figure historians deal with most easily, one who fits his surroundings closely. Henry Adams did not fit his Massachusetts surroundings well at all and by 1877 had moved to Washington, D. C., where he could research Albert Gallatin and be freer from the Adams family expectations. Already Henry Adams was a sort of modernist in a context where modernism was unintelligible, while Lodge was subject to the cultural expectations of his immediate cultural and social moment.

While Lodge was launching himself on a course that would eventually propel him into the U.S. Senate for thirty-four years, Henry Adams went off to Washington determined to have no further role in the quotidian political events that then and now are the most common aliment of that city. In June 1876, writing to Lodge about details concerning the number of the *North American* that was going to press, Adams pronounces that

> Politics have ceased to interest me. I am satisfied that the machine can't be smashed this time. As I feared, we have ourselves saved it by a foolish attempt to run it, which we never shall succeed in. The caucus and the machine will outlive me, and that being the case I prefer to leave this greatest of American problems to shrewder heads than mine. When the day comes on which it will be considered as disgraceful to be seen in a caucus as to be seen in a gambling-house or brothel, then my interest will wake up again and legitimate politics will get a new birth.[77]

NOTES

1. Henry Adams, *The Education of Henry Adams*, ed. Ernest Samuels (Boston, 1973), 31–32.
2. Henry Adams to Charles Milnes Gaskell, Dec. 7, 1869, in *The Letters of Henry Adams*, ed. J. C. Levenson et al. (Cambridge, Mass., 1982–1988), 2:54.
3. HA to William Dwight Whitney, Oct. 25, 1870, in *Letters*, 2:85.
4. John T. Morse, Jr., tribute to Henry Cabot Lodge, *Proceedings of the Massachusetts Historical Society* 58(1924–1925):100.
5. John A. Garraty, *Henry Cabot Lodge: A Biography* (New York, 1953), 35–36.
6. HA to Henry Cabot Lodge, June 2, 1872, in *Letters*, 2:138–139.
7. Garraty, *Henry Cabot Lodge*, 29.
8. Edward Chalfant, *Better in Darkness: A Biography of Henry Adams: His Second Life, 1862–1891* (Hamden, Conn., 1994), 315, 773. On the other hand, in his recently completed final volume *Improvement of the World: A Biography of Henry Adams: His Last Life, 1891–1918*, Edward Chalfant notes that as of 1915, "Adams had long despised [Lodge]" (487), but Chalfant is not explicit about the origins of that feeling.
9. Chalfant, *Better in Darkness*, 287, 315.
10. Henry Cabot Lodge, *Early Memories* (1913; New York, 1975), 240–241.
11. Henry Cabot Lodge, *The Life and Letters of George Cabot* (1878; New York, 1974), v.
12. Chalfant, *Better in Darkness*, 294; Ernest Samuels, *The Young Henry Adams* (Cambridge, Mass., 1948), 266–267.
13. HA to Charles W. Eliot, Mar. 2, 1877, in *Letters*, 2:301.
14. HA to Henry Cabot Lodge, Aug. 25, 1876, in *Letters*, 2:288–289.
15. Arguably the only election an Adams ever really struggled to win was the 1824 presidential election, when John Quincy Adams converted a losing electoral college total into election by the House of Representatives through a series of adroit tactical outflankings of Andrew Jackson's forces.
16. Henry Adams accurately reports only John Adams's final views of Pickering, because Adams did not fire his first secretary of state until May 1800, less than a year before the end of his term of office.
17. HA to Henry Cabot Lodge, Sept. 4, 1876, in *Letters*, 2:291. Carl Schurz, former German revolutionary, Union general, and senator from Missouri, had served as the leading political figure in the Independent movement. Earlier in the year he had convened a large gathering of leading Independents in New York City in the anticipation that the Independents might have some leverage in the presidential election of 1876. After the Repub-

licans bypassed James G. Blaine and nominated Rutherford B. Hayes, Schurz returned to Republican Party loyalty, a move that appalled Adams.

18. Henry Cabot Lodge, review of *The Life of Alexander Hamilton*, by John T. Morse, Jr., *North American Review* 123(1876):113.
19. Lodge, review of *Life of Alexander Hamilton*, 118.
20. Lodge, review of *Life of Alexander Hamilton*, 113.
21. HA to Henry Cabot Lodge, May 15, 1876, in *Letters*, 2:267.
22. Lodge, Journal, Feb. 7, 1876, Henry Cabot Lodge Papers, Massachusetts Historical Society.
23. Lodge, Journal, Mar. 2, 1876, Lodge Papers, MHS.
24. Lodge, Journal, Jan. 22, 1876, p. 71, Lodge Papers, MHS.
25. William Lawrence, *Henry Cabot Lodge: A Biographical Sketch* (Boston, 1925); Morse, tribute to Lodge, 99–110.
26. Lodge, Journal, p. 74, Lodge Papers, MHS.
27. Lodge, *George Cabot*, 193–215.
28. Lodge, *George Cabot*, viii.
29. HA to Henry Cabot Lodge, June 12, 1877, in *Letters*, 2:306.
30. HA to Henry Cabot Lodge, June 29, 1877, in *Letters*, 2:308.
31. Chalfant, *Better in Darkness*, 346–347.
32. Lodge, *George Cabot*, 417.
33. Lodge, *George Cabot*, 417n.
34. Henry Adams, "Lodge's Cabot," *Nation*, July 5, 1877, p. 13.
35. HA, "Lodge's Cabot," 13.
36. HA, "Lodge's Cabot," 13.
37. HA, "Lodge's Cabot," 13.
38. Lodge, *George Cabot*, 551–559, 563.
39. HA to Hugh Blair Grigsby, Aug. 20, 1877, in *Letters*, 2:315.
40. James M. Banner, Jr.'s *To the Hartford Convention* includes an excellent concluding note on sources, although Banner mistakes the 1905 second edition of *Documents* for the first edition and thus fails to place the publication in what he aptly describes as "a decorous but always sharp historiographical war of ancestral vindication" between Adams and Lodge. Banner, *To the Hartford Convention: The Federalists and the Origins of Party Politics in Massachusetts, 1787–1815* (New York, 1970).
41. Henry Adams, *Documents Relating to New-England Federalism* (1877; New York, 1969), v.
42. HA, *Documents*, 6.
43. HA, *Documents*, 12.
44. HA, *Documents*, 23–26.
45. HA, *Documents*, 109.
46. HA, *Documents*, 108.
47. HA, *Documents*, 118.
48. Edmund Quincy, *Life of Josiah Quincy*, 6th ed. (Boston, 1867), 250–251.
49. Samuel Eliot Morison, *The Life and Letters of Harrison Gray Otis, Federalist, 1765–1848*, 2d ed. (Boston and New York, 1913), 1:265–269.
50. For the majority view, see Morison, *Harrison Gray Otis*, 2:110–122, 156–159; David Hackett Fischer, *The Revolution of American Conservatism: The Federalist Party in the Era of Jeffersonian Democracy* (New York, 1965), 176–179; and Banner, *To the Hartford Convention*, 294–350.
51. Quincy, *Life of Josiah Quincy*, 358; also cited in Banner, *To the Hartford Convention*, 334.
52. HA, *Documents*, 109.

53. HA, *Documents*, 339–341.
54. HA, *Documents*, 346.
55. HA, *Documents*, 108. Samuel Dexter, father of Franklin Dexter, had even been drafted by the Republicans in 1814 as their candidate for Massachusetts governor. Banner, *To the Hartford Convention*, 320.
56. Samuels, *Young Henry Adams*, 84–90.
57. Edward Chalfant, *Both Sides of the Ocean: A Biography of Henry Adams: His First Life, 1838–1862* (Hamden, Conn., 1982), 322–379.
58. [Henry Cabot Lodge], "New England Federalism," *Nation*, Jan. 3, 1878, p. 11.
59. Lodge, "New England Federalism," 11–12.
60. Lodge, "New England Federalism," 11.
61. Lodge, "New England Federalism," 11.
62. HA to Henry Cabot Lodge, Jan. 3, 1878, in *Letters*, 2:331.
63. HA to Henry Cabot Lodge, Jan. 6, 1878, in *Letters*, 2:332.
64. Edward Chalfant, "Lies, Silence, and Truth in the Writings of Henry Adams," in *Henry Adams and His World*, ed. David R. Contosta and Robert Muccigrosso (Philadelphia, 1993), 8–9.
65. HA to Henry Cabot Lodge, Feb. 1, 1878, in *Letters*, 2:333.
66. "Independents in Massachusetts," clipping inserted in Lodge Journal between pages 93 and 94, Lodge Papers, MHS.
67. Pickering's son Octavius had begun a biography of Timothy Pickering which had been concluded by Nathaniel Hawthorne's feckless Salem rival Charles W. Upham in his dual capacity as town pastor and antiquarian historian. In his biography Upham carefully drains out the fiery old Federalist's life's blood.
68. Henry Cabot Lodge, "Timothy Pickering," *Atlantic* 41(1878):740.
69. Lodge, "Timothy Pickering," 740.
70. Garraty, *Henry Cabot Lodge*, 3; Lodge, *Early Memories*, 18.
71. George Bancroft, quoted in Garraty, *Henry Cabot Lodge*, 55.
72. George Bancroft to Henry Cabot Lodge, May 25, 1878, George Bancroft Papers, MHS.
73. Henry Cabot Lodge to George Bancroft, May 28, 1878, George Bancroft Papers, MHS.
74. Lodge, "Timothy Pickering," 753.
75. Lodge to Bancroft, May 28, 1878, George Bancroft Papers, MHS.
76. HA to Henry Cabot Lodge, June 30, 1876, in *Letters*, 2:281.
77. HA to Henry Cabot Lodge, June 24, 1876, in *Letters*, 2:279.

Investigating the "Great American Mystery"

Theory & Style in Henry Adams's Political Reform Moment

LESLIE BUTLER

THE FAMOUSLY "INQUIRING MIND" of Henry Adams extended into the realm of politics no less than history, art, architecture, and technology. Like Madeleine Lightfoot Lee, the protagonist in his novel *Democracy*, Adams's "restlessness, discontent, ambition" eventually led him to Washington, D.C., in 1868. There he embarked on his brief but compelling reform career, which might be said to have culminated twelve years later in the publication of *Democracy* in 1880. Like a "passenger on an ocean steamer whose mind will not give him rest until he has been in the engine-room and talked with the engineer," Adams found himself unsatisfied with the merely theoretical study of politics he had begun while in England during the Civil War. His "need to know" drove him straight to the national seat of power, where he hoped to touch, hear, and see American politics for himself.[1]

Adams's firsthand investigation of "the great American mystery of democracy and government," like Madeleine Lee's, was short-lived, but in the two decades following the Civil War he became a significant voice for liberal reform and an important bridge between British and American liberalism. His education in liberalism was emphatically transatlantic, involving intensive study in European and British political thought while living in London during an American national crisis. His diplomatic and social experience during the war reinforced his view of the historic importance of American democracy for the world. His course of study, especially in the works of Alexis de Tocqueville and John Stuart Mill, led him to undertake a more comprehensive exploration of that system's promises and perils. Together, this wartime experience and study shaped his vision of the American polity and encouraged him to construct a role as a political reformer and independent critic upon returning to the United States. Despite relative neglect in recent scholarship on Adams, his political thought and work forms a compelling chapter in his life. It also reveals much about the political theory and political style of late-nineteenth-century liberal reform.[2]

Adams, like Tocqueville and Mill, understood democracy as the inevitable next phase in Western history, a development to which all three men were committed, though with varying degrees of trepidation. Popular government had had no shortage of critics throughout the nineteenth century, and all eyes in Europe watched the United States to see if this system could survive a massive civil conflict. Adams wondered too, and discovered a newfound commitment to "the American experiment" in the process. As the nation weathered the storm, with its system of self-government still intact, he saw a new opportunity. "The great principle of democracy" was "still capable of rewarding a conscientious servant," he told his brother Charles in 1863, believing he saw "in the distance a vague and unsteady light in the direction towards which I needs must gravitate, so soon as the present disturbing influences are removed."[3]

The vague and unsteady light guiding him was a vision of a reformed democracy that would serve as an increasingly important model to the Western world. This vision, sharing much with the analyses of Tocqueville, Mill, and the younger British Liberals, imagined a political life based on intellect and education. With cultivated intelligence, the polity could discuss and decide public issues on principle, not partisanship or private interest. Similarly, an emphasis on education might insure a place for the "best"—or wisest—in governing. Furthermore, education would be just as crucial for the led as for leaders, precisely because democracy had so dramatically altered the meaning of those terms and the traditional relationship between them. Democracy required an educated and intellectually engaged citizenry—one that could discern principles and judge wisely.

Adams's emphasis on civic acuity inclined him more and more to view parties and partisanship as destructive forces in late-nineteenth-century American politics. The great machines that parties had become, Adams thought, obstructed the free play of ideas by subordinating the public good to party advantage. Worse, they deadened the intellectual capacities of citizens by asking them to do nothing more than ratify decisions made by a small group of "bosses." In stressing the importance of active minds and engaged knowledge in politics, Adams generalized from his own experience, turning his personal "need to know" into a veritable political style.

London

We "are democrats," Henry Adams wrote home to his brother Charles in 1863, "and you may be sure that in Europe a democrat is never and never can be really received into the circle of monarchists."[4] Adams's ideology and identity as an American democrat shaped the contours of his entire experience in England. Most obviously as a member of the American legation, but also socially, politically, and intellectually, his wartime world was bound by that fact. British and American attitudes towards each other had always included ideas about democracy as the subtext, and the war years only intensified this dynamic. Throughout the nineteenth century, Americans had boasted of the superiority of their political and social institutions, but their boasting barely masked their insecurity about the supposed vulgarity, commercialism, and mediocrity of their culture. Meanwhile British observers had long commented on the inferiority of American culture and, more devastatingly, mocked the hypocrisy of chattel slavery among America's purportedly "free" institutions.[5]

British opinion was extremely divided on the question of the American Civil War. Officially and diplomatically, Britain remained neutral, having declared neutrality on the eve of Charles Francis Adams's arrival at his post as minister in May 1861. Such a position conferred belligerent status on the Confederacy, which many Unionists feared would be the first step towards full recognition of the Confederacy as an independent nation.[6] As a firsthand observer of events and diplomacy, Adams believed the initial move had resulted from a diplomatic misunderstanding, and in letters to the *New York Times* and his brother Charles he tried to calm American outrage. Though recognition of the Confederacy never came, relations between the two countries were severely tested during the crisis.

The hostile opinion expressed by members of the government and ruling class in particular pained Unionists like Adams and his family. The British foreign secretary, Lord John Russell, for example, declared in October 1861 that the North and the South were merely "contending, as so many States in the old world have contended, the one for empire and the other for independence."[7] Between the outspoken Confederate sympathies of the London *Times* and the frequent ridicule and anti-Unionist comments overheard in society, Adams and his father felt overwhelmed by hostility, at least until Abraham Lincoln proclaimed emancipation in 1863. Adams complained often about the "mortification" of his situation, especially during the early Confederate victories when, already ambivalent about his decision to serve his father rather than the Union army, he had to "stand the taunts of everyone without being able to say a word in defence."[8]

The Adamses, like many other Unionists, interpreted the Confederate sympathies of England's governing class as the result of its hostility to democracy and its belief that democracy itself was on trial in the American Civil War. From his firsthand, albeit highly selective, observations, Henry Adams sensed that "the American question is organizing a vast mass of the lower orders in direct contact with the wealthy." His father agreed. He too thought that "the great body of the aristocracy and the wealthy commercial classes are anxious to see the United States go to pieces," while "the middle and lower class sympathise with us, more and more as they better comprehend the true nature of the struggle." This "true nature" of the struggle, which father and son believed divided British opinion ideologically, comprehended as they understood it the essential principle of the Union cause. As Henry Adams interpreted it, the Union supporters in Britain "go our whole platform and are full of the 'rights of man.' . . . You can find millions of people who look up to our institutions as their model and who talk with utter contempt of their own system of Government." From this perspective a formal British-Southern alliance made sense; Britain's traditional hostility to slavery gave way before the fear and loathing its ruling class felt for popular government. Surveying a radical pro-Union rally in London, Henry Adams claimed finally to understand "the cause that the privileged classes in Europe have to fear us."[9]

The addition of aristocratic England as at least an ideological opponent further imbued the war with transcendent meaning for the young Adams. The fate of democracy in the modern world was at stake. If it were to disappear in the United States, who knew when or even if it would reappear? "I see in America the trial of Democracy and its failure," the Earl of Shrewsbury ominously put it. "I believe that the dissolution of the Union is inevitable, and that men now before me will live to see an aristocracy established in America."[10] Such an interpretation obviously raised the stakes of the democratic experiment for Adams, as Union victory and national cohesion took on world-historic importance. This sentiment was of course not unique to Adams; it would become Lincoln's most powerful message in his address at Gettysburg. But living in Britain during the crisis perhaps gave the idea more direct meaning for the young Adams: victory was crucial to ensure that democracy would not perish and would continue to inspire others abroad. Adams believed he saw signs of this inspiration at work even before Union victory looked inevitable. Not long after the Emancipation Proclamation, he wrote his brother Charles about the "'moral influence' of American democracy" already evident in England. Attending an antislavery rally, he perceived the "symptoms of a great popular movement peculiarly unpleasant to the upper classes here because it . . . has a pestilent squint at sympathy with republicanism." He marveled at the power of such a "great republic" that could "shake the very crown on the Queen's head" and "threaten to tear down the rulers of the civilised world, by merely assuming her place at the head of the march of democracy."[11]

In the midst of this world-historic battle, however, Adams found allies sympathetic to the Union cause among the ruling classes. Several voices, in both political and intellectual circles, spoke in support of the Union. These friends included such figures as John Bright and Richard Cobden, John Stuart Mill, William E. Forster, Thomas Hughes, Robert Browning, John Elliott Cairnes, Harriet Martineau, Charles Lyell, Thomas Huxley, Charles Darwin, Goldwin Smith, and Leslie Stephen. Adams, in his capacity as private secretary and son of the minister, tried to cultivate these allies, requesting copies of diplomatic documents for them as supplements to the British Government's "blue books" and circulating useful newspaper articles from home among British periodicals. Relieved for the social, as well as political, acceptance, Adams peppered his letters to his brother Charles with references to "the literary and progressive set," the "cultivated radicals of England," and the "advanced minds" of the country.[12]

Adams again connected the fate of the Union and the international fate of liberal-democratic principles, characterizing these "friends" of the Union as part of a liberal movement in their own country. "There are all the elements of a great, reforming, liberal party at work here," he told his brother, and he followed their course with high interest.[13] Adams sensed the dawn of a new, liberal age across Europe, feeling himself, "by tastes and education," a part of this "Young England, Young Europe," indeed the "young world." He found evidence of this new era dawning in both intellectual and political life. Even Oxford University, he remarked, "that most Catholic of conservative places, has become strongly tinged with the ideas of the new school. John Stuart Mill ranks even there rather higher than the authorities of the place itself, with which he is waging internecine war."[14] Adams detected Liberal progress on another front as well, witnessing the parliamentary election of 1865 that returned several Liberal supporters of the Union, including Thomas Hughes and John Stuart Mill—"a new set of men, too strong to be kept quiet," he declared.[15] "Our friends everywhere show very strong," he wrote Charles, "and so far as America is concerned we have nothing to do but to restore peace and arrange our finances, and our influence on England will be strong enough to carry a new reform through within ten years. . . . Then there will be another long step forward here."[16] The reunification of the American republic would lead inexorably to political reform in Britain, Adams thought, as the Atlantic tide turned decisively towards liberal democracy.

As this political prognostication suggests, Adams did not pass his time in Britain exclusively in diplomatic missions or London social life. He also entered on a rigorous course of study, particularly in political and economic theory. "I pass my intervals from official work in studying De Tocqueville and John Stuart Mill," he wrote Charles in 1863, moving from "International Law to our foreign history . . . [to] the philosophic standing of our republic" and "the advance of the democratic principle in European civilization." Perhaps out of defensiveness about his comparative idleness, Adams repeatedly assured his army officer brother of his intensive mental labors. "My candles are seldom out before two o'clock in the morning," he wrote, "and my table is piled with half-read books and unfinished writing." He found himself drawn primarily to history, political economy, and philosophy. "I write and read; read and write," he explained, staying only as "calm as the philosophic mind within me will allow."[17]

John Stuart Mill held a special place in Adams's curriculum. Adams considered him, along with Tocqueville, one of the "two high priests of our faith." But unlike Tocqueville, who had died in 1859, Mill served not just as an intellectual oracle but as a prominent and forceful presence throughout the war. Taking "particular pains" to arrange an introduction in early 1863, Adams described him as "about the ablest man in England . . . and a mighty weapon of defence for our cause in this country."[18] Adams would have been familiar with and appreciative of Mill's many public pronouncements in support of the Union, notably his 1862 article in *Fraser's* on "The Contest in America" and his review of *The Slave Power*, a book by the Irish political economist John Elliott Cairnes. Mill shared Adams's view of the Civil War as a great struggle over the fate of democracy. He recalled later in his *Autobiography* how he had seen it as his "obvious duty to be one of the small minority who protested against this perverted state of public opinion" in Britain by writing in support of the Union cause. He believed his writings had "helped to encourage those Liberals who had felt overborne by the tide of illiberal opinion, and to form in favour of the good cause a nucleus of opinion which increased gradually, and after the success of the North began to seem probable, rapidly."[19] Adams became a student of Mill's during the "final, and in some ways quite distinct, phase of his career," when, in Stefan Collini's words, he most clearly acted as a "public moralist." In the 1860s, Mill was at the height of his intellectual authority, entering debates on leading public issues, especially through the periodical press, and serving from 1865 to 1868 as a member of Parliament.[20]

It is not hard to imagine why Adams would have found his reading in European political theory compelling. As countless scholars have pointed out, Mill and Tocqueville would have appealed to the young New Englander in their defense of intellectual authority and their belief in the need for educated intelligence in a representative government. Both thinkers privileged intellect and worried about the leveling effects democracy might have on culture and thought. Tocqueville most famously articulated (and named) this fear that democracies would inevitably tend to the mediocre and banal, all genius or originality being snuffed out by "the tyranny of majority." Politics would also suffer from this leveling effect. As Tocqueville pointed out in 1835, only in highly unusual times were political parties "more attached to principles than to consequences . . . to ideas rather than to personalities." In quiet times, such as when "a time of calm succeeds a great revolution," parties were "not elevated and sustained by lofty purposes" but strove only for power. Tocqueville looked to the saving efforts of an intellectual elite to guide and elevate public life, pointing to New England as a crucial example of this kind of guidance and elevation.[21]

Mill's *On Liberty*, which appeared just two years before Adams's arrival in England, picked up where Tocqueville left off and presented an impassioned brief for freedom of thought and especially for "genius." He, too, made a case for an intellectual elite to guide the public, making a number of unconventional recommendations intended to safeguard the place of intellect in his *Considerations on Representative Government*, which appeared the very year Adams came to London. Suffrage, Mill believed, must extend widely but still only to those "able to read, write, and . . . perform the common operations of arithmetic."[22] He also proposed a complicated system for a "graduated suffrage," arguing that citizens command "plural" votes according to their level of intelligence.[23] Mill's most dramatic suggestion in this regard involved the formation of a special, appointed "Commission of Legislation" that would draft laws. Elected bodies would continue to represent the will of the people and maintain the power of *enacting* laws, in Mill's proposal, but the Commission would "embody the element of intelligence in their construction."[24] In a stance sure to please the young Adams, Mill, like Tocqueville, also believed New England played an indispensable role in softening the hard edges of democratic equality. "Democracy has been no leveler there," he wrote an American correspondent in 1865, "as to intellect and education, or respect for the true personal superiority."[25]

Tocqueville's and Mill's fear of tyrannical majorities and emphasis on the leadership of an intellectual elite is an oft-repeated theme in Adams scholarship. Brooks Simpson has recently summarized this influence: "Mill's insistence that a democratic society must be overseen by an intellectual elite willing to restrain its excesses and guide it down proper paths outlined a role for Adams to play in the American experiment, one similar to his forefathers."[26] Indeed, as we have seen, Adams did begin to glimpse a "vague and unsteady light" in the direction of a public career in 1863 as he pursued his course of intensive reading. With the very future of democracy at stake during the war, Adams no doubt stood ready to receive a call to action from Tocqueville and Mill. A public role for educated men seemed not just imperative but even possible. "What we want," he wrote Charles, "is a school . . . a national set of young men like ourselves or better, to start new influences not only in politics, but in literature, in law, in society, and throughout the whole social organism of the country."[27]

Nonetheless, while clearly an important part of the Tocqueville-Mill-Adams connection, the emphasis on an intellectual elite does not tell the whole story. What it leaves out reveals a crucial, though often neglected, component of Victorian liberal thought: that is, its concern with public morality and civic spirit as well as with individual liberty and elite leadership. Tracing out this component helps us better understand Adams's thought and offers a fuller and more balanced account of late-nineteenth-century liberal reform.

As Seymour Drescher has argued, Tocqueville's fears about democracy underwent an important shift between the printing of the first and second volumes of *Democracy in America*. While in 1835 liberty and principled statesmanship seemed to Tocqueville threatened by omnipotent majorities jealous of any claim to superiority, by 1840 that threat had receded in the face of an even more troubling one: an enfeebled and inactive citizenry. The locus of tyranny in this latter case "was no longer in the majority of acting unthinking citizens," in Drescher's words, "because Tocqueville's democratic citizens no longer acted or thought."[28] The concerns of private life had overridden those of public life and the increasing bureaucratization and centralization of political power made participation less necessary and more difficult for a new middle class that had no conception of civic spirit. Albeit more "gentle" than tyrannical, according to Tocqueville, governmental power in this guise nevertheless "hinders, restrains, enervates, stifles, and stultifies so much that in the end each nation is no more than a flock of timid and hardworking animals with the government as its shepherd." Equality again took the blame here, Tocqueville explained, believing it "easier to establish an absolute and despotic government among a people whose social conditions are equal than among any other."[29]

Reviewing Tocqueville's second volume, Mill picked up on this theme of an enfeebled citizenry, but he disagreed that democracy or equality *per se* necessarily produced this passivity. The crucial factor, he believed, was civic participation, which he illustrated in the distinction between France and the United States, both nominal democracies, but with very different political cultures. In France, Mill wrote, "everything was done *for* the people, and nothing *by* the people," but in the United States, the people took as active an interest in civic affairs as they did in their own private affairs. As long as the political system encouraged participation in self-government, Mill thought, democracies could escape the fate Tocqueville envisioned for them. Indeed, it was this very widespread participation that made democracy a desirable form of government.[30]

Civic virtue became a main theme of Mill's own analysis of democracy, the condition of the citizenry sharing equal importance in his mind with the intelligence of its leaders.[31] Mill enumerated two criteria for a good form of government: how well it promoted "the virtue and intelligence of the people themselves" and how well it brought "the general standard of intelligence and honesty existing in the community, and the individual intellect and virtue of its wisest members," to bear on governance.[32] The one was as important as the other; all political schemes in the world were useless—even those assuring elite influence—if the people were passive, apathetic, or stupid.[33] Mill, therefore, favored representative government precisely because of its educative effect on the whole people. A wise and benevolent despot might make good laws and administer them efficiently but, Mill asked, "what sort of human beings can be formed under such a regimen?" Their mental and moral capacities would be "equally stunted." In a passage that has particular resonance in light of Adams's impending reform moment, Mill sympathized with "impatient or disappointed reformers, groaning under the impediments opposed to the most salutary public improvements by the ignorance, the indifference . . . [and] perverse obstinacy of a people, and the corrupt combinations of selfish private interests armed with the powerful weapons afforded by free institutions." He understood why those reformers might "sigh for a strong hand to bear down all these obstacles" and compel a people to be well-governed in spite of itself. But he cautioned that any such notion left "out of the idea of good government its principal element, the improvement of the people themselves." Reform, to be worthwhile and enduring, must come from the people. Participation in self-government itself provided an indispensable political education.[34]

Mill's insistence on the importance of civic participation drew from the lessons of classical republicanism. He derived many of his prescriptions for modern democracies from his understanding of ancient Athens, particularly through the work of his friend George Grote.[35] His enthusiasm for the direct democracy of the polis tempered his liberalism, if we understand liberalism to be concerned only with the private rights and enlightened self-interest of individuals. For example, Mill conceived of the franchise not as a private right at all but as a public trust, in the same manner as service on juries. A vote "is strictly a matter of duty; [the citizen] is bound to give it according to his best and most conscientious opinion of the public good."[36] Part of the reason Mill found Athenian direct democracy so attractive, as Eugenio Biagini has recently argued, was its supposed openness to the leadership of intellectual elites. For "the multitude have often a true instinct for distinguishing an able man" as long as he received a fair hearing. While in "the old democracies there were no means of keeping out of sight any able man," in modern democracies all kinds of barriers stood between the able man and his "natural" constituency. As the United States and Britain both demonstrated, he claimed, one who has "only talents and character" to offer could rarely compete with those who had great wealth or the support of party machines behind them. Indeed, it was precisely because large, modern democracies obstructed what was formerly a fair field for the exchange of ideas that Mill believed special provisions like plural voting and proportional representation were necessary.[37]

During Adams's residency in Britain, Mill proved himself an exception to the general rule of modern representative politics by winning election to Parliament in 1865—an event Adams noted with enthusiasm. Mill used this opportunity to extend his influence as a public intellectual, or public moralist, explaining that he valued his position as an M.P. less as an entry into practical politics than as "an elevated Tribune or Chair from which to preach larger ideas than can at present be realized." His subsequent defeat in 1868 allowed him to continue his preaching unfettered by party concerns, and as his disillusionment with the Liberal Party increased, he bypassed it and appealed directly to "the people" both in speeches and in print. Such appeals reflected Mill's belief in the importance of independent and elevated journals of opinion as the only means of obtaining a hearing for "advanced" views. As Stefan Collini has argued, Mill demonstrated a sophisticated appreciation of the power of the periodical press throughout this last phase of his career.[38] The mode of engagement also enacted his insistence that reform must come from the people.

Adams failed to record the precise lessons he drew from Tocqueville and Mill, but his later political analyses reveal evident and substantial connections. His reading in political thought came at a propitious time, both for himself and the American nation. As the country weathered a crisis and then negotiated reunion, Adams, like many of his class and generation, cast about for a career. With the example of Mill and the young college-educated Liberals before him, he thought seriously about a career in journalism.[39] He laid the groundwork for this new role while still in England, writing articles on history and political economy for the *North American Review*, which James Russell Lowell and Charles Eliot Norton had taken over in 1863, and cultivating his public voice. He and his brother criticized each other's work ruthlessly and engaged in lengthy epistolary discussions over style and audience. He dreaded the dullness of some of his essays, and though he confessed to Charles that "the public is a pretty contemptible thing . . . [and] I've no very high opinion of it myself," he insisted that liveliness and clarity were crucial to "men who propose to influence the public."[40]

In tandem with discussions over style came debates over the appropriate stance towards American politics as presently arranged. Adams professed only hostility for the Radical Republicans who had taken control of Reconstruction and seemed, to Adams, bent on destroying the Constitution. Entirely unsympathetic to the cause of newly freed African Americans, he viewed black suffrage and military occupation as dangerous departures from American traditions. He registered his alarm in language and concepts borrowed from Tocqueville and Mill, fearing that Radicals such as Massachusetts senators Charles Sumner and Henry Wilson had become "utterly savage, intolerant and intolerable towards minorities now that they have themselves become a majority." With unintentional irony, Adams concerned himself with the treatment not of the black minority in the South but of the minority of self-styled political moderates, including his brother John, newly defected from the Republican Party. "The tyranny of majorities in our country must be tempered by resistance," he declared, "and I believe it would be a good policy to support the most profligate political opposition rather than allow one party to rule unchecked"—thereby articulating a working credo for his new career.[41]

Though Adams's views were extreme, his dissatisfaction with the Radical Republicans and his defense of moderation would soon find companionship at home, especially in the body of opinion developing around the New York *Nation*, the new weekly to which Henry asked Charles to subscribe him in 1866. As editor, E. L. Godkin maintained a similar line against party discipline, if not yet against Reconstruction, and would become one of Adams's contacts when he returned home. In December 1867, Adams admitted the future still seemed "misty," but his wartime experience in Britain as an American democrat and his studies as a young liberal helped guide his path. "I have a few more articles in view for future use, but I mean to change their purpose a little," he wrote his brother. "There are still heads to hit in the world." Adams returned home in the summer of 1868, looking for targets.[42]

Washington

"There is much reason to regret that every voter in the US cannot be compelled, at some period of his life, to visit Washington," Adams wrote in 1869, six months after he had begun his own such visit. The first fruits of Adams's extended Washington "visit" came in the guise of a feisty article on the congressional session (titled, simply, "The Session") for the *North American Review* and an economical analysis, "American Finance, 1861–1869," for the *Edinburgh Review*. With these transatlantic productions—or "fire-crackers," as he called them—Adams hope to establish his intellectual authority and build a reputation for himself as a bold and independent critic. The "Session" article gave him an opportunity to diagnose America's political ills and begin to articulate a cure. Unsurprisingly, given his family history and his initial views on post-war politics, he identified the overweening power of parties as the main problem with American political life. "The condition of parties," he announced, "precludes the chance of reform."[43]

Parties, as they existed in the late 1860s, irked Adams for a number of reasons. He charged them, most importantly, with hampering individual action and the free play of ideas. As evidence of this, Adams cited the experience of his new friend and ally David A. Wells, special commissioner of the revenue, whose annual report had demonstrated, "in a way so clear that no one could misunderstand the evidence," the mischief wrought by the present tariff and the need for reform. Adams gave "hearty support" to Wells's free-trade principles, as he would "to every liberal and honest movement," but tariffs or even economic policy in general did not constitute his real concern. He wished instead to call attention to the "debauching effect of the system upon parties, public men, and the morals of the State." While Wells himself, Adams explained, "has no party to serve, no interest to enrich, nor any 'ring' to work for," his report unleashed a "swarm of stinging insects" from special interests determined to kill the document. The special interest "rings"—iron, whiskey, railroad, and others—controlled legislation because they paid "liberally towards the support" of both party organizations. Tempering his assault, Adams conceded that "Congressmen, themselves, as a class, are not venal" and that "Congress itself still has a sense of honor." Party organizations, however, had "no decency or shame," and dependent on the interests for financial support, they paid for that support with control of policy. Wells's report, therefore, went unnoticed as parties prohibited the free play of ideas. "A network of rings controls Congress, and forms a hedge which marks the limit within which argument and reason may prevail." As Mill had written, the most powerful elements in modern democracies contrived ways, through money and organization, to stifle ideas they did not favor.[44]

To win a fair hearing for one's ideas, a free agent like Wells had only one strategy at his disposal: to place "his arguments before the people" and wait "until some party finds its interest involved in supporting him." Meanwhile, something had to check the increasingly "dictatorial power of parties," and Adams looked to both free trade and reform of the civil service as ways of breaking down party control by removing the main sources of their power: special protection and patronage. Because parties had so much stake in the system, reform would never come from them. Indeed every measure they touched "seems to have this inevitable result, of swelling the blind, unreasoning vote which follows mechanically a party standard, and thus encourages and protects party corruption." If the public waited for Congress to reform itself, "it will wait long, and it will wait in vain," and Adams feared the government would ultimately break down under the weight of this system. Reform, to be effective, must come from the people. An individual leader like the new president could only provide temporary relief, as his successor would simply revert to the old ways. Unless the "public takes its stand upon some solid principle" against party spoils, reform would never occur. Parties would elude control "until the natural good sense of the people, acting over the heads of all party organizations," reasserted itself.[45]

Adams sharpened his attack on parties and corporate interests in the following years with, again, a double-barreled, transatlantic assault: he wrote "Civil Service Reform" for the *North American* and "The New York Gold Conspiracy" for John Stuart Mill's old journal, the *Westminster Review*. Pursuing further his previous argument, he argued that corruption stemmed from the unbridled and mutually beneficial power that parties and corporations shared. This time, he proposed a solution, arguing that some kind of reform of the civil service could limit the power of parties, which would in turn limit the power of corporations on government.[46] He offered a constitutional argument for reform of the patronage system, claiming that the massive hunt for spoils had unintentionally allowed Congress to usurp executive authority—a theme he would treat humorously in *Democracy*. Again he sounded his emerging themes: the parties were too vested in the system to change it and reform must come from the people. "Whatever troubles distract the state, public opinion is first responsible either for creating or tolerating them," he explained. The solution was not only clear but simple: "whenever public opinion has once declared itself in favor of civil-service reform, and against the corrupt use of patronage by politicians, the evil will cease."[47]

Adams was pleased with his initial foray into political reform, telling his good friend Charles Gaskell he had "smashed things generally and really exercised a distinct influence on public opinion by acting on the limited number of cultivated minds." His work received notice in the leading papers and periodicals of the day, which commented at times on his slash-and-burn style as much as his argument. Adams's efforts reveal a number of interesting things about his emerging reform strategy and the political style it implied. First, Adams, like Mill during this same era, had resolved to construct a public role as independent critic acting through periodicals and not party organizations. He conceived of his journalism and political commentary as, in William Merrill Decker's words, "a form of statecraft." In the heady days of 1869, he imagined transforming his annual "Session" articles into their own "institution and . . . power in the land," capable of framing public debate or even shaping policy. [48] Second, to gain influence he sought the public's attention more than the ear of any political leader.

"The true policy of reformers," he wrote, "is to trust neither to presidents nor to senators, but appeal directly to the people." This is an important point, especially as scholars have, at times, faulted Adams for not cultivating relations with politicians like Pres. Ulysses S. Grant. Though Adams enjoyed the lobbying and intrigue of Washington life, and sent copies of his "Civil-Service Reform" to Grant's cabinet and to all members of the House and Senate, the thrust of his reform work was always public, if not "populist."[49] Restoring virtue to the American republic by breaking the stranglehold of power would require a change in sentiment among the citizenry. Influencing a few congressmen or cabinet members would not be enough; he wanted also to influence the people, by which he meant the middle-class, newspaper-reading public.

The third, and here most relevant, aspect of Adams's reform career is that his belief in the authority of "aroused public feeling" and "sound public opinion" dictated his reform strategy. The public's need to know became the reformer's mission. Only by telling the public the truth about the system could the reformer hope to precipitate the outrage that would put an end to corruption. "The public must be convinced that reform is a vital question," Adams explained, "that the evils and dangers are real, and not mere inventions of a lively fancy." Only with this knowledge would the public have the power to impose its will on its representatives. Inspired by the zeal of a missionary, Adams allowed his language to overcome him: "There is no way but to attack corruption in all its holes, to drag it before the public eye, to dissect it and hold the diseased members up to popular disgust, to give the nation's conscience no rest nor peace until mere vehemence of passion overcomes the sluggish self-complacency of the public mind." Adams believed that in fighting against self-complacency and civic sluggishness, reformers would be doing noble and important work. "To build by slow degrees this deep foundation of moral conviction, to erect upon it a comprehensive and solid structure of reform, and to bequeath the result to posterity as a work not inferior in quality to that of the Republic's founders," he considered "an aim high enough to satisfy the ambition of one generation."[50]

Nevertheless, the flood of outrage failed to descend on Washington. Adams's rhetoric was apparently unequal to the task of jolting the citizenry out of their apathetic stupor. Consequently, Adams and his reforming set decided more aggressive measures were in order. If the public knew the extent of the problem, knew the stranglehold that special interests had on parties, knew that "argument and reason" were circumscribed within strict party-determined limits, and still did not act, then things were worse than Adams had imagined. "The American public crouches," Henry and Charles wrote in 1876, "in a sort of good-natured ignorance of its dignity." The situation demanded more dramatic tactics. Ensconced in Cambridge as professor at Harvard and editor of the *North American Review*, Adams conspired in a more direct assault on parties through the Independent movement. He appealed now to a more select group: the "Independent voters and thinkers," something between the general "public" and the "limited number of cultivated minds" he had formerly hoped to influence. They would lead the charge, as "one by one the great organs of public opinion have assumed the Independent position . . . [and] on this steady growth of Independent opinion the hopes of reformers are built." Independence from parties offered citizens a more intensive kind of political education, according to Adams. Voters would have to be vigilant, weighing the rhetoric of platforms against the practices of parties. When parties fall short of their professions, voters must be unsentimental about "bolting" them and throwing them out of office. Parties would also benefit, at least morally, from such civic independence. Only when out of power, Adams argued, could a party devote itself to a principle, become "educated up to it in opposition," and come back "into power prepared and pledged to accomplish it."[51]

Although Adams kept up the good fight through 1876, he grew increasingly disillusioned with reform. All his efforts at forcing knowledge on an indifferent public seemed in vain. While he believed the Independents had done some good in exposing "the awful corruption of our system in root and branch" and attacking the most "powerful scoundrels," he feared that exposure would prove insufficient. "Our people as yet seem quite callous," he wrote Gaskell in the months before the ill-fated election of 1876, adding, "if any storm of popular disgust is impending, no sign of it as yet darkens the air." The public's callousness, in turn, affected his own attitude. "Politics have ceased to interest me," he declared to Henry Cabot Lodge. "Satisfied that the machine can't be smashed this time," Adams decided to "leave this greatest of American problems to shrewder heads than mine." Only when the day arrived when it would "be considered as disgraceful to be seen in a caucus as to be seen in a gambling-house or brothel" would his interest "wake up again" and "legitimate politics . . . get a new birth." Until then, Adams focused on more rewarding pursuits.[52]

"NO REPRESENTATIVE GOVERNMENT can long be much better or much worse than the society it represents," Silas P. Ratcliffe explains in *Democracy*. "Purify society and you purify the government. But try to purify the government artificially and you only aggravate failure." Putting these words in the mouth of the amoral senator from Illinois, Adams revealed the cynicism of a system that relied on the shortcomings of its citizens to shield itself from its own corruption. One might read Adams's novel as the last act of his political reform moment, his final and most aggressive attempt to expose the evils of American politics and wake the nation's conscience. The novelistic form, the witty sketches of Washington political society, and the who's who parlor game it generated all ensured the book a larger and broader circulation than any of his earlier reform productions had.[53]

Adams gleefully depicted Ratcliffe's corruption, from his election-stealing in Civil War Illinois to his bribe-taking as senator. Adams portrayed as insidious the depraving effect of a political system dedicated to power above principle. To Ratcliffe, "the pleasure of politics lay in the possession of power," and nothing more: "He had very little sympathy for thin moralizing, and a statesmanlike contempt for philosophical politics. He loved power, and he meant to be President. That was enough." Leadership, ideas, and philosophy are all shut out from political life in Adams's fictional capital; politicians soon lose any moral compass they may have had. Ratcliffe justifies his behavior through an amoral defense of party, frequently conflating the interests of his party with the public good. "He talked about virtue and vice," Madeleine concludes at the end of the novel, "as a man who is color-blind talks about red and green."[54]

Democracy is a far more nuanced, even conflicted, work than any of his earlier reform declarations. While Ratcliffe comes in for scorn and ridicule, so too do reformers like Mr. C. C. French, Nathan Gore, and even Madeleine Lee herself. French seems hopelessly out of touch; Gore practically prostitutes himself for office. Madeleine finds herself nearly seduced by power, making all kinds of moral compromises in the process. Adams seems to mock the ideals not just of reformers but of Americans more generally, who, as the world-weary Baron Jacobi contends, imagine themselves "to be excepted from the operation of general laws" by believing that Washington alone among capitals might be pure. Madeleine echoes the Baron's sentiments at the end of the novel, once her political education is complete: "She had got to the bottom of this business of democratic government, and found out that it was nothing more than government of any other kind." Adams leaves the reader less with an earnest call to action than with sober acquiescence. The Massachusetts historian and would-be diplomat Nathan Gore sounds the new theme: "I believe in democracy. I accept it. . . . I believe in it because it appears to me the inevitable consequence of what has gone before it. . . . I grant it is an experiment, but it is the only direction society can take that is worth its taking; the only conception of its duty large enough to satisfy its instincts; the only result that is worth an effort or a risk. Every other possible step is backward, and I do not care to repeat the past."[55]

Adams and Madeleine gained knowledge of politics during their brief reform moments, and both gained self-knowledge as well. "If I do not yet know about politics all that is to be known," Madeleine tells Ratcliffe as she refuses him, "I have learned enough to prove that I could do nothing sillier than to suppose myself competent to reform anything." The objects of politicians were "not her objects," she realizes, "and to join their company was not her ambition." Instead she escapes to Egypt, declaring "Democracy has shaken my nerves to pieces." Adams remained in Washington, but fled into history. Having seen, touched, and measured American politics, Adams, like Madeleine Lee, turned away: "To protect herself was the only right [Madeleine] claimed. If this view of her duty was narrow, it was at least proof that she had learned something."[56] Their need to know satisfied, both gave up the fight. One could hardly blame the American people for doing no more.

NOTES

1. This was not Adams's first time in Washington. He had spent Secession winter there both as private secretary to his congressman father and as anonymous Washington correspondent for the *Boston Daily Advertiser*—an experience he described as one of "continual intoxication." See Ernest Samuels, *The Young Henry Adams* (Cambridge, Mass., 1967), 81–95.
2. Interest in Adams's political thought seems to have waned in tandem with general interest in him among historians. Most recent scholarship has come from literary scholars. Some notable exceptions include Ari Hoogenboom, "Henry Adams and Politics," in *Henry Adams and His World*, ed. David R. Contosta and Robert Muccigrosso (Philadelphia, 1993); Brooks P. Simpson, *The Political Education of Henry Adams* (Charleston, 1996); and James P. Young, *Henry Adams: The Historian as Political Theorist* (Lawrence, Kans., 2001). The latter, a political theorist, makes a persuasive case for a reexamination of Adams's political thought.
3. Henry Adams to Charles Francis Adams, Jr., May 1, 1863, in *The Letters of Henry Adams*, ed. J. C. Levenson et al. (Cambridge, Mass., 1982–1988), 1:350. A glance at the contemporary periodical debate, with such titles as "Democracy on Its Trial" and "Democracy Teaching by Example," reveals the interest of Britons in the fate of democracy

during the Civil War. See also Christopher Harvie, *Lights of Liberalism: University Liberals and the Challenge of Democracy, 1860–86* (London, 1976); Christopher Kent, *Brains and Numbers: Elitism, Comtism, and Democracy* (Toronto, 1978); Donald Bellows, "A Study of British Conservative Reaction to the American Civil War," *Journal of Southern History* 11(1985):506–536; James McPherson, "'The Whole Family of Man': Lincoln and the Last Best Hope Abroad," in *The Union, the Confederacy, and the Atlantic Rim*, ed. Robert E. May (West Lafayette, Ind., 1996); and R. J. M. Blackett, *Divided Hearts: Britain and the American Civil War* (Baton Rouge, 2001).

4. HA to Charles Francis Adams, Jr., Nov., 13, 1863, in *Letters*, 1:406.

5. On the attitudes towards American democracy in 19th-century England, see Benjamin Lippincott, *Victorian Critics of Democracy: Carlyle, Ruskin, Arnold, Stephen, Maine, Lecky* (Minneapolis, 1938); G. D. Lillibridge, *Beacon of Freedom: The Impact of American Democracy upon Great Britain, 1830–1870* (Philadelphia, 1954); Frank Thistlethwaite, *The Anglo-American Connection in the Early Nineteenth Century* (Philadelphia, 1959); David Paul Crook, *American Democracy in English Politics, 1815–1850* (New York, 1965).

6. Recognition would have been disastrous for the Union. It would have flouted the North's arguments about the sanctity of the Constitution, given the Confederacy the right to make treaties, and made Confederate independence far more possible. France would no doubt have followed Britain's lead, as Napoleon III seemed already eager to recognize the Confederacy. As Howard Jones points out, distinct advantages accrued to the Union by virtue of belligerent status for the Confederacy. Specifically, it absolved the Union of any responsibility for the actions of the Confederacy and granted it the right to establish a blockade that foreign states were compelled to honor. Still, the Lincoln administration, and the North at large, "mistakenly regarded the decision as purposefully partial toward the South, if not in motive than surely in consequence," *Union in Peril: The Crisis over British Intervention in the Civil War* (Chapel Hill, 1992), 28–29.

7. Earl Russell, quoted in James Ford Rhodes, *History of the United States from the Compromise of 1850* (New York, 1904), 3:504. A host of motives factored into British attitudes towards the American war, from humanitarian outrage at the bloody conflict to economic worries over the languishing cotton industry in Lancashire to national jealousy about a large and growing rival.

8. HA to Charles Francis Adams, Jr., Aug. 5, 1861, in *Letters*, 1:248.

9. HA to Charles Francis Adams, Jr., Jan. 23, 1863, in *Letters*, 1:327; Charles Francis Adams, Sr., to Charles Francis Adams, Jr., Dec. 25, 1862, in *A Cycle of Adams Letters, 1861–1865*, ed. W. C. Ford (Boston, 1920), 1:221; HA to Charles Francis Adams, Jr., Mar. 27, 1863, in *Letters*, 1:339. The debate on British opinion towards the American war is a long one that begins, if not with the Adamses and other firsthand Northern observers, with the Progressive-era historians Ephraim Douglass Adams, *Great Britain and the American Civil War* (New York, 1925), and Donaldson Jordan and Edwin J. Pratt, *Europe and the American Civil War* (New York, 1931), who argued that British and European attitudes towards slavery and democracy determined sympathies with the North and South. For the argument that Britain acted pragmatically and in response to American *events*, rather than *ideals*, see Max Beloff, "Historical Revision No. CXVIII: Great Britain and the American Civil War," *History* 37(1952):40–48; and David Paul Crook, *The North, the South, and the Powers: 1861–1865* (New York, 1974). Others have challenged the notion that the British working class favored the North, such as Mary Ellison, *Support for Secession: Lancashire and the American Civil War* (Chicago, 1972). More recent accounts suggest that after the effect of the Emancipation Proclamation had sunk in, the working class did in fact support the North, and that the cause of freedom and that attitudes towards democracy helped

determine pro-Southern or pro-Northern sympathies. See Philip S. Foner, *British Labor and the American Civil War* (New York, 1981); McPherson, "'The Whole Family of Man'"; and Blackett, *Divided Hearts*. From his survey of conservative British opinion during the war, Donald Bellows has argued that "antidemocratic attitudes . . . may have been more pervasive and more influential than previously thought." "A Study of British Conservative Reaction to the American Civil War," 507.

10. The quotation from the Earl of Shrewsbury appears in Adams, *Great Britain and the American Civil War*, 2:282.
11. HA to Charles Francis Adams, Jr., Jan. 23 and Mar. 27, 1863, in *Letters*, 1:327, 339–340.
12. HA to Frederick William Seward, Jan. 9, 1863, and HA to Charles Francis Adams, Jr., Mar. 20, 1863, in *Letters*, 1:325, 336. Adams requested copies of documents for the Liberal statesmen John Bright, W. E. Forster, and Monckton Mills, explaining "there are many good friends of ours with whom a copy would be well invested."
13. HA to Charles Francis Adams, Jr., Mar. 20, 1863, in *Letters*, 1:336. On the importance of the American Civil War as a means of unifying and rallying young British Liberals, see Harvie, *Lights of Liberalism*, and Kent, *Brains and Numbers*. Charles Milnes Gaskell, who became Adams's closest and most enduring friend from Britain, was the son of a Liberal M.P.
14. HA to Charles Francis Adams, Jr., Oct. 23, 1863, in *Letters*, 1:402. On the acceptance of Mill at Oxford, see Eldon J. Eisenach, "Mill and Liberal Christianity," in *Mill and the Moral Character of Liberalism*, ed. Eisenach (University Park, Penn., 1998), 191–230.
15. HA to William Evarts, July 14, 1865, in Edward Chalfant, *Better in Darkness: A Biography of Henry Adams: His Second Life, 1862–1891* (Hamden, Conn., 1994), 108.
16. HA to Charles Francis Adams, Jr., July 14, 1865, in *Letters* 1:498. Curiously, Adams makes no mention of two causes célèbres of Liberal England in these years: that of Gov. Edward Eyre in Jamaica in 1865 and the campaign for suffrage reform, which eventually culminated in the 1867 Reform Act. While his silence is curious, it may owe in part to the fact that his brother—his main correspondent while in England—was traveling in Europe on honeymoon from Nov. 1865 to Sept. 1866. Young college Liberals rallied to both causes, boldly asserting their arrival on the public scene with their *Essays on Reform* in 1867. Adams never mentioned but was certainly familiar with this volume, as his friend Richard Monckton Milnes was a contributor. See Samuels, *Young Henry Adams*, 143.
17. HA to Charles Francis Adams, Jr., May 1, July 23, Oct. 23, 1863, in *Letters*, 1:350, 375, 401.
18. HA to Charles Francis Adams, Jr., Feb. 13, 1863, in *Letters*, 1:330.
19. John Stuart Mill, *Autobiography* (1873; New York, 1989), 200–201.
20. Stefan Collini, *Public Moralists: Political Thought and Intellectual Life in Britain, 1850–1930* (Oxford, 1991), 122 and chapter 4. See also Bruce L. Kinzer, Ann P. Robson, and John M. Robson, *A Moralist in and out of Parliament: John Stuart Mill at Westminster, 1865–1868* (Toronto, 1992).
21. Alexis de Tocqueville, *Democracy in America* (1841; New York, 1966), 1:175.
22. Mill coupled this recommendation with an equally insistent demand for universal, free education, so that to him the restriction was never elitist, simply principled. He further wished "that some knowledge of the conformation of the earth, its natural and political divisions, the elements of general history, and of the history and institutions of their own country, could be required from all electors." But he conceded that this level of knowledge was not generally accessible to the whole people anywhere, "save in the Northern United States" perhaps. J. S. Mill, *Utilitarianism, On Liberty, and Considerations on Representative*

Government, ed. H. B. Acton (London, 1987), 304 (cited hereafter as *Considerations*).

23. As a measure of one's intelligence, Mill looked to occupation, though he admitted the imperfections therein. In this scheme a man who employs labor might get three votes to the two votes given a skilled laborer and the one vote for an unskilled laborer. Those in the "liberal professions" would receive even more votes. He was, however, adamant that this "plurality scheme" remain open to the "poorest individual in the community to claim its privileges, if he can prove that, in spite of all difficulties and obstacles, he is, in point of intelligence, entitled to them." *Considerations*, 310. Mill's complicated suffrage discussion also advocated the "proportional representation" scheme put forth by Liberal writer Thomas Hare, which would allow citizens to vote for candidates outside their own district. This system would, in theory, protect minorities, especially that minority of the highly educated who were often swamped in their own districts. Charles Francis Adams, Jr., picked up on this scheme in the 1880s and '90s. See his *Individuality in Politics* (New York, 1880) and his *Emancipation of the Voter* (Boston, 1895). No discussion of Mill's views on the suffrage is complete without acknowledging that he urged the enfranchisement of women on the same terms (that is, with the same requirements, restrictions, and privileges) as men. In spite of Adams's extensive relationships with and comments on women, he did not follow Mill on the issue of woman suffrage. See Young, *Henry Adams*, 127–135.
24. Mill, *Considerations*, 256; Alan Ryan, *J. S. Mill* (London, 1974).
25. John Stuart Mill to E. L. Godkin, May 24, 1865, in E. L. Godkin Papers, bMS Am 1083, Houghton Library, Harvard University. Mill explicitly linked his own opinion of the region to Tocqueville's, saying "If any encouragement were required by those who hope the best from American institutions, the New England States as they now are would be encouragement enough. If Tocqueville had lived to know what those States have become, thirty years after he saw them, he would, I think, have acknowledged that much of the unfavourable part of his anticipations had not been realized."
26. Simpson, *The Political Education of Henry Adams*, 20. See also J. C. Levenson, *The Mind and Art of Henry Adams* (Boston, 1957), 18–20; David R. Contosta, *Henry Adams and the American Experiment* (Boston, 1980), 31–33; Robert Dawidoff, *The Genteel Tradition and the Sacred Rage: High Culture vs. Democracy in Adams, James, and Santayana* (Chapel Hill, 1992), chapter 2; and the more detailed (and nuanced) discussions in Samuels, *Young Henry Adams*, 136–140. Chalfant acknowledges Adams read Mill and Tocqueville but does not credit them with much impact on his ideas of government. *Better in Darkness*, 143.
27. HA to Charles Francis Adams, Jr., Nov. 21, 1862, in *Letters*, 1:316.
28. Seymour Drescher, "Tocqueville's Two Democraties," *Journal of the History of Ideas* 25(1964):204–205. As Drescher argues, the change in Tocqueville's thinking had much more to do with sociological and historical changes in France than conditions in the United States. But much of the language Tocqueville used to describe passivity in the second volume resembles Adams's assessment of post-war America. Adams also seemed directly to echo Tocqueville in the *History*, where he wrote "If at any time American character should change, it might as probably become sluggish as revert to the violence and extravagances of Old-World development. The inertia of several hundred million people, all formed in a similar social mold, was as likely to stifle energy as to stimulate evolution." *History of the United States during the Administrations of Thomas Jefferson and James Madison*, ed. Earl N. Harbert (New York, 1986), 1345. For a discussion of Tocqueville's emphasis on voluntary associations as crucial to a vital democracy, see James T. Kloppenberg, "Life Everlasting: Tocqueville in America," in *The Virtues of Liberalism* (New Yok, 1998), 71–80.
29. Tocqueville, *Democracy in America*, 2:692, 695. Tocqueville pointed out here one of the

"strangest paradoxes," in which a democratic people combined freedom with dependence, consoling themselves for their complete subordination to "administrative despotism" by thinking that they have brought it into being: "Under this system the citizens quit their state of dependence just long enough to choose their masters then fall back into it." He saw this periodic choosing of masters as little consolation, however: "This brief and occasional exercise of free will will not prevent them from gradually losing the faculty of thinking, feeling, and acting for themselves, so that they will slowly fall below the level of humanity." *Democracy in America,* 693–694.

30. Mill, quoted in Eugenio F. Biagini, "Liberalism and Direct Democracy: John Stuart Mill and the Model of Ancient Athens," in *Citizenship and Community: Liberals, Radicals, and Collective Identities in the British Isles, 1865–1931*, ed. Eugenio F. Biagini (London, 1996), 31.
31. As Dennis F. Thompson has argued, the challenge of *Considerations on Representative Government* is to strike a balance between these two concerns (participation and competence). See his John Stuart Mill and Representative Government (Princeton, 1976).
32. Mill, *Considerations*, 207, 209. After decades of conventional wisdom holding Mill confused or inconsistent in his political views, recently more scholars have found unifying themes in his work, from a concern with virtue to an emphasis on character to a conception of Athenian active citizenship. See Bernard Semmel, *John Stuart Mill and the Pursuit of Virtue* (New Haven, 1984); Stefan Collini, *Public Moralists*; H. S. Jones, "John Stuart Mill as Moralist," *Journal of the History of Ideas* 53(1992):287–308; and Biagini, "John Stuart Mill and the Model of Ancient Athens."
33. Semmel, *John Stuart Mill and the Pursuit of Virtue*, 115.
34. Mill, *Considerations*, 219; Ryan, *J. S. Mill*, 202–203.
35. Biagini, "John Stuart Mill and the Model of Ancient Athens," 21–44; Dale E. Miller, "John Stuart Mill's Civic Liberalism," *History of Political Thought* 21(2000):88–113. Grote's and Mill's liberal interpretation of Athens was part of a much larger, heavily politicized conversation about ancient Greece throughout the 19th century. See Frank M. Turner, *The Greek Heritage in Victorian Britain* (New Haven, 1981).
36. Mill, *Considerations*, 324; Biagini, "Mill and the Model of Ancient Athens," 36–37. This interpretation explains Mill's hostility to the secret ballot, which he believed gave the false impression that one's vote was simply a matter of private concern. The logical extension of calling the suffrage a private right, he argued, was that citizens could freely sell their votes to the highest bidder. E. L. Godkin picked up on Mill's interpretation of the ballot in an article for the *North American Review*. The franchise, Godkin wrote there, was "but a trust committed to each individual still more for the benefit of the rest of the nation than for his own, and to be used solely for the promotion of the general progress of the community in virtue and knowledge." Godkin, "The Democratic View of Democracy," *North American Review* 101(1865):103–133.
37. Mill, *Considerations*, 289. "In the context of the polis, elitism and participatory democracy coincided." Biagini, "John Stuart Mill and the Model of Ancient Athens," 38.
38. Mill, quoted in Collini, *Public Moralists*, 162, 126, and see all of chapter 4. Mill supported independent journals both at home and in the United States, including the journal Adams was about to choose to launch his journalistic career in politics and history: the *North American Review*. John Stuart Mill to E. L. Godkin, May 24, 1865, in E. L. Godkin Papers, bMS Am 1083, Houghton Library, Harvard University.
39. Here Adams was an important part of that transatlantic phenomenon, the "higher journalism," which was just then remaking print culture. See Christopher Kent, "Higher Journalism and the Mid-Victorian Clerisy," *Victorian Studies* 13(1969):181–198; and Da-

vid D. Hall, "The 'Higher Journalism' and the Politics of Culture in Mid-Nineteenth-Century America," unpublished paper in author's possession.

40. HA to Charles Francis Adams, Jr., Oct. 22, 1867, in *Letters*, 1:555. On Adams's relation to his imagined audience, and his construction of an authorial role in general, see William Merrill Decker, *The Literary Vocation of Henry Adams* (Chapel Hill, 1990).
41. HA to John Gorham Palfrey, Aug. 23, 1866, in *Letters*, 1:509. He accused Charles of being too fearful of public opinion to speak his mind on the matter and believed John was the only one willing to live up to the family name.
42. HA to Charles Francis Adams, Jr., Dec. 24, 1867, in *Letters*, 1:561–562.
43. Henry Adams, "The Session," *NAR* 108(1869), reprinted in *The Great Secession Winter of 1860–61 and Other Essays*, ed. George E. Hochfield (New York, 1958), 63, 70.
44. HA, "The Session," 69–71. Interests in politics were, of course, not new. Indeed Henry's grandfather had struggled against the efforts of a powerful interest—slavery—to limit "argument and reason." But Adams and other reformers saw new cause for concern in the expansion of the state and the explosion of industrial capitalism during the war and post–war period, which thereby multiplied both the rewards and the tools of parties.
45. HA, "The Session," 71–73. Stephen Skowronek offers an excellent discussion of the futility of relying on parties to limit their own power. See *Building a New American State: The Expansion of National Administrative Capacities, 1877–1920* (Cambridge, 1982), especially chapter 3. See also Ari Hoogenboom, *Outlawing the Spoils: A History of the Civil Service Reform Movement, 1865–1883* (Urbana, 1961); and Mark Wahlgren Summers, *The Era of Good Stealings* (New York, 1993).
46. Simpson seems to miss this crucial connection between corporate power and civil service reform, faulting Adams for not sticking to the issue of corporate power and instead subordinating it to civil service reform. *Political Education*, 59. Reform of the civil service, for Adams, was more a means to an end than an end in itself.
47. Henry Adams, "Civil-Service Reform," in *Great Secession Winter*, 127.
48. HA to Charles Francis Adams, Jr., May 17, 1869; HA to Gaskell, May 17, 1869, in *Letters*, 2:31, 32; Decker, *Literary Vocation*, 13.
49. HA, "Civil-Service Reform," 127. Simpson repeatedly faults Adams for alienating Grant, saying Adams's attacks on him in the press ended "any hope of exercising influence in high places." *Political Education*, 70. The influence Adams sought, however, was a public one, which James Young makes clear by arguing that his reform strategy "reflects some real confidence in the people, since it is essentially populist in character." *Henry Adams*, 96. Far from a populist by ideology or temperament, however, Adams's notion of public influence relied precisely on the "limited number of cultivated minds" he thought he could reach through the *North American* and the *Nation*.
50. HA, "Civil-Service Reform," 128.
51. [Henry Adams and Charles Francis Adams, Jr.], "The Independents in the Canvass," in *Great Secession Winter*, 331. See Chalfant, *Better in Darkness*, 327–328, for claims Charles Francis Adams, Jr., wrote the whole piece himself. In pointing out the power of a principled opposition, Adams evinced a distaste (common to many liberal reformers) for the moral compromises that actual governing involved.
52. HA to Charles Milnes Gaskell, June 14, 1876; HA to Henry Cabot Lodge, June 24, 1876, in *Letters*, 2:276, 279. Adams felt particularly embittered by how Carl Schurz had abandoned the Independent movement in his haste to return to party regularity once Rutherford B. Hayes was nominated.
53. Henry Adams, *Democracy: An American Novel* (1880; New York, 1994), 47–48.
54. HA, *Democracy*, 54, 182.

55. HA, *Democracy*, 176, 48, 50.
56. HA, *Democracy*, 185, 176.

"No traces of a beginning, no prospect of an end"

Henry Adams, Charles Lyell, & the Politics of Uniformity

CROSBIE SMITH & IAN HIGGINSON

IN THE SPRING OF 1868, a young Henry Adams, seeking to build his authorial reputation, wrote to Charles Eliot Norton to offer to prepare a piece for the *North American Review.* He proposed, specifically, "some thirty pages in the North American, for a review of Sir Charles Lyell's 'Principles of Geology. Tenth Edition,'" published in two volumes in 1867–1868. Adams's review followed in October 1868.

In the early 1830s, Lyell had built a model of the geological economy that reflected Enlightenment values of stability and perfection. Just as late-eighteenth-century French astronomers such as Pierre Simon de Laplace had represented the sun and its planets as an eternally stable solar *system* in a state of dynamic equilibrium, so too did Lyell view the terrestrial order as one that, despite continual change and rearrangement, showed no tendency to decline or failure. Indeed, the same kinds of models could also serve as goals for the "improvement" and even "perfection" of human society through the new science of political economy.[1] Hostile to all notions of "progressive" change in the physical world, Lyell remained for three decades skeptical of any evolutionary theory of the animal economy. But by the 1860s Charles Darwin's theory of evolution by natural selection finally persuaded Lyell to admit fully such a radical notion of species progression into the penultimate edition of his *Principles.* Adams's reading of Lyell thus took place at this significant juncture whereby Enlightenment stability met nineteenth-century progression.

Adams opened his review, which finally amounted to thirty-five pages, with the words of the eighteenth-century Scottish geologist James Hutton:

> "*Nunc naturalem causam quaerimus, et assiduam, non raram et fortuitam.*—In the economy of the world, I can see no traces of a beginning, no prospect of an end." Dr Hutton used this language in announcing his famous theory of the earth eighty years ago. The choice of words was unfortunate, and theological wrath burst upon him with true Scotch energy in consequence. . . . Dr Hutton maintained only that geology had nothing to do with first causes, or with the origin of matter . . . but though he would not even discuss the world's beginning, the world's economy was a different thing.[2]

As a product of a very well-known gentlemanly professional, *Principles of Geology*, in both its first edition of 1830–1833 and its tenth, offered a model of the terrestrial economy in which Lyell unashamedly declared its Enlightenment pedigree, most famously in the form of its Huttonian maxim: "no traces of a beginning, no prospect of an end." Permeated by notions of a *balanced* and *stable* (though not static) economy of nature, by the adequacy of *ordinary* agents of change, and by the refusal to introduce miraculous or arbitrary *interventions*, the model appeared *prima facie* one that would appeal to New England Unitarians, whose culture of gentlemanly professionalism also promoted a "democratic" ethos.

This compatibility persisted despite the significant scientific controversies that had intervened between 1833 and 1868. Much had changed since the first edition, in which Lyell appraised and rejected the developmental doctrine of French naturalist Jean-Baptiste Lamarck. By the 1860s, Lyell recognized the extent to which Charles Darwin had based his theory of evolution by means of natural selection upon Lyellian geology, and especially upon the vast resources of geological time that it seemed to offer. As a result, Lyell became, in Adams's later judgment, "the geological champion of Darwin." Not only did Lyell publish his *Antiquity of Man* (1863) "in order to support Darwin by wrecking the Garden of Eden," but with the tenth edition of the *Principles* "the Darwinian doctrine grew in stature" as "Natural Selection led back to Natural Evolution, and at last to Natural Uniformity."[3]

Indeed, for anyone looking for a science of history and human society, the grafting of Darwinian evolutionary doctrine, read as "progressive development," onto the tenth edition of the *Principles* seemed to offer a perfect antidote to John Quincy Adams's earlier verdict on the consequences of democratic principle, namely, that a system of natural laws with democratic agencies led not to improvement and progress but to plunder and greed. For Henry Adams, however, this early familiarity with Lyellian and Darwinian doctrines became the route back to his grandfather. The hints of skepticism in his review presage his subsequent "conversion" to a set of highly anti-Lyellian perspectives, most notably those of Lord Kelvin's energy physics and geological dynamics.

Through his well-known empathy with the work of his close friend Clarence King, Adams became committed to a "catastrophic" model of nature and society. Reacting against "progressive" readings of Lyell and Darwin, Adams aligned himself with Lord Kelvin's heat-engine model, which posited that physical changes were driven by the transformations of energy from states of greater to lesser intensity. This model also readily assimilated American "catastrophist" doctrines in geology and political economy and provided Adams with the foundation for his later perspectives on the possibilities for a science of history.[4]

IN 1868, HOWEVER, Adams still found himself drawn to Lyell's models, and he offered to write his review with an eye to promoting himself and Lyell, who was already a friend of the family. Lyell had proven himself a true ally with his support of the Union cause in the Civil War, during which Charles Francis Adams, with son Henry as his personal secretary, served in London as the American minister. In that situation, the American Legation found itself largely alienated from the English establishment, including *The Times* and much of the aristocracy, who were ambivalent if not outright hostile about the goals of the North. A celebrated geological visitor to North America on four occasions between 1841 and 1853, Lyell, together with his wife Mary, was a firm supporter of the Union through the Civil War and had become a close friend of the Adams family.

Lyell made use of this connection himself around 1868, when he paid a personal visit to the U.S. Legation in London "to inquire about getting his 'Principles' properly noticed in America." This visit became the immediate occasion for the ensuing review. Henry Adams "found nothing simpler than to suggest [to Sir Charles] that he could do it himself if Sir Charles would tell him what to say." Less concerned to educate American geologists "about the principles of their profession" than to educate himself, and above all to get himself properly noticed in America, the young

Adams was, however, far from allowing himself to become a mere mouthpiece for the "great Uniformitarian."[5]

In *The Education of Henry Adams*, Adams identified the shortcomings of a Harvard graduate's education as those of "self-criticism and self-consciousness. . . . Afraid of serious risks, and still more afraid of personal ridicule, he seldom made a great failure of life, and nearly always led a life worth living," socially or intellectually. Since Adams already had all the social status he would ever need, and since he always tended toward self-deprecation of his own academic qualities, he instead "betook himself to the single ambition which otherwise would scarcely have seemed a true outcome of the college, though it was the last remnant of the old Unitarian supremacy. He took to the pen. He wrote." Having contributed to the college magazine as an undergraduate in the late 1850s and written much for others in his capacity as private secretary at the legation, he became increasingly eager to establish himself in the republic of letters.[6] Lyell's desire for a review to promote the new edition of his work provided an ideal opportunity, and Henry sounded out *North American* editor Norton on the proposal.

The plan was not without its risks, however. The scientific theories engaged had advocates and detractors, as well as very controversial implications for politics and religion. Keenly aware that he was treading a tightrope, Adams addressed the issue directly with Norton:

> I ought perhaps to add that I shall try to express more valuable opinions than my own, though I don't wish to be controversial. As it is long since I have had the pleasure of talking with Mr [James Russell] Lowell [editor-designate], and neither your opinions nor his are very well known to me, I would rather run no risk of offering to you anything which might seem not conservative enough for your united tastes. Therefore if you are afraid of Sir Charles and Darwin, and prefer to adhere frankly to Mr Agassiz, you have but to say so, and I am dumb. My own leaning, though not strong, is still towards them, and therefore I should be excluded from even the most modest summing up in the Atlantic [*The Atlantic Monthly*], I suppose. It is not likely that I should handle the controversy vigorously—the essay should rather be an historical one—but I should have to touch it.[7]

Adams managed his task with care, and publication of the review served him well. Settled in Washington, D.C., by November 1868, he informed his brother Charles Francis of Lyell's seal of approval and instructed him to pass on the news to the new co-editor (with Lowell) of the *North American*: "Should you see [E. W.] Gurney you may tell him I have a very handsome letter from Sir Charles about my article, which he calls 'the most original he has yet seen on his new edition, and the only one which has called due attention to what is new in it.'" To his English friend Charles Milnes Gaskell he predicted that "In about five years I expect to have conquered a reputation."[8] The *North American* accepted two new articles on political economy for publication soon after.

Privately, however, Henry told Charles Francis early in 1869 of his dissatisfaction: "My article on Lyell humiliated me. It was so damn neatly put together and not an original idea in it." By that time he had begun to throw caution to the winds: "I want to be advertised and the easiest way is to do something obnoxious and do it well":

> I am going to make it [an article on commercial "rings"] monumental, a piece of history and a blow at democracy. I mean to put into it all I've got in matter, thought and style, so that I may be a year or two in working it up, but the return in public horror and disgust will I hope make me a "degenerate son," and a "traitor," a "cynical sceptic," and a "person whose career is closed before it has begun." Damn the idiots, how I do hate 'em! . . . I have however another idea which is to write a popular article showing the practical expedients by which traders make a profit out of the currency. Oh my boy! these fields are gloriously rich and stink like hell if we were only of the force to distil their flowers.[9]

Yet such a radical strategy proved unnecessary, at least in the short term. Adams's credibility was now rising faster than he himself had imagined. By 1870 he took over editorship of the *North American* and almost simultaneously was appointed to a chair of history at Harvard.

The Politics of Uniformity

"Sir Charles thinks the secret of the ill will to us here," Charles Francis Adams confided in his diary in January 1862, "is to be traced to the terror of democratic movement entertained by the aristocracy. They feel it hanging over their heads, and think they may evade it by appealing to the example of our failure." He pondered, specifically, the apparent lack of sympathy for the United States in some establishment circles, most notably in *The*

Times. Lyell, conversely, was "one of the most liberal men in Europe" and "one of our best and most reasonable friends." Both families regularly attended the Unitarian Chapel in Little Portland Street where Reverend James Martineau delivered sermons with such high philosophical content that the elder Adams eventually severed his connection to seek more practical spiritual succor elsewhere in the capital. But Enlightenment liberalism, both in religion and in politics, maintained a strong bond between the Lyells and the Adamses throughout the latter's years at the legation. In May 1863, for example, Charles Francis recorded in his diary Sir Charles's account of a recent visit to Queen Victoria at Windsor Castle during which a conversation with Prince Albert "about America and government generally" did not inspire Lyell "into any great admiration of the monarchical form."[10]

Henry understood these shared values—non-dogmatic Christianity and anti-aristocratic politics—as the product of a common Enlightenment heritage, embraced by the intelligentsia in Boston and in European capitals such as Paris and London. "If the world in London grows old and wanes towards its dotage," Henry Adams wrote to Gaskell in June 1876, "the world here stands still. Boston is a curious place. Its business in life is to breed and to educate." In Boston both parent and teacher reproduced themselves in child and scholar, who repeated the cycle in the next generation:

> Nothing ever comes of it all. There is no society worth the name, no wit, no intellectual energy or competition, no clash of minds or of schools, no interests, no masculine self-assertion or ambition. Everything is respectable, and nothing amusing. There are no outlaws. There are not only no convictions but no strong wants. . . . [W]hen a society has reached this point, it acquires a self-complacency which is wildly exasperating. My fingers itch to puncture it; to do something which will sting it into impropriety. I want to tweak its nose.[11]

Boston, in short, had come to embody the Enlightenment values that made it seem as if reasonableness, balance, and uniformity had smoothed over all those differences of religion and politics that gave purpose and vitality to a culture. Two years on, and he confessed to Gaskell that the sins of "bourgeois ease and uniformity" afflicted him as well in the neighborhood of his native city.[12]

In his *Education*, Adams affirmed that, up to midcentury, "New England society was still directed by the professions. Lawyers, physicians, professors, merchants were classes, and acted not as individuals, but as though they were clergymen and each profession were a church." The Bostonian belief in the classical republican values of "government by the best" had "produced the long line of New England statesmen," not politicians, who "guided public opinion, but were little guided by it." Such values, which exemplified Samuel Coleridge's notion of a "clerisy," or the rule of an elite intelligentsia, did not promote or favor a radical democracy in which mass public opinion dictated policy. Immersed in such an elite liberal culture, Adams "took for granted that this sort of world, more or less the same that had always existed in Boston and Massachusetts Bay, was the world which he was to fit."[13] By the early nineteenth century, the harsh dogmas of the old Puritanism in Boston had yielded to latitudinarian Enlightenment religion. Unitarianism in particular served to express an optimistic faith in human advancement grounded on belief in a natural and moral order.

Adams recognized that this world too had its counterparts in Paris and London: "The Paris of Louis Philippe, Guizot, and de Tocqueville, as well as the London of Robert Peel, Macaulay, and John Stuart Mill, were but varieties of the same upper-class *bourgeoisie*. . . . England's middle-class government was the ideal of human progress."[14] Sir Charles Lyell, he might have added, also fitted such a gentlemanly world, in which men pursued not financial profit but the building of professional reputations in the name of public service. This general consanguinity of European and Bostonian, of political and scientific, made a welcome place for some of Boston's leading residents in British scientific organizations and for European gentlemen of science among American scientific communities.

As Jack Morrell and Arnold Thackray have shown, Boston residents (especially medical men) had been prominent among U.S. visitors to the early meetings of the British Association for the Advancement of Science (BAAS) in the 1830s. Following the failure of an initial attempt by John Collins Warren, professor at the Harvard Medical School and New England's leading surgeon, to create an American Association for the Promotion of Science along the lines of the BAAS, a later campaign established the Association of American Geologists (AAGN) in 1840.[15] The arrival of Louis Agassiz in Boston in 1846 to take up the professorship of zoology and geology at Harvard's new Lawrence Scientific School added European authority to the association, whose core members, like those of the BAAS, tended to be gentlemanly professionals. At the AAGN's Boston meeting in 1847 a proposal to create an American Association for the Advancement of Science succeeded.[16]

When he made his midcentury visits to the United States, Charles Lyell had the opportunity to interact with many of his American counterparts, who greeted him with pleasure but also viewed him with some trepidation. During Lyell's extensive travels around North America, local field-workers and geologists of every variety received him warmly. Indeed, many aspiring New World geologists hoped for a mention in one of Lyell's publications, which could confer on its recipient the considerable credit of a foremost European authority. Conversely, as Robert H. Silliman has demonstrated, American geologists worried that Lyell's appropriation of data and information in the cause of uniformitarian principles might undermine their own status and hinder the cause of nascent national science in the United States.[17] Although Silliman has suggested that Lyell's relations improved in the latter half of the century, the Adams-Lyell interaction shows that Lyell used his most diplomatic efforts "to get his Principles properly noticed in America."

Lyell chose well. Adams felt, at that moment, a particular comfort with these models. Recapturing the period later in the *Education*, he explained the original appeal of the Lyellian (and Darwinian) economy of nature and made explicit the link with the democratic politics and Unitarian religion of New England:

> Unbroken Evolution under uniform conditions pleased every one—except curates and bishops; it was the very best substitute for religion; a safe, conservative, practical, thoroughly Common-Law deity. Such a working system for the universe suited a young man who had just helped to waste five or ten thousand million dollars and a million lives, more or less, to enforce unity and uniformity on people who objected to it; the idea was only too seductive in its perfection; it had the charm of art. . . . One had been, from the first, dragged hither and thither like a French poodle on a string, following always the strongest pull, between one form of unity or centralization and another. The proof that one had acted wisely because of obeying the primordial habits of nature flattered one's self-esteem. Steady, unbroken evolution from lower to higher seemed easy.[18]

Despite the kernels of skepticism the printed review would contain, Henry Adams in 1868 could present Lyell's principles thoroughly and sympathetically.

As Lyell represented his model in the tenth edition of the *Principles*, it featured six interlocking premises. First, he portrayed a world that was rational and reasonable in character, rejecting all arbitrary agencies of a supernatural and mysterious kind to account for geological phenomena. No sudden cataclysms or catastrophes disturbed the terrestrial economy. Second, the same causal agencies at work at the present time had been at work in the past and as such were alone adequate to operate the terrestrial economy. Because these causes were known to produce visible effects, they constituted *verae causae.* A weaker reading in terms of "methodological" (rather than "ontological') uniformitarianism specified that "ordinary" agencies held methodological priority in geological explanations. If, and only if, these agencies proved inadequate, would "catastrophic" agencies be invoked.

Third, Lyell's agents lacked dramatic or theatrical spectacle, representing as they did the ordinary and the natural. No agent was better or worse than any other: they were "democratic" rather than "hierarchical" in nature. Just as a professional society boasted different kinds of expertise and a division of professional labor (such as lawyers or medical men), so the geological economy operated with different kinds of agency (such as water or heat). But just as a professional group did not differentiate its members by birth, class, or creed, neither was there distinction of status within each kind of geological agency. Nonetheless, these "democratic" agencies, acting within a system of division of labor, worked spectacular results very gradually over immense periods of time.

Fourth, the "uniformity" of these agents inhered in their obedience to *natural* laws with no arbitrary or ad hoc behavior and in their unvarying intensity. Fifth, the terrestrial economy functioned as a self-regulating, dynamically balanced, and stable unity, with no inherent tendency to decay or fail over time. Sixth, within this economy vast geographical and environmental change occurred, making possible a progressive development of living organisms from the lowest to the highest (man). Lyell's premises also allowed for the most significant innovation of the tenth edition: it accepted Darwin's perspective on a common origin of species, including man.[19]

Echoing the thesis of the ninth and tenth editions of the *Principles*, Adams's review articulated the extended Lyellian model as one in which the geological conditions of uniformity had made possible the "progressive development" of species up to and including man. Equal in intensity (relatively minor fluctuations averaged out over the long run) and ordinary in character, these natural agencies produced not only change but improvement. While the agencies themselves remained unchanged and operated according to uniformitarian principles, they allowed progressive organic development over time by means of natural selection. Nature itself, therefore, requiring no arbitrary, extraordinary, or revolutionary powers, was "democratic" and "egalitarian." The metaphor did not encompass, however, a concept of mass democracy in which vast numbers of individual human beings acted like equally endowed and freely competing atoms to produce particular results. Instead, the action of different and opposing powers of equal intensity (rather than the action of equal powers) permitted improvement, if not perfection, of the animal economy. This model offered to the heirs of John Quincy Adams an alternative to his pessimistic conclusion that the democratic principle of equality would generate only greed, slavery, and war.[20]

In the immediate context of American politics in the 1860s, Lyell's most recent works made a friend of Union goals, as we shall see below in his critique of Agassiz's theory of human origins. Lyell explicitly rejected Agassiz's view of different "human" races deriving from different quadrumina in different regions of the globe. While Agassiz did not support slavery, his theory opened up opportunities for any society keen for political reasons to separate the races by kind and degree. Darwin's version, conversely, supported the antislavery line that generations of Adamses so vigorously pursued. By giving all the varieties of humanity a single, common ancestor, Darwin implicitly placed all humanity on an equal, democratic footing.[21]

Despite these attractive features of the Lyell/Darwin model of the natural economy, the young Adams revealed in his review some deep reservations. From a geological point of view, he remained highly skeptical of Lyell's account of global changes in climate, which presented geographical shifts in the distribution of land and sea as the explanation of glacial epochs. In the *Education*, Adams pointed to this as the principal weakness in uniformitarianism: "If the glacial period were uniformity, what was catastrophe?" Those insights would mirror his growing doubts about the stability of the United States itself.[22]

Adams had seen from the inside of the legation that the Union was not a balanced and stable "natural" system operating in true uniformitarian fashion through routine agents and unvarying intensity. Instead, the Union had come perilously close to self-destruction when it unleashed the catastrophic forces of civil war, a conflict that "cost a million lives and ten thousand million dollars, more or less, North and South, before the country could recover its balance."[23] Now, post–Civil War, the old fears of John Quincy Adams once more haunted the family: "democratic" agents did not necessarily produce either stability or progress. As Henry wrote to John Gorham Palfry in February 1869:

> How a mere change of administration is to help us, I cannot see, and am rather inclined to think that it will only improve our affairs as far as to make the system endurable, and so blind our people to the necessity of true reform. The idea that democracy in itself, by the mere fact of giving power to the masses, will elevate and purify human nature, seems to me to have now turned out one of those flattering fictions which have in all ages deluded philanthropists. The great problem of every system of Government has been to place administration and legislation in the hands of the best men. We have tried our formula and find that it has failed in consequence of its clashing with our other fundamental principle that one man is as good as another. How to escape the logical consequences of this failure, common to all systems yet invented, I confess I do not see.[24]

An increasing concentration of wealth and power in the hands of the few—the bankers, the capitalists, and ultimately perhaps J. P. Morgan—would itself be enough to suggest that catastrophism in some form would be a more realistic model for the New World disorder than that of gentle and gentlemanly Lyellian uniformitarianism.

Reviewing the "great Uniformitarian"

"I read your ms with much pleasure," Lyell began his first letter to Adams in May 1868. "It seems to me geologically correct in the main & much better calculated to set people thinking than if you had attempted to embrace a greater number of themes, old & new, treated of in my first volume." Thereupon Lyell launched into a page-by-page commentary, offering suggestions, amplifications, and amendments, which Adams for the most part incorporated into his published review.[25] At several points, however, as we will demonstrate in what follows, Adams chose to diverge from the wishes of his subject and even cast a skeptical eye upon the methodological assumptions of the "great Uniformitarian." Those moments, in particular, would shape Adams's "science of history" in the decades that followed.

At the very outset of his review, Adams noted that James Hutton's famous theory of the earth had avoided all questions of first causes, origins of matter and beginnings to earth history. Focusing on the world's economy, Hutton had "been unable to detect any sign that the natural influences now at work had not always been in action or would ever cease to be active; nor would he consent to imagine extraordinary agents in order to account for geological phenomena, until it could be proved that ordinary agents were unequal to the task." As Adams perceived it, there seemed "nothing unreasonable or extravagant in these views, unless it be their very bald and prosaic stamp." But, he asserted, "they were in absolute contradiction to the scientific theories most in fashion, and they were peculiarly obnoxious to religious prejudices." The result was "a combination of scientific and religious intolerance [against which] no power on earth could prevail. Dr Hutton was suppressed."[26]

The "theological wrath [that] burst upon him with true Scotch energy" vividly expressed early-nineteenth-century Scottish religious opposition to Huttonian doctrines. Not everyone in Scotland, however, manifested such hostility. Known for his very liberal theological views, John Playfair, Edinburgh professor of natural philosophy, published his celebrated *Illustrations of the Huttonian Theory* in 1802. He thereby not only rendered Hutton accessible to a wide audience but also stressed the way in which the Huttonian terrestrial economy reflected the balanced perfection of all Nature's economies, none of which manifested any tendency to decline or decay:

> In the continuation of the different species of animals and vegetables that inhabit the earth, we discern neither a beginning nor an end; and, in the planetary motions . . . we discover no mark, either of the commencement or the termination of the present order. It is unreasonable, indeed, to suppose that such marks should any where exist. The Author of nature has not given laws to the universe, which, like the institutions of men, carry in themselves the elements of their own destruction. He has not permitted, in his works, any symptom of infancy or of old age, or any sign by which we may estimate either their future or past duration. He may put an end, as he no doubt gave a beginning, to the present system, at some determinate period; but we may safely conclude, that this great *catastrophe* will not be brought about by any of the laws now existing, and that it is not indicated by any thing which we perceive.[27]

To assert, Playfair concluded, that "in the economy of the world, we see no mark, either of a beginning or an end, is very different from affirming, that the world had no beginning, and will have no end." Complementing Laplace's celestial mechanics, Huttonian theory testified for a "moderate" Scottish Presbyterian like Playfair to the wisdom of the Creator in designing a stable economy of nature. A far more aggressive response, however, arose from a new generation of evangelical Presbyterians led by Thomas Chalmers. These men saw in the Huttonian and Laplacian economies a self-sustaining universe without beginnings or endings—one in which the Christian God had been banished to the margins. Small wonder, then, that Scotland's Free Church Colleges listed Hutton alongside Laplace and Hume as "infidels" to undermine at every opportunity.[28]

With the first printing of his *Principles* in 1830, Lyell "reopened the old controversy," Adams wrote, "by asserting and developing Hutton's theory." Hutton's affirmation of "ordinary agents" became with Lyell the basic rule of geological science, "fixing limits beyond which it has no right to pass, connecting all phenomena in an unbroken series, and applying to them all the known laws of the existing world." In all this, Lyell was "thoroughly methodical in his science," seeming to take "pleasure in lopping away fanciful excresences which other men foster, and . . . treating the earth's marvellous history in that coldly scientific spirit which admits only what is enough, and no more than enough, to produce the result observed." Rigorous and lifelong adherence to a strictly defined method rendered Sir Charles "essentially a conservative philosopher . . . advancing so cautiously as often to lean, in his friends' opinion, somewhat too strongly towards negation." Lyell's tendency to hold steady against the avant-garde of science stood out specifically regarding three contemporary and contentious areas of discussion: the potential for science to grasp or even posit an original world, the glacial theory, and the theory of progressive development.[29]

Of the first, Adams wrote that, "Like Hutton, [Lyell] has always maintained that geology has nothing to do with the origin of things. There is no original world, he says." Thus the "theory of the earth's igneous origin is especially his aversion." The globe's original fluidity or solidity made no difference to the form: it "must inevitably have assumed, sooner or later, the same form as now, from the mere action of atmospheric and astronomical causes." Similarly, because of its association with original fluidity, Lyell would not admit the presence of a fluid nucleus or core below the earth's solid surface. Second, when Louis Agassiz and his friends "introduced into the science the glacial theory, certainly the most brilliant geological discovery of the last half-century, Sir Charles was slow to accept it until the accumulation of evidence overpowered all possibility of resistance."[30] And third, up to and including the ninth edition of the *Principles*, Lyell had "contested energetically the theory of progressive development, maintaining that there was no evidence to justify the common assumption that earlier forms of existence were necessarily simpler than later forms, the more complex making their appearance in an ascending scale till the arrival of man at last." Adams pointed out that before the ninth edition, Lyell met Lamarck's argument in particular with the assertion that "species have a real existence in Nature, and each was endowed at the time of its creation with the attributes and organization by which it is now distinguished." As a consequence of "this scientific spirit of caution, or to this national characteristic of hostility to theories," Adams remarked, Sir Charles's views possessed a certain solidity "which gives them high authority." Always the gentlemanly specialist, Lyell was never one to make concessions to popular beliefs.[31]

Adams now introduced a note of skepticism toward uniformitarian geology with the remark that "Perhaps only the most sanguine geologists feel even now any strong confidence that the truth of this theory can ever be proved by demonstration." He noted, for example, that the diversity was "so enormous between fossils of so-called successive strata, and the quiet of our earth since historical times contrasts so strongly with the evidence of wide and laborious convulsion offered by mountain ranges like the Alps." In particular, "Mont Blanc is but a young mountain, which owes at least two thirds of its upheavals to periods later than the older tertiary. The strata about it are tortured, twisted, folded over and over, the oldest above the newest . . . yet we are required to believe that this process may be, and most probably is, actually going on at some spot in the world, under our very eyes, without our perceiving it."[32]

In an earlier draft of the review, "reading" the natural history of Mont Blanc in particular had become a point of negotiation between him and Lyell. In a letter written in May, Lyell had suggested this revision: "Page 5. Modern origin of Mont Blanc. I believe this mountain must owe more than two thirds of its height to a period of post-eocence date, because Eocence [the term that Lyell introduced for the earliest of four Tertiary epochs] marine strata are found at that height in some of the Alps not far distant but as Mont Blanc is 15000 ft high it might be desirable to moderate your statement and it would serve your purpose to say it owes at least two thirds or more of its upheavals to periods later than the older tertiary." These remarks suggest that Lyell wanted his reviewer to play the role of "independent" critic before an American readership in such a manner that ultimately the critic (and his audience) would be compelled by its *reasonableness* to assent to the Lyellian case, despite the possibility of reading the natural history of Mont Blanc through catastrophic spectacles.[33]

The printed review met Lyell's wishes. Adams reviewed and considered "the rival [catastrophist] hypothesis," which "asserts a series of grand catastrophes, by which all life was extinguished only to be incorporated again in new forms,—and of prodigious, but apparently rare, convulsions of Nature, which have transformed by sudden paroxysms the appearance of the world." Although not identified as such in Adams's review, this theory is usually linked to the work of French naturalist Georges Cuvier. Against this, however, Adams found for the Huttonian principle that Lyell favored: "Of the two theories, Hutton's was certainly the most reasonable. That all life has ever been extinguished on the earth at any one moment . . . is too violent an hypothesis to be accepted without irrefragable proof." On the contrary, some species such as the small marine shell known as the *Terebratula striata* had apparently "lived undisturbed through some of the worst of these catastrophes."[34]

Thus far, Henry Adams appeared to be playing on Sir Charles's team. Where doubts over uniformity opened up, he weighed the "rival view" in the balance of reasonableness and found it wanting, while passing over more sophisticated catastrophist perspectives (linked to Agassiz's glacial theory, for example) then on offer. When Adams turned to the subject of climate, however, his tone became altogether more skeptical. He made a full confession in his later *Education*:

> At the very outset Adams struck on Sir Charles's Glacial Theory or theories. He was ignorant enough to think that the glacial epoch looked like a chasm between him and a uniformitarian world. If the glacial period were uniformity, what was catastrophe? To him the two or three laboured guesses that Sir Charles suggested or borrowed to explain glaciation were proof of nothing, and were quite as unsolid as support for so immense a superstructure as geological uniformity. If one were at liberty to be as lax in science as in theology, one might better say so, as the Church did, and not invite attack by appearing weak in evidence. Naturally a young man, altogether ignorant, could

> not say this to Sir Charles Lyell . . . but he was forced to state Sir Charles's views, which he thought weak as hypotheses and worthless as proofs. Sir Charles himself seemed shy of them.[35]

Hinting "his heresies in vain," Adams admitted that he had inserted in the draft review a sentence "intended to provoke correction": "The introduction [by Agassiz] of this new geological agent seemed at first sight inconsistent with Sir Charles's argument, obliging him to allow that causes had in fact existed on the earth capable of producing more violent geological changes than would be possible in our own day." Lyell apparently said nothing, and Adams "never knew whether the great Uniformitarian was strict or lax in his uniformitarian creed; but he doubted." He must have recognized the parallels between Lyell's flexibility and Boston Unitarianism, where doctrine had been so relaxed as to avoid all controversy: if uniformitarianism could accommodate Agassiz, what constituted catastrophe? The skeptical Adams thus posed questions as to the fruitfulness of a creed without strict doctrine, which could accommodate anything and everything.[36]

In his review, Adams observed that Agassiz's case had been so persuasive that "the question is now no longer whether very astonishing revolutions in climate have taken place, but rather why they have taken place, and how often." In grappling with the question of causes, Adams drew upon a wider field of debate. At this point in his discussion, therefore, Adams also invoked the doctrine of *verae causae* to argue that "Whatever can be proved to have happened once on the earth will probably be found to have happened frequently, since we have no right to assume that any true cause has acted only in a single instance." Partly for this reason, and others besides, Lyell had rejected "as untenable the favorite theory, that the radiation of internal heat, while the earth was still cooling from a liquid state, raised the temperature on its surface throughout the primary period to a higher point than would now be possible." By making this argument, Adams explained, Lyell precluded the possibility of deploying the theory of a cooling earth to explain phenomena such as the apparently higher average warmth of Paleozoic times.[37]

In the absence of reliable knowledge of the primary period, Adams chose to focus on the much more recent and better-known Tertiary period. If a particular pattern of phenomena could be explained for such a period, then the doctrine of *verae causae* meant that the same causes could be invoked to explain phenomena in other, earlier periods such as the Paleozoic. Adams therefore deployed the findings of Prof. Oswald Heer, the

Swiss geologist and a friend of Agassiz, to test for the Tertiary period the efficacy of Lyell's views on climate. Heer's researches, Adams explained, had yielded a "rich harvest of fossils buried almost at his own door in the miocene [Lyell's term for the second Tertiary epoch] deposits of Oeningen." Arguing from the characteristics of present-day species most closely allied to species of the miocene period, Heer had reconstructed a picture of the miocene Swiss climate that resembled present-day Madeira or the Canaries. Heer's further comparative work on fossil collections drawn from Arctic regions yielded proof in high latitudes of a rich miocene vegetation more typical of California or Louisiana. In contrast, evidence from the later pliocene period [fourth and last of the Tertiary epochs] suggested that species of marine shells peculiar to warmer seas "began slowly to disappear [from high latitudes], supplanted by northern forms." The result was that glaciers "poured down the mountains, eroding, polishing, scouring with long grooves the hardest rocks, and carrying boulders and drift over hill and valley."[38]

With these phenomena now firmly set forth, Adams subjected each of three possible explanations to critical scrutiny: a "great ever-recurring winter"; major shifts in land mass—the theory Lyell favored; and astronomical causes associated with the earth's orbit around the sun. Rehearsing all three in rigorous detail, Adams used the occasion to challenge Lyell. The first and third he rejected more soundly, albeit giving extensive consideration to the last.

He treated with maximum skepticism the first of these, offered by "nine in every ten" of "the mass of imaginative human beings." Adams summarized this view as the belief that "this apparition which we call the glacial epoch is but the world's great ever-recurring winter, as the warmer age that preceded it was the world's summer." While there was "much to be said in its favour," Adams asserted unequivocally that "Nature does not necessarily revolve in cycles."[39]

The third theory, nurtured in Scotland and explicated in two widely read papers by James Croll that appeared in the *Philosophical Magazine* in 1867–1868, posited that the eccentricity of the earth's orbit could "seriously affect the distribution of heat" received by a planet from the sun. After giving the hypothesis a thorough review, Adams concluded that the astronomical explanation, "certainly attractive and perfectly philosophical," failed to accord with the facts, notably in accounting for the antecedent warm Tertiary period. He did observe, however, that if science could overcome such objections, "Only the recurrence and the effects of these revolutions in the earth's economy would remain to be studied, and we venture to think that not a long time could elapse before every geologist would find the basis for a new science in the history of climatic variations."[40]

Adams understandably directed most of his readers' attention to addressing the theory of geographical shift as a determinant of climatic change, since Lyell promoted it in the *Principles* in order to win over the skeptics, including the astronomer Sir John Herschel.[41] This view, as Adams summarized it, asserted that "these climatic variations may be sufficiently explained by assuming corresponding changes in physical geography." A globe with "all the dry land massed about the poles" and acting as a storehouse for ice would have a climate "far cooler than one on which all the dry land were massed under the equator," where the land would act as "a furnace for the distribution of heat." Conversely, water at the poles would check and moderate the accumulation of ice, and water about the tropics would absorb and moderate heat. "Calculations had been made," Adams suggested, "to prove that a comparatively small amount of geographical change would be sufficient to produce climatic variations fully as great as those we have stated."[42]

Although this theory ultimately had more credibility in Adams's assessment than the other two, it did not come out unscathed: he deemed it one of those geological theories, necessary to the science, without "the proper number of legs to run upon; the facts, if not contradictory, are wanting." He argued, specifically, that evidence from the miocene period contradicted Lyell's hypothesis. The latter posited less land at the poles than at present and more land within the tropics during the warm phases: "In proportion to these oscillations of land and sea was the greater or less degree of cold; but increased warmth was always the sign of more sea about the pole, or fewer mountains there, or of less sea within the tropics; while increased cold was always preceded by an elevation of polar land, or an extension of tropical ocean." Adams had little opportunity to debate Lyell's view of the tropics, since scientists knew so little of the history of the three-quarters of the globe now sea. More substantial evidence of the polar region, however, made it possible to assert that in miocene times there had existed a "wide extent of firm dry ground." Indeed, Heer's research implied that "a continent existed precisely where according to theory there could not have been any land at all." Similarly, the tropical region now contained an unusually high proportion of land, and to "assume that it contained still more land in the tertiary period is contrary to the geographical theory itself."[43]

Adams also read the evidence of the glacial period in opposition to Lyell's theory. Far from there being an additional elevation of land at the pole as the glacial epoch approached, the evidence pointed to "a remarkable depression beneath the water . . . far and wide throughout the northern hemisphere" amounting to "a submergence of fourteen hundred feet, proved by upraised marine shells, in the latitude of Wales." Lyell had already commented that in the draft Adams had spoken "of Whales [sic] being submerged 2,000 feet in the glacial period. It may be well to remind them that 1400 feet of this is positively proved by upraised marine shells in Moel tryfane. See my 'Antiquity of Man.'" Lyell, however, did not allow this instance to undermine the model; he urged his reviewer not to "forget that when there are proofs of parts of the Welsh or White Mountains being submerged this by no means shows that the quantity of land was less in a given latitude." Lyell attributed such cases of depression to local causes, "counterbalanced by great local elevations." Adams would have none of it. "So far as there is any evidence at hand, both the depression of land and its subsequent emergence about the pole were general, not local," he asserted. "[And they] took place in an order directly the reverse of that which the theory requires."[44]

THIS PORTION OF ADAMS'S REVIEW also provides the segue to the most controversial subject matter of the surrounding discussions: the age of life and the evolution of species. Adams broaches this topic by drawing attention to Sir Charles's "curious attempt" to deploy Croll's theory of eccentricity to calculate the age of organic life on earth. The formula went, in summary, thus: since about 5 percent of marine shells peculiar to the northern hemisphere had disappeared since the beginning of the glacial period and assuming the time elapsed to be 1 million years, then a complete change in the existing testacea shells would require 20 million years. Given that the range of modern shells extended back to early miocene times and given twelve such complete cycles back to the Laurentian epoch, Lyell arrived at a figure of 240 million years as the limit of life on earth. Adams, however, qualifies the conclusion:

> Sir Charles does not, however, mean his estimate to be taken strictly. He would probably be fully as willing to assume a thousand million of years for the development of organic life as a quarter of that time. Nevertheless we may hope that scientific data for a closer calculation may possibly be discovered, and,

> were this once effected, that another step would enable science to fix the limits within which species have flourished, and the race of man among the rest may expect to carry on its development.[45]

"Subjects more and more delicate": The Doctrine of Progressive Development

"Geology is bearing the fruits predicted by Hutton's religious opponents," Adams observes in his review. "It is dealing, for good or evil, with subjects more and more delicate." He therefore turns to Sir Charles Lyell's opinions on the history of organic life on earth, "a subject which involves the fate of all mankind." He begins by noting the parallels between the geological reforms of Hutton and those of Lamarck: "As Hutton maintained that there had been no break of continuity in the earth's economy, but that causes still existing had made the world what we see it, so Lamarck affirmed that there had been no want of continuity in organic existence, but that every shape endowed with life had been derived by the ordinary process of reproduction from shapes previously existing."[46]

Addressing the debate around the origin of species directly later in the review, Adams delineates two scientific theories as the rival answers, one identifiable in shorthand as the theory of special creation and the other as progressive development:

> On this subject the difference of opinion has now become irreconcilable; for, while all the highest authorities in physiology, with but few exceptions, maintain, that, notwithstanding the existence of a limited faculty for self-adaptation in the organism, every separate form has yet its own precise and unvarying boundaries, and had its origin in a distinct, physical, external act of creation, the followers of Lamarck and Darwin affirm no less positively that no such boundaries exist, but that every form of organic life owes its peculiarities of structure to an innate capacity for change. . . . [T]he controversy has now gone so far that it becomes every day more and more difficult for any scientific man to escape committing himself either to the one theory or to the other.[47]

Lyell's position vis-à-vis these two theories demanded substantial consideration in Adams's review, especially because the geologist had made a significant shift. Whereas in his earlier editions of the *Principles* Lyell had avowed that "Lamarck was wrong," Adams explains that now "he recants his former opinion as formally as he then announced it, and declares his belief that Lamarck was right."[48]

In more than fifteen pages of the review, Adams elucidates the change in detail, at times following Lyell's agenda and at others adopting again the stance of independent critic. He also presents himself as mediating between the "high authorities" of science and the "public." In the latter capacity, he cautions his readers, advising them to withhold judgment until they have the full narrative of the current theories offered up for advocacy. "When the leading authority in any branch of science announces that the basis upon which one half, and that the most important half, of his science rested, is insecure, and must be removed in order to substitute another, constructed on an opposite principle," Adams observes with a tone of detached authority, "the public cannot be too cautious in avoiding to take sides in the dispute, nor can it be too rigorous in exacting an explanation of the reasons which have caused such a revolution in opinion." It was now the reviewer's task, "without pretending either to justify or condemn him, . . . to show by what process he has reached his conclusions."[49]

Of course, in the preparation of the review, Adams had a privileged view of that process in the comments that Lyell made on the draft. Lyell used these opportunities to expand on his understanding of the fine points of the emerging map of species development, particularly concerning Charles Darwin's place in that landscape. In a letter of June 1868, for example, Lyell responded to Adams's assertion that the new *Principles* favored both Lamarck and Darwin:

> You represent me as declaring that Lamarck was right, but it would be desirable in this & the next page to keep in view the great difference between Lamarck & Darwin. Both may be right in what may be considered the main point the derivation genealogically of living organic forms from those extinct types which have passed away. Yet when we ask why Darwin suddenly made so many more converts than Lamarck had done, the answer is the discovery of the theory of Natural selection, independently worked out by Darwin & Wallace. Instead of Lamarck's giraffe getting a longer neck by stretching up to reach the foliage of lofty trees the neck of no individual was ever elongated but individuals having the longest necks survived and perpetuated

> or improved the breed. . . . All that you have to guard against is, in speaking of Lamarckian and Darwinian doctrines as one & the same is to take care that you are referring simply to the fact of transmutation & not to the manner in which it is brought about so far as that depends on Selection.[50]

In the printed essay, therefore, one finds Adams reminding his readers that "in referring to the theories of Lamarck and Darwin as one, we speak merely of their common starting-point, transmutation, not of the development which each writer has given to the principle." He furthermore explained that "Mr. Darwin has gained more supporters than Lamarck, because he has pointed out and argued with extraordinary ability an explanation of the phenomena more reasonable than Lamarck's."[51]

Adams recognized that he could not engage the debate about species origin without addressing how the physiologists—as he designated those professional men most closely associated with these issues—chose to define the term *species* and classify their variety. He notes, first, that the question of definition divided the public from the physiologist and also divided physiologists into two contending schools or parties. "The common reader," he suggests, was satisfied with defining "species to be collections of individuals which reproduce their like by generation, and are averse to sexual union in proportion as they are remote from each other in structure." As self-evident as that may seem, it "would probably satisfy no scientific physiologist." Indeed, he suggests further that "Few scientific men would to-day venture to risk their reputation by defining absolutely the meaning of this [*species*], the commonest and most elementary term in their vocabulary, upon which the whole question in dispute between the two schools of physiologists depends."[52] Adams therefore portrays physiologists as an elite scientific and social priesthood, concerned with individual reputation and power, and unable to agree on matters of the most fundamental doctrines.

"Every physiologist has enjoyed a delicate sense of his own omnipotence over [organic] forms which have had the misfortune to be discovered for the first time," Adams insists. "He is at liberty to class them as varieties, or invent for them a new species, according to his individual views of their—and of his own—importance." As for anything approaching an exact estimate of the number of species in existence throughout nature, science was no more "absolute on this point than we have found it to be in dealing with other essential matters." Most strikingly, man "does not know and cannot learn whether he is himself one species or a dozen. . . . All the varieties of human beings have usually been classed in one species; but so great a zoölogist as Professor Agassiz . . . recognizes in the different races of mankind, such as the negro, the Indian, and the European white, the distinctive characteristics of as many true species."[53]

The question of differentiation among human species, of course, provoked the most debate, and Lyell had singled out Agassiz's theory in his letter of June 1868, expressing his approval of Adams's representation: "You do well to nail Agassiz to this theory of races such as the Indian, Negro & White corresponding to species of animals in zoological systems. See his 'Journey in Brazil' p. 297 Boston 1868—He has cut off all retreat & must have numerous distinct Adams & Eves created, or, if he grants that they all come from one stock he cannot escape from Lamarckian transmutation." Two days later, Lyell elaborated his (and Darwin's) objections to such an interpretation:

> In your M.S. you alluded to a notion which Agassiz has thrown out in one of his papers that the black negro occurs where the black gorilla is indigenous in Africa & the copper colored man where the brown ourang outang is a native or some statement of this kind. I wish you to guard against its being supposed by a careless reader that any advocate of Lamarckian or still more of Darwinian transmutation would for a moment attach the slightest importance to such a geographical coincidence as countenancing a theory of different human races coming from different existing species of quadrumana. The chances according to Darwin would be millions of millions to one against two species having as much in common as the negro & white man coming from independent stocks as distinct as the chimpanzee the gorilla & the Sumatran ourang—The common ancestor from which they must have branched off must have been very nearly allied both to one & the other if we adopt Darwin's views.[54]

In the final review, however, Adams omitted any detailed, still less controversial, discussion of the issue. At one level, he had a good personal reason not to wish to take sides with Lyell and Darwin against Agassiz. As he noted in his *Education*, the only teaching at Harvard College "that appealed to his imagination was a course of lectures by Louis Agassiz on the Glacial Period and Palaeontology, which had more influence on his curiosity than the rest of the college instruction altogether." Lyell therefore had to remain content with Adams's diplomatic neutrality with respect to the Harvard professor. "I was glad you did not omit to cite Agassiz for his belief in there being several species of man," he told Adams in November after reading the published review. "In that belief he is at least logically consistent."[55]

In the same letter, Lyell reiterated his support for the progressive development theory. He drew Adams's attention to Ernst Haeckel's new work, *Natürliche Schopfungsgeschichte*, which "makes out ten distinct species of man." Although he had not yet had time to read the work, Lyell affirmed that Haeckel "is all for the ape origin of our ancestors." Furthermore, as Haeckel "is to be depended upon as an embryologist, his pictures of the foetus of a dog & of a man when they have advanced six weeks from the egg or germ surprise me a good deal by their identity." While "the dog's tail is one-third longer, . . . that of the embryo lord of creation is of a most respectable length & there seems to be very little difference between the size of their skulls." If, Lyell added facetiously, "we had to trace our genealogy to dogs instead of apes there would not I think be such reluctance to admit such development."[56]

Rather than dwell in his review upon the specific doctrinal differences between Agassiz and Darwin, Adams chose to insist that science had only two theories to offer with respect to the origin of species. On the one hand, what he termed "a distinct, physical, external act of creation" (some form of special creation) resulted in each species having "its own precise and unvarying boundaries." On the other hand, Lamarck and Darwin had been affirming the contrary view of development, that "every form of organic life owes its peculiarities of structure to an innate capacity for change." Adams settled on "external act of creation" to replace the phrase "interference of external creative force," which had appeared in the draft. In his letter of June 10, 1868, Lyell had drawn Adams's attention to two possible readings of the word *creative*, referring either to divine creativity or to creative forces *within* the natural order: "'Interference of external creative force.' This expression may I suppose pass, as the word external may distinguish special creation from that exertion of a creative force which may be at work in what has been called spontaneous variation." Lyell explained further in the same letter: "It is very difficult if one adopt the doctrine of progressive development & an ascensive [that is, rising, progressive] scheme to exclude the term creation from that force or causation which is capable in the course of ages of turning a fish into an ape or an ape into a man or evolving one out of the other." Adams thus substituted "external act of creation," which seemed to bring the interpretation into line with Lyell's concern to differentiate all form of special creation (as causation *outside nature*) from "creative force" (as causation *within nature*).[57]

The tenth edition of the *Principles* affirmed what Lyell had for many years denied: a doctrine of progressive development. The popular view of this doctrine, Adams explained, held that "geological science" had, in the fossil record, discovered a sequence of organic beings on the earth "in the order of their relative perfection." Indeed, Adams might have cited the opinions of several elite British geologists, notably the Cambridge-based professor Adam Sedgwick, who combined a progressive earth history (beginning with an originally molten globe) with a progressive series of special creations timed by the Creator to suit the changing (cooling) terrestrial environment. In the earlier editions of his *Principles*, however, "Sir Charles boldly denied the fact" of any such progressive development of organic beings. He had further asserted that "geology furnished no argument whatever in favor of the fancied evolution of one species out of another." The original Lyellian economy of nature permitted neither progressive special creation nor transmutation.[58]

Lyell's change of view began with his investigations in the early 1860s into the antiquity of man when he had found "all the geological evidence pointing, not to the original creation of man in his highest type, but to the gradual evolution of that type from one less perfect." Lyell now had two choices: to follow a version of Sedgwick's progressive special creation or to begin to recant his old opposition to transmutation. As Adams noted, however, even a determination to preserve his own consistency failed to force Lyell into acceptance of "the doctrine [of progressive special creation] peculiarly disagreeable to his special cast of mind, that the creative energy which shaped the world had not yet ceased to act, and that when active it moved still by leaps, creating new forms at will."[59]

Left only with recantation, Lyell "reconsidered the reasons on which his opposition to the theory of progressive development was founded," leading him, with characteristic caution, to accept that "there is fair ground for believing the invertebrate animals to have flourished before the vertebrata, and, in the latter class, fish, reptiles, birds, and mammalia to have made their appearance in a chronological order analogous to that in which they would be arranged according to an advancing scale of perfection in their organization." In Adams's view, Lyell had now rendered "progressive development" a "fact" to his own satisfaction, independent of speculations about creative energy, and "the first step towards [his acceptance of] Lamarck's doctrine of transmutation."[60]

Before the tenth edition, Lyell had followed the evidence that suggested limits to variation from original types and had used this argument to reject Lamarck's theory. In the tenth edition he admitted that he had been, as Adams summarized, "mistaken in supposing that the limits of variability had ever been reached, or that any peculiarities which actually exist in Nature might not be produced by the process of selection." This shift, then, marked Lyell's most dramatic about-face.[61]

The evidence for such transmutation that Lyell cited as persuasive still did not derive from geology: "there was nothing in geology to forbid such a belief [in transmutation of species]," Adams wrote, "and Sir Charles ultimately found in the study of insular floras and faunas a very ingenious line of reasoning against the opposite doctrine of special creation; but so far as positive evidence of transmutation was concerned, geology had nothing to offer." Instead, Lyell "had no choice but to depend upon Mr. Darwin" for evidence from the animal economy, and especially upon Darwin's "train of argument by which he shows the probability that all the one hundred and fifty named races of domestic pigeons are the true descendants from one original type, the rock-pigeon."[62]

Adams notes in particular Lyell's new arguments on the insular floras and faunas of the Madeiras and Canaries, which had been thrown up by volcanic action in the miocene age. Discussing them at some length in the review, he treats these issues according to Lyell's prompting: "As my Chapter on 'Insular Faunas & Floras' is thought the best & most original in the new edition by Hooker, Darwin, & others in reference to the theory of the creation of species by variation, I hope you mean to allude to it." Most significantly, Lyell found the evidence of the distribution of organic forms largely compatible with transmutation and incompatible with special creation. The examples posed some specific difficulties for the transmutation theory, however, in accounting for the distributions of different species of land-shells among neighboring islands. While presuming a common ancestor from the African continent some three hundred miles distant, the inter-island distributions pointed to few species in common, suggesting that thirty miles of ocean could form an effectual barrier to transportation. Despite such unresolved issues, Adams concludes that "it would be still more difficult, in fact it would verge very closely on the ridiculous, to argue that the omnipotent and beneficent creative power was exercised on behalf of certain [shell] species of Helix, Bulimus, Pupa, and on their behalf alone."[63]

With these conclusions, Adams completes his task, summarized toward the end of his review: "to state as clearly as possible the process of reasoning by which so conservative and so eminent a writer as Sir Charles Lyell has been led to adopt opinions which many excellent men consider revolting." Adams, through Lyell, had an opportunity to demonstrate what this new theory might have to offer to even the most cautious of scientific men. He stresses that Darwin had announced only a theory, "supported . . . by the greatest ingenuity of reasoning and fertility of experiment, but in its nature incapable of proof." Adams also took the opportunity to explicate Lyell's loss of confidence in the old theory, which he described as invoking "an apparently arbitrary and supernatural interference." Even the "idealist" reshaping of the old theory "in the hands of its great and brilliant supporters" such as Karl Ernst von Baer and Agassiz would not "win the sympathy of a mind so practical as Sir Charles Lyell's," the whole strength of which "lies in the direction of Realism."[64]

As far as the public was concerned, Adams concludes, the "high authorities of science" still did not agree on the "meaning of their own discoveries." To date, "Extremely little is as yet known with certainty on the subject, too little to warrant any unscientific person in becoming a partisan of either opinion, and far too little to justify one party in announcing dogmatic conclusions, or in excommunicating its opponent." Moreover, with regard to "a subject which involves the fate of all mankind," neither party had "fairly met the problem" of origins, beginnings, and first causes. "Here Mr Darwin's theory explains nothing," Adams observes, adding, "it merely records a fact. We here step beyond the range of science, and begin a hopeless struggle with first causes." Indeed, Darwin remained vulnerable to the charge that his theory of natural selection bore "too close a resemblance to an actual originating force," while Lyell, dealing only in "facts," chose "to guard himself most carefully on the question, as on similar questions [of first causes] in pure geology."[65] Sir Charles had written to Adams to this effect in June 1868:

> What you say of my avoiding to commit myself to questions of origin is perfectly true. It is a popular but unfair way of attacking Lamarck or Darwin to say how did the system begin, when the question for the geologist is, were the recent species derived from tertiary forms & these from types of antecedent geological

> periods made known to us by palaentology. If we want to prove that the Italian language grew out of the Latin & the modern Greek out of the ancient we are met by the question how did language begin & was there one original tongue or several distinct languages. You will do well to point to the unreasonableness of such a line of argument or objection.[66]

Lyell, like Hutton, as Adams points out, "sought a permanent and natural, not a rare and fortuitous development." Adams would pursue this uniformitarianism "in kind" in his own quest to comprehend the nature of human history, but he would soon find himself consciously rejecting that uniformitarianism "in degree" that characterised the geological economy of this "geological champion of Darwin."

Conclusions

Henry Adams undertook his major review of the penultimate edition of Sir Charles Lyell's *Principles of Geology* in 1868 at the celebrated geologist's own bidding. Though introducing a note of skepticism concerning Lyell's doctrine of strict uniformitarianism, Adams recognized the manner in which Lyell grafted Darwin's evolutionary biology onto a Lyellian geological foundation: while the latter continued to represent the earth as a balanced, steady-state system, that economy became compatible with the model of a living world that evidenced upward progression. After Adams assumed the editorship of the *North America Review* in 1870, Darwinism, natural selection, and human progress dominated its pages. Confidence in natural progression seemed to go hand-in-hand with political progress, especially in the New World. Readers of the *North American* could therefore feel reassured and comfortable as to the *inevitability* of natural and human progression, whatever the apparent evidence to the contrary.[67]

As Adams himself became increasingly disillusioned with the prospects for a rapid cure of the nation's chronic ills of political corruption and material self-interest, he turned to "history" as the means by which to judge the "true" value of men and nations. Only in the production of such books would the historian construct enduring monuments to human thought and action in a world prone to "decay, disaster or collapse."[68] By the 1890s he was increasingly drawn to the possibilities of a "science of history" based on the energy physics of Lord Kelvin and inspired by the geological perspectives of his friend Clarence King, whom he had first met in the early 1870s.

King, a New Englander with strong commitments to evangelical Christianity, had led the Fortieth Parallel geological survey along the approximate route of the first transcontinental railroad; he later became first director of the U.S. Geological Survey. As a result, he played a leading role in mapping the mineral resources of the American West.[69] King had an unbounded enthusiasm for Lord Kelvin's energy physics, which the Scottish physicist had begun theorizing in the 1840s. By the 1860s, Kelvin entered formally into the discussion about the earth's age and geophysical change, which he related to the same energy laws—transformations from states of greater to lesser intensity—that he believed drove all physical change. Earthquakes and volcanoes, for example, represented intensive forms of terrestrial energy. Kelvin also argued that the intensity of the earth's energy was diminishing over geological time. In opposition to the "steady-state," gradualist uniformitarianism of British geologists such as Lyell, Kelvin's model appealed to American "catastrophist" geologists like King who believed that the geological evidence in the New World pointed to anything but gradualist action.[70]

Although Adams, unlike King, grew up with a Puritan heritage that had turned away from its Calvinist foundations, he nonetheless—like King—shared several of the cultural values of the original North British group of energy physicists. From John Quincy Adams in particular he inherited a rejection of the optimistic and progressive Unitarianism of enlightened Bostonians. Both men instead adopted a characteristic skepticism towards all doctrines of human perfectibility. They saw, like their Calvinist ancestors, a world infected with decay, sin, and death. In contrast to the onward and upward faith of many Darwinian disciples, therefore, Kelvinism spoke authoritatively of a universe ruled by the Universal Dissipation of Energy.[71]

Adams's perspective highlights a profound shift from the Scottish founders and their Christian conception of a universe of beginnings and endings, of nature's perfection and man's limitations, to a godless world in which "the tyranny of thermodynamics" redefined man as "a bottomless sink of waste unparalleled in the cosmos" and beside which even the wasteful sun was "a model economist." "We have created and established a new philosophy and religion, which I think will endure; the religion of Energy with a very big E, and of man with a very small m," Henry Adams told a Bostonian clerical friend in 1902.[72] These words effectively encapsulate the conclusions Adams had reached by the 1900s: the ideals of the founding fathers of the United States, offering visions of an enlightened and rational society, served only decorative roles. In contrast, by 1902 the United States had become not a community driven by ideals but a nation that worshiped material power. Faith in progress yielded to the uncertainties of massive power.[73]

NOTES

The authors gratefully acknowledge the valuable assistance of Ondine Le Blanc of the Massachusetts Historical Society. They are also endebted to the Leverhulme Trust for the support of their work through a Special Research Fellowship (Ian Higginson) and a one-year Leverhulme Fellowship (Crosbie Smith).

1. See especially M. Norton Wise (with the collaboration of Crosbie Smith), "Work and Waste: Natural Philosophy and Political Economy in Nineteenth Century Britain (parts I–III)," *History of Science* 27(1989):1–38, 391–449; 28(1990):221–261.
2. Henry Adams, "The Principles of Geology," *North American Review* 107(1868): 465–466.
3. Henry Adams, *Novels, Mont Saint Michel, The Education*, ed. Ernest Samuels and Jayne N. Samuels (New York, 1983), 925–926. All references below are to this "Library of America" edition containing *The Education of Henry Adams* (hereafter *Education*).
4. For a summary, see Crosbie Smith and Ian Higginson, "Consuming Energies: Henry Adams and 'the tyranny of thermodynamics,'" *Interdisciplinary Science Reviews* 26(2001):103–111. We are currently preparing a full-length study of Henry Adams's readings of 19th-century science, especially thermodynamics.
5. HA, *Education*, 927–928. See also Leonard G. Wilson, *Lyell in America, 1841–1853* (Baltimore, 1998).
6. HA, *Education*, 779–780.
7. Henry Adams to Charles Eliot Norton, Apr. 10, 1868, in *The Letters of Henry Adams*, ed. J. C. Levenson et al. (Cambridge, Mass., 1982–1988), 1:569.
8. HA to Charles Francis Adams, Jr., Nov. 23, 1868; HA to Charles Milnes Gaskell, Nov. 5, 1868, in *Letters*, 2:9, 6.
9. HA to Charles Francis Adams, Jr., Jan. 27, 1869, in *Letters*, 2:14.
10. Charles Francis Adams, Sr., Diary, 1862–1864, Adams Family Papers, Massachusetts Historical Society, especially entries for Jan. 19, Feb. 7, May 11, Oct. 19, 1862, May 19, 1863, and Sept. 13–15, 1864. Adams initially described Martineau as "a very good writer, and at times eloquent but a little too abstracted in his speculation to keep the attention fixed" (Jan. 19, 1862). He terminated occupation of his pew toward the end of 1863, writing of Martineau being open to "the objection so often made to the Unitarians at home, of cold, abstract speculation" (Nov. 8, 1863). At Lyell's suggestion to the mayor, Adams was invited to the Bath meeting of the British Association for the Advancement of Science to hear Lyell's presidential address centered on the antiquity of creation (Sept. 13–15, 1864).
11. HA to Charles Milnes Gaskell, June 14, 1876, in *Letters*, 2:275.
12. HA to Charles Milnes Gaskell, Aug. 21, 1878, in *Letters*, 2:344.
13. HA, *Education*, 749–750. On Coleridge's notion of a "clerisy" or rule of an elite intelligentsia with a strong moral agenda, see Jack Morrell and Arnold Thackray, *Gentlemen of Science. Early Years of the British Association for the Advancement of Science* (Oxford, 1981), especially 17–29.
14. HA, *Education*, 749–750.

15. Morrell and Thackray, *Gentlemen of Science*, 411–423. See also Sally G. Kohlstedt, *The Formation of the American Scientific Community: The American Association for the Advancement of Science, 1848–1860* (Urbana, 1976); and Robert V. Bruce, *The Launching of Modern American Science, 1846–1876* (Ithaca, N.Y., 1987). Although Warren's proposal obtained strong support from the American Academy of Arts and Sciences in Boston, as well as support from Benjamin Silliman (Yale) and William Ellery Channing, the hostility of the American Philosophical Society in Philadelphia (America's oldest learned society) killed the scheme. The AAG attached the word "Naturalists" to its title two years after the founding.
16. The Bostonian geologist Henry Darwin Rogers, professor at the University of Pennsylvania and head of the Pennsylvania state geological survey, had been instrumental in shaping the AAGN from the start and would play the lead role in drafting the AAAS's constitution.
17. Robert H. Silliman, "The Hamlet Affair: Charles Lyell and the North Americans," *Isis* 86(1995):541–561.
18. HA, *Education*, 926–927.
19. See especially Martin J. S. Rudwick, "The Strategy of Lyell's Principles of Geology," *Isis* 61(1970):4–33; Rudwick, "Uniformity and Progression: Reflections on the Structure of Geological Theory in the Age of Lyell," in *Perspectives in the History of Science and Technology*, ed. D. H. D. Roller (Norman, Okla., 1971), 209–237; Rudwick, "Poulett Scrope on the Volcanoes of Auvergne: Lyellian Time and Political Economy," *British Journal for the History of Science* 7(1974):205–242.
20. See especially the interpretation of John Quincy Adams offered by Henry's brother Brooks Adams, "The Heritage of Henry Adams," in Henry Adams, *The Degradation of the Democratic Dogma* (New York, 1920), 1–122, especially 77–86, 109. For a recent study of John Quincy Adams and government funded science, see Marlana Portolano, "John Quincy Adams's Rhetorical Crusade for Astronomy," *Isis* 91(2000):480–503. See also Paul Nagel, *John Quincy Adams: A Public Life, a Private Life* (Cambridge, Mass., 1997).
21. Elizabeth Cary Agassiz, ed., *Louis Agassiz: His Life and Correspondence* (Boston and New York, 1895), especially 497.
22. HA, *Education*, 926.
23. HA, *Education*, 819.
24. HA to John Gorham Palfrey, Feb. 19, 1869, in *Letters*, 2:18–19.
25. Sir Charles Lyell to HA, May 28, 1868, Theodore F. Dwight Papers, Massachusetts Historical Society. We thank the Massachusetts Historical Society for permission to quote from the Dwight and Adams Family Papers.
26. HA, "Principles of Geology," 466.
27. John Playfair, *Illustrations of the Huttonian Theory of the Earth* (Edinburgh, 1802).
28. See Crosbie Smith, *The Science of Energy: A Cultural History of Energy Physics in Victorian Britain* (Chicago, 1998), 15–30, 115; and Anne Scott, "Practices of Witnessing in Victorian Science and Religion: The Heresy Trial of William Robertson Smith and the Development of Henry Drummond's Evolutionary Scientific Theology" (Ph.D. diss., University of Kent at Canterbury, 2001), chapter 1.
29. HA, "Principles of Geology," 466–468.
30. HA, "Principles of Geology," 468. See especially Philip Lawrence, "Charles Lyell versus the Theory of Central Heat: A Reappraisal of Lyell's Place in the History of Geology," *Journal of the History of Biology* 11(1978):101–128; Stephen G. Brush, "Nineteenth-century Debates about the Inside of the Earth: Solid, Liquid or Gas?" *Annals of Science* 36(1979):225–254; Mott T. Greene, *Geology in the Nineteenth Century: Changing Views of a*

Changing World (Ithaca and London, 1982); and Martin J. Rudwick, "The Glacial Theory," *History of Science* 8(1969):135–157.

31. HA, "Principles of Geology," 468–469.
32. HA, "Principles of Geology," 469.
33. Sir Charles Lyell to HA, May 28, 1868, Dwight Papers, MHS.
34. HA, "Principles of Geology," 469–470.
35. HA, *Education*, 927–928.
36. HA, *Education*, 928.
37. HA, "Principles of Geology," 471.
38. HA, "Principles of Geology," 474.
39. HA, "Principles of Geology," 475.
40. HA, "Principles of Geology," 480. James Croll, former janitor of the Andersonian Museum in Glasgow, became assistant geologist for the Geological Survey of Scotland thanks to the influence of the director Archibald Geikie and the support of Lord Kelvin and Sir Roderick Murchison. He published two widely read papers in the *Philosophical Magazine* in 1867–1868, in which he concluded that while the eccentricity of the earth's orbit did not affect the total annual quantity of heat received from the sun, "yet it may seriously affect the distribution of heat." Over a 5,000-year period, for instance, the hemisphere that had its winter when the globe was farthest from the sun would lose one-fifth of the whole winter's heat, while the summer would gain the same amount. The process could create, Croll argued, the long seasons of fog, clouds, and rain that would check the melting of ice. On Croll, Lyell, and Darwin, see especially J. D. Burchfield, *Lord Kelvin and the Age of the Earth* (London, 1974), 62–70, 75–76. On Croll and Kelvin, see Crosbie Smith and M. Norton Wise, *Energy and Empire: A Biographical Study of Lord Kelvin* (Cambridge, 1989), 593–595, 599–600. Sir Charles informed Adams that he had included a table, due to Croll and Stine, showing that over the last million years there had been four periods when the eccentricity exceeded 10 million miles, the most striking being 850,000 years ago when the equivalent of 36 days would have extended the winter. He also emphasized that, despite his preference for the second explanation, he had nevertheless "been desirous to give these latter [astronomical] causes as they are vera causae fair play but I think them very subordinate. I shall be glad however to see you make the most of them." Sir Charles Lyell to HA, May 28, 1868, Dwight Papers, MHS. Adams considered that astronomical causes involved a recognition that the earth's orbit was not constant but was so "acted upon by the planets that during long periods the earth may be drawn no less than 14,500,000 miles farther from the sun than at other periods." HA, "Principles of Geology," 479.
41. As Lyell told Adams, a key to persuasion lay in the continuing development of visual representations: "I have repeated my old map of putting all the land about the Poles to produce the great winter & about the Tropics to produce the summer, the Annus Magnus, but in the new edition p.263 I have for the first time given an ideal map of a normal distribution of land to show how much warmth might be produced by a slight change instead of those extremes or caricatures which are given at p.266. Now by looking at the new map p. 263 you may see how easily a little more land in the north polar region taken perhaps from the Antarctic latitudes or from the Northwest part of asia might satisfy all that Heer can demand & yet leave a warm climate according to my geographical principles to which I firmly adhere & to which as the chief cause I have brought round Herschel after reading my new chapters although he was much inclined at one time to go very far with Croll in the direction of the preponderating influence of astronomical causes." Sir Charles Lyell to HA, May 28, 1868, Dwight Papers, MHS.

42. HA, "Principles of Geology," 475–476.
43. HA, "Principles of Geology," 476–478.
44. HA, "Principles of Geology," 478–479; Sir Charles Lyell to HA, May 28, 1868, Dwight Papers, MHS.
45. HA, "Principles of Geology," 480–481.
46. HA, "Principles of Geology," 482. The reception of Lyell's *Antiquity of Man* (1863) is examined in William F. Bynum, "Charles Lyell's *Antiquity of Man* and its Critics," *Journal of the History of Biology* 17(1984):153–187. Lyell's *Antiquity* was also reviewed rapidly, at length, and anonymously in the *NAR* 97(1863):451–483.
47. HA, "Principles of Geology," 485.
48. HA, "Principles of Geology," 483.
49. HA, "Principles of Geology," 483.
50. Sir Charles Lyell to HA, June 10, 1868, Dwight Papers, MHS.
51. HA, "Principles of Geology," 482. At the end of his formal comments on Adams's draft review, Lyell returned to the distinction between Lamarck and Darwin: "you will observe in my 34th chap. on Lamarck's doctrine of transmutation that I mention in a note p. 246 that I have re-printed my abstract of it as it was drawn up by me in 1832. I really should have suspected myself of having sketched a point to make Lamarck seem to anticipate Darwin if I had not before my eyes this chapter which was written as you now see it & printed before Darwin had begun his studies on this subject. You will see in the following chapter that in some respects—see p. 265—I hardly did justice to Lamarck & this I have still more shown at p. 274. I am sure that most of Darwin's enthusiastic followers would not have believed that Lamarck went so far in the right direction as few of them will turn to his work unless I was able to point to my chapter published in 1832 & written a year or two previously." Sir Charles Lyell to HA, June 10, 1868, Dwight Papers, MHS. Responding, Adams incorporated in his review the remark that "we doubt whether even Sir Charles Lyell would believe that Lamarck's decried and ridiculed theory had so closely anticipated Mr. Darwin, had not his own chapter in the 'Principles,' written in 1830, to explain and oppose Lamarck, been still before his eyes." HA, "Principles of Geology," 482.
52. HA, "Principles of Geology," 484.
53. HA, "Principles of Geology," 484–485.
54. Sir Charles Lyell to HA, June 10 and 12, 1868, Dwight Papers, MHS.
55. HA, *Education*, 774–775; Sir Charles Lyell to HA, Nov. 8, 1868, Dwight Papers, MHS.
56. Sir Charles Lyell to HA, Nov. 8, 1868, Dwight Papers, MHS.
57. HA, "Principles of Geology," 485; Sir Charles Lyell to HA, June 10, 1868, Dwight Papers, MHS.
58. HA, "Principles of Geology," 487. See also Crosbie Smith, "Geologists and Mathematicians: The Rise of Physical Geology," in *Wranglers and Physicists. Studies on Cambridge Mathematical Physics in the Nineteenth Century*, ed. P. M. Harman (Manchester, Eng., 1985), 49–83.
59. HA, "Principles of Geology," 487.
60. HA, "Principles of Geology," 487.
61. HA, "Principles of Geology," 488.
62. HA, "Principles of Geology," 488–489.
63. Sir Charles Lyell to HA, June 10, 1868, Dwight Papers, MHS; HA, "Principles of Geology," 493–494.
64. HA, "Principles of Geology," 494–496. The embryologist Karl Ernst von Baer (1792–1876) viewed the development of individuals as a gradual process of differentiation,

shaped by the interaction of the living matter with its external environment.

65. HA, "Principles of Geology," 498.
66. Sir Charles Lyell to HA, June 10, 1868, Dwight Papers, MHS.
67. See especially Crosbie Smith and Ian Higginson, "'Improvised Europeans': Science and Reform in the North American Review 1865–1880," in *Science Serialized: Representation of the Sciences in Nineteenth-Century Periodicals*, ed. Geoffrey Cantor and Sally Shuttleworth (Cambridge, Mass., 2004), 149–179. During Adams's editorship, the *NAR* published well over 200 pages of reviews concerned with Darwin and Darwinism.
68. HA to Charles Milnes Gaskell, May 24, 1875, in *Letters*, 2:225–227, on 225.
69. See, for example, Thurman Wilkins, *Clarence King: A Biography* (New York, 1958).
70. Clarence King, *Catastrophism and the Evolution of Environment: An Address by Clarence King Delivered at the Sheffield Scientific School of Yale College, on its Thirty-first Anniversary. June 26th 1877* (n.p., n.d.), 23–24. Pamphlet in possession of the Massachusetts Historical Society. Also published as Clarence King, "Catastrophism and Evolution," *The American Naturalist* 11(1877):449–470. See also Clarence King, "The Age of the Earth," *The American Journal of Science* 45(1893):1–20, especially 1; and Burchfield, *Age of the Earth*, 107, 115–117.
71. HA, *Education*, 40; Brooks Adams, "The Heritage of Henry Adams," in Henry Adams, *The Degradation of the Democratic Dogma* (New York, 1920), 1–122, especially 77–86, 109. On the British story of energy physics, see, for example, Crosbie Smith, *The Science of Energy*.
72. Henry Adams, *A Letter to American Teachers of History*, in *The Degradation of the Democratic Dogma*, 218; HA to Edward Everett Hale, Feb. 8, 1902, in *Letters*, 5:336–337.
73. See especially Henry Adams, "Prayer to the Virgin of Chartres," in *Letters*, 5:208. See also Smith and Higginson, "Consuming Energies," 103–111.

Massachusetts to Virginia

Knowing Henry Adams's "John Randolph"

RICHARD G. ANDRONE

What asks the Old Dominion? If now her sons have proved
False to their fathers' memory, false to the faith they loved;
If she can scoff at Freedom, and its great charter spurn,
Must we of Massachusetts from truth and duty turn?
—*John Greenleaf Whittier, "Massachusetts to Virginia"*

I

IN THE LARGER CONTEXT of Henry Adams's need to know, what did he hope to learn from researching and writing a biography of the Virginia statesman John Randolph of Roanoke? At first glance, the answer would seem to be, not very much. The surviving evidence suggests that Adams thought he knew quite enough about the essential contours of Randolph's character and historical significance when he undertook the project offered to him by J. T. Morse, Jr., editor of Houghton, Mifflin and Company's "American Statesmen" series of biographies, "on April 1, 1881, or thereabouts."[1]

By that time, Henry Adams already seems to have formed most of his opinions and even to have had at hand many of the necessary source materials. Work proceeded swiftly. Adams declared himself finished by July 9 and ready to do another volume for the series on Aaron Burr. Less than a month later on August 6, Adams wrote to E. L. Godkin that he had "written two whole volumes in exactly two months," so he spent about two months in preparation and roughly a month in the composition of *John Randolph*.[2] Furthermore, as he did this research and writing, he must have been researching the never-published and now-lost *Aaron Burr*, because the composition of that book followed swiftly on the heels of *John Randolph*. This pace suggests the work of a person who knew his own mind, at least about the Virginian.

As early as 1862, when he was working on "Captain John Smith," Henry Adams had already conceived of "Randolf," who claimed descent from Pocahontas, as a figure in opposition to himself and his values. He revealed this sense of opposition in two different letters to the historian John Gorham Palfrey. In both, he depicts the Virginian as a comical specter, hostile but impotent. In the first letter, Adams anticipates "that the ghost of John Randolf will haunt you and Mr Deane and me" for the "impiety" of investigating Randolph's famous ancestress. In the second, Adams delights "to imagine to myself the shade of John Randolf turn green" at his revelations debunking the romantic story of the dashing English soldier saved by the noble, Native American princess, and he describes the early Virginia colonists whom Smith served as the "'decayed serving-men's' sons of Jamestowne."[3] Written when he was only twenty-four, these two passages show Adams already imagining John Randolph as a Gothic grotesque, a threatening but ultimately comic being associated with a Virginian "aristocratic" past that needed demythologizing, and they demonstrate that Henry Adams was more than willing to do it. All of these elements appear in the biography written nineteen years later.

Despite the firmness and consistency of his judgments, however, when Adams began work on the life and papers of Albert Gallatin in 1877, he knew little enough about Randolph that he found it necessary to question the president of the Virginia Historical Society, Hugh Blair Grigsby, concerning the location of Randolph's papers: "John Randolph was in close relations with Gallatin down to 1807 or thereabouts. I have a number of his letters. Can I ascertain where J.R.'s papers are . . . ?" As the research on Gallatin continued, Adams commented to Grigsby regarding Hugh A. Garland's 1850 *The Life of John Randolph of Roanoke*, "I much regret that Mr Garland, the author of the life of Randolph, did not add a little more to our historical knowledge than he has done," showing an increased interest in more detailed information about Randolph, at least as regards his political connections to Gallatin. By the time Adams accepted Morse's offer to write Randolph's biography in 1881, moreover, as Edward Chalfant noted, "Since 1877, Henry Adams had been telling Henry Cabot Lodge that he was finding John Randolph papers, first among Gallatin's papers, later among those of Jefferson, Madison, and others." So Adams was becoming something of an expert on Randolph, even if his primary interests lay elsewhere. Increased knowledge did not breed acceptance, however, and Adams wrote to Grigsby on May 30, 1878: "I have unearthed much private correspondence of that time, including masses of John Randolph's and [Nathaniel] Macon's letters. I fear that they will not give our generation any extravagant opinion of their predecessors."[4]

In his April 9, 1881, letter accepting Morse's request to write on Randolph, Adams allowed the Virginian the merest edge of his approval, "Randolph is the type of political charlatan who had something in him," but in a letter to John Hay of September 3, 1882, written as he corrected proofs of the completed the biography, Adams's opinion had worsened, and he called Randolph "a lunatic monkey." *John Randolph* contains extensive extracts from Randolph's speeches and letters, including some of those that Adams had turned up, and one of Adams's stated motives in writing the book was, on the evidence of the same letter to Hay, "to print some of his letters and those of his friends." Adams continued, "in order to do so, [I] was obliged to treat him as though he were respectable." Even if one discounts here the mixture of modesty and irony with which Henry Adams sometimes described his own work, and the equally characteristic humorous and hyperbolic denigration that he applies to the famous Virginia statesman, it should be noted that Adams refers again to "the papers we have printed" in a letter to Morse a week later.[5] So putting some of Randolph's words before the public, despite Adams's low opinion of their author, may indeed have been a partial motive for writing *John Randolph*.

After publication, Adams repeatedly dismissed the book, as well as its subject, calling it a "brat" and "an unpleasant book" too full of "acidity." He confided to Henry Cabot Lodge that it was "but a feeler" and "a preliminary essay" for his projected *History of the United States of America during the Administrations of Thomas Jefferson and James Madison*, and he firmly put aside Lodge's compliments: "it does not please me." At best, *John Randolph*'s negative portrait of the subject and, to a lesser extent, of his Virginia might stimulate interest in the issues and personalities of the *History*'s period: "I want the mud it stirs."[6]

Despite Adams's formidable array of insults, ironies, and disclaimers concerning both subject and book, however, Henry Adams needed very much to know John Randolph in 1881, and we need to know *John Randolph* to know as much as we can about its author. Henry Adams needed to express, in a signed and published volume, what he already knew, or thought he knew, about the character and ideas of this adversarial figure at this point in his own career. The kind of moral, social, political, and historical knowledge, moreover, that Adams managed to impart in *John Randolph* is of interest in itself, and it presages certain characteristics in Adams's later, more famous books. The most interesting aspect of *John Randolph*, however, may be what Henry Adams managed to project about what he did not yet know, or fully know, about himself and would spend the rest of his life trying to discover.

Possibly due to *John Randolph*'s swift composition, Henry Adams fell back on traditional ideas drawn from his classical education and reading of literature in shaping the portrait of Randolph as a satire, a debate, and a moral study of character in relation to a defective ethos. Or, perhaps, the sometime scientific historian thought that a familiar, classical approach to character would appeal more directly to the broadest range of the "American Statesmen" series' readers. Whatever Adams's conscious motives, however, an unusually intense, probably unconscious mixture of attraction and repulsion toward its subject drove this witty and satirical contribution to the postbellum, national dialogue over the merits of the republic's founders and their ideas. Close scrutiny of John Randolph's background, career, and writings reveals a surprising number of parallels to Henry Adams's own situation. Yet Randolph moved in directions forbidden to Adams at the time he wrote the biography, and Randolph's horrifying degeneration may have seemed a kind of caricature of what the successful, middle-aged, patrician writer might become at his worst. Whatever its cause, a powerful animus, including but extending beyond intellectual opposition, energizes Henry Adams's satirical portrait.

II

In many respects, *John Randolph* is Henry Adams's most interesting and readable historical work on the period of Jefferson, Madison, and Monroe. The biography is as well written as the *History*, albeit stylistically quite different, and it escapes the *History*'s forbidding immensities. Adams had learned much about how to write history for a broader readership, and how to characterize a historical figure, since completion of the ponderous *Gallatin* in 1878. The encouraging sales and reviews of his first novel, *Democracy*, written before *Gallatin* but published later in 1880, may have encouraged him to take greater creative chances in a historical work.[7] Relatively brief, *John Randolph* offers a complex but clear point of view, a rapid pace, a fluent and concrete style, and *Democracy*-like touches of humor and irony. In a sense, in *John Randolph* Henry Adams applied some of the techniques of the novelist to the writing of history.

Adams's treatment of Randolph involved another new step in his relationship to his readers. That is, he risked signing his name to a book-length work employing the supple, witty, and opinionated narrative voice—a voice sometimes conversational and sometimes ironically oratorical—that he was to perfect in his late works. This voice is richer in character, imagery, and allusion than the narration in earlier journalistic, economic, and historical works. Hitherto, he had reserved this voice for private letters and the anonymously published *Democracy*, although he had allowed brief hints of it in his articles and reviews of the later 1860s and 1870s. Why did Henry Adams begin publicly to acknowledge and use his more private voice at this time? Despite his disclaimers, was he trying to reach a wider audience, whether to promote his projected *History* or for some other reason? Did a deepening sense of the interconnections of historical knowledge with the subjectivity of the historian force Adams out of the mingled shadows of initially anonymous and then more distant and formal expression in his signed works? Or was what Adams called the "eccentric" Randolph the catalyst?

From the very beginning of Henry Adams's career as an adult writer, he had shown scruples about various aspects of publication so numerous and convoluted as to constitute a substantial block to his literary development. Nonetheless, he also had demonstrated his desire—equally intense, if usually ironically expressed—to "make a position for himself" by his writing, to "attract . . . attention," and to "break as much glass" as he could, recalling this period much later in *The Education of Henry Adams.*[8] He was cautious and highly self-critical—which can be great virtues in a writer and scholar if not carried too far—but also extremely ambitious, sometimes iconoclastic, and even what today would be called transgressive. He wanted to operate behind the scenes, but he also wanted to strut the stage, in a sense, as he had done in a college performance as Sir Anthony Absolute in Sheridan's *The Rivals*, a prophetic role in many ways. The younger Henry Adams had shelved at least two extended articles of some merit, "Two Letters on a Prussian Gymnasium" and "The Great Secession Winter of 1860–1861," and he did not publish under his own name as an adult until January 1867, a month before his twenty-ninth birthday, when "Captain John Smith" appeared in the *North American Review.*[9] He actually had written "John Smith" in 1862 and decided put it aside in 1863, leaving it in the keeping of his brother John for over three years before deciding to publish. Writing in London during the difficult days before the Union victories at Vicksburg and Gettysburg, Adams had composed the essay in the hope that the "Virginia aristocracy," and particularly the shade of "John Randolf," would be "utterly graveled by it." It was a complex mixture of scholarship and aggression, a historical "flank, or rather a rear attack" on two of the earliest Virginians by a restless and ambitious young man employed as his father's secretary far from the battlefield.[10] So at least some of what he had desired to express in the article was lost through his reticence.

This is not to say that the aspiring writer did not publish anything. Modern scholarship has demonstrated that Adams's pen was active during the London years in producing journalism that his father's diplomatic position, and sometimes the publishing conventions of the day, forced him to leave unsigned. He enjoyed the secrecy imposed by his situation, but he yearned to go on the record. After seeing "John Smith" into print in 1867 and before writing *John Randolph* in 1881, Adams did advance as a political journalist and establish a new career as an academic and professional historian. He published numerous articles, reviews, and editions of essays, which included his own work and that of others. He put his name to some of these compositions, but none of the signed works released the iconoclastic and transgressive impulses—confessed at the beginning of his career—as fully as would *John Randolph*. To put it differently, there were kinds of knowledge that he had not yet been able to reveal in print under his own name. Moreover, the kinds of historical knowledge he had been publishing had not attracted the response he had hoped for.

During these years, the four *Gallatin* volumes of 1879 constituted Adams's major claim to public attention as a historian, but clearly the work did not "break glass," and some of the notices and reviews were sharp enough to have piqued writers much less sensitive than Henry Adams. Allen Thorndike Rice, Adams's possibly jealous successor as editor of the *North American Review*, printed only "an insultingly brief squib," as Ernest Samuels has called it, and Adams's good friend E. L. Godkin of the *Nation* did him an ill turn by publishing a most severe anonymous review by Henry's brother Charles Francis. Henry Adams could draw some comfort from two more-favorable reviews, Henry Cabot Lodge's in the *International Review* and J. Lawrence Laughlin's in the *Literary World*, but praise from one's own former Harvard history students hardly amounted to the acclaim Adams sought.[11]

A description of Nathan Gore, the fictional historian in *Democracy* whom Adams had created before he saw the reviews of *Gallatin*, may hint at high hopes at least partially frustrated:

> [Gore had been] a deep student in Europe for many years, until his famous "History of Spain in America" placed him instantly at the head of American historians, and made him minister at Madrid, where he remained four years to his entire satisfaction, this being the nearest approach to a patent of nobility and a government pension which the American citizen can attain. (23)

Despite the characteristic irony in this passage and the fact that Henry Adams did not necessarily aspire to succeed such scholarly diplomats as his friends James Russell Lowell and John Lothrop Motley, not to mention three Adamses before him, his conception of Gore's leap from the historian's study to a great government office suggests a desire for public and professional responses much different from those that *Gallatin* had attained. Of course, *Democracy*'s Nathan Gore does not get the reappointment to his old position that he has come to Washington to seek, and the changes in American society that determine his failure are part of the point of the book. *John Randolph*, moreover, was hardly calculated to display Henry Adams's credentials as a diplomat. Indeed, it is almost as if Henry Adams decided to hazard any hope he may have had of political preferment, or even popularity of the more general sort, in the interests of truth, self-expression, and vigorous discussion. Adams did not write the biography to be a balanced piece of historical and biographical work. It does not fish for compliments from readers of all beliefs and from all parts of the United States. In fact, one of the few things he liked about the book was that the introductory chapter made "the Virginians . . . red-hot."[12] *John Randolph* was partly written to reveal what Adams knew and believed about the sources of current problems in sectional and ideological differences during the early years of the republic. It was not designed to be popular, but profiting by what he had learned from tepid reactions to *Gallatin*, *John Randolph* was written to elicit a warmer response from those who read it. Employing every technique of satire, irony, and high rhetorical flourish that Adams could muster, *John Randolph* was intended to be part of a debate on the fate of the nation, a case for the negative against the most extreme member of what Adams called "the Virginia school."

III

John Randolph of Roanoke (1773–1833) was one of America's more colorful political figures during the first three decades of the nineteenth century.

He sat in the House of Representatives for most of the years from 1799 to 1829, represented Virginia in the U.S. Senate from 1825 to 1827, and was minister to Russia for a brief period in 1830. Toward the beginning of his career in Congress, he was Ways and Means Committee chair (1801–1805) and House leader for the first administration of Thomas Jefferson. Despite both ideological and blood relationship to Jefferson, however, he went into opposition in 1805, and remained there as an "Old Republican" defender of states' rights and limited federal government to the end of his days.

Randolph opposed Jefferson in his second administration, and he opposed Madison. He opposed the War of 1812 and the Missouri Compromise. He reserved his most intense antagonism, however, for the two Adams presidents, and especially for John Quincy Adams. As a statesman whose career was spent almost wholly in opposition, and in a number of other respects, Randolph's role in government roughly parallels that of the great British parliamentary figure Charles James Fox (1749–1806), whose grand but stormy career was one of the models for American legislators of Randolph's period. Both were high born in their respective societies, both made their reputations as orators despite the handicap of a shrill voice, both were highly independent, and both were odd looking, although Fox was as fat as Randolph was lean—"this lean, forked figure, pointing at the objects of his aversion as with a stick . . . this parchment face, prematurely old and seamed with a thousand small wrinkles . . . that bright, sharply sparkling eye . . . the flattering, caressing tone and manner, which suddenly, with or without provocation, changed into wanton brutality," as Henry Adams wickedly if vividly describes Randolph's unusual appearance and manner.[13]

Given Henry Adams's highly critical stance and John Randolph's peculiarity, it may seem surprising today that Adams did not mention directly the bachelor Randolph's chief weakness, his probable impotence, about which he was taunted publicly. Indeed, in the post-Freudian world, even so sympathetic a biographer, and so conservative a one, as Russell Kirk thought it necessary to discuss its significance, at least briefly, in his *Randolph of Roanoke*.[14] One might even develop a theory connecting Randolph's pattern of opposition to legislative action with his own inability to act sexually. Adams did make a few, highly oblique references to this alleged problem, suggesting, for instance, that Randolph "seems to have been suffering under a complication of trials, the mystery of which his biographers had best not attempt to penetrate" (44–45). A master ironist, Adams may have intended the sexual innuendo here, and the book includes a few other such possible but indirect references.[15] William Merrill Decker has theorized that "Insofar as he portrays Randolph as crushed by the masculine intellectuality of Luther Martin, Adams hardly needs directly to invoke Randolph's alleged sexual weakness."[16]

The knowing reader will observe *John Randolph*'s definite but brief allusions to the once-famous scandal surrounding John Randolph's older brother, Richard, and Nancy Randolph, Richard's wife's sister. In 1793, Richard and Nancy Randolph were accused of murdering their newborn, illegitimate child, although they may instead have aborted and disposed of a fetus. Both were acquitted, however, partly because of the brilliant legal maneuvering of their attorneys, Patrick Henry and John Marshall, and partly because Richard's outwardly loyal wife, Judith, seems to have perjured herself in his defense. The matter cast a permanent shadow over Richard's life, and he died four years later. The tougher Nancy faced down society and went on to become the wife of Gouverneur Morris.[17] John Randolph cherished an intense and lasting hatred for her, and he blamed her alone for the murder of a Randolph child. Considering this reaction in the context of John Randolph's probable sexual incapability and consequent frustration, a post-Freudian could see a psychological transference, an identification with the potency and paternity of his brother (or actually two brothers, because Randolph believed that another brother, Theodorick, had actually fathered the child). In a letter to Nancy that Adams does not quote, John Randolph called her a "vampire . . . sucking the best blood of my race," and today's reader can see the physical identification of John Randolph with his brothers.[18]

To what extent was this understanding the case with Henry Adams in 1881? In contrast with his usual critical stance in *John Randolph*, Henry Adams treated John's response to Richard's death with sympathy and insight, indicating considerable psychological feeling. He commented, for example, that "Richard's last years had been embittered by a strange and terrible scandal, resulting in a family feud, which John, with his usual vehemence, made his own. These complications would have been trying to any man, but to one of his *peculiar temper* they were a source of *infinite depression and despair* [italics mine]" (*Randolph* 24). The reader who is familiar with nineteenth-century circumlocutory usage in sexual matters, and with Henry Adams's level of sophistication, may recognize in "peculiar temper" and "infinite depression and despair" an intentional reference to Randolph's probable impotence and even to his sexual identification with his brothers.

While Henry Adams's capacity for this kind of verbal subtlety should not be precluded, both the infrequency and the obliquity of such passages suggest that one should look elsewhere for an understanding of what is central and most successful about *John Randolph*'s approach to the character and significance of a political and historical personage and to the kinds of knowledge Adams's book can impart.

In the "Political Morality (1862)" chapter of the *Education* dealing with the period when Henry Adams began his adult career as a writer, he states that "Henry James had not yet taught the world to read a volume for the pleasure of seeing the lights of his burning-glass turned on alternate sides of the same figure. Psychological study was still simple" (869). In "Darwinism (1867–1868)," he suggests that psychology had become more problematical: "Psychology was to him a new study, and a dark corner of education" (931). The statement is thrust rather abruptly into a passage on the Darwinian idea of natural selection, and Adams's use of the word "psychology" does not resonate with the meanings it has for us in the wake of the rise and fall of various schools of depth psychology and a complex array of other academic approaches to the mind. Adams immediately precedes it with the statement that "what he valued most was Motion, and . . . what attracted his mind was Change," and he uses "psychology" to signify both "the study of the mind" and "introspection," but both are conceived as static and as opposed to the spheres of moral and intellectual action. This is clear a bit later when he states, "He had no notion of letting the currents of his action be turned awry by this form of conscience. To him, the current of his time was to be his current, lead where it might. He put psychology under lock and key" (932). The "Adams" who narrates the *Education*, then, associates "psychology" with something "dark" and, for him, at least some of the time, to be locked up. It might be intriguing, as the intense "burning-glass" image suggests, but it is primarily for "Henry James." "Adams" is interested in "action." These ideas are consistent with, if simpler than, those in the more extended passage on "the new psychology" of William James and others in "The Abyss of Ignorance (1902)" (1114–1116). Here, the narrator equates "introspection" with "tragedy," and although "Adams" in 1902 reflects a more complex notion of the "sub-conscious chaos," he states that this "newest science" is moving in the direction of "a dissolving mind." What "Adams" craves is "unity" of psychological force so he can "measure motion."

Henry Adams begins the "Eccentricity (1863)" chapter of the *Education* with the statement, "Knowledge of human nature is the beginning and end of political education" (885). The kind of "human nature" that will enable us to understand politics and history in *John Randolph*, however, is not "psychology" but "character," a word Adams uses in a variety of ways, but it reflects more of his classical education,[19] and his self-professed identity in the *Education* as "an eighteenth-century child," than it does the new psychology (730). Before turning to this older conception of human nature in detail, however, it should be noted that "character" in *John Randolph* also does not reveal a much closer relationship to another aspect of "newest science" in 1881, Darwinism, than it does to what Adams calls "psychology."

In *The Metaphysical Club*, Louis Menand gives his version of the invention of much twentieth-century American thought, with special emphasis on a group of young American intellectuals who came of age during the violent 1860s, were influenced by Darwin, and compared their developing ideas in Cambridge of the 1870s, when Henry Adams was an associate professor at Harvard. Henry Adams does not seem to have been a part of the short-lived, ironically named "Metaphysical Club," but some of its membership crossed over with a larger group, "The Club," that included Adams. He was very much a part of this significant and innovative community of thought, and he was not among those least affected by Darwin. In his comparison of William James's and Henry Adams's differing reactions to Darwinism, for example, Menand argues that Adams took Darwinism more seriously as "Law," if only "for fun," than did James.[20]

One can find slight traces of Darwinism in *John Randolph*. The most extended example is in the "Eccentricities" chapter:

> To the cold-blooded New Englander who did not love extravagance or eccentricity, and had no fancy for plantation manners, Randolph was an obnoxious being. Those traits of character and person of which he was proud, as evidence of his Pocahontas and Powhatan ancestry, they instinctively attributed to an ancestral type of a different kind. It was not the Indian that they saw. . . . The Indian owns no such person or such temperament, which, if derived from any ancestry, belongs to an order of animated beings still nearer than the Indian to the jealous and predaceous instincts of dawning intelligence. (255–256)

This is not very Darwinian, and it is very close to metaphor used for satiric purposes. There is a nod toward a misunderstood, or ironic, version of evolution in the idea of beings "still nearer than the Indian" to the period of "dawning intelligence," but Adams questions whether Randolph's "temperament" is "derived from any ancestry." Furthermore, the initial criticism of "manners" and Randolph's ancestral pride, treated derisively as a slur on the Indian, owes more to the moral and conceptual structure of Jane Austen's *Persuasion* than it does to the biological framework of the *Origin of Species*. The word "jealous" also suggests a moral rather than a biological concept, and "animated," which can mean possessed of a soul, contains spiritual as well as physical overtones. In short, Adams did not build his overall treatment of Randolph on the notion of his being a biologically primitive type of humanity.

The biography's method of portraiture largely looks backward to literary sources rather than forward to scientific ones. Part of the reason for this may have been Adams's desire to suit his approach to Randolph, who was a true "child of the eighteenth-century," but Adams's conception of character in *John Randolph* also reveals the persistence of the classics in Adams's own pattern of thought and in the intellectual culture of his time, perhaps especially when it came to biographical study. In 1881, Henry Adams was a thoroughly modern historian, but when it came time to characterize this historical figure and to shape a narrative around him, he fell back on the classics rather than the "newest science."

IV

In the *Education*'s "Harvard College (1854–1858)" chapter, Henry Adams observes of his intellectual formation, "Beyond one or two Greek plays, the student got nothing from the ancient languages" (774). Often missed beneath this famous, ironic dismissal of his classical education is his acknowledgement of the enduring power of "one or two Greek plays." As readers of Aristotle know, character in literature, generally, and in drama, particularly, is evaluated morally and is expressed in action (*Poetics* 2.15).[21] Character is, in a sense, repeated or habitual action. Groups can have character as well as individuals.[22] In conceiving of literary character somewhat along these lines in *John Randolph*, Henry Adams was not necessarily an Aristotelian per se, although *Mont Saint Michel and Chartres* reveals that he knew his Aristotle. In his approach to character, Aristotle had expressed ideas common in the ancient world that still were alive in the reading and study of a classically educated, "eighteenth-century child" even in the 1840s and 1850s. As such, Adams tends to shy away from amoral depth psychology, to associate psychology in a somewhat old-fashioned way with "a form of conscience" in the "lock and key" passage, and to prefer "Motion," "Change," and "action" in the public world of moral choice to static introspection.

In the *Education*'s "Eccentricity" chapter, Adams also refers to "national character," and he chiefly discusses the character of the English. He uses phrases such as the "English mind," "the American Mind," and "the French mind," and he emphasizes "British self-assertion, bluff, brutal, blunt" (885–886). "Eccentricity" can refer either to individual or group character, as when a whole people deviates too far from the norms of human nature. "Eccentricity" may also refer to small groups that reflect, in exaggerated form, some of the characteristics of larger groups. The English as a nation are eccentric in a special way because they tolerate, even enjoy, an unusual number of individual eccentrics and eccentric "types." Adams sees Thackeray and Dickens as creating individual characters that are actually English eccentric types, but they did not see it themselves because of the national tendency toward a high tolerance of eccentricity (886). The important thing about this pattern of thought is the classical emphasis on the general as something higher than the particular, and any reader of Henry Adams soon becomes used to his categorization of persons with such words as "class," "race," "party," and "caste." In the chapter in question, young "Adams" is concerned to know whether eccentricity, which is associated with the groups supporting the Confederate cause, is a "force," but the acute reader knows long before being told at the chapter's end that, quite apart from the specific historical context, "Adams" will eventually see that "eccentricity is a weakness," and so he does (897). This is because the usual tendency of Henry Adams's value system is toward the concentric and not the eccentric, toward the form rather than the individual instance, toward unity rather than multiplicity. There are a number of reasons why this is the case, of course, but it is a classical pattern of thought, and Aristotle would have approved.

Eccentric characters may be amusing, and eccentricity's grotesque exaggeration, especially of defects, is associated in classical tradition with comic characters (*Poetics* 5). This is so in Adams's sometimes-comic treatment of Randolph. Of course, humorous effects are not used in Adams's references to his heroes. In *John Randolph*, George Washington, Patrick Henry, and John Marshall are not characterized as either comic or eccentric. Also, these "good" Virginians are often associated with their "country," in the sense of the whole United States, rather than with their state. One does not find lots of endearing foibles in Adams's treatments of his heroes. Foibles are eccentric.

Adams treats Virginia as having an overall character, the planter class as having character, and the Jeffersonian Republicans as having character. John Randolph starts well as a sometime "Centralizing Statesman," the title of Chapter IV, but increasingly exhibits "Eccentricities," the title of Chapter X. Overall, Adams treats him as an eccentric character and as having in exaggerated form certain Virginian characteristics. He is "an exaggerated type recognized and understood by Virginians [,] . . . a representative man, with qualities exaggerated but genuine" (12). Unfortunately, as does the English national character in the *Education*, the Virginia gentry's regional character encourages eccentricity, or "individuality," which is not always negative, but it contains risks, such as aristocratic high-handedness (*Randolph* 7). To encounter the word "individuality" used even partly negatively may be surprising to us in a postmodern era that encourages self-expression and has largely substituted "personality" for the older "character," with its generalizing and moral overtones. But Henry Adams's skeptical usage of "individuality" is closer to the classical pattern of thought than is ours. The highly unusual, eccentric, and "individual" character of John Randolph, then, can be used in good classical fashion to criticize moral and political defects in his class, native state, and region: "*ab uno disce omnes*," from one man learn about all, as Virgil put it (*Aeneid* 2.65–66).[23]

John Randolph's "Eccentricities" chapter is, in many ways, a precursor to the "Eccentricity" chapter in the *Education*. In the latter, the narrator presents the South and Southern sympathizers during the Civil War as eccentric and in opposition to Northern sympathizers, who are not eccentric. In *John Randolph*, the eccentric Randolph and his Virginia, which itself has the potential to be eccentric in comparison with the nation as a whole, oppose an identifiably Northern narrator, often tied to New England, to Massachusetts, and sometimes explicitly or implicitly to the Adams family. Because this Northern narrator embodies a blend of Northern character varieties, he can provide the non-eccentric, or less-eccentric, standard of judgment. The Northern narrator's standard is regional, but Adams presents it as more closely and effectively connected to the whole United States than is Virginia's: "To a New England man, [Randolph's] . . . type was unintelligible and monstrous. The New Englander had his own code of bad manners, and was less tolerant than the Virginian of whatever varied from it" (*Randolph* 12). It is in character for the narrator to be "less tolerant" than the Virginian, but this is less eccentric than to be "monstrous." Henry Adams does not insist that his narrative voice provide an absolute standard. Indeed, to do so would be "eccentric." The narrator assumes the stance of Cicero and not of an omniscient Jove. *John Randolph* is the case for the negative in a debate, and Adams's narrator uses, and acknowledges, some of the polemical tactics and highly colorful language of the classical rhetorician, but he never poses as an oracle, a very different kind of ancient discourse.

According to Adams, then, Virginia, Randolph, and Adams's own rhetorical or narrative stance all have character. Randolph and his Virginia are strongly conceived, so Adams needed the character and vivid language of an opinionated and eloquent narrator to balance them. The continuing intellectual value of *John Randolph*, and much of the historical knowledge it can still impart, lies in the strength of the case that Adams's narrator can make for the negative. The continuing literary value lies in the richness of the interplay Adams achieved, first, between the characters of Randolph and his Virginia, and, second, between both of those and the character of the narrator.

John Randolph is an openly polemical book, and it is part of a larger dialectic. This extended biographical essay on a "representative man, with qualities exaggerated but genuine," presents the negative side of "Virginia school" education, deportment, and statesmanship that Henry Adams had recently treated so positively in *Democracy*, with its constant, affirmative references to Virginian historical figures and family names— "Lee," "Washington," and "Carrington." In the novel, "educated Virginians of the old Washington school," and their names and houses, become a pole of value opposed to a corrupt and debased post–Civil War democracy epitomized by the venal Silas P. Ratcliffe (*Democracy* 12). In the novel's Mount Vernon scene, the historian Nathan Gore describes George Washington as an "abstract virtue," but to Ratcliffe, Washington was "no politician at all, as we understand the word" (70–71). After publishing *John Randolph*, Henry Adams would strive to treat Virginia and Virginians more impartially in his *History*, which is, in this way, the synthesis of a dialectical pattern. In *Democracy*, Adams allowed the Virginia of Washington and the Lees to respond to postbellum democracy, and *John Randolph* is Henry Adams's reply—an identifiably Northern and New England one—to that lost Virginia world. To borrow the title of Whittier's antebellum poem, *John Randolph* is Henry Adams's reply of "Massachusetts to Virginia."

V

In 1881, Adams liked neither Randolph's tactics nor his rhetoric, for the most part. He found Randolph's arrogance and intemperance offensive, and he disagreed with many of Randolph's points of opposition to the two Adams presidents. He criticized Randolph's bending of legitimate states' rights protections in the Constitution to the uses of the slave power, and Adams asserted that, in this matter, Randolph was twisted tutor of Calhoun (*Randolph* 91, 197).

Adams opened his biography with a brief account of Randolph's ancestry and a characterization of Virginia colonial society. Randolph belonged to the fourth generation of his branch of the Randolphs in Virginia. The family lines descended from William Randolph of Turkey Island (1650–1711) were not the oldest in Virginia, but from the first, Adams noted, they were among the "most successful" (2). By line of descent from his paternal grandmother, Jane Bolling, however, John Randolph was a great-great-great-great-grandson of Pocahontas and John Rolfe (1585–1622), who had discovered a method of curing tobacco that made it the exportable commodity upon which colonial Virginia's wealth was founded. In addition to being both numerous and rich, Randolphs distinguished themselves in law, scholarship, and public service. In short, John Randolph's family was long descended and well established during "the Golden Age of Virginia," the middle half of the eighteenth-century, and he was born toward the end of that period. Despite the fact that the Randolphs were more numerous and richer, they occupied a position, when John Randolph entered the world, somewhat akin the Adamses' in Massachusetts about two generations later at the time of Henry Adams's birth. Beneath the negative perspective that Henry Adams assumed in *John Randolph*, then, there were many aspects of the Virginian's situation with which Henry Adams could have felt kinship—or which might have excited feelings of rivalry.

Adams characterizes the ethos of Randolph's family as aristocratic in its fundamental feelings—whatever the professions of some of its members—and as English in its "tastes, fashions, theories" (4). This society was highly privileged yet still in its prime, "supported by tobacco plantations and Negro labor, by colonial patronage and royal favor, or to do it justice, by audacity, vigor, and mind" (4). Adams stresses the rural simplicity of this gentry rather than elegance or the artistic accomplishments of high civilization. For a Randolph boy, Virginia in the 1770s and 1780s was a "paradise of indulgence" (6): "Schools there were none, and stern discipline was never a part of Virginian education" (6). The freedom of the Virginia gentry, however, might well become laxity and looseness: "The life of boyhood in Virginia was not well-fitted for teaching self-control or mental discipline, qualities which John Randolph never gained" (6). All about one there were temptations to drink, to violent behavior, and to "talking as freely as the utmost license of the English language would allow" (7). The gentry might have fine manners, but society also contained "coarse and brutal elements" best exemplified by the "old-fashioned rough-and-tumble fight, where the champions fixed their thumbs in each other's eye-sockets and bit off each other's noses and ears" (7). While John Randolph's class did not brawl in this fashion, the freedom that it allowed its sons would have permitted him to "look on, with as much interest as an English nobleman felt at a prize ring" (7).

In these and many other details in his description of the Virginian aristocratic ethos on the eve of the Revolution, Henry Adams mixed fact drawn from documentary evidence with personal opinion and moral judgment. What kind of discourse about late eighteenth-century Virginia is this, to whom is it directed, and what kind of knowledge of Randolph can one draw from it? Clearly Adams did not write primarily as a scholar, much less as a "scientific historian." He did not seem to aim toward comprehensive, "definitive" treatment, and he certainly did not claim any status as a discoverer or editor of any collection of Virginia documents or papers. He included no notes of any kind, and while he usually appended the place of composition and date of letters quoted in the text, he did not always do so. Sometimes when he first mentioned a historical figure, such as "Giles" in Chapter III (53), he did not bother to give his full name, and frequently he did not introduce the players in his drama with any kind of background description.

Clearly, Adams created his characterization of Randolph's Virginia ethos for a readership—whether of historians or general readers—that already knew something about the subject and was interested in an interpretative study, a readership accustomed to informed moral debate on historical and cultural matters. This readership cared less about information, much less comprehensive detail, than it did about coming to terms with things, possibly in order to make moral choices in the world of action or to ratify choices already made. It was a readership that would have seen intellectual and moral relevance in Mrs. Lee's statement in *Democracy*, "I must know whether America is right or wrong" (39). In the biography, the question concerns the Virginia of the Jeffersonian Republicans, of whom John Randolph was the slightly younger, eccentric representative. While Henry Adams varied in his opinion about the possibility of ever answering such questions, in the classical moral and polemical atmosphere of *John*

Randolph Adams allowed Massachusetts to make its case for the wrongness of Virginia and its historical legacy. Massachusetts may speak legitimately with solemn authority of "the awful judgment which fell upon this doomed region" in the Civil War (29), if its indictment of John Randolph is strong enough.

The case against Randolph begins with the statement that "the only well-authenticated fact about his infancy is that before his fifth year he was known to swoon in a mere fit of temper, and could with difficulty be restored" (6). A bit later, Adams notes of Randolph's "character," "His mind was always controlled by his feelings; its antipathies were stronger than its sympathy, it was restless and uneasy, prone to contradiction" (14). While such qualities of character, among others, appear in the documents from which Adams quotes, he selects those qualities that suggest the young Randolph's vulnerability to the "license," poor "discipline," "temptation," and "rough-and-tumble" violence that were parts of the slave owner's ethos as Adams evoked it. The book casts Randolph, then, as temperamentally inclined to realize fully the negative opportunities present in his native culture, and it indicts that culture for allowing the opportunities. This temperament and these opportunities, furthermore, reappear in Randolph's adult actions—his opposition, quickness to attack, emotional speeches and behavior, and inconsistent views on political matters. Such behavior, in turn, foreshadows future rebellion and war, led by Randolph's class and fought on their home ground, which will bring on the "awful judgment" of defeat and disaster for Virginia.

Adams's analysis of the character and career of the eccentric Randolph ultimately criticizes the social system that created him, allowed him, and sent him to congress. It also attacks the anti-federal, states' rights political philosophy developed by Randolph's Virginian contemporaries, a philosophy that Randolph both carried to absurd lengths and contradicted in his own inconsistent and unstable career. Finally, it indicts Randolph's fellow Virginia Republicans, not only the other extreme "Old Republicans" but even Jefferson and Madison, who shared with Randolph common aspects of background, behavior, and belief even though he eventually broke with them all. This whole case, furthermore, emerges as far more than a mere matter of antiquarian interest. It is Adams's position in *John Randolph*, whatever he argued elsewhere in his historical writings, that this person, this social system, these ideas, and these more rational but related contemporaries all paved the way for later civil war and, through it, consequences at the time of Adams's writing. The biography's narrator makes a highly aggressive case against Virginia, and he wants approval or an answer. The aesthetically, historically, and intellectually proper way to get the most out of *John Randolph* is not to ask Adams to be more polite, or more balanced, or to give us still more documents or detail. It is to engage in debate. Cicero has spoken against Cataline. Can Cataline be defended?

VI

The purpose of this attempt to know *John Randolph*, however, is not to condemn or defend Randolph's Virginia but to understand the case that Henry Adams made. Ultimately, the effectiveness of Adams's character studies of Randolph and Virginia rests on "Massachusetts," the narrative voice on the opposing side.

The first thing one notices is the unusual rhetorical strategy. The narrator is far more humorous and satirical than is customary in a historical work. One of the best treatments of *John Randolph* as a complex and coherent whole is J. C. Levenson's *The Mind and Art of Henry Adams*. In his chapter "Satiric Virtuosity," he employs such terms as "satiric," "light comedy," and "bitter irony," as well as "burlesque" shadowed by "more complicated feelings," to characterize *John Randolph*'s rich and unusual narrative tone.[24] Levenson also found occasional evidence of the "lurid" and "unscreened hostility" in the narrative line, but he did not connect these bold and broad effects with Adams's occasional oratorical pose, a pose appropriate in the analysis of a famous orator. Such effects, moreover, often mimic Randolph's own highly colored speaking style.

The distinctive character of Adams's satirical narrative voice derives in part from a number of techniques that he had perfected when writing *Democracy*, in which he used recurrent names, labels, phrases, and image patterns. By a stroke of luck, the name of Randolph's late brother's principal plantation was "Bizarre." Although John Randolph's own large estate was at Roanoke, there was no manor house, and it was at Bizarre that he often resided with his deceased brother's family. Given the choice of names, Adams seized upon "Bizarre," and he repeats it as often as possible, augmenting his portrait of Randolph as an eccentric type.[25]

In addition to playing upon "Bizarre," Henry Adams takes up the eccentric slave holder's notion, as a youthful Radical Republican, that he was an "ardent *ami des noirs*" (*Randolph* 21), and Adams repeats the phrase throughout the book with ever more damning effects. At the end of the final chapter, Adams applies it with great, accumulated power to an extract from one of Randolph's late speeches:

> "There is a meeting-house in this village, built by a respectable denomination. I never was in it, though, like myself, it is mouldering away. The pulpit of that meeting-house was polluted by permitting a black African to preach in it. If I had been there, I would have taken the uncircumcised dog by the throat, led him before the magistrate, and committed him to jail. I told these ladies, they, sweet souls, who dressed their beds in the whitest sheets and uncorked for him their best wine, were not far from having negro children." (304)

To appreciate fully Adams's selection of this passage, one should note that, while expressing attitudes hardly appropriate to a professed *ami des noirs*, it also concludes patterns of reference throughout the book to religion, violence, drink, sex, and children. After youthful "over-vehement and unhealthy" antireligiosity, Randolph reverted to "religious spasms" (14); the text presents Randolph's violent language and behavior in every chapter; after Randolph went into opposition, "his habits became bad, and at intervals, until his death, he drank to excess" (236); he could employ "coarseness that would have sickened a Connecticut peddler" (256–257); and proud of family as he was, Randolph died childless. Henry Adams also exposes another of Randolph's unconscious references to impotence, transferred to hatred for the "uncircumcised" "black African" for whom women may spread their "whitest sheets" and "uncork." Finally, one may see displayed, to satirical effect, the "learning" of an orator deemed literary. Randolph misquotes Shakespeare, "uncircumcised dog" (*Othello*, 5.2.355), as he attempts to dignify his lewd remarks. Shakespeare's dog is "circumcised."[26] Ultimately, then, Adams puts before the reader the spectacle of a broken and degenerate politician unconsciously revealing his own flaws and inconsistencies in a public address, and Adams systematically prepares the reader for this final demonstration.

Henry Adams reserves sharper satire, however, for the more formidable Randolph in his prime. Adams regarded the self-described *ami des noirs* as violent, haughty, and overbearing, a tyrannical driver both of slaves and of his colleagues in the House. Hence, there could be no more appropriate image for Randolph than the whip or riding crop, and Adams uses it repeatedly. When the younger Randolph, as a congressional leader, "saw that the Committee of the Whole showed signs of evading a vote on his resolutions, he stood over them like an Egyptian taskmaster, and cracked his whip as though they were his own negroes" (107). The fact that Randolph sometimes entered the House still dressed for riding in boots and spurs with crop in hand was very much to Adams's literary purpose, and he keeps this image before the reader. Sometimes, Adams uses it as a source of satire, as when he states, "no comic dramatist, neither Sheridan nor Mark Twain himself, could represent with all the humor of the reality . . . the queer figure of Randolph, booted, riding whip in hand, flying about among the astonished statesmen" (166). Classical satire has an ethical base, however, and Adams's caricature exposes the moral incongruity of the aristocratic pose in a democratic assembly. Adams regarded the paradox that the Virginia Republican "democrats" were also landed, slaveholding aristocrats as a flaw in the characters of both Virginia society and, particularly, Randolph (26). The Virginians professed democratic principles but held on to the whip and could not bear it in the hands of others.

With high rhetorical coloring, Adams relates an incident from the time of Washington's administration when John and his brother Richard were at school in New York, then the national capital, and John Adams's coachman snapped a whip over Richard Randolph's head. John Randolph seems deeply to have resented the high-handedness of what he called the "vice-regal" coachman. "Of course the sting did not lie in the coachman's whip," Henry Adams's narrator responds.

> Had the carriage been that of a Governor of Virginia or a Lord Chancellor of England or had the coachman of his own old-fashioned four-horse Virginian chariot been to blame, John Randolph would never have given the matter another thought, but that his brother, a Virginian of ancient family and large estates, should be struck by the servant of a Yankee school-master, who had neither family, wealth, nor land but was a mere shoot of a psalm-singing democracy, and that this man should lord it over Virginia and Virginians, was maddening; and the sight of that Massachusetts whip was portentous, terrible, inexpressible, to the boy. (19–20)

To heighten the contrast, Henry Adams chooses the briefest and least significant of all of John Adams's careers, that of "Yankee school-master," and he exaggerates the plainness of the Adamses—"neither family, wealth, nor land"—even in 1755, when John Adams, a recent Harvard graduate, rode off to keep school in Worcester before studying law.[27] Vice President Adams in the 1790s was considerably better off, moreover, than was the family in 1755. A "mere shoot of a psalm-singing democracy" also simplifies and democratizes John Adams's religious tradition. Overall, Henry Adams's rendition of the incident emphasizes the contrast between more egalitarian Massachusetts and much less egalitarian Virginia, despite the democratic protestations of the Jeffersonians.

It is significant in a deeper way that John Randolph was a schoolboy at the time of the whip incident and that John Adams had been a schoolmaster. Not only did schoolmasters whip schoolboys, it was one of Henry Adams's chief criticisms of Randolph that the supposedly literary statesman was a bad student, and he hated worst of all whips the cane of intellectual discipline.[28] Whenever possible, Massachusetts chips away at Virginia's reputation for learning. Many among the landed gentry had placed a lower value on systematic learning, or at least the appearance of it, than did the New England clerisy. John Randolph seemed to demonstrate this once when he stated bluntly, "I am an ignorant man, sir" *(Randolph* 13), and Adams took him at his word, despite Randolph's attendance at Princeton, Columbia, and William and Mary.

Henry Adams's set piece to display John Randolph's intellectual shortcomings is the latter's handling in 1804 and 1805, as leader of the House, of the impeachment and trial of Judge Samuel Chase, an outspoken Federalist who had criticized the Jeffersonians and their policies in an 1803 address to a grand jury. In this and other matters of Jeffersonian opposition to an entrenched judiciary, Randolph came up against Chief Justice John Marshall, and, as Adams metaphorically puts it, the combative Randolph "clutched with both hands at Marshall's throat, but to be victor in such a contest he needed Marshall's mind" (130). If Randolph could prevail in the House, the "as yet undefined" power of impeachment might be radically expanded, and he had a precedent for this action since Congress had just impeached, convicted, and removed from office an easy target, the "friendless, absent, unknown, and imbecile New Hampshire district judge," Judge Pickering (134). From the start, Randolph overreached, drawing up the charges badly and "demanding the conviction of Chase as a criminal" (134). In this he was opposed by "the notorious reprobate genius," defense attorney Luther Martin (141), who was long celebrated for his defenses of Chase and, later, of Aaron Burr at his 1807 trial for treason.[29]

In contrasting the minds of Randolph and Luther Martin, Henry Adams emphasizes the difference between "show and strength, between intellectual brightness and intellectual power" (147). According to Adams, "On no other occasion in Randolph's life was he compelled to follow a long and consecutive train of thought within the narrow bounds of logical method, and his arguments at the trial are therefore the only exact test of his reasoning powers. His failure was decided" (143). In his closing speech to the Senate, the "ill and unprepared" Randolph "broke down," was "forced to apologize," said he had lost "voluminous notes," and in general "betrayed his own weakness" (148–149).

The contrast between Martin, Attorney General of Maryland, and Randolph is not a clash between Massachusetts and Virginia, but Henry Adams introduces his theme by allowing John Quincy Adams's words to conclude the chapter "Yazoo and Judge Chase." Henry Adams quotes a severe but finely written criticism of Randolph's climactic speech from the diary of his grandfather, who would soon after become Boylston Professor of Rhetoric and Oratory at Harvard:

> On the reopening of the court . . . he began a speech of about two hours and a half, with as little relation to the subject-matter as possible,—without order, connection, or argument; consisting altogether of the most hackneyed commonplaces of popular declamation, mingled up with panegyrics and invective upon persons, with a few well-expressed ideas, a few striking figures, much distortion of face and contortion of body, tears, groans, and sobs, with occasional pauses for recollection, and continual complaints of having lost his notes. He finished about half-past two. (149–150)

It would be difficult for any but the most vigorous partisans of Randolph not to see a certain justice in allowing John Quincy Adams to sink the scholarly and oratorical reputation of the Virginian who had so often and so bitterly vilified him, and who would continue to do so after Adams wrote these words in 1805. Later in the biography, Henry Adams quotes his grandfather's elegant Latin reply, a couplet from Ovid's characterization of Envy, to Randolph's famous characterization of J. Q. Adams and Henry Clay as "the coalition of Blifil and Black George," and he comments that Randolph's quip was cribbed from Lord Chatham (289). As if to emphasize his identification with his grandfather, Henry Adams adds further lines from Ovid in a quotation of his own.

Earlier in *John Randolph*, Henry Adams had allowed John Adams a similar opportunity to criticize Randolph's use of language. Randolph, who shared the Jeffersonian opposition to standing armies in times of peace, had once referred to soldiers as "ragamuffins" in a speech in the House. Later, a pair of young marine officers taunted and jostled him in public at the theater. Randolph took the unusual step of writing a florid letter of complaint, including a demand for punishment "commensurate with the evil," to President Adams. Adams ordered an investigation, but he also returned the letter to the House with the dry comment, "I have thought proper to submit the whole letter and its tendencies to your consideration, without any other comments on its matter or style" and announced that an investigation had been ordered (42–43).

VII

Henry Adams, of course, does not hide behind Martin's and the two elder Adamses' criticisms of Randolph's uses of language. On one level, *John Randolph* is literary criticism. Extracts from Randolph's letters and speeches make up a large portion of the book, and Henry Adams analyzes their style and content for revelations of character as well as historical substance. Here, he puts himself on equal ground with Randolph as one writer to another. Randolph had an obvious flair for language as well as a reputation for learning, and Henry Adams confesses a grudging appreciation for the former if not the latter.

Adams's opening chapter includes an analysis of Randolph's youthful reading, noting the books one was most likely to have found "in the cupboards of Virginian houses." He then lists what Randolph is known to have read before his eleventh year: "the Arabian Nights, Shakespeare, Homer, Don Quixote, Gil Blas, Plutarch's Lives, Robinson Crusoe, Gulliver, Tom Jones." In addition to this creditable catalogue, albeit a secular one, Adams asserts that the "chances are a thousand to one that to this list may be added Peregrine Pickle, the Newgate Calendar, Moll Flanders, and Roderick Random," a somewhat morally more questionable series "found in every Virginian country-place." Adams speculates further that "Randolph never learned to love two books which made the library of every New England farmhouse, where the freer literature would have been thought heathenish. If he ever read, he must have disliked the Pilgrim's Progress and the Saint's Rest" (9–10). This unsubstantiated attribution is a highly questionable scholarly technique and a bit disingenuous. Adams, himself, enjoyed many of the books on the Randolph list, and one can certainly forgive an Anglican boy in the 1780s for not learning to "love" Richard Baxter's puritanical *The Saint's Everlasting Rest* of 1650. The passage is clever cultural criticism and fine rhetoric, however. The reading Adams attributes to Massachusetts, and the farmhouse, contrasts sharply with that of Virginia, and the "country-place." Randolph's list, made up mostly of literature, does not suggest hard study, and Adams observes of his later speeches that Randolph's "cleverest illustrations were taken from Shakespeare and Fielding" (10).

As time advanced, the eccentric and emotional Randolph developed an often-grandiloquent writing and speaking style characterized by "egotism" (119), according to Adams, but in letters among friends, the usually critical biographer conceded that Randolph could sometimes give "an agreeable impression" (159). Adams asserted, however, that many of Randolph's Virginia political associates also had a weakness for "magniloquence," and "Bombast . . . was a fault of the young Virginia school. John Thompson, one of Randolph's intimates, the author of Gracchus, Cassius, Curtius, and Heaven knows how many more classical effusions, wrote in the same stilted and pseudo-Ciceronian sentences" (46). After Randolph went into opposition to his party, however, a speech could become a "violent harangue" (120). Echoing language from his earlier description of the fighting style of the Southern poor, Adams stated that Randolph's "method of attack was always the same: to spring suddenly, violently, straight at the face of his opponent was his invariable rule; and in this sort of rough-and-tumble he had no equal. In the white heat of passionate rhetoric he could gouge and kick, bite off an ear or a nose, or hit below the waist; and he did it with astonishing quickness and persistence" (172). The image of Randolph at a "rough-and-tumble" fight, first as a youthful observer, then as an adult participant (in metaphor), and finally, years later in 1909, as equaled in this capacity by J. Q. Adams, seems to have fascinated Henry Adams.[30] In 1881, however, he could not openly identify his grandfather, much less himself, with John Randolph engaged in this kind of public speaking and employing this kind of language.

Throughout *Randolph*, Henry Adams displays a genius for turning Randolph's words to Adams's own literary purposes. For example, he quotes a wildly self-dramatizing description of a scene of physical violence in an 1811 letter that Randolph wrote to his friend Joseph Nicholson about a run-in with fellow representative Willis Alston of North Carolina:

> This poor wretch, after I had prevailed upon the House to adjourn, uttered at me some very offensive language, which I was not bound to overhear; but he took care to throw himself in my way on the staircase, and repeat the foul language to another in my hearing. Whereupon I said, 'Alston, if it were worth while, I would cane you,—and I believe I will cane you!' and caned

> him accordingly, with all the nonchalance of Sir Harry Wildair himself. (265)

As a young man, Henry Adams had deeply resented the caning of Massachusetts's senator Charles Sumner by Preston Brooks of South Carolina, and he was not about to let Randolph's self-association with Southern violence go unrecorded.[31] Adams also uses Randolph's allusion to Sir Harry Wildair to enrich the biography's central dialectic. John Randolph refers to two plays by restoration dramatist George Farquhar, *The Constant Couple* (1699) and *Sir Harry Wildair* (1700), and Randolph's identification in 1811 with a gentleman rake in two old-fashioned English plays provides another contrast between the Virginia gentry and the pious, theater-shunning world of "Massachusetts" as earlier characterized by the farmhouse, *The Saint's Everlasting Rest*, and *Pilgrim's Progress*.

The cultivated Henry Adams does not confine his Northern perspective to these rustic examples, however, and he employs a number of more urbane literary references to undermine Randolph's use of language and inflated sense of himself. Randolph may have seen himself as the dashing Sir Harry Wildair, but Adams characterizes him as Sir Percie Shafton, a proud, fantastical character with a pretentious style of speaking in Sir Walter Scott's *The Monastery* (1820): "At his coolest moments, the word Yazoo was to him what the sight of a bodkin was to Sir Percie Shafton" (125–126). One of Adams's most perceptive satirical references is to *Don Quixote*: "As the character of Don Quixote was to Cervantes clearly a natural and possible product of Spanish character, so to the people of Virginia John Randolph was a representative man" (12). The comparison is apt on a number of levels, and Adams returns to it several times. Not only did the gaunt, sallow Randolph look something like the haggard Quixote, Randolph's imagination, too, had fed much on tales of nobility and chivalry. He was half a madman, who was ever ready to clap on his own "helmet of Mambrino"—the doctrine of states' rights—and ride furiously forth to tilt with the windmills of federal power (32, 254).

This image of Randolph takes the reader into the realm of caricature and creates the verbal equivalent of a political cartoon. One finds a similar effect also when Adams likens Randolph to a monkey (6). In making this comparison, the narrator both strikes the Darwinian pose and alludes to eighteenth-century *singerie* or *babouinerie*, the rococo use of the monkey for humorous or satirical effect. Adams had already begun to blend these two associations of the monkey in *Democracy*, where Ratcliffe both scoffs at the notion of mankind as descended from monkeys and also sees "the impenetrable eighteenth century cynic," Baron Jacobi, as a mocking "monkey-faced foreigner" (51, 56). Another cartoon-like animal image, lifted from one of Randolph's own speeches, presents him as a butterfly "with a secret sting" (18). At the end of Randolph's life, he is included among the hoard of showy "opal-winged dragonflies of politics that from the moment their wings become tarnished and torn . . . become objects of disgust" (194). Given Adams's rhetorical mode, these stylizations do not diminish the book. Satirical political cartoons in the classical moral tradition can be great art as they are in the work of Randolph's contemporary, James Gillray (1757–1815).

Although Henry Adams sometimes reduces Randolph to a caricature, he acknowledges the "brightness" of some of Randolph's speeches, and he even notes that they were "full of astonishingly clever touches." Adams also observes that much of Randolph's "best wit was in parentheses," and he could inject "very clever, keen, terse, vivacious" language into dull debate (279, 280). By focusing his appreciation on the aside and the interjection, however, Adams further supports his contention that Randolph was not capable of "a long and consecutive train of thought" structured by "logical method," as was proven in the Chase fiasco, and his larger conception of Randolph as eccentric, a man of the part and not of the whole. Adams argues, however, that Randolph's wit improved as he degenerated in morals and influence: "Randolph was a worse man than in his youth, but a better rhetorician," and his "epigrammatic" effects were good, but he could not rise to the "great elevation of tone" of a "man of true character" (292). Randolph's eloquence haunted Adams, however, and at the end of the *History*, when he describes American oratory in the period of Jefferson and Madison as still imitating the grand models of "Fox and Burke," he remarked that "even" their follower John Randolph had "style."[32]

VIII

In his last chapter, "Faculties Misemployed," Henry Adams describes the aged Randolph, who gave long and rambling speeches, as "broken to pieces by disease, and in the last stages of consumption" (303). Randolph was probably insane toward the end of his life, and a jury posthumously judged him as such after a long dispute over which of two extant wills was valid. Adams was too good a historian not to note the verdict of insanity (305), but he dissented, choosing instead to describe the older Randolph as "partially insane" and "half-insane, half-intoxicated" (296–297). Adams also observes that "there is no apparent proof that he was less sane in 1831 than he was in 1806, except that he was weakened by age, excesses, and disease" (306). The book closes with Randolph's own words, "Time misspent, and faculties misemployed, and senses jaded by labor or impaired by excesses, cannot be recalled" (306).

A number of scholars have commented on Adams's lack of sympathy for John Randolph, especially at the end of the biography. For example, Eugenia Kaledin found the sentence just before the final one "self-righteous": "Neither sickness nor suffering, however, is an excuse for habitual want of self-restraint." Kaledin asserted that at this time in Adams's life, "Henry found it difficult to articulate deep feeling." Robert A. Hume called the ending of *John Randolph* "a less than chivalrous summation, this apt employment of an unhappy, broken man's words against himself, and one must say at last that *John Randolph*, though historically informative and stylistically skillful, is deficient in pity."[33] This is not an unfair comment, because it grants Adams credit for his literary skill in the book, as some have not, while noting that Adams is not "chivalrous" and lacks "pity." The standards of Christian chivalry that Hume invoked do not apply here, however, since Adams treated Randolph in classical fashion as "worthy of the satire of Juvenal," and satire is deficient in pity (296). So is the literary theory of Aristotle, which famously praises tragedy for purging pity and fear (*Poetics* VI), counterproductive emotions in the classical conception of civic life, which emphasizes dispassionate judgment, and classical satire can have a similar social function. Adams did not write the biography of a private individual but rather a partially satirical study of a person who had held the public's trust nearly to the end of his days and whose acts had political consequences. Adams is consistent throughout the book in his condemnation of "excess," a violation of the classical virtues of prudence, temperance, and fortitude. *John Randolph* is not just a satire, moreover; it is a debate, and the point of a debate is to win.

More interesting than criticism of a satire's deficiency of pity or condemnation of excess, or of a debater for trying to win, is the question of Adams's refusal to judge Randolph insane. Given Adams's moral treatment of psychology using the older concept of character, and his classical connection of individual character to social character, Adams could have treated Randolph's alleged final insanity as a logical and moral consequence of the eccentric and excessive course of life that he had pursued—a "terrible judgment." This would remove some of Randolph's responsibility for his acts, however, and it would tend to exculpate Virginia, which was not responsible for what Adams calls Randolph's "nature" and "temperament." It would also tend to make Randolph a tragic figure, and Adams chose to treat him as comic and grotesque. Finally, it would allow partisans of Randolph's ideology to separate his "good" ideas from his broken mind and body. Randolph's sympathetic biographer, Russell Kirk, who treats Randolph as a Burkean conservative, granted Randolph "fits of madness" and concluded that "his life had tragedy strongly imprinted on it." Kirk argued, however, in stated opposition to Adams, that "Whatever the eccentricities of his private character, they did not affect his political beliefs" and that Randolph's philosophy was "internally consistent," an assertion of intellectual coherence that Adams is at pains not to grant to the Virginian.[34]

One can see, then, that the internal logic of Adams's *John Randolph* calls for a judgment of sanity and moral responsibility, but how can Henry Adams credibly make such a judgment? What concept of sanity did he use in 1881, and how does it relate to the biography's concept of knowledge? First of all, at the end of *John Randolph*, Henry Adams asserts that the distinction between "self-indulgence" and insanity is "a question for experts to decide," differentiating himself largely from the world of "psychology," as he did later in the *Education*. Furthermore, any diagnosis of Randolph as insane must rest on other than functional grounds, because he held office, made speeches, and participated in the business of government. He was not dysfunctional and could act in public life. This is the central aspect of the classical concept of character that Adams employs in *John Randolph*. Randolph "suffered" (306), but he was able to make moral choices in the world of action, and he did so; therefore, Adams holds him morally responsible.

In the passage in *The Education of Mrs. Henry Adams* in which she discussed the ending of John Randolph, Eugenia Kaledin made the following observations about Henry Adams's treatment of the wild Mrs. Wharton in his later novel, *Esther*:

> Adams' early writing often reveals a vital flaw—inability to communicate compassion for human suffering. The artist Wharton's wife in *Esther*, for example, who had attempted suicide in sheer disgust of life, emerges as "coarse and melodramatic," not pathetic. When Adams tried to account for her hysteria by writing that "doubtless this excellent woman [had] faults, owing to a defective education," he almost seemed to be

> mocking the educational concerns of all his Hooper in-laws, rather than providing insight into, or understanding of, his character's tension.[35]

Whether or not Henry Adams is to be judged deficient in this passage from *Esther*, he refused also to see the "pathetic" in Randolph, and this is not necessarily a flaw in the satirical biography, whatever its effect in the novel. In classical character psychology, pathos moves "the very young," according to Francis Fergusson, and when the moral character of an adult such as Oedipus is destroyed through failure, pathos takes over.[36] Fergusson notes that Shakespeare follows in this tradition when he depicts the fallen Lear as initially resisting pathos: "Hysterica passio! Down thou creeping sorrow, / Thy element's below." Lear is noble for resisting hysteria and pathos. He is not "pathetic," in our sense, but he eventually becomes "pathetic," in the classical, partially pejorative sense, in spite of himself. The attribution of Mrs. Wharton's defects to "education" is in keeping with Adams's treatment of Randolph, moreover, and with his treatment of himself in the *Education*, "Whatever was peculiar about him was education, not character" (726). For Randolph and Adams, education after their earliest days contained an element of choice. Perhaps this was not the case with Mrs. Wharton, whose education may have been "defective."

In suggesting that Henry Adams "almost seemed to be mocking the educational concerns of his Hooper in-laws," Kaledin made an interesting contrast between the Adams and Hooper ways of looking at the world as regards sanity, among other things. Earlier in her book, she had discussed at considerable length Mrs. Adams's father's work at the Worcester Asylum for the mentally ill. Because of Dr. Hooper's visits, "an awareness of deep irrationality and instability was a part of the Hooper children's education," and this is contrasted with instances of less sympathy for psychological disorders in the Adams family (33–35). Certainly Hooper interest in the asylums in Worcester and Somerville is commendable and seems more progressive than the Adamses' view, at least as Kaledin described it in 1981, although recent changes toward the outpatient treatment of the mentally ill may provide some unexpected support for the Adamses.[37]

Perhaps Henry Adams's most famous picture of the psyche functioning properly, of sanity, is the image of the moving bicycle rider in "The Abyss of Ignorance" chapter of the *Education* in which he confronts the new psychology of William James: "To his mind, the compound φυχη took at once the form of a bicycle-rider, mechanically balancing himself by inhibiting all his inferior personalities, and sure to fall into the subconscious chaos below, if one of his inferior personalities got on top" (1116). Later on, he expresses the precariousness of sanity in a grotesque complication of the bicycle image: "His artificial balance was acquired habit. He was an acrobat, with a dwarf on his back, crossing a chasm on a slack rope, and commonly breaking his neck" (1116). For Henry Adams, the important thing was not to look down and to keep moving.

IX

Gamaliel Bradford, who included a portrait—or "psychograph," as he would have called it—of Randolph in his *Damaged Souls*, referred to Henry Adams's earlier biography as "really a profound and brilliant book."[38] If this description fits a book that is a satirical and sometimes denunciatory study applying an old-fashioned method of character analysis to a historical figure the author regarded as a failure, there must be some hidden source of energy. Without discounting Henry Adams's impressive verbal dexterity, or the extraordinary sweep of his historical imagination, that source seems to be his deep identification with John Randolph. Adams appears to have been largely unaware of this identification in 1881, and he never changed his low opinion of Randolph as a statesman, but years later, Adams had mellowed to the extent that he confessed to taking pleasure in John Randolph's letters, and he ventured the qualified praise that they stood up well in comparison with certain kinds of bloated epistles produced by fame-conscious politicians. In a 1901 letter to Kemp P. Battle, an editor of the letters of Randolph's friend Nathaniel Macon, Adams wrote, "Macon's letters are always good-writing, no matter how bad their grammar. As reading, one of Macon's, or John Randolph's, is more entertaining and closer to the point than dozens of those of the great statesmen who wrote for the public."[39]

As an old man, Henry Adams compared John Randolph favorably with the elderly John Quincy Adams as a fierce debater. Writing to his brother Brooks in 1909, Henry Adams says of their grandfather's "rhetoric, his satire and humor, his readiness in debate, and his superiority to his opponents" that no one else "in our political history, except John Randolph, has approached him in the rough-and-tumble fight of savage prize-fighting."[40] He also expresses admiration for the kind of verbal behavior that he had once censured, applying almost the same language once negatively associated with Southern violence and Randolph: "[John Quincy

Adams] hit and bit without scruple, and gouged, too, when he could. This was a field where his temper stood him in good service. Damn it! I can scarcely keep my own, when I think of it. I take keen pleasure in every outburst of his malignant tongue, and I only wish that it had been more malignant still." He attributes his pleasure to his "own wicked nature," but a moral and political tie-in is not far off. He likes Randolph's style, but he likes John Quincy Adams's use of the same verbal violence against "that cotton-planting gang of brutes." The Civil War had left scars that would never heal for Adams, but he was capable, in old age, of admiring the eccentric scrapper on the other side, at least as a fighter.

If the sources of Henry Adams's long-term identification with Randolph include both attraction and repulsion, the latter at first would seem to dominate. The deep involvement of self with subject needed to produce this "profound and brilliant book" is partly what Joseph Conrad called "the fascination of the abomination" in *Heart of Darkness*. In the biography, Adams was consciously and morally opposed to Randolph. Randolph was the abomination, yet there was much even in this abominable Randolph to transfix Adams's eye. First of all, there was Henry Adams's fascination with Randolph's much higher level of tolerance for violence, a kind of behavior to which Henry Adams was clearly attracted, at least verbally, but a trait in himself that he came only slowly to acknowledge and accept. Randolph's open expression of a quality foreign to the kind of classical balance that was Henry Adams's conscious approach to character, at least in this biography of 1881, brought with it a whole host of other transgressive behaviors: Randolph's fearlessness, despite frequent defeats and humiliations, in confronting others both verbally and physically; his open expression of emotion; his impulsiveness; his public yielding to forbidden appetites such as drinking in excess, openly bringing his jug of porter on to the floor of the House; and his unregulated social aggression and open expression of class feeling and family pride. All of these things were more or less problematical for Henry Adams in 1881, and while he saw Randolph as a grotesque in all of these behaviors, the passionate but highly regulated Adams must have seen, to some extent, in Randolph's grotesque visage, his own face in a distorting glass.

There was much in the life of John Randolph with which Henry Adams could legitimately identify consciously, however. In Henry James's *The Portrait of a Lady* of 1881, the year in which Henry Adams wrote *John Randolph*, Mrs. Touchett states in her abrupt way to Isabel Archer,

"There are only a dozen American names."[41] "Randolph" and "Adams" both were on almost any version of such a list in the lifetimes of John Randolph and Henry Adams. Both men felt strongly the pride and the burden that comes with what Earl Harbert called "the great inheritance."[42] Furthermore, Henry Adams could have felt some intellectual and emotional connection to the son of a family that had risen to prominence in the eighteenth century and felt alienated in the nineteenth. Randolph opposed the irresistible tendencies of the United States toward increased federal power and social equality. Adams expressed his somewhat different alienation in much more complex ways in the *Education*, and close comparison of it with *John Randolph* reveals that the earlier book was, whether consciously or unconsciously, in some ways, a rough draft for the later.

John Randolph is more like the *Education* than are any of Adams's other books. Both works open with references to long American ancestry and allusions to colonial dignities. The sense of place, too, is strong in *John Randolph*'s "Youth" and in the *Education*'s "Quincy" chapters, and it is evoked in a similar fashion. A glance at the first two paragraphs of both books will reveal the same mingling of the names of persons and places, Henry Adams's distinctive poetry of historical particularity. Both books, also, dwell more or less affectionately and nostalgically on the vanished freedoms and simplicities of "eighteenth-century" American country life, and both books lean heavily on references to eighteenth-century English literature, and other books popular in eighteenth-century England, to characterize the lost way of life of a rural gentry. When one reads in "Quincy" of the "writing desk with little glass doors above and little eighteenth-century volumes in old binding, labeled 'Peregrine Pickle' or 'Tom Jones' or 'Hannah More'" (16) one might recall the description in "Youth" of the "cupboards of Virginia houses" containing a longer but similar list (9).

John Randolph and the *Education* both conjure up a sense of privilege and protection by contrasting images of a vulnerable, newborn child with a surrounding network of powerful institutions:

> The world upon which the last Randolph baby opened his eyes was, so far as his horizon stretched, a world of cousins, a colonial aristocracy all its own. (*Randolph* 4)

> First Church, the Boston State House, Beacon Hill, John Hancock and John Adams, Mount Vernon Street and Quincy, all crowding in on ten pounds of unconscious babyhood. . . . (*Education* 3–4)

Adams, moreover, chooses to portray both babies as born at unrecognized junctures in history, as born just before deluges overwhelmed the eighteenth-century, privileged societies that bulked so seemingly massively about them. One passage from *John Randolph* that recalls many in the *Education* captures Adams's sentiment with particular poignancy: "This small cheerful world . . . was about to suffer a wreck the more fatal and hopeless because no skill could avert it, and the dissolution was so quiet and subtle that no one could protect himself or secure his children" (4). He envisions John Randolph, and later himself, as caught up in tremendous and unexpected historical forces, and we find related forms of thinking in his other works.[43]

Henry Adams suggested in the *Education* that his childhood bout with scarlet fever had affected his character. Whether it did so or not, one notes that Adams thought that "his character and processes of mind seemed to share in a fining-down process of scale . . . and his nerves were more delicate than a boy's nerves ought to be. He exaggerated these weaknesses as he grew older" (6). Adams could not decide whether "the change of character was morbid or healthy." To the slender Randolph, Adams decides in favor of attributing a "morbid constitution" (15), and, accordingly, the character is not "healthy." Adams never calls himself "eccentric," but he describes himself as a "variation from a normal type" as he does Randolph. Henry Adams inherited his share of the famous Adams testiness, and he criticizes Randolph most severely for irritability.

Parallels of form, diction, and characterization between the *Education* and *John Randolph* could be extended much farther, but there is enough evidence of Adams's affinity for his subject, and also of negative employment of his own traits, to hazard some speculations about the Randolph portrait. Henry Adams was forty-four when he published the biography in 1882, and he was working diligently toward what he hoped would be major achievement and belated celebrity. It is possible that he responded to the Virginian so intensely because he saw in Randolph an explorer of forbidden emotional territory and a kind of caricature of what he could become at his worst. Here was another nervous, sensitive, proud, bright patrician who, through lack of self-discipline and self-control, significantly damaged himself and his career.

John Randolph shares an overall structure with many of Adams's larger works, a pattern of early hope and then decline and fall. Adams never employed the "comic rise." *John Randolph* is largely a satire, and Adams avoids a clear potential for tragic treatment, but unlike classical comedy the action of satire falls, and the satiric figure draws society down with him. Henry Adams's hero Albert Gallatin lived to see the early hopes of the Jeffersonians disappointed. Madeleine Lee's early enthusiasm for democracy ends primarily in horror and flight, although there is a concluding hint that she may return to marriage to the Washington lawyer Carrington. Esther Dudley is left with the thundering sound of Niagara Falls in the distance and an expression on her face that is "infinitely dreary and absent." *Mont Saint Michel and Chartres* is a study of medieval unity, but the reader's delight in this unity is shadowed by the knowledge that "Nothing is sadder than the catastrophe of Gothic art, religion, and hope."[44] The *Education* ends with the desire that, should Adams return to life in 1938, he would "find a world that sensitive and timid natures could regard without a shudder."

X

When *John Randolph* was published in 1882, the perceptive reader could encounter Henry Adams's most ambitious and complex attempt up to that time to create a character on the printed page and to set that character against the backdrop of history. Despite Adams's reticence, antagonism, and satirical flights of fancy, his *John Randolph* is a rich and suggestive portrait that continues to provoke controversy. Henry Adams achieved this feat largely without the use of contemporary psychological or scientific perspectives, and he did so through deep feeling for various classical conventions of character study, rhetorical strategy, and moral analysis. Adams, perhaps, was never again to confine himself so strongly to classical patterns of thought and composition, but they eminently suit the decorum of one child of the eighteenth century confronting another.

Although the evocation of character in *John Randolph* may show Henry Adams at his most classical, it foreshadows future treatments of character in many ways. Adams tended not to pose the self against a backdrop of dreams and desires but rather against a dark mass of other selves, some contemporary with his subject and others ranging both back and forward through time. Beyond these human groups lay an outer darkness of natural forces. Adams's sensibility was moral, social, historical, political, and scientific. It tended, moreover, to reach for abstract explanations, laws, and first principles. Adams usually followed the thread of character not within but without—out first to family, then to class and regional culture, still farther out through "national character" to the broad ranges of history, and finally out to the cosmos, toward ultimate abstraction and all-embracing theory. There are few interconnections in *John Randolph* of the self with metaphysical and cosmic matters such as we find in *Chartres* and the *Education*, yet what we do have at this stage of Adams's development in the treatment of human character is something rather rare in American literature and historical writing, a literary fusion of personal, moral, cultural, political, historical, scientific, and theoretical insight that fulfills the promise of the brilliant, early letters and of *Democracy*.

For the first time in Adams's work, in *John Randolph* of 1882 the narrative voice occasionally gives us that shock of uniting nearly all aspects of the reader's mind and sensibility that so few writers can provide. Henry Adams can sweep the reader, albeit intermittently, through the full range of literary responses as can only those writers who combine powerful intellect, mastery of ideas, human insight, intense emotion, comprehensive reading, and superior gifts of expression with matter of epic proportions.

To know *John Randolph*, then, is to know much about Henry Adams's way of knowing human nature. It is also to witness a bravura demonstration of Adams's mastery of one kind of historical knowledge. *John Randolph* shows the sometime scientific historian primarily in a traditional, classical mode, connecting an individual character and his ethos with historical causes and historical consequences in a framework of complex and thoughtful moral analysis.

NOTES

1. Edward Chalfant, *Better in Darkness: A Biography of Henry Adams: His Second Life, 1862–1891* (Hamden, Conn., 1994), 415.
2. Henry Adams to E. L. Godkin, Aug. 6, 1881, in *Letters of Henry Adams*, ed. J. C. Levenson et al. (Cambridge, Mass., 1982–1988), 2:434.
3. HA to John Gorham Palfrey, Feb. 12, Mar. 20, 1862, in *Letters*, 1:280, 287.
4. HA to Hugh Blair Grigsby, Aug. 20, Sept. 29, 1877, May 30, 1878, in *Letters*, 2:314, 321, 339; Chalfant, *Better in Darkness*, 415.
5. HA to John T. Morse, Jr., Apr. 9, 1881; HA to John Hay, Sept. 3, Nov. 19, 1882; HA to Morse, Nov. 19, 1882, in *Letters*, 2:424, 468, 479.
6. HA to John Hay, Oct. 8, 1882; HA to John T. Morse, Jr., Nov. 19, 1882; HA to Henry Cabot Lodge, Oct. 31, 1882; HA to Robert Cunliffe, Nov. 12, 1882; HA to Lodge, Dec. 26, 1882, in *Letters*, 2:475, 479, 476, 477, 485.
7. Chalfant, *Better in Darkness*, 137, 326–328, 398–399.
8. Henry Adams, *Novels, Mont Saint Michel, The Education*, ed. Ernest Samuels and Jayne N. Samuels (New York, 1983), 924. Each title referred to separately in subsequent notes; *Education* cited in text.
9. Edward Chalfant, *Both Sides of the Ocean: A Biography of Henry Adams: His First Life, 1838–1862*, 70, 120, 248.
10. HA to John Gorham Palfrey, Mar. 27, May 29, 1863, Mar. 20, 1862, in *Letters*, 1:340, 359, 287.

11. Ernest Samuels, *Henry Adams: The Middle Years* (1958; Cambridge, Mass., 1965), 62, 64–65, 63, 66–67.
12. HA to Lodge, Oct. 31, 1882, in *Letters*, 2:476.
13. Henry Adams, *John Randolph* (1882; Boston, 1895), 255–256. All subsequent references will be to this edition, with page numbers cited parenthetically in the text.
14. Russell Kirk, *Randolph of Roanoke: A Study in Conservative Thought* (Chicago, 1951), 8.
15. Edward Chalfant mentions a note that Henry Adams "inserted into his copy of *John Randolph*, 1883," to the effect that "[Randolph] was secretly married to Hester Mensgrewe [spelling unclear], the daughter of his boarding-house mistress, authority Joseph Bryan." Chalfant, *Better in Darkness*, 832. Perhaps Henry Adams was not possessed of this information when he wrote the book in 1881, or did not trust it entirely, or decided that it did not refute necessarily the charge of impotence, or saw that such a *mésalliance* for the proud Randolph might have been entered into for a variety of reasons too broad to interpret without further information. See also William Cabell Bruce, *John Randolph of Roanoke* (New York, 1922); and Robert Dawidoff, *The Education of John Randolph* (New York, 1979).
16. William Merrill Decker, *The Literary Vocation of Henry Adams* (Chapel Hill, 1990), 303. Luther Martin was Judge Chase's defender in the famous impeachment trial that Randolph mismanaged.
17. Richard Brookhiser, *Gentleman Revolutionary: Gouverneur Morris, the Rake Who Wrote the Constitution* (New York, 2003), 180–185; H. J. Eckenrode, *The Randolphs: The Story of an American Family* (Indianapolis, 1946), 172–181; Robert McColley, introduction to *John Randolph* (Armonk, 1996), 9–11.
18. Brookhiser, *Gentleman Revolutionary*, 199; Eckenrode, *The Randolphs*, 183–184.
19. Ernest Samuels, *The Young Henry Adams* (1948; Cambridge, Mass., 1967), 6, 32.
20. Louis Menand, *The Metaphysical Club* (New York, 2001), 201, 216, 140–143.
21. The edition referred to is Hill and Wang's 1961 *Aristotle's Poetics*, translated by S. H. Butcher.
22. See *Aristotle on Rhetoric: A Theory of Civil Discourse*, trans. George A. Kennedy (Oxford, 1991), 2:12–17.
23. Quoted from *The Aeneid of Virgil, Books 1–6*, ed. R. D. Williams (London, 1972).
24. J. C. Levenson, *The Mind and Art of Henry Adams* (Palo Alto, Calif., 1957), 105, 100.
25. Eckenrode, *The Randolphs*, 170–171, 192–194; Samuels, *The Middle Years*, 195. Henry Adams was to become one of the American writers most responsive to architecture. Toward the beginning of his literary career, one notes the tendency to use the names of buildings as symbols—"Bizarre" in *John Randolph* or "Arlington" and "Mount Vernon" in *Democracy*, the latter also very lightly sketched visually—and a movement through the joint use of verbal and architectural symbolism in *Esther*'s St. John's Church to the complex uses of the abbey at Mont-Saint-Michel and Chartres Cathedral.
26. Randolph's reference to Othello's words are laden with erotic and racial overtones. In the same letter in which he called Nancy Randolph a vampire, John Randolph charged "that she had had an 'Othello' (a slave lover) at Bizarre." Brookhiser, *Gentleman Revolutionary*, 199.
27. See David McCullough, *John Adams* (New York, 2001), 37.
28. The only time Adams associates the schoolmaster role with Randolph, on the other hand, is when his influence is waning in Congress at the end of 1804, and he begins to "lecture" and "worry" his colleagues "with the pragmatic air of a pedagogue" *(Randolph* 123).
29. Martin died at Burr's house in 1826. One wonders what Adams made of the "rollicking, witty, audacious . . . drunken, slovenly, grand" Martin in the lost *Aaron Burr* manuscript

(141). The two famous trials would seem to call for parallel treatment. Both the decorum and larger scope of the *History* would ensure more restrained evocation of Martin than the amusing references to him that appear in *John Randolph* (141–148), although Adams does note Martin's idolization of Burr's daughter, Theodosia. *History of the United States during the Administrations of Thomas Jefferson*, ed. Earl Harbert (New York, 1986), 909.

30. HA to Brooks Adams, Mar. 13, 1909, in *Letters*, 6:239.
31. Samuels, *Young Henry Adams*, 41.
32. Henry Adams, *History of the United States during the Administrations of James Madison*, ed. Earl Harbert (New York, 1986), 1329.
33. Eugenia Kaledin, *The Education of Mrs. Henry Adams* (Amherst, 1994), 220; Robert Hume, *Runaway Star: An Appreciation of Henry Adams* (Ithaca, 1951), 83.
34. Kirk, *Randolph of Roanoke*, 12, 1, 163, 157, 2. See also McColley, introduction to *John Randolph*, 13–14.
35. Kaledin, *Education of Mrs. Henry Adams*, 220. The brackets are in Kaledin's text.
36. Francis Fergusson, introduction to *Aristotle's Poetics*, trans. S. H. Butcher (New York, 1963), 22–23.
37. Alex Beam's *Gracefully Insane: The Rise and Fall of America's Premier Mental Hospital* (New York, 2001) examines one of the Boston area's more noteworthy institutions, McLean Hospital, which was settling into its beautiful, new 240-acre campus in Belmont about the time that Henry Adams wrote *John Randolph*. Founded in 1817 as the Charlestown Asylum, the future McLean shared a board of trustees with Massachusetts General Hospital. John Adams moderated the first meeting of a board that also included John Quincy Adams (Beam 20), so the Adamses contributed in the administrative and leadership capacity that they knew best. At midcentury, the asylum had moved to Somerville, becoming one of the mental hospitals sometimes alluded to by Clover Hooper Adams in her letters. By 1875, Frederick Law Olmstead, who later became a patient, was sketching designs for the new site in Belmont (10). Beam treats McLean as a "living museum" of changing attitudes toward mental health (4), and the hospital has provided a complex variety of treatments over the years. In Henry Adams's day, McLean was beginning to become especially associated with an expensive and comfortable variety of long-term, even lifetime, care in handsome surroundings for the affluent.

    Setting aside the genre of *John Randolph*, Henry Adams's "eighteenth-century" moral severity regarding some of the more extreme varieties of "eccentricity" in the book may seem wanting by some standards of the 1880s and many today. The concept of sanity as something that can be restored (as opposed to insanity contained) in the static atmosphere of the 1880s asylum, however, runs directly counter to Adams's classical emphasis on the importance of action in the world of moral choice. Although Henry Adams hardly posed as an expert on mental illness, one might note that, today, due both to rising costs and recent changes in the laws governing involuntary confinement, the asylum model of long-term confinement for all but the most serious cases of mental illness has fallen on hard times. "Warehousing" has given way to "mainstreaming" whenever possible, and contemporary respect for the civil rights of the mentally ill has also forced upon them many legal responsibilities that the asylum movement of the nineteenth and early twentieth centuries sought to spare them. To sum up metaphorically, contemporary society has decided that the mentally ill should have Hoopers as therapists but Adamses as lawyers.

38. See Samuels, *The Middle Years*, 190–191, 456.
39. HA to Kemp P. Battle, Apr. 6, 1901, in *Letters*, 5:229.
40. HA to Brooks Adams, Mar. 13, 1909, in *Letters*, 6:239.
41. Henry James, *Portrait of a Lady*, ed. Leon Edel (1881: Boston, 1963), 277.

42. Earl N. Harbert, *The Force So Much Closer Home: Henry Adams and the Adams Family* (New York: 1977), 18.
43. As Ernest Samuels has demonstrated, Henry Adams had much more difficulty in giving up the geological catastrophism he had learned at Harvard from Louis Agassiz than the "Darwinism" chapter of the *Education* would seem to indicate. Samuels, *Young Henry Adams*, 163. One could argue that catastrophism in many forms was congenial to his nature, and that he always remained a "biographical catastrophist."
44. HA, *Mont Saint Michel*, 383.

Portraits & Privacy

Henry Adams & John Singer Sargent

BARRY MAINE

JOHN SINGER SARGENT, American expatriate and the most celebrated and sought-after portrait painter of his day on both sides of the Atlantic, arrived in Washington, D.C., in February 1903 to paint Pres. Theodore Roosevelt and Secretary of State John Hay. It was the middle of a triumphant homecoming for Sargent, who had been born abroad to expatriate Philadelphians, educated in Italy and France, trained in the atelier of Carolus-Duran in Paris, and attracting scores of lucrative commissions in London. He came to the United States in 1903 for a working tour of cities along the East Coast, painting portraits of wealthy financiers and industrialists, their wives and families, and other shining ornaments of what passed for fashionable society in America. To have one's portrait painted by Sargent at the beginning of the new century was to court fame and to seek immortality. The American Century had arrived, and with it came notoriety as the measure of achievement. Sargent's fame made a celebrity of each sitter who submitted to his judgment. Many paid dearly for the privilege.[1]

Roosevelt and Hay were a different breed of horse. They did not need Sargent to make them famous; they suffered themselves to be so immortalized out of respect for the dignity of the offices they held. In Washington that March, Henry Adams met Sargent and reported to Elizabeth Cameron that he found him "stodgy" and "as unresponsive as ever" to his social solicitations.[2] Begrudgingly, he added that Sargent's portrait of Hay was "good, but as I tell Hay, it will take a few years to show me just what meanness I hadn't in forty years' intimacy, fully recognized in him."[3] A month later he reported (again to Elizabeth Cameron) that Sargent's portrait of Roosevelt, which still hangs in the White House in Washington today, conceals "with diabolical cunning" the "depth of its malignity towards Theodore."[4] Such moody, "interested," idiosyncratic, and thus perplexing responses bring to mind what Adams had once observed of the St.-Gaudens Adams Memorial in Rock Creek Park, which Henry had commissioned in memory of his wife, Marion (Clover) Adams: "The interest of the figure was not in its meaning, but in the response of the observer."[5] Roosevelt's portrait also, Adams wrote, "calls out curious traits in [its] observers."[6]

Before 1903, Adams already knew what it felt like to have a Sargent portrait call out his own "curious traits." A decade earlier, Adams likened his response to the World Columbian Exposition in Chicago to his response to a Sargent painting that he had seen in London the previous summer of fashionable London hostess Mrs. Hugh Hammersley: "was it," he asked his friend Hay, "a defiance or an insult to our society, or a rendering in good faith of our civilization, or a conscious snub to French and English art, or an unconscious revelation of the artist's despair of reconciliation with the female of the gold-bug? Well, the Chicago architecture is precisely an architectural Mrs. Hammersley!"[7] Evidently, Adams did not know what to make of a portrait that appeared, to him at least, to honor its subject while poking her in the ribs, so to speak, for believing she was worthy of the honor. Likewise, the Chicago Exposition, while surpassing even Paris in "scenic display," displayed most of all its pretentiousness.[8] Portraits by Sargent often called forth from Adams such vexing questions about meaning and intention.

On the subject of art generally, Adams was characteristically coy: "for some things ignorance is good, and art is one of them. He knew he knew nothing, and had not the trained eye or the keen instinct that trusted itself, but he was curious."[9] His interest in Sargent in particular reflected his curiosity about portraiture in general, about what the artist saw in his subject, about what the subject revealed to the artist, about the truth in art, and about what his friend Henry James termed "the force and beauty of its process."[10] His reactions to Sargent's portraits of Hay and Roosevelt demonstrate that he had put his finger on a question about Sargent's portraits that continues to perplex us today: what was this sphinx-like artist's attitude toward the people he painted?

Adams purposefully sought out Sargent's work whenever he visited the Salons in Paris, the Royal Academy in London, or gallery exhibitions in Boston and New York, as if in search of answers to questions about himself and his milieu. Sargent was often the only artist he mentioned in his accounts of these exhibitions in letters written to friends, and he measured all other portraits by Sargent's work. He brooded over Sargent's portraits of friends and acquaintances, hooted and howled with delight over Sargent's portraits of social types he found much more amusing than his own, and theorized about Sargent's motives in painting people as he did. As much as Adams admired Sargent's talent, he clearly mistrusted the artist's motives. Just as importantly for our purposes, his responses to Sargent's rendering of his contemporaries, many of whom he painted while Adams was writing his own group portrait and memorial to his generation in *The Education of Henry Adams*, speak to the principles of portraiture Adams himself observed as a historian and a biographer. Adams believed that historical contexts and backgrounds were essential to one's understanding of any public figure or private personage. Accordingly, he believed that whatever Sargent's motives might be, his approach to portraiture was often too personal, too focused on the subject's character as defined by personality rather than social identity. Such portraits tantalized the public, and catered to its increasing voyeurism, but offered, to Adams's way of thinking, ultimately misleading representations of the figures he painted. Adams did not wish to make the same mistake in portraying himself and his contemporaries in the *Education*.

I

Henry James once insisted that there is no greater work of art than a great portrait, and he made that observation in reference to Sargent, whose work he championed in an essay written for *Harpers Magazine* in October 1887. John Singer Sargent was the last great portrait artist in the tradition of Van Dyck, Rembrandt, and Reynolds. A painter of unmatched technical facility in his day, Sargent presented prize-winning portraits at the Paris Salons that brought him fame at a young age. As his biographer Stanley Olson has put it, "the portrait ruled the Academy and Sargent ruled the portrait. It was an uncontested fact."[11]

Nonetheless, Sargent painted at a time when traditional assumptions about art were beginning to crumble under the pressure of modernism. Since his death in 1925 there has been a continuous debate over the value and quality of his work. His talent has never been in question, only what he chose to do with it. A traditional function of portraiture (to capture and preserve a "likeness") was gradually being usurped by photography during his career, while another (to memorialize and pay tribute to the subject) became less and less defensible when the subjects were self-aggrandizing bourgeoisie.[12] Sargent himself admitted that he painted far too many portraits, yet some of these—such as his portraits of the daughters of Edward Darley Boit; Lady Agnew of Scotland; Parisian beauty Virginie Gautreau; Mrs. Henry White, friend of the Adamses and wife of the American diplomat; and members of the Wertheimer family, a socially prominent Jewish family in England—are among the most daring, provocative, and celebrated paintings of the period. Nevertheless, portraits that some critics admire for bringing cultural commentary and psychological complexity to a genre better known for obsequious flattery, others see only as examples of Sargent fawning before rich and powerful patrons. What Sargent actually set out to paint in any given portrait—a likeness, a subject's performance of a public persona, a psychological study, a social type, an advertisement for the bourgeoisie or a satire of it—is no easy affair to determine, and Sargent left no trail to follow.[13]

Portraits more than any other artistic genre are bound to the moment of their execution. They bear the stamp of date, cultural milieu, and material culture. They both reflect and record the subject's reputation, the particular circumstances of the sitting, and the artist's and sitter's responses to each other's physical presence. As artifacts, as products of highly charged moments of perception and performance shared between artist and subject occurring in a dense yet ephemeral social atmosphere, portraits can be notoriously difficult to read. Norman Bryson has argued that we tend to see in them supporting evidence for the existing "archive" of information about the subject, for what the viewer already knows, or thinks he knows, about the subject. Any response to a portrait reveals as much about the viewer's attitudes toward the subject as it does the painter's. Adams describing his reaction to a portrait by Sargent was certainly no exception.

Adams's responses were eccentric and motivated by personal concerns. He reacted most favorably to what he perceived as Sargent's talent for capturing or even defining a social type.[14] He suspected Sargent of harboring feelings and attitudes toward his subjects that found their way into the style of the portrait and the pose of the sitter. Adams thought he saw "condescension" there, condescension that took the form of playing up or exposing the most damning (in Adams's mind at least) attributes of Sargent's subjects.[15] When the individual exposed for a type was one he disliked for some reason or held prejudices against, Adams howled in delight. When it was someone he knew or a type he identified with, he grumbled. To "out-Sargent" Sargent was, in Adams's mind, to expose the truth about a subject in some brutal or scandalous fashion; for example, in 1900 he commented that "Boldini's portrait of Whistler . . . actually beats Sargent for sheer audacity."[16]

Although Adams relished the unmasking in such portraits, he also resented it, as he resented the brutal invasion of privacy enabled and enforced by the public's voyeurism and the growing popularity of photography. A portrait by its very nature must reveal something of its subject. But Adams believed a portrait by Sargent stripped its subject naked. Adams delighted in the exposure of transgressions against time-honored hierarchies of social class in portraits of the Jewish nouveau riche. To his niece Mabel Hooper he wrote archly from London in 1897 that there was "nothing better" than Sargent's portrait of Mrs. Carl Meyer, and he reported a few years later to Elizabeth Cameron that "The Wertheimer girls [figure 1] are stupendous. . . . Sargent must be put to death instantly or he will libel us all to eternity."[17] But he could also take offense at paintings of his friends whether or not he could detect what it was exactly that Sargent sought to expose. To Elizabeth Cameron he wrote, "Sargent gibbets us all with his everlasting British condescension and patronage. We bore him. He paints it."[18]

In a letter of June 1896, Adams complained to Elizabeth Cameron that he "loathed" society on both sides of the Atlantic, without being able to explain why, and noted that somehow "Sargent expresses it best in his awful tale-telling portraits."[19] Adams does not say exactly what "tales" Sargent "told" about his

Figure 1. Ena and Betty, Daughters of Asher and Mrs. Wertheimer *(1901), by John Singer Sargent. Copyright Tate Gallery, London / Art Resource, NY.*

subjects, but one may surmise that he felt they exposed either something personal about them or something derogatory about the social type or class to which they belonged. For example, he pronounced Sargent's portrait of the Duchess of Sutherland "an absolutely fiendish caricature."[20] The "awful" in "Sargent's awful tale-telling portraits" is less an aesthetic judgment than a sign of his distaste for Sargent's "telling tales" in public about people in high social positions. As much as Adams took pleasure in the "exposure" of people and social classes he despised, he evidently believed that Sargent's portraits committed unsavory violations of privacy. Despite his own confessed loathing for the perennial parade of social dignitaries, such as those lining up to be murdered by Sargent (and paying a high price for the privilege!), Adams insisted—to Elizabeth Cameron—that as for himself he could not "throw bombs" at society "like Sargent did."[21] It would appear that Adams believed Sargent was guilty of making too freely with people who, whatever their faults or the sins of the social class they represented, were in most cases "better" than the stream of gawkers and critics who paraded by their portraits to pass judgment on them.[22]

As unsupportable as such accusations against Sargent may be, it is clear that Adams characterized Sargent's approach to portraiture as aggressively judgmental and psychologically probing and invasive: "Never did an artist paint with such psychology as Sargent."[23] Adams's well-documented personal aversion to public exposure of any kind may help to explain his objections to Sargent's work.[24] He often refused to allow photographs to be taken of himself, and he shied away from portrait painters, Sargent in particular. He urged Henry James to take his own life by writing his autobiography rather than submit to assassination by someone else, and he followed his own advice. Spurred on by reading a recently published collection of letters by Robert Louis Stevenson, he urged Elizabeth Cameron to burn his letters: "Don't leave them knocking about as mush for pigs to root in for scandal and gossip." He observed that volumes of personal letters represent the author "like a portrait by Sargent: they betray one's besetting vices in youth, one's worst selfishness in middle age," and eventually "one's senility." Not only are they too personally revealing, but "they exaggerate all one's bigness" and in this regard they are susceptible to "egotism and error." Personal letters, in other words, are too self-interested and too self-involved to represent the subject fairly or accurately, and they "do not leave enough for" the reader to interpret without the subject's ego getting in the way.[25] Likewise, in posing for their portraits, Sargent's subjects attempted to craft a public persona, and in painting it, Sargent exposed his subject's aspirations—who and what they wanted to be or how they wanted to be known. William James once observed to his brother Henry that Sargent "sees the mask rather than the inside of people, but how he hits it off!"[26] By "painting the mask," Sargent allowed himself and the public to be manipulated by the subject's posing and, paradoxically, violated the subject's privacy by putting the subject's ego on display. This is what Adams meant by Sargent's psychological approach to portraiture.

Sargent's portrait of Theodore Roosevelt [figure 2, next page] provides a case in point. Adams's first impression of the portrait had been mostly positive: "The portrait is good Sargent and not very bad Roosevelt. It is not Theodore, but a young intellectual idealist with a taste for athletics, which I take to be Theodore's idea of himself. It is for once less brutal than its subject. It offers nothing to criticize except Sargent."[27] A month later, after subsequent viewings, Adams evidently saw more in it than he had at first glance: Sargent "flings raw mud in our faces," Adams claimed, implying that the portrait, as part of its "diabolical cunning," "maligned" not only Roosevelt but also the class of Americans he represented (which certainly included Adams). "All the worst is there, paraded and flaunted before one's eyes, but one does not see it," presumably because of the difficulty of achieving the detachment from one's own class necessary to recognizing Sargent's judgment on it.[28] Nevertheless, he was deeply suspicious. In Adams's eyes, what was "cunning" about this portrait was Sargent's sly form of simultaneously pandering to and poking fun at his subject, as Adams believed Sargent had in his portrait of Mrs. Hammersley. Sargent captured Roosevelt's "intellectual idealism" and "athleticism" in his confident, imperial pose as he grasps the banister knob as if it were the great round globe itself.[29] Sargent painted the pose and exposed Roosevelt's egotism at a single stroke. Does that make the portrait malicious? Sargent himself claimed that in every portrait he painted, he painted only what he saw. "I do not judge," he claimed. "I only chronicle."[30] But Sargent's eye was not innocent, what he saw was never simple, and not all of what he saw was necessarily posed. The eyes in the Roosevelt portrait, for example, suggest a wistful melancholy, which qualifies the self-assurance of the imperious stance. The portrait can be viewed as sympathetic toward its subject; Roosevelt and his family and closest friends certainly believed it was. This was no gibbeting. Adams's defensive reaction may reflect how much he feared exposure of his own person as he convinced himself he was witnessing it in the portrait of a compatriot.

Figure 2. Theodore Roosevelt *(1903), by John Singer Sargent. White House Collection, Courtesy White House Historical Association (56).*

If it is true, as Rudolph Arnheim has observed, that the subject of a portrait gives permission to the artist and the viewer to stare, to judge, to dissect, to study, to objectify, to regard their person as a thing or a type, then it is understandable that Adams bristled at such treatment of his friends and would not brook it for himself. According to Ernest Samuels, "all his life Adams lived in terror of clacking tongues. Unfavorable publicity made him miserable."[31] Adams's anxieties over privacy originated in family pride and class prejudices more so than in personal modesty or any belief in the "rights" of individual citizens. However, Adams's objection to what he termed Sargent's "psychological" approach to portraiture was not based solely or even primarily on concerns for the subject's privacy. Adams's "terror" of publicity reveals not only his aversion to gossip at his own expense but his fear of others characterizing him on the basis of isolated pieces of personal information or judging him in isolation of historical context. In a letter to his brother Brooks in March 1900, in reference to their elder brother Charles's recently published biography of their father, Charles Francis Adams, Henry lamented over what such a biography had done to his father:

> the stale smell of dead anxieties makes me sick, and that history bores my life out. That we saved our skins in London was God's mercy, and the work of blind forces that no one understood or measured. Looking back I grovel in the dust, and shake with terror at the immensity of the danger and the impotence of our efforts. I want to say nothing about it. The effect of reading Charles' book is only to make this feeling keener, and to stimulate my twelfth-century instincts. I should prefer not to dissipate the atmospheric effects of time and distance, and not to bring our figures too near for perspective. Our father would stand out better, larger and even truer, without definition. I do not like the microscope, or even the telescope as a family ornament, and I loathe the photograph and Sargent's analysis of character.[32]

It would appear that Adams's confidence in writing diplomatic history had waned considerably since he wrote his *History of the United States during the Administrations of Thomas Jefferson and James Madison*. Here he reveals that the bafflement he would later express in the *Education* over the motives of British statesmen in response to his father's diplomatic mission to keep England neutral in the American War between the States would be more than just a pose. Yet the historical sense in him ran as strong as ever, and he realized that his father could not be understood except by revealing him in the context of his particular time and place.

According to Adams, photographs and portraits appeared to offer characterizations of subjects, yet they promised more than they delivered by failing to provide sufficient backgrounds for knowing or judging anyone. In his brother's biography of their father, he objected not to the exposure of his father's person but to the failure to reveal it. That failure had little to do with however much of their father's personality Charles succeeded in revealing under the "microscope" of personal reminiscence. What he objected to was his brother's failure to dramatize the relationship between figure and historical background necessary to understanding their father, not as a contemporary (which he was not) "brought too near for perspective" or as a personality or study in psychology, but as a historical figure caught up in the historical currents of his time. This view was central to Adams's approach to writing history and biography.

II

Adams's own historical practice leaves little doubt that he believed no biography or historical portrait could succeed without placing the figures in the context of what he called historical atmosphere.[33] The most vexing (and most intriguing) problem for Adams was the problem of inventing and sustaining a narrative form that could do justice to the subject as a historical figure. Writing to his brother Brooks about the biography Brooks was writing of their grandfather John Quincy Adams, Henry observed that

> you are, in reality, writing a romance, a Political novel, and you need above all else, Form. There has always been my own gallows! All my life I have labored and sweated to get Form, and always I have failed, because . . . I could never get to the point of seeing a big book as a whole. . . . My mind cannot carry it as a whole, but my eyes can see where the modeling, or drawing, or color, or conception, fails.[34]

He knew that to separate the figure from the background was one sure way to lose the figure altogether. He thought the memoir, for example, a narrative form too limited in point of view to provide a satisfying portrait of anyone, for reasons similar to those cited by Henry James for shying away from the first-person point of view in his fiction: the figure or subject is better understood observed in relief against the background of the history that aids in explaining who he or she is. Without that, Adams explained to Elizabeth Cameron, biographies "are like bad photographs and distorted perspectives." The challenge for the biographer, given that "the modern public is as dead to the feeling of historical atmosphere as it is to the color of the Chartres window," was to invent a form in which figure and background were interdependent.[35]

Adams's solution to the problem in writing the *History* had been to portray the early years of American democracy as a drama of political figures classified as representative types by region, party affiliation, religion, and social class. Adams leaned particularly heavily on the concept of regional types. For example, he wrote that "in the best and greatest Virginians, the virtues which always stood in most prominence were those of the field and farm—the simple and straightforward mind, the notions of courage and truth, the absence of mercantile sharpness."[36] The Federalist New England type was guided neither by reason nor by experience but rather by "narrow theological prejudices," a lack of faith in democratic government, and a self-righteous sense of mission.[37] The use of regional types prefigured Adams's ultimate concern with national character. As futile or as pointless as it may seem to us in the twenty-first century to attempt to define such a thing as "The American Character" (the title Adams gave to the final chapter of his *History*), Adams insisted that "of all historical problems, the nature of a national character is the most difficult and the most important."[38] His efforts to understand American history as a development of American ways of thinking help to explain his obsession with it. Accordingly, by the time Adams wrote the *Education*, in spite of his increasing skepticism with regard to history conceived as a sequence of events, the taxonomy of national and regional types survived as an ordering principle. Sen. James Donald Cameron, for example, was "the Pennsylvania type": "The Pennsylvania mind, as minds go, was not complex; it reasoned little and never talked, but in practical matters it was the steadiest of all American types; perhaps the most efficient; certainly the safest."[39] This passage begs the question of why this type is "safest"; in the text that follows, Adams characterizes it, rather brutally, as violently prejudiced in its own favor. He sees the Pennsylvania type as narrow minded and bigoted but also more effective at achieving its ends than idealistic, wavering, or self-distrustful New Englanders. His habit of classifying public figures throughout his writing career as representative of social forces at work over time in a region or nation provided the essential balance he sought between figure and background.

How does this manner of representing his contemporaries compare with Sargent's manner of painting portraits? Although Adams clearly disliked portraits that purported to reveal the character of the subject, he was quite carried away by Sargent portraits that portrayed the subject as a representative social type (except of course when it happened to be his own!). To make his portraits more expressive of his subjects, Sargent often exploited contemporary assumptions about and attitudes toward race, class, gender, profession, and cultural identity. He often sought to capture, define, and dramatize in a pronounced way a social type that his audience might easily recognize. (Consider for example his portraits of the British aristocracy, such as his portrait of Lord Ribblesdale [figure 3]) His success at this depended on commonly recognized visual codes concerning the dress, accessories, bearing, and setting of his painted subjects. He painted the daughters of American art dealer Edward Boit in poses and dresses expressive of their ages and social identities within the family in a room in which the prominence of oversized vases suggests a role for these daughters as precious objects imprisoned in a dollhouse.[40] The visual codes in the picture evoke this response and provide the background in which to "place" the figures.

Sometimes Sargent painted a subject—often an American subject—without an established set of visual codes to draw upon, because neither he nor his subject could supply them. In such cases Sargent would typically resort to expressing something of the subject's personality, as in his portrait of Mrs. Boit (which even Henry James, who admired Sargent greatly, took exception to). Without a strong, visible personality to paint, or a background of assumptions or a reputation to exploit, he devoted his energy and talent to representing the subject's physical appearance, to getting the hair, the flesh tones, the texture of the dress on canvas to match what he saw in life. He became, as Olson has observed, completely absorbed in the visual challenge. Yet his subjects and critics expected more.

Sargent's trip to America (only his second) in 1903 capitalized on his growing reputation for painting dazzling portraits. Yet Adams reported to Elizabeth Cameron that "Sargent himself feels that his work here [in Washington] has not been good."[41] William James repeated a rumor to brother Henry that Sargent's portrait of Henry Lee Higginson, also

Figure 3. Lord Ribblesdale *(1902), by John Singer Sargent. Courtesy of the National Gallery, London.*

painted in Washington that year, was "esteemed to be a failure."[42] Neither the relative quality of the work nor Sargent's supposed disappointment in it is easy to ascertain or verify, but if what Adams and James said was true, it could be because the atmosphere in Washington was too thin for Sargent, the social backgrounds less clearly definable to him than in London or even Boston or New York. Adams willingly conceded that Sargent was very good at catching "English manners" and "English minds," but his portrait of John Hay, he came to realize, was "as bad as well can be."[43] We may safely assume that he meant it captured nothing at all about Hay as an American type or American mind. Apparently a British lord or even a Boston society hostess (such as a Mrs. Fiske Warren) was easier to characterize as a type than a midwestern, American secretary of state. The problem would be the same one Adams noted in his brother's biography of Charles Francis Adams: the problem of missing backgrounds. In English society, where even in the nineteenth century class distinctions were fairly rigid and observable, Sargent's portraits of the British aristocracy or mercantile class were easily understood as advertisements for social privilege, paid for by the subjects themselves. There was little question about the content expressed in such portraits. The ego's claim to distinction on social grounds was visible and legible.

Not so in many of Sargent's American portraits. Neither the subject, the painter, nor the viewer could supply the visual codes necessary to social interpretation. Many of these portraits—and the portrait of John Hay [figure 4] offers a good example—appear rather flat and inexpressive. American politics was, for Sargent, a foreign subject bereft of the exotic. Faced with an American figure that did not lend itself easily to his talent for capturing social types, Sargent could only resort to painting a personality, as Adams believed he had in his portrait of Roosevelt, or a painting a visual likeness without cultural markers or psychological depth, as in his portrait of Hay. Adams responded to Hay's portrait as if it represented some kind of comment on his character ("it will take a few years to show me just what meanness I hadn't in forty years intimacy fully recognized in him") because he thought he knew Sargent's work well enough to expect it and because the portrait offered nothing else to interpret. Skeptical of any reading of Hay's character based on the quick and summary judgments of a portrait painter guilty not only of "British condescension" but of paying disproportionate attention to the subject's ego as the register of character, Adams also resented the presumed invasion of his friend's privacy. Adams much preferred portraits expressive of cultural identity because they

Figure 4. John Hay *(1903), by John Singer Sargent.*
Brown University Library.

ministered to his understanding of individuals as "channels of force" in a historical process.

As he turned his thoughts to his own time in planning the *Education*, Adams began to conceive of his generation as "channels of force" as well—channels of ego and ambition to be sure, but also channels of broad social movements and historical change. Adams's reaction to Henry James's biography of William Wetmore Story offers a revealing glimpse of Adams's classifying habit of mind. He appears to praise James for placing the American sculptor in a social milieu and defining him as a social type:

> The painful truth is that all of my New England generation, counting the half-century, 1820–1870, were in actual fact only one mind and one nature. . . . Type bourgeois-bostonien! A type quite as good as another, but more uniform. What you say of Story is at bottom exactly what you would say of Lowell, Motley, and Sumner, barring degrees of egotism. . . . So you have written not Story's life but your own and mine, pure autobiography,—the more keen for what is beneath, implied, intelligible only to me, and half a dozen other people still living. . . . Improvised Europeans we were, and—Lord God!—how thin![44]

Whether or not Adams truly liked the book for doing what he said it did for Story and his generation, and whether or not he was serious about including himself in the category of "Improvised Europeans," what he says here about Story, Charles Sumner, John Lothrop Motley, and James Russell Lowell is certainly consistent with what he says elsewhere. Even if we cannot entirely trust the sincerity of Adams's praise for the book, it is clear that he read the book through the lens of his own preoccupation with classifying individuals as social types.[45] As a biographer and historian, rather than speculating upon the "personal motives and idiosyncrasies" of his subjects, Adams had committed himself to discovering social and economic forces that gave meaning and direction to historical events.[46] Although the forces became more elusive and complicated in the *Education*, and went beyond the individual agent's ability to control or the historian's ability to understand, Adams never varied his approach to history as a manifestation of developments in thought or relinquished his fascination with defining what was American (or British or Russian or so on) about it.

Ernest Samuels has described the *Education* as, among other things, a series of "portraits hung on the wall."[47] Since Adams and Sargent offered up portraits of some of the very same people, the *Education* affords an opportunity to make direct comparisons. In doing so, it is important to keep it in mind that most often Sargent did not choose his subjects so much as they chose him. Adams faced the historian's challenge of having to decide who should be remembered and for what. In the *Education* he acknowledged that "of all branches of education, the science of gauging people and events by their relative importance defies study most insolently."[48] Moreover, Sargent's style of portraiture reflects his classical training, his sensibility, his perception and talent for expressing what he perceived, the very lucrative market for his work, and what his patrons—often people of considerable power and influence—were willing to pay for. Adams, on the other hand, though not without personal motives, did not seek to curry favor, attract commissions, or otherwise earn a living by his pen. He was interested in learning and revealing what he could about himself and his contemporaries and the history they shared.

Although Sargent did not always choose his subjects, by painting them he did contribute to their relative importance. Both Adams and Sargent would have been acutely aware of the stakes involved for the people they portrayed. Finding oneself the subject of one of Adams's heavily ironic portraits in the *Education* was likely to be a decidedly mixed blessing; these subjects did not enjoy the opportunity Sargent's did to negotiate their image for posterity. Samuels has claimed that "Adams knew his victims so surely that they dared not show a sign of offense at the irony that lurked in the shadows of some of his portraits."[49] Adams offered to delete anything anyone found objectionable but probably knew in advance that pride would not permit objections.[50] His contemporaries may have recognized the invitation as no more than a clever ruse by which Adams inveigled them to take their medicine without choking on it—which is precisely how Adams regarded the intent of portraits painted by Sargent. Perhaps in this regard Adams himself succeeded in "out-Sargenting Sargent."

Adams's portraits of his contemporaries in the *Education* are Sargent-like in other respects as well. The style of such portraits, characterized by bold strokes of imagination and perception and by biting analysis compressed into vivid images, mirror those by Sargent that Adams had observed with a mixture of horror and glee. Persuaded as I am by Samuels's argument that the wider play of language in the *Education* (in comparison to the *History*) arose in large measure from the freedom of expression Adams developed in his letters, relieved of the conventional tone and restraint of writing biography and history, I hesitate to make too great a claim for

Sargent's "influence" on Adams's literary style of portraiture in the *Education*, especially given the frequency of Adams's complaints about his work. But in light of such complaints one may speculate that Sargent's work was in the back of his mind as he completed his own portraits. The boldness of Sargent's impressions had certainly caught Adams's attention and may have contributed to the impressionistic style of his own portraiture in the *Education*. For example, in Adams's characterization Grant was "a mere cave dweller." Swinburne resembled "a tropical bird, high-crested, long-beaked, quick-moving, with rapid utterance and screams of humor." Whistler exhibited "a willingness to seem eccentric where no real eccentricity, unless perhaps of temper, existed." William C. Whitney "satiated every taste, gorged every appetite."[51] These are really sketches rather than full-blown portraits, and quoted out of context, they leave the mistaken impression that historical backgrounds are absent. Such is not the case. Adams's gallery of portraits also includes cultural and national types extending all the way from British "eccentricity" to Russian "inertia." Closer to home, the American male, for example, "thought of himself as a restless, pushing, energetic, ingenious person, always awake and trying to get ahead of his neighbors." The American woman had "failed as a force, and was left with only a decorative role."[52] Clearly Adams claimed the very privilege he wanted to deny Sargent, the privilege of judging his contemporaries. The most telling difference in the nature of the judgments rendered is that Adams's are explicitly historical.

Two of the most striking full-scale portraits of public figures in the *Education* are those of Theodore Roosevelt and Henry Cabot Lodge, both of whom Sargent had painted. If Adams did not intend to "expose" each for a type, I do not know what else he could have intended. Roosevelt, he wrote, "more than any other man living within the range of notoriety, showed the singular primitive quality that belongs to ultimate matter—the quality that medieval theology assigns to God—he was pure act." In the context of Roosevelt's responsibilities and opportunities as president, Adams worried about his "abnormal energy": "Roosevelt enjoyed a singularly direct nature and honest intent, but he lived naturally in restless agitation that would have worn out most tempers in a month, and his first year of Presidency showed chronic excitement that made a friend tremble." Adams bears witness to what he had seen before in the White House—the "effect of unlimited power" on a "limited mind"—and accepted with regret the unhappy postulate that "a friend in power is a friend lost."[53] Here and elsewhere Adams elevates his concerns and disappointments to the level of general truth reserved for aphorism. Accordingly, his portrait of Roosevelt reproduces Sargent's with one essential difference: whereas Sargent's portrait appears to invite the viewer to enter (or intrude upon) the subject's "penetrable, interior, psychologized space," Adams's portrait restricts the reader's view of his subject to the type, a type the world had seen before and will see again, a type that responds in predictable ways to laws of politics and exhibits laws of human nature familiar to readers of Seneca and Shakespeare.[54] The only thing "personal" about his portrait is the personal loss Adams suffered as a result of the type's manifestation in Roosevelt.

Adams's portrait of Henry Cabot Lodge follows closely on the heels of his Roosevelt. Of the two men, Lodge was the more "interesting" to Adams: "Roosevelts are born and never can be taught; but Lodge was a creature of teaching—Boston incarnate—the child of his local parentage."[55] His ambition to become more than that Adams characterizes as "virtuous," but "restless." Lodge was "an excellent talker, a voracious reader, a ready wit, an accomplished orator, with a clear mind and a powerful memory," but he "could never feel perfectly at ease whatever leg he stood on," not knowing whether to pose as "uncompromising Yankee," "American patriot," or "a scholar and historian of Harvard College." Adams casts his former pupil and now senator from Massachusetts, despite the pose, as "English to the last fiber of his thought." His standing in Massachusetts "highly insecure," Lodge gave his first and only loyalty to his Anglo-Saxon race: "He betrayed the consciousness that he and his people had a past, if they dared but avow it, and might have a future too, if they could but divine it."[56] Lodge was playing a dangerous game, pretending to be and to stand for something he was not. "Double standards," Adams argues, "are inspiration to men of letters, but they are apt to be fatal to politicians." "Modern politics," he insists, "is a struggle not of men but of forces" and "the motors that drive them."[57] The motor driving Lodge was his identification with the history and achievements of his race and class.

Owen Wister has written of Henry Cabot Lodge that "[John Singleton] Copley, and only Copley" would have been the right man to paint his portrait, because he remained "unmitigated Boston to the end," with Boston's self-righteous air of cultural and political superiority.[58] Sargent's portrait of Lodge [figure 5, next page] bears little resemblance to the one Wister imagined for him. Sargent painted Henry Cabot Lodge in 1890 looking more like the academic he had been than the congressman he was or the senator he was soon to be. The averted eyes suggest evasive-

Figure 5. Henry Cabot Lodge *(1890), by John Singer Sargent. National Portrait Gallery, Smithsonian Institution; gift of the Honorable Henry Cabot Lodge.*

ness, though one could just as easily read into them intellectual curiosity or restlessness, the latter reading supported by the right hand fidgeting with his watch chain. An air of youthfulness escapes from this portrait of Lodge at age forty, and the averted glance is less commanding, less forceful, and less assertive than that of Sargent's Roosevelt. Sargent clearly had not found a way to portray Henry Cabot Lodge as the New England type Lodge represented to Adams and Wister. Perhaps he had no means at his disposal of picturing him that way. Instead, he brings the subject "too near for perspective," communicating through the pose the very quality Adams was to emphasize: his never feeling "at ease whatever leg he stood on."[59] Sargent's portrait of Lodge is Adams's portrait without the cultural backgrounds and political analysis that lend social dimension and historical significance to the pose. Instead, this portrait of Lodge, like so many portraits by Sargent, invites the viewer to enter the private psychological space of the subject and participate in the illusion of catching a glimpse of the subject unawares. In that sense, the portrait invites the viewer to participate in what Michel Foucault has defined as not merely the pleasure in learning something about someone we would like to learn more about but the pleasure in overcoming their resistance to being known.[60] Adams's avowed distaste for such "tale telling" portraits helps us to understand his divergence from Sargent in the manner in which he chose to portray his contemporaries in the *Education.*

III

In this context we may turn now to Adams's portrait of himself in the *Education*. Barrett Wendell, a former pupil of Adams, professor of English at Harvard, and one of the *Education*'s earliest readers, recognized that "as a work of art, *The Education* is wonderful in precision of perspective. Hardly any other book in my experience at once so places individual consciousness in its environment."[61] Adams wanted to frame his experiences against the background of the history of his times. William James wrote to Adams that he had succeeded best in the early chapters. The "boyhood part" and "the London part," he wrote, "should become classic historic documents."[62] Not coincidentally, these are the chapters in which "the contrasts and backgrounds" of social and political history are most vividly portrayed and dramatized. In the second half of the book, the emphasis on science and economics is too abstract to provide a social milieu as historical background to the protagonist Henry Adams conceived as a representative type (the nineteenth-century American with an eighteenth-century education unprepared for the challenges of the twentieth century). Instead Adams places himself as a subject against the background of intellectual history by joining in the discussion, weighing in on debates over evolution and theorizing over the nature of history, and by inviting a comparison between his mind as representative of twentieth-century multiplicity and the unity of the medieval mind in his *Mont Saint Michel and Chartres*.[63] Although Edward Chalfant has argued that Adams himself is "present" in the *Education* not as the manikin protagonist of the book but in the voice that narrates his experiences, I do not believe Adams wanted his own voice to portray him. That would fly in the face of his characterization of Rousseau's *Confessions* in the preface to the *Education* as "a monument against the ego" and render meaningless his decision to write about himself in the third person.

Writing about himself in the third person permitted Adams at one and the same time to portray himself as a historical subject and to subordinate his personal life to his life as a historical subject. As a historian, a biographer, a correspondent, a political insider and advisor, a guardian of his family's reputation, and a writer who played at autobiography in the *Education*, Adams dutifully observed a distinction between private life and public history. As a biographer, for example, he believed he was entitled to all materials pertaining to the life of a subject, once deceased, but he considered "private" anything that did not pertain to public life. He was not interested in satisfying any reader's voyeurism or taste for gossip. Matters of an intimate nature he would not have considered fit for publication even if he had known about them. If Henry Commager is right that "Henry Adams at Monticello is the most pregnant problem . . . in American History," Sally Hemmings's pregnancies would not have figured at all in the problem for Adams, even if he had known about them.[64] In his first book-length work, his biography of Albert Gallatin, Jefferson's secretary of the Treasury, Adams did little more than hint at his subject's personal or family life. It was his public life that mattered because it alone, from Adams's perspective, had something important to teach.

Yet Adams wrote at a time when privacy had come under siege by newspapers in which the "newspaper interview" had become a popular feature. He could see that the private lives of public figures were swiftly becoming a commodity, and he protected his own privacy by denying "the public" (which for Adams meant, simply, people he did not know) access to anything of an intimate nature, including even his person in portraits or photographs. There have been many theories advanced to explain why

Adams did not write about his marriage to Clover in the *Education* (including Andrew Delbanco's contention that he wanted to spare Clover the heavily ironic treatment he gave everyone else in the book, including himself), but surely his need for privacy, developed partly in response to assaults against it, played a significant part.[65] Adams proved himself a master at manipulating his relationship to the reading public by carefully controlling how his works were published; taking at times extraordinary precautions to conceal and disguise his identity and elude detection, all the while teasing his audience and inviting curiosity; and pretending not to care, but caring very much indeed. The *Education*, for example, was both a "private letter" addressed to friends and acquaintances for their revisions and comments, and a public portrait of himself and his contemporaries executed with posterity in mind. What kind of self-portrait are we likely to get from a man who wanted fame so long as he did not have to court it, who wanted to be known but was unwilling to appear that he cared one way or the other? One characterized by false modesty, disarming self-deprecation, pervasive irony, and playful belittlement of the very audience he wished most to please. Adams was well aware of the gap between self and performance. Like subjects posing for posterity in Sargent's portraits, he wanted to control his own image in the public mind.

In an often-quoted and much-discussed 1907 letter to William James, Adams refers to the *Education* as "a stack of rubbish meant only to feed the foolish," save for "a hundred pages" (he does not say which hundred) that he wrote to complete the last hundred of *Mont Saint Michel and Chartres*.[66] What Adams might have meant, and the extent to which we should take any of it seriously, has been much debated, as has his admission, in the same letter, to a fear of William James's judgment. [67] Receiving much less attention in the rather extensive debates over the significance of this letter is Adams's pronouncement in the penultimate paragraph that everything "personal to me" in the *Education* is all in the final chapter: "I meant to bid goodbye with graceful and sympathetic courtesy. The devil take it. I feel that Sargent squirms in the portrait. I am not there."[68]

These are cryptic pronouncements, even by Adams's standards. By "the portrait," did he mean the final chapter or the entire book? If he meant the final chapter, how could it contain "everything personal to me" and Adams himself remain absent ("I am not there")? And why is it Sargent who squirms in the portrait? Could he have meant that his own efforts at portraying himself had been influenced by Sargent's style of portraiture, or did he mean that he recognized an unfortunate similarity after the fact? I believe he meant the latter. Whatever he did not like about Sargent's work had somehow found its way into his own self-portrait. It was Adams who had implied that Sargent *exposed* what his subjects thought of themselves and thus allowed the ego to rule the pose and stand for posterity. When he complained to William James "the devil take it. . . . Sargent squirms in the portrait. . . . I am not there," he certainly did not mean that he had failed in the final chapter to get his ego into his self-portrait, for in no chapter in the book does Adams speak more personally about himself or others. From the opening to the closing lines of "Nunc Age," Adams takes his readers on a sentimental journey, laying bare his bewilderment in the face of a New York City (and America) utterly transformed by corporate power, material prosperity, and immigration; his melancholy sense of himself as an anachronism; his resignation to the fact that he would not live long enough to see if future events would prove his dynamic theory of history; and, most of all, his misanthropy and sense of purposelessness at the end of his life. He likens himself and John Hay to seals in the Antarctic that drag themselves thousands of feet above the water "to die in peace." He laments that Hay, his closest friend, has been "worried to death" by "creatures that have not the strength or the teeth to kill him outright." He sees himself as having lived beyond his time, bidding goodbye to dying friends. Even his final tribute to Hay is not without a touch of self-pity over what could never be his own fate: "he was satisfied to have his friend die, as we all would die if we could, in full fame, at home and abroad, universally regretted, and wielding his power to the last."[69]

In short, Adams's personal feelings about Hay and about himself dominate his self-portrait in the final chapter. There was plenty to "squirm" over, including the maudlin character of his farewell ("it was time to go"). He exposed too much of himself, too much of his personal disappointments, ennui, and despair. Self-pity he no doubt felt, but to allow self-pity to stand as the final note in his self-portrait reminded him of what he liked least about "psychological" portraits by Sargent. He had ended his book on too personal a note. There was too much ego in the final chapter, too much of his own revealed view of himself that Sargent specialized in. Private emotions had little if any place in Adams's idea of history, less so out of respect for the subject's personal privacy than because Adams believed human lives are best understood in terms of the social backgrounds and historical forces that define them. By saying "I am not there," he meant that he had failed to maintain the balance between figure and background, in particular the balance between the Henry Adams foregrounded as character and/or narrating voice, and the social, economic, political and intellectual history of the moment in which he lived and spoke, which alone could offer a true and meaningful portrait of himself, John Hay, or anyone else. Adams's practice of historical biography and autobiography was indeed predicated on a distinction between public and private life that continues to frustrate those who would like to know and understand him in ways that he cared not to be known.

"Poets and painters," Horace remarked in a famous passage, "have always had the right to dare what they want." Historians heed a muse more jealous of empirical truth. Adams sought the truth wherever he might find it, and in the chapter of the *Education* entitled "The Abyss of Ignorance," he confessed that the new science of psychology was a source of truth that he could intuitively accept, insofar as it confirmed that "the only absolute truth" about human consciousness was "the sub-conscious chaos below, which everyone could feel when he sought it."[70] Sanity was only an acquired habit of managing the mind's "want of balance." Following the lead of William James in his *Principles of Psychology*, Adams acknowledged the unity of the individual consciousness in maintaining (or losing) its balance, but he could not see how psychology unified anything larger than a single mind. A world of separate unities solved nothing for Adams, for whom history was a collective affair—even the history of thought—so he preferred history to psychology as a framework for understanding and judging human behavior and achievement. Portraits that offered studies in character or depictions of personality brought the subject "too near for perspective" and not only misrepresented but usually diminished the subject. To his brother Brooks he wrote, "I have never known a biography which raised the reputation of its subject" except for Hay and Nicolay's *Abraham Lincoln*, which "was properly called . . . a History."[71] Accordingly, he pictured himself and his contemporaries not as the personalities Sargent was sometimes driven to paint but as the bold examples of cultural "types" that Sargent had daringly executed and exhibited as emblems of their age. As early as 1903 Adams boasted "if I can hang onto my memory five years more, . . . I can live forever, and we shall all perish at once."[72] Adams was already planning his gallery of portraits. If he could "live forever," he wanted to choose the manner in which he would be remembered. He wanted to be known and remembered in the same way that Henry James remembered John LaFarge, shortly after his death—as "that rare thing, a figure."[73]

NOTES

1. John D. Rockefeller, Jr., offered Sargent $100,000 to paint portraits of five members of his family. (Tired of painting portraits, Sargent painted only two.) Others offered similar sums. For some, an additional price was silent suffering over bruised egos.
2. Henry Adams to Elizabeth Cameron, Mar. 1, 1903, in *The Letters of Henry Adams*, ed. J. C. Levenson et al. (Cambridge, Mass., 1982–1988), 5:464.
3. HA to Elizabeth Cameron, Mar. 1, 1903, in *Letters*, 5:464.
4. HA to Elizabeth Cameron, Apr. 5, 1903, in *Letters*, 5:480.
5. Henry Adams, *The Education of Henry Adams* (Boston, 1918), 329.
6. HA to Elizabeth Cameron, Apr. 5, 1903, in *Letters*, 5:480.
7. HA to John Hay, Oct. 18, 1893, in *Letters*, 4:134.
8. HA, *Education*, 339.
9. HA, *Education*, 215.
10. Henry James to H. G. Wells, July 10, 1915, in *Henry James Letters*, ed. Leon Edel (Cambridge, Mass., 1974–1984), 4:770.
11. Stanley Olson, *John Singer Sargent: His Portrait* (London, 1989), 205.
12. There may be a veiled reference to Sargent in the character of Wharton in Adams's *Esther*, described as a painter who would paint "a tailor . . . as though he were painting a doge of Venice." Henry Adams, *Esther* (New York, 1884), 30.
13. Henry James's description of the title character in his short story "John Delavoy" (1898), if not a veiled reference to Sargent, could easily serve as one: "was he not the man of the time about whose private life we delightfully knew least?" *The Complete Tales of Henry James*, ed. Leon Edel (New York, 1961–1964), 9:405.
14. I say "capturing" rather than caricaturing a social type because there is little if any explicit satire in any of Sargent's portraits of wealthy men and fashionable ladies. He no doubt knew he would run short of patrons if he bit the hands that fed him. If anything, according to Stanley Olson, his biographer, he "polished egos" (205). Olson writes, "His sitters were those who had a willingness to spend time and a lot of money; to Sargent, each sitter presented new but usually unexciting problems, and his solution, in keeping with his development as a painter, was the urge not to disturb convention, but to adapt it, modernize it to make his subjects a little more vital." Olson, *John Singer Sargent: His Portrait*, 205. Olson claims that the "brilliant shine" of the portraits and the attention to material wealth should not be read as social commentary or overvalued as historical document, for such trademark characteristics only reflect Sargent's love of visual splendor. Visual content, according to Olson, was Sargent's only interest. For reasons that may tell us more about Adams than Sargent, Adams did not hold this view.
15. "Condescension" may be too strong a term if what Sargent did was allow each subject's view of him or herself to stand as the defining image; nevertheless, there is a certain degree of exposure even in that and, for all we know about Sargent, condescension as well.
16. HA to Lady Mary Leiter Curzon, May 27, 1900, in *Letters*, 5:123.
17. HA to Mabel Hooper, May 2, 1897, in *Letters*, 4:469; HA to Elizabeth Cameron, May 25, 1901, in *Letters*, 5:253.
18. HA to Elizabeth Cameron, Apr. 26, 1903, in *Letters*, 5:493.
19. HA to Elizabeth Cameron, June 26, 1896, in *Letters*, 4:392. Without a clear reference we can only surmise that Adams is referring to portraits he had heard about or seen of well-known figures in British or American society, such as the wife of New York banker and collector Henry Marquand, Boston society hostess Mrs. Charles Inches, the Vickers sisters in England, Mrs. William Henry Vanderbilt, or Elsie Palmer, daughter of railroad

promoter Gen. William Jackson Palmer. He may not have seen the latter portrait, but he is likely to have read about it. The reviewer in the *London Times* (May 8, 1891) was one of many who shared Adams's concerns, professing astonishment at Sargent's "merciless analysis of character." Quoted in Richard Ormond and Elaine Kilmurray, *John Singer Sargent: The Early Portraits* (London, 1998), 191.

20. HA to Elizabeth Cameron, May 7, 1905, in *Letters*, 5:655. He added that Sargent could not have managed the caricature without the duchess "helping him to it." Here again he emphasizes the role that the subject's ego plays in the portrayal.

21. HA to Elizabeth Cameron, June 26, 1896, in *Letters*, 4:392.

22. Augustus St.-Gaudens seems to have felt the same way, suggesting to Adams in April of 1903 that Sargent didn't give a damn about the people he painted or what his paintings revealed about them. HA to Elizabeth Cameron, Apr. 5, 1903, in *Letters*, 5:480.

23. HA to Elizabeth Cameron, May 7, 1905, in *Letters*, 5:655. Adams was not alone in assuming this, for the term appears in many contemporary reviews of Sargent's work.

24. Adams's refusal to allow himself to be photographed is of a piece with his refusal to permit any photographs to appear in his many volumes of history and biography. "I hate photographs abstractly," he wrote, "because they have given me more ideas perversely and immoveably wrong than I ever should get by imagination. They are almost as bad as an ordinary book of travels." HA to Elizabeth Cameron, Feb. 13, 1891, in *Letters*, 3:408.

25. HA to Elizabeth Cameron, Mar. 5, 1900, in *Letters*, 5:103.

26. William James to Henry James, June 24, 1893, in *The Correspondence of William James*, ed. Elizabeth Berkeley et al. (Charlottesville, 1994), 2:270.

27. HA to Elizabeth Cameron, Mar. 8, 1903, in *Letters*, 5:472.

28. HA to Elizabeth Cameron, Apr. 5, 1903, in *Letters*, 5:480.

29. The pose was suggested by Roosevelt himself, as revealed in this account by James G. Barber: "The choice of a suitable place to paint, where the lighting was good, tried Roosevelt's patience. No room on the first floor agreed with the artist When they began climbing the staircase, Roosevelt told Sargent he did not think the artist knew what he wanted. Sargent replied that he did not think Roosevelt knew what was involved in posing for a portrait. Roosevelt, who had just reached the landing, swung around, placing his hand on the newel, and said 'Don't I!' Sargent saw his opportunity and told the President not to move; this would be the pose and the location for the sittings." James G. Barber, *Theodore Roosevelt: Icon of the American Century* (Seattle, 1998), 48–50.

    Whether Roosevelt knew it or not, Henry James for years had been advising Sargent's sitters "to be as difficult for him as possible," for "the more difficult you are the more the artist will be condemned to worry over you, repainting, revolutionizing, till he, in a rage of ambition and admiration, arrives at the thing that satisfies him and that enshrines and perpetuates you." Henry James to Mrs. Mahlon Sands, Jan. 1894, in *Henry James Letters*, 3:456.

30. Evan Edward Charteris, *John Singer Sargent (*London, 1927), 107.

31. Rudolph Arnheim, *New Essays on the Psychology of Art* (Berkeley, 1986), 103; Ernest Samuels, *Henry Adams* (Cambridge, Mass., 1989), 201.

32. HA to Brooks Adams, Mar. 4, 1900, in *Letters*, 5:100. Emphasis mine.

33. In Mar. 1900, Adams quipped, "French society is like a Watteau that has been cleaned and scraped down to the canvas. American society is like a Whistler that never had any atmosphere to scrape." HA to Elizabeth Cameron, Mar. 12, 1900, in *Letters*, 5:105. See also HA to Barrett Wendell, Mar. 12, 1909, in *Letters*, 6: 237–238.

34. HA to Brooks Adams, Feb. 18, 1909, in *Letters*, 6:227.

35. HA to Elizabeth Cameron, Mar. 5, 1900, in *Letters*, 5:102.

36. Henry Adams, *The History of the United States during the Administrations of Thomas Jefferson and James Madison* (New York, 1930), 1:32.
37. HA, *History*, 1:87.
38. HA, *History*, 1:176.
39. HA, *Education*, 333.
40. See David Lubin's *Act of Portrayal* (New Haven, 1985) for a fuller discussion of this aspect of the painting.
41. HA to Elizabeth Cameron, Apr. 19, 1903, in *Letters*, 5:488.
42. William James to Henry James, May 3, 1903, in *Correspondence*, 3:235.
43. HA to Elizabeth Cameron, Mar. 1, Apr. 19, 1903, in *Letters*, 5:464, 488.
44. HA to Henry James, Nov. 18, 1903, in *Letters*, 5:524. Edward Chalfant has called into question the sincerity of these remarks, arguing that by calling what James had produced in the book an "autobiography," Adams meant to chide him for not writing a biography at all. That Adams was less than sincere in his praise for the book is confirmed in a letter to Brooks in Feb. 1909: "Failure matters little when it concerns only oneself. Henry James can fail as often as he likes in novels, but when he fails in biography, he leaves mighty little of William Story. In biography we are taking life." HA to Brooks Adams, Feb. 18, 1909, in *Letters*, 6:227.
45. Curiously but not uncharacteristically, Adams claims a privileged view of the subject, begging the question of what it is that art (the art of biography, the art of portraiture) communicates and to whom. Chalfant's assertion that this letter to Henry James does not mean what it says, or rather that its meaning is subtly coded, its nuances readable only to an "insider" familiar with Adams's peculiar habits of expression, mirrors Adams's conviction that the portraits he saw and the biographies he read had their own "private" meanings for those who were qualified to read them. Edward Chalfant, "Lies, Silence, and Truth in the Writings of Henry Adams," in *Henry Adams and His World*, ed. David Contosta and Robert Muccigrosso (Philadelphia, 1993), 8–22.
46. Henry Adams, quoted in Samuels, *Henry Adams*, 114.
47. Samuels, *Henry Adams*, 369.
48. HA, *Education*, 391.
49. Samuels, *Henry Adams*, 380.
50. "Thus far they have dared not squeak! Even the President and Cabot Lodge bow their necks in submission." HA to Charles Milnes Gaskell, May 10, 1907, in *Letters*, 6:63. Was it Sargent or Adams who "gibbeted" their subjects?
51. HA, *Education*, 260, 139, 371, 347.
52. HA, *Education*, 297, 442.
53. HA, *Education*, 417, 418.
54. Richard Salmon, *Henry James and the Culture of Publicity* (Cambridge, 1997), 86.
55. HA, *Education*, 419.
56. HA, *Education*, 420.
57. HA, *Education*, 412, 422. Adams admits that his own theory and practice were also at variance, as he preferred continental standards of art and order but recognized that "English disorder approached nearer the truth" HA, *Education*, 420.
58. Owen Wister, *Roosevelt: The Story of a Friendship* (New York, 1930), 153.
59. HA to Brooks Adams, Mar. 4, 1900, in *Letters*, 5:100; HA, *Education*, 420.
60. Michel Foucault, *History of Sexuality* (New York, 1978), 1:45.
61. Barrett Wendell to Henry Adams, Mar. 10, 1909, Henry Adams Papers, Massachusetts Historical Society.
62. William James to Henry Adams, Feb. 9, 1908, in *Correspondence*, 11:536.

63. Adams was well aware of this problem in form, admitting to Barrett Wendell that "uniting drama with what is essentially undramatic" is "unpleasantly evident" in the *Education*, so much so that "I had to write a long supplementary chapter to explain in scientific terms what I could not put into the narration without ruining the narrative." HA to Barrett Wendell, Mar. 12, 1909, in *Letters*, 6:238. The "supplementary chapter" Adams makes reference to is "The Rule of Phase."
64. Henry Commager, introduction to *History*, 1:x.
65. Andrew Delbanco, *Required Reading: Why Our American Classics Matter Now* (New York, 1997), 83–100. Ironically, the subject's resistance to penetration is now regarded as confirmation of something important to know. Whatever is kept "private" is often presumed to be the most valuable and accurate knowledge one could acquire of anyone. Richard Salmon has claimed that by resisting biographical investigation, Henry James, for instance, only "confirmed the privileged status of privacy as a domain of revelatory signs." Salmon, *Henry James and the Culture of Publicity*, 86. Whether the *Education* is an autobiography at all has been the subject of much debate. See, for example, Chalfant, "Lies, Silence and the Truth in Henry Adams."
66. HA to William James, Dec. 9, 1907, in *Letters*, 6:91–92. In this letter, Adams agrees to loan James the so-called "proofsheets" of his *Education* in return for corrections and revisions (which he could hardly expect to get). Adams contextualizes the book as the modern half of a literary experiment that had begun with his *Mont Saint Michel and Chartres*. He casually (and disingenuously) dismisses the latter as no more than an unsuccessful effort to "clean off a bit of the surface of my own mind," then makes high claims for it as a text that could not be understood by more than "a hundred people in America."
67. See, for example, Loren Glass, "Giving Thought to the Adience: A Response to Paul Bové," and Paul Bové, "Policing Thought: On Learning How to Read Henry Adams," *Critical Inquiry* 23(1997):933–946.
68. HA to William James, Dec. 9, 1907, in *Letters*, 6:92.
69. HA, *Education*, 502, 504.
70. HA, *Education*, 433.
71. HA to Brooks Adams, Feb. 18, 1909, in *Letters*, 6:226.
72. HA to Elizabeth Cameron, Feb. 22, 1903, in *Letters*, 5:462.
73. Henry James to Margaret LaFarge, Nov. 15, 1910, in *Henry James Letters*, 4:566.

Mr. Secrets

Henry Adams & the Breakdown of the Exemplary Tradition in American Autobiography

JOANNE JACOBSON

SINCE THE LATE EIGHTEENTH CENTURY, American autobiography has celebrated both America and the form itself as the ideal grounds of personal transformation. Enlightenment individualism found in personal narrative its perfect medium and its perfect champion—the means both to portray the autonomous protagonist on a trajectory of self-improvement and, at the same time, to showcase the writer's success in the project of self-invention. From the disparate, raw materials of private experience, American autobiography has forged a series of exemplary success narratives—"fit," as Benjamin Franklin famously put it, "to be imitated"—and modeled those narratives publicly.[1]

Yet if autobiography remains the podium from which many well-known Americans (from Monty Hall, Loretta Lynn, and Lee Iococca to Colin Powell and Bill Clinton) continue to align themselves with the rags-to-riches model of public achievement, much of American autobiography has now turned away from the exemplary voice. Neither America nor American autobiography has retained its confident hold on exemplary status. Nor has narrative's potential for transparency—its gift for revealing in the fragments of private experience the potential for public wholeness and meaning—retained its credibility, especially during recent years. Instead, many American autobiographers of the final decades of the twentieth century reveal about themselves information that refuses to unknot into linear narrative and that resists serving public utility. These writers uncover information about their families that casts a shadow not only over their own identity but also over their ability to author, and obscures the power to shape memory in the self-creating act of narrative that is essential to the exemplary autobiographical tradition. In these texts, the hold of the past is darkly confirmed rather than victoriously broken. These narratives call into question autobiography's great promise to make "America" come true—the ability to start new, tabula rasa.

When we track this late-twentieth-century retreat from the eighteenth-century exemplary voice in American autobiography, one text appears poised at a pivotal turn-of-the-twentieth-century moment: *The Education of Henry Adams*. Adams backed steadily away from the Enlightenment tradition of cultural stewardship to which his ancestors had been loyal and, simultaneously, from the projection in autobiography of an exemplary national model. Secretive and suspicious, the *Education* seems to take pleasure in undermining the Enlightenment's regenerative hopes both for America and for American authorship, and in rendering its cantankerous author *not* "fit to be imitated." Those doubts have sown Henry Adams's own ironically exemplary public legacy—a century after the private publication of the *Education*—on one of the most prolific generations of writers of autobiography in U.S. history.

MORE THAN A CENTURY before Adams, there was Franklin. Benjamin Franklin's *Autobiography* has for more than two centuries stood out among the origin narratives of an unusually articulate generation of writer-politicians, as an American *Genesis*, for in it both Franklin and Franklin's text emerge as national exemplars.

In the *Autobiography*, Franklin chronicles his victorious liberation from a pre-Enlightenment past that he frames with increasing drama and sharpness—and significance—as pre-"American." Franklin aggressively wrote the members of his family into his own success story, where they serve as strategic resources in his acquisition of personal power—an acquisition that comes to exemplify America's human potential. Franklin characterizes his father and mother as relics, however well meaning, of a static Puritan past. They are made complicitous in the apprenticeship to his older brother, whose abusive conditions justify Franklin's flight from Boston. His future wife's first impression of him in Philadelphia—"dirty from my Journey" and struggling awkwardly up Market Street with his "three great Puffy Rolls"—becomes, subsequently, the point against which Franklin the protagonist marks his new trajectory of upward moblity and Franklin the writer sets in motion his newly imagined life.[2] Like the early employers and sponsors (Keimer, Keith, Merideth) whose false mentorship provides a backdrop for Franklin's growth, family members are introduced and then dropped from the narrative to highlight, in their wake, Franklin's own dynamically independent destiny.

Individualistic though this story is, of course, it is far from personal. It does not reveal much feeling (about for example, the losses Franklin endured, alone, when he was young and vulnerable). And while his autobiography shamelessly advertises for posterity Franklin's own ability to master through the application of intellect and industry every challenge he encounters—from setting up a subscription library to paving and cleaning and lighting the streets of Philadelphia—in these victories it also advertises an America that puts such mastery within the reach of every reader. While the autobiography dramatizes his own successes as arbiter and paragon of virtue—experimenting with vegetarianism, mounting his "bold and arduous Project of arriving at moral Perfection"—it also dramatizes an America where such personal initiative will almost inevitably yield empowering results.[3] Even as Franklin's autobiography showcases his ability to overcome the mistakes that youthful inexperience and indiscretion led him to commit, it also showcases his newfound ability to name the "great Errata of my Life," to locate them in a narrative of self-improvement, and to write away on American ground the Puritan vision of human depravity, powerlessness, and immobility.[4]

Conflating his own origin narrative with the origin narrative of "America," Benjamin Franklin modeled both autobiography and America as the quintessential forms of modernity: at once epitome and instrument of the human potential for self-invention and transformation.[5] The then new American conditions of self-authorship that Franklin modeled in the *Autobiography* paralleled the new American conditions of selfhood that he championed; both would set human beings free from the static past. Like autobiography, the "America" that Franklin proclaimed would rise on the world stage as human-centered and anti-authoritarian; like Franklin's autobiography, Franklin's America exemplified a viable alternative to the past's oppression and trauma.

More than a century later, Henry Adams looked back toward his family legacy and toward his autobiographical predecessors with a sense of burden and loss that profoundly challenged Franklin's optimism. In effect, Adams announced as his subject in the *Education* the eroded credibility of the exemplary tradition in American autobiography—and, ultimately, of the Franklinian models of selfhood, of authorship, and of America itself.

The preface to the *Education* introduces the reevaluation of that legacy of Enlightenment initiative and mastery as the occasion of Adams's writing:

> The student must go back beyond Jean-Jacques [Rousseau], to Benjamin Franklin, to find a model . . . of self-teaching. Except in the abandoned sphere of the dead languages, no one has discussed what part of education has, in his personal experience, turned out to be useful, and what not. This volume attempts to discuss it. (xxix)

Adams's retreat from the first-person and from the Enlightenment's most fundamental assumptions about human significance, human knowledge, and human power put him on provocative ground, modeling the "faults of the patchwork" of his ancestors on an anonymous "manikin" (xxx). Envisioning that figure in the new language in which the new science of physics was acknowledging new difficulties in apprehending the world, Adams challenged the rational, empirical foundations of Enlightenment individualism:

> The manikin, therefore, has the same value as any other geometrical figure of three or more dimensions. . . . [I]t is the only measure of motion, of proportion, of human condition; it must have the air of reality; must be taken for real; must be treated as though it had life. Who knows? Possibly it had! (xxx)

In turn, in his first chapter, "Quincy," Adams posited the defining characteristic of his life as disjunction and suggested the inadequacy of narrative as a strategy for countering either momentum or unity. Between Quincy and State Street, between Adams on his father's side and Brooks on his mother's, "From earliest childhood the boy was accustomed to feel that, for him, life was double. Winter and summer, town and country, law and liberty, were hostile" (9). And rather than setting this gnarl of family as a point out of which he would, like Franklin, write himself free, Adams projected it as his destiny. "What could become of such a child of the seventeenth and eighteenth centuries," Adams queried, "when he should wake up to find himself required to play the game of the twentieth?" (4) As beached at the cusp of the modern age as his aged grandmother; "Louis Seize, like the furniture" (19); "distinctly branded . . . heavily handicapped" (3) by an inherited past, Adams would be, he responded, as disempowered by cultural change as Franklin had been empowered by it.

Adams made a pair of radical literary decisions in the *Education* that set in angry relief his doubts about the viability of the exemplary autobiographical tradition in playing "the game of the twentieth" century. Burdened by a sense of alienation and isolation, Adams turned his back on the public, cutting off access to his autobiography and limiting *audience* to the hundred or so kindred spirits whom he counted on to share his estrangement. "I knew that not a hundred people in America would understand what I meant. . . . I need not publish when no one would read or understand," Adams lamented in the letter that accompanied William James's copy of the *Education*.[6] And—witness to a lost America of possibility, continuity, and community—Adams turned his back on *narrative* as well, leaving a twenty-year gap in the *Education*, between "Failure (1871)" and "Twenty Years After (1892)," around the excruciatingly private heartache of his wife's suicide. In one of his few even oblique references to Clover Adams's death, Adams recalled at the end of the chapter his 1892 return from Europe to Washington to her memorial statue, "to the cemetery known as Rock Creek, to see the bronze figure which St. Gaudens had made for him in his absence" (329). But he never even once put her name or his own feelings into words. Instead, Adams stood as usual aside, watching others, voyeur rather than Franklinian actor: "The interest of the figure was not in its meaning, but in the response of the observer" (329). While the exemplary voice and narrative had promised to carry Franklin out of the past's traumas, trauma brought Adams up short, in ironic silence: "At past fifty, Adams solemnly and painfully learned to ride the bicycle. . . . Nothing else occurred to him as a means of new life" (330).

Of course, the *Education* did go forward out of this vortex of silence. One might in fact argue that the *Education* constitutes Henry Adams's greatest victory as a writer, for in it he grappled openly with a bewildering set of challenges to language and to narrative that Franklin's visionary text never imagined, admitted his own confusion and pain—and continued to write. Just two chapters before the twenty-year collapse of language in the *Education*, Adams forced himself back—in language—to the bedside of his much-loved sister, for "ten days of fiendish torture" (287) as she died a slow, gruesome death from lockjaw. There Adams took his own lingering, rhythmic stock of the taunting contradiction between nature's undisturbed sensuality—"the soft shadows . . . of the Italian summer, the soft, velvet air" (288)—and the shattering of the confidence in empiricism on which his eighteenth-century forebears, as well as Franklin, had counted: "For the first time, the stage-scenery of the senses collapsed; the human mind felt itself stripped naked, vibrating in a void of shapeless energies, with resistless mass, colliding, crushing, wasting, and destroying what these same energies had created and labored from eternity to perfect" (288). Ultimately, just two chapters in the wake of his twenty-year silence, "The Dynamo and the Virgin" generated a set of metaphors for cultural unity and historical evolution that offered an ingenious solution to the authorial crisis that Adams encountered, "aching to absorb knowledge, and helpless to find it" (379), at the 1900 Paris Exposition. Early in the *Education* Adams had set "this problem of running order through chaos" (12) as a daunting, lifelong task for himself. In framing as symbolic figures the very "supersensual" (381) forces that continued to stymie him, he managed to rewrite his own confusion into a form of rhetorical mastery: "to Adams the dynamo became a symbol of infinity. As he grew accustomed to the great gallery of machines, he began to feel the forty-foot dynamos as a moral force, much as the early Christians felt the Cross" (380).

Although in the culmination of the *Education* Adams proved himself as aggressive a master of language as Franklin—and the greater artist, belying his own relentless claims to failure as an author—he nonetheless never abandoned the critical stance from which the *Education* initially had sniped at the exemplary tradition. "The Dynamo and the Virgin" aimed its critique directly at the Enlightenment belief in the shaping power of individuals and in narrative progress, in "sequences,—called stories, or histories—assuming in silence a relation of cause and effect" (382); the chapter thus contradicted the public model of Franklin's *Autobiography*. "His historical neck broken by the sudden irruption of forces totally new" (382), Henry Adams positioned himself as an anti-model, sidestepping the possibility either of attaining mastery or of starting fresh on the modern American stage that Franklin's autobiography had glowingly promised.

Moreover, the epiphanies to which language brought Henry Adams, in Italy at his sister's deathbed and in Paris at the Great Exhibition, were for him writerly solutions that remained private. While Franklin overcame every obstacle that he faced, Adams left questions hanging in the air all around the problems that he raised, to the very end of the *Education*. "No scheme could be suggested to the new American. . . . [T]he next great influx of new forces seemed near at hand, and its style of education promised to be violently coercive" (498), Adams warned in the late chapter "A Law of Acceleration." When he stepped off stage in his final paragraph, into the circle of his close friends, Adams hung in the shadow of his disappointment with the life that he had lived in an increasingly alien world:

> Perhaps some day—say 1938, their centenary—they might be allowed to return together for a holiday, to see the mistakes of their own lives made clear in the light of the mistakes of their successors; and perhaps then, for the first time since man began his education among the carnivores, they would find a world that sensitive and timid natures could regard without a shudder. (505)

Adams's final appeal to those treasured allies—his carefully hoarded audience—softened the refrain of loneliness repeated throughout the *Education*, just as his rhetorical prowess called into question his claim of helpless submission to a set of dehumanizing modern forces. Yet together these rhetorical gestures evidence the fact that Adams remained at odds with his American world rather than adopting the Franklinian pose of spokesman for it. In them we see as well that writing autobiography remained for Adams, in turn-of-the-twentieth-century America, a subversive rather than an exemplary act.

AT THE TURN of the twenty-first century, autobiography retains its status as a premier, even defining, genre of American writing—so widely practiced that it has acquired its own "backlash."[7] Yet the exemplary stance that for Benjamin Franklin gave autobiography its authority as the defining medium of "America" and American-ness seems to have receded into a long gone, inaccessible national moment. It is Henry Adams's subversive stance—rooted in a sense of disjunction between private and public, between self and world—that has, instead, acquired greater credibility for many American autobiographers. Franklin's vision of "America" as a site for throwing off the past and beginning again tabula rasa, and of authorship as the means of self-invention, has given way to Adams's experience of the past as a source of dissonance, even burden, and of self-authorship as problematic.

An especially striking feature of American autobiographies of the past decade is the frequency with which they revolve around the revelation of family secrets and, consequently, call into question key aspects of the exemplary tradition. In *The Shadow Man* (1996), Mary Gordon unlayers her rediscovery of her father: rather than the Ohio-born, Harvard-educated Catholic poet whom she had known—the devoted father who told her that he loved her "more than God"—David Gordon turns out to have been a Jewish immigrant from Vilna; a high school dropout who published a crudely antisemitic, pornographic magazine called *Hot Dog*; a supporter of fascism and McCarthyism. In *The Color of Water*, also published in 1996, James McBride tells of his discovery that his mother, who had "raised twelve black children" in a Brooklyn housing project, was actually the run-away daughter of an abusive Orthodox rabbi. And in *My Brother*, published the following year, Jamaica Kincaid returns to Antigua to face her brother's secretive battle with AIDS: "Who is he?" she has to ask herself. "How does he feel about himself, what has he ever wanted?"[8]

In each of these memoirs, secrets render opaque the family past on whose transparency Benjamin Franklin had counted—as both protagonist and author—in dramatizing his exemplary mastery. In each, the narrator is thrown from the start into a passive, even defensive, position rather than an initiating posture, constantly anticipating knowledge that never becomes complete. And in each of these texts "America" shifts under the feet of the writer—from an ideal location on which to make a fresh start, unencumbered by past or restraint, to a source of lurking trauma, inadequately anticipated and comprehended.

James McBride and his siblings "traded information on Mommy the way people trade baseball cards."[9] Who then exactly is Mommy's son, the author of *The Color of Water*, whose story is still uncoiling? Jamaica Kincaid's helplessness as a protagonist, paying out of pocket at her home pharmacy in Vermont for medications that will only postpone her brother's fated death in Antigua, is paralleled by the impasse that she reaches as an author in *My Brother*. Even when Kincaid finally discovers, through a chance encounter in Chicago, that her brother had been a gay man, this hidden knowledge comes too late to complete Kincaid's task as an author, too late to illuminate anything except the lack of closure that she feels at her brother's death:

> That night as he lay dying and calling the names of his brothers and his mother, he did not call my name, and I was neither glad nor sad about this. For why should he call my name? I knew him for the first three years of his life, I came to know him again in the last three years of his life. . . . I had never been part of the tapestry, so to speak.[10]

To control, to shape—and to complete—the disparate elements of personal experience in narrative was the empowering Enlightenment discovery that Franklin modeled for posterity in his autobiography. But none of these contemporary writers can get a sufficiently firm grip on the elements of their own stories to move forward with Franklin's unifying, exemplary confidence.

Just as the narrative "tapestry" remains impossible for Jamaica Kincaid to salvage, so Mary Gordon's hold on her own narrative gives way in the face of revealed family secrets. The more deeply her narrative enters into her father's hidden story, the more vulnerable, rather than masterful, Gordon feels. She is frightened when she realizes that her father, instead of studying at Harvard as she had thought,

> was working at the Baltimore and Ohio Railroad. Reading on his own time. Furtive. Yearning.
>
> It is unbearable for me to think of him in this way. If he is yearning, then I am unsafe.[11]

These writers become "unsafe" in their personal narratives because the discovery of secrets long, and deliberately, kept from them undermines their own sense of identity. They experience the revelation of family secrets in adulthood as disempowering, disordering, dislocating. *Telling* plunges each text into a realm of un-wholeness rather than bestowing the whole-making momentum of exemplary autobiographical narrative. Susan Bergman's 1994 memoir, *Anonymity: The Secret Life of an American Family*, evokes the splitting effect that followed her discovery that her father—whom she had known as a devoted husband and strict Christian—had for many years, like Kincaid's brother, led a secret life as a gay man: "It was not until my father died [of AIDS] that we found out about his other life. Then our other lives began." Unlike Franklin, Bergman does expect personal narrative to write away the traumas that family can impose on children; instead, personal narrative takes her back to the un-rooted life in which family locked her into dissonance, made her feel "other" to herself, as though she were not "the same as myself all the way through."[12]

In another kind of recent American memoir, adult children of famous parents reveal in public the secret truths of their parents' rage and alcoholism and substance abuse that they had preserved throughout their own childhoods. In such "tell-all" volumes, many of them bestsellers, the daughters and sons of Joan Crawford, John Cheever, and James Dickey find the opportunity to unburden themselves in public, and, one suspects, the primal satisfaction of revenge. But the relief experienced by those who break their own silence is not so easily shared by those writers who discover as adults that they have been shut out of their own family story. James McBride is the exception here in that he closes the circle of his mother's puzzle with a peacemaking return to her hometown, and he consolidates his story around his mother's racially transcendent formulation: "God is the color of water."[13] Mary Gordon's decision to disinter her father and to re-bury him in the presence of her new knowledge does not bring her to the same unifying clarity. The final pages of *The Shadow Man* teeter instead, uncertainly, between the satisfying closure of her son's conclusion that "Love is stronger than death" and her friends' lingering concern that "what I'm doing is crazy."[14]

Ultimately, these texts tell their most powerful emotional truths in the narrative limits that they expose. Mary Karr's *The Liars' Club* opens with a scene that hovers in incompleteness even as it takes haunting hold of the entire text: "My sharpest memory is of a single instant surrounded by dark. I was seven, and our family doctor knelt before me where I sat on a mattress on the bare floor. . . . 'Show me the marks,' he said. 'Come on, now. I won't hurt you.'" Karr's loyalty to absence itself—to "the missing story"—as an element of experience produces a text that conveys childhood as a condition of silence, of incompleteness, of being buffeted by a world that never ceases to be mysterious and inexplicable.[15] Nor does Karr allow narrative to relieve the trauma of remembered pain or to force festering, killing illness into the background. Her grandmother's cancer proves as relentless and as dehumanizing as Henry Adams's sister's lockjaw, so much so that her grandmother actually reeks "from her open mouth, from deep inside her where the cancer was doubtless eating out whatever was human."[16] Like Bergman and Gordon and McBride and Kincaid, Karr unmasks memory's unreliablity and instability; she exposes it even as an occasion of betrayal. When her mother eventually reveals her secret past of marriages and abandoned children, her "line-up of wedding rings," it is much too late for memory to be redemptive: "It's only looking back that I believe the clear light of truth should have filled us, like the legendary grace that carries a broken body past all manner of monsters."[17] Neither can confronting the losses that proliferate in the suddenly cracked silence of Kathryn Harrison's memories of incest in *The Kiss* bring back the innocence that her father's seduction forever cost her: "once upon a time I fell from grace, I was lost so deeply in a dark wood that I'm afraid I'll never be safe again." She is left to mourn "for me, the lost child, the child snatched away." Speaking publicly the unspeakable and un-linking herself from her father liberate Harrison, enabling her at the end of *The Kiss* to give herself to her own children and to begin healing her relationship with her mother. But Harrison's un-parenting will be permanent—"The loss of my father will haunt me as it did in the days long past"—and no narrative will be able to rewrite those private losses and make them yield wholeness.[18]

WHAT SHOULD WE SAY about the American autobiography—and the America—left in the wake of the receding exemplary voice? What does the ebbing, for so many American writers since Adams, of confidence in American lives' "fit-ness to be imitated" tell us about early American autobiography's hopeful intertwining of national idealism and personal experience?

A considerable amount of criticism has been heaped on the revelation of the better-left-private in the contemporary memoir. From the Franklinian peak of emulation and inspiration, American autobiography seems, to many observers, to have declined to the current low of a television talk show: voyeuristic, predictable, emotionally greedy, out for profit, barely literary. Paul John Eakin has suggested that in at least one 1990s autobiography, Howard Stern's *Private Parts*, "self-revelation becomes a form of flashing."[19] "As for the gentle reader of the present," one reviewer recently complained in the *New York Times*,

> they may be forgiven for feeling a little memoired-out—for suspecting that if they consume one more lyrical, ever-so-writerly account of a lousy childhood involving incest, physical abuse, alcoholism, poverty, anorexia, bulemia, drug addition, sexual perversity, they might just pop.[20]

Nor would Henry Adams likely have disagreed about either the self-indulgence or the pandering of the mass culture tell-all paperback. It was Adams, after all, who chose not to tell, not to breach the boundary between the private and the public where his deepest alienation lay.

Nonetheless, Adams's reluctance to tell everything to everyone also testifies to the complications of negotiating that boundary and, especially, of negotiating the boundary between personal experience and cultural consensus. In fact, the doubts that many late-twentieth-century American writers of belletristic autobiography share with Adams represent several kinds of reckoning that the exemplary tradition in American autobiography has not been prepared, or willing, to undertake.

The public disclosure of previously unfaced truths about personal experience—and about personally experienced America—has shaped and freighted a significant amount of *telling* in American autobiography. Long before *The Education of Henry Adams*, African American autobiographers made it their business to expose the distortions of the exemplary tradition's universally constructed "America." In Frederick Douglass's *Narrative*, America constitutes more of an obstacle—to human dignity as well as to personal transformation—than an opportunity. And the silence that Douglass was obligated to preserve around the climactic moment of his escape from slavery stands as a powerful reminder of the limits of American authorship under the Fugitive Slave Law: "It would afford me great pleasure indeed, as well as materially add to the interest of my narrative, were I at liberty to gratify a curiosity, which I know exists in the minds of many . . . ," Douglass told his reader, "but I must deprive myself of this pleasure."[21] A century later, in *Manchild in the Promised Land*, Claude Brown exposed the betrayal of the generation of rural blacks who migrated to the urban North: "It seems that Cousin Willie, in his lying haste, had neglected to tell the folks down home about one of the most important aspects of the promised land: it was a slum ghetto."[22] What better way to call America to task for failing to make good on its promises than to turn autobiography itself against the exemplary "America" that had spawned the form?

Yet in a medium that has tended to expect the writer to exemplify a cultural type, whether of liberation or of oppression, Adams's evocation of alienation remains in important ways more stubbornly personal. This resistance to driving personal experience into seamless, publicly palatable form has emerged as Adams's most compelling legacy among contemporary American writers of autobiography.

Both Richard Rodriguez's 1982 *Hunger of Memory* and Art Spiegelman's 1986 *Maus* echo Henry Adams's sense of family as an arena of unresolved tension and unfulfilled longing. In his subtitle, *The Education of Richard Rodriguez*, Rodriguez refers explicitly to Adams's legacy and thus emphasizes his thematic debt to Adams's alienation from the exemplary tradition of personal freedom, rhetorical mastery, and public self-projection. That alienation resonates in Rodriguez's decision—never peeled free from ambivalence—to be the teller of his mother's family secrets: "I am writing about those very things my mother has asked me not to reveal. Shortly after I published my first autobiographical essay . . . my mother wrote me a letter pleading with me never again to write about our family life."[23] Rodriguez never quite makes peace with the sacrifice of intimacy that his parents made when they gave up Spanish for the sake of their children's upward mobility in the English-speaking United States. Like *The Education of Henry Adams*, *Hunger of Memory* never breaks free of the conflicted relationship between the writer and his America. Moreover, for Richard Rodriguez language remains—like family and like America—the ground both of his hopes for the future and of irreconcilable conflict. Loss and incompleteness hang over Rodriguez through the final paragraph of the book—as lonely a conclusion as Adams's—in which Rodriguez vainly attempts on a chilly Christmas night to warm his father with his jacket: "I take it to my father and place it on him. In that instant I feel the thinness of his arms. He turns. He asks if I am going home now too. It is, I realize, the only thing he has said to me all evening."[24]

Like Rodriguez's mother, Art Spiegelman's father beseeches his son to respect his secrets: "I can tell you other stories, but such private things, I don't want you should mention"; and like Rodriguez, Spiegelman never quite resolves this question of *telling*. The layers of hiding and secrecy that made possible his father's survival during the Holocaust make it impossible for Spiegelman's father to start new in America.[25] And they leave a painful, dissonant legacy for the American son who emerges—framed, provocatively, in comic strip form that never congeals into seamless narrative—as a different kind of "Holocaust survivor." In writing of his own suffering as the child of a survivor of so much suffering, Spiegelman breaks through the taboo of family silence surrounding his mother's suicide and his father's lack of trust and generosity, and challenges a set of hallowed notions about portraying the Holocaust. In fact, Spiegelman's "survival" remains ambiguous, for he bears the scars of both his father's past and his own. Rather than writing his own liberation from those losses as Franklin had, Spiegelman is left, like Rodriguez and Adams, to mourn the losses of his innocence and his childhood.

The emotional damage to which the revelation of private family information testifies in all these recent American autobiographies cuts deep, in layers at once personal, literary, and cultural. These revelations seem essential in coming to terms with emotional truths that the exemplary tradition never faced. Rodriguez and Spiegelman in the 1980s, Kincaid and others in the 1990s, all these writers have dared to admit the reality of trauma and loneliness beneath the victorious upward trajectory of the immigration narrative that Franklin pioneered and mythologized in the eighteenth century. In their "America" we see neither the Franklinian model of autonomy, independence, and self-sufficiency that became polished into a national ideal nor even the systemic oppression of the African American slave but, instead, the raw personal face of isolation and confusion. In these texts we see the seductiveness of the promise to start new, tabula rasa, that autobiography made for the American individual, for the American author, and for America. And in the claustrophobic embrace of family we see what Henry Adams saw at the turn of the twentieth century: that the past never fully unburdens the present, even on the ostensibly healing ground of America.

In short, the breakdown of the exemplary autobiographical tradition has—in the long wake of *The Education of Henry Adams*—decisively exposed as illusory that tradition's notions of "America," of Enlightenment individualism, and of narrative. Adams could not have anticipated the great, inconsolable American traumas of the twentieth century—World War I, the Holocaust, Vietnam, AIDS; traumas incomprehensibly beyond the power of narrative to resolve.[26] Yet he clearly saw the world ahead as different, and he saw clearly the strain that that world's difference would apply to the exemplary tradition's faith in human beings' order-making potential and in the transformative power of American conditions. In evoking a level of alienation that neither narrative nor America could heal, the *Education* called for and modeled a new kind of American text—one that recognized the arrogance and the naivete of modernity.

The American writers of autobiography who have followed Adams have lived with his reservations. As the American world and the American families into which they were born have left them scarred and doubting, they are unlikely to imagine starting from scratch. Nor can they trust the benign plasticity of memory and of narrative on which the exemplary tradition counted. In a terrible sense, recent American writers have had to consider a possibility that Franklin never seemed to imagine: the potential for their own voices to be hurtful. In a world where parents' hold on love has become fragile—"I thought you wouldn't like me anymore," Mary Karr's mother explains in defense of her decision to keep her past secret—or where parents themselves endanger their children—"I had to stop talking," Maya Angelou realized after her stepfather raped her and threatened to kill her beloved brother if she told anyone—lying and forgetting seem safer than memory and speech.[27] To reveal family secrets is to put others' pride and dignity at risk: a father humiliating himself and his son in front of a teenage gas station attendant, making English "sounds as confused as the threads of blue and green oil in the puddle next to my shoes."[28] Could it have been his fear of his own hurtfulness that made Henry Adams choose silence when his wife ended her life after a long, inaccessible depression, his reluctance to leave to posterity his memory of Marian Adams's despair and desperation, and of his own sense of abandonment?

While the erosion of the "exemplary" aura of America and American authorship might be read as a cultural disappointment, it ought also to be read as a coming of age. This more mature reckoning is the legacy not only of Adams but of Adams's literary milieu, the legacy of realism that has moved American writing—and American individualism—past its early, ideological obligations to nation. Although we may have lost the sense of Enlightenment experimentation and idealism that shaped so much of American literature and American autobiography from Franklin through Thoreau, we may have gained the ability to see "America" as an experienced thing of the present and the past, rather than an imagined thing of the future. Now we can give fuller voice to the fears and insecurities that have stubbornly dogged Americans' spinning of national myths, to the anxieties that quietly trail even the loudest American dreaming. Arthur Miller's *Death of a Salesman* set *that* literary agenda half a century ago with Linda Loman's quiet, insistent refrain: "attention must be paid" to the bewildered Willy Lomans, whose expectations of success on Franklinian terms are unlikely to be met by twentieth-century corporate America. And to the Jay Gatsbys, whose abstract, inflated hopes for an America "commensurate to [their] capacity for wonder" have left them fumbling—"it was just personal"—when the real emotional world has pressed upon them.[29] Henry Adams saw the potential for heartbreak—*that* well-kept secret!—beneath the surface of modern America, and Adams recognized the hardening fact that neither America nor narrative could necessarily make the world new. Nearly a century after the *Education* it seems a victory, rather than a diminishment, for American autobiography to be able to face up, finally, to that legacy.

NOTES

1. Benjamin Franklin, *The Autobiography and Other Writings*, ed. Kenneth Silverman (1793, as *The Private Life of the Late Benjamin Franklin*; New York, 1986), 3.
2. Franklin, *Autobiography*, 27.
3. Franklin, *Autobiography*, 90.
4. Franklin, *Autobiography*, 37.
5. See James Cox, "Autobiography and America," *Virginia Quarterly Review* 47(1971):252–277; Robert F. Sayre, "Autobiography and the Making of America," in *Autobiography: Essays Theoretical and Critical*, ed. James Olney (Princeton, N.J., 1980), 146–168; and Karl J. Weintraub, "Autobiography and Historical Consciousness," *Critical Inquiry* 1(1975):821–848.
6. Henry Adams to William James, Dec. 9, 1907, in *The Letters of Henry Adams*, ed. J. C. Levenson et al. (Cambridge, Mass., 1982–1988), 6:91–92. Subsequent citations will appear in the text.

7. Brent Staples, "Hating It Because It Is True: The Backlash against the Memoir," *New York Times*, Apr. 27, 1997, p. 14.
8. Mary Gordon, *The Shadow Man: A Daughter's Search for Her Father* (New York, 1997), xviii; James McBride, *The Color of Water: A Black Man's Tribute to His White Mother* (New York, 1996), xiii; Jamaica Kincaid, *My Brother* (New York, 1997), 69–70.
9. McBride, *Color of Water*, 15–16.
10. Kincaid, *My Brother*, 174–175.
11. Gordon, *Shadow Man*, 128.
12. Susan Bergman, *Anonymity: The Secret Life of an American Family* (1994; New York, 1995), vii, 183.
13. McBride, *Color of Water*, 39.
14. Gordon, *Shadow Man*, 274, 260.
15. Mary Karr, *The Liars' Club: A Memoir* (New York, 1996), 3, 10.
16. Karr, *Liars' Club*, 78–79.
17. Karr, *Liars' Club*, 310, 320.
18. Kathryn Harrison, *The Kiss: A Memoir* (New York, 1998), 174, 176, 202.
19. Paul John Eakin, *How Our Lives Become Stories: Making Selves* (Ithaca, 1999), 143.
20. Zoë Heller, "No Incest, and Only a Little Drink," *New York Times Book Review*, Mar. 15, 1998, p. 10.
21. Frederick Douglass, *Narrative of the Life of Frederick Douglass, An American Slave* (1845; New York, 1982), 137.
22. Claude Brown, *Manchild in the Promised Land* (New York, 1965), viii.
23. Richard Rodriguez, *Hunger of Memory: The Education of Richard Rodriguez* (New York, 1983), 175.
24. Rodriguez, *Hunger of Memory*, 195.
25. Art Spiegelman, *Maus: A Survivor's Tale* (New York, 1986), 1:23.
26. See Lawrence Langer, *Holocaust Testimonies: The Ruins of Memory* (New Haven, 1993); and Arthur W. Frank, *The Wounded Storyteller: Body, Illness, and Ethics* (Chicago, 1995).
27. Karr, *Liar's Club*, 318; Maya Angelou, *I Know Why the Caged Bird Sings* (1970; New York, 1993), 73.
28. Rodriguez, *Hunger of Memory*, 15.
29. Arthur Miller, *Death of a Salesman* (1949; New York, 1976), 56; F. Scott Fitzgerald, *The Great Gatsby* (1925; New York, 1995), 189, 160.

Henry Adams

Travel as Episteme

PIERRE LAGAYETTE

EPISTEMOLOGY, THE THEORY OF KNOWLEDGE, evolved throughout the nineteenth century at a quickening pace, producing tremendous agitation among scientists and theologians that baffled historians who tried to account for these changes and evaluate their scope and implications. Henry Adams stood in the center, spanning the century—not chronologically but intellectually—and trying desperately to bridge the gap between the safe, reason-based age of Enlightenment and the turbulent, multifaceted modern world with its profusion of challenges and uncertainties. He assigned himself the task of establishing some degree of continuity in history and of turning history towards the future using the past as a measurement of progress. Despite his repeated admissions of being utterly bored by life and the world, despite his well-rehearsed act of arch-skepticism or -cynicism, Adams knew intuitively that history *had* direction, although he lacked the appropriate tools to demonstrate it. He always professed to be no more than a teacher and a storyteller, but one with epistemological ambitions. He had an imperious desire to improve knowledge and bring history closer to the realm of final, scientific explanations.

Someone indeed had to tackle the leap in epistemology that such theories as Charles Darwin's or Karl Marx's imposed on the historian, lest history simply miss the train of intellectual evolution. Someone had to look for and provide directions and arguments so that society could be subject to the same explanation that the physical world and man himself were. Society had its movements, changes, and restlessness. With what degree of predictability could the scholar chart them? What navigational instruments could he use on this adventurous voyage? How would the historian—forever caught, it seemed, between fable and fact, explicit and latent contents, the sensual and the conceptual—deal with the temptation of scientific universalism?

To these questions, to the need for general explanations in social and intellectual history, to the movements of Western society, Adams responded with "a formula of his own" that made movement and travel a constant experiment of life. He could have remained a sedentary student/teacher of history, as caught in the intellectual comfort of Boston and his family as Emily Dickinson was in her readings ("There is no frigate like a book / To take us lands away . . .").[1] But Adams, even in his worst moments of pessimism or despair, never was an anchorite. He traveled—never alone—because travel constituted education and enhanced his sense of belonging to an age that had produced the most fantastic revolution in transports and communication.[2] The extent of the gap between past and present manifested itself in this tremendous change and in the ensuing transformation of the very idea of distance. For Adams, time and space converged to link history and travel irremediably.

From the onset, travel held for Adams a didactic interest. It provided on many occasions a litmus test of his own intellectual capacities and—even though he would often deny it—of the historian's legitimate need to expand his investigations into such alien disciplines as ethnography, geology, or architecture. Travel became a response to mental restlessness, to an uncontrollable curiosity, to a natural attraction to novelty and surprise. Nonetheless, Adams started on the trail as an ordinary tourist, education in the early years of contact with Europe being, he claimed, merely "accidental." *The Education of Henry Adams*, for example, chronicles his first practical approach to Italy as almost purely dilettantish, based on a conventional fascination for sights, the emotion of difference, and the pleasure to experience beauty firsthand, like other tourists, without further investigation beneath the surface of things. But tourism taught little else than that Rome was "pure emotion," and thirty years later, the weathered traveler who looked for ultimate meanings among twelfth-century cathedrals resented the proximity of those whom he had emulated when in his own barbarian youth.[3] The obnoxious tourist in Mont-Saint-Michel or Coutances simply incarnated ignorance and lack of taste. "He comes in processions and armies," Adams complained to John Hay in 1895, "like the old pilgrims. When the head of such a column enters where you are, it is like an advancing flood. It rolls you over, and crushes you. The tourists themselves are what pilgrims always were, only without the slightest glimmer of an idea which faith gave."[4]

The idea of travel as youthful adventure still lingered when Adams set off for Japan with John LaFarge in 1886. "If you and King were with us," he told Hay from the ship bound for Tokyo, "we would capture the ship, turn pirate, and run off to a cocoa-nut island."[5] Japan was gay, healing, reassuring. It talked to the senses, turned history into a "nursery-tale," provided a vantage point from which to evaluate the Western world, European art, American manners, and Adams's own conceptions of color, nature, and sex. It also told of possible historical vistas into a mysterious, distant past where the very notion of history (Western, Aryan history) dissolved.[6]

Traveling to the Far East confirmed Adams's suspicion that European-centered and even American-centered history—both entangled in their cultural conventions—had begun to sediment. Adams declared the need for a new history, and he believed that traveling to exotic places could give fresh direction to his historical enterprise. What he called his "instinct of wandering" offered him opportunities to break with the past, including past notions of history. "Society is getting new tastes," he told Gaskell upon his return from Japan, "and history of the old school has not many years to live. I am willing enough to write history for a new school."[7] No doubt that with the last part of his multivolume *History of the United States* a manner of writing history ended for him. And the resources for a new life, and a new writing, he discovered again in travel, this time to the South Seas.

Adams's voyage to the Pacific islands responded, in his own words, to "a longing to try something new and different," thus expelling the nausea created by absorbing too much "kerosene of American ideas and interests," as he told his brother Charles Francis.[8] To consider the South Seas voyage as a total break with traditional conceptions of history would be inaccurate. Adams expected to find in the Pacific the often-desired, and often-promised, extension of the American dream of Paradise, the lost golden age, an Arcadia that served primarily to reconcile history and eternity. When he dove into that archaic world, however, he discovered that it challenged him to acknowledge the inadequacy of his favorite epistemological tools. They could not help him interpret this archaism.

With his natural intellectual resiliency, Adams resorted to as-yet untested devices, explored as-yet untried instruments of knowledge or representation. Under LaFarge's guidance, he experimented with watercolor, which predictably threw him back upon his stark ignorance.[9] Yet LaFarge taught him to "see," to look for beauty and meaning beneath the surface of things. LaFarge showed him the peculiar charm of the Polynesian woman, who carried Adams back to the myth of the "old-gold girl" and the archaic, idyllic world introduced in exotic literature and pregnant with historical significance. Along this path to ancient society, Adams encountered the history of origins, naturally drifted towards geology, and looked for scientific explanations for the very existence of these islands. Accordingly, his travels assumed an epistemological turn: he undertook a study of Darwin's geological hypotheses about the Pacific and sought to confirm or deny them. A description of the attempt and its results are consigned in a long letter to Clarence King, which Adams wrote from Tahiti and in which he blandly expressed his puzzlement and admitted to his lack of qualification as a scientist.[10] He subsequently transferred this constant need to understand to the safer grounds of family history, when he undertook to tell the story of the Tevas, his adoptive Tahiti clan, and through them the island's history.

What happened between Adams, the Salmon family, and their Teva ancestors in the island of Tahiti was, in many respects, exceptional. The need to recompose the history of the island turned his attention towards autobiography, but autobiography of a particular kind, reinvented, based on a past vicariously relived and reconstituted by a devoted, yet distant, chronicler. The more Adams felt physically stranded in Tahiti, expecting the next steamer to leave the island, the more he focused on this bizarre task of salvaging family history through the recollections of an aging lady who considered herself entitled to his interest due to a vaguely felt natural nobility (the Arcadian dream again), dignified behavior, and a friendly concern to draw him into the narrow circle of native royalty.[11] Surely enough, the Tevas bore (at least he felt) a striking resemblance to the Adamses. They had suffered at the hands of an adverse fate and failed to go down in history as the true, legitimate leaders of their nation. Contrary to his earlier experience in Samoa, where he had turned ethological historian, inquiring essentially about customs and religion and wondering about the morality of the "old-gold girl," here he discovered an opportunity to rescue and rehabilitate a vanishing past.

The endeavor itself betrayed Adams's temporary abandonment of any pretension to objectivity or accuracy. His interpretation of Teva history became even more genuinely introspective and biased when Queen Marau's mother, Arii Taimai, formally adopted him into the clan. And his usual historian's tools aided him very little in his efforts to handle the kind of material his new Tahitian family supplied. An uneasiness prevailed, all along, in the relationship of the historian to his sources, a reluctance that, at times, verged on distrust. The complexity of the challenge soon struck him. First, the language gap presented myriad problems. Adams never mastered Maori, as had scholarly missionaries such as John Davies, John Orsmond, or Henry Nott. Arii Taimai told the old native legends in an archaic tongue that puzzled even the younger Salmons. "She talked by the hour," he once told Hay, "bothering her daughter and grandson terribly because they did not understand her old-fashioned Taïtian words, and scolding them because they did not know their own language."[12] In addition, Adams accessed Tahitian oral tradition only through Tati Salmon's or Marau's translations, so that he eventually gave up trying to render in English the beauties of the Tahitian tongue or even to reach a reasonable level of accuracy in reporting ancestral stories. "Paraphrase is all one can try for, where languages are so hopelessly different," he complained candidly in the *Memoirs of Arii Taimai*.[13] Oral tradition, he found out, was an "open" system of interpretations that assumed an infinity of shapes with an infinity of narrators.

The core of Tahitian oral tradition, and Tahitian history, were the island's genealogies, which established lines of descent. Handed down from one generation to another in oral form, they indicated which chiefs (*ari'is*) should prevail over others and played a key role in the distribution of social status and political power among the living. At the time that Adams landed in Tahiti, the French government had started to straighten out the many contradictory claims to hereditary property. The Tevas were literally fighting for political survival, desperate to establish some traditional supremacy among the Tahitian clans and especially anxious to legitimize their claims to native leadership against their traditional rivals, the Pomares. The Salmons, on behalf of their Teva forebears, needed to cement their rights to ancestral lands without further delay. The Teva and Pomare lines of descent, however, were so intricately connected that the Tevas needed, to win their cause, either the disappearance of former King Pomare V or the customary weight of an official chronicle.[14] Adams's visible appreciation of their hospitality and company could easily further these short-term political ambitions, and *The Memoirs of Marau* (privately printed in 1893) served the purpose. Even John LaFarge, whose sensibility to aristocratic status was far less developed than Adams's, recognized the book's efficacy:

> Now the French Government, in its anxiety to extend all benefits of civilization, and to make all its peoples equals has desired to have everything put into proper shape; and as in Samoa, so everybody here must put in his claim to the land, which thus will be duly recorded for good and all. For never again will be the time when a family might claim the fruit of a branch of a given tree. These genealogies, kept by hearsay, will be unfolded to the public, so far as needed, and claims settled. . . . Everything conspires for getting some definite record just before the last veil closes over a past already dim enough. And Marau and Moetia [her sister] are writing out songs and legends, and may be inspired, if their ardour can continue, to help save something.[15]

Fifteen years after leaving Tahiti, some time after the publication of *Memoirs of Arii Taimai* (1901), Adams told Margaret Chanler: "You shall have the volume if you want it, but it was not made to be read. It was made only for my brother Tati to offer the French Government as basis for a family pension. At least for that it was printed."[16] Epistemology became, in the end, the instrument of a local coterie, and the historian's need to know was incorporated into a broad scheme of intellectual and sentimental barter.

Adams recognized the purpose that his work served for the Tevas, and he recognized the limits of the oral tradition that transmitted the genealogies to him. He repeatedly lamented their lack of historical accuracy and the liberties oral tradition took with chronology: "as usual tradition is indifferent to dates and details," he observed in the *Memoirs of Arii Taimai*, "joins together what was far apart and cares only for what amuses it."[17] Of course, one must note Edward Chalfant's remark that "Adams was not disinterested" in fully assuming his Tahitian identity, after being renamed Taura atua i Amo.[18] Nonetheless, as the backbone of island history, genealogies constituted the only reliable epistemological tool Adams had at hand for investigating the Tahitian past. Furthermore, Adams went to considerable lengths to exercise full authority over his material.[19] He put the genealogies that the Salmon family provided him to comparative tests; sent lengthy and detailed questionnaires to family members, especially Tati and Marau, for corroboration; and read extensively in explorers' and missionaries' accounts. To claim that Adams pioneered modern Polynesian ethnography would be excessive, but in later years, ethnographers in the Pacific would use such genealogies extensively to study native societies.

Behind the utilitarian purpose of the *Memoirs of Arii Taimai* lurks Adams's personal need to come to terms with a so-called "primitive" world that neither philosophy nor science seemed capable of explaining. Adams deemed modern science helpless before the contradictions and mysteries of Polynesia. Its shortcomings symbolized the collapse of rationality and abstractions. Polynesia proposed more riddles than solutions, more paradoxes than comforts; to understand it required more sensibility than sense and a capacity for civilized man to look back into his origins—a deliberate jump that most Europeans had been reluctant to take. For the historian willing to look, however, Tahiti offered a brief insight into a forgotten world of instinct and imagination that modern civilized man had resolutely dismissed as primitive and left mostly undeciphered.

Adams, against all expectations, given his background and his training, discerned in this "primitive" Polynesian society an art of living, a philosophy of being that could match all the wisdom of Buddha or Confucius. He found elements of refinement that the modern cultures of Europe and America had stifled and lost—traces of which he would later see in the windows of Chartres. "Our age," Adams complained in an 1896 reference to Greek temples and Gothic cathedrals, "is too thoroughly brutalized to approach or understand any of these creations of an imagination which is dead."[20] The Tahitian legends, like twelfth-century glass, prompted Adams to find a way to bring that imagination into the historian's work. They left Adams to ponder the true nature of historical dynamics and to wonder about that "vital energy" that lay behind the rise and fall of civilizations. He considered that his main task might well be to expand the province of history to incorporate artistic expression whenever it could help trace and measure cultural changes. In both the *Memoirs* and *Mont Saint Michel and Chartres*—which he intended as a sequence—he sought to recover that "essential instinct" that could revolutionize the historian's epistemological condition.[21]

The results of the South Seas travels were varied and pointed towards seemingly opposite directions. On many accounts the pilgrimage—as Adams would later recognize—brought him into contact with an archaic environment, with earlier stages of social development, such as the Western world had known, but directly available to the historian-turned-eyewitness.[22] Epistemologically, the confrontation was invaluable. At the same time, as he was led to reflect on social evolution, to draw parallels between the primitive South Seas conditions and Western civilization, Adams was undergoing a personal change: "This long year of tropical life . . . ," he wrote Lucy Baxter, "has broken the old habits of life and given me new ones."[23] As he had expected, his former self was gone, his old life was closed, and he experienced a sense of renewal that opened his eyes and mind to the power of Art, to the aesthetic experience. Not that he had ignored or been insensitive to Art before, but the part to be played by the aesthetic emotion in what he called his "adventures in search of knowledge" might have to be reconsidered.[24]

To the uninformed observer, the transition between Tahiti and Chartres might look like a gigantic epistemological leap from the architectonics of coral reefs or lava beds to those of the Gothic arch and stained glass windows. The scheme, however, is less arbitrary than it might seem. Historians, thus far, in their wish to separate fact from fable, had attempted, and managed, to separate trace from emotion, the document from a possible reconstruction of its meaning. Nonetheless, circumstances can push the historian beyond that boundary: some vestiges of ancient times—including artistic traces—provide such fragmentary, lacunary representations of the past as to make the loss of meaning crippling. They require the use of entities—structures, epistemes, paradigms—larger in scope and effect than the individual traces and capable of helping historians explain the state and/or evolution of a whole period.

The well-known example of the Ara Coeli, which Adams repeatedly visited throughout his life, provides a good demonstration: what the historian expected from Cola di Rienzo's fourteenth-century experience had little to do with the architectural design of the stairs. Adams concerned himself with that extraordinary fascination for the past splendor of Rome expressed through Cola's folly, which could inspire the historian to measure the degree of growth or decline of a whole society or of civilization. In this specific case, Adams saw in the Ara Coeli, with the memory attached to it of Cola haranguing the mobs in a Roman emperor's garb, a paradigm of degradation that perfectly contradicted the elevation it proposed to the eye. The same methodology would serve for Chartres and Gothic architecture. The Middle Ages held up signs to the historian's eye that directed him to explanations much broader than the signs themselves. Another voyage of discovery.

In the 1902 chapter of the *Education*, Adams suggested a link between travel and epistemology with his metaphor of the pilgrim: "the pursuit of ignorance in silence had, by this time, led the weary pilgrim into such mountains of ignorance that he could no longer see any path whatever, and could not even understand a signpost."[25] Adams's self-deprecatory tone should not blind us to the fact that he saw more in medieval architecture and art than did any of his fellow historians, including Europeans. His successive visits to Amiens, Coutances, Mont-Saint-Michel, Chartres, and other marvellous examples of the Gothic monuments taught him that Western civilization had changed for the worse. His vision ran counter to the prevailing, progressive vision of Euro-American history: it postulated loss, not gain; perversion, not improvement of the aesthetic emotion; movement, indeed, but backwards and downwards. After his long peripatetic voyage over the world, Adams came back to the Middle Ages with a mind changed from the days when he had taught and written about Anglo-Saxon law. His thinking now bore the marks of having gone into and seen for himself primitive, instinctual societies, those "fragments of the past" that still existed on earth in defiance of chronology.

History was definitely a matter of motion; so was travel; so was, in fine, epistemology, always dynamic in its objectives and procedures. Yet Adams could not rest with simply observing and acknowledging the reality or the direction of movement, be it his own across the seas or that of human societies through the ages. He needed to identify the forces that impelled the changes. He realized that, epistemologically, the study of "dregs and fragments" had no value if disconnected from the study of cultural and social change, if dissociated from the appreciation of movement—which mechanical scientists call "moment."

The project of explaining the movement of societies certainly became clearer with *Mont Saint Michel and Chartres* and with the subsequent historical essays: "The Tendency of History," *A Letter to American Teachers of History*, and "The Rule of Phase Applied to History." Adams explicitly offered each of these pieces as epistemological endeavors, but we can also see them, in spite of the scientific rhetorical style, as metaphorical representations of a traveler's quest. By the turn of the century, however, Adams hardly needed to employ such tropes to establish a parallel between scientific/historical inquiry and a traveler's movements. The didactic, epistemic character of travel had, over the years, become part of the fabric of his professional activities as teacher and historian.[26]

Travels not only provided the mind with vantage points from which and standards by which to evaluate the gap between different stages of human development; they also supplied proof that, as Benedetto Croce indicated, all history is contemporary and shaped by its environment. The more Henry Adams attempted to escape physically from his familiar world, the more he saw the futility of his efforts to ignore his social and cultural training. "I find that I carry myself with me," he wrote Lucy Baxter in 1894, "and that my Ego is the very product of the age I am trying to fly from."[27] His epistemological pursuits also proved therapeutic: they, like travel, aimed at generating a new man, one who would not "reason too much," as LaFarge's friendly reproach went.[28] Adams could hope that this new man, after undergoing a sort of mild brainwashing in the hands of the Polynesian "old-gold girl" or the medieval Virgin, would find himself secluded and protected from the habits of thought of contemporary American historians.

In the *Education*, Adams often indicated that the renewal of his vision of Western historiography depended on the practice of travel. Here he put forward the idea that travels should become integral to a wholly new conception of history; he also suggested, subtly but forcefully, that the failure to open itself to the rest of the world had brought American history to a dead-end. Finding a way out of that dead-end would require new ways of thinking. In the chapter "Silence," Adams appears to be looking for a formula that will combine the lessons of travel, the emotions of art, and the assurances of science. The metaphor of voyage as he uses it, with its challenges and discoveries along the way and its promise of a final destination, held sufficient didactic and teleological interest to deserve a radical expansion: "he hoped, if he rode long enough in silence, that at last he might come on a city of thought along the great highway of exchange."[29]

But silence was not the proper condition for an epistemological revolution, as Adams dreamed of it, unless it served as background for the throwing of intellectual bombs, such as his 1910 *Letter*. Having despaired of the historian's narrative powers, having thrown into the world highly unusual texts, like *Mont Saint Michel* and the *Education*, which sought to end the war between the "narrative and the didactic" (which he told Barrett Wendell in 1909 had been lost), he turned finally to scientific discourse as a means to blast the last strongholds of antiquarianism and intellectual inertia and provoke some reaction from his fellow historians.[30] "What I have wanted, for the last twenty years," he wrote Yale physics professor Henry Bumstead, "was to force some sign of activity into my own school of history, which seems to me as dead as the dodos. In my despair of galvanizing it into life by any literary process, it occurred to me that some little knowledge of physico-chemical processes might show me a means of acting on it from the outside."[31]

Characteristically, Adams held science in high esteem, but scientists he found unreliable, as most of their intuitions led nowhere (as far as the historian was concerned), as their conclusions offered blatant contradictions, and as none seemed applicable to society—which proved utterly frustrating to someone who desperately sought to extract latent meaning from social evolution.[32] In private, he sniffed at mathematicians, "who are truly the bottom of all possible depths of imbecility," and time and again complained that physical and geological theories were of little help to him, chiefly because of his own ignorance.[33] As regarded physics or mathematics, he confided to his old friend Raphael Pumpelly, "The only thing of which I am positively assured by internal consciousness and objective evidence is that I am incapable of comprehending the simplest, as the most complex reasoning."[34] As a pioneer in the field of social history, Adams enjoyed considerable leeway to propose explanations for the state of society, past, present, and future. Yet the traveler of knowledge had become tired of wandering through the wilderness of speculative science or philosophy. He asked for proofs of a tendency, a direction, permanence and unity in the history of modern society. Although his visit to the 1893 Chicago Fair had supplied more questions than answers, it had also initiated the quest that by 1910 extended far beyond the limits of American society.[35] Describing the experience in the *Education*, Adams acknowledged his younger self's search for "a historical formula that should satisfy the conditions of the stellar universe"—a search that represented for the traveler the scientific equivalent of going to the desert of Gobi, a dream of solitude and perfect wisdom that Adams had often expressed.[36]

It was the epistemological challenge posed by this quest for a direction and a theory of direction that brought the curious traveler-historian in contact with disciplines hitherto unexplored by his colleagues. He would therefore attempt to process into intelligible equations the motions of mass, man, and mind, intuitively positing that the forces at play in the physical world might, under proper conditions of transfer, also be applied to the evolution of human societies. What he called "thought power" must follow some physical laws—and Adams was all too happy to find comforting parallels with electric mass as described in Gustave Le Bon's *Evolution des Forces*.[37] If societies did not follow similar paths and lend themselves to systematic explanation, history would reach a dead-end. The historian, then, might as well pack his bags and return home.

Explanation, however, stumbled on quantification. Adams suspected that what he sought to prove could only be shown or described. The historian was compelled to rely on similes, metaphors, and other literary devices; scientific formulas would not serve his purpose. If, as Adams said, "all the steam in the world could not . . . build Chartres," then all the words in the universe would fail to provide an epistemological construct to account for thought power. Before an ever-receding horizon of knowledge, Adams, the "navigator of ignorance," was thrown back on merely manipulating the sails of language. "Endless displacement," he wrote, "promised eternal bliss to the mathematician, but turned the historian green with horror."[38] The historian needed a mooring, which he found in adjusting the powers of narration to the requirements of "representing" historical evolution instead of explaining it.

In the same way that Adams's physical travels led him to distant, almost unexplored places (especially in the South Seas) and forced him to confront primitive life and primitive art as proofs of what he called "thought-motion," his inquiry into "the laws of historical evolution" turned into an epistemological voyage to the shores of physics and mathematics, using the full metaphorical power of narrative language. His "navigator of ignorance," his "weary pilgrim," and his voyager exploring "the shores of Multiplicity and Complexity" are all metaphors that borrow from the lexicon of travel.[39] They also seem to signal Adams's renunciation to the denotative function of language, to point to a certain "truth" of the metaphor as a mode of access to an indescribable reality.

The "Tendency" and the *Letter* bear the mark of Adams's ultimate attempt to make personal and universal movement converge, if only rhetorically. And it is not difficult to perceive that the movements of a constantly shifting world replicate Adams's own restless, lifelong traveling; that the American school of history represents that power of inertia, that "resistance to deflection" that prevents intellectual and social change; and that Adams, the instructor, the teacher, the active pioneer unafraid of motion and ready to question all accepted theories for the sake of epistemological progress, saw himself as a new Galileo, dreamed of becoming a new Darwin, fantasized over his own capacity to measure the movement of humanity. His enterprise amounted to much more than an epistemological wreck, yet Adams had *in fine* to admit that as "a true traveller on the highways of history" he was bound endlessly to follow the paths that his need for intellectual adventure and his thirst for knowledge always opened before him.[40]

NOTES

1. Emily Dickinson, *Collected Poems* (New York, 1982) 34.
2. See Henry Adams, *The Education of Henry Adams* (Boston, 1961), 5.

3. HA, *Education*, 87–90.
4. Henry Adams to John Hay, Sept. 7, 1895, in *The Letters of Henry Adams*, ed. J. C. Levenson et al. (Cambridge, Mass., 1982–1988), 4:320.
5. HA to John Hay, June 11, [1886], in *Letters*, 3:13.
6. See also Adams's intention to explore China, "the great unknown country of the world." HA to Charles Milnes Gaskell, Dec. 12, 1886, in *Letters*, 3:49.
7. HA to Charles Milnes Gaskell, Dec. 12, 1886, in *Letters*, 3:49.
8. HA to Charles Milnes Gaskell, Apr. 13, 1890; HA to Charles Francis Adams, Jr., July 3, 1890, in *Letters*, 3:235, 246.
9. HA to Elizabeth Cameron, Aug. 26, 1890, in *Letters*, 3:271.
10. HA to Clarence King, Mar. 3, 1891, in *Letters*, 3:435–444.
11. "By way of excitement," he wrote E. Cameron, "or something to talk about, I sometime ago told Marau [Tati Salmon's sister and ex-wife of King Pomare V] that she ought to write her memoirs, and if she would narrate her life to me, I would take notes and write it out, chapter by chapter. To our surprise, she took up the idea seriously, and we are to begin today, assisted by the old chiefess mother, who will have to start us from Captain Cook's time." HA to Elizabeth Cameron, May 10, 1891, in *Letters*, 3:471.
12. HA to John Hay, Mar. 2, 1891, in *Letters*, 3:433.
13. Henry Adams, *Memoirs of Arii Taimai* (Paris, 1901; reprinted as *Tahiti, Memoirs of Arii Taimai* [Ridgewood, N.J., 1968]), 38.
14. The former king happened to die in June 1891, only a few weeks after Adams had left the island.
15. John LaFarge, *Reminiscences of the South Seas* (New York, 1912), 344–345.
16. HA to Margaret Chanler, Jan. 27, 1905, in *Letters*, 5:630.
17. HA, *Memoirs*, 18.
18. Edward Chalfant, *Improvement of the World: A Biography of Henry Adams: His Last Life, 1891–1918* (North Haven, Conn., 2001), 57.
19. For more details on this question, see my discussion of Henry Adams's treatment of Tahitian genealogies in my Ph.D. dissertation: "The Edge of Life: Henry Adams in the South Seas" (University of Michigan, 1978).
20. HA to Elizabeth Cameron, Aug. 6, 1896, in *Letters*, 4:412.
21. "My idea is that the world outside—the so-called modern world—can only pervert and degrade the conceptions of the primitive art and feeling. . . . In other words, I am a creature of our poor old Calvinistic, St Augustinian fathers, and I am not afraid to carry out my logic to the rigorous end of regarding our present society, its ideals and purposes, as dregs and fragments of some primitive, essential instinct now nearly lost." HA to Albert Stanburrough Cook, Aug. 6, 1910, in *Letters*, 6:357. On the two books as a sequence, see his remarks about the "Chartres volume" to Cook in this letter (*Letters*, 6:356) and his statement that "I wanted to show the intensity of the vital energy of a given time, and of course that intensity had to be stated in its two highest terms,—religion and art."
22. "It is quite impossible for our society, young or old, to get its intellectual processes back to the state of mind in which society naturally expressed itself in the Iliad, or the Chanson, or the temple, or the church, and sang, or built, or fought, or loved, as a habit, without necessary reference to practical use. I've seen such societies in the South Seas, but they would be as impossible to our students as the habits of butterflies or beetles." HA to Frederick Bliss Luquiens, July 5, 1910, in *Letters*, 6:351.
23. HA to Lucy Baxter, Sept. 30, 1891, in *Letters*, 3:552
24. HA, *Education*, 98.
25. HA, *Education*, 433.

26. Of his illuminating first architectural escapade in Normandy and Brittany he said to Elizabeth Cameron "the trip was really an education." HA to Cameron, Aug. 29, 1895, in *Letters*, 4:311.
27. HA to Lucy Baxter, Sept. 26, 1894, in *Letters*, 4:213.
28. HA, *Education*, 370.
29. HA, *Education*, 361.
30. Referring to his brother Brooks's, Wendell's, and his own "literary" achievements, Adams reflected: "We have all three undertaken to do what cannot be successfully done—mix narrative and didactic purpose and style. . . . My conclusion is that we need far more art than ever before." HA to Barrett Wendell, Mar. 12, 1909, in *Letters*, 6:237–238.
31. HA to Henry A. Bumstead, Feb. 1, 1910, in *Letters*, 6:305
32. In the *Letter*, Adams noted that "the violent contradiction between Kelvin's Degradation and Darwin's Elevation was . . . profound, . . . flagrant, . . . vital . . ." and remarked, further on: "Unless the inquirer is full of courage, he will be aghast at the confusion of responses which his prayer disturbs." Henry Adams, *The Degradation of the Democratic Dogma* (New York, 1969), 162, 171.
33. HA to Charles Milnes Gaskell, Mar. 14, 1910, in *Letters*, 6:323.
34. HA to Raphael Pumpelly, May 19, 1910, in *Letters*, 6:341.
35. "Chicago asked in 1893 for the first time the question whether the American people knew where they were driving." HA, *Education*, 343.
36. HA, *Education*, 376.
37. "With the effort of a few logarithms," he wrote happily to Oliver Wendell Holmes, "I am driven to the conclusion that the law of mind in motion follows the same formula as the law of electric mass." HA to Holmes, Dec. 31, 1907, in *Letters*, 6:97.
38. HA, *Education*, 388, 455.
39. HA, *Education*, 456, 455, 433, 449.
40. HA, *Education*, 499.

Henry Adams's Unwritten American Travels

CHARLES VANDERSEE

Of all American travellers {in the late eighteenth and early nineteenth centuries} President {Timothy} Dwight {of Yale} was the most experienced; yet his four volumes of travels were remarkable for no trait more uniform than their reticence in regard to the United States. Clear and emphatic wherever New England was in discussion, Dwight claimed no knowledge of other regions. Where so good a judge professed ignorance, other observers were likely to mislead; and Frenchmen like {the Duc de} Liancourt, Englishmen like {Isaac} Weld {Jr.}, or Germans like {H. W.} Bülow, were almost equally worthless authorities on a subject which none understood.

—*Henry Adams, "History of the United States of America during the First Administration of Thomas Jefferson"*[1]

The West caught the vision of the nation's continental destiny. Henry Adams, in his History of the United States, *makes the American of 1800 exclaim to the foreign visitor, "Look at my wealth! See these solid mountains of salt and iron, of lead, copper, silver, and gold. See these magnificent cities scattered broadcast to the Pacific! See my cornfields rustling and waving in the summer breeze from ocean to ocean, so far that the sun itself is not high enough to mark where the distant mountains bound my golden seas. Look at this continent of mine, fairest of created worlds, as she lies turning up to the sun's never failing caress her broad and exuberant breasts, overflowing with milk for her hundred million children."*

—*Frederick Jackson Turner, "The Problem of the West"*[2]

> *I will come home {to Washington from Paris}, and immediately, if you will join me in writing, under any assumed name or character you please, a volume or two of Travels which will permit me to express my opinion of life in general. . . . I wont do it alone. Such a book, to be amusing needs variety of treatment and experience. . . . If {Clarence} King could be induced to join, so much the better; but I would do it with you alone, and put into it all the vinegar, pepper and vitriol necessary to make it a success of scandal if nothing else. . . . Travels that say anything are nowadays read. . . . We could start with San Francisco and go through America to England and France. . . . My notion of Travels is a sort of ragbag of everything; scenery, psychology, history, literature, poetry, art; anything in short, that is worth throwing in.*
>
> —*Henry Adams to John Hay, Jan. 9, 1892*[3]

I

THIS "SUBJECT WHICH NONE UNDERSTOOD" (epigraph one), the expanding United States, drew Henry Adams out on the road, the railroad, sporadically during some thirty years of his adult life, from 1871 when he reached Utah to 1886 when he first saw San Francisco and then to 1904 when at age sixty-six he visited his third American world's fair, the Louisiana Purchase Centennial Exposition in the "poor, little, German, half-baked city" of St. Louis.[4] These were famously decades of growth: in 1860 already 31 million people and thirty-three states established, while the 1900 census showed 75 million people in the forty-five states, with another million in Oklahoma, Arizona, and New Mexico. When Adams said of himself in the *The Education of Henry Adams* that in 1901 he picked up "his vague trail across the darkening prairie of education," this prairie metaphor applied as much to his previous geographical experience as to his general intellectual forays.[5] But the literary consequences of Adams's literal travels consist only of tantalizing fragments—a far remove from the two solid volumes of Alexis de Tocqueville, who in 1830–1831 had found in Andrew Jackson's America "[t]he longest railroads that have been constructed up to the present time" but whose nine-month sojourn left him unacquainted with the Louisiana Purchase, the seaboard below Norfolk, and (except for Cincinnati) the states of Ohio, Indiana, and Illinois.[6]

My thesis has to be double. First, Henry Adams, avidly deploying vinegar and vitriol (epigraph three) but who as traveler was also gregarious and indeed flirtatious, missed a calling both authentic and important while doing other things. Therefore readers lack one or more great travel books, one of which, as noted in epigraph three, would have boldly read the United States by starting not with New England or Virginia or New York but with California, moving east. Historian and autobiographer, reform journalist, political analyst, novelist, and letter-writer, Adams came of age in 1859, which was Charles Darwin's year, of course, but of more practical importance, the year of petroleum—the first producing oil well in the United States. In 1903 Adams would envision a nation of "three hundred million people running an automobile . . . at full speed."[7] At times in his adult life Adams functioned informally as a travel counselor, his letters describing unconventional itineraries in places like Colorado and Wyoming, South Carolina and Florida, a kind of travel different from joining sheeplike in one of Thomas Cook's flocks. As observer and recorder, Adams resisted the Baedeker formula of viewing obligatory sights, and though often traveling in comfort, he also relished the difficulties and inconveniences of roughing it. My second and more speculative thesis, left merely adumbrated: his travels in the United States and in the Americas—he examined Mexico, Cuba, and the Caribbean more than casually, eventually claiming to know Havana "as well as I do Washington"—help clarify why, in the *Education*, Adams seems in command of American realities rather than viewing them peripherally or parochially.[8] The character of "Henry Adams" talking about national failures and trends, and the equivocal future, is much larger than an Atlantic self, constructed by Boston and Quincy, London in his twenties, Washington for fifty years, and long stretches in Paris.

Precisely how travel experience feeds the writing of books that are outside the genre of travel-writing is not easy to establish; the *Education*, for example, famously erased the chronological center of Adams's life, not only his teaching and writing years between ages thirty-three and fifty-two, but his three months in Japan in 1886 and his thirteen-month trip in 1890–1891 to Samoa, Tahiti, and Fiji. His letters in these thirteen months constitute more or less a coherent travel book.[9] Since thoughtful Americans generally in Adams's day were riven by anxieties over regions—the established old East, the brash new West, the chastened and surly Confederacy, the culturally challenged Mark Twain country—did his own travels make him uncommonly attentive not only to these distinctions but to preoccupations overriding them? In the *Education*, an otherwise glib phrase, "the American mind," suddenly becomes particularized in Adams's wariness toward universals: "The American mind—the Bostonian as well as the Southern or Western—likes to walk straight up to its object, and assert or deny something that it takes for a fact."[10] At the least, his travels complemented his scholarship, enabling him on occasion to challenge received wisdom. In *A History of the United States during the Administrations of Thomas Jefferson and James Madison*, for example, his urbane demythologizing of Lewis and Clark upsets the romantic vision of schoolbooks and national epic-making by emphasizing big doings back East:

> The[ir] crossing of the continent was a great feat, but was nothing more. The French explorers had performed feats almost as remarkable long before . . . While Lewis slowly toiled up the Missouri River. . . . the engine which Robert Fulton had ordered from the works of Watt and Bolton in England had been made, and Fulton returned to New York to superintend its use.[11]

In other words, the American future depended on new technology enabling mobility on the continent. Exploration beyond the Missouri, meanwhile, would continue, as in other times and places, through the application of conventional human energy, whether by Lewis and Clark or by others.

Habitually the quizzical historian, Adams disrupted received wisdom concerning his own century: "The 19th century moved fast and furious . . . ," he wrote in *Chartres*, "but the eleventh century moved faster still." Habitually the resourceful traveler, Adams could not help seeing his own country in global terms because he had seen much of the globe, eyes undistorted by visions of personal gain or professional advancement. He was sixty years old when he asserted from Beirut to his chief confidante, Elizabeth Cameron: "You will never believe it, but I am a good traveller. I don't mean good in the sense of putting up with hardships. Any fool can do that. I mean that in a given situation, I generally am more comfortable than my neighbors."[12] Comfort implies a quelling of agitation that prevents reflection, and of course cash helps. To endure a violent storm on the Mediterranean between Alexandria and Beirut, Adams had "bought out the second engineer's room," situated at the ship's center of gravity "in among the engines," and thus smoked and read and dozed in peace. As for other passengers—well, as he told Mrs. Cameron, "The seasickness of that set of tourists had been something awful. I spare you the details."[13] On an earlier trip, an 1894 exploration into Mexico and Puerto Rico, an outlay of $300 hired him a small steamer for reaching the island of St. Thomas (in what are now the Virgin Islands), otherwise inaccessible.[14] These assertive maneuvers spring from desire and determination, a capacity for ingratiating oneself, and a worldly savoir faire—present already in 1865, when at age twenty-seven he shepherded his fretful mother, his younger sister, and his younger brother around France and Italy for three months.[15] While "the charge of a family has made me prematurely grey and bald," travel itself was exhilarating: "What a good time one can have in Italy, though, if one goes the right way about it. This traveling in one's own carriage is luxury itself."[16]

II

Concerning Adams's other global travels, everybody knows that he assiduously explored France, especially its medieval churches and cathedrals, issuing in 1904 *Mont Saint Michel and Chartres*, subtitled "Travels—France," a warmly personal guide for his wife's five nieces and for posterity, "nieces-in-wish," though they may be suspected of not cherishing every sentence of Adams's Thomist metaphysics. What almost everybody knows: Adams's two long trips with the artist John La Farge were aesthetic as well as ethnographic adventures. La Farge "has taught me to feel the subtleness and endless variety of charm in the color and light of every hour in the tropical island's day and night."[17] Besides Japan in 1886, their longer trip in 1890–1891 to the South Seas became a circumnavigation that eventually returned Adams to Washington by way of Australia, Bali, Singapore, Ceylon, the Suez Canal, and Marseilles. What some few readers recall, from eight of the *Education*'s five hundred pages: Adams reached not only the tropics but the Arctic. In 1901, a "tourist-student" at age sixty-three, he took the train from Bayreuth to Moscow and St. Petersburg, with Sen. and Mrs. Henry Cabot Lodge, then went on alone, "happily," the senator being something of a pompous bore, to Stockholm, and then, lured by "a cheerful New England landscape and bright autumn," reached Hammerfest, in Norway, well above the Arctic Circle, which surprised him by having "permanent electric lights."[18] He returned to Paris through Hamburg, Bremen, and Cologne, seeing "a Germany new to mankind," the Rhine "more modern than the Hudson."[19]

What almost no one notices (two cryptic paragraphs in the *Education*): Adams spent thirty days in "the wilderness" of Yellowstone in 1894, riding "three or four hundred miles on ponies through trails or trailless country, over mountains and in cañons," with the companionable John Hay and two other men of their generation, "making twentytwo different camps."[20] From there Adams went regretfully alone to Seattle and Vancouver, "to inspect the last American railway systems yet untried" by him, returning to Washington (too impatient to await the Alaska steamer) after "two days of ocean," meaning Lakes Superior, Huron, and Erie.[21] "I have just put in two months in the north-west," he wrote to Charles, his older brother, "which pretty well fills out my outlines on that side. The West Indies, Mexico, and South America are still on my horizon, and I shall devote this autumn and winter to bagging portions of those regions. Beyond all, is Asia, which will, I think, satisfy and satiate my last small appetites."[22] By Asia he meant mainly China, "the great unknown country of the world," which he long craved to visit, but never did, though he started learning Chinese characters, hoping to master one thousand.[23] He did reach Constantinople, Sofia, and Belgrade; "I wanted to see these so-called Balkan states in order to complete my knowledge of Europe," he reported, on his way to Budapest in 1898.[24] The grand idea was this sense of *completion*—direct, unshepherded experience of the whole accessible globe—an aesthetic satisfaction in its own right and a sort of muted cantus firmus for use when elaborating on any local part. His eye and mind would be very ready indeed to interrogate his own nation in the nineteenth century when in the new century he wrote the *Education*.

III

Adams's travels and his thinking about American travel do not necessarily emerge most clearly in a chronological account, but glances at two early fraternal utterances serve well as previews of things to come. In 1859, barely out of Harvard College, Adams was living in Dresden, to learn German, when he presumptuously advised brother Charles: "if you mean to travel, . . . do it first in America. . . . Go out into the wilds, boy; pass a month round among the Mormons and then come back with a clear head and a little practical knowledge."[25] Henry himself did not proceed this way; he spent nearly ten years in Europe before venturing west of Boston or south of Washington. Charles meanwhile, patriotic and intrepid, got out and about as a cavalry officer during the Civil War.[26] Indeed, after seeing the sea islands of South Carolina and camping for the winter in the mud of Virginia, Charles in 1863 fired back advice of his own:

> [W]ait until you can honorably leave your post [as private secretary to their father in London] and then make a bolt into the wilderness, go to sea before the mast [referring to their family's close friend Richard Henry Dana], volunteer for a campaign

> in Italy, or do anything singularly foolish and exposing you to uncalled for hardship. . . . I tell you I know you and I have tried the experiment on myself, and I here suggest what you most need. . . . If you joined an expedition to the North pole you might not discover that terra incognita, but you would discover many facts about yourself which would amply repay you the trouble you had had. All a man's life is not meant for books, or for travel in Europe.[27]

If they seemed to agree, there was one minor divergence. Travel for Henry would seldom include exposure to unwanted "hardship" but instead offered hardship as welcome escape—comic relief even—from the pale cast of thought and the propensity of civilization to express itself in plunder and war. Three decades later, his exuberant letters record travel by mule in Mexico and Cuba, stopping in native huts overnight. From Barbadoes in 1895, eight words that in effect served as his motto: "I mind dirt much less than English neatness."[28]

Leaving aside the well-traveled Samuel Clemens, two of Adams's illustrious literary contemporaries, William Dean Howells and Henry James, both committed to characterizing "the American" (title of a James novel), had virtually no direct nineteenth-century contact with the American West, much less Mexico and the Caribbean. Howells, Ohio-born, got west of Chicago only at age sixty-two, in 1899. Lecturing, his itinerary set by a booking agent, he did not reach Denver, refusing even to consider California. He had no leisure for observing and recording, being harassed at every stop—in places like Topeka, Emporia, Grinnell, and Ottumwa—by small-town literati and their smaller talk, obliged to confess to reporters that, yes, this was his "first trip to the West."[29]

Henry James learned Europe well, but for the first sixty years of his life remained a greenhorn in his native land. As Sheldon Novick has written, "the great artery of his America" early on was a well-known Eastern river, the Hudson. In the early 1870s, James's American travel pieces for the *Nation* depicted Saratoga Springs, Quebec, and Niagara. Though fascinated at Saratoga by the somewhat boorish "western men" on holiday, he would still, ten years later, lay down in his notebook the famous rule that an American writer "*must* deal, more or less, even if only by implication, with Europe: whereas no European is obliged to deal in the least with America."[30] Until 1903, when he began a ten-month American visit, James's West consisted of Milwaukee, once, for four days, where his two younger brothers lived.[31] Finally, in 1904, James's American lecture tour yielded his nuanced and enduring "impressions," in that startling and ever-provocative book *The American Scene*. James stopped in unfamiliar Richmond, Charleston, St. Augustine, and Palm Beach, and wrote them up, but he tired before inscribing Chicago, Los Angeles, San Diego, Portland, and Seattle. He was now passionately ready for America; Europe by then "had taken to writing itself plain to him"—she "had been romantic years before, because she was different from America; wherefore America would now be romantic because she was different from Europe."[32]

Henry Adams, by contrast, though also born a peripheral man—a Boston Brahmin—had discovered romantic America much earlier, especially the American West, both before and after completing his *History*. Adams first left the Eastern periphery in 1871, at age thirty-three, when after his first year of Harvard teaching, he embarked on "an expedition which will lead me for the next six weeks into paths unknown to European blokes . . . an absolute wilderness." Leaving Cambridge early in July, he was aware of his status at the center of things there: "I have managed to get into the 'inside ring,' as Americans say, the small set of men who control the University."[33] The wilderness trip famously reintroduced him, in Colorado, to geologist Clarence King, thereafter a close friend; equally important, it set Adams to pondering the nation's future from a new angle.

"In the year 1871," Adams recalled in the *Education*, "the West was still fresh, and the Union Pacific was young. Beyond the Missouri River, one felt the atmosphere of Indians and buffaloes." Arriving by rail in Cheyenne, Wyoming Territory, he went off for a month, and "several hundred miles," with mule, rifle, and leather breeches, accompanying the twenty men of the Fortieth Parallel Survey who were working in the Colorado Rockies. Returning to Cheyenne and the railroad in mid August, he pushed farther west, to Fort Bridger in the far southwest corner of present-day Wyoming, then with boyhood friend Frank Emmons and Clarence King explored the Uintah Mountains in northern Utah "till the frosts became sharp." "I enjoyed the life and learned a great deal about my own country," he wrote from Wyoming, "and forgot all the [medieval] history I had studied for a year."[34]

Despite learning well these portions of Wyoming, Colorado, and Utah, he did not range the West widely—as had his younger brother the year before. Brooks Adams in 1870, the week after his Harvard graduation (and barely a year after the transcontinental Golden Spike), had headed west with two friends to St. Paul. From there, they proceeded down the Mississippi in a stern-wheeler, then by train from St. Louis to San Francisco. They saw the remote Yosemite Valley and returned east by way of Salt Lake City, there meeting Brigham Young and seeing "a good deal of the Mormon community not normally accessible to strangers," writes Brooks's biographer (Brooks vigorously reminding the Mormons that his father as U.S. minister in London had helped their people relocate from Europe). From Denver, Brooks and his companions had hired a guide and horses to explore Ute country, and like Henry a year later found Native Americans paying friendly visits to their camp.[35]

In 1871, "he came out [to the West] to spy on the future," Adams would recall of himself in the *Education*. The men of the survey, insiders in their special way, "held under their hammers a thousand miles of mineral country with all its riddles to solve, and its stores of possible wealth to mark. They felt the future in their hands."[36] By July of 1871, the Union Pacific had connected East and West for a mere twenty-two months. Like Brooks a year earlier, Henry returned East without writing an essay or monograph about the American future, despite his professed investigation of the subject. Except for a long letter to an English friend, and five tantalizing pages in the *Education*, the region west of the 100th meridian represented the first of his American travels left uninscribed.

Then, for the next decade and half, no American travels. Adams, himself the American of the future (having become a workaholic), made himself too busy to travel in his native land, first as professor, then as writer: editor of *Essays in Anglo-Saxon Law*, biographer of Albert Gallatin, author of nine volumes on Jefferson and Madison. Life was books, and life was Europe, both of which brother Charles had warned against: this entrepreneurial war veteran who had become a Kansas City stockyards developer and land speculator in cities such as Denver, San Antonio, Salt Lake City, and Seattle.[37] Charles, a Greeleyan opportunist in the West, from 1870 to 1890 made at least one trip west from Boston every year, sometimes staying for months at a time and covering ten thousand miles. When Henry married in 1872, he and Clover headed the other direction, to Europe and Egypt for their wedding trip, stopping at archives in Paris and Madrid. Ironically, it was Clover's suicide, late in 1885, that turned Adams back westward, unable to stay at home in Washington but realizing that for now he simply could not "go to Europe. It is full of ghosts."[38] Choosing remote Japan because of both curiosity and contacts there, he and artist John La Farge traveled almost the entire distance across the United States (Albany to San Francisco) in relaxed splendor: the Union Pacific directors' car provided by brother Charles, lately (in 1884) become president of the road. But heartsick and grimly anticipating weeks of his usual seasickness, Henry put on record very little of what he saw and heard. San Francisco "looks to me as if its glories had passed; and everyone tells me that the two Oregon lines have diverted a large part of the Californian trade, and that the last three years have been very hard ones."[39]

Returning from Japan, he and La Farge made sure to visit picturesque Monterey, south of San Francisco, which Richard Henry Dana had seen in 1836–1837 and called "the prettiest town on the coast."[40] Then (thanks again to Charles's Pullman palace car) they returned to the East not directly but via Los Angeles, Albuquerque, Dodge City, Kansas City, Chicago, and Albany.[41] Two years later, in 1888, when Sir Robert Cunliffe, an old friend from England, paid an American visit, Adams dragged him nine thousand miles back and forth across the United States, taking in Chicago, Laramie, Salt Lake City, the Shoshone Falls of Idaho ("which tourists have hardly yet discovered"), Portland via the Columbia River steamer, Mount Shasta on a railroad just built, and San Francisco, with side trips to the Yosemite Valley ("the whole valley for near twenty miles up and down and sideways") and Menlo Park, where Sen. Leland Stanford was establishing a university with his fortune amassed as builder and president of the Central Pacific Railroad.[42] They returned to Washington by way of Santa Barbara ("a sort of Sorrento"), Los Angeles, Yuma, and El Paso, spending three days in New Orleans.[43] Not pioneers—Yosemite had been set aside already in 1864 as a public park—Adams and Cunliffe were also not tourists, though Thomas Cook had opened U.S. offices by 1872.[44] They were independent travelers in a land fast changing and not yet well known. Adams glimpsed Los Angeles twice in three years, 1886 and 1888, precisely at the time of the city's boom driven by railroad competition (briefly in 1886 the fare from Kansas City was $1). Land prices in Los Angeles County in 1887 soared from $100 per acre to $1,500, and the city population, 11,000 in 1880, reached 50,000 ten years later.[45] The desert city was an economic dynamo at the very moment that the new national virgin came into being: that is, at the time of Adams's first quick stop in Los Angeles the *Times* there reported the dedication of the Statue of Liberty.[46]

IV

Start of work on the *Education,* though not the start of his thinking about it, was at least seven years in the future when in 1894 Adams confided to Elizabeth Cameron what it had felt like, traveling alone, after leaving

John Hay and his other Yellowstone companions—the Yellowstone a "lost Eden"—to go first to the West Coast and then lazily take ten days on the Canadian Pacific eastward before embarking on his Great Lakes passage, which terminated in Buffalo. It was late summer, and Adams at age fifty-six insisted he had "seen or done nothing but what the tourist sees or does." This is unusual, since he usually either roughed it or rode in luxury. But he quickly corrected himself: "I pass invariably as a drummer. I am only happy to shelter myself under the disguise of so respectable a class."[47] Whether tourist or salesman (rather different constructions of the self in motion), he rendered thus "[t]he people one meets":

> The most varied type was one "professional drunken tourist," rather curious. . . . The other types have been all commonplace; much youth travelling apparently to find a living; some few simple travellers for instruction and improvement. Oh, I talk with them! You'll not believe it, but I do; and flirt with all the ladies who sell photographs and curios, and keep the hotels; and who are, by the bye, much the most amusing and instructive people I meet. With them I begin to feel the advantages of my years. They see they can trust me, and they talk without being silly. When the youth chips in, I step out, but the silliness begins at once. I listen to it with more interest than it ever before roused in my once impatient breast.[48]

This is a voice on the periphery speaking, seeking to understand the center, the strangeness of the American ordinary, both serious and silly. It is also the voice, the stance, the attractive openness to experience that exactly one year later will start making him an insider in the France of the twelfth century.

The previous year, 1893, he had twice visited bustling Chicago, for its incongruously ethereal Great White City of the Columbian Exposition, spending "a fortnight absorbed in it" the second time. "[I]f we ever write those Travels of ours, I've a volume or two to put in for the Fair," he told Hay.[49] The Exposition did eventually prompt an extended meditation in the *Education*: "Chicago asked in 1893 for the first time the question whether the American people knew where they were driving. Adams answered, for one, that he did not know, but would try to find out."[50] At the end of those four pages on the Chicago Exposition Adams ventured the conclusion that "Chicago was the first expression of American thought as a unity," a curious statement, as historian William McFeely has observed, since among the variety of peoples and achievements in the various pavilions, one American people had been ill-represented: slaves and their descendants. Frederick Douglass, McFeely remarks, "had he been alive to read *The Education of Henry Adams*, would have recognized with infinite sadness, that his own thought—his concept of human oneness—was excluded; Adams' unity did not transcend the denigrating divisiveness of race."[51] Yet while in quarantine on the island of St. Thomas the next year, in his third month of "wandering in Spanish countries," chiefly Mexico, Adams noted sardonically that American unity was a matter of some complexity. Triumphalist commerce imposed on the modern world a unity in its own inexorable terms, enforcing the divisiveness of race:

> Always mankind is absorbed with more or less success in the same solemn human duty of making money. The tiller of the soil is always being exploited by the trader and the money-lender. . . .
>
> . . . The negro, the half-breed, and the broken planter are the results of Columbus and the four hundred years of triumphant civilisation which we celebrated at Chicago the other day.[52]

The *Education* famously leaves out so much, and while Adams's letters at the time of the Chicago fair say nothing of the African condition, they tantalize with his sense of uncertainty about what the Great White City added up to: "I am puzzled to understand the final impression left [by the Fair] on the average mind of the ignorant rich and the intelligent poor, as to the inward meaning of this dream of beauty." This he wrote to a woman two years older than he, Lucy Baxter, for whom, unlike Elizabeth Cameron, he had no romantic feelings. Former companion to Adams's mother, and outside Adams's social circle, Miss Baxter typically received the honor of Adams's unguarded candor. Don't show this letter or repeat it "to any human being," but burn it, he demanded. "I wonder whether the twenty million visitors carried off the same sense that I did. Probably not. . . . They will think it education. Perhaps it is. Precisely what education is, I don't know. Perhaps to learn chaos when one sees it."[53]

But what had he meant, "You'll not believe it," when telling Elizabeth Cameron that he flirted with talkative sales clerks? What did he mean, "You will never believe it, but I am a good traveller"? He and the charming Ohio-born senator's wife knew each other well; indeed, she was the romance of his life. Why did she not know what he was like, when footloose? Possibly he meant that sometimes he reveled in seeming vexed and even contemptuous. "Why did Matthew Arnold see nothing to interest him in our civilisation?" he wrote, not without irony, just after visiting her in Pennsylvania in 1888. The train between Harrisburg and New York was itself a wonder, "entirely intended and used for the conveyance of Chicago German Jews."[54] Only rarely, when Mrs. Cameron's husband and daughter and friends were along, as in a trip to Mexico City in 1896, did Henry and Elizabeth travel together, enabling her to watch him.[55] In fact, his travels were attempts to put safe distance between them, lest his adoration exceed propriety. Beginning in the mid 1890s they both frequented Paris, but seldom at the same time, Adams occupying Mrs. Cameron's flat there during her absences. He may also have meant that even before the Panic of 1893, the world's lust for wealth had commanded his attention and his epistolary pen. To make too big a thing of pure enjoyment in travel, especially American travel, in the face of mammon-madness, was perhaps to seem frivolous. In London during the Civil War, not knowing if the next letter would tell of the death of his brother in the Army of the Potomac, Henry had forever accepted the burden of his generation's future: "We cannot be commonplace." From Banff Springs in late summer 1894, with the Panic in full sway, the "unlucky hotels all over the Northern and Canadian Pacific routes, are ending a season which has been pure loss from beginning to end."[56] Where, as Adams asked in Chicago, were the American people driving, within their borders and outside?

As to the capacity for enjoyment of travel, not necessarily the physical movement itself but the aesthetic and human surprises, possibly travel was not only in Henry Adams's blood but his eyes and ears from infancy. In childhood he had indelibly taken in "the intense blue of the sea, as he saw it [in summers] a mile or two away, from the Quincy hills." Lawyer Richard Henry Dana, Pacific coast adventurer, was one of his father's three closest friends; Dana "talked well," and at the dinner table "he affected to be still before the mast, a direct, rather bluff, vigorous seaman." Adams's maternal grandfather, Peter Chardon Brooks, had amassed "the largest estate in Boston," largely from the Asia trade and then maritime insurance. And suddenly, in Adams's own teenage years, Americans had been granted permission to enjoy themselves. "Sport as a pursuit was unknown" to Bostonians in Henry Adams's childhood. "Boat-racing came [only] after 1850," when Adams was twelve; much later a nephew would compete in America's Cup trials.[57] If in the 1850s young Henry saw strenuous leisure becoming acceptable among Puritan descendants, in the year 1892 the middle-aged scholar perceived another marker of luxury owing to technology. Returning to Washington after eighteen months around the globe, Adams embarked from Southampton on the *Teutonic*, "an ocean steamer of the new type. . . . That he should have a deck stateroom, with fresh air, and read all night, if he chose, by electric light, was matter for more wonder than life had yet supplied."[58] Twenty years later, as valetudinarian, he would book passage on another advanced liner, the *Titanic*, for its return passage to England from New York.

V

There were three points in his life when Adams's career path became a sort of crossroads, summoning him for the time being at least into serious experimentation as American travelist, if one may coin that term for the travel writer as uncommonly serious inquirer. Three times he had the chance to become the nation's preeminent travel counselor, expositor, ragbag-maker, vinegarist, illustrator.

Adams encountered his first such crossroads in 1867, when, soon to return to the United States after eight years in London, he faced the choice of an occupation. Adams chose freelance Washington journalism—not day-by-day reportage but a "literary career," the observation and historically informed analysis of men in power. He was determined to remain "an independent cuss."[59] Twice for the *North American Review* he produced summary accounts of "The Session" in Congress. The frenetic expansion of the nation beyond the Potomac could not help catching his attention, as it did that of Mark Twain, who in 1873 would designate the era the Gilded Age. Adams's close friend John Hay, in *Abraham Lincoln: A History*, would later point to unbelievable national growth—a net worth in 1870 of $30 million compared to $16 million the year before the Civil War—while the burgeoning of local-color writing showed an array of exotic cultures in the United States.[60] Tycoons coped with sudden new wealth, while struggling "far in the rear" were "millions of immigrants, negroes, and Indians."[61] Adams in 1868 was a well-educated Washington journalist who wanted attention, craved "to be advertised"; he could not go everywhere in the nation but could at least think about it.[62] "[N]ature, geology and Canada" were his prospects (unfulfilled) for a "few weeks" in summer of 1869, while he hoped to go "to the Pacific" two summers hence.[63] Indianapolis and Cincinnati occupied his thoughts sporadically, owing to a dubious railroad investment, important enough for him to confer about it in New York with "the Treasurer of the competing road to St. Louis."[64] With his brother Charles he carried on extended arguments about western investments. Did

"Boston capitalists think that by building railways for Chicago, or sinking copper-mines in Wisconsin, they can double their money"?[65] What we ourselves notice, whether or not Adams yet did: out in Arizona John Wesley Powell was mapping the Grand Canyon, and construction on the Eads Bridge—first span over the Mississippi at St. Louis—had begun in 1867.

In the first of his two "Session" essays Adams briefly considered the question of national scope. America of the future was wider than the actual political boundaries of the nation; the day was "already so near" when the nation would "have to support" first 50 million people and then 100 million, a population now "tolerably homogeneous" but destined to be less so if "popular feeling" in the United States remained as strong as ever for "the absorption into our system of Canada, Mexico, and the West Indies." "[T]he imagination is dazzled" already by Lincoln's acquisition of "Russian America [Alaska], St. Thomas [the future Virgin Islands], and the Isthmus of Darien [Panama]."[66] But the road that Adams took after those two "Sessions" went up from Washington to the city of Boston, his birthplace, where across the river at his alma mater he started teaching young men who wanted Harvard degrees because the diplomas were "worth money" in Chicago.[67]

The second point in Adams's life for delineating the nation in Travels occurred nine years later, in 1877, when, tired of prepping young philistines for the boom years following Chicago's Great Fire, he found himself suddenly handed a treasure, the Albert Gallatin papers. Here, with Jefferson's secretary of the Treasury, a Swiss immigrant who became one of the few exemplary "practical statesmen" of the republic, Adams faced a road difficult not to take. After first compiling Gallatin's *Writings*, he would write Gallatin's life, then tackle the formidable project of creating a historical monument: an account both comprehensive and definitive of the nation's formative years, under Jefferson and Madison. In the passage that Frederick Jackson Turner would quote at length (second epigraph), there had been nature's abundance and exuberance but not exactly a sense of nationality when in 1801 the Monticello Virginian had succeeded Henry's great-grandfather as president. But by 1817, when another Virginia president, James Madison from Montpelier, left office, the country had attained not only a sense of unity but unheard-of power and opportunity. To gather, organize, and contextualize all this—eschewing for the most part vinegar, pepper, and vitriol—meant years at his Washington desk and months in European archives rather than weeks in rail cars or on horseback or aboard river steamers.

A further consideration in 1877, conceivably a deterrent to certain kinds of travel, was marriage. Marian (Clover) Hooper Adams on their wedding journey in 1872 had observed, from Geneva, that "Travelling would be quite perfect if only one could go home at night," and her half-anguished quip of ten years later, concerning the condition of Gilded Age America, would resonate in every book about either Henry James or Henry Adams.[68] James, Europe-bound for good, had bid Clover good-bye by calling her (she reported) "the incarnation of my native land." "Am I then," she jested to her Boston father, "vulgar, dreary, and impossible to live with?"[69] She and Henry read books by travelists; annoyed by a bad one in 1882, she announced that "[i]f we get out of health, or money, or both, we'll go to Spain and write a charming book of travels or die in the attempt."[70] If at all serious—and why not?—this otherwise passing remark, in a letter to her father, represents an early indication that Clover had re-imagined the genre of Travels—even if only in Europe—as a site for literary adventuring. Henry had said as much himself, at Greenwich in 1873, Clover reported; called on for a brief speech at the Bohemian Club, he wryly expressed "the hope that he might some day write a book about England corrresponding to Hepworth Dixon's book on America." Henry's "piece of impertinence was received as a compliment by the thick-skinned Britisher," noted Clover, adding to her father: "Do you remember his [Dixon's] nasty book?"[71] A "nasty" book would be vulgar, different from a vinegary or vitriolic one; in *New America* (1867) Dixon had relished—in page after compulsively readable page—exposing to Britain, as if routine behavior, such salacious American phenomena as free love in the Oneida colony and Mormon marriages, which he characterized as not only polygamous but incestuous.[72]

Indeed, already in 1860 Adams had experimented, writing nine long travel pieces from Italy for a hometown paper, the Boston *Courier*.[73] His wife apparently complaisant, Adams's main deterrent from writing Travels in the 1880s was the disciplined and demanding work of writing history. Clover claimed to crave an excursion into the American West, stimulated by their friend Raphael Pumpelly, geologist and world traveler, who dined with them one April night in 1883. She wrote her father with enthusiasm about Pumpelly's current work with the transcontinental railroad of the North:

> His account of the Great Northwest on the line of the Northern Pacific is like a fairy tale. The line at this end is finished as far

> as Bozeman [south central Montana], near which he has found a great coal field on a mountain; myriads of first-class emigrants are crowding up from California—Germans and Swedes. . . . I've no desire to go abroad again, but should like to go in a director's car over that line to the Pacific when the country is a little more settled up and to the west coast of Mexico in winter, when that country is a little more settled down.[74]

The Northern Pacific would be completed within the year, with Tacoma its Pacific coast terminus, but the road to Mexico (reported Clover in a letter the following week) would not be ready for "three or four years," at which time she and Henry would "take a summer there instead of Beverly," on Boston's North Shore, where they had a summer house.[75] Two years later, in July 1885, five months before she killed herself, she and Henry made plans to camp out in Yellowstone, taking their own horses and tents.[76]

The third point at which Adams should have become an American travelist was the year 1892, when circumstances pushed him in that very direction rather than, as before, deflecting him. Pausing in Paris after his circumnavigation of the globe via Tahiti, he needed fresh work to do to distance himself from the failure of his romance with Elizabeth Cameron. His magisterial *History* had been published, that too a failure in terms of sales, and the natural next step was to turn to the project advanced in his letter to John Hay (third epigraph to this essay): plunge into writing American travels, informed, amusing, scandalous, varied, and inevitably enriched by history and politics. As J. C. Levenson has observed, commenting on Adams's Travels project, he surely, so soon after writing his *History*, had "not unlearned his discipline of scholarly responsibility."[77]

These Travels would ideally be not a solo engagement with the nation but a collaboration with Hay, or, with both Hay and King. Could they be persuaded? "Travels that say anything are nowadays read." King in particular was a plausible collaborator, author twenty years earlier of *Mountaineering in the Sierra Nevada* (1872), the book that pushed Yosemite toward park status, a man always on the go, persona grata with people of all levels in various countries and languages, as Adams later testified, not only in the *Education* but in a warmly anecdotal posthumous tribute to King put together by the Century Club. The formidable difficulty was that King followed geology exclusively, or rather the mining money that followed geology; this meant scrambling unsystematically about the West, the Southwest, the Caribbean, and the wild Wall Street region of

New York, with no time for the richly vulgar, dreary, and unmineraled hinterlands. As for John Hay, difficulty also. He too, twenty years earlier, had published a spirited travel book, *Castilian Days* (1871), on Spain.[78] Adams had pleaded with him in the summer of 1890 to come along to the South Seas, making a threesome with La Farge, bringing if necessary Mrs. Hay and the four children. To this summons the strenuously domesticated Hay responded with a woebegone rejection for not only the present but the future: "I now feel that I shall never go west, and thence east. I shall never see California nor the isles of the sea."[79]

VI

So if undertaken it would have to be done alone, this project of a ragbag of Travels starting with San Francisco and eventually proceeding to England and France. Such a west-to-east itinerary is particularly arresting for several reasons, which may or may not correspond to Adams's thinking. One can see clearly enough, however, how the course would build to an unexpected anticlimax.

First, there was that prominent Boston precursor, the West Coast adventurer Richard Henry Dana, of *Two Years Before the Mast*, intimate friend of the Adams family, not easily erased from childhood impressions. Dana especially resonated with the "future-mindedness"—in William Decker's words—that Adams as a student of Alexis de Tocqueville, John Stuart Mill, and Jefferson "had long made it his business to exemplify."[80] He had already made a study of this Tocqueville who in *Democracy in America* had, except for one synoptic chapter, told readers nothing about *places*. And he had chosen to read the American future into Clarence King's Colorado surveyors when he traveled with them in 1871. The American future had made an appearance in Dana's text some thirty years earlier, captured in the author's view of the Pacific coast in 1835 as he left San Francisco Bay, a passage that one imagines as an irresistible point of departure for Adams's unwritten book of American travels:

> We sailed down this magnificent bay with a light wind, the tide, which was running out, carrying us at the rate of four or five knots. . . . We passed directly under the high cliff on which the presidio is built, and stood into the middle of the bay, from whence we could see small bays making up into the interior, large and beautifully wooded islands, and the mouths of several rivers. If California ever becomes a prosperous country, this bay

> will be the centre of its prosperity. The abundance of wood and water; the extreme fertility of its shores; the excellence of its climate, which is as near to being perfect as any in the world; and its facilities for navigation, affording the best anchoring-grounds in the whole western coast of America—all fit it for a place of great importance.[81]

The future prosperity that Dana envisioned had arrived by the time Henry Adams planned his eastward journey, and so it provides the second excitement in starting American Travels with San Francisco, especially since it was producing appalling results well suited to Adams's mordant irony. Mining wealth and railroad wealth had egregiously encrusted that moist green promontory upon which San Francisco built. "Probably, since human society began," Adams would write in the *Education*, "it had seen no such curious spectacle as the houses of the San Francisco millionaires on Nob Hill."[82] Adams and La Farge had beheld them in 1886, before embarking for Japan; in his *Artist's Letters from Japan*, La Farge referred incisively to "the preposterous dwellings, the vulgar adornments" of San Francisco's elite. In 1888, taking Sir Robert Cunliffe around the country, Adams performed deeper incision, noting that Leland Stanford's house was "astonishing beyond the Yosemite or all the wonders of the wild west. The world never saw such glory. An insane tomcat would be sobered by the Governor's furniture."[83] The editors of Henry Adams's *Letters* could not resist a footnote elucidating what magazine readers of the 1880s had marveled at: "Stanford's two-million-dollar palace on Nob Hill had an Indian room, a Pompeiian room, and a Chinese room. A feature of the art gallery was a circular velvet seat with plants filling the center and, perched on the plants, mechanical birds that sang at the touch of a button."[84] Whatever is overdone is right—that is, fitting and suitable material for Travels—when marinated in the mind of a sojourner who knows his Europe and has seen much of Japan and the South Seas.

Third, to begin his American Travels with San Francisco meant that Adams would go Mark Twain one better. *Roughing It*, twenty years earlier (1871), had brilliantly—if breezily and nostalgically—caught the boomtown at a moment of feverish activity precipitated by the Gold Rush. Now in 1892 arose the moment not only to see the city growing, inflating even, but to situate it as well as satirize it. Beyond the mechanical birds of Nob Hill spread resources Dana had detailed as the necessary future of the city: forests, fishing grounds, climate, shipping facilities. At least some of this Adams could incorporate into his ragbag of "scenery, psychology, history, literature, poetry, art."[85] In particular, literature; no less an authority than William Dean Howells would declare that San Francisco had special standing in the nation's literary history. It was "only after the Civil War that we really began to have an American literature," he would note in 1902, and this literature spoke "in the varying accents of all the different sections—North, East, South, West, and Farthest West." "The San Francisco school [of writers] briefly flourished from 1867 till 1872 or so," he continued, "and while it endured it made San Francisco the first national literary centre we ever had, for its writers were of every American origin except Californian."[86]

Howells named Bret Harte, Mark Twain, and Charles Warren Stoddard as the central figures in the San Francisco school, Harte being of course the writer Adams would famously cite in the *Education* as the only American writer of the century, besides Whitman, who "insisted on the power of sex, as every classic had always done."[87] The companionable Stoddard, least known today of these three, became the best known to Adams. By 1890 Stoddard had moved to Washington, where he taught at the Catholic University, and though not entirely clandestine in his irregular fondness for young men, he quickly became intimate enough with Henry Adams's circle to drop in at those famous noon breakfasts in H Street, even bringing Church dignitaries.[88] His book *South Sea Idyls* served as one of Adams's guides to the South Seas, and when Stoddard left Washington in 1902, Adams twice in letters mentioned publication of Stoddard's "little volume of sketches of his best time."[89] In *Exits and Entrances*, reminiscing about Harte, Stoddard recalled "the halcyon days [of the 1860s] before California had become a health resort and been 'railroaded' to the depths of the commonplace."[90] The three middle terms undergirding Adams's proposed Travels in the letter to Hay—"psychology, history, literature"—set his project up as a balance between the "opinionated" on the one hand and the closely observed and historicized on the other, Adams being uncommonly well equipped for both.

Once having served up San Francisco to his taste, by which of several appealing routes would Adams in 1892 have proceeded eastward across the continent? From the letter of 1894 already cited we know that at that later date he wanted to visit Alaska, his "Russian America" of 1869, but could not wait a fortnight to sail.[91] Now, in no apparent hurry to reach England and France, he could take a railroad car or steamer due north from San Francisco. Equally or more attractive would have been a retracing of the southern route he had taken with Robert Cunliffe in 1888, down to frenzied Los Angeles and then eastward. This would allow for a side trip into Grand Canyon country, the region that had made famous his Washington friend John Wesley Powell, now head of the U.S. Geological Survey.[92] Had he been unwilling to struggle up and down Powell's Colorado River canyons, as with Cunliffe he had "clamber[ed] down and up" the ravine at Idaho's Shoshone Falls, Adams would have found the route due east from San Francisco equally promising, if only because of special connections.[93] Like his brother Brooks twenty years earlier, Henry presumably would have had privileged access to Mormons, owing to his father's aid to them in the 1860s. Kansas City would have welcomed him as the brother of Charles Francis, builder of their great stockyards and prominent real estate developer.[94] In Chicago he still had a friend, civic leader Franklin MacVeagh, grocery wholesaler and litterateur, whose "exquisite house," designed by Adams's Harvard classmate Henry Hobson Richardson, Adams had taken Cunliffe to see in 1888.[95] Cleveland was another city of easy access; John Hay had there met and married his wife Clara and thereafter maintained such close ties that he would be one of the kingmakers when Mark Hanna decided that William McKinley, a fellow Ohioan, should be president. The ungregarious Adams would not, in these cities, have submitted to parties and receptions; instead, his acknowledged status as historian and his contacts in each city would have combined to command a meeting with just about anyone he might have cared to listen to, for views on current matters and on his beloved future.

All this is speculative, these three different American itineraries featuring sublime natural sites and booming cities. We know with certainty, however, the contrast Adams wished to draw to England and France—the aforementioned anticlimax. For American readers, especially Europhiles, the book would end with something of a shock: the Old World cast as hopelessly backward. Adams's literary construction of the ancestral continent would thus salute the irrepressible *Innocents Abroad* (1869) of Mark Twain rather than the stately appreciations of Adams's friend Henry James. "The comforts of European travel in winter fill me with admiration for America," Adams wrote John Hay, continuing on January 11 the letter of 1892 in which he had laid out his "notion of Travels." It had been too cold to sleep on the Calais steamer across the Channel, and the Charing Cross customhouse had "a chill like salted ice." "I can understand that their art should be bad and their literature rotten and their tastes mean, but why the deuce they should inflict on themselves cold and hunger and discomfort, hang me if I can understand." "This is the end!" he continued. "If nothing more has been done in these last thirty years, that have produced our Atlantic steamers and our railway system in America, nothing more need be expected from Europe. The people are stupid. They grow stupider and coarser as their aristocracies disappear."[96] For Mrs. Cameron the same day he undertook vitriolic expansion:

> Thirty years have not made a change in the discomforts of European travel; I should not have known, from anything but the electric light, that our [Civil] war was over, and that I had ceased to belong to the London legation [quitted in 1868]. The Frenchman and Englishman are just where they were thirty years ago, with a certain halo of vulgarity and commonness added to their stupidity. If they had taste! but what little taste they then had has vanished and vulgarised. Thank Christopher Columbus and George Washington who gave us a country where there was nothing to spoil and where man can play what antics he likes without disturbing the ghost of an artist. Well! I am here at last, in Clarges St, with three inches of thick mud everywhere.[97]

Hardships if truly necessary, in unmechanized, unelectrified regions like Cuba and Mexico, were tolerable and even savory; beyond patience, however, were mud and chills persisting unnecessarily in so-called modern Europe. Paris, four years later, still provoked Adams to wrath when he could not find a good breakfast or dinner at restaurants catering to mere American and English palates. "Last year, in the black cañons of the Yellowstone, I was in a better place than this."[98]

So for a travelist the choice evidently was plain. Do either *old* Europe, a pandering and primitive civilization, or tackle a vigorously transitional America, which, like the Jefferson-Madison era before Henry Adams addressed it, still did not have its needed and acute native inscriber.[99] Adams for now, in 1892, was keen for the contemporary—call it transitional or call it chaotic—as the next three years demonstrated when he spent nearly six months in Mexico and the Caribbean. In October 1894, soon to "start for Mexico and the West Indies," he tried once again to rouse a phlegmatic Hay: "Be a hero in the strife! My old idea of writing travels has come back on me. Privately printed."[100] Only the accident, in 1895, of abduction by Cabot and "sister Anne" Lodge, who took him into unexplored regions of old Europe, the Norman churches of France and their Gothic successors, would close out hopes for Travels in America. One hardly wants to charge a major national political figure and his pertinacious wife with nefarious acts, but for the Lodges to drag Henry Adams backward in time, reducing vinegar to the merely avuncular, in *Mont Saint Michel and Chartres*, rather than urge him in the full vigor of his writing life to fix his attention on Frederick Jackson Turner's West, on McKinley and empire, seems nearly impeachable. What spares Nannie and Cabot from calumny is Adams's discovery, to his considerable satisfaction, that old France presaged modern America. "The ultimate cathedral of the 13th century," he told Elizabeth Cameron, " . . . was a Chicago Exposition for God's profit."[101] Four times in the opening paragraph of *Chartres*, Adams put forth the cathedral and the world's fair as representing the "energy" and "industries and interests" of their respective centuries.

VII

His native Boston in desuetude fascinated Adams in the later years of the nineteenth century, as did the rise of Washington, D.C. "One of these days this will be a very great city if nothing happens to it," he wrote to an English friend just after moving back to the nation's capital in 1877. "Even now it is a beautiful one, and its situation is superb."[102] The city's legendary improver, Alexander "Boss" Shepherd, had worked at it imperiously, inspiring one newspaper to predict in 1875 that "Washington is at the beginning of a long period of growth and prosperity, which in a few years will make it one of the most important, as it will be one of the most beautiful, cities in the Union."[103] One might have argued that a travelist in one's own country needs, if not exactly a home, or home base, then at least a place of calm between travels. Washington provided this for Adams, though political strife and posturing, especially in the 1890s, often set his vitriol flowing. By the last of his American travels, his visit to the St. Louis world's fair in 1904, Washington was again on the verge of major improvements, the famous McMillan Commission (which included Adams's friend Augustus Saint-Gaudens) having persuaded Congress to remove unsightly buildings from the Mall and in other respects to attain some of Pierre-Charles L'Enfant's original grandeur. The work was needed; Adams in 1903 complained, "I can't walk half a mile beyond Boundary Street [today's Florida Avenue], in the capital of eighty million people, without getting up to my ankles in mud and breaking my springs in ruts. As for pavements, our great [American] cities are mediaeval." The Rock

Creek area of Washington, wrote Adams in the *Education*—admiring, not objecting—"is as wild as the Rocky Mountains," though admittedly that landscape "carried no hidden horrors of glaciers."[104]

When in 1904 Adams rode in style from Washington to St. Louis with John and Clara Hay (Hay as secretary of state making an official visit), he saw America's modern ugliness from the train window. He had first stayed in St. Louis in 1894, en route to Mexico.[105] Now, as he would report in the *Education*, "Ten years had passed since he last crossed the Mississippi, and he found everything new. In this great region from Pittsburgh through Ohio and Indiana, agriculture had made way for steam; tall chimneys reeked smoke on every horizon, and dirty suburbs filled with scrap-iron, scrap-paper, and cinders, formed the setting of every town. Evidently, cleanliness was not to be the birthmark of the new American."[106] Insistent American contradiction—as at Chicago in 1893, lavish spectacle splashed down in a cultural wasteland—continued to fascinate Adams:

> The St. Louis exposition was [the new American's] first creation in the twentieth century, and, for that reason, acutely interesting. One saw here a third-rate town of half-a-million people without history, education, unity, or art, and with little capital—without even an element of natural interest except the river which it studiously ignored—but doing what London, Paris, or New York would have shrunk from attempting. . . . The world had never witnessed so marvellous a phantasm; . . . as one wandered among long lines of white palaces, exquisitely lighted by thousands on thousands of electric candles, soft, rich, shadowy.[107]

As usual, in his letters Adams was less complimentary and more vinegary. The "insides [of the buildings at St. Louis] were empty. The management was the interest." "The architecture is interesting, but comes straight from the Beaux Arts." Seen from their rooms in a new apartment building, the Buckingham Club, the buildings of the exposition were "recklessly illuminated at night." Adams's young niece Abigail, guest of Hay's guest Henry Adams, remembered having "several good laughs over the art exhibitions" with her uncle. From Abigail we learn that Adams, while with Hay's entourage, saw on a river excursion the site north of St. Louis where the grand Missouri River joined the epic Mississippi.[108]

St. Louis, viewed skeptically by Adams in 1904, had decades earlier suggested itself as a locus for his whole future life: Adams the lawyer, he had anticipated, would grow up with the West. "As for my plan of life, it is simple," he had written brother Charles in 1858,

> and . . . I see no reason why it should not be carried out. . . . Two years in Europe; two years studying law in Boston; and then I propose to emigrate and practice at Saint Louis. What I can do there, God knows; but I have as theory that an educated and reasonably able man can make his mark if he chooses.[109]

This "theory" of personal westward settlement and success may have been only a passing notion, the zeitgeist speaking through a human subject, as theories sometimes do. But reasons emerge for thinking it more than casual in Adams's mind. Historian John Brinckerhoff Jackson sums up St. Louis in the years immediately after the Civil War:

> St. Louis had many claims to being the largest truly American city, though fourth in rank in population after New York, Brooklyn, and Philadelphia. In many respects it was indeed the center of the nation; it stood in the midst of the very richest and most productive agricultural country; it was the terminus of routes from the West and Southwest, and the Mississippi linked it with the Northwest and the South. . . . [I]ts cultural activity was distinguished. Its fine botanical garden, the "wonder of the West," was widely known; its parks—including the oldest public park west of the Mississippi—were not surpassed by those of any other city.[110]

Moreover, these river cities were not remote, as Henry's own father, hardly an adventurer, had long ago proven. In 1844, in slavery days, traveling as the self-described "passive" companion of future Boston mayor Josiah Quincy, Charles Francis Adams had taken a Mississippi River steamboat from Quincy, Illinois ("inhabited mainly by New England people," situated just above Hannibal, Missouri), to Davenport, Iowa, stopping in Nauvoo for an interview with the Mormon leader Joseph Smith and a tour of his massive new "stone temple."

Sixty years later, in 1904, Henry's journey through fin-de-siècle smoke and suburbs to St. Louis, the last of his journeys away from the East, again made it clear that Adams's need to know his North America had much to do with its fast-increasing accessibility. "The generation between 1865 and 1895 was already [in 1868] mortgaged to the railways," he would observe in the *Education*, "and no one knew it better than the generation itself." He himself "had been born with the railway system; had grown up with it; had been over pretty nearly every mile of it with curious eyes, and knew as much about it as his neighbors."[111] Seductive and myth-making, rails and locomotives had linked East Coast and West successively in 1869, 1881, 1883, and 1889. One exuberant modern historian proclaims that the Golden Spike at Promontory Point "ranks with the signing of the Declaration of Independence in American history."[112] Yet of course few Americans were as privileged as Adams, who, as neither drummer nor developer, indulged a disinterested curiosity to see exactly where these rails led, mile after Pullman mile. The trip with John Hay to St. Louis employed a private car provided by Alexander Cassatt, president of the Pennsylvania Railroad.[113] Adams when finishing his *Education* could not resist a sly rebuke to his comparatively untraveled host. Though raised in Lincoln's Illinois, Hay visiting St. Louis had been "as strange to the Mississippi River as though he had not been bred on its shores," referring to the village of Warsaw, forty miles north of Sam Clemens's Hannibal.[114]

BEWARE, as travel theorist Caren Kaplan has advised, of some universal model of the travel experience: "[T]he tourist is as time bound and historically constructed as any other trope."[115] Indeed, Adams, born 1838, dying in 1918, was poised to experience American regions during various phases of startling change. As we have seen, Adams's need to know his America had surely something to do with the passions of men such as Clarence King and John Wesley Powell; also his Quincy boyhood friend, the geologist Frank Emmons (member of King's survey); also Adams's entrepreneurial brother Charles, who had his own need to know—to read decisively those cities where Americans would be fruitful and multiply, in order that he might develop and promote them. On the emerging maps of this vast land, new marks rapidly appeared, to stand for rails, concrete, smokestacks. Remote places suddenly became familiar, while familiar places took strange shapes. One railroad historian, Sarah H. Gordon, opens her book, about railroads transforming American life for a century, with an epigraph by Henry Adams (from the *History*) and goes on to acclaim his accurate reading of the future. While Adams in the *Education* saw the railroad system as "on the whole . . . satisfy[ing] the wants of society better than any other part of the social machine," he also "predicted the demise of the railroad at a time when most people were still 'satisfied' with it."[116] Moreover, his remark about the century being "mortgaged" to the railroads has since become "famous," another railroad historian notes approvingly.[117]

In the American past, men—and a few women—had made marks that remained visible as traces only by the era of Adams's adulthood, such as the journey of the celebrated Lewis and Clark, of course, and historian Francis Parkman, a family friend who laid out routes Adams apparently took no interest in following. Instead, one glimpses the cryptic but easily forgettable figure of Laura Towne, a woman of consequence left without a voice in an unwritten chapter of Adams's Travels. Such a volume should have emerged from Adams's several visits—at least five, by 1896—to Sen. James Donald Cameron's South Carolina folly, the old plantation known as Coffin's Point, on the sea island St. Helena, east of Beaufort. In 1862, Miss Towne, thirteen years older than Adams, had boldly ventured from Philadelphia to St. Helena to set up Penn School for the slaves abandoned on the plantations as their masters went to war. Henry's future brother-in-law, Ned Hooper, age twenty-two, also "volunteered to work without pay at the Port Royal Experiment," in Eugenia Kaledin's words, "where the most sober members of the Boston anti-slavery community" worked with other Northerners "to try to establish a working example of successful Negro independence . . . by reorganizing agriculture and educating everybody in a systematic manner."[118]

Miss Towne had stayed on St. Helena, and thirty years later Ned Hooper was corresponding with her. In 1893, when Hooper and two of his daughters went with Henry Adams to spend a week at Coffin's Point, they planned to visit her.[119] But did they follow through? If so, what did Henry's two nieces think, and how did the uncle as historian explain what the agonizing years of the 1860s meant in South Carolina, to both blacks and whites? Some hints crop up in other sources, such as a footnote in John Hay's history of Lincoln. The note records an anecdote passed on "immediately after it happened" by Ned Hooper—a story from the sea islands that became oft-told, of how a young African American wished to gaze upon Lincoln, savior: "A gray-headed negro rebuked the rash aspiration: 'No man see Linkum. Linkum walk as Jesus walk—no man see Linkum.'"[120] How then would all this fit into Adams's unwritten Travels in South Carolina, together with such St. Helena exotica as "roasting oysters and potatoes in bonfires" and catching crabs in the creek, digging in ancient mounds and "Indian shell-heaps," and rising to dress in an unheated beach cottage in forty degree weather—acted out on the estate of a Pennsylvania Republican senator who favored Cuban independence from Spain but who also tried to gratify every wish that captains of American industry might express?[121]

One could similarly flesh out other traces. That historical adventure of 1888, adumbrated by John Hay, in a letter to W. D. Howells: "[Clarence] King, Adams and I have been making a little trip into Virginia—which was extremely enjoyable. At Williamsburg our hotel-keeper showed us some charming old family portraits. . . . We spent a day at Fredericksburg also, and 'realized' that horrible battle field." That visit a year later to North Carolina, with two male friends, passing "ten days knocking about Body [Bodie] Island Light, and investigating Raleigh's lost colony."[122]

VIII

Adams in the prime of life had experienced not only Oregon mountain summits, southwestern deserts with air "like champagne" and "with devils standing over them with arms stretched out, calling themselves some kind of cactus," and the Teton range in Wyoming where "[f]ew travellers, and probably no tourists have ever been," but also the beginning of one of the great American land booms, the parceling of Florida "forest and swamp" into lots for bungalows and for extravagant faux European hotels.[123] He had stayed four nights at the huge Ponce de Leon Hotel in St. Augustine the year it opened, 1888, and had gone on to Winter Park, Kissimmee, remoter Narcoosee to visit friends of his late wife, and then to Tampa, John Hay accompanying him as far as Winter Park.[124] With Theodore Dwight, former State Department librarian (and one of Charles Stoddard's gay confidants), he went on to Cuba, returning through Key West and again Tampa.[125] In 1893, two years after the huge fake-Moorish Tampa Bay Hotel opened, he stayed there after another ramble in Cuba.[126] In 1894, after relishing Cuba once again, especially the high coffee plantations, but being bored in Nassau, he stopped in Jacksonville before dining in Savannah with relatives of a friend and then joined Clarence King to see the "phosphate works" in Charleston, South Carolina.[127]

Clearly this America, this "subject which none understood" in 1800, had become more adequately pieced together by the time Adams in 1907 privately printed his *Education* in Theodore Roosevelt's Washington. Yet without articles or essays or monographs from Adams we have only a rudimentary sense of how, inimitably, he as coast-to-coast travelist would have made the nation understood—and perhaps even made it understand. Inferences drawn from his letters and from the *Education* do not suffice, since neither epistolary writing nor autobiographical writing is necessarily an adequate vessel for the travelist sensibility. Both tone and content in Travels, as in other genres, need to be custom-crafted, subordinated neither to one's life trajectory (the *Education*) nor to a correspondent. An autobiography, for example, should not have illustrations, if we can generalize from Adams's instructions to Henry Cabot Lodge, barring "the introduction of all illustrations" when the *Education* was published in a trade edition. "Always" in his writings, he told Lodge, he had wanted to make the reader "think only of the text."[128] By contrast, Travels offered Adams the chance, at least, for experiment. Possibly American Travels needed some sort of visual element either integrated or accompanying, as Adams seemed to indicate in 1894 to one of his wife's nieces, Mabel Hooper, who became a painter and would marry a painter, a son of John La Farge. "You ought to have been with us in the Yellowstone country this summer. . . . I wanted you there to sketch for me. I was quite sick in spirit that I could not catch a tone of the country, for it was American to the very snow. I was amused to find that when I went round through Canada to see the Selkirk glacier, it turned out to be distinctly European,—very fine indeed, but not in the least like the American. I wanted awfully to be an artist."[129]

In Adams's unwritten travel book(s) of America there would likely have been at least a few of the esthetic touches that he craved from Canada's Selkirk Glacier, since he moved about with an alert eye, dexterous hand, and—sometimes—a box of paints. The editors of his *Letters* reproduce in color seven of his watercolors from South Carolina, Cuba, and Wyoming.[130] With Clarence King as collaborator, he would have had an alert eye as well as able language; biographer Thurman Wilkins has noted of *Mountaineering in the Sierra Nevada* that "King's descriptions read like the prose of an articulate art historian writing of richly executed landscape paintings."[131] One word-picture in Adams's *Education* paints the dogwood, judas-tree, azalea, and laurel during the month of May, in Maryland near Washington, an "intermixture of delicate grace and passionate depravity"—the passage famously drawn upon by T. S. Eliot in writing "Gerontion."[132] In one letter, Adams described to Scots friends the woods of the Washington area "all painted by Turner in his late period"—a world "all the more [lovely] because no painter ever discovered it."[133] In his pseudonymous novel of 1884, *Esther*, one of Adams's two heroines is a charming and good-natured daughter of the West, Catherine Brooke, who possesses her creator's alert eye. Bantering with bright and artistic new friends, young men and women of New York City, with whom she "became a favorite on the spot," she makes a vow not entirely comic: "When we come home from Europe," she tells them, "I am going to buy a cattle ranche in Colorado and run it myself. . . . I mean to have ten thousand head, and when you see them you will say that they are better worth painting than all the saints and naiads round the Mediterranean."[134]

NOTES

1. Henry Adams, *History of the United States of America during the First Administration of Thomas Jefferson* (1889; New York, 1930), 1:4. "One of the few books of travel which will always retain value for New Englanders," said Adams in the *History*, "was written by President Dwight to describe his vacation rambles; and although in his own day no one would have ventured to insult him by calling these instructive volumes amusing, the quaintness which here and there gave color to the sober narrative had a charm of its own" (1:100).
2. *Atlantic Monthly* 78(1896):293
3. In *The Letters of Henry Adams*, ed. J. C. Levenson et al. (Cambridge, Mass, 1982–1988), 3:598f.
4. Henry Adams to Elizabeth Cameron, May 22, 1904, in *Letters*, 5:588.
5. Henry Adams, *The Education of Henry Adams* (Boston, 1918), 396.
6. Alexis de Tocqueville, *Democracy in America*, 2:166.
7. HA to Charles Milnes Gaskell, June 14, 1903, in *Letters*, 5:501. Adams did not use an automobile while in Washington, as shortly after the turn of the century the vehicle began to gain general use. But as early as 1901, and for several years thereafter, he did have one in Paris, where he spent some portion of of the year. His motoring adventures are recounted by Viola Hopkins Winner, who points out that the auto began infusing his letters with new imagery. Adams, as Winner wrote, applied his future-oriented mind to the automobile, insisting not only that the United States needed more and better roads but that mere widening would not serve; the auto "must have its own roads, not on grade." HA to Gaskell, June 18, 1903, in *Letters*, 5:504. In the last summer of his life, 1917, he did make use of an automobile and chauffeur while at his cottage in Beverly Farms, Massachusetts. HA to Mabel Hooper La Farge, May 23, 1917, in *Letters*, 6:753. In the month of his death, March 1918, he complained that his "once quiet study" on H Street in Washington was "pervaded by rampant automobiles." HA to Elizabeth Cameron, Mar. 1, 1918, 6:789.
8. HA to John Hay, Jan. 27, 1895, in *Letters*, 4:252.
9. In 1974 the Société des Océanistes in Paris published a 450-page volume, *Lettres des Mers du Sud*, printing Adams's letters from the South Seas, demonstrating their coherence as a narrative.
10. HA, *Education*, 369.
11. HA, *History*, 3:216.
12. HA to Elizabeth Cameron, Mar. 12, 1898, in *Letters*, 4:547.
13. HA to Elizabeth Cameron, Mar. 12, 1898, in *Letters*, 4:547.
14. HA to Elizabeth Cameron, Feb. 8, 1895, in *Letters*, 4:253.
15. HA to Charles Francis Adams, Sr., Feb. 4, 1865, in *Letters*, 1:468–469.
16. HA to Charles Milnes Gaskell, Apr. 23, 1865; HA to Charles Francis Adams, Jr., May 10, 1865, in *Letters*, 1:492, 495.
17. HA to Elizabeth Cameron, Sept. 13, 1890, in *Letters*, 3:280.
18. HA, *Education*, 410, 412, 413.
19. HA, *Education*, 414, 415.
20. HA to Elizabeth Cameron, July 29, 1894, in *Letters*, 4:206.
21. HA, *Education*, 350; HA to Elizabeth Cameron, Sept. 25, 1894, in *Letters*, 4:208–211.
22. HA to Charles Francis Adams, Jr., Sept. 24, 1894, in *Letters*, 4:209.

23. HA to Charles Milnes Gaskell, Dec. 12, 1886; HA to Ward Thornton, Aug. 11, 1888, in *Letters*, 3:49, 134.
24. HA to Louisa Hooper, May 5, 1898, in *Letters*, 4:584.
25. HA to Charles Francis Adams, Jr., Apr. 22, 1859, in *Letters*,1:39.
26. Charles Francis Adams, Jr., to Charles Francis Adams, Sr., Nov. 26, 1861, in *A Cycle of Adams Letters, 1861–1865*, ed. Worthington Chauncy Ford (Boston, 1920), 1:72.
27. Charles Francis Adams, Jr., to HA, Jan. 23, 1863, in *Cycle*, 1:240.
28. HA to Lucy Baxter, Mar. 11, 1895, *Supplement to the Letters of Henry Adams: Letters Omitted from the Harvard University Press Edition*, ed. J. C. Levenson et al. (Boston, 1989), 1895:12.
29. Robert Rowlette, "William D. Howells' 1899 Midwest Lecture Tour," *American Literary Realism* 9(1976):5; Thomas Wortham, "W. D. Howells' 1899 Midwest Lecture Tour," *American Literary Realism* 11 (1978):266. For Howells's 1899 lecture tour rendering him "perfectly astonished at the vastness and extent of this great west" (Rowlette, "Lecture Tour," 19f.), see also Harrison T. Meserole, "The Dean in Person: Howells' Lecture Tour," *Western Humanities Review* 10(1956):337–347; and Wortham, "Lecture Tour." Howells acknowledged himself a belated Western traveler to an interviewer from the Topeka *State Journal*, Nov. 8, 1899. Robert Rowlette, "Addenda to Halfmann: Six New Howells Interviews," *American Literary Realism* 8(1975):102.
30. Sheldon Novick, *Henry James: The Young Master* (New York, 1996), 227, 229; Henry James, Nov. 25, 1881, *The Complete Notebooks of Henry James*, ed. Leon Edel and Lyall H. Powers (New York, 1987), 214 (emphasis in original).
31. In January 1883 the temperature was twenty below, but their father's estate needed settling, Henry as executor. William James, *The Correspondence of William James*, ed. Ignas K. Skrupskelis and Elizabeth M. Berkeley (Charlottesville, Va., 1992), 1:357. The Europeanized Henry James needed temporary behavior modification, as William James in London had briskly advised: when in Milwaukee, "[b]e as American & homely as you can in your ways, & it will go off best." William James to Henry James, in *Correspondence*, 1:347.
32. Henry James, *The American Scene* (1905; Bloomington, Ind., 1968), 366.
33. HA to Charles Milnes Gaskell, June 20, 1871, in *Letters*, 2:112.
34. HA, *Education*, 309, 313; HA to Charles Milnes Gaskell, Aug. 13, 1871, in *Letters*, 2:114–115.
35. Arthur Beringause, *Brooks Adams: A Biography* (New York, 1955), 47f.
36. HA, *Education*, 309.
37. Edward Chase Kirkland, *Charles Francis Adams, Jr., 1835–1915: The Patrician at Bay* (Cambridge, Mass., 1965), 72–74.
38. HA to Charles Milnes Gaskell, Apr. 25, 1886, in *Letters*, 3:8.
39. HA to Theodore F. Dwight, June 11, 1886; HA to John Hay, June 11, 1886, in *Letters*, 3:10, 11, 12.
40. Richard Henry Dana, Jr., *Two Years Before the Mast* (1840; New York, 1936), 244–248, 419.
41. Edward Chalfant, *Both Sides of the Ocean: A Biography of Henry Adams: His First Life, 1838–1862* (Hamden, Conn., 1982), 521.
42. HA to Charles Scribner, Nov. 29, 1888; HA to Charles Milnes Gaskell, Oct. 28, 1888; HA to Abigail Brooks Adams, Nov. 14, 1888, in *Letters*, 3:159, 150, 155.
43. HA to Abigail Brooks Adams, Nov. 14, 1888; HA to Charles Scribner, Nov. 29, 1888, in *Letters*, 3:155, 159.
44. John F. Sears, *Sacred Places: American Tourist Attractions in the Nineteenth Century* (New York, 1989), 130, 123.

45. *Los Angeles: A Guide to the City and Its Environs* (New York, 1941), 43f.
46. On both the 1886 and 1888 rail trips across the country Henry's brother Charles Francis was at times with or near the party, in 1886 making the entire trip back to Boston from San Francisco with Henry Adams and La Farge. Because of Charles's national prominence, newspapers often noted his sojourn in town. One item appeared in the "Personal News" column of the Los Angeles *Times*, Oct. 17, 1886:

    > Hon. Charles Francis Adams, President of the Union Pacific Railroad Company, is expected to arrive by to-day's steamer from the north with C. A. Whittier and E. Canfield of Boston in his party [these are railroad men, not Henry Adams and John La Farge incognito]. They stopped at Santa Barbara a couple of days on their way down. Their private car arrived from San Francisco yesterday, and was sent down to San Pedro [the port of Los Angeles] to meet them. The distinguished party will go east by the Atlantic and Pacific line to-morrow. (5)

    On Oct. 12, 1888, as Adams and Cunliffe headed west, the Chicago *Tribune* devoted two column inches to Charles Francis Adams's presence "in the city yesterday," en route back to Boston after visting Omaha on Union Pacific affairs (9). Five days later, on Oct. 17, Henry Adams explained in a letter that he and Robert Cunliffe had been picked up in Chicago by Charles's railroad car, which "happened to be returning empty from Boston" after delivering Charles there (HA to Elizabeth Cameron, Oct. 17, 1888, in *Letters*, 3:149).
47. HA to Elizabeth Cameron, Sept. 13, 25, 1894, in *Letters*, 4:208, 211.
48. HA to Elizabeth Cameron, Sept. 13, 1894, in *Letters*, 4:208.
49. HA, *Education*, 339; HA to John Hay, Oct. 18, 1893, in *Letters*, 4:134.
50. HA, *Education*, 343.
51. Willam McFeely, *Frederick Douglass* (New York, 1991), 369f.
52. HA to Charles Milnes Gaskell, Feb. 16, 1895, in *Letters*, 4:259.
53. HA to Lucy Baxter, Oct. 18, 1893, in *Letters*, 4:132–133.
54. HA to Elizabeth Cameron, June 10, 1888, in *Letters*, 3:120. Matthew Arnold's posthumous article "Civilisation in the U.S." (*Nineteenth Century* 134[1888]:481–496) received considerable response from the U.S. literary and journalistic press. Arnold addressed seriously the commonplace word *interesting*, proposing that "the great sources of the *interesting* are distinction [or 'elevation'] and beauty" (488), which American civilization lacked (495). "He might have found new things to say," Adams complained to an old friend, Sir Robert Cunliffe (soon to tour the United States with Adams), "for there are many things to observe here, but he was past the age of observation and reproduced only his own formulas." HA to Cunliffe, May 27, 1888, in *Letters*, 3:115. Arnold's impressions of the United States derived from his 1883–1884 lecture tour, his only visit to the United States, a five-month exploration taking him westward as far as Detroit, Chicago, and St. Louis. See John Henry Raleigh, *Matthew Arnold and American Culture* (Berkeley, 1957). The Arnolds had dined in the Adamses' house in Washington on Christmas Day 1883. HA to Elizabeth Cameron, Dec. 25, 1883, in *Letters*, 2:524. The article, drawing belatedly on Arnold's impressions, judged that "[i]n the long-settled States east of the Alleghanies the landscape in general is not interesting, the climate harsh and in extremes," while

    > [i]n the valley of the Connecticut you will find farm after farm which the Yankee settler has abandoned in order to go West, leaving the farm to some new Irish immigrant. The charm of beauty which comes from ancientness and permanence of rural life the country could not yet have in a high degree, but it has it in an even less degree than might be expected.

Arnold went on with qualms of deprivation long since expressed by Hawthorne and Henry James:

> If we in England were without the cathedrals, parish churches, and castles of the catholic and feudal age, and without the houses of the Elizabethan age, but had only the towns and buildings which the rise of our middle class has created in the modern age, we should be in much the same case as the Americans. We should be living with much the same absence of training for the sense of beauty through the eye, from the aspect of outward things. The American cities have hardly anything to please a trained or a natural sense for beauty. They have buildings which cost a great deal of money and produce a certain effect—. . . such as our Midland Station at St. Pancras. (488)

55. HA to Anna Cabot Mills Lodge, Apr. 25, 1896, in *Supplement*, 1896:12.
56. HA to Charles Francis Adams, Jr., July 17, 1893; HA to Elizabeth Cameron, Sept. 13, 1894, in *Letters*, 1:371, 4:209.
57. HA, *Education*, 8, 29f., 23, 38; HA to Elizabeth Cameron, Apr. 5, 1914, in *Letters*, 6:647.
58. HA, *Education*, 318f.
59. HA to John Bright, Feb. 3, 1869; HA to Charles Francis Adams, Jr., Dec. 24, 1867, in *Letters*, 2:18, 1:561.
60. John G. Nicolay and John Hay, *Abraham Lincoln: A History* (New York, 1890), 10:340.
61. HA, *Education*, 237.
62. HA to Charles Francis Adams, Jr., Jan. 22, 1869, in *Letters*, 2:13.
63. HA to Charles Milnes Gaskell, Mar. 30, Sept. 13, 1869, in *Letters*, 2:23, 44.
64. HA to Charles Francis Adams, Jr., Nov. 23, Dec. 13, 1861, Apr. 21, 1868, Jan. 8, 18, 22, June 22, 1869, in *Letters*, 1:570; 2:8–10, 13, 38.
65. HA to Charles Francis Adams, Jr., July 30, 1867, in *Letters*, 1:542.
66. Henry Adams, "The Session," in *The Great Secession Winter of 1860–61 and Other Essays*, ed. George Hochfield (New York, 1958), 64, 80. First published in *North American Review* 108(1869):610–640.
67. HA, *Education*, 305f.
68. Marian Hooper Adams to Robert William Hooper, Aug. 23, 1872, in *The Letters of Mrs. Henry Adams, 1863–1883*, ed. Ward Thoron (Boston, 1986), 29.
69. Marian Hooper Adams to Robert William Hooper, May 14, 1882, in *Letters of Mrs. Henry Adams*, 384. The running exchange between Clover Adams and Henry James, as to the propriety of his becoming even more Europeanized (likely to be "spoiled by injudicious old ladies in London"), had produced at one point her suggestion, expressed in a letter to her father, that Henry James "had better go to Cheyenne & run a hog ranch." Marian Hooper Adams to Robert William Hooper, Aug. 31, 1879; Eugenia Kaledin, *The Education of Mrs. Henry Adams* (Philadelphia, 1981), 161.
70. Marian Hooper Adams to Robert William Hooper, May 7, 1882, in *Letters of Mrs. Henry Adams*, 381f.
71. Marian Hooper Adams to Robert William Hooper, June 29, 1873, in *Letters of Mrs. Henry Adams*, 124.
72. William Hepworth Dixon, *New America* (London, 1869), 2:179, 190. Adams's metaphors of vitriol and vinegar, like his motoring tropes, hint that his unwritten Travels might have explored new frontiers of imagery. "You and I have had our minds fairly soaked," he wrote his brother Charles, finishing his *History* before leaving for the South Seas, "with the kerosene of American ideas and interests, until we can neither absorb more, nor even retain what we have. Nausea has set in, and we might as well wash the nasty stuff out of

us now, as let it make us sick. . . . I should be mighty glad to be certain that one form of nausea [i.e., experience with a different culture] would drive away another, and that in six months I should come back fit and good for ten years more work." July 3, 1890, in *Letters*, 3:246f. His absence extended thirteen and a half months, and it was at the end of this time that he proposed to Hay that they collaborate on American Travels. Kerosene, trade mark for an early petroleum derivative, had been first distilled in Boston (though not named there) in 1852, when Henry was in his early teens.

73. For a discussion of these, see Ernest Samuels, *The Young Henry Adams* (Cambridge, Mass., 1948), 69–74; Chalfant, *Both Sides of the Ocean*, 144–180; and William W. Stowe, "Henry Adams, Traveler," *New England Quarterly* 64(1991):181–185. Samuels has suggested that a book by Henry's grandfather John Quincy Adams, *Letters on Silesia: Written during a Tour of That Country in the Years 1800, 1801*, is a possible model for Henry's Italian letters (34). Chalfant has proposed that these numbered letters of Adams constitute a travel book, *A Journey to Italy* (158).
74. Marian Hooper Adams to Robert William Hooper, Apr. 22, 1883, in *Letters of Mrs. Henry Adams*, 442.
75. Marian Hooper Adams to Robert William Hooper, Apr. 29, 1883, in *Letters of Mrs. Henry Adams*, 444.
76. Patricia O'Toole, *The Five of Hearts: An Intimate Portrait of Henry Adams and His Friends, 1880–1918* (New York, 1990), 152. Marian Hooper Adams on her mother's side had a notable West Coast adventurer as grandfather, as Ward Thoron explains in appendix 1 of *The Letters of Mrs. Henry Adams*. Capt. William Sturgis (1782–1863) at age sixteen "decided, like his father, to 'follow the sea' as a profession," and after five years on the Pacific coast and in China he returned to Boston as a ship's captain, soon returning to sea until 1810. He then formed a business partnership "which for the next forty years did more than half the trade from the United States with the coast of the Pacific and China" (466). Clover's father, Dr. Robert Hooper, owned Sturgis's journal, which in 1883 she lent to John Wesley Powell, head of the U.S. Geological Survey in Washington, who wished to publish extracts concerning "vocabulary" (of Native languages, presumably) and "the value of fur trade" (405).
77. J. C. Levenson, *The Mind and Art of Henry Adams* (Boston,1957), 235.
78. Adams may or may not have considered the extent to which defamiliarizing would be a project of his proposed Travels: the rendering of U.S. politics and ideologies and social formations as exotic to some degree, or as less exceptionalist than American readers might generally take them to be. In the *History* his diminishing of the great Lewis and Clark expedition had shown him willing to be a provocative defamiliarizer. The same is true of John Hay in *Castilian Days* (1871; Boston, 1903), who had included a passage in which Europe sees the United States as a strange and volatile place, politically wholly illegible: I fell into conversation with Señor ———, one of the best minds in Spain, an enlightened though conservative statesman. He said: "It is hard for Europe to adopt a settled belief about you. America is a land of wonders, of contradictions. One party calls your system freedom, another anarchy. In all legislative assemblies of Europe, republicans and absolutists alike draw arguments from America. But what cannot be denied are the effects, the results. These are evident, something vast and grandiose, a life and movement to which the Old World is a stranger." (191)
79. HA to John Hay, July 14, 1890, in *Letters*, 3:252; John Hay, *Life and Letters of John Hay*, ed. William Roscoe Thayer (New York, 1915), 2:80.
80. William Merrill Decker, *The Literary Vocation of Henry Adams* (Chapel Hill, 1990), 223.
81. Dana, *Two Years Before the Mast*, 243.

82. HA, *Education*, 328.
83. HA to Elizabeth Cameron, Aug. 19, 1888, in *Letters*, 3:135.
84. Levenson et al., *Letters*, 3:155–156n.
85. HA to John Hay, Jan. 9, 1892, in *Letters*, 3:599f.
86. William Dean Howells, *Literature and Life: Studies* (New York, 1902), 175, 176.
87. HA, *Education*, 385.
88. Roger Austen, *Genteel Pagan: The Double Life of Charles Warren Stoddard*, ed. John W. Crowley (Amherst, Mass., 1991), 132–135, 140f.
89. HA to Elizabeth Cameron, Mar. 29, Apr. 5, 1903, in *Letters*, 5:479, 481.
90. Charles Warren Stoddard, *Exits and Entrances* (Boston, 1903), 239. The Henry Adams library at the Massachusetts Historical Society includes a presentation copy of *Exits and Entrances*, which librarian Mary E. Fabiszewski has kindly located: "To Henry Adams with the love of his devoted friend Chas. Warren Stoddard."
91. HA to Elizabeth Cameron, Sept. 13, 1894, in *Letters*, 4:208.
92. It was an intellectual friendship; the two men had been among the founders of the Cosmos Club in Washington, a gathering of men in the capital taking an interest in science. It is Adams, in fact, long interested in geology, whom a western writer, Wallace Stegner, admiringly pairs with Powell throughout his vigorous narrative, *Beyond the Hundredth Meridian*, depicting Powell's explorations and his later role in conceptualizing and advancing "government science." "Adams saw more, and saw it more acutely, than any of his contemporaries," explains Stegner, of this important meeting of the minds in dispassionate service of the future. "He was one of the few non-scientists who understood the importance and the implications of the developing scientific bureaus in Washington." Stegner, *Beyond the Hundredth Meridian: John Wesley Powell and the Second Opening of the West* (1954; New York, 1992), 249.
93. HA to Elizabeth Cameron, Nov. 4, 1888, in *Letters*, 3:152.
94. Daniel Serda has recently concluded that "[h]ad {Charles Francis} Adams failed to take a personal interest in the stockyards, St. Joseph {Missouri} or Omaha would surely have surpassed Kansas City as the nation's second largest meat-packing center." Serda, "Boston Investors and the Early Development of Kansas City, Missouri," lecture in "Midcontinent Perspectives" series, Midwest Research Institute, Kansas City, Jan. 23, 1992; PDF available at Western Historical Manuscript Collection-Kansas City, http://www.umkc.edu/whmckc/publications/mcp/mcppdf/serda-1-23-92.pdf, p. 10 (accessed Nov. 10, 2004). Adams "began investing in Kansas City in 1869," and in 1874 purchased controlling interest in the stockyards (4); he remained a company director till 1913 (10). So strong was his commitment to the West that he sent his twin sons to Idaho (after their 1898 Harvard graduation) to manage a real estate development project there (8). Walt Whitman, who admired really big things, had in 1879 enthused over the stockyards: "In Kansas City I had visited a packing establishment that kills and packs an average of 2,500 hogs a day, the whole year round, for export." Whitman, *Speciman Days* (1882; New York, 1961), 210.
95. HA to John Hay, July 1, 1892, in *Letters*, 4:36; Levenson et al., *Letters*, 3:148n; HA to Elizabeth Cameron, Oct. 17, 1888, in *Letters*, 3:149. Franklin MacVeagh, later secretary of the Treasury in William Howard Taft's administration, had settled in Chicago in 1866 and by 1874 was president of the Chicago Citizens' Association, devoted to civic improvement. That same year he became a founding member of the Chicago Literary Club, delivering eight papers before the group from 1884 to 1906, and serving as president in 1906–1907; his membership extended sixty-one years. Adams's letter to MacVeagh, May 26, 1893, in *Letters*, 4:102f, on first looking into Chicago's heroic fair, is perhaps his most vigorous confession of amazement. On Apr. 28, 1919, a year after Adams's death, the

Literary Club heard a paper on "The Work of Henry Adams," by Edwin Herbert Lewis, professor at a small Chicago college.

96. HA to John Hay, Jan. 9, 1892, in *Letters*, 3:599–600.
97. HA to Elizabeth Cameron, Jan. 11, 1892, in *Letters*, 3:601.
98. HA to Elizabeth Cameron, Sept. 3, 1895, in *Letters*, 4:317.
99. Why old Europe had become increasingly less attractive as a subject for Travels would receive thoughtful treatment from W. D. Howells ten years later:

> There are some sorts of of light literature once greatly in demand, but now apparently no longer desired by magazine editors, who ought to know what their readers desire. Among these is the travel sketch, to me a very agreeable kind, and really to be regretted in its decline. There are some reasons for its decline besides a change of taste in readers, and a possible surfeit. Travel itself has become so universal that everybody, in a manner, has been everywhere, and the foreign scene has no longer the charm of strangeness. We do not think the Old World either so romantic or so ridiculous as we used; and perhaps from an instinctive perception of this altered mood writers no longer appeal to our sentiment or our humor with sketches of outlandish people and places. (Howells, *Literature and Life*, 26–27.)

100. HA to Charles Francis Adams, Jr., Nov. 30, 1894; HA to John Hay, Oct. 12, 1894, in *Letters*, 4:227, 225. In the first clause here, Brooks quoted from Longfellow's "A Psalm of Life."
101. HA to Elizabeth Cameron, Sept. 18, 1895, in *Letters*, 4:326.
102. HA to Charles Milnes Gasekll, Nov. 25, 1877, in *Letters*, 2:326.
103. Michael Farquhar, "The City's Pretty New Face: 'Boss' Shepherd Got the Job Done—at a Steep Price," *Washington Post*, Nov. 28, 2000.
104. HA to Brooks Adams, Mar. 8, 1903, in *Letters*, 5:469; HA, *Education*, 268.
105. HA to Elizabeth Cameron, Dec. 12, 1894, in *Letters*, 4: 234.
106. HA, *Education*, 465f. American river cities as eerily equivocal, both anachronistic and modern (fine material, therefore, for the travelist), are suggestively adumbrated by W. D. Howells in 1902, after "a voyage on the Ohio River from Pittsburg to Cincinnati and back":

> Through veils of smoke I saw the ugly house, in the ugly little town [Martins Ferry, Ohio], where I was born, the steamboat not staying for me to visit it. The boat did, however, let me visit a vanished epoch in the life of the shores, where the type of Americanism, for good and for bad, of fifty years ago, still prevails. It is all, where man could make it so, a scene of hideous industrialism, with topless chimneys belching the fumes of the bottomless pit; but thousands of comfortable farmsteads line the banks . . . and the diabolical contrasts of riches and poverty are almost effaced. I should like to write a book about it. (William Dean Howells, *Life in Letters of William Dean Howells*, ed. Mildred Howells [Garden City, N.J., 1928], 2:154.)

The fog of "The Love Song of J. Alfred Prufrock," T. S. Eliot would explain, "is the fog that blew from the factory chimneys across the Mississippi." Peter Ackroyd, *T. S. Eliot: A Life* (New York, 1984), 26f. Age sixteen in the year of the Louisiana Purchase Exposition, Eliot would leave St. Louis for good the next year.

107. HA, *Education*, 466f.
108. HA to Elizabeth Cameron, May 22, 15, 1904, in *Letters*, 5:587; Abigail Adams Homans, *Education by Uncles* (Boston, 1966), 139f.
109. HA to Charles Francis Adams, Jr., Nov. 3, 1858, in *Letters*, 1:4.

110. John Brinckerhoff Jackson, *American Space: The Centennial Years, 1865–1876* (New York, 1972), 58–60.
111. HA, *Education*, 240, 330.
112. Albro Martin, "Union Pacific Railroad," *Reader's Encyclopedia of the American West*, ed. Howard R. Lamar (New York, 1977), 1205.
113. Homans, *Education by Uncles*, 139
114. HA, *Education*, 466.
115. Caren Kaplan, *Questions of Travel: Postmodern Discourses of Displacement* (Durham, Vt., 1996), 63.
116. Sarah H. Gordon, *Passage to Union: How the Railroads Transformed American Life, 1829–1929* (Chicago, 1996), 315.
117. Albro Martin, *Railroads Triumphant: The Growth, Rejection, and Rebirth of a Vital American Force* (New York, 1992), 78.
118. Kaledin, *Education of Mrs. Henry Adams*, 89.
119. HA to Lucy Baxter, Apr. 30, 1892, in *Letters*, 4:8.
120. Nicolay and Hay, *Abraham Lincoln*, 10:347. The Penn School archives today preserve an letter from Ned Hooper commenting "on the condition of the freemen." Edward Hooper, Feb. 23, 1863, Penn School Papers, Southern Historical Collection, Manuscripts Department, Library of the University of North Carolina at Chapel Hill.
121. HA to Mabel Hooper, Feb. 21, 1892, in *Letters*, 4:2; HA to Elizabeth Cameron, Mar. 16, 20, 1893; HA to Mabel Hooper, Mar. 15, 1896, in *Supplement*, 1893:8, 10, 1896:7.
122. John Hay, *John Hay-Howells Letters: The Correspondence of John Milton Hay and William Dean Howells, 1861–1905*, ed. George Montiero and Brenda Murphy (Boston, 1980), 92; HA to Theodore F. Dwight, Feb. 17, 1889, in *Henry Adams and His Friends: A Collection of Unpublished Letters*, ed. Harold Dean Cater (Boston, 1947), 183; Chalfant, *Better in Darkness*, 560.
123. HA to Elizabeth Cameron, Nov. 4, 1888; HA to Abigail Brooks Adams, Nov. 14, 1888; HA to Charles Milnes Gaskell, Mar. 8, 1888, Sept. 27, 1894, in *Letters*, 3:152, 155, 107, 4:215; HA to Mabel Hooper La Farge, Aug. 20, 1890, in *Henry Adams and His Friends*, 195.
124. HA to Charles Milnes Gaskell, Mar. 8, 1888, in *Letters*, 3:107.
125. HA to Elizabeth Cameron, Mar. 7, 1888; HA to Charles Milnes Gaskell, Mar. 8, 1888, in *Letters*, 3:100f, 104, 108.
126. HA to Elizabeth Cameron, Mar. 3, 1893, in *Letters*, 4:91.
127. HA to Elizabeth Cameron, Mar. 16, 1894; HA to John Hay, Apr. 11, 1894, in *Letters*, 4:176, 180; HA to Elizabeth Cameron, Apr. 16, 1894, in *Supplement*, 1894:13.
128. HA to Henry Cabot Lodge, Mar. 1, 1916, in *Letters*, 6:725.
129. HA to Mabel Hooper, Oct. 6, 1894, in *Letters*, 4:220.
130. Levenson et al., *Letters*, 4: after 150.
131. Thurman Wilkins with Caroline Lawson Hinkley, *Clarence King: A Biography* (Albuquerque, 1988), 159.
132. HA, *Education*, 268.
133. HA to Sir John Clark, May 2, 1892, in *Letters*, 4:10.
134. Henry Adams, *Esther: A Novel* (1884; New York, 1982), 208, 324.

"I measured her as they did with pigs"

Henry Adams as Other

JOHN C. ORR

HENRY ADAMS ROUTINELY referred to his life after 1885 as his "posthumous" years, but a better descriptor might be "amateur." In the best sense of the word, he explored areas of knowledge that lay outside of his training as an historian/author and immersed himself in them with a fervor available only to the leisure class. In the worst sense, he tended to adopt as his own and to speak from and for identities he could never truly claim. His knowledge of modern physics, Buddhism, watercolor, and anthropology came primarily from reading numerous books, but they also involved what might be called field work: visiting world's fairs to study the universe of force, stopping in Ceylon to sit under the sacred Bo tree, painting with John La Farge during their South Seas idyll, measuring the bodies of natives on those same islands. These passionate exercises afforded Adams the material for some of his late, cranky works, a failure to obtain Nirvana, a few score of paintings, and a strange sense of revulsion from and occasional near-identity with those same natives. He learned, as he said about the painting lessons, to "look at painting rather from the inside, and see a good many things about a picture that I only felt before."[1] He learned, in other words, to see enough from another perspective to confirm intellectually his preconceived nebulous inklings.

My title references a moment from Adams's excursion to the South Seas, where he early on measured and charted natives' bodies in part to demonstrate the degeneration of modern Western man. He reported that after he took exhaustive measurements of a Samoan chief's daughter, she responded "with a laugh that I measured her as they did with pigs."[2] I take that scene as my starting point because it readily signifies how, in the South Seas, Adams employed a rational process of investigation that involved collecting and analyzing data. Confronted with an alien culture, he ultimately could not function outside of the investigative methodology afforded him by his cultural heritage and professional training. Yet in a very real sense, the amateur Adams at times attempted to cast off the tools of reason and scientific investigation and embrace his, admittedly skewed, version of alternative epistemologies even as he sought to comprehend them analytically. His effort was, of course, a failure—as is evident in the above quotation. His desire to know about the natives ultimately rendered the objects of his investigation, as the Samoan woman recognized, little more than animals.

Nonetheless, from this sojourn in the relatively non-Westernized South Seas archipelago began Adams's journey towards a recognition of other ways of knowing, ways that he could imagine but never inhabit. In addition to native means of cultural and historical explanation, he also pursued what he understood to be a female epistemology. This journey offered him evidence for his nascent valorization of the feminine that would reach its maturity in the figure of the Virgin. Not surprisingly, his versions of these alternative epistemologies were often fraught with his characteristic attitudes of superiority and disdain. It is, therefore, overly simplistic to argue that he was attempting to position himself in the role of the Other, yet he did indeed identify with aspects of subaltern groups—albeit perhaps most often when they confirmed his preconceptions. He also tried, however condescendingly, to valorize those subjectivities as means to overcome what he regarded as the failures of Western rationality, though he could never truly adopt them. In at least one instance—his ghostwritten Tahitian memoirs—he attempted to place his Western reader in the position of Other to a puzzling episteme based on genealogy and legend rather than history and chronology. The result is to expose the Western reader to the effects of Western imperialism and at the same time to confront that same reader with his own imperialist perspective and cultural dominance. Recent criticism of this era in Adams's career has tended to investigate either his complicity in imperialist ventures or the effects of his gender politics.[3] Perhaps the two are not so easily separable.

I

The terms most often associated with the mature Adams—*unity* and *multiplicity*—and their accompanying metaphors, the Virgin and the dynamo, signify the dilemma at the heart of each of his late works. *Tahiti*, *Mont*

Saint Michel and Chartres, and *The Education of Henry Adams* each in its own way tells the story of a once stable and unified culture's decent into instability and multiplicity. The two terms referred, as he suggested in the *Education*, to a changing world order that his training poorly prepared him to understand. Moreover, his varied attempts to capture the vestiges of a lost unity through the totalizing systems of genealogy, history, and science all ultimately failed, since, like the dynamo, each finally spun itself out of his control. Unity represented, in part, a philosophical program able to contain virtually all signifiers in a single unit of signification. Conversely, the multiplicitous world resembled what has come to be called modernism: signification continued unabated, but in no unified totality of meaning. No longer did a metasystem hold the various signifiers together.

But just as more recent critics have debated whether postmodernism is a new world order or simply one which prior generations failed to grasp, so also do the dialectics of unity and multiplicity operate not simply on a historical continuum but also on a more personal axis for Adams.[4] The crisis represented by the two terms resonated for Adams, as it did for virtually all the great nineteenth-century thinkers, as the dilemma of the subject/object split endemic to Western philosophy, not simply the transmogrification of a culture from one state to its opposite. What finally is multiplicity but a state of separation between subject and object? In *Mont Saint Michel and Chartres*, Adams identified that the "attempt to bridge the chasm between multiplicity and unity is the oldest problem of philosophy, religion, and science."[5] But Adams was no Hegel or even, finally, another Emerson. The dialectic of self and Other failed to lead him to a synthesis of the two, a realization of self in the Other.[6] Instead, Adams could not negotiate a position outside of the logic of domination inherent to Western rationality, in which the perceiving/acting subject asserts itself on its Other, the perceived/acted-on object.[7] This duality remains by definition a power relationship, one offering no union, since the subject and object are realized only through their difference. There can be no unity under Western rationality, only continual multiplicity, and as a thinker, Adams was inextricably locked into the polarity of Western thought. Because he reasoned the world in binary oppositions—male/female, civilized/savage, dynamo/Virgin—he could not help but view the Other, whoever it might have been, as something of an absolute opposite to himself. He thus routinely failed to recognize and value the commonalities of diversity.[8]

As a function of the subject/object split, the disparity between unity and multiplicity operates on a synchronic axis rather than the diachronic axis of the pervasive societal movement towards modernity. Thus, the unity of the individual and the Other could exist, Adams seemed to hope, but only in certain non-Western or nonmasculine mind-sets, even at the same time that the Western world continued its acceleration towards total multiplicity under the aegis of rationality.[9] His intellectual and spiritual dyspepsia led him on a worldwide quest, though he eventually glimpsed the grail of unity—both cosmic and personal—in his idealized French twelfth century. But the restless traveling that the amateur Adams adopted following his wife's suicide suggests the very real urgency of his search. It was no accident that he made his first two major excursions after 1885 to the Far East, locales that offered Americans sites for their Orientalist projections.[10]

Although never a tourist in the sense of breathlessly following guidebooks from site to site, Adams carried with him to Japan and the South Seas all of the reprehensible and racist attitudes of Westerners towards non-Western cultures. Despite a growing awareness of the effects of Western imperialism on native cultures, he could not divest himself of his own imperialist mind-set. He found Japan "a child's country," where the "whole show is of the nursery"; he determined that Polynesians, "like all orientals, are children, and have the charms of childhood as well as the faults of the small boy." Samoans "are the happiest, easiest, smilingest people I ever saw, and the most delightfully archaic. . . . They have virtues of healthy children."[11] Undoubtedly, Adams is guilty of the worst kind of Orientalism: the process that uses "the people of the non-West as convenient objects of analysis for the social sciences but ignores their intellectual and ethical existence."[12] At his best, he might be accused of exhibiting towards Japan what Kojin Karatani has called "aestheticentrism," a reverence for the aesthetic of a non-Western culture while ignoring the lived reality of the people who actually inhabit the space. Of Polynesians, however, he noted that, beyond their aristocratic social schema, they "have no other arts worth mentioning."[13]

The impetus for the extended trip to Polynesia stemmed from two related urges: the desire to know and the desire to forget. He wanted to know and experience cultures far removed from Western, masculine rationality, and he wanted to forget his sorrow over his wife's death and his growing affections for Elizabeth Cameron. These desires overlap in his attempt to come to an understanding of modern woman in relationship to her archaic past. Duco van Oostrom has argued that Adams "sought to flee the disrupted gender roles of modern America and transport himself into a primitive culture to see the essence of womanhood."[14] His quest for the "archaic woman," beginning with his 1876 lecture on "The Primitive Rights of Women," was fueled by Clarence King's stories of the Hawaiian "old-gold girl" who playfully cavorted, semi-nude, in waterfalls.[15] That image offered Adams a concept of woman "very different from the neurasthenic American woman of the late nineteenth century."[16] But the women he found did not exactly comport with his fantasy, so Adams in essence reads them through the image that King presented. He "measures Woman according to his standards, and fails to see differences between his standards and the women's personal lives and interests."[17] The lived experience of the natives was relatively unimportant to him; his image of what the natives should be dominates all that he sees. Consequently, the natives simply confirmed some felt sense that he brought with him.

At the same time, Adams does step beyond the standard Victorian response: he searches for a sense of identity—however misperceived—with the very cultures he otherwise disparages. He wants to undertake two contradictory programs at once: to view the Other as object for investigation using the tools of Western analysis and to claim kinship with the Other even in the process of examining her. In one sense, this paradox constitutes yet another example of what Carolyn Porter has identified in Adams, among others, as an attempt to be both participant and observer.[18] Despite this broader cultural valence, this need for identification apparently had a personal impetus for Adams: despite all of the evidence to the contrary, he desperately wanted to claim a position within American culture as an outsider.[19]

Adams valorized what he conceived of as female consciousness as an antidote to the logic of domination. Like many Victorians, he uncritically accepted that women did not reason as men but were instead moved by their instincts, the irrational feminine intuition. "The charm of women," he once remarked, "is the Hegelian charm of the identity of opposites. You can assume nothing regarding them, without assuming the contrary to be equally true."[20] Conversely, unlike most of his contemporaries Adams found in this epistemic distinction something of a utopian possibility. If not finally capable of bridging the split in consciousness engendered by masculine rationality, women at least offered an alternative to it as a consequence of their lack of rationality and their position as object for male subjectivity. His experiences in Polynesia confirmed that "man is pretty vile, but perhaps woman might partly compensate for him."[21] His idealization of women led not to support for the burgeoning women's rights movement but to contempt for the New Woman, whom he considered a failure, since she forfeited her natural power—primarily her fecundity—by seeking to thrive in the arid world of masculine rationality.[22]

The personal crisis for Adams signified by his gender distinctions was his inability to approach the irrational rationally. In the *Education* he recognized this dilemma when he noted that the "mind resorts to reason for want of training." In his most naturalistic moments, he claimed that Polynesia convinced him that "sex is altogether a mistake, and that no reversion to healthier conditions than ours, can remove the radical evils inherent in the division of the sexes."[23] That division may not have been repairable, but the question of dominance apparently was. In his "Prayer to the Virgin of Chartres," he asks the Virgin's forgiveness for following the Father and for all the baleful effects his choice engenders, noting,

> So I too wandered off among the host
> That racked the earth to find the father's
> clue.
> I did not find the Father, but I lost
> What now I value more, the Mother,—
> You!
>
> I thought the fault was yours that foiled my
> search;
> I turned and broke your image on its throne,
> Cast down my idol, and resumed my march
> To claim the father's empire for my own.
>
> Crossing the hostile sea, our greedy band
> Saw rising hills and forests in the blue;
> Our father's kingdom in the promised land!
> —We seized it, and dethroned the father
> too.[24]

Clearly here, the choice to follow the Father—the male principle as well as the Trinity—terminates in the destructive pursuit of empire. But curiously, by equating the Mother with irrationality, Adams implies in the final line that vanquishing the imperial figure leads to downfall, obviously of a God-head (the following line, "And now we are the Father," indicates Oedipal complications) but also of the feature most representative of the masculine: rationality. Masculine rationality ends inevitably for Adams in tragedy. His eventual entropic historical perspective turns on the causal breakdown between intention and effect, since in an entropic universe, a positivist causality no longer exists.

For my purposes, the significant feature of the gender split detailed in the poem is the economic component and its correlation with the logic of domination. Adams's ambiguous opinion of women functioned within the context of the nineteenth-century polarization of home and work, with women serving as the assigned arbiters of religion, culture, and morality. Thus, they readily functioned as symbols of a pre-industrial past, a past that ultimately afforded Adams the illusion of a cultural unity antedating modern multiplicitous dissipation. The economic element implicit in his genderized ideology of unity and multiplicity emerged most distinctly at the turn of the century, after his meanderings in the South Seas and his search for the "archaic woman," in the irrational, generative power of the Virgin, decidedly opposed to economic power and rational systematizing. But the roots of his feminine principle had appeared some twenty years earlier.

On December 9, 1876, Adams delivered at the Lowell Institute his only known public lecture, "Women's Rights in History," which he later revised as "Primitive Rights of Women" for inclusion in *Historical Essays*, the tenth and final volume of his *History of the United States of America during the Administrations of Thomas Jefferson and James Madison*, published in 1891.[25] He pursues a rather modest goal in the essay: to counter the theory that "the original position of married woman was one of slavery, or akin to slavery"—a theory based on the premise that she was subject not only to the superior force of men "but to legalized force."[26] The corollary to this theory "attributed the complete triumph of women to the influence of Christianity" (336). Drawing on a variety of examples ranging from American Indians to Egyptians to Greeks and Romans, Adams rather artlessly identifies numerous legal constraints in each culture regarding the treatment of women in order to argue that *de jure* women were not slaves. Even though they might have been "treated without much regard to" laws, "violation of law never was law" (357).

As an indication of the direction his later thought would take, the essay offers valuable insight. Primitive cultures, according to Adams, were communistic and, thus, matrilinear. Only with the rise of property, which he claims attracts mankind by "the strongest human instinct" (338), is matriarchal culture overthrown. But he takes great pains to point out how even in early forms of the more advanced, patriarchal cultures, women still maintained a strong legal status that protected them from complete subjugation by their husbands. The most interesting and inspired aspects of this demonstration are his readings of Homer's *Odyssey*, which he considers "little more than a running commentary on the Greek law of marriage" (345), and the Icelandic saga *Njalsaga*. In both cases, the extraordinary status accorded the key women characters speaks plainly to their legal rights, as both Penelope and Hallgerda are free to choose their suitors and to leave them when they desire. Likewise, in a statement that contains the germ of *Chartres*, Adams notes that "Christian philosophers of a later period . . . adopted the trinity, and in adopting it, dethroned the woman from her place," though the "irresistible spread of Mariolatry . . . proved how strongly human nature revolted against the change" (343). The paradoxical effect Christianity had on women's status is that the religion only partially restored "rights which the Church herself had a principal share in taking away" (357), since the Church evolved from Roman forms that degraded woman's position.

In this essay, the particles of Adams's thinking clearly begin to orbit the Manichean poles that inform so much of his late work. In advanced, masculine cultures, such as the Roman, reason dominates instinct, leading to ordered, militaristic societies devoid of artistic imagination. Cultures in which women enjoy more freedom from masculine control—Greek, Icelandic—develop stunning artistic expression, since imagination is inherently less constricted by masculine rationality. Yet Adams persists here in establishing a qualitative distinction between the more "advanced" masculine cultures and the prior "primitive" structures. While the opposition between masculine and feminine was far from complete at this early stage in Adams's thought, the outline of the duality was coming into focus.

Equally important is the explicit connection between the degradation of woman's position and the rise of property relations. Like Marx and Engels, Adams was enormously influenced by the anthropological investigations of his longtime acquaintance Lewis Henry Morgan.[27] Consequently, the narrative in "Primitive Rights of Women" relates the decline of matrilinear communistic societies at the moment when private property emerges with its requisite patrilinear descent. In that conception one finds the key to the gender dialectic that ultimately informs Adams's understanding of the Other's displacement from dominant culture and his reservations regarding imperialism. Women become but another form of property, another object of patrilinear society. In Adams's scheme, that domination destroys the cultural unity and balance that existed in the more primitive society because that unity cannot survive the split between subject and object endemic to a culture ordered by masculine rationality.

Consequently, since Adams lived in the apex of what his brother Brooks called "commercial society," the feminine ideal offered a means both of escape and critique. Adams found in woman the embodiment of nonrationality and nonproperty, both residing in the object position. Ultimately, the perfect realization of this schema was the Virgin of *Mont Saint Michel and Chartres*, whose downfall was significantly precipitated by the rationality of Aquinas and the power of the growing bourgeoisie. Likewise, his critique of the correlation between gender relations and property extends beyond *Mont Saint Michel and Chartres* to include the imperialism of the turn of the twentieth century, which was from this gendered perspective an extension of masculine assertion of power over a primitive, balanced culture composed of childlike natives. The imperial ventures of Adams's adult years, patriarchal control manifest in economic exploitation of native cultures, was being replayed all over the globe. Only the object to be subdued changed.

Years after his lecture on primitive women, the antipodes undergirding Adams's work emerged more clearly. William Jordy has sketched the preliminary terms orbiting each pole: "Unity, intuition, art, woman, Madeleine, Esther, the Virgin, and Mrs. Adams: these formed one pole. The other: multiplicity, science, man, Ratcliffe, Hazard, and finally Henry Adams."[28] Including characters from Adams's two novels, Jordy's list is relatively complete. Unity and multiplicity, female and male, body and mind, intuition and reason. Adams's thought rotated around these oppositions, and while, as with any thinker, he occasionally contradicted himself, on the whole he remained remarkably true to this severe split, symbolized most famously by the Virgin and the dynamo. Consequently, since for Adams primitive peoples also represented nonmasculine epistemology—identifying the natives as children places them along with women in opposition to men—that operated on instinctual drive, he assigned to all women the potential for the same kind of unified, non-Western thought pattern he observed in native peoples.

If we carry Jordy's schema a bit further, the pole containing masculine rationality also encompasses imperialism and the dynamo, a partnership whose interrelationship reveals another dimension of Adams's thought.[29] What these terms in the second category share is a valorization of abstraction, from abstract reasoning to the unmanageable power of the dynamo operating outside the pale of direct and constant human control.[30] Both appealing and appalling to Adams, Polynesian cultural unity presented a seeming dearth of abstract reasoning among the natives, who produced no "arts or literature" and whose "intellectual existence is made up of concrete facts."[31] Adams's ambivalence toward native cultures over this very issue aids his readers in grasping his complicated response to American imperialism, since it is both a product of abstract reasoning inherent in Western thought and a representation of that abstraction. As Fredric Jameson has pointed out, the significant feature of a colonial economy is that essential aspects of it "are located elsewhere . . . outside the daily life and existential experience of the home country." The actual colonies, which "remain unknown and unimaginable for the subjects of the imperial power," are in lived experience abstract, beyond the realm of immediate apprehension.[32] Thus, the reification of the worker inherent in any capitalist endeavor assumes a hyperspatial dimension in imperial economy. The key element for Adams's critique of these shared abstractions is the loss of human capacity to control the forces set into motion. Eventually such a concern would lead him to posit his infamous theories of abstract force as the causal agent in human history. Adams identified at times with the victims of imperialism, the invisible people in international debates, the natives of the South Seas in particular. First, however, it required his journey there in order for him to recognize them and their plight.

II

In the fall of 1890, with the *History* behind him, Adams persuaded La Farge to accompany him (all expenses paid) on an extended and scheduleless voyage that would eventually take them around the globe. He was absent from Washington for over seventeen months. In addition to awakening a new aesthetic sensibility in the exhausted historian under the tutelage of the artist, the trip to the South Seas confronted Adams for the first time with the degrading effects of economic and cultural imperialism on native culture, played out in various stages of development on the different islands.[33] Hawaii was most severely altered by the combined force of Christian missionaries and sugar planters. "The old-gold girl, and all King's illusions of 1872," Adams wrote John Hay, "belong to a region of youth and poetry which no longer exists in 1890," since the few natives who remained "are much more Americanised." In addition to the ideological power of the missionaries, the sugar plantations were "absolutely extinguishing the natives."[34]

Samoa, where he arrived in October, proved a distinctly more exciting experience in part because the hegemony of the missionaries was not so entrenched there. Although he later claimed that on the islands he had "been living in communistic societies . . . such as I used to lecture about so learnedly," the "archaic woman" he found there did not comply with his expectations. He found the position of women in Samoan society to be "the strangest compound of laxity and strictness, of absolute freedom and rigorous restraint, of charm and repulsion." Women maintained a socially conspicuous place in Samoa, but their realm of actual power was not limited to the social sphere. The *taupo*—village maiden—"in war-times, leads the warriors even to battle." Adams left the island amazed at "how large a share woman plays in this archaic society." He also left the island convinced that the foreign governments controlling Samoa were effectively destroying native culture. Thus, he firmly declared, "My sympathies are all Samoan."[35]

Although Samoan culture was far less damaged by Western influences than was Hawaiian culture, Adams recognized that the "curse of money has touched here, but is not yet deep." Because American trade was rapidly becoming normal, the Samoans received Adams and La Farge as oddities, "the first Americans who ever travelled here for pleasure, without a business object."[36] The potential exploitation that loomed drove Adams to a vitriolic outburst:

> I am inclined to profanity when I think that religion, political economy and civilisation so-called, will certainly work their atrocities here within another generation so that these islands will be as melancholy a spectacle as Hawaii is, and the dignity of [contract] labor will be asserted as God's lesson to Polynesia.[37]

He predicted that within "five-and-twenty years, all the lingering remnants of archaic society, in its higher forms, will probably have disappeared."[38]

Tahiti proved to be the realization of that dire forecast, and Adams soon found the French colonial atmosphere oppressive. When he landed in February of 1891, the island seemed "tinged by a South Sea melancholy, a little sense of hopelessness and premature decay," and Tahitians were "still, silent, rather sad in expression, like the Hawaiians, and they are fearfully few in number." Like Hawaii, Tahiti exhibited signs of dissipation and disease: rum and leprosy. "Rum is the only amusement which civilisation and religion have left them," Adams noted, since they "are forbidden to dance or to keep any of their old warlike habits." Even the archaic woman exhibited "pretty near the European standard of female faults," though she was as yet "not nervously diseased." Consequently, no people ever "seemed so hopelessly bored as the Tahitians." Had he not seen Samoa before Tahiti, Adams "could not even have put together the fragments of Taïti so as to make them intelligible."[39]

When confronted with Tahiti, Adams found a culture already soiled, irrevocably damaged by its contact with the Western world, and that intermingling of cultures extended to the clan he eventually claimed as his own. Some few days after arriving, he and La Farge were introduced to Tati Salmon, head of the Teva clan, the dispossessed island aristocracy. Tati's father, Alexander Salmon, had married Arii Taimai, heiress of the Tevas, and his sister Marau was divorced from the head of the rival Pomare clan—the reigning king of the island. Even the Tevas had intermarried with a Westerner, a Jew no less. Thus, Adams's search for a primitive present to serve as antidote to Western malaise ended initially in contradiction, and when read through the lens of his nascent antisemitism, his eventual adoption into the clan is fraught with ironies that Adams would have appreciated had he not chosen to overlook them.[40]

Nonetheless, his introduction to Arii Taimai, the matriarch of the Tevas and widow of Alexander Salmon, revealed to Adams the strain of primitive purity he sought. Adams met Arii Taimai when with Tati he and La Farge traveled to Papara, ancestral home of the Tevas. His first impression of Arii Taimai indicated his fascination and how readily she matched the preconceptions he brought with him:

> The old Chiefess talks nothing but Taïtian, and old Taïtian at that. She will sit at none of your vulgar tables, on chairs, but on mats on the ground, like a true princess; and I, who like lying on mats, was glad to sit by her side and ask her about her ancestors and race. . . . Only one generation separates the old chiefess—who is only sixtyeight—from her pagan temple on the neighboring point, and from human sacrifices to your choice.[41]

Appreciative of his attention, Arii Taimai told him to ask questions, which he did, "especially about the women of pagan times."[42]

Adams casually suggested to Marau that if she would write her memoirs, he would serve as her amanuensis. To his great surprise, she accepted the offer, and on May 10, 1891, they began. Within a week, he reported that he was "rather amused and occupied. My 'Memoirs of Marau, Queen of Tahiti' give me a sort of excuse for doing nothing." Eventually, Arii Taimai became interested and "astonished her children by telling me things she would never tell them" while they served as translators. Soon the entire family was providing him with material. Swamped with "new stories, legends or songs," Adams recognized the stylistic difficulties such a work would entail; twenty years of writing political history had ill-prepared him for the task, rendering his hand "too heavy for such work." His methods were "all intellectual, analytic and modern."[43] It required a distinctly original approach to write the history of Tahiti, one that intertwined island history and politics with legends and poems. If that methodology appeared somewhat amateurish in his Tahitian memoirs, it clearly proved adaptable for *Chartres*.

Although Adams hyperbolically claimed after completing the *History*, "With the year 1890 I shall retire from authorship," work on the memoirs apparently rekindled his literary aspirations. Shortly after arriving in France in December 1891, he suggested that Hay join him "in writing . . . a volume or two of Travels which will permit me to express my opinion of life in general." He conceived of the book as "a sort of ragbag of everything; scenery, psychology, history, literature, poetry, art; anything in short, that is worth throwing in."[44] *Tahiti*, as the book came to be known, stands as an initial excursion into that realm of ragbag compilation, one that despite its weaknesses excited Adams. After producing the first edition in 1893, he confessed that "I really enjoy writing that kind of history," since unlike American history, "Tahiti is all literary." The result of his labors "amused me much more, and is much better reading, than my dreary American history."[45] At the end of 1893, Adams privately published ten copies of *Memoirs of Marau Taaroa, Last Queen of Tahiti*. Robert Spiller has pointed out that, despite the title, the memoirs were "always Arii Taimai's, never Marau's."[46] Adams acknowledged the true genesis of the book in 1901 when a new private edition appeared as *Tahiti: Memoirs of Arii Taimai e Marama of Eimeo, Teriirere of Tooarai, Terrinui of Tahiti, Tauraatua i Amo*. In addition to listing all of Arii Taimai's landed titles in the subtitle, the new edition also included an epilogue: the story of how she saved the island from French wrath in 1846 by convincing tribal chiefs and Queen Pomare to accept status as a French protectorate.[47] The primary difference between the two editions, however, is one of perspective.

The span of years bookended by the two editions encompasses the era of Adams's increased clandestine political activity, brought on by the financial crisis of 1893, the economic and political philosophy of his brother

Brooks, and his close personal relationship with the architects of American diplomatic policy, especially John Hay.[48] His forays into politics include ghostwriting at least one speech and resolution for Elizabeth Cameron's husband, Donald, and meeting privately in the years surrounding the Spanish-American War with the Cuban emissaries who sought public support for their struggle for independence from Spain. Adams's ambivalence towards the United States was nowhere more profoundly evident than in his often contradictory attitudes about his country's emergence as a world power. Torn between a nationalistic longing to observe it finally freed from European domination and a nostalgic wish for a return to a limited, decentered government, Adams saw the Spanish-American War as a harbinger of a new world order purchased at the expense of republican government.[49] Likewise, that form of government was threatened by finance capitalism. Earl Klee has argued that beginning with "The New York Gold Conspiracy" in 1870, the "subterranean stream" running throughout Adams's work followed the course of his fear that modern financial transformations had outstripped his family's republican values. The keenness of Adams's insights originates in his having been "caught in limbo between . . . the republican ideal and the new force of centralizing, industrial capitalism." Consequently, Adams saw the modern danger not in the huge fortunes corporate capitalism permitted but instead in "the odd public-private hybrid which the modern state has become."[50] That hybrid quality extended to foreign policy, as financiers sank enormous amounts of capital into long-term projects—railroads, mines, and governments themselves—that required continual stability in undeveloped countries. Maintaining stability too often required the direct intervention of the U.S. government.[51]

Situated somewhere between his brothers—Brooks the militaristic imperialist and Charles the early and vocal anti-imperialist—Henry initially "followed Brooks's lead," according to Jackson Lears, "in seeking a revitalized identity through a racist cult of violence"; all the while, he privately acknowledged the validity of the anti-imperialist position. But imperialism only "temporarily leavened his despair."[52] By 1901, with the bloody war to suppress the Filipino rebellion limping to a conclusion, Adams had become almost thoroughly estranged from his younger brother over his increasingly venomous imperialism. Likewise, his close relationship with John Hay suffered from Adams's clandestine efforts on the part of the Cuban revolutionaries—although he still served as the secretary of state's confidential sounding board during their daily strolls up 16th Street. Due to that friendship, Adams remarked to Brooks at the end of 1901, he had "followed the Philippine procession in silence, and must continue to follow it, but that is quite a different thing from believing it."[53] Earlier that year he had declared wearily for continental isolationism:

> I incline now to anti-imperialism, and very strongly to anti-militarism. I incline to let the machine smash, and see what pieces are worth saving afterwards. I incline to abandon China, Philippines and everything else. I incline to let England sink; to let Germany and Russia try to run the machine, and to stand on our internal resources alone.[54]

Appearing in the same year that Adams rearranged and expanded *Tahiti* while toiling in his Paris apartment over a draft of *Mont Saint Michel and Chartres*, this anti-imperialist proclamation represents the culmination of a long intellectual journey, one whose manifestations emerge clearly in *Tahiti* as a narrative of conflicting epistemologies brought about by Western colonial and imperial aggressions. His revisions heighten the tragic consequences of that conflict and force readers to recognize themselves in the imperial epistemology.[55]

He had opened the 1893 edition with the 1767 arrival of Capt. Samuel Wallis on board H.M.S. *Dolphin*, thus giving that edition a decidedly European slant. A few chapters later, Adams presents island legend that predates Wallis. In the second edition, the first chapter of the original edition becomes the sixth. The first five chapters in the second edition recount island prehistory, primarily the ascension of the Tevas, accessible solely through legend and genealogy, since Tahitians had no history in the Western sense of the word. Besides reorienting the book on a strict chronology, this alteration forces readers to recognize the initial balance among rival tribes as well as to confront their arcane customs and mores. Consequently, the arrival of the Europeans in chapter 6 makes the reader more conscious of the multiple errors they made in treating island politics and customs as derivations of a European model.

With these strategies, Adams dramatizes how Western rationality failed to grasp a different kind of pattern—seemingly chaotic or irrational—behind island customs, leading inevitably to tragic consequences. Adams emphasizes this perspectival dysfunction in the concluding sentence of chapter 5 of the second edition: up to that point, the reader notes that he has depended "mainly on tradition, but here Captain Wallis and Captain Cook begin their story from the European stand-point."[56] Surely

Adams realized that this rearrangement makes the volume more difficult to read, for the labyrinthine genealogical structure of the first five chapters challenges even the most dedicated reader. Nonetheless, it clearly forces the reader to identify with the Tahitians and their ordered, if seemingly irrational, society and to recognize the destruction of that society at the hands of the Europeans.[57]

Adams remarked in 1886 that "genealogy has a curious, personal interest, which history wants."[58] Even before the South Seas sojourn, he saw in genealogy a more material approach to a past than rational, abstract history can afford. He was predisposed, then, to write the history of Tahiti, where "genealogy grew into a science" and "swallowed up history" (17). To an extent, the genealogical emphasis in Tahiti constituted its fascination for Adams. It predates Western history, it offers him a recognizable methodology for working within an alien epistemology, and it inevitably relates the narrative of the rise and fall of great families, primarily the Tevas of Papara with whom the displaced Adams identified. But the genealogical perspective also makes the book initially so challenging to read—if not, in places, indecipherable. Living, as Stanley Fish might argue, in a postlapsarian print culture complete with linear, chronological history, the modern Western reader is inevitably mystified by the Tahitian oral culture and its esoteric genealogical mappings and their occasional capriciousness.[59] Even Adams appears to throw his hands up in frustration at one point, noting that one generational progression leaves behind "one of the most complicated puzzles in genealogy that ever perplexed a succession" (38).

What these difficulties highlight are the competing cultural mindsets that so interested Adams. The native manner of organizing past experience appears less than rational to a logical Westerner; thus Adams's text mediates between the two worlds.[60] From the outset Adams indicates the difficulty facing him as he attempts to negotiate between the competing epistemologies when describing the shape of the island in the first chapter. A Westerner, most likely, sees it as "an hour-glass or figure 8; but as the native knew neither hour glasses nor figures, they used to call the island a fish, because it had a body and a tail" (1). In the native oral culture, they neither mark time in the Western manner nor do they have abstract symbols for their language or mathematical system. While Adams's desire to represent native culture for his readers may finally fail, what he structurally implies by opening with genealogy before switching to European history is the ultimate dominance of the agents of Western rationality over their native object. Moreover, in the reader's failure to comprehend fully native culture, Adams forces him to confront his own logic of domination, which ultimately leads to his longing for the arrival of the Europeans in the narrative in order to supply it with a recognizable telos.

What emerges from the ragbag combination of Byzantine genealogies with passages from travel logs and memoirs of European explorers and missionaries is a recognizably tragic narrative of decline and fall of both the Tevas and the old island culture. Spiller has noted that in *Tahiti* is found "the great theme of modern history in capsule form,"[61] but Adams adapted that theme to his own ends. His is not Gibbon's story of a great civilization corrupted from within by its wealth and power. That story would have to wait for his subsequent books. The decline and fall of Tahiti came not at the hands of Tahitians. The initial chapters of *Tahiti* comport with subsequent accounts of the island in describing a place that was "less than perfect" but had nonetheless "established a balance with itself." That balance was, however, destroyed by the forces that accompanied Western intervention: "firearms, disease or alcohol, or . . . an alien code of laws and morals."[62]

Since all linear island history dates from the June 1767 arrival of Capt. Samuel Wallis, events occurring before his arrival are either dated backward from it or are consigned to mythology and genealogy. In his most trenchant criticism, Adams asserts that the Europeans "not only upset all [the Tahitians'] moral ideas, but also their whole political system" (138). Before their appearance, island politics operated under a balanced system of mutual retribution. A number of tribal chiefs ruled the island, and "whenever a single chief became intolerably arrogant or threatened to destroy the rest, the others united to overthrow him," thereby "restoring the balance" (138). Tahiti was not a bloodless paradise—tribal wars were relatively common—but the system whereby the collective political body worked to thwart the aspirations of any one chief maintained a high degree of stability.

Into this system blundered the British in 1767. Early on, Adams remarks that to tell Tahiti's history, one must "struggle with this idea of kingship" (6–7) among the Tahitians, which he suggests Europeans have yet to understand. There was no monarchy on the island, but the British could conceive of no other political system. Thus, Wallis, after a brief battle, designated the first person who approached the ship in something resembling a royal party "my princess, or rather queen" (48). The woman's name was Purea and, while as chiefess of the Tevas she had "no serious rival in the island" (42), she was no queen. In fact, her power was being challenged at that very moment, for in a show of intolerable pride she had demanded a general *Rahui* (year of obeisance) for her son, Teriirere.

In the intervening years between Wallis's discovery and Cook's first appearance in April 1769, Purea's hubris led to her downfall at the hands of various cousins who refused to acquiesce to her efforts to elevate Teriirere above all others. Though Purea and her family survived the ensuing war of December 1768, their wealth was effectively removed and their power weakened in what was undoubtedly an adjustment of the island's political balance. Unfortunately, into these island politics "Captain Cook was suddenly thrown, with the effect of confusing and irritating him and all the chiefs he had to deal with" (61). A sailor who had been aboard the *Dolphin* and returned with Cook recognized Purea among a gathering of islanders and identified her as Wallis's "queen." Cook immediately received her in a formal recognition of her royalty, exchanging gifts and compliments. Cook's initial errors were compounded on his second voyage in 1773. When he saw Purea dispossessed of much of her wealth, he was convinced that civil war had broken out, a perfectly rational conclusion for an eighteenth-century Englishman. Adams remarks that "having made a queen of Purea in 1768, [the British] were determined to regard her as a beggar in 1773" (92-93). But Western logic failed to grasp tribal relations on the island as well as the degraded position a parent assumed (often with a new name) upon a child's ascension. Further British errors and interventions ensued, including the introduction of missionaries and of firearms.

In March 1797 the first representatives of the London Missionary Society arrived on board the *Duff*. Some of Adams's most caustic criticism is reserved for the missionaries. He seems more willing to forgive the explorers their errors; their rigid military training evidently limited their ability to adapt to new contingencies. With the missionaries, though, he has much less patience, at least partially because they better understood island politics. Upon arrival, the missionaries faced a difficult situation. When the *Duff* sailed for England, it left them "to be plundered or murdered by the rival factions" (123). Consequently, they became dependent upon the established "king"—Pomare—for their safety. For example, after intervening in a local dispute, two missionaries were stripped of their clothes and roughed up by some natives. Pomare avenged them in an action that cost fifteen native lives. Although this affair "was not calculated to make the missionaries popular," it did make them "more than ever dependent on Pomare" (124). When the chief of the Paparas was gravely injured in an explosion, the missionaries came to treat him. But the natives immediately interpreted their feeble attempts to aid the dying man as part of Pomare's plot to kill his rival. Quoting from the missionaries' journals, Adams ridicules their comparison of island politics with court intrigues in England. Instead, by reversing the poles of sophistication and simplicity, he presents the perspective of the natives, who "looked at the missionaries as a kind of children, or idiots, incapable of understanding the simplest facts of island politics or society, and serving only as the unconscious tools of the Tu family" (128).

The missionaries' innocence resulted in more unintended consequences. Although "Pomare was vicious and cruel," he was "an angel compared with his son Tu" (143–144). The missionaries were, however, so dependent upon them for their well-being that they found themselves forced at times to beg weapons for the Pomares from ships at anchor. The irony of the missionaries' situation leads Adams to remark that "alternately praying for peace and helping Pomare and Tu to make war, the missionaries innocently hastened the destruction of the natives, and encouraged the establishment of a tyranny impossible for me to describe" (143). He goes so far as to suggest that some of their actions indicate that they were "glad to see the natives fighting together" (142), perhaps because they felt it distracted the Tahitians from uniting against external forces. Whatever the motivations, "the only winner in this tragic game was the worst and most bloodthirsty of all—Tu," known as "the first Christian king" (133). As was true in "Prayer to the Virgin of Chartres," following the Father in Tahiti ironically results in the brutal establishment of empire and the downfall of all prior forces of stability.

The book concludes with assertions of the Tevas' social superiority over the Pomares, even though they no longer dominated island politics, before Adams turns the narrative over to Arii Taimai and her efforts to reconcile Tahitians to the necessity of accepting French status. As the history of the transformation of a stable, balanced society into entropic degradation, the tragedy of *Tahiti* results from the agents of Western imperialism who, in a little over thirty years, effectively destroyed native Tahitian life. Noting that the Tahitians were "a great people," Adams praises their culture for making them "better fitted than any other possible community for the conditions in which they lived" (136) before summing up the culpability of the Europeans by listing the modes of destruction they intentionally and inadvertently wrought on the island. Disease, the first among these, desolated the once populous island. He asserts that for "this, perhaps, the foreigners were not wholly responsible, although their civilization certainly was; but for the political misery the foreigner was wholly to blame, and for the social and moral degradation he was the active cause" (137).

Ever the quester for forces of change, Adams ascribes the greatest responsibility for the destruction of the island to the firearm, the perfect symbol of masculine dominance. Like the dynamo, the gun is a coldly scientific agent, a product of rationality, efficiently enforcing a new order of meaning but always carrying the potential to operate in ways unintended by its creator. The role of firearms in the overthrow of Polynesian order became abundantly clear to Adams in a story told him by a Samoan chief:

> Gunpowder and missionaries have destroyed the life of the nobles. In former times a great chief went into battle with no thought of the common warrior. He passed through a herd of them, and none presumed to attack him. Chiefs fought only with chiefs. The idea of being killed by a common man was sacrilege. The introduction of fire-arms has changed all this, and now, as one of the chiefs said with a voice of horror, any hunchback, behind a tree, can kill the greatest chief in Samoa.[63]

The final event that destroyed the balance of forces on Tahiti and established a European-style monarchy was the death of the great warrior Opuhara at the hands of a native convert armed with a gun.

Although no Virgin functions as counterweight to the emergence of the masculine firearm in Adams's telling of this history, he does address the alteration in Tahitian culture with gendered terminology echoing the distinctions he delineates elsewhere between masculine rationality and feminine irrationality. In the first chapter of the 1901 edition, the narrator mentions that women played "an astonishing part in the history of the island" (10). They could inherit property, serve as clan leaders or chiefesses, and apparently divorce their husbands—even the chief of a clan—almost at will. They were "much the same sort of personages as female sovereigns in Europe" (10). In a schema reflecting the overthrow of matrilineal culture by the patrilineal, island unity is initially identifiable by its communal nature, while the transformation that occurs leads to individual acquisitive desire.

The epistemological distinctions that Adams assigns to gender identification result in part from limited perception. Curiously, he can identify the perceptual predisposition in others while remaining blind to his own. The first Europeans to land at Tahiti, all familiar with the teachings of

Jean-Jacques Rousseau, thought that in the natives they had found Rousseau's "natural man." But the Tahitians did not live in a state of nature or an instinctual, lawless ether. It simply appeared that way to the Europeans. "The real code of Tahitian society," Adams claims, "would have upset the theories of a state of nature as thoroughly as the guillotine did" (56). The Europeans failed to grasp the operative code, instead seeing in native life only what appeared to be no order whatsoever. Adams implies that even had they understood Tahitian social order, they would have still found it irrational. By imposing European structure onto the island order, the interlopers could not avoid regarding island codes as childish and in need of correction.

In the narrative voice, we witness yet another example of Adams's attempts to maintain two perspectives at once: the position of the female Tahitian combined with the avuncular Westerner observing the "primitive" culture.[64] Nonetheless, it certainly sounds like Henry Adams. *Tahiti* shares a number of stylistic elements with the *History*, as Daniel Manheim has demonstrated,[65] and clearly some of the most powerful prose of the book belongs to the mature Adams:

> In these thirty years [1767–97] Europe had also passed through the experience of centuries; the dreams of Rousseau and the ideals of nature were already as far away as the kingdom of heaven. In 1797 the philosophers were dead; the guillotine had disposed of the innate virtues of the human heart; and war had swept away most of the landmarks of old Europe, with much of its old population; but the wreck of society that had occurred in Europe was not to be compared with the wreck of our world in the South Seas. (136)

In addition, Adams occasionally departs from his assumed Tahitian persona, reverting to the bemused amateur anthropologist who notes, "Primitive people seem to have kept certain stock-stories . . . which represent the sharp points of their history and the names of their heroes" (21). He wants to keep one foot in each camp. Having been formally adopted into the Tevas, a status he clearly held in high regard, Adams would have felt it appropriate to write their history in the first person. La Farge wryly noted that after his adoption, Adams became "more Teva than the Tevas," once even refusing to discuss a poem praising the Pomares, the Tevas' rival ruling clan.[66] The question of voice, however, is not so simply resolved with the answer that Adams tried on a female persona while continuing to write in his own voice. That he clearly does, particularly when he brings in a Western understanding of the island and its history, complete with literary and historical references to the Western canon. But the Tahitian lore depends on Arii Taimai and her family for its very presence and, one would assume, aspects of its presentation, since the children translated the material for Adams before he ordered it into his narrative. The piecemeal collaborative nature of the book is evinced by the concluding section describing Arii Taimai's efforts to negotiate a peace between the Tahitians and the French.[67] Clearly, Adams speaks for the Tahitians, but without their assistance in the process, he would have nothing to say.

Tahiti, the first production of the amateur Adams, suffers from all of the limitations one would expect of such an experiment. Louis Auchincloss has called it "little more than an interesting failure," one that "nonetheless marks an important step in Adams' career" as his initial attempt to approach a subject with the combined skills of artist and historian. Likewise, J. C. Levenson has noted that the book and Adams's letters from the South Seas "point the way to Adams's extremely personal expression of an historical subject" in *Chartres*, though Levenson's final appraisal is that *Tahiti* is "the most esoteric book he [Adams] ever wrote." In addition to *Chartres*, *Tahiti* also formally prefigures the *Education* as Adams's earliest attempt at a posed autobiography.[68]

Despite its weaknesses, *Tahiti* delineates the powerful degrading force of Western imperialism as an act of masculine rationality. More clearly than anywhere else, here Adams explains the transformation from unity to multiplicity as at least partially the product of a specific economic aspect of rationality. Moreover, in the revisions for the 1901 edition, Adams forces readers of *Tahiti* to confront their own cultural imperialism, as the complex island genealogy ultimately gives way to the more familiar and understandable historical progression. Of course, Adams was not innocent in this entire affair and is as guilty of a kind of cultural imperialism as anyone. He clearly found in the destruction of Tahitian society a convenient version of what he perceived to be his family's history. Likewise, no matter how much he loathed the destructive influence of Westerners on native cultures, he obviously never considered those cultures equal to his own. They were, in a word, primitive. Despite his demands that Western nations cease their interference in the South Seas, he never considered applying the same restrictions to travelers such as himself who ultimately reconstructed the natives into little more than manikins in a tragic drama of decline and fall.[69] He wanted it both ways, just as he wanted to inhabit alternative identities simultaneously, never wholly a part of either, but speaking through and for both.

NOTES

1. Henry Adams to Elizabeth Cameron, Mar. 16, 1891, in *The Letters of Henry Adams*, ed. J. C. Levenson et al. (Cambridge, Mass., 1982–1988), 3:448.
2. HA to Mabel Hooper, Nov. 2, 1890, in *Letters*, 3:322.
3. The recent work of John Carlos Rowe has most seriously questioned Adams's relationship to American imperialism. See "Henry Adams's *Education* in the Age of Imperialism," in *New Essays on "The Education of Henry Adams,"* ed. John Carlos Rowe (New York, 1996), 87–114. For an argument that responds to Rowe's, see Daniel Manheim, "The Voice of Arii Taimai: Henry Adams and the Challenge of Empire," *Biography* 22(1999):209–236. Recent evaluations of Adams's gender politics include Martha Banta, "Being a 'Begonia' in a Man's World," in *New Essays on "The Education of Henry Adams,"* 49–86; and Duco van Oostrum, *Male Authors, Female Subjects: The Woman Within/Beyond the Borders of Henry Adams, Henry James and Others* (Amsterdam, 1995).
4. E. Ann Kaplan, introduction to *Postmodernism and Its Discontents*, ed. E. Ann Kaplan (London, 1988), 3–5.
5. Henry Adams, *Mont Saint Michel and Chartres* (Garden City, N.Y., 1993), 337.
6. Joseph G. Kronick, "The Limits of Contradition: Irony and History in Hegel and Henry Adams," *Clio* 15(1986):404–405. Kronick identifies Adams's contradictory attitude with Hegel's concept of the unhappy consciousness.
7. I derive my term from Herbert Marcuse's "Logos of domination" in *Eros and Civilization: A Philosophical Inquiry into Freud* (New York, 1962), 114. In this vein, Alan Trachtenberg regards the dynamo as a symbol of "the refinement of power, the domination of nature, parallel to the dominance of ruthless, acquisitive, and repressive behavior in modern society." *Brooklyn Bridge: Fact and Symbol* (New York, 1965), 138. For an extended treatment of the genderized relationship between subject and object see Susanne Kappeler's *The Pornography of Representation* (Minneapolis, 1986).
8. I am indebted to J. C. Levenson for helping me clarify this point. His essay "The Etiology of Israel Adams: The Onset, Waning, and Relevance of Henry Adams's Anti-Semitism," *New Literary History* 25(1994):569–600, explores this issue by detailing Adams's evolving attitude towards Jews.
9. *Unity* is a purposefully slippery term for Adams, but as it functions on a synchronic axis, it signifies something akin to Freud's "oceanic feeling," clearly a feminine image. The dilemma for Adams was essentially the same for Freud, who admitted that he could not "discover this 'oceanic' feeling in myself," for it is difficult "to deal scientifically with feelings." Sigmund Freud, *Civilization and Its Discontents* (New York, 1961), 1–2.
10. Edward W. Said, *Orientalism* (New York, 1979), 1. By looking to the East, Adams, like many of his contemporaries, followed in the footsteps of the Transcendentalists. Ferner Nuhn suggests that "Concord . . . might have saved Adams a trip back to the twelfth century," since there he might have found that "Man's conscience and his nature work best together, not at cross-purposes." *The Wind Blew from the East: A Study in the Orientation of American Culture* (New York, 1940), 190–191. While the Transcendentalists' quest led to India and Hinduism for "glimpses of the Over-Soul, of mystic insights and illumination" in the material world, the latter generation's search "for a true spiritual home" focused on Japan and China and the Buddhist insight into the truth beyond the sensory world that is Nirvana. No longer capable of recognizing the beautiful and divine in the crass material-

ism of Gilded Age America, the later pilgrims looked to Asia as a means of escape. Arthur E. Christy, "The Sense of the Past," in *The Asian Legacy and American Life*, ed. Arthur E. Christy (New York, 1942), 43, 47; Eusebio Rodrigues, "Out of Season for Nirvana: Henry Adams and Buddhism," in *Indian Essays in American Literature: Papers in Honour of Robert Spiller*, ed. Sujit Mukherjee and D. V. K. Raghavacharyulu (Bombay, 1968), 182.

11. HA to John Hay, July 9, 1886, Oct. 16, Nov. 16, 1890, in *Letters*, 3:17, 302, 346.
12. Kojin Karatani, "Uses of Aesthetics: After Orientalism," in *Edward Said and the Work of the Critic: Speaking Truth to Power*, ed. Paul A. Bové (Durham, 2000), 140.
13. HA to Elizabeth Cameron, Oct. 2, 1890, in *Letters*, 3:293.
14. Oostum, *Male Authors, Female Subjects*, 197.
15. HA to Elizabeth Cameron, June 4, 1891; HA to John Hay, Sept. 15, 1890, in *Letters*, 3:485, 282.
16. Oostum, *Male Authors, Female Subjects*, 202.
17. Oostum, *Male Authors, Female Subjects*, 216.
18. Carolyn Porter, *Seeing and Being: The Plight of the Participant Observer in Emerson, James, Adams, and Faulkner* (Middletown, Conn., 1981). In a similar vein, Robert Dawidoff, attributing the dual perspective to a Tocquevillian point of view that allows one to rise above the rabble of democracy while remaining somewhat of a participant in it, calls Adams "The First American Tocquevillian." Robert Dawidoff, *The Genteel Tradition and the Sacred Rage: High Culture vs. Democracy in Adams, James, and Santayana* (Chapel Hill, 1992), 31.
19. Paul A. Bové, "Anarchy and Perfection: Henry Adams, Intelligence, and America," in *America's Modernisms: Revaluing the Canon*, ed. Kathryne v. Lindberg and Joseph G. Kronick (Baton Rouge, 1996), 47–48. It is entirely feasible that his attempted identification with the Other at times stems from his perverse urge to find a means to counter the prevailing culture that spawned him.
20. HA to Lucy Baxter, Mar. 25, 1890, in *Letters*, 3:231.
21. HA to Elizabeth Cameron, Sept. 13, 1890, in *Letters*, 3:280.
22. Elaine Showalter, *Sexual Anarchy: Gender and Culture at the Fin de Siècle* (New York, 1990), 8–12. Kim Moreland asserts that his idealization of medieval woman augmented his harsh criticism of modern women for failing to sustain their true femininity. Kim Moreland, "Henry Adams, the Medieval Lady, and the 'New Woman,'" *Clio* 18(1989):292.
23. Henry Adams, *The Education of Henry Adams*, ed. Ernest Samuels (Boston, 1973), 370; HA to Clarence King, Apr. 22, 1891, in *Letters*, 3:467.
24. Henry Adams, "Prayer to the Virgin of Chartres," in *Letters to a Niece and Prayer to the Virgin of Chartres* (Boston, 1920), 126–127.
25. Levenson, *Letters*, 2:271, n. 1.
26. Henry Adams, "Primitive Rights of Women," in *The Great Secession Winter of 1860–61 and Other Essays*, ed. George Hochfield (New York, 1958), 335. Subsequent references will be noted parenthetically in the text.
27. For an interesting intellectual background of Adams's essay along with an analysis of how it confronted aspects of American culture at the time, see David Partenheimer, "Henry Adams's 'Primitive Rights of Women': An Offense against Church, the Patriarchal State, Progressive Evolution, and the Women's Liberation Movement," *New England Quarterly* 71(1998):635–642.
28. William H. Jordy, *Henry Adams: Scientific Historian* (New Haven, 1952), 277.
29. Kenneth Burke's distinction between the Virgin as an emblem of *reproduction* and the dynamo as one of *production* implicitly speaks to this point. *A Grammar of Motives* (1945; Berkeley, 1969), 120–121.

30. If we pursue this abstract connection further, we arrive finally at the abstraction of money and commodity exchange. Though never explicitly approached as such by Adams, money undoubtedly lines up in this thinking with masculine rationality, since particularly in *Chartres*, "political economy, which analyzes the relation between value and prices, is a practical, masculine discourse totally at odds with Mary's feminine concept of value, where love and pity reign." Nancy R. Comley, "Henry Adams' Feminine Fictions: The Economics of Maternity," *ALR* 22(1989):13. For an interesting, if somewhat flawed, discussion of the connection between abstract reasoning and commodity exchange, see Alfred Sohn-Rethel, *Intellectual and Manual Labour: A Critique of Epistemology* (New York, 1978).
31. HA to John Hay, Dec. 7, Nov. 16, 1890, in *Letters*, 3:363, 346. Bové says bluntly, "Adams is a materialist," and then explores the implications of that claim in "Anarchy and Perfection," 43–47.
32. Fredric Jameson, "Modernism and Imperialism," in *Nationalism, Colonialism, and Literature*, by Jameson, Terry Eagleton, and Edward Said (Minneapolis, 1990), 50–51.
33. Levenson, among others, places enormous emphasis on La Farge's painting lessons as crucial elements in Adams's artistic development that would make *Chartres* and the *Education* possible. J. C. Levenson, *The Mind and Art of Henry Adams* (Boston, 1957), 209–211.
34. HA to John Hay, Sept. 15, 1890, in *Letters*, 3:282–283.
35. HA to Henry Cabot Lodge, Aug. 4, 1891; HA to Lucy Baxter, Nov. 4, 1890, in *Letters*, 3:518, 324–327.
36. HA to John Hay, Nov. 16, 1890; to Anna Cabot Mills Lodge, Oct. 21, 1890, in *Letters*, 3:342, 306–307.
37. HA to John Hay, Oct. 16, 1890, in *Letters*, 3:302 (brackets in original).
38. HA to Elizabeth Cameron, Nov. 8, 1890, in *Letters*, 3:337.
39. HA to Elizabeth Cameron, Feb. 6, 1891; HA to Clarence King, Apr. 22, 1891; HA to John Hay, Mar. 2, 1891, in *Letters*, 3:405–406, 466, 431.
40. I am indebted to William Decker for pointing out the importance of the intermarriage in complicating Adams's search for the primitive Other.
41. HA to Charles Milnes Gaskell, Mar. 1, 1891, in *Letters*, 3:428.
42. HA to John Hay, Mar. 2, 1891, in *Letters*, 3:433.
43. HA to Elizabeth Cameron, May 17, 1891; HA to John Hay, Mar. 2, 1891, in *Letters*, 3:477–479, 434.
44. HA to Henry Holt, Mar. 5, 1890; HA to John Hay, Jan. 9, 1892, in *Letters*, 3:225, 598–599.
45. HA to John Hay, Jan. 16, 1894; HA to Charles Milnes Gaskell, Jan. 23, 1894, in *Letters*, 4:156, 157.
46. Robert Spiller, introduction to *Tahiti*, by Henry Adams (New York, 1947), iv.
47. Manheim reads the appearance of Arii Taimai's voice in Adams's narrative as complicating Adams's complicity in Hay's imperial agenda, thus, reacting to Rowe's thesis. See Manheim, "The Voice of Arii Taimai," 218–227.
48. For a more detailed examination of this activity and the way it affects our understanding of Adams, see Manheim, "The Voice of Arii Taimai," 215–218. See also my article "Beneath the Manikin's Clothes: Displacement and Engagement in the Biography of Henry Adams," *Genre* 31(1998):33–54.
49. Richard Hofstadter identifies two primary "moods" in the American psyche in the 1890s: sympathy and power. "The capacity for sympathy and the need for power existed side by side," both of which manifested themselves in the Spanish-American War, as the effort to free Cuba became an assertion of American force in world affairs. Adams clearly

participated in this duality. Richard Hofstadter, "Manifest Destiny and the Philippines," in *America in Crisis: Fourteen Crucial Episodes in American History*, ed. Daniel Aaron (New York, 1952), 175–182.

50. Earl Klee, "Henry Adams and the Patrician Response to the Liberal Polity," *Humanities in Society* 3(1980):252–261.
51. Robert H. Weibe, *The Search for Order, 1877–1920* (New York, 1967), 231–232.
52. T. J. Jackson Lears, *No Place of Grace: Antimodernism and the Transformation of American Culture, 1880–1920* (New York, 1981), 275.
53. HA to Brooks Adams, Nov. 3, 1901, in *Letters*, 5:307.
54. HA to Brooks Adams, Feb. 7, 1901, in *Letters*, 5:194.
55. That the book was privately printed with no intention of public release must be kept in mind when discussing the rhetoric of its arrangement. Adams acquiesced to a friend's request for a copy in 1905, though he claimed that "it was not made to be read." "It was made," the letter continued, "only for my brother Tati to offer to the French government as basis for a family pension" (HA to Margaret Chanler, Jan. 27, 1905, in *Letters*, 5:630). Perhaps this letter does not understate the book's intended readership, though I am hard-pressed to understand why he would revise the book for such a limited audience. Running counter to that point is his earlier claim that the book would serve to introduce his American associates to "what the archaic woman was" (HA to Elizabeth Cameron, June 4, 1891, in *Letters*, 3:485). In either case, the intended reader of both editions was clearly occidental, a crucial element of my argument.
56. Henry Adams, *Tahiti* (1901; New York, 1947), 46. Subsequent references will be noted parenthetically in the text.
57. Although he directs his argument elsewhere, Manheim nicely summarizes that "Adams attempted to tell a story of colonial conflict from the point of view of the colonized as well as from the point of view of the colonialist, and in doing so he attempted to begin to resolve his own fundamentally divided allegiances." "The Voice of Arii Taimai," 211.
58. HA to Paul Leicester Ford, Mar. 22, 1886, in *Letters*, 3:6.
59. I am referring to Fish's reading of Milton's *Paradise Lost* in *Surprised by Sin: The Reader in "Paradise Lost"* (New York, 1967). For a brief and brilliant introduction to the transformations from oral to print cultures, see Walter J. Ong, *Orality and Literacy: The Technologizing of the World* (London, 1988).
60. In *Mediation in Contemporary Native American Fiction* (Norman, Okla., 1995), James Ruppert says that a "mediational text attempts to maneuver readers into taking a series of regenerated socio-political positions" (15). Through his manipulation of point of view and the rearrangement of the chapters in the book, Adams is attempting something similar for his Western readers.
61. Robert E. Spiller, "Henry Adams: Man of Letters," in *Literary History of the United States*, ed. Robert Spiller et al., 3d ed. (New York, 1963), 2:1088.
62. Alan Moorehead, *The Fatal Impact: The Invasion of the South Pacific, 1767–1840* (1966; Sydney, Australia, 1987), 20, 13.
63. HA to John Hay, Nov. 16, 1890, in *Letters*, 3:342.
64. See Banta, "Being a 'Begonia' in a Man's World," 70–71, for a discussion of the many female roles Adams adopted.
65. Manheim, "The Voice of Arri Taimai," 222.
66. John La Farge, *Reminiscences of the South Seas* (New York, 1916), 350. Adams's obvious partiality to the Tevas led Robert Langdon to comment on the one-sided nature of the book in "A View on Arii Taimai's Memoirs," *Journal of Pacific History* 4(1969):162–165.
67. The collective nature of the books is further complicated by another memoir, *Mémoires*

de Marau Taaroa, Dernière Reine de Tahiti, written some twenty years later by the original "voice" of the first version of Adams's book. Marau's book draws directly from Adams's memoir, relying on or mirroring exact passages from his earlier work. The question of who relies on whom is not clear. Ariimanihinihi Takau Pomare, *Mémoires de Marau Taaroa, Dernière Reine de Tahiti* (Paris, 1971).

68. Louis Auchincloss, *Henry Adams* (Minneapolis, 1971), 7–8; Levenson, *Mind and Art*, 217, 216; John Carlos Rowe, "Henry Adams," in *Columbia History of American Literature* (New York, 1988), 661; William Merrill Decker, *The Literary Vocation of Henry Adams* (Chapel Hill, 1990), 228–231.
69. In the same way, modernist writers relied on the very imperial aggression they deplored to reach formerly unknown sites that then served as the settings for their works. John A. McClure, "Postmodern Romance: Don DeLillo and the Age of Conspiracy," in *Introducing Don DeLillo*, ed. Frank Lentricchia (Durham, 1991), 100–101.

From True Woman to New Woman to Virgin

CINDY WEINSTEIN

When Madeleine Lightfoot Lee decides to leave New York for the more exciting pastures of Washington, D.C., her horrified friends ask that famous Freudian question, "what does the woman want?"[1] In the opening chapter of Henry Adams's *Democracy*, the narrator gives us a variety of possible answers. We are told that "what she wanted was POWER" (18). To be sure, this motive seems quite plausible given the fact that throughout the novel Madeleine surrounds herself with some of the most powerful people in government, seeking to understand their actions with the hope of eventually gaining some influence. We also learn that she is "tortured by *ennui*" (13), suggesting that Madeleine visits Washington less for the acquisition of power and more for a change of scenery, a means of escape. Madeleine simply wants something to do, and so she goes to the center of government to "see, she thought, the clash of interests, the interests of forty millions of people and a whole continent" (18). What she thinks her motives are and what the narrator imagines them to be are clearly different. Indeed, her movements and motives seem even more complicated once we learn that she has "lost a husband and a baby" (17–18). That she seeks something other than power becomes further evident when her friends chide her for leaving New York with assurances that she will find in Washington only an "illiterate swarm of ordinary people." She replies that if this proves to be the case, "it would be a pleasure to return,—precisely the feeling she longed for" (18). Here, then, is yet another answer to the question of what Madeleine wants. She wishes for the "pleasure" of a return. But a return to what?

Madeleine is in a predicament. No longer mother and wife, and yet uninterested in "lectur[ing] for women's rights" or "go[ing] on the stage" (17)—two options that present themselves only to be summarily dismissed—Madeleine finds herself in the position of having lost her hold on the private sphere and not knowing how to proceed with a career in the public sphere. She is, to use the terms bequeathed to us by nineteenth-century authors on the woman question and taken up by contemporary scholars of the period, neither a true woman nor a new woman. Her relation with Ratcliffe, the senator from Illinois, initially promises a happy combination of the two. She imagines that she can find the satisfaction of participating in the public world of politics through her influential position as confidante and soon-to-be wife at the same time that she "sacrifices" her public ambitions on the altar of "her duty" (99) as a woman. Carrington skillfully and fortunately interferes with Madeleine's plans for sacrifice and success, and her journey to Washington concludes with yet another journey to Egypt. Although she had claimed that she would return with pleasure if Washington proved every bit as dreary as her New York friends had predicted, she chooses to continue her wanderings. Thus, there is no return. But no return to what?

Madeleine's ambivalence with respect to the future that lies before her bespeaks a broader sense of liminality felt by many women of the time, who found themselves caught between two paradigms of female identity: the true woman of the antebellum period and the new woman of the late nineteenth century. Madeleine does not know where to go, geographically, psychically, or professionally. Through the deaths of her husband and child, she has been painfully separated from an older ideal of a woman's place that was aligned with the private, domestic world, and yet she is hesitant to embrace the newer model of female identity associated with the public world. Adams situates Madeleine, and Esther Dudley of *Esther*, precisely at the moment when they and their nonfictional counterparts have the option of choosing a professional identity—in the novel, specifically that of political maverick or artist—or an identity defined by one's position in the home. Adams seems to portray the first option as unfulfilling, if not impossible, for women whose "tendency towards asceticism, self-extinction, [and] self-abnegation" (99) makes a professional career implausible; the second option appears equally unrealizable because the home has become the place of loss, whether of husband and child in Madeleine's case or of the father in Esther's or of Marian in Adams's life. For Adams and the women with whom he identifies, a return to family is impossible because it has been destroyed, and an embrace of professionalism is undesirable because reproduction becomes impossible. Thus, Adams eventually makes his way to the Virgin of Mont-Saint-Michel and Chartres in order to return to a dream where families are whole and the spirit of motherly love guides one's professional undertakings.

MARIAN ADAMS COMMITTED SUICIDE by ingesting potassium cyanide, a chemical used to develop photographs. The combination of this tragedy and Adams's own uneasy relation to his professional life makes the dilemmas of his female characters all the more pointed, relevant, and self-revealing. If one cannot return to an immediate past, one can always go further back to a less remembered, perhaps more malleable past—to Egypt, to Mont-Saint-Michel and Chartres, to the twelfth-century home of the Virgin—in the hopes of finding (or constructing) an ideal home, an ideal woman, to make one's experiences of loss less painful. Adams's paradoxical return to and invention of the Virgin in *The Education of Henry Adams* as "the greatest force the Western world ever felt . . . [in that she] had drawn man's activities to herself more strongly than any other power, natural or supernatural" provide the cure for the psychic malaise of his heroines. His spiritual relation to the Virgin also assuages his own manikin-like relation to the human condition, which he formulates in the preface.[2] Whereas paralysis rather than praxis awaits the female protagonists of the novels, Adams creates in the *Education* another fictional woman who not only saves herself but Adams and the entire human race from what he sees as a cultural paralysis. This woman represents the power of "reproduction—the greatest and most mysterious of all energies" (384). "All she needed," Adams writes, "was to be fecund" (384) because her fecundity functions as an assurance against and an antidote to loss. It is this return to an original source of life figured in the female body, essentialist and reductive as one might argue it to be, that is denied to Madeleine, to Esther, and, most lamentably, to Marian, and which Adams proposes as the solution to his heroines', his culture's, and his own "helpless" sense of being (*Education* 111, 385). The Virgin both combines and transforms elements of the true woman and the new woman ideologies of the nineteenth century. She offers a cure for Adams's experience of professional and personal dissatisfaction at the same time that she provides Adams with a more secure sense of his male identity by establishing a female identity over which he has ultimate control.

My reading has thus far invoked two stereotypes of female identity, the true woman and the new woman, that help situate an analysis of Adams's relation to women in an historical, economic, and cultural context. A closer examination of these female stereotypes will help us sort out Adams's use of them, although we must keep in mind that the invocation of a particular stereotype does not deny exceptions to it. Adams was no stranger to stereotypes. They appear throughout the *Education*: "the machine-made collectivist female" (446), "the Bostonian [who] had always been noted for a certain chronic irritability" (419), "the Southerner [who] had no mind; he had temperament" (57), "the Jew Banker" (285), or the Virgin and the dynamo, to which all analyses of Adams inevitably return. He finds stereotypes useful as points of departure, cultural meditation, and personal intervention that enable him to construct his own ideal of womanhood. The "true woman," as delineated by Barbara Welter in "The Cult of True Womanhood," upheld values in the home antithetical, though complementary, to those that organized behavior outside the home, specifically in the developing antebellum marketplace. Her attributes, according to Welter, could be "divided into four cardinal virtues—piety, purity, submissiveness and domesticity."[3] Thus we see Catharine Beecher's *Treatise of Domestic Economy* advising women on the religious and national significance of a well-ordered household, or Lydia Sigourney in *Letters to Mothers* urging "submission to parents, teachers and superiors, harmony with brothers, sisters, and friends [which] prepare the way for those more arduous relative duties which devolve upon our sex."[4]

Even as Welter powerfully argues for the restrictive logic of an identity harnessed to the home, however, she also suggests that the very category of "true woman" carried within it the potential for its own undoing, "for if woman was so very little less than the angels, she should surely take a more active part in running the world, especially since men were making such a hash of things."[5] The new woman, by contrast, rejected the promise of power within the home in favor of power outside of it. Carroll Smith-Rosenberg, in an essay that does for the new woman what Welter's does for the true woman, has defined the new woman of the 1870s through the turn of the century as "single, highly educated, [and] economically autonomous. . . . Eschewing marriage, she fought for professional visibility, espoused innovative, often radical, economic and social reforms, and wielded real political power."[6] The breadth of this change became evident in the proliferation of women's colleges, such as Bryn Mawr and Wellesley; the expansion of teaching opportunities for women at these colleges; and the establishment of settlement houses, such as Jane Addams's Hull House. Women had access to sections of the public sphere that had heretofore been closed to them, and they entered those arenas in numbers indicating that significant cultural changes had indeed taken place since the antebellum period.

Adams may have considered himself married to a new woman. After all, upon her death, Marian was described in the *Boston Transcript* as a woman who "came nearer being the head of an intellectual coterie than any woman [in Washington]." According to the obituary in the *New York World*, she had been "a very skilful amateur photographer . . . and has made a number of very artistic negatives of distinguished people among her friends and acquaintances."[7] From Henry Adams's point of view, the new woman's potential power in the public sphere came at the enormous cost of her power as a sexual (and married) being. Did Adams think that Marian had paid that price? They had married, but the marriage proved infertile, marking yet one more failure, perhaps the most significant one, in a life Adams would represent as a series of repeated failures.

Kim Moreland has shown that "while Adams's dedication to the medieval ideal provided the dispensation for his attractive celebration of female sexuality, it also less attractively justified his reaction of distaste to the so-called 'New Woman.'"[8] Madeleine and Esther, both new women in their intellectual vigor and personal ambition, illustrate this point as they find themselves sad and alone, one looking for answers in the Great Pyramids, the other searching for meaning at Niagara Falls. In contrast to these dispirited and exhausted women, the Virgin is a wondrous and vitalized combination of true and new womanhood. She is the true woman in that she is the Virgin, whose power rests in the home. Her piety is unquestionable, given her domain in the church, and her virtue is untarnished. After all, she did immaculately conceive. As a distillation of true womanhood, however, the Virgin's home appears conceptually redecorated to meet the personal and cultural needs of Adams's and, by extension, America's sense of homelessness. Her home transcends the boundaries between private and public, so that comfort is never far away. She and her home (the two are inextricable) are ubiquitous and timeless, transcending the boundaries between private and public. But she is also the new woman who wields a tremendous amount of political power, who has the capacity to effect social reform, and who remains free from marital attachments, all the while able to shower her maternal love upon her son, who happens to be the savior.[9]

Thus, as much as Adams appropriates elements of these stereotypes, his own representation of womanhood radically differs from them in his understanding that "sex is a vital condition" (441) to be acknowledged and even celebrated. Heterosexual sex, as represented by the admittedly very peculiar figure of the Virgin, is not only present in Adams's work but is omnipotent and ubiquitous. In contrast, the true woman, as cultural critics have pointed out, was to a large extent defined by her commitment to discipline, and that discipline applied not only to the care of her children and the maintenance of her home but also to the expression of her own passions and desires. The true woman, unlike the Virgin, represented a sexual force to be harnessed, not honored. Similarly, the "vital condition" of the new woman, unlike the Virgin, had to be reanimated not for the purposes of celebrating her sexual powers but because her accession to the public sphere had allegedly diminished her capacity to master the reproductive duties of the private sphere. For all of the new woman's differences from her antebellum predecessor, a woman's desire for something other than a life organized around the domestic sphere nevertheless continued to demand concern and containment.

Medical debates raged about the new woman's growing incapacity to bear and care for children. S. Weir Mitchell, perhaps most famously known as Charlotte Perkins Gilman's doctor, whom she denounces in "The Yellow Wallpaper," and less famously as Marian Adams's acquaintance, anxiously watched "the increase of nervous diseases . . . and the dying out of the maternal instinct." Similarly, George Beard, medical specialist in nervous disorders, described the increasing difficulty American women had during childbirth: owing to the pressures of "modern civilization . . . the simple act of giving birth to a child opens the door to unnumbered woes; beginning with lacerations and relaxations, extending to displacements and ovarian imprisonments, and ending by setting the whole system on fire with neuralgias, tremors, etc., and compelling a life-long slavery to sleeplessness, hysteria, or insanity."[10]

Like Mitchell and Beard, Adams feared the atrophying of the maternal instinct, and the painful fact that he and his wife could not have children surely had a great deal to do with his interest in the subject.[11] In the "Vis Inertiae" chapter of the *Eduation*, for example, Adams writes that "so far as she succeeded, she must become sexless like the bees, and must leave the old energy of inertia to carry on the race. . . . [B]ut the American woman had no illusions or ambitions or new resources, and nothing to rebel against, except her own maternity" (446). For Adams, this rebellion against maternity amounted to a denial of "the power of sex" (385). He made no distinction between marriage and maternity, let alone between marriage and sex. To be sure, sex is the subject of Mitchell and Beard's tracts, though they relegate its "power" to their textual margins, effectually silencing it.[12]

In the *Education*, Adams invokes this erasure of female sexuality as the source of his personal and his culture's woes; without it, there is no productive, indeed reproductive, force to counter the antiproductive, "parricidal" (381) mechanical forces, which Adams describes as creating "a universe of motions . . . of vertiginous violence" (495). Rather than advocating the infamous "rest cure," a disciplined cessation of everything including sexual desire, Adams has something far more radical in mind when he calls upon women to recreate themselves in the image of the Virgin, so as to be "potent, not merely as a sentiment, but as a force" (384). His invocation of force places him squarely in the naturalist literary tradition of Theodore Dreiser, Frank Norris, and Charlotte Perkins Gilman, but it also indicates Adams's attempt to overcome the constraints of its deterministic underpinnings by suggesting that women's force, once marshalled and enacted, has the capacity to inspire "the highest energy ever known to man" (385). Adams's Virgin recalls the energizing aspects of female sexuality, whether in aiding economic, aesthetic, or spiritual production.[13]

Inasmuch as desire, sexuality, and fecundity provide the foundations for Adams's ideal womanhood, they are all but absent from his self-construction in the *Education*. Adams's own desire appears nowhere in the text, except perhaps in the profound ellipsis at the center, where the very stillness and silence speak of Marian Adams's suicide and his wish to keep that loss private. If the question that begins *Democracy* is "what does the woman want?" then "what does the man want?" might be the appropriate question with which to begin any discussion of the *Education*. Adams wants an education (for he, ironically, finds himself sorely lacking one), as well as the opportunity to educate others so as to transcend his experience of "the sheer chaos of human nature" (153). He ascribes this chaos simultaneously to the individual and to a collective "flounder[ing] between worlds passed and worlds coming" (83). For Adams, such floundering initially has little to do with the inadequacies of female force and everything to do with an overwhelming sense of his own shortcomings as his father's underling: "the young man knew no longer what character he bore. Private secretary in the morning, son in the afternoon, young man about town in the evening, the only character he never bore was that of diplomatist, except when he wanted a card to some great function" (194). Adams understands neither society nor his place in it: "he never felt himself in society, and he never knew definitely what was meant as society by those who were in it" (197). Again and again, Adams calls attention to a confusion about "his identity, if one could call a bundle of disconnected memories an identity" (209), the source of which lies in his inability to understand his value as a professional: "by courtesy [he was] allowed to go to Court as Attaché, though he was never attached. . . . In society, when official, he was attached to the Minister; when unofficial, he was a young man without any position at all" (145).[14] It hardly matters whether the reader agrees with Adams's consistent representation of himself as "consciously pursu[ing] nothing, but drift[ing] as attraction offered itself" (366–367)—an assertion that seems disingenous given that by this time in his narrative he has written several books, edited the *North American Review*, and taught medieval history at Harvard. His portrayal of himself as "drift[ing] into the mental indolence of history" (36) is intimately tied to his experience of professional helplessness.

One might suppose that a proper education would lead to mastery rather than drift, but Adams's education has only given him a heightened knowledge of his own "mental indolence," the sense that he is "a vagrant as well as a pauper" (93) and "a beggar" (337)—not at all the "economy of force" he claims to desire in the preface to the *Education*. What Adams means by economy of force becomes clear in the chapter "Berlin," when he characterizes German state education as "a sort of dynamo machine for polarizing the popular mind; for turning and holding its lines of force in the direction supposed to be most effective for State purposes" (78). He concludes this laudatory account with damning praise: "The German machine was terribly efficient. Its effect on the children was pathetic" (78). Adams claims to want an education in economy and efficiency, but when he gets it he runs the other way. In a letter to Mabel Hooper La Farge, Adams went so far as to say that any education is doomed to failure: "the only well-educated and successful boys I ever knew were those who were kicked and cuffed most, and least educated."[15]

It would seem that Adams both wants an education and cannot find a teacher who knows what the lessons are, let alone someone who is able to teach them. What, then, does Adams want? In the chapter "Diplomacy," the narrator explains that "the kind of education he most required was that of a charming woman" (122). This woman will be the Virgin: she will educate him, and she will rescue him from the professional restlessness and personal chaos, which are the legacies of his attachment to his father and to which he returns even more painfully with the suicide of his wife. The Virgin, as Adams constructs her, provides a solution to his professional dilemma as author. In the editor's preface, which Henry Cabot Lodge signed but Adams wrote, he discusses the composition of *Mont Saint Michel and Chartres*, as well as the *Education*, and calls attention to the issue of aesthetics: "the point on which the author failed to please himself, and could get no light from readers or friends, was the usual one of literary form" (xxvii). If Adams "could not satisfy himself with his workmanship" (xxviii), it is perhaps because he did not have the proper muse to inspire him, someone to help him see the larger significance of his work. In the windows of Chartres described in *Mont Saint Michel and Chartres*, Adams keenly felt both the guiding transcendental spirit of the Virgin and what Thorstein Veblen had called the "instinct of workmanship." "We see," Adams wrote, "and the artists meant that we should see, only the great lines, the colour, and the Virgin."[16] In contrast to the ideal of workmanship represented at Chartres, where "the work shows blind obedience, as though he [the architect] were doing his best to please the Virgin without trying to please himself" (112), Adams's aesthetic labors in the *Education* betray the author's torment during the process of composition: "the pencil or pen runs into side-paths and shapelessness, loses its relations, stops or is bogged" (389). Like Madeleine, Adams, while studying the windows in *Mont Saint Michel and Chartres*, wishes for the pleasure of a return to "some controlling hand" (172)—a hand, perhaps, not unlike that offered him by John Quincy Adams in "Quincy," the opening chapter of the *Education*: "he took the boy's hand without a word, and walked with him, paralyzed by awe, up the road to town" (13).

At the same time that the Virgin promises Adams a literary or professional salvation, she is also a personal savior, and I would like briefly to consider how the Virgin as an ideal of female sexuality might relate to the Adamses' experience of childlessness. We can, at best, glean the impact of their inability to have children from scattered, though profound, references. Eleanor Whiteside, Marian's lifelong friend, wrote that although the latter wanted children, "not having any was a greater grief to Mr. Adams than to her." In response to the news of Charles Milnes and Catherine Gaskell's first child, Adams offered his congratulations "on getting happily over this first great condition of marriage," implying (retrospectively) that his marriage had failed in that it had not met that essential condition. Adams ended with the bittersweet acknowledgment that "one consequence of having no children is that husband and wife become very dependent on each other and live very much together."[17]

Adams's sense of his own failures, whether aesthetic or reproductive, requires divine female intervention. No real person could heal his psychic wounds. In an often-quoted letter to Margaret Chanler, written in 1905, Adams asserted that "the American woman is a failure; that she has held nothing together, neither State nor Church, nor Society nor Family. She is more of a failure when she tries a mission than she is when she doesn't. On the whole I think she is a worse failure than the American man who is surely failure enough."[18] As a contrast to the terrific failure of American women (and men), Adams explains the consoling and unifying power of the Virgin in *Mont Saint Michel and Chartres*: "She never calls for sympathy by hysterical appeals to our feelings; she does not even altogether command, but rather accepts the voluntary, unquestioning, unhesitating, instinctive faith, love, and devotion of mankind" (148). In this passage, Adams celebrates the gentle power of the maternal Virgin and the sexuality that inheres in her identity as a mother.

To state the obvious, he has chosen an extremely unusual woman to represent his ideal of female sexuality, since the Virgin immaculately conceived her child and gave birth without pain. Given Adams's exhaustive education (deplorable as he finds it), he would surely have known Aquinas's views about the Virgin in *Summa Theologiae*. Here Aquinas presents a scene of parturition radically different from the one that Beard imagined at Adams's time; Aquinas believed that "the pangs of childbirth are caused by the baby opening the passage from the womb. Now we have said that Christ came from his mother's closed womb without forcing a way. Consequently there was no pain in the birth and no injury done."[19] Her fecundity thus has nothing to do with her biological body. Indeed, it is ironic that even as Adams laments the fact that American "society regarded this victory over sex as its greatest triumph" (385), he presents as ideal a version of sexuality that would seem to be one of the greatest victories over sex imaginable. The woman's body in Adams's representation of perfect sexuality is actually the closest thing possible to the dynamo. Like the dynamo, which creates force without sexuality, so too the Virgin produces children and forces with little, if any, help from the body.

In a letter Adams wrote to Elizabeth Cameron about his infatuation with babies, this fantasy of childbirth takes a somewhat different form. Adams recounts a dream in which he has given birth: "One of my minds was rather surprised, and asked, in a puzzled way, whether men had babies as a rule; and my other mind at once replied with my usual positiveness and passion for generalisation, that men always had babies."[20] Adams's imaginative appropriation of female reproductive labor is witty and touching. This letter not only speaks to a desire to do what his wife could not—bear children—but it also speaks to an ongoing identification with women.[21] He published *Esther*, for example, under the female pseudonym of Frances Snow Compton. In the *Education*, he confesses his deep, though unselfconscious, kinship with his grandmother Louisa Catherine Adams: "He never dreamed that from her might come some of those doubts and self-questionings, those hesitations, those rebellions against law and discipline, which marked more than one of her descendants; but he might even then have felt some vague instinctive suspicion that he was to inherit from her the seeds of the primal sin, the fall from grace, the curse of Abel, that he was not of pure New England stock, but half-exotic" (19). These words, which speak to Adams's sense of personal and professional dislocation, could just as easily have come from Madeleine.

Adams, however, had a fondness for occupying the identities of those with whom he had very little in common or with whom he feared he had all too much in common, be they Jews (in a letter to Brooks, he compared himself to "a cautious and somewhat cowardly Scotchman or Jew"), vagrants, paupers, or women.[22] This strategic self-fashioning, to use Stephen Greenblatt's term, allowed Adams to position himself as victim (of prejudice, of the market economy, of chaotic masculine forces or inert female ones) and to claim the sympathy reserved for victims while continuing to enjoy the privileges of an Anglo-Saxon, upper-class male. His disaffection with his labor, for example, led him to claims about work in the *Education* that made him sound far more pro-labor than he was: "if the world wants hard work, the world must pay for it; and, if it will not pay, it has no fault to find with the worker" (257). This sentence, let us remember, came from someone who "if he worked at all, it was for social consideration, and social pleasure was his pay" (257). His self-portrait of helplessness and incessant victimization throughout the *Education* is a fiction he generated by appropriating identities not his own.[23]

The case of women in this regard offers particular complexities: while Adams consistently indicates a desire to submit to their reproductive and sexual power, his willingness to do so depends on the implausibility of his wish that women resume their rightful place as "the highest energy ever known to man" (*Education* 385). Passages such as "an American Virgin would never dare command; an American Venus would never dare exist" (385) demonstrate the relatively safe position from which Adams launches his attack on American sexlessness and his campaign for the reorganization of American culture around female force. Only because an American Venus would not dare to exist does Adams plead with her to appear. Moreover, Adams is willing to submit to female power as long as it accords with his notions of what that power should be—that is, as long as it fulfills his needs. In an 1883 letter to John Hay, Adams reported that "there are pleasant new women always coming and going, but no new men. . . . Man delights me not. Woman is my only solace."[24] As deeply as Adams identified with women, he also identified them as sources for solace and sympathy—the most conventional of all female roles. Women such as Elizabeth Cameron and her daughter, Martha, were important figures in Adams's life, but specifically in the context of helping him to feel less alienated, more important, more powerful. As much as Adams confided in, sought out, even worshipped women, he still valued his more powerful position as a man.

One passage from *Democracy* manifests this aspect of his representation of women with particular clarity. In the middle of the novel, Madeleine and Ratcliffe engage in a conversation about how best the senator might promote the public good. Up until this point, their relationship has remained relatively impersonal, but when Ratcliffe demands that Madeleine own up to the extent to which her influence has become indispensable to him, and therefore instrumental to his promotion of the public good, Madeleine "for the first time began to feel his power" (97). She temporarily fends off his advances, contemplating her next move. "Was not his career a thousand times more important than hers? If he, in his isolation and his cares, needed her assistance, had she an excuse for refusing it? What was there in her aimless and useless life which made it so precious that she could not afford to fling it into the gutter, if need be, on the bare chance of enriching some fuller existence?" (99) Madeleine's thoughts resound with Adams's own anxieties about his career, his usefulness, and the relative emptiness of his existence. As analogous as Adams's situation was to Madeleine's, as often as the *Education* presents his insecurity about the "useful[ness]" of his professional life (117), the "shapeless[ness]" (389) of his education, and the "futil[ity]" of his "pursuit of power" (389), the fact is that Adams's worries are rhetorical conceits aimed to evoke a sympathetic response in the reader. Like it or not, Adams did have a career, certainly as a writer, if nothing else. And this is quite a lot, for, as William Decker has reminded us, "it is Adams's compulsive authorship, belying the conceit of an already posthumous author, that emerges as the *Education*'s grandest symbol, or, if one prefers, example."[25] In "The Dynamo and the Virgin," for example, when he mourns the fact that "the secret of education still hid itself somewhere behind ignorance" (389), he nevertheless has his "pen [which] becomes a sort of blind-man's dog, to keep him from falling" (389). Madeleine, on the other hand, has no career. She has no pen. Neither private secretary to the head of the American legation nor editor of a prestigious magazine, neither Harvard professor nor writer of fiction, history, letters, essays, or autobiography. Madeleine's power is only her power to sympathize with Ratcliffe. She *is* aimless, as is Esther, and the only option they have to correct the problem is marriage, which they ultimately refuse, and thus are left feeling just as aimless and useless as when they began. To be sure, Adams would like us to apply this narrative to his own case, and he does so quite powerfully in the *Education*. In a 1903 letter to George Cabot Lodge, Adams lamented, "Unluckily I was never an American woman."[26] So this is what Adams wanted. To be Madeleine, Esther, his wife. One might indeed wonder just how lucky he would have felt had he switched places with them.

NOTES

I would like to thank Henry Wasser of CUNY for the invitation to present my work on Adams at the graduate school, Bill Decker for the opportunity to include it in this collection, Ondine Le Blanc for her editorial skills, and Jim Astorga for his many comments on this reading.

1. Henry Adams, *Democracy* (New York, 1983), 17. All further quotations will be from this edition and will be noted in the text.
2. Henry Adams, *The Education of Henry Adams*, ed. Ernest Samuels (Boston, 1973), 388–389. All further quotations from the *Education* will be from this edition and will be noted in the text.
3. Barbara Welter, "The Cult of True Womanhood, 1820–1860," in her *Dimity Convictions: The American Woman in the Nineteenth Century* (Athens, Ohio, 1976), 21.
4. Lydia Sigourney, *Letters to Mothers* (New York, 1846), 210. Such an understanding of female identity has met with recent challenges from historians and literary critics who have argued that a greater permeability of boundaries existed between home and the market, between the private and the public. This scholarship posits a culture that opened up the possibility of female empowerment. There is a considerable archive of feminist scholarship that challenges the private/public divide. See, for example, Mary P. Ryan, *Women in Public: Between Banners and Ballots, 1825–1880* (Baltimore, 1990); Nina Baym, *American Women Writers and the Work of History, 1790–1860* (New Brunswick, 1995); and the *No More Separate Spheres!* volume of *American Literature* 70(1998).
5. Welter, "The Cult of True Womanhood," 41.
6. Carroll Smith-Rosenberg, "The Woman as Androgyne: Social Disorder and Gender Cri-

sis, 1870–1936," in her *Disorderly Conduct: Visions of Gender in Victorian America* (Oxford, 1985), 245.

7. Quoted in Ernest Samuels, *Henry Adams: The Middle Years* (Cambridge, Mass., 1958), 276.
8. Kim Moreland, "Henry Adams, the Medieval Lady, and the 'New Woman,'" *Clio* 18(1989):300.
9. On the maternal function of discipline in the antebellum home, see Richard Brodhead's "Sparing the Rod: Discipline and Fiction in Antebellum America," *Representations* 21(1988):67–96.
10. Samuels, *The Middle Years*, 39; George M. Beard, *American Nervousness and Its Consequences* (1881; New York, 1972), 76–77. Smith-Rosenberg discusses how the true woman not only raised concerns about heterosexuality and reproduction but also about lesbianism and what Havelock Ellis famously called sexual "inversion."
11. In *Better in Darkness: A Biography of Henry Adams: His Second Life, 1862–1891* (Hamden, Conn., 1994), Edward Chalfant argues that the Adamses' childlessness was intentional. Chalfant, however, does not account for Mrs. Adams's acquaintance with Mitchell, nor for the presence of James Marion Sims's *Clinical Notes on Uterine Surgery—With Special Reference to the Management of Sterile Conditions* in the Adamses' library. I would like to thank Professor Chalfant for his careful and helpful reading of this paper.
12. See Howard Kaplan, *Power and Order: Henry Adams and the Naturalist Tradition in American Fiction* (Chicago, 1981), especially 37–64.
13. Adams's interest in force suggests his affinity with much naturalist fiction, but his work is distinctive by virtue of the central place accorded to the Virgin—his religious icon, his heroine, and his exemplar of female sexuality. The Virgin, as an incarnation of ideal womanhood, is quite different from Dreiser's Carrie in *Sister Carrie*, Norris's Trina in *McTeague*, or the unnamed narrator in Gilman's "The Yellow Wallpaper." For the best account of the place of sexuality in naturalist fiction, see Walter Benn Michaels's *The Gold Standard and the Logic of Naturalism: American Literature at the Turn of the Century* (Berkeley, Calif., 1987).
14. For an enlightening discussion of Adams's complex relation to authority, particularly his biological and philosophical fathers, see John Patrick Diggins, "'Who Bore the Failure of the Light': Henry Adams and the Crisis of Authority," *New England Quarterly* 58(1985):165–192. Also see T. J. Jackson Lears, *No Place of Grace: Antimodernism and the Transformation of American Culture, 1880–1920* (New York, 1981), to which my own reading of Adams is deeply indebted.
15. HA to Mabel Hooper La Farge, Mar. 9, 1902, in *The Letters of Henry Adams*, ed. J. C. Levenson et al. (Cambridge, Mass., 1982–1988), 5:352.
16. Henry Adams, *Mont Saint Michel and Chartres* (Princeton, 1981), 195. All further quotations will be from this edition and will be noted in the text.
17. Quoted in Katherine Simonds, "The Tragedy of Mrs. Henry Adams," *New England Quarterly* 9(1936):577; HA to Charles Milnes Gaskell, Nov. 25, 1877, in *Letters*, 2:327.
18. HA to Margaret Chanler, Aug. 11, 1905, in *Letters*, 5:701.
19. Thomas Aquinas, *Summa Theologiae* (New York, 1972), 52:101. Adams's knowledge of Aquinas is demonstrated in "Saint Thomas Aquinas," the final chapter of *Mont Saint Michel and Chartres*, though his focus is not as much on the Virign as it is on Aquinas's theory of the Trinity, which Adams characterizes in the following way: "God, as a double consciousness, loves Himself, and realizes Himself in the Holy Ghost. The Third side of the triangle is love or grace" (355).
20. HA to Elizabeth Cameron, Feb. 8, 1903, in *Letters*, 5:452.

21. Martha Banta goes so far as to say that a "bisexual imagination authors *The Education of Henry Adams*," in "Being a 'Begonia' in a Man's World," in *New Essays on The Education of Henry Adams*, ed. John Carlos Rowe (Cambridge, England, 1996), 62. My argument differs from hers in that I believe Adams's identification with women to be one element in a larger strategy of identifying with less powerful members of his culture as a means of obtaining sympathy and power.
22. HA to Brooks Adams, Aug. 10, 1902, in *Letters*, 5:400.
23. Gregory Jay makes a similar point: "the symbolic figure of the Virgin turns out to be Adams's first major experiment in ironic self-fashioning. . . . The outlaw characteristics he ascribes to the Virgin and her worshipers will be those given, in *The Education*, to the rhetorical figure, spoken always in the third person, of 'Henry Adams.'" *America the Scrivener: Deconstruction and the Subject of Literary History* (Ithaca, 1990), 234–235. For a fuller discussion of Adams's appropriation of worker's identity, see chapter 5 in my *The Literature of Labor and the Labors of Literature: Allegory in Nineteenth-Century American Fiction* (Cambridge, Eng., 1995).
24. HA to John Hay, May 20, 1883, in *Letters*, 2:502.
25. William Merrill Decker, *The Literary Vocation of Henry Adams* (Chapel Hill, 1990), 271.
26. HA to George Cabot Lodge, Apr. 27, 1903, in *Letters*, 5:497.

A Martyr to the Disease of Omniscience

WILLIAM MERRILL DECKER

THE INQUIRING MIND OF HENRY ADAMS counted among its chief fascinations the martyrdom of the mind that inquires. Early and late, his writings examine men and women engaged in ambitious intellectual tasks: to create a new order of civilization (Albert Gallatin, Thomas Jefferson), to diagnose the malaise of popular government (Madeleine Lee), to reconcile theology with intuition (Esther Dudley), to propound the bond between humankind and God (Pierre Abélard, Thomas Aquinas), to predict the course of events leading up to a new millennium (Henry Adams). Whereas heroes cast in the military or political mold count little in Adams's historiography, he was always ready to exalt the inquirer who interrogates the world with the heroic conviction that mind can draw within reach of some ultimate knowledge of itself and its universe. How, once achieved, such knowledge might apply to daily life remained for Adams a troubling issue, and he often hesitated when it came to defining the pragmatic implications of an evident truth. Yet knowledge per se received from Adams less attention than the effort to know, and ideas for him were seldom more interesting than the people who produced them under specific historical conditions. How individual thinkers and their societies process the fresh, paradigmatic, dangerous idea constituted his true focus. Ever a biographer and inevitably an autobiographer, Adams perceived the life of the mind as the highest form of human endeavor and his narratives bear regular witness to the drama of intellection. Such narratives may not always support the conclusion he draws in chapter 29 of *The Education of Henry Adams*—that "the highest intelligence known to history had drowned itself in the reflection of its own thought"—but Adams's inquirers must generally settle for a qualified success and routinely answer for venturing beyond the dogmas of their time.[1]

My essay concerns the intellectual protagonist in the work of Henry Adams and what he regards as the unique *agon* of the inquirer's calling. Beginning with the profile of the innovative thinker that occurs in his 1868 review of Charles Lyell's *Principles of Geology* and concluding with the autobiographical personae who appear in *The Education of Henry Adams* and *A Letter to American Teachers of History*, I will consider various personalities whose compulsion to inquire Adams contemplates: James Hutton, Albert Gallatin, Thomas Jefferson, Madeleine Lee, Esther Dudley, Pierre Abélard, Saint Thomas Aquinas, and (last but ever first) Henry Adams "himself." I begin with the assumption that these figures serve as alter egos by which Adams attempts, at a strategic remove, to decide his role as an intellectual in post–Civil War America. My guiding questions are these: What affinities draw Adams to specific protagonist personalities? How does he perceive the relation between innovative thought and the conventional wisdom of the time? What for Adams is at stake in the human and intellectual drama that accompanies the birth of ideas? For whom or for what does the inquirer work? And finally, on what premises and in what form is Adams prepared to recognize truth? As will be obvious, my questions reflect the hypothesis that the conflicts generated by human intellection have for Adams less to do with issues pertaining to discipline-specific inquiries than with matters of a more ideological character; accordingly, I seek answers of a sort that Adams's narratives tend to mystify. The continuing interest in Henry Adams owes much, I believe, to the occasions he provides latter-day intellectuals for assessing their role in a culture that marginalizes humanist thought. As I examine the ways in which Adams searches for usable images in the mirror held up by his fellow inquirers, I hope to promote a similar self-reflexivity among those for whom Adams represents an inspiring and yet ever cautionary example.

ADAMS'S CAREER AS AN ACTIVE INQUIRER spanned half a century and only briefly conformed to anything conventionally academic. His conception of his calling proved to be exceptionally fluid and persistently aloof. Impervious to official honors and recognitions, Adams resisted settlement in institutional contexts and avoided protocols of scholarly publication. In some respects he exemplified a high Romantic conception of the thinker as Prometheus or Faust at a time when intellectuals were becoming academic professionals, submitting increasingly to institutional vassalage. In other respects he pioneered a kind of interdisciplinary inquiry that puts the thinker in position to perform syncretistic and deconstructive procedures.

This public persona of the intellectual who refuses to conform to standard expectations is one of his most enduring achievements as well as a source of difficulty for his interpreter. It is very much a constructed persona, and it has a history.

How did Henry Adams envision the inquirer's role as he stood at the threshold of adult life? For the young man obliged to spend the war years in London as his father's private secretary, he had full range to invent the role, although his New England background provided definite leads. Growing up in antebellum Boston, Adams was exposed to alternative and overlapping models of intellectual life: the Unitarian clergy (of whom Ralph Waldo Emerson and Man Thinking constituted a variation), the Harvard faculty (generally more conservative than its British counterpart), and the philosophical statesman embodied by his own male forebears. As an Adams he was predictably eager to contribute to the shaping of public life, but even before the war broke out he had surmised that his path lay in journalism and scholarship rather than in law and elective office. Recognizing that the war must wholly unmake the America of his youth, Adams spent much of his time contemplating the part he might play as a public intellectual in a post-war America. Anticipating the expansions that would soon transform American life, he meditated the reestablishment of a constitutional democracy purged of the slave power and the abuses of the party system. But he also imagined the formation of an elite that could foster an American cultural life by diffusing virtue and intellect throughout the general population. The conception was at once academic, clerical, and political. "What we want . . . is a school," Adams wrote in November 1862 to his brother Charles in view of the challenges at hand. "We want a national set of young men like ourselves or better, to start new influences not only in politics, but in literature, in law, in society, and throughout the whole social organism of the country." His idea reflects a nostalgic, ideal vision of the American Republic, one whose antiquity Adams himself acknowledged when he doubted the possibility "of combined action for any unselfish end."[2] Still, in thinking about the American prospect, Adams was encouraged by his readings in Tocqueville and Mill inasmuch as they identified democratization as the inevitable tendency of civil society. The trend did not have to lead to wholesale corruption if the "social organism" would submit to proper schooling.

For his model of inquiry, however, Adams turned less to Tocqueville and Mill, whom he identified in a May 1863 letter to Charles as "the two high priests of our faith," than he did to the scientists—geologists, botanists, physicists—prominent in nineteenth-century England.[3] Social philosophers, early and late, existed for Adams as derivative thinkers. Recalling the London years in the *Education*, he would identify the doctrine of evolution as providing the bedrock for such faith in human perfectibility as the social philosopher might develop, and as Adams himself would want to affirm at various stages of his early and middle career. What else he derived from his readings in the scientific literature of the day is evinced by an October 1863 letter that exhibits his perennial susceptibility to determinist explanations of phenomena—one that would ever vie with his democratic leanings: "The truth is," he remarked to Charles, "everything in this universe has its regular waves and tides. Electricity, sound, the wind, and I believe every part of organic nature will be brought some day within this law. But my philosophy teaches me . . . that the laws which govern animated beings will be ultimately found to be at bottom the same with those which rule inanimate nature, and, as I entertain a profound conviction of the littleness of our kind, and of the curious enormity of creation, I am quite ready to receive with pleasure any basis for a systematic conception of it all." Such "philosophy," Adams went on, prepared to superimpose Calvinist theology on an empiricist model of truth, "whether it calls itself submission to the will of God, or to the laws of nature, rests in bottom simply and solely upon an acknowledgement of our own impotence and ignorance."[4] It should not surprise us that the author of this statement will look both to scientists and theologians as model inquirers, and even claim that the theology of Thomas Aquinas prophesied modern science.

Adams's first sustained consideration of the social context of the innovative thinker occurs in his 1868 review of Sir Charles Lyell's *Principles of Geology*. A friend of the United States legation during the Civil War, Lyell sought Adams's help in arranging for an American review of the tenth edition of the *Principles*, and Adams responded by volunteering his own services. The opportunity came just when the former private secretary prepared to return to the United States and, having published several scholarly articles already in the *North American Review*, was in a position to promote what in America might pass as "new influences." Writing as a nonspecialist for the conservative and largely Harvard-educated readership of the *North American*, Adams's task was to summarize Lyell's uniformitarian argument (that the earth evolved under uniform conditions over the course of millions of years) and to compare the virtues of Lyell's thesis with those of rival arguments, notably that of Harvard geologist Louis Agassiz, built on the supposition that the earth evolved in response to abrupt and catastrophic changes of condition. The catastrophic school provided a ready explanation for glaciation, but the theory had the retrograde feature of lending itself to creationist accounts of the earth's origin.

In comparing the uniformitarian with the catastrophic persuasion, Adams is obliged to acknowledge Lyell's challenge to a biblical cosmogony and address the opprobrium most of his readers associated with Darwinian theory. Throughout the review, Adams is eager to depict Lyell as not so much hostile to religious orthodoxy as rigorously aloof from theological discourse. As a geologist, Sir Charles "deals only with the facts before him" and hence does not answer to metaphysical objections. To the question of whether his science supports the doctrine of one or multiple acts of creation, for instance, "he would reply, that, for his own part, it was personally a matter of indifference to him whether he assumed that the first cause had acted once or ten million times, or was acting without repose."[5] Lyell's modernity, for Adams, consists precisely in his willingness to ask some questions and not others.

In Lyell, then, Adams has something of a heretic, and hence someone about whom it might be exhilarating to write, but Lyell's heresy took the self-effacing form of a refusal to engage methodologically irrelevant questions. Such practice had long since gained currency in a society that had become irrevocably secular and that valorized the very scientific inquiry that tended to abandon theological dispute. The price of such heresy would not be martyrdom; the *Principles*, then in its tenth edition, had made Lyell an institution in British scientific circles. In Adams's commentary, Lyell appears as a disciplined researcher, and the review celebrates his methodological caution by affecting to find fault with his insistently prosaic approach to the subject. "Sir Charles," we are told, takes "pleasure in lopping away fanciful excrescences which other men foster, and in treating the earth's marvelous history in that coldly scientific spirit which admits only what is enough, and no more than enough, to produce the result observed." The geologist becomes in this view a comic figure wandering "among the monotonous and flowerless forests of the coal-measures without saddening our spirits, and describes the enormous reptiles of the lias in language as calm and little sensational as though ichthyosauri were still gambolling in shoals along the banks of the Thames."[6] In departing from the fanciful, marvelous, and biblical, Lyell presents a serious case of iconoclasm, but there is nothing of the firebrand insurgent to his character, which is above all cautious and arrives at his theories in reasoned pursuit of empirically supportable truth.[7]

Adams's review of the *Principles of Geology* features a second inquirer, and it is really this other who makes the piece noteworthy. In Lyell's shadow stands a predecessor, James Hutton, the first geologist to propose a uniformitarian explanation of the earth's formation and thus the first to deny the biblical scheme of creation. If Adams's review required a martyr—a role that the controversial but institutional Lyell could not fill—Hutton met the need. In fact the Scottish geologist stands in Adams's writing as a signal instance of intellection running afoul of social, political, and ecclesiastical authority: "Against a combination of scientific and religious intolerance," Adams affirms, "no power on earth could prevail. Dr. Hutton was suppressed. His theory was dropped."[8] Hutton is the first of several figures, including Abélard and Galileo, whom Adams would identify as subjecting themselves to general censure in pursuit of an uncanonized but evident truth, a fate that the scientific historian, as Adams announced to the American Historical Association in 1894, would likewise have to face—a fate indeed *sought* by the autobiographical persona of *A Letter to American Teachers of History*. If Lyell presents the comic face of heresy, Hutton represents the path-breaking thinker who pays the price of telling a society what it does not want to hear. From the perspective of the essayist writing in 1868, Hutton is not so much an example of the perennial intellectual martyr as a figure suppressed in an age that would not have been receptive to the kind of reasoned assessment that Adams's review aspires to epitomize. Implicitly, Lyell's success exists as a measure of how scientific inquiry has come to lead society in spite of the fact that it cannot be counted on to support received truth.

Adams's assessment refrains from adjudicating between rival geological schools. Although it defends Lyell's rigor, it expresses a marked dissatisfaction with the reductive manner with which he supposedly treats "the earth's marvelous history." But the review fully champions the free inquiry and scientific method unfettered by theological opinion that Lyell's work exemplified; it also honors the great principle of evolution, for which the geologist provides support. For the Henry Adams of the late 1860s, attached to the old-fashioned republicanism of his forebears but open to progressive thought, Lyell exists as an attractive compromise figure: cautious, disciplined, middle-class, his uniformitarianism proceeding from a temper that was also pro-Union and that marked him as a friend of the United States. As iconoclast he was safe for progressive conservatives eager to step from an outworn, theological way of regarding the world to one that may have been no less metaphysical but that was material and methodological in its affirmations. As Adams would put it in chapter 15 ("Darwinism") of the *Education*, he and his contemporaries were happy to embrace, in the order suggested by the theories of Lyell and Darwin, "the very best substitute for religion; a safe, conservative, practical, thoroughly Common-law deity" (926). Whether Adams fully desired a substitute for religion is debatable. As his attraction to determinism suggests, he wanted to depend on a supreme will outside the sphere of human direction and seemed ever ready to decry the inherent weakness and nescience of humankind. But he resisted views of human possibility constrained by the doctrine of innate depravity; he believed that humanity on its best behavior could intervene in its own worldly behalf, and he was susceptible to the idea that a society can create the world it would inhabit in accordance with distinctly utopian specifications.

In the dispassion and intellectuality of its basic idea, the Darwinian "Common-law deity" is in keeping with the deism associated with the generation of Jefferson and John Adams and the Enlightenment thought that produced the American republic. Although evolutionary theory represents a break with the Calvinist past, it is by no means incompatible with what Adams characterizes in the *Education* as the republicanism and Unitarianism of his mostly secular homelife. Even though he was not averse to the residual Puritanism of his regional culture, Adams equated truth seeking with the freest possible inquiry. He may strike an apologetic tone in his review of Lyell's *Principles*—"we have endeavoured to state . . . the process of reasoning by which so conservative and so eminent a writer as Sir Charles Lyell has been led to adopt opinions which many excellent men consider revolting"—but Adams would have faced a more formidable challenge trying to make Jefferson palatable to those same excellent men.[9] Although he plays up Lyell's iconoclasm, the geologist's doctrines had become mainstream; they formed the conventional wisdom of the late-nineteenth-century Anglo-American intelligentsia. If, as Adams tells us in the *Education*, his early education sought a "great generalisation which would finish one's clamor to be educated" (925), evolution—of earth, life forms, and human institutions—served in that capacity. The progressive, evolutionary, and scientific outlook that Adams associated with Darwinian thought allowed him to lay claim to Gallatin and Jefferson and encouraged him to understand their vision as one in which uniform conditions provide for the progressive amelioration of average human aptitude. In spite of their sardonic cast of mind, the Adamses actually coveted opportunities to view the future optimistically. And such opportunity as Henry

Adams would seize offered itself in the shape of a mythic Jeffersonian America. Between his return to the United States and his absorption in the literary discipline that produced *The Life of Albert Gallatin*, *John Randolph*, *History of the United States during the Administrations of Thomas Jefferson and James Madison*, and the two novels, Adams went through several short-lived professional incarnations—political journalist, editor, and professor. Despite his disgust with the Grant administration and the tenor of public life, he remained committed to the study of the evolution of American character and institutions. Commitment hardly meant uncritical promotion, however, and the impression one would form from the Gallatin and Randolph biographies is that America had long since lost its opportunity to achieve a culture exempt from the corruption of immemorial experience—if in fact it ever existed. Yet Adams made his way through the immediate post-war period without losing sight of a visionary America, and in his Jefferson the figure of the inquirer achieves its most sanguinary cast.

In Gallatin and Jefferson, Adams examines philosophical inquirers who were also statesmen, possessed of opportunities to shape public life after the image of their utopian speculations. Both carried on active if not frequently dramatic public lives, but it is as men of thought, and as men who thought elusively and in private, that Adams wishes to present them, investing them with his own elusive dream life—his own consciousness of the line between private and public, thought and act. Gallatin and Jefferson allied in the same visionary project and through much of their careers proceeded on the assumption that American society, breaking from the European past, could evolve its own order, favorable to the full development of average human capacity. Nonetheless, the two men offer contrasting occasions for Adams to consider the fate of the inquirer. And here I refer both to the inquirer as protagonist (Gallatin, Jefferson) and the inquirer as moralizing historical narrator (Adams). In depicting Gallatin and Jefferson, Adams experiments with different formulations of what the historian can accomplish in writing about the past and arrives at different conclusions as to whether the office of historical narrative is elegiac or prophetic in emphasis. The question is all the more weighted inasmuch as this historian—descendent of philosophic statesmen who encountered memorable setbacks in the public service—himself rejected statesmanship as a field in which his own inquiry could overtly unfold.

One cannot create a protagonist in any kind of narrative without investing something of one's own interior life in the character and thereby fashioning a hypothetical self. Gallatin never quite achieves the status of alter ego that Jefferson does. Whereas Jefferson appeals to a Henry Adams who sought to step free of an overdetermined family personality, Gallatin is more of a projection of the ancestral component of Adams's selfhood. To appreciate Jefferson's place in Adams's thought, and Adams's tentative willingness to consider the world of possibility that Jefferson represents, one must note the occasion for cathartic lamentation that his study of Gallatin affords him. *The Life of Albert Gallatin* (1879), Adams's first full-length book, would seem to repudiate anything like the enthusiasm for new ideas and receptivity to the upwardly evolutionary outlook that the Adams of the *Education* reads back into his salad days. The narrative is ironic (Ernest Samuels has described it as Greek in its tragic reversals) and its tone elegiac.[10] An intelligent and principled participant in democratic process, Gallatin the naturalized citizen rises from state to national politics, and his appointment as Treasury secretary in Jefferson's administration would appear to vindicate a political system open to individuals on the basis of merit. According to the thesis developed in both *Gallatin* and the *History*, the ideals of strict constructionism that formed the basis of Jefferson's political identity were immediately if necessarily abandoned in favor of a federal system that made possible, among other things, the Louisiana Purchase and Jefferson's ill-fated Embargo.

Adams provides a double perspective on the Jefferson administration's implicit repudiation of ideology. On the one hand, he underscores the irony that Jefferson and Gallatin worked against their stated principles, exhibiting the blindness with which even enlightened men act. On the other, he commends the pragmatism with which this administration met the most basic national exigencies. Adams depicts Gallatin, an able administrator of the nation's Treasury, as participating willingly in some but not all of Jefferson's federalizing strategies. His moments of signal defeat come when he is forced to frame an enforcement act to support Jefferson's embargo and when Congress, jealous of federal power, refuses to recharter the U.S. Bank. Assessing Gallatin at the end of his tenure as Treasury secretary, Adams supplies a suitably gloomy moral. "Riper, wiser, and infinitely more experienced than in 1800, Gallatin had . . . outgrown the convictions that had made his strength." On the subject of Gallatin the public servant whose action takes instruction from his thought, Adams is even more reductive. For his "statesmanship had become, what practical statesmanship always has and must become, a mere struggle to deal with concrete facts at the cost of philosophic and *a priori* principles."[11]

Having forsaken the world of politics, Gallatin shifts to "the study of social and economical principles, to purely scientific methods and objects, to practical commerce and the means of obtaining wealth." Adams's narrative thus implies that practical politics ultimately repels intelligent guidance and the philosophical temper—that a fundamental incompatibility cleaves politics from thought. With relief the elderly statesman turns "away from that political life which no longer represented a single great political conception" that he might "grapple with the ideas and methods of the coming generation."[12] He thus quits the public world of an ascendant Andrew Jackson. And yet his sense of duty recalls him to that world toward the end of his life to protest the Mexican War and thus make common cause with John Quincy Adams. Indeed, Gallatin becomes increasingly identified with the principled disaffection of the house of Adams as well as with the engagement-in-estrangement that all the Adamses practiced and that Henry, as scholar, was already practicing in Washington on his own terms as he wrote the Gallatin biography. Gallatin is thus absorbed into the family martyrology. Nevertheless, however much this image of the inquirer presages the aging Henry Adams—and however much the aged Henry Adams lurks with all his cranky skepticism within the young Henry Adams—it does not represent the full range of the biographer's midlife susceptibilities.

If Adams's conception of Gallatin owes much to his sense of the public fate of John and John Quincy Adams, his portrait of Jefferson proceeds from a sensibility closer to his own.[13] His description of Jefferson as a man who above all takes pleasure in private intellectual pursuit approaches self-portraiture: "The rawness of political life was an incessant torture to him, and personal attacks made him keenly unhappy. His true delight was in an intellectual life of science and art. To read, write, speculate in new lines of thought, to keep abreast of the intellect of Europe . . . were pleasures more to his mind than any to be found in a public assembly." As inquirer, Adams's Jefferson possesses intellectual virtues that Adams particularly admired; moreover, he possesses intellectual vices with which Adams sympathized. Never a provincial thinker, Jefferson could not help but transcend the limitations of the states'-rights school that found expression in the Virginia and Kentucky Resolutions. "His instincts led him to widen rather than to narrow the bounds of every intellectual exercise," Adams writes, "and if vested with political authority, he could no more resist the temptation to stretch his powers than he could abstain from using his mind on any subject merely because he might be drawn upon ground supposed to be dangerous." His federalism, then, whether or not it counted as an unauthorized arrogation of power, was the reflex of a liberally active mind. To that mind religious dogma offered no impediment. "He was a deist, believing that men could manage their own salvation without the help of a state church." Boldness of speculation at once constituted the strength and weakness of his thought; such boldness sought justification in an exalted vision of human capacity alien to the Adams temperament but distinctly appealing to Henry. "Prone to innovation, he sometimes generalized without careful analysis. He was a theorist, prepared to risk the fate of mankind on the chance of reasoning far from certain in its details. His temperament was sunny and sanguine, and the atrabilious philosophy of New England was intolerable to him." Finally, there is the singularly empathetic insight of one compulsive inquirer into another: "He was superficial in his knowledge, and a martyr to the disease of omniscience."[14] Jefferson has become Henry Adams's secret sharer.

These well-crafted sentences measure the admiration and sympathy, if also resistance, Adams bore Jefferson and provide the best indication of what he believed to be the vocation and occupational hazards of inquiry. They make the martyrdom of intellect sound like a delightful fate compared with the trials of a public life. This is a heroic if also a cautionary portrait. If the story of Gallatin illustrates "the inevitable isolation and disillusionment of a really strong mind," the story of Jefferson—as disappointing in many respects as that of his colleague—establishes that the strong mind will aspire to the point of failure to prove what it can achieve.[15] It articulates the principle of speculative utopianism that Adams celebrates in the prologue to the *History*, the exuberantly inventive capacity of common Americans and their ability to transform their world materially beyond the expectations of European observers and atrabilious New Englanders. Although little remains of the celebratory tone in the epilogue nine volumes later, Adams never withdraws the icon of Jefferson as Man Thinking. Isolation and disillusionment, Jefferson's no less than Gallatin's fate, might be inevitable. But to be pronounced a martyr is to have one's failure exalted into a kind of success.

The *History* never entirely negates Jefferson even though it makes clear that his theories, at least in the short run and in certain key facets, fail with disastrous consequence. His pacifism could not avert the War of 1812, left to the hapless Madison to oversee, and the British burning of the capital constitutes the narrative's absolute nadir. Yet the resourcefulness of American naval intelligence (evidence of the democratic genius of Jeffersonian

America) ultimately saves the day, and the epilogue frames the America of 1817 as one that is peaceful, materialist, secular, and scientific, tending toward a steady development that presages a trend in universal human development. The War of 1812 may prove that the United States will not elude the fate of nations, but the success of the republic in cohering as a nation places American society at the vanguard of human progress. In the end the *History* is both elegy and prophecy. It laments the passing of the popular vision associated with Jefferson, but while the epilogue expresses skepticism as to whether the United States can develop a high culture (an "America of thought and art"), it expresses confidence in the general intelligence and adaptability of the people. The more far-reaching prophecy of the epilogue concerns what the historian believes to be the ultimate predictability of a democratic nation of average people developing under uniform conditions, an opportunity in which the laws of human history may appear and the destiny of human experience known in advance as so much science, or omniscience.

Jefferson is a pivotal figure in Adams's work inasmuch as he embodies Adams's own best hopes for an American civilization and sets an example of how one inquires boldly, extravagantly, and with visionary faith. Creating an "America of thought and art" that would reflect "the differentiation" in the United States "of a higher variety of the human race"—motives that Adams, drawing on Darwinian phrasing, ascribes to Jefferson—are of course the highest of all possible expectations. For the historian to state that "nothing less" was required for the "complete success" (*History* 1:125) of the Jeffersonian experiment focuses attention less on the time period of the narrative (1800–1817), in which there could be no definitive success or failure, than on the post–Civil War present in which the *History* becomes available for contemporary and future readerships. Adams passes immediate and rather harsh judgments on Jefferson's effectiveness as an administrator and character as a public man, even as he affirms that evaluation of his success as a thinker and prophet requires the perspective of at least a century. Given the extended period during which critics must afford Jefferson the benefit of the doubt, his steady diminution throughout the narrative as the presiding genius of American democracy contributes much to the *History*'s moral ambiguity. Cover-to-cover readers of the *History* know that the long work conforms throughout to an aesthetic of cautious tonality. Moods of lyric celebration and outbursts of satiric disgust occasionally jostle the equanimity of Adams's prose but remain otherwise in check, and after building to a constrained exuberance in the prologue,

Adams narrates the triumphs, struggles, and mounting fiascoes of the Jefferson and Madison administrations with Olympian composure. By the time one reaches the epilogue, however, the sympathy evident in the prologue chapters, which affirmed above all the fantasy life of a whole society united in a single ideal, with Jefferson at the head and the frontier squatter at bottom, has vacated the work, and the typical American figures more as a statistical datum, subject in the mass to quantitative analysis (were the formulas available), than as a new man with a significant life of thought. What is not obvious, in the beginning or at the conclusion of the *History*, is how Adams intends this narrative to speak to the United States of the post-war period and to what sort of politics he would commit this extended inquiry into American character. If this is the past, what is its use? What sort of lasting relevance might Jefferson possess? What office does Adams, as admirer and critic of Jefferson, perform in presenting to his country the portrait of American national character with which the *History* concludes?

The answers to such questions are complicated by the fact that Adams's own persuasions evolved as he composed the *History*. At the outset he affirms that the past can exist as a moral resource; at the end he is less sure. The celebration of popular activity and initiative that reaches a climax in "American Ideals," the prologue's concluding chapter, serves as a refutation of European and New England critics of the American democrat circa 1800 who saw nothing in the average citizen but ignorance and greed. In the epilogue, the more reserved but still affirmative descriptions of the national character as energetic and scientific evince the American's exceptional viability in the struggle for existence. Whether that existence will be ennobled and justified by something beyond material interests is left as an open question. In his most direct reference to post–Civil War America, Adams suggests that the people's affability may foster corruptions that the nation will lack the machinery to purge, but the notable absence of enthusiasm pertains more to what he does not say. Whereas at the outset the *History* had projected an "America of thought and art" as the final measure by which this people must be judged, this idea appears nowhere toward the end. Beneath the aspiration to a scientific historiography that would absolve itself of moralizing, the *History* exhibits a jeremiadical reflex in positioning its analysis between past and future.

The quasi-jeremiadical, quasi-scientific historiography speaks to what we but not Adams can recognize as a restrictive vision of an American people and national past. Ideologically, the *History* does much to reinforce the primacy of political, diplomatic, and military history, as though the activities of powerful men provide the core sequence of human experience. But Adams's express interest in inquiring into national character, and his attempt, in prologue and epilogue, to frame the narrative with demographic portraits, qualifies somewhat the traditional emphasis, and the work as a whole dismisses the importance of the great man as an action figure. The great man as thinker whose ideas materialize over the course of centuries is another, undecided matter.

Although the *History* can see beyond the patriarchal and national biases that dictate its historiography, and although it distinctly privileges the American citizen as a national type to end all others (defining the American narrowly as those with northwestern European ancestry), it is difficult to state more specifically whose interests the *History* serves, or even how it might have served anyone in 1891 as an unequivocally usable representation of the past. Against its own ambition to construct a predictive model it exposes the shortcomings of highly educated conservative observers who repeatedly underestimated the American democrat. Such perception might logically align the historian with underprivileged but emerging constituents of the late-nineteenth-century American populace. Yet the *History*'s postulation of a national type obscures the class divisions that characterized earlier and later American social life, and this could only have served a status quo that wished to ignore the glaring inequities of the Gilded Age. Still, the *History* does nothing to exalt the antebellum background of post-war capitalism. It does not endorse a jingoist American destiny. Adams withholds detailed prognostications regarding his nation's future. Nevertheless, he ventures the prophecy that historians will one day discern laws of necessary social change and thus be able to know that future. Grim expectation inheres in his contention that human experience conforms at some level to laws of force. However, in asserting that answering the most crucial questions regarding national destiny needed a hundred years of experience beyond 1817, Adams suggests that the world in which he is publishing his magnum opus cannot be seen with clarity sufficient for assessment. By ending with an open inquiry, the *History* artfully obscures where its author stands and would appear to support no particular interest.

FROM HIS NOVELS we may form some idea of what Adams saw as he looked into the post–Civil War America that rapidly evolved during the years (1877–1891) he wrote the *History*. Both *Democracy* (1880) and *Esther*

(1884) feature female inquirers interrogating a culture in crisis. In *Democracy*, Madeleine Lee moves to Washington "to see with her own eyes the action of primary forces" as those forces relate to "the great American mystery of democracy and government" (7). Because she is cast as an innocent abroad, the results of her inquiry are never in doubt: beneath the mystery is a corruption more serious and systemic than she had surmised in coming to the capital or in allowing herself to be courted by Senator Ratcliffe, whom she suspects initially of simply being a crude if fascinating western politician rather than the election stealer and acceptor of bribes that he turns out to be. While acknowledging the inevitability of democracy as a stage in human civilization, the novel ends implicitly with the questions that the *History* would also raise: By what means, if any, were such corruptions to be purged? What ideals would rescue this materially affluent society from the decadence of a banal self-satisfaction, the parody of a visionary republic? The second novel is less obviously political in its orientation. Like *Democracy*, *Esther* makes an attempt to determine where American society may be headed, but Adams frames the issue as the more private concern of a young woman in search of belief on which to structure her life. Repelled by church doctrine because of its emphasis on the self's stakes in an eternal afterlife, and equally repelled by scientific methods that never really permit the inquirer to step from piecemeal truths to a bold metaphysical idea, Esther has nothing to give her life motive and direction. The men in the novel, the Reverend Stephen Hazard, Prof. George Strong, and the painter Wharton, who respectively voice ecclesiastic, scientific, and pre-Raphaelite dogmas, are unable to demonstrate ways in which their beliefs afford anything like a passionate reason to live. Hazard, with whom Esther falls in love, cannot be true to both Esther and his church, since the latter regards Esther as female and weak, a thoroughly preordained quantity. Without an innovative occasion, an America of thought and art, Esther's materially privileged existence has no meaning; in the final scene set by Niagara Falls she envisions death as the great discloser and eagerly anticipates contact with a "next world" conceived as "a sort of great reservoir of truth" into which the little intuitions that mortal beings entertain pour "like raindrops" (321).

Both Madeleine and Esther inquire with an urgency prompted by a near experience of death. Prior to her Washington adventure Madeleine incurs the loss of her husband and infant, and in the course of her narrative Esther, already motherless, loses her father. For both characters, the great questions of life proceed with reference to the American project of reinventing civilization and human possibility, but the millennial nation is slow to materialize and each regards herself as a mortal in need of answers that one cannot wait a century to frame. Less educated than the men in their lives and only superficially conversant with the ideas of the day, Madeleine and Esther do not possess the inquirer's usual qualifications; as intellectual but by no means feminist women, they inquire intuitively and pose questions normally repressed by the reigning conventional wisdom. More clairvoyant than the men who surround them, they ask ultimate questions that expert scrutiny prefers to suspend or avoid. Neither can abandon her ultimate question; each rejects the opportunity to marry a prestigious male who represents a definitive and comfortable if entirely false answer. Isolated by their concerns and marginalized within the confines of a privileged but spiritually vapid existence, each comes up against a solid dead-end. Inasmuch as their respective narratives offer neither a philosophical nor a social avenue of escape, each suffers a kind of martyrdom in her pursuit of truth.

Democracy and *Esther* indicate that, for Adams, the search for "the great generalisation" that would complete his continuing quest for education would not rest with evolutionary theory, not, at least, as uncertainly evinced in the American democratic experiment. The novels demonstrate that his own inquiry, as reflected in his fictional female inquirers, had become intuitive and metaphysical in what it asked and that it did so in accord with a tragic sensibility that had always formed part of his temperament but that had deepened with the passage of time. As a member of the generation that fought the Civil War, Adams had an intimate acquaintance with public tragedy, but his more personal initiation into tragic experience, as he would represent it in the *Education*, came with the shock of his sister Louisa's death by lockjaw in 1870. The death of Marian Hooper ("Clover") Adams in 1885, just after publication of the oddly premonitory *Esther*, followed and certainly exceeded this experience; in writing about Louisa's death he inevitably if tacitly referred to Clover's. Evidence of the parricidal and suicidal inner life of the evolutionary process—as he would take the deaths of these women to be—challenged the validity of progressive views of history and set Adams to the task of theorizing a catastrophic human fate.

"For the first time, the stage-scenery of the senses collapsed," Adams writes in one of the key passages of his entire oeuvre; "the human mind felt itself stripped naked, vibrating in a void of shapeless energies, with resistless mass, colliding, crushing, wasting and destroying what these same energies had created and labored from eternity to perfect" (*Education* 983). Given Adams's nostalgia for some principle of divine omnipotence with which to upbraid human folly, and given his skepticism of the evolutionary "Common-law deity," which persisted even as he fulfilled what he thought to be his generational duty to promote such idols, the passage suggests the degree to which progressive doctrine was undone by events like the accident that led to his sister's death and the self-murder of his wife. The phrase "for the first time" implies a sequence, and it is precisely the force of the second example that informed readers are expected to feel. Not only does the "Common-law deity" perish in these confrontations with death but also the orthodox divinity that it had tentatively replaced. Any thought that a "personal deity could find pleasure or profit" in such misery as Adams saw his sister and wife endure "could not be held for a moment. For pure blasphemy, it made pure atheism a comfort" (983). Behind these failed god-concepts rose the specter of "a chaos of anarchic and purposeless forces" imaged in Mont Blanc—the dystopic, alternative "great generalisation" that haunts all of Adams's later work.

If disasters in his personal life impeached working doctrines, so too did the geopolitical world that held for him an obsessive interest and that seemed to him increasingly subjugated to the predatory design of international finance capital. For Adams, capitalism took form as an elusive, London-based banking conspiracy that sapped the vigor of post–Civil War America and devastated the non-Western world under European colonial rule. The differentiation in America of a higher species of humanity—an idea that, in one form or another, Adams could never easily discard—was blighted by the globalizing reach of the European gold broker. The panic of 1892 demonstrated to him that a call for specie in London could paralyze industry in the American hinterland as though the U.S. economy lingered in its historically colonial position. Adams's circumnavigation of 1890–1891 put him in touch with actively colonized worlds, the leading edge of the expanding European capitalist system, and although his letters from the South Seas bear the florid signature of the Western male gaze, they also document his remarkable capacity to see the moral deficiency of the West in its rapacious contact with precapitalist culture. Everywhere Adams saw what he took to be evidence of new centralizations of power, international in scope and totally unanswerable to popular government, American or European. The progressive, democratic, middle-class model of social order seemed decreasingly viable as the world polarized and as opposing forces took the forms of tyrant and anarchist.

In the 1890s, with Karl Marx as a point of reference, inquiry for Adams became increasingly politicized, as we may see in the letter—afterward titled "The Tendency of History"—that he addressed to the attendees of the December 1894 American Historical Association convention. As the reluctant president of the AHA, Adams chose to avoid the social horrors of attending a learned conference and so planned a trip abroad to coincide with the annual meeting. In the epistle datelined Guadalajara he speaks with the bluntness his absence enables. His message is somber. In view of heightened rivalries among European powers and among the class interests within Old World society, and in view of the inability of the United States to develop an economic life independent of Europe, Adams informs his colleagues that the old evolutionary synthesis no longer holds.

> I cannot be wholly wrong in thinking that a change has come over the tendency of liberal thought since the middle of the century. Darwin led an intellectual revival much more hopeful than any movement that can now be seen in Europe, except among the socialists. Had History been converted into a science at that time, it would perhaps have taken the form of cheerful optimism which gave to Darwin's conclusions the charm of a possible human perfectibility. . . . If a Science of History were established today, on the lines of its recent development I greatly fear it would take its tone from the pessimism of Paris, Berlin, London and St. Petersburg, unless it brought into sight some new and hitherto unsuspected path for civilization to pursue.[16]

Adams encourages little hope that a science of history will bring to view a redemptive "unsuspected path." Determinist in nature, the science Adams envisions can only confirm the gloomy continental outlook. Historians may have professional reasons to be excited about the fruition of long-pursued research: Adams reports that nearly any serious inquirer into historical process will have felt that he has stood "on the brink of a great generalisation that would reduce all history under a law as clear as the laws which govern the material world."[17] But a great generalization with power to refute the prevailing optimism of progressive historical models must meet with a cold reception; the bearer of this knowledge must fully expect censure.

Adams allows fifty years for the profession to arrive at the formulation of such "law" but is already prepared to outline the risks incurred by the supposedly disinterested historian:

> I ask myself what shape can be given to any Science of History that will not shake to its foundations some prodigious interest? . . . Any science assumes a necessary sequence of cause and effect,—a force resulting in motion which cannot be other than what it is. Any Science of History must be absolute, like other Sciences, and must fix with mathematical certainty the path which human society has got to follow. That path can hardly lead towards the interests of all the great social organizations. We cannot conceive that it should help at the same time the Church and the State, Property and Communism, Capital and Poverty, Science and Religion, Trade and Art.[18]

This statement is noteworthy because it absolves the scientific historian of any ideological basis or bias, while at the same time affirming that whatever the historian publishes by way of findings is effectively political inasmuch as it indicates "the path which human society has got to follow." While Adams predicts conflict between vested interest and the disciplined inquiry that would result in a true science of history, he claims for his profession and for himself a perfectly neutral stance. Like the *History*'s concluding paragraphs, the "Tendency" engages a prophetic rhetoric that defers disclosure of the great generalization for another half-century—beyond the lifetime of Adams and his middle-aged academic colleagues. He is thereby able to retain his position of ostensible uncommitment and to avoid having to suggest which interest will (or should) prosper at another's expense. Should his equivocal suggestions prove obnoxious to his hearers he asks that his remarks be struck from the public record and taken only "in the paradoxical spirit of private conversation."[19]

As in the concluding paragraphs of the *History*, Adams herein assumes the role of prophet, foreseeing the perfection of a historical science still in its formative stage, but his emphasis on the hostility this science must encounter and the martyrdom the historian must suffer is new. The historian who transforms history into a predictive science will find himself in the position of Galileo inasmuch as that science must inevitably contest the official narratives of the powers that be. For Adams to proclaim that a formulation of historical law is imminent and that the law will shake certain great but as yet unspecified interests means that he can challenge everyone's complacence without forfeiting what he conceives as his neutrality. The lawgiver Adams imagines works for no object but the glory of subjecting phenomena to unitary rule, and the fact that he may serve one interest rather than another is purely coincidental. This view represents a refinement of what had long been Adams's paradoxically engaged detachment, his role as observer-advocate. Indications that Adams did not conceive the *History* in a cold spirit appear in *Democracy*, as when Nathan Gore, a New England historian who speaks more nobly than he acts, remarks, "I am glad to see society grapple with issues in which no one can afford to be neutral" (40). As the writing of the *History* moved forward, however, and as Adams became less able to affirm progressive doctrines, he increasingly insisted on the neutrality of his inquiry's platform. "No honest historian can take part with—or against—the forces he has to study," he states toward the end of the *Education*. "To him even the extinction of the human race should be merely a fact to be grouped with other vital statistics" (1128).

This attitude eventuates in the elaborate bluff of *A Letter to American Teachers of History* (1910). Adams can never demonstrate that the pursuit of truth in actual practice stands apart from interventionist motive. In the *Education* he manages to avoid the issue by writing history in a genre that is not strictly history. Rather, in his frankly autobiographical bildungsroman he embraces a genre that proceeds on admittedly subjective claims and that enacts the conviction that historians (scientific or otherwise) have to account for themselves as instruments of inquiry actuated by the forces they would study. The *Education* documents a mind formed by specific beliefs, biases, and values. By announcing in the preface that he intends the work for "young men, in Universities or elsewhere" (*Education* 722) who will need to react to a world of radically novel forces, Adams reaffirms that "no one can afford to be neutral" (*Democracy* 40) and commends his inquiry to pragmatic if ever uncertain application. He may abstractly project a value-free lawgiver but he cannot write about actual thinkers, least of all himself, without contextualizing them among specific times, places, and interests. Indeed, Adams habitually merges the story of the inquirer with the knowledge that the inquirer seeks. He began work on the *Education* having erased such distinction in the recently completed narratives of Abélard and Aquinas, inquirers whose thought was an extension of their lives and whose lives were embedded in their historical moments. As protagonists in Adams's ongoing narrative of intellection, Abélard and Aquinas serve as precursors to the third-person "Adams" of the *Education*, and the later chapters of *Mont Saint Michel and Chartres* provide Adams an occasion to interrogate the (engaged) inquirer's polar personae.

As scholastic philosophers, Abélard and Thomas Aquinas exemplify disciplines of knowing that have little in common with the empirical methods of the natural and human sciences practiced in the nineteenth and twentieth centuries. But this does not mean that the issues besetting medieval thought—the many and the one, the real and the nominal—had lost their relevance. Adams in any case is prepared to create such relevance: just as he asks traditional philosophical questions of post-Newtonian physics, so he imposes upon medieval inquiry a contemporary frame of reference. Abélard and Aquinas engage in the timeless and perennially dangerous enterprise of formulating generalizations that would unite all humanity in a large, God-informed purpose without fatally offending vested interests. In telling their stories Adams draws his readers' attention as much to the effort as to the result and to irreducible personal contrasts: the distinct motives that impelled their inquiry, the difference in their styles of thought, the contrasting relationships each bore to the society of his time. He presents one thinker as determined to offend and the other as prepared to comply, and yet he demonstrates that neither succeeded fully in perfecting a system of thought or in avoiding official condemnation. The thinker is at least as interesting as the thought; each is celebrated and each is commended to the reader's sympathy.

In the scheme of *Mont Saint Michel and Chartres*, Abélard is identified as the "Portal of approach to the gothic thought and philosophy" (607) of the twelfth century, and hence an entrance into the system of thought perfected by Aquinas. The text thus unites Abélard, despite a career of egoism and eccentricity, with Aquinas in a single project. Although Adams apologetically refrains from retelling the story of Abélard's love affair with Héloïse, emotional volatility is always a part of this predominately intellectual narrative. Abélard's famous association with Héloïse is cited as his link to the romance and emotional life of the age. Adams's account fully integrates Abélard in the life of his twelfth-century world despite the introduction of a discordant note when Adams attempts to specify Abélard's motives—that he philosophized not for the glory of Héloïse (or Mary) nor because he believed in the philosophy but "because he believed in himself" (607). Abélard, in Adams's characterization, is a prototype of the freethinker devoted to the performative side of intellectual exercise. He works for no end beyond his immediate satisfaction and proceeds in the conviction that the coherence of the world reflects the symbolic capacity of his own mind. Abélard thus enacts the principle of anarchy, preferring his own truth and vision of order to what he looks upon as the false official versions, and in this he anticipates the subjective reference and intellectual improvisation of the *Education*'s protagonist. Something of a Byronic hero, Abélard figures as the intellectual on the margin of society convinced of the mendacity of sanctioned formulas. In his virtuoso practice of philosophical discourse, in his insistence on treating the Holy Trinity as open to logical scrutiny, and in his refusal generally to honor official mystery, he is not afraid to reduce church and state to absurdity. He thrives on intellectual danger. And yet the moral of his story is that church and state, unable to tolerate what they perceive as his anarchy, win out in the end. The institutions suppress him, not however as reprobate ironist but as errant intellectual child. Adams's only direct quotation of Abélard draws on the latter's autobiography, an account of his persecutions written late in life after the condemnation of his writings. His martyrdom may not be a high one, but readers are asked to sympathize with it on the grounds that Abélard takes delight in the exercise of mind—a mind that naturally resists official dogma. Like any truth seeker, he is vulnerable to the politicians who surround him.

The tolerance that Adams displays toward Abélard as one more multiple in the flexible social wholeness of the twelfth and thirteenth centuries attenuates dramatically in his meditation on Aquinas, which marks the transition of his own inquiry from its lyric retrospection of an idyllic medieval society to the dour apprehension of a modern world. Had Adams wanted to do so, he could have demonized Abélard by charging him with conspiracy to depose the Virgin in favor of a logician's Holy Ghost, but his contradictory susceptibility to Héloïse and the suggestion of their abiding relationship redeem him. Adams emphasizes the importance of this aspect of the story by quoting Peter the Venerable's prediction that Abélard and Héloïse will reunite in heaven. Aquinas, unlike Abélard, does not possess this romantic, sexual, and vulnerable side nor does he work for the childish glory of his own ego and personal celebrity. He singlemindedly pursues his task: to affirm God as unity, and humanity as a multitude that achieves unity with God through the necessary institution of the church, and to do so without reducing God to a pantheistic substance or humanity to a predetermined entity incapable of willing its submission to God. On the basis of the persevering massiveness of this doctrine, Adams pronounces Aquinas a success: "The hive of Saint Thomas sheltered God and Man, Mind and Matter, the Universe and the Atom, the One and the Multiple, within the walls of a harmonious home" (665). Taking the side of the church and state and what he looks upon in this chapter as their legitimate mandate to impose order on society, Adams increasingly faults a humankind that would reject the structure Aquinas has created in order to exert its own perverse willfulness. Conceding that humanity must assert its freedom or admit that it is merely a machine, Adams claims that "Thomas's settlement could not be a simple one or final, except for practical use, but it served, and it holds good still" (685).

Abélard and Aquinas provide Adams with a means of thinking through distinctly alternate roles the inquirer may play in society; that he can characterize such contrasting personalities with sympathy measures his own ambivalence. According to Adams, both lived in an age in which the doctrine of organic unity held, but we may suspect that "organic unity" is something that mostly exists in the eye of the beholder looking nostalgically to the past (Adams similarly beholds the initial years of Jefferson's ascendancy in the prologue of the *History*). Given his sometime evasion of the pragmatic considerations of knowledge, it is telling that Adams in turning to Aquinas should make such conspicuous reference to "practical use." Throughout the chapter, Adams speaks frequently of the structural strength and architectural beauty of Thomas's theology; the theology is verily an art form. The genius of a Thomas transcends time; it consists in "the power of broad and lofty generalisation" (689). Yet the art has a decidedly ideological intent, and with perhaps no other thinker in Adams's oeuvre is it more clear what interest intellection serves: "Saint Thomas was working for the Church and the State, not for the salvation of souls, and his chief object was to repress anarchy" (685). As though to make the point perfectly clear, Adams explains the doctrine of grace by an electrical analogy in which 99 percent of the human components burn out in confrontation with a moral crisis and are thus lost to such divine assistance as might rescue them. This is Thomism read in a distinctly Calvinist as well as scientific light. It begs the question with respect to where Adams stands, temperamentally, ideologically, the heir to Puritan and Enlightenment thought, in relation to a world that he finds increasingly alien. If Aquinas's solution is as successful as anyone's, and if it "holds good still," why inquire further?

"ONE WOULD HAVE BEEN GLAD to stop and ask no more, but the anarchist bomb bade one go on, and the bomb is a powerful persuader" (*Education* 1114). On such emphatically political terms does Adams explain the incessant inquiry that preoccupies his retirement. "To repress anarchy" figures among the motives that impel Adams's late activity, but the *Education*, "The Rule of Phase Applied to History," and *A Letter to American Teachers of History* by no means constitute a *Summa Theologiae* sponsored by church and state. On the contrary, these texts—the productions of a self-styled Conservative Christian Anarchist—do much to resist ideological positions and specific political commitments. Although their author speaks as the prophet of a postdemocratic dystopia, he never abandons the office of Socratic ironist whose skepticism ridicules the human presumption to knowledge of any sort. Despite the compulsive prognostication and persistent desire to catch hold of a generalization that would confer omniscience on the inquirer, Adams's late writings consistently emphasize the false knowing and partial seeing that typify human experience. Disabused of the grand Darwinian generalization, he knows that the most persuasive theory may well be a form of false consciousness and that the best-informed mind is susceptible to ideas that subsequent thinkers will dismiss as ignorance. All forms and means of knowledge become subject to Adams's suspicion. Conceding the relative nature of what we assert to be true, he recognizes that the linguistic apparatus of inquiry and the psychology of the inquirer constrain and predetermine the object known.

Partial knowledge becomes for Adams a real and humbling experience in this period inasmuch as his non-mastery of mathematics, "the only necessary language of thought" (*Education* 1088), made current scientific discussion inaccessible to his direct scrutiny. Formerly confident of his ability to follow and assess scientific discourse, he now felt barred from these important conversations and his sense of exclusion contributed greatly to the deprecation with which he portrayed the *Education*'s protagonist. "Perhaps," Adams speculates, "the effect of knowing no mathematics is to leave the mind to imagine figures,—images,—phantoms" (1109). Although he readily admits that "images are not arguments" (1167), it is from precisely such nonscientific imaginings that he constructs "A Dynamic Theory of History" and "A Law of Acceleration." He does so for their heuristic merit, ready always to defer to those who can compute what he imagines to be the precise values beyond his calculus. Adams's prophetic statements draw upon various analogies—magnetic attraction, phase theory, the second law of thermodynamics. Lacking any valid applicability to the unfolding of human events, these analogies are the mental toys of an apprehension of imminent thresholds, generalized catastrophe, and hairbreadth escapes. Recognizable as tropes, they require considerable work on the reader's part to determine what if anything they convey as knowledge—scientific, historical, or moral. Because Adams evades ideological binaries, because he speaks and publishes in ways that disavow an obvious political identity, because he writes in literary genres that elude protocols of standard interpretation, readers understandably struggle to discern the platform from which he speaks, the interests his inquiry serves, the church in which his martyrdom should be celebrated.

Not that it is difficult to identify Adams as a member of a specific class or to read his analysis as enabled by privilege and haunted by class anxieties. Throughout this later period, as throughout his life, Adams maintained close ties with a power elite and moved among social circles that had unquestioned access to high office, elective or appointive. Leading a life of material advantage, and enjoying the company of the Hays, Lodges, Camerons, and many other wealthy and influential individuals, Adams cultivated a sense of himself as the antiquated survivor of an old-fashioned professional class associated more with virtue and intellect than with wealth. As a member of an extinct caste that defined itself against various tyrannies (Charles I, George III, the Slave Power, Old World autocracy, militarism, capitalism), he persisted in his aversion to banking interests and his passionate antipathy to European imperialism. He contributed to the presidential campaign of William Jennings Bryan. Yet, fierce as Adams's enmity may have been toward the multinational capitalism represented by the single gold standard, and as much as he abhorred the tendency of State, Wall, and Lombard Street bankers to place narrow interest above communal ideals, when McKinley and the gold standard triumphed he accepted that triumph as inevitable. And under the McKinley administration Adams prospered; at no other time did he enjoy closer relations with John Hay, McKinley's minister to Great Britain and later secretary of state.[20] Through Hay, Adams could take vicarious pleasure in watching England come into an Atlantic alliance with the United States in the lead. Recalling the British insolence personally endured by four generations of Adamses, the pleasure had much to do with seeing a partial realization of his ancestors' foreign policy aspirations and little to do with the prospect of an American empire imposing its rule in violation of the democratic principles for which his family stood. In the horror of rapid geopolitical change, he was sentimentally happy to see the United States rise as a world power with some idealism in its tradition to counter what it was capable of doing as the world's emerging creditor nation. Even so, he remained doubtful that any great massing of power can have benevolent issue.

Aside from social ties and material interests, what permitted this accommodation of Capital Triumphant was Adams's deepening suspicion—always a part of his intellectual reflex but never quite a full-fledged conviction—that human society had all but evolved beyond the point at which individuals and groups may choose their paths and that the conflicts organizing conventional discussion were not the real ones. The speculative chapters of the second half of the *Education* establish various inertial forces—ethnic, sexual, technological—as the true determinants of social direction. The pantomime of democratic process masks the true internal workings of state power. Adams never abandons his eighteenth-century republican values but cannot in good conscience insist on their inevitable triumph. Indeed, he suggests that the dystopian future has already arrived. "The work of domestic progress is done by masses of mechanical power," the narrator explains, and such power has "to be controlled by a score or two of individuals who have shown capacity to manage it. The work of internal government has become the task of controlling these men, who are socially as remote as heathen gods, alone worth knowing, but never known" (1105). Suggesting that occult forces unleashed by human acquisitiveness have overruled democratic process, Adams asserts that the "conflict is no longer between the men, but between the motors that drive the men" (1105). In such a world, ideological distinctions collapse, and the "capitalistic scheme of combining governments, like railways or furnaces, was in effect precisely the socialist scheme of Jaurès and Bebel" (1107). While Adams never wishes to declare participatory democracy dead, or otherwise rule out humanity's ability to intervene intelligently in its own destiny, he looks upon conventional political understanding as naïve. In bold strokes that allow him to avoid the detail work of social analysis, he represents the world as dissolving into large tyrannies and petty anarchies; such representation allows little possibility for a hands-on political praxis. Eighteenth-century models of political action cannot leverage a world projected as moving in accord with unintelligible forces.

Yet it is precisely the spectacle of violent hands-on political action that spurs inquiry: "The anarchist bomb bade one go on." The bomb persuades the inquirer that he must continue to search out some principle of unity on which to rebuild social and political life, even as evidence supports the hypothesis that such a principle does not exist and that any plausible principle will turn out to be false in substance and pernicious in effect. For purposes of human formulation, truth for Adams has become merely provisional. Because he cannot adjust his eighteenth-century politics to a world of provisional unities, the protagonist of the *Education* is doomed to inquire after a situation beyond recuperation. Given an irreducible multiplicity of phenomena, which Adams looks on allegorically as unbridled, self-serving willfulness—anarchy animate and inanimate—he will hazard only the following generalizations: "He could not deny that the law of the new multiverse explained much that had been most obscure, especially the persistently fiendish treatment of man by man; the perpetual effort of society to establish law, and the perpetual revolt of society against the law it had established . . . the perpetual victory of the principles of freedom, and their perpetual conversion into principles of power; but the staggering problem was the outlook ahead into a despotism of artificial order which nature abhorred" (1138). The "organic unity" of a Gothic Europe or Jeffersonian America could absorb individual expression, but militarist collectivisms of the right and left are another matter, especially in view of the technological enhancement of modern armaments.

Simply to control the vast forces that had increasingly become available to society, the human mind, in Adams's view, would have to evolve. In not discounting the possibility of a spontaneous increase in human capacity, he allows a little of the old Darwinian reflex to surface. "Thus far," Adams writes toward the conclusion of "A Law of Acceleration," "since five or ten thousand years, the mind had successfully reacted, and nothing yet proved that it would fail to react" (1175), but his conviction is tenuous and the evolutionary leap that he imagines constitutes at most the precondition of a political solution. He has reached a formidable impasse. Speaking for his protagonist, he concedes that "an ignorant old man felt no motive for trying to escape, seeing that the only escape possible lay in the form of *vis a tergo* commonly called death" (1114).

From the acceleration hypothesis that concludes the *Education* Adams moved to the "The Rule of Phase Applied to History" and *A Letter to American Teachers of History*. Both of these works present attempts on the part of a self-styled "by-stander" to conclude inquiry in a great generalization derived from post-Newtonian physics.[21] Continuing the line of argument begun in "A Dynamic Theory of History," "Rule" tries to specify a law of transformation by which thought, responding to pressures in its world, becomes capable of the higher powers requisite to the task at hand (no less than survival of the human species), and this essay celebrates thought as a material force in itself. For an inquirer who has experienced the sensation of thought perishing in its own reflection, "Rule" holds out the prospect of a kind of afterlife in which the energies of mind transform the thinker just at the moment when thought and thinker are about to succumb. Despite the catastrophic mood of the essay, its thesis is speculative and life affirming in its assertion of the mind's powers of adjustment.

It is in the *Letter*, however, that Adams arrives at his final position, as willfully oppositional as he can make it. This text embraces what he had identified in the *Education* as "the only escape possible." Privately printed and self-published as was all the later work, the *Letter* announces the long-sought "great generalisation": it is none other than the second law of thermodynamics, formulated in the glory days of Darwin and Lyell and serving to invalidate the whole evolutionary program before it had fairly begun, thus rendering in retrospect the progressive outlook of the nineteenth century a charade. The historian emeritus boldly asserts that most of his own and his contemporaries' intellectual life has proceeded on false premises; further, he asserts that intellection itself, as part of an irreversible dynamic process, dissipates energy and realizes death. The radical oppositionality of the argument consists in its rejection of the doctrine that "the flower of vital energy is Thought," its repudiation of the dogma that thought is "incapable of degradation or dissolution."[22] On the contrary, according to this argument, thought manifests a degradation of instinct and facilitates the process of cosmic decomposition. Inquiry culminates in the recognition of the mortal condition of all existence and in so doing hastens its realization. To think is to commit suicide, and indeed the voluntary death of highly evolved life forms—a motif seen elsewhere in Adams's life and work—becomes the master motif of the essay. The "joke" of the *Letter* is that he has dispatched it as a collegial proposal to reorganize university study around the second law as the great generalization.

Thus martyrdom to the disease of omniscience takes on final and, assuming the validity of Adams's trope, literalized meaning. It is as though in this, his last performance before his peers, he would insist that ultimate knowledge, as much as we can aspire to it in absolutely certain form, concerns what we begin life suspecting and that only ambition and pride allow us to forget: that we are limited, that we are dependent, and that we die, as individuals and as a species. The bearer of such tidings knowingly courts martyrdom as a public intellectual in a culture that has apotheosized the positive outlook. The message, as Adams himself points out, is as old as the biblical prophets, but by identifying the physicist (specifically, William Thompson, Lord Kelvin) as the one who confirms humankind's innate and irredeemable fallibility, and by identifying this condition as material rather than moral in nature, he adumbrates a heretofore-unsuspected level of depravity. He contrives a discussion that implicitly denies the compensatory strategies of ethical discourse, strategies that assume that even the harshest jeremiads lend themselves to a pragmatic moral application with a prospect of atonement and redemption. The text, intelligible only as allegory, does what it can to withhold itself from any reading that would mitigate the prolix and clausal death sentence it seeks to pronounce.

Certainly Adams must have recognized that at most a writer can only deflect a readership from recourse to such anodynes, and that his anti-sermon would be absurd if not interpreted at some remove as moral discourse. Read with due attention to its call for curricular reform, the *Letter* achieves a seriousness belied by its appearance as a cynical practical joke. As a critique of the perennial conspiracies of silence that suppress dangerous truth-seeking, the text probes basic premises concerning not only what we know and what we do with our knowledge, but also how knowledge is dominated by institutions that serve power rather than truth. Formulating the most discouraging truth imaginable, Adams is especially eager to challenge progressive views of history and the confident embracing of new technologies and wealth: those vast unreckoned capabilities that the twentieth century brought within reach. In his last act as a public intellectual, on the brink of a world war that anyone with a shred of intelligence could see coming, Adams sought to publicize hypocrisy—the mindlessness and moral bankruptcy of institutions of higher learning that readily submit to the dictates of wealth and power—and did so with an outrage consistent with American intellectual traditions.

Our acceptance of the *Letter* does not depend on our conceding the second law as the great generalization. Nor does it require us to forget that Adams's cultivated, if warranted, pessimism depended on a material affluence that discouraged an oppositional political activism and that equated activism with purposeless anarchy. Nor does it mean that we must disregard the offense of the book's disingenuous manner. We accept it if we recognize the authentic menace Adams steadfastly discerned: the arrogating nature of "mainstream" thought, the tendency of the day's conventional wisdom to legislate and give marching orders on the basis of falsehood supported by powerful interests. One might wish that Adams's engagement with contemporary life had permitted a franker analysis of those interests and more forthright condemnation of the corporate structure of academic life, yet the allegory achieves singular cogency. In the counter-arrogance of the *Letter*, Adams the inquirer stands in memorable opposition to the unreflecting hubris of American learned culture and its perennial cooptation by more and less visible concentrations of power. Given the persistent presence of the bomb (whether detonated by a terrorist or a hegemonic state) and the ever more sophisticated ways by which rigid ideology generates plausible truth, the message is as relevant to our own time as it manifestly was to his.

NOTES

1. Henry Adams, *Novels, Mont Saint Michel, The Education*, ed. Ernest Samuels and Jayne N. Samuels (New York, 1983), 1115. Page reference to the works in this volume will hereafter be cited in text by individual title and page number.
2. Henry Adams to Charles Francis Adams, Jr., Nov. 21, 1862, in *The Letters of Henry Adams*, ed. J. C. Levenson et al. (Cambridge, Mass., 1982–1988), 1:315.
3. HA to Charles Francis Adams, Jr., May 1, 1863, in *Letters*, 1:350.
4. HA to Charles Francis Adams, Jr., Oct. 2, 1863, in *Letters*, 1:395–396.
5. Henry Adams, "The Principles of Geology," *North American Review* 107(1868):498.
6. HA, "Principles of Geology," 467.
7. Adams's review is not without criticism of Lyell's theories: the uniformitarian view of the earth did not, in Adams's view, satisfactorily account for periods of glaciation. Moreover, it fell short on less tangible grounds in its failure to appeal to the imagination. But these objections do not make common cause with the theologically motivated rejections of Lyell and the Darwinian view of the world for which Lyell's theories provide a framework.
8. HA, "Principles of Geology," 466.
9. HA, "Principles of Geology," 494.
10. Ernest Samuels, *Henry Adams: The Middle Years* (Cambridge, Mass., 1958), 52.
11. Henry Adams, *The Life of Albert Gallatin* (1879; New York, 1943), 559–560.
12. HA, *Life of Albert Gallatin*, 635.
13. See Samuels, *The Middle Years*, 388–389; and J. C. Levenson, *The Mind and Art of Henry Adams* (Boston, 1957), 124.
14. Henry Adams, *History of the United States during the Administrations of Thomas Jefferson*, ed. Earl N. Harbert (New York, 1986), 99, 100.
15. HA to Henry Cabot Lodge, Oct. 6, 1879, in *Letters*, 2:376.
16. HA to Herbert B. Adams, Dec. 12, 1894, in *Letters*, 4:231.
17. HA to Herbert B. Adams, Dec. 12, 1894, in *Letters*, 4:229–230.
18. HA to Herbert B. Adams, Dec. 12, 1894, in *Letters*, 4:231.
19. HA to Herbert B. Adams, Dec. 12, 1894, in *Letters*, 4:233.
20. For a detailed discussion of Adams's relations with John Hay in the capacities of minister to Great Britain and secretary of state, see Edward Chalfant, *Improvement of the World: A Biography of Henry Adams: His Last Life, 1891–1918* (North Haven, Conn., 2001), chapters 7–9.
21. Adams applies this term to himself in "The Rule of Phase Applied to History," collected in *The Degradation of the Democratic Dogma*, ed. Brooks Adams (1919; New York, 1949), 270.
22. Henry Adams, *A Letter to American Teachers of History*, collected in *The Degradation of the Democratic Dogma*, 206.

Henry Adams, U. S. Grant, & Evolution

Practicing History in the Age of Darwin

J. C. LEVENSON

The progress of evolution from President Washington to President Grant, was alone evidence enough to upset Darwin.
—Henry Adams, "The Education of Henry Adams"[1]

EARLY IN *THE EDUCATION OF HENRY ADAMS,* readers are told what the book is about. Adams declares that the lifelong problem of education, "as it is the moral of religion, philosophy, science, art, politics, and economy," can be summed up as "running order through chaos, direction through space, discipline through freedom, unity through multiplicity."[2] The statement sounds forthright, but in the narrative it quickly becomes equivocal. For one thing, it is prologue to an incident which seems to contradict it. A memorable scene brings together the child Henry Adams, heir of the American Enlightenment, and his president grandfather John Quincy Adams, son of John Adams and sometime protégé of Washington, later the ally of Jefferson, Madison, and Monroe and their successor in the presidency, and now in the 1840s a congressman and the heroic champion of free speech for the antislavery cause. Six-year-old Henry learns that the Laws of Nature and of Nature's God do not extend to him when he stands up to arbitrary power and resists going to school. His resistance is loud enough to embarrass his mother in the house of her parents-in-law, and he counts on that tactical advantage. In the event, the old President descends from his study as from Olympus, takes the misbehaving child by the hand, and with silent authority leads him to school. The established order of the Founding Fathers evidently runs discipline through freedom like a knife through watermelon. So much for the social contract!

In a way, the whole book is an exposition of this parable and, incidentally, of the rhetorical ambiguity of the prefatory statement. The task of running order through chaos, which as a verbal formulation may sound easy, turns out to be more difficult than the labors of Hercules, especially if one mistakenly reads the precept as a call to *imposing* order on chaos, unity on multiplicity. Young Henry Adams, the more or less guileless protagonist of the first part of the *Education*, seems prone to that mistake. His overconfidence with respect to making, or even finding, order leads repeatedly to failure. As the story proceeds, there is a shrinking gap of age and irony between narrator and protagonist. The young man's naïveté counts less and less in explaining the discrepancy between rational anticipation and baffling outcome, and the difficulties look more and more like the way the world actually works. What may have seemed special to Henry Adams with his unique eighteenth-century inheritance, is by no means merely personal to him.

The push-pull of order and mess, direction and drift, purpose and bafflement is partially resolved by the shape of Adams's narrative. The shrinking gap between narrator and protagonist disappears as the author skips the twenty years of his professional career, the years when the actual life story turned from learning to doing. Once the active career is over, the learning process resumes—with a disinterestedness that could not have been claimed before. In the last part of the *Education*, the roles of narrator and protagonist converge, and the Adams in the text becomes the "historian" who perceives contradictions as he encounters them. Despite Adams's provisional subtitle for the book ("a study of twentieth-century multiplicity"), the epithet "historian" rightly suggests that "twentieth-century multiplicity," set forth as a distinctly modern condition, is also a name for age-old problems of historical study and historical writing. The historian confronts the unlimited welter of the past, which is too much for the human mind to know, and deals with selections from that past that seem to hang together. Sequences that take unexpected turns, become tangled, or simply break off, constantly challenge historians. Retroactively this historical consciousness of anomalies, snarls, and extinctions helps explain the "failures" of the young protagonist whose story differs from conventional narratives of education, in fiction or autobiography, that relate a young man's progress to maturity and wisdom. Young Henry Adams does not outgrow his mistakes, much less put them behind him all at once; he repeats them in different contexts. And yet his story is far from being a pointless repetition of trials and errors, and though his problem is finally seen to lie in the nature of things, bafflement is hardly the last word of the book.

For many readers, supposed axioms that turn out not to be dependable, as in the anecdote of what happened to "the inalienable rights of boys," provide lessons enough to justify the word *education* in Adams's title. As the narrative moves along, a response of condescension at the child's gullibility turns into something like shared liberation from common errors. There is a kind of comic release when Adams the narrator sums up what Adams the ambitious young journalist learned from his two years of covering national politics in the late 1860s: "The progress of evolution from President Washington to President Grant, was alone evidence enough to upset Darwin" (266). The sentence has difficulties, but its rhetorical purpose seems clear. Adams was ridiculing the straight-line historical "grand narrative" that had widest currency in his lifetime, the idea of progress, as reinforced by the authority of science. The belief that historical sequence means improvement and that the ultimate stage of improvement is here and now is so familiar that he can invoke it as premise. And it fails the test of direct observation with flying colors. The debunking of progress that goes on throughout the *Education* helps explain why, when the book was published posthumously in 1918, it became a best seller. A reading public for whom the horrors of the First World War had undone a prevalent belief in progress could well respond to a narrative that threw light on just such experience. In this respect, Adams was providing fuel for a major shift in popular sentiment.

But there is a historical crux in the epigram on the progress from Washington to Grant, in that it would not have fazed Charles Darwin in the least. Adams explicitly acknowledged that Darwin did not belong with the popularizers of evolution who were making it into the idea of progress writ large. Evidently the difference did not matter enough to keep him from conceding the name of Darwinism to the popularizers. Unlike his friend William James, who first read Darwin at about the same time as Adams did, he was not swept away by *The Origin of Species*. James, destined to be a scientist and a philosopher, seized at once on its scientific and philosophic importance. Adams had already used up his capacity for transformative intellectual enthusiasm a few years earlier when he was reading Tocqueville and Mill, who were to be informing presences in his historical career, and Auguste Comte, closest of the three to being an evolutionist. At first he had been excited by Comte's promise of a social science that would make human history as predictable and ineluctable as the course of the planet. He could even imagine that the determined course of progress might end in apocalypse, that science and technology were in the saddle and riding mankind towards an ultimate collapse. These ideas subsided to dormancy and were least in evidence during the years of Adams's active career as a historian, though they were to recur later and become, after the writing of the *Education*, crankily obsessive. Cynthia Russett, whose authoritative *Darwin in America* tracks the spread of evolutionary ideas from *The Origin of Species* into the twentieth century, gives a chapter to Henry Adams on the basis of his early and late speculations, and she also notes that these themes do not affect his remarkable work as a historian. I would press the point further. The intelligent practice of history was one way in which Adams was protected from the hazards of imagining cosmic scenarios. The discipline of the profession offered protection from the vagaries of free-wheeling among imaginable possibilities. Adams's other great protection was his readiness to go beyond Comte's general proposition that humankind had arrived at an ultimate scientific stage of development and actually study the new sciences.

Adams still subscribed to Comte's positivism in thinking that religion and metaphysics had lost their authority in the matter of belief and that science had now become the best source of truths about the world. But when he called himself in the *Education* "a Comteist, within the limits of evolution" (225), he implicitly qualified his allegiance to Comte by his acceptance of Darwin. Not in so many words, to be sure, for as we have seen, he used the word evolution equivocally. Nevertheless, in undermining a grand narrative—call it *progress*, call it *evolution*—that would encompass the end of history, he was in fact allying himself with Darwin and the great intellectual revolution of his time. He understood the momentous choice he was making. In calling himself "a Darwinist before the letter" (224), he absolved himself from having to be a Darwinist by the book. What kept him from the grand teleological simplifications of the evolutionary theorists was not only the high intelligence of his historical practice, but also his direct grasp, albeit as an amateur, of the scientific issues Darwin raised. His language sometimes played on the vague boundary between popular evolutionism and Darwin's theory of evolution by natural selection, but the distinction he himself made between the two is crucial to discriminating the argument of both Adams the professional historian and Adams the "historian"—telling epithet—who takes over in the last fifteen chapters of the *Education*.

THE WORLD OF *THE ORIGIN OF SPECIES* is one of flux and multiplicity, where novelties constantly occur and some phenomena pass irrevocably into extinction. There are stories with beginnings and endings, but there is no single grand story with an end to which all the parts have been inevitably leading. The fluid, changeable, multiple world of Darwin succeeded the mathematically neat universe of Isaac Newton as the most powerful statement of what our world is like, and his book is still a primary text by which we can get our intellectual bearings. In some respects, the revolution was less than total. The old regime could be said to have survived in that physics is still the queen of the natural sciences: it remains the most general science, the most inclusive, the most "objective" in its validation by elaborate mechanical devices and abstruse mathematics. But present-day physics seems unlikely soon to become a usable present for the popular imagination, since the means of its demonstrability are beyond the grasp of most non-physicists. As for Newton's physics, it constitutes less and less of the field for practicing scientists, and even in the layman's world, where the anecdote of the falling apple is still cherished, it no longer exerts hegemony over the imagination.

We still live in the age of Darwin, even though he has in many ways been left behind by later advances in his science. Reading him today, we recognize the severe handicaps under which he labored. He had to work without the physiology and without the genetics that nowadays even the layman knows to some degree. Lacking the sciences he helped call into being, he had to derive his argument simply from natural history. One consequence is that there are no prerequisites to the study of *The Origin of Species*. Apart from the wonderful clarity of his writing, readers then and now could get directly to his main theses without having to go down byways that might confuse the half-informed. Darwin's great advantage, arising directly from his handicap, is that history, natural or otherwise, is where we live our lives. One may concede to professional philosophers that a historical frame of mind originates with Hegel and others still further back in time, but John Dewey, who began as a Hegelian idealist, shifted the focus from origins to endings when he declared that it was Darwin who finally, decisively, put time into the study of human life.

In *The Origin of Species*, Darwin covered an expanse of time that geologists had recently lengthened from a few thousand to millions of years. He needed such a span in order to show how incremental changes like those which breeders use to improve their strains, could work far greater changes, given time enough. Within that span, time meant change. Given that organisms reproduce everywhere with random variations and that environments (both geological settings and competing species in the neighborhood) allow more survival space to some variants than to others, these interacting histories in the long run evolve new species and extinguish old. In his demonstration of how the process goes on by itself, Darwin explicitly tried to purify his language of animistic metaphors. When he used expressions like *struggle* for existence and natural *selection*, he cautioned readers against the linguistic traps whereby such turns of phrase seem to imply an agent. He warned that, hard as it is to avoid personification with a word like nature, "I mean by Nature, only the aggregate action and product of many natural laws, and by laws the sequence of events as ascertained by us."[3] The tone of austerity could not conceal the scale of his conception. He regarded the domain of science as coextensive with the natural world, every bit as wide as that world—and not concerned to go beyond. Here the cultural difference between Darwin and Newton proves crucial. *Principia Mathematica* resolved the anomalies and intricate complexities of Newton's scientific world in formulas that were seen as elegant, stable, rational, and confirming the age-old argument that the order of the world was the effect of supernatural design. The teeming life of Darwin's world flouted all such assumptions. The tangled bank that he invited his readers to contemplate, however much it stood for a wonderful expansion of human knowledge, required giving up old ideas of orderliness. To those who could not make the intellectual leap, it simply seemed inelegant, unstable, irrational.

Worst of all, Darwin evidently attacked the foundations of religion. He acted on the premise that science ceases to be science when extranatural causes are called upon for explanation, and so his narrative admits no *deus ex machina*. In his theory, natural causes sufficiently accounted for natural effects, even on the grand scale of evolution. The theological argument from design had to be abandoned. These claims for science remain the most contested of his principles even today—not in the scientific laboratory, to be sure, but in the political forum. They testify to his daring. When Dewey applied Galileo's defiant disavowal of his forced recantation—"E pur si muove" (nevertheless it moves)—to Darwin and species, he caught the connection between scientifically positing a world everywhere in movement and having to defend oneself against the anathema that his findings evoked.

In writing natural history, Darwin wrote history. He showed, for one thing, that a general comprehensive work of history need not imply a universal progress culminating in the present. Unlike other big generalists—Auguste Comte, Karl Marx, Herbert Spencer—who wrote as if we have arrived at a final stage of human development or at least have the end in sight, Darwin forbade such a belief. In his words, natural selection "does not necessarily include progressive development."[4] Moreover, since variability, adaptation, and extinction continue to function as they have done, the future remains open to becoming what we cannot foresee. The principles on which Darwin's world worked operate for Adams, too, though in Adams's historical career they must be inferred as tacit premises. In *Darwin's Plots*, Gillian Beer's brilliant book on implicit narrative in *The Origin of Species*, she looks closely at virtual contemporaries who seem independently to envision a world of flux and multiplicity and web-like interconnectedness much like Darwin's—Dickens is her great example—and later writers who, having read Darwin, had him as part of their cultural inheritance. Henry Adams belongs ambiguously in both categories. He had read Darwin when he embarked on his career as a historian, but his narrative principles and his conception of the world were sufficiently accounted for by his professionalism alone. When he came to write the *Education*, where he touched on Darwin directly, he argued resistance to Darwin almost as persuasively as the need for reasoned acceptance. The multiple relations become more easily understood when we recognize that *The Origin of Species* is a dense representation of the world, more immediately available to a wide public than other texts that try for the same scope, functioning in a literate and scientific society like a founding epic in an oral or prescientific culture. For many people, in varying degrees, reading Darwin was a transformative experience, but philosophers thinking about the principles by which Darwin's world works and historians using analogous principles in their day-to-day work could do so quite independently of the book. A look at Adams's *History of the United States* shows how comfortably such independent practice fits both with Darwin's text and with its theoretical implications.

THE TRADITIONAL TOPICS OF HISTORY—both the study of the past and writing about it—bear a likeness to what Darwin called a "varieties." Darwin defined the term as "one arbitrarily given, for the sake of convenience, to a set of individuals" that is less distinct and more fluctuating than "species."[5] But the various kinds of writing are more fluid than the analogy suggests, for serious work in history—or other forms—is rarely reducible to a single category and is usually best understood in a multiplicity of relations. The westward movement of European civilization, dating from the Fall of Constantinople, say, or from Columbus's first voyage is the grand topic of demographic, and ultimately ecological, change. The material that might supply a narrow political account of wars and diplomacy could also serve to illuminate Ranke's magisterial precept that a national history had to be international before it could qualify as general history. In his *History*, Adams made the rise of American democracy his theme, and he gave the story of national development its epic significance by placing it in these two broad contexts.

The big-scale topics of westward movement and of diplomacy and war are central to Adams's *History of the United States during the Administrations of Thomas Jefferson and James Madison*, to give his work its full title. The span of time—four four-year presidential administrations—sounds extremely short, and the blatant claim to write a merely political history sounds narrow, but the comprehensiveness that requires nine volumes shows that the apparent self-limitation can serve to focus a narrative in which every detail enlarges the general themes. Just when the rising star of American Western historians, Frederick Jackson Turner, was preparing to celebrate the moving frontier as the deep source of American character, Adams spoke for an older generation and a more critical view of westering. The single most important event in the *History* is the Louisiana Purchase, far more important in Adams's argument than the low point of the British burning of Washington or the high point of Andrew Jackson's victory over Wellington's veterans at New Orleans. As a political historian, Adams accepted Jefferson's view that the election of 1800, with the nation committing itself to popular democracy, enacted a democratic revolution. But the great question remained as to whether a democratic republic could establish a nation-state over the formidable expanse of American territory. The Louisiana Purchase of 1803 doubled the territory and more than doubled the challenge. Just a dozen years after the purchase, the young nation's survival in war and success at peacemaking were evidence that the challenge could be met. A nation was founded, a democracy was established, and, something very different from either of those two propositions, the American democracy had taken on a character of its own, a character based on political experience and not on some ultimate contact with the wilderness. To be sure, any writing about national character, any suggestion that one nation is different from another, is open to the easy charge that an exception to the common human lot is being claimed. However, compared to Turner's natural causes that seemed in their workings to be very like supernatural causes, Adams dealt with questions that the rest of the world could understand.

Was democracy primarily a matter of how a state is governed, or did it go deeper into the way people conduct their lives? Questions like these took the political historian far beyond the superficial limits that his announced subject matter might seem to allow. Even within the usual boundaries of what is called political, Adams questioned Jefferson's claim that the democratic revolution of 1800 abolished forever the monarchic and arbitrary powers that Federalists had supposedly exerted when they were in office. He found, first of all, that the "reign of politics" did not end with the swearing in of a Republican administration. As Jefferson—like Madison later—got used to his presidential role, he learned to trust himself with the active exercise of government power. His most positive act was the Louisiana Purchase, which entailed presidential prerogative hardly envisaged in the Constitution. It was an assertion of national sovereignty such as Jefferson had denounced as monarchical and arbitrary when he went into opposition in the 1790s. Now, aside from questions of legality and propriety, the purchase made immediate and pressing the physical and economic problems of expanding American society westward. In Adams's telling, the Burr conspiracy showed how hard it would be to hold the country together, especially since Jefferson's adaptability on the occasion of the Louisiana Purchase had not led to his revising the doctrine of negative government. Popular indifference to imperial dreams rather than vigorous government kept Burr from succeeding. However, a further layer of Adams's irony suggests that popular democracy could in a surprising new way accomplish acts of self-preservation that government had historically been established to do, that is, the novel Jeffersonian idea of a democracy without a polity seemed in this first trial to work.

Even so, distances that far outran existing means of communication meant that the danger of the United States breaking up was real. The Burr conspiracy was not the only instance in which the danger of geographic overextension would be surmounted, but not by political means. Adams conceived that water transport was the essential lifeline of social organization as of commerce, and he saw that in the new continental nation the problem was one of mastering rivers, not oceans. In his account, the problem was to be solved—without encouragement from government or from public opinion—by a handful of "visionaries" such as America seemed sporadically to produce. In this case, the visionaries included the inventor Robert Fulton and the venture-capitalist who backed him, Robert

Livingston. The voyage of the steamship *Clermont*, though it commanded little public or official attention at the time, was for the historian far more important than the vicissitudes of naval warfare. Although keepers of the political record, official and journalistic, took little note of what decisively mattered to the national future, there were other Americans who made it happen.

War itself, the deadly game of states, was for Adams an occasion for seeing how social arrangements took on political meaning. As he saw it, war set up "international tests of popular intelligence." He debunked the legend that the Americans' quick mastery of artillery, crucial to Jackson's victory at New Orleans, resulted from the frontiersman's habitually targeting the eye of the squirrel. Instead, he presented it as evidence of an American technological bent, the handiness that developed in a new country short of artisans. In technology worthy of the name, handiness showed itself as inventiveness. Adams rated the torpedo and the screw-propeller as American inventions more original than the steamboat, but he gave the place of pride to that anonymous invention "the fast-sailing schooner with its pivot-gun—an invention that grew out of the common stock of nautical intelligence."[6] The democratic and the technological revolutions were deeply interwoven, both in the matter of westering and in the trial by combat that was forced upon the young nation.

Adams's *History* is in some ways an epic of national origins, and despite such counter-themes as the end of statecraft and the persistence of the "reign of politics," the rise of the American democracy could possibly be taken as the American story. Indeed I have argued so myself. What I see today is how complexity and open-endedness keep that from being the only story. The *History* concludes with a series of questions as to what the republic might become after the passage of, say, a century. How would new vices be purified? How would new powers be curbed? How would material content be kept from deadening intellectual life? But the refusal to suggest finality is not just in the coda. Complexity, multiplicity are present from the beginning. The opening chapter of the *History*, squarely in the tradition of Tocqueville's *Democracy in America*, names relative equality of condition as the great political asset of American society in 1800, but Adams puts the qualifier before the proposition itself. On the very opening page, he makes it clear that political society and society were not congruent, that almost one-fifth of the American people were Negro slaves. Later, he shows how the Louisiana Purchase came about only because Napoleon's imperial plans in the New World were thwarted by the

Haitian revolution. As the first historian to make this point, he goes on to declare that "prejudice of race alone blinded the American people to the debt they owed to the desperate courage of five hundred thousand Haytian negroes who would not be enslaved."[7] In the great moment of the rising action, Adams noted the tragic theme that shadowed the national future.

The other major event of the *History*, the great international test of war, is similarly entwined both with the matter of westering and with the matter of racism. The War of 1812, and the European wars of which it was part, began on the Indiana frontier. Adams describes in detail the clash of cultures between American settlers and native hunter-warriors. American settlers poached game and stripped the hunting-grounds of the Indians. They trafficked in whiskey and, as part of such commerce, bought land at depressed prices from tribes near the line of settlement. The federal government piously encouraged the hunting peoples to become agricultural and thus end the most obvious form of cultural clash. But Adams pointed out that if, contrary to reasonable expectation, they had done so, they would have thwarted the other Jeffersonian policy of buying up Indian rights in order to make room for American settlement.

Effectual anarchy prevailed on the frontier. One-sided anarchy, that is: natives were subject to severe and inflexible justice. On the other hand, random murder of natives was condoned, and when Indian-killers were apprehended, no jury would convict. The minimal state of Jeffersonian democracy released energies it could not control. Neither treaties nor laws could be enforced on the Americans. Eventually the territorial governor, William Henry Harrison, pressed by local militants and under ambiguous orders from Washington, attacked the vacated Indian village of Tippecanoe, declared victory, and in effect started a general war. Indian reprisals looked to "civilized" settlers like terrorist attacks and redoubled the element of fear that was mixed with blood-thirst and racist moral blindness. But the worst of it was that there seemed to be no policy that could change the course of events. The historian's simple statistics tell the story: the census of 1800 reported 2,500 Americans in Indiana, that of 1810, nearly 25,000.

Adams does not rely on the bare statistics of tenfold population growth to convey the lethal effect of Euro-American expansion on indigenous peoples. Characteristically, he keeps his "objective" distance by framing his comment as a political historian on the official documents at hand. He cites Harrison as his "highest authority" on northwestern Indians and as spokesman for a well-disposed Jeffersonian point of view:

> His account of Indian affairs offered an illustration of the law accepted by all historians in theory, and adopted by none in practice; which former ages called "fate," and metaphysicians called "necessity," but which modern science has refined into "survival of the fittest." No acid ever worked more mechanically on a vegetable fibre than the white man acted on the Indian. As the line of American settlements approached, the nearest Indian tribes withered away.[8]

With the briefest mention of the popular metaphor that implied a we-are-the-fittest celebration of national triumph, he drops it as insufficient to convey the enormity of cultural conflict that is a tragic cross-weave in his national epic. The rise of a peace-loving, hardworking, apolitical American democracy is not the uncontested last word of a grand universal story. The rich inclusiveness of the narrative brings in stories of a very different order.

IN THE WHOLE NINE-VOLUME *HISTORY*, Adams made that one brief mention of "survival of the fittest," only to drop it as being a wrong figure of speech. The *History* has a Darwin plot, so to speak, a web of relations rather than an argument of straight-line cause and effect, but it gives scarcely a hint of Darwin's doctrine. By contrast, the *Education* is loaded with explicit reference and doctrinal exposition. But plot and rhetoric and argument sometimes seem to say conflicting things. For instance, when the young protagonist first visits Rome, where the great figures of the past "might be mixed up in any relation of time . . . and never lead to a sequence," the narrator observes that "Rome could not be fitted into an orderly, middle-class, Bostonian, systematic scheme of evolution" (91). But the word *evolution* as thus used stands for the orderly, systematic scheme that Herbert Spencer popularized, and that the nineteenth-century non-scientific public liked to call Darwinism. Ten years on in the narrative, Adams himself invokes the name of Darwin as he puts evolution at the center of Victorian complacency: "Never had the sun of progress shone so fair. Evolution from lower to higher raged like an epidemic. Darwin was the greatest of prophets in the most evolutionary of worlds" (284). This optimistic progressivism similarly misappropriated the name of Darwin to describe the popular ideology. Darwin's scientific ideas were subject to testing and subject also to use and development by workers in adjacent fields, like Adams's contemporaries William James and Thorstein

Veblen. Darwin's conception of a constantly changing world and how to write about it showed how easily his natural history fitted with the practice of history. But the relation of Darwin's science to the ordinary world that nonprofessional readers inhabit, is subject to drift; patent implication veers over by degrees to free analogizing. The distinction between Charles Darwin's science and Herbert Spencer's evolutionism becomes central not only to what Adams was writing, but also to the way we read him, since the two are profoundly at odds. For this reason it is necessary to disentangle Adams's engagement with Darwin and with the Spencerian heresy.

Adams read *The Origin of Species* when he was in London as private secretary to his father, the American minister to Great Britain. The apprentice diplomat read widely, but with *Origin* he was an amateur venturing beyond his field. Another important book led him to closer study. When Sir Charles Lyell, a good friend of the Union and of the Adams family, expressed hope of having the new tenth edition of his *Principles of Geology* reviewed in America, young Adams volunteered— provided Sir Charles would help him on theoretical questions. This was the first edition of *Principles* in which Lyell, after earlier skepticism, fully supported Darwin's theory of evolution by natural selection. Adams's volunteering was a mixture of intellectual boldness and social timidity. Whereas William James, on reading Darwin, saw at once that his teacher Louis Agassiz was a far inferior scientist, Adams's reaction was tempered by his knowing that Agassiz, Darwin's foremost antagonist in America, was social Boston's favorite scientist. When he offered his review to Charles Eliot Norton, editor of the *North American Review* and a full-fledged Brahmin, he volunteered that if the article proved "not conservative enough," he would withdraw it without a word.[9] He confessed to a "leaning" towards the new views, and in the review he treated Lyell's momentous conversion as the matter to be explained. He understood that evolution by natural selection accorded with Lyell's "uniformitarian" principle that natural causes operated constantly and consistently through time and that first causes, divine or otherwise, were beyond the reach of geological inquiry. He affirmed that the new views adhered to "the first principle of philosophy," that of economizing "forced suppositions," but he for his part hung back.[10] Scientists had to say aye or nay to Darwin's hypothesis, he said, but laymen might be more or less neutral bystanders until fuller scientific explanations came into being. As late as 1890, traveling in the South Seas and examining coral reefs firsthand, Adams reread Darwin and could not reconcile the argument for elevation of landmasses and subsidence of the ocean floor with his own observations. In short, his interest in Darwin the scientist was still conditioned by his geological point of view. Following his own advice, he remained a neutral bystander.

Neutral but not uncurious. Long before he was able to check Darwin against his own independent observations, he followed sound scholarly procedure and made sure he knew some of Darwin's material from more than one source. He took his lead from *The Origin of Species*, to be sure, where Darwin addressed two major objections to his theory: first, despite the strong inference that life forms become more complex as they evolve, there are complex forms for which no prior, simpler stages can be shown; and secondly, despite the assertion that random variation takes place constantly, some simple forms have not changed at all since the earliest fossil record. To look further into these questions, Adams went to Lyell for help. Lyell sent him to the *Paleontology* of Sir Richard Owen (who was Darwin's leading scientific opponent in England, but whose egregious display of professional rivalry in no way diminished his authority as a paleontologist). The American student did his homework. In the *Education*, the ancestorless *Pteraspis*, which comes in as the first vertebrate (though it has since been demoted to a more primitive order of fish), and the do-nothing *Terebratula*, a primitive mollusk unchanged over successive geologic eras, figure importantly in both argument and rhetoric. Although neither appears in *The Origin of Species*, they represent what Darwin himself recognized as difficulties for his theory. They were difficulties for Darwin, to be sure, but they pose insuperable questions for the simplified evolutionism of Spencer.

Adams's cautious acceptance of Darwin was genuine, even as he followed his own advice and declined to say more than he knew. He kept to the scientific conservatism of the Lyell review during his Harvard years from 1870 to 1877. As part of his appointment, the assistant professor doubled as editor of the *North American Review*, and as such he could demonstrate most publicly what those scientific standards were. In a journal that tried to cover intellectual activity worldwide, the continuing controversy over Darwin was bound to come up. Adams particularly relished joining the controversy when it gave him a chance to show that American scholarship could match and even surpass that of British universities. Thus when the Oxford philologist Max Müller developed an anti-Darwin argument that language-using human beings were the crucial instance of special creation, Adams solicited a review by the Yale philologist W. D. Whitney. In "Darwinism and Language," Whitney defended Darwin and the natural evolution of language even though he carefully warned readers that the theory was by no means definitively proven. When it came to Müller, however, he felt no such need to qualify his criticism, and he dismantled the creationist argument both for its reasoning and for its citation of supposed facts. Neutrality was not the same as not judging at all, and conservatism was by no means a covert attempt to go back to the theological geology of Agassiz. Whitney's neutrality was clearly of a kind with Adams's. For once, the editor broke his rule against sponsoring running battles, and he asked Whitney for more.

In time the reward for Adams's relatively neutral open-mindedness came from his geologist friend Clarence King, whose "Catastrophism and Evolution," originally a lecture at Yale in 1877, gave the debate over Darwin a new turn.[11] King offered a way of accepting Agassiz's scientific breakthrough on glaciation quite apart from the religious and political-racist entanglements of "special creation" that Agassiz embraced, and he did so without giving up evolution by natural selection. What he gave up—enthusiastically—was English uniformitariansim, both Lyell's and Darwin's. As head of the United States Geological Survey, he was aware of earth changes that did not fit with Lyell's incrementalism, and he took a hyperbolic American pride in them. His American evidences were quite off the scale of "poor, puny little Vesuvius" or "the feeble energy of a Lisbon earthquake." As he put it more prosaically, the Tertiary period of geologic history bore the marks of volcanic activity so sudden, intense, and massive that it "cannot be explained away upon any theory of gradual action." While agreeing that there were periods of "geological serenity" in which change took place by "insensible gradations," he affirmed that geology showed more: "then all at once a part of the earth suffered short, sharp, destructive revolution unheralded as an earthquake or volcanic eruptions." Catastrophic changes had disastrous effects on organic life, but they were also creative since in the changed environment the process of organic evolution speeded up. The observable evidence required a radical rethinking of basic principles such as has been at the forefront of paleontology in our own time. King somewhat heavy-handedly argued that environmental catastrophe rather than incremental variation was "the major cause of the Evolution of life," but he also made the important case that science itself must be allowed to evolve. He argued that the British uniformitarians, by assuming "unlimited time" and "inch-by-inch process," had "tied the hands of science." He himself envisioned a science with a future. He expected that "Rosetta Stones" would be found to enable geologists to interpret phenomena that currently resisted explanation.[12] In his natural history, grand-scale changes had in fact occurred, and the story perforce remained open-ended. For Adams, about to undertake the great project of writing his *History*, both the substance and the vision of King's lecture helped clarify ideas that he had been thinking about since he first undertook his studies under Lyell. The plot of his *History*, beginning with the Jeffersonian revolution of 1800 and concluding with unanswered questions about the American democracy, bore a generic likeness to the natural history that King expounded and to the "punctuated evolution" that today addresses variable rates of change.

For more than thirty years Adams's relation to Darwin was as a student of science, and never more so than in 1890 and 1891 when he matched his observations of volcanic islands and coral reefs with those of Darwin. Direct observation made him chary of the speculative regions of Darwin's science, the "nice explanations of everything he didn't see." Darwin's best response to objections had been the incompleteness of the geologic record, but negative arguments can never be conclusive. As for positive evidence that didn't fit, it seemed to suggest any number of theories "equally reasonable and untenable." For Adams as an observer on the scene, the multiplicity of patterns to be found in natural history made a self-evident case against a unified theory: "The Pacific swarms with paradoxes as numerous as the islands. No general rule will hold, not even Darwin's."[13] The idea that unified theories were not safe from future revision, even as anomalies might be resolved by future Rosetta Stones, was fully in the spirit of the science he had been studying. No doubt Adams enjoyed playing the game of falsifiability in which even an amateur could score points at the expense of the foremost naturalist of the age. In doing so, nevertheless, he confirmed his belonging to the age of Darwin.

Within a few years, however, he was speaking of Darwin at a very different level of generalization. In his 1894 Presidential Letter to the American Historical Association (his professional colleagues could make him president, but they could not make him attend their convention), he viewed publication of *The Origin of Species* with the eye of a social historian. He recalled the midcentury when Buckle's history and Darwin's natural history made it seem as if scientific laws would soon extend to the historian's domain. Efforts along that line had proven quixotic, and it is hard to assess how much irony was intended as he pictured his professional colleagues still waiting for "some new Darwin . . . to demonstrate the law or the laws of historical evolution." The prospect seemed dim compared to the might-have-been of the earlier generation: "Darwin led an intellectual revival much more hopeful than any movement that can now be seen in Europe. . . . Had history been converted into a science at that time, it would perhaps have taken the form of cheerful optimism which gave to Darwin's conclusions the charm of a possible human perfectibility."[14] This is the point at which he conceded the Darwin of social history to the Darwinists who subscribed to that grand narrative of progress, the evolutionism of Herbert Spencer. Moreover, he put himself into that history—his was the irony of a social observer, not that of an amateur of science.

THE DARWIN OF SCIENCE was indeed different from the Darwin of popular intellectual history, and Spencer more than anyone else made that difference. Spencer prided himself on having been the philosopher of evolutionism from before the publication of *The Origin of Species*, and he looked down on Darwin somewhat for dealing only with the evolution of organic beings. He himself covered physics and astronomy and sociology and politics as well. In an age that valued science as explaining almost everything, his self-styled "synthetic philosophy" brought together all the sciences in explanations that laymen could adapt to their own views of the world. One of his formulas was "persistence of force," a rephrasing of the physicists' "conservation of energy" whereby, as Chauncey Wright pointed out, Spencer takes scientific terms out of context and "adds a new sense, or rather a vagueness, so as to make them descriptive of as much as possible."[15] The sweep of generalization was dazzlingly interdisciplinary. Thus Spencer illustrated the way "every living body exhibits . . . the balancing of mechanical forces"[16]:

> When, for instance, there is a great expenditure of motion through muscular activity, there arises a re-active demand on those stores of latent motion which are laid up in the form of consumable matter throughout the tissues: increased respiration and increased rapidity of circulation are instrumental to an extra genesis of force, that counterbalances the extra dissipation of force. This unusual transformation of molecular motion into sensible motion, is presently followed by an unusual absorption of food—the source of molecular motion.

And if the marathon runner or tennis player becomes too exhausted to eat or sleep for the time being, "an equilibration is still eventually effected."[17] Eating and sleeping catch up in time—unless the effort kills the athlete, in which case another sort of equilibration balances the books. Such an all-embracing philosophic redescription of the world could be endlessly elaborated without regard to verification or measurement or specific cases. Wright, the mathematician-philosopher whom William James, Charles S. Peirce, and Oliver Wendell Holmes regarded as their mentor, reviewed in 1865 the eight works of "synthetic philosophy" that had so far appeared and entered his interim judgment without fudging. He declared that scientific terms, wrenched from context, "lose their definiteness and utility" and "become corrupting and misleading ideas."[18]

Spencer's evolutionism invites the same strictures as his physics. Spencer defined evolution as "an integration of matter and concomitant dissipation of motion; during which the matter passes from an indefinite, incoherent homogeneity to a definite, coherent heterogeneity," a formula that extended back past paleontology to the origins of the cosmos and forward to the advent of Victorian society.[19] Spencer mostly wrote as a materialist. On the much-discussed question of environment versus inheritance, for instance, Spencer kept his distance from the openness of genetic variation and often plumped for environmental determinism. Even so, he offered something for everyone. Whatever was beyond the range of his determinist materialism, he named the "unknowable," and, sounding like a philosophical idealist, he posited the unknowable as the ground from which the phenomena dealt with by science ultimately come. He was similarly equivocal on social issues. Given that he believed profoundly in "survival of the fittest" (he invented the phrase, though Darwin made it widely known) and in laissez-faire economics, he was the prophet of "Social Darwinism," the ideology of jungle competition that hailed the most successful acquisitors as the most valuable members of society. On his other, milder side, he argued that the ferocious militarism of past humanity was giving way in the Victorian era to a pacific industrialism, an environment that would in time change human nature and make altruism our dominant characteristic.

This domestic-sentimental reading of current history led William James to scoff at "the ladylike tea-table elysium" that was for Spencer "the final consummation of progress."[20] Adams expressed a similar view without James's aggressive masculinism, replacing it with the anti-hometown animus of his "orderly, middle-class, Bostonian, systematic scheme of evolution" (*Education* 91). One might say that Adams was of the anti-Spencer party without knowing it, while James was four-square in the explicitly anti-Spencer line of criticism that Chauncey Wright had founded. But the anti-Spencer critics were in their time no more than a countercurrent of social history. The running of the tide was with Spencer, whose books were to sell half a million copies in the United States. Henry Holt, an *homme moyen intellectuel* and sometime publisher of both William James and Henry Adams, declared that Spencer's "synthetic philosophy" was the greatest intellectual feat since Aristotle, and other enthusiasts tried to match the hyperbole.[21] Much as in Henry Adams's view of the Jeffersonian era, the late nineteenth century showed a great gap between popular consciousness and the intellectual events that would matter most to a later time. Statistically speaking, it was the Age of Spencer rather than the Age of Darwin.

An obvious reason was that Darwin required study of *his* science whereas Spencer required mainly a susceptibility to language games. The gist of Spencer could pretty much be taken in by osmosis, and so Henry Adams for a long time contented himself with hearsay. His hearsay, however, was remarkably instructive. In 1870, back in Cambridge to teach and edit, he took up bachelor quarters in a college building and boarded out. He regularly took his meals at table with Chauncey Wright, who had early recognized that to be pro-Darwin entailed being anti-Spencer, and John Fiske, the leading American expositor of Spencer's evolutionism. Fiske had seen how easily one could transform Spencer's "unknowable" into a God of intelligent design, and so he made "cosmic evolution" his own variety of natural religion. The dinnertime dialogues were by no means one-sided: both the principals relished the continuing argument and often pursued it at length. Darwin was deeply grateful to Wright for his defense of *Origin* against the first major religious onslaught in Britain. But Darwin also wrote to Fiske about his *Cosmic Philosophy*, "I never in my life read so lucid an expositor (and therefore thinker) as you are."[22] And indeed the amiable Fiske had a tough-minded scientific side. He wrote a scathing attack on Louis Agassiz's religious anti-Darwinism that cost him all chance of a regular appointment to the Harvard faculty.[23] Adams, though he considered himself a Comteist and a stern adherent of the criteria and practices of modern science, was only theoretically in Wright's positivist camp. He exercised his layman's privilege of remaining technically neutral. Given the staggering campaign of reading by which he was making himself an authority on medieval history, he simply skipped reading Spencer. He made a partial concession in 1874, when Henry Cabot Lodge, his student and his assistant on the *North American Review*, enthusiastically recommended Spencer's *Philosophy of Style* and thrust a copy upon him. The professor dutifully read, and his response was strong and forthright. He found it "neither philosophical nor accurate." Given the quality of the thinking, he declared, "I am not encouraged to read his larger works."[24] He seemed to put the matter aside indefinitely.

Adams had left Harvard and Cambridge for Washington and sustained work on his *History* before there was any sign of his shifting from a scientific interest in Darwin to a historical interest in "Darwinism" and Spencer. The indirect evidence involves William James, who, after Chauncey Wright's early death in 1875, became the leading resister of the rampant Spencerian ideology. James's first major professional article, "Remarks on Spencer's Definition of the Mind as Correspondence" (1878), was a devastating critique, which incidentally served as the occasion for a radical overturning of cognitive psychology since John Locke. A few years later, in 1882, he sent his friend Adams two recent pieces in which he touched on the historian's field. In both essays, he made shrewd citations of Darwin and shrewder animadversions on Spencer. Adams, however, recoiling from what he took to be James's soft romanticism, seemed not to notice these aspects of the essays. "Rationality, Activity, and Faith" set out an early version of James's thesis that will and belief, since they can make a psychological difference in how human effort turns out, may count as positive elements in any rational activity. Adams judged that this "microscopic" gift to orthodox believers in free will did little to change the ever-unsettled debate with unbelievers.[25] The more important article, "Great Men, Great Thoughts, and the Environment," might well have interested Adams if the title had not begun with "Great Men." Against the fallacy of treating intellectual history as if it went on independent of human effort, James argued that individual thinkers originate important hypotheses by a kind of "spontaneous variation," that the best of these ideas find a niche in the historical environment, and that, as a result of this "selection," they become the heritage of a succeeding time and instigation for further thought. The concomitant attack on Spencer for attempting a "science of history" extended to all who spoke of "the 'laws of history' as of something inevitable, which science has only to discover."[26] James's quarrel with "positivists" provoked Adams's resistance. His immediate response was to lecture James on the wrongheadedness of Thomas Carlyle's hero worship, and his one saturnine concession to James's argument was that "you could doubtless at any time stop the entire progress of human thought by killing a few score of men," hardly the kind of agreement that James was looking for.[27]

James's piece may have had a further effect. Adams went on to read Spencer. There is no telling when or why he read *First Principles*, but his copy is of the 1882 printing. And Spencer's language made its way into the *History*. As Ernest Samuels notes, Adams adopted the figure of Spencer's "equilibration" in the concluding chapter of the final volume. There, in an epic simile, he compares American history to the course of the Rhine river, flowing briefly through a picturesque medieval landscape, then becoming a highway of industry, ending in the ocean that science alone could sound, measure, and assess: "In a democratic ocean science could see something ultimate. Man could go no further. The atom might move, but the general equilibrium could not change."[28] It is curious that Spencer's version of entropy, the persistence of force even as it runs down in dead-ends where further development is impossible, should have beguiled Adams more than two decades before his own interest in thermodynamics took him on a similar path. But Spencer's permissive reasoning allowed a choice of interpretations: an equilibrium reached at the ultimate point of differentiation and development might be locked in the virtual death of entropy, it might revert to simplicity and start the cycle again, or it might arrive at a "dynamic equilibrium" like the river-ocean-cloud-rain system that looked very like a perpetual-motion machine. Moreover, Adams's beguilement should not be overstated. The content of his figure came more from Tocqueville's notion of the efficacy of individuals in ages of equality than from any other source. (Tocqueville's argument is that in democratic times, as more people affect political events, the power of any individual becomes less—and the sense of individual power declines even faster.) In that final chapter Adams immediately goes on to say that the establishment of the American democracy is a beginning and not an end. The figurative ocean in which democratic society could develop no further was an ending for one strand of the story, but American society goes on and its future history is undetermined.

It is Adams's reasoning, not his scientific analogizing, that puts him in the constellation of Darwin rather than Spencer. When the vehicle of his figuration comes from the vocabulary of natural science, the implicit argument is still that of a historian who invites examination of his facts. This is obvious in a discursive work like the *History*. In the *Education*, it is equally true and, given the multiplicity of story lines, it is even more important. Thus the *Pteraspis*, a complex organism for which no incremental prior development can be found, balks any effort to follow genealogy back to the simple beginnings that Spencer posited. Stretching the meaning of "genealogy" hardly at all, Adams designated *Pteraspis* the earliest of man's progenitors—a much more unsettling ancestor than the primates that disturbed, and continue to disturb, anti-Darwinians. Cousin to the dogfish, a kind of shark, it comes also to stand for the sharklike heredity to which its human descendants sporadically revert (229–230). Unlike the many "Darwinian" expressions that have been absorbed into trite common usage, Adams's chief Darwinian image remains uniquely his and, despite the revisions of later science, it remains clear in its multiple meanings.

As a professed Comteist in an age of science, Adams drew his vocabulary of reference and metaphor as readily from the sciences as from other cultural fields. His respect for science was very different from worship of it. He saw the irony that the scientist who was seen as attacking religious belief became, not by his own doing, the prophet of a quasi religion: "To other Darwinians—except Darwin—Natural Selection seemed a dogma to be put in place of the Athanasian creed; it was a form of religious hope; a promise of ultimate perfection" (231). Satirical as he was about the secular cult, he himself had grown up with a belief in progress, and so he could in some part feel the attraction of a naturalized teleology like Spencer's. The positivist student of biology and history won out. Against what he took to be the dominant thought of the age, he took his stand. Where evolutionists saw progress, he saw none: "All he could prove was change" (230). If every line of descent supposedly led back to simplicity and uniformity, he pointed to *Pteraspis* as a case where "complexity precedes evolution" (302). These two maxims—"All he could prove was change," "complexity precedes evolution"—were enough to undo Spencer's mythology of progress while in no way subverting Darwin's science. Even so, there is an emperor's-new-clothes tone of surprise in the pronouncements, which suggests how strenuous an effort it took to free oneself from the simpler, all-embracing, popular story.

From his engagement with Darwinism, Adams reached conclusions that did not require biological analogies. "All he could prove was change" and "complexity precedes evolution" could stand apart from any scientific reference as maxims for the historian dealing with a world of flux and multiplicity. The corollary Adams drew was a rather cheerless version of the web-figure: "History is a tangled skein that one may take up at any point, and break when one has unravelled enough" (302). The same argument need not sound so disillusioned. Henry James, schooled all his adult life by his brother William's letters and published writings, took the Darwinian worldview much more in stride. Precisely at the time that the sexagenarian Adams was writing the *Education*, the sexagenarian James was writing prefaces for the New York edition of his work, and in the very first of these prefaces he declared with masterly assurance: "Really, universally, relations stop nowhere, and the exquisite problem of the artist is eternally but to draw, by a geometry of his own, the circle within which they shall *appear* to do so."[29] James's formulation helps explain the plurality of stories, like the plurality of periodizations that could be made of the past—like dating the modern world from the Fall of Constantinople or Columbus's first voyage, from Newton's *Principia* or Darwin's *Origin*. Adams's way of putting it helps explain why the historian claims to have a harder time than the fictive artist: the historian's commitment to accuracy means that he cannot look away from the places where such lines of narrative run parallel, or diverge, or snarl.

FROM THE TANGLED SKEIN OF THE PAST, Adams took up in the *Education* strands that he had developed in the argument of the *History*. In the *History*, the invention of the steamboat was presented as taking place below the threshold of public consciousness, an ironic unconscious history that contrasted with the politicians', the journalists', and evidently the people's preoccupation with elections, wars, or simply making a living. The narrator of the *Education*, taking up the American story a generation after the earlier work left off, describes the world that lay ready at hand for the child "Henry Adams" and his contemporaries. The first great ocean liners, so different from the *Clermont*, could be seen steaming into Boston Harbor, tying America more closely to the transatlantic world and soon to tighten bonds across the Pacific as well. Any thought that the country could have a history apart from the international scene was even then an illusion. As for internal development across continental distances, the mastery of river transport by means of the steamboat was already being overshadowed by the opening of the first railroads. The westward movement that began with covered wagons was consolidated by heavy transport and heavy industry. Apart from its economic significance, Adams saw the railroad system as the single most durable artifact that the country had produced in his lifetime, a cultural monument for future historians to assess. Finally, there was a conquest of both distance and time, the telegraph that brought hot news of the 1844 presidential nominations all the way from Baltimore to Washington. No more ironies like Jackson's great victory at New Orleans coming after the peace treaty had been signed. But progress? The telegraph would bring word of assassinations and disasters of war to Henry Adams on the upper Nile, at Hammerfest above the Arctic Circle, or in provincial France.

The child of 1844, who might have been a witness to what the historian knows, is for practical purposes unconscious of all these phenomena. As facts or as symbols, they are meaningless to him not only in childhood and youth, but even when he is a young scholar teaching history at Harvard. Paradoxically, so long as he pursues an active career, he remains a representative figure of unconscious history. Accepting the conventional truths of his time, he explores some of the ways in which inherited categories like reason, unity, or progress fail to make sense of experience. That negative education proves to be a necessary clearing of the ground. Then, when the historian has completed his great project and retired from his profession, in the complex and difficult latter part of the *Education*, the protagonist of the narrative turns from trying to shape history to contemplating it. In turning to the study of science, technology, multiplicity, he begins trying to interpret experience for which he has not hitherto had categories. Old topics such as continual movement to the West or the necessity of international perspective by no means disappear, but the protagonist-narrator-author perforce becomes a maker of new topics that can stand with the old and may even alter their meaning.

With his shift of interest from organic evolution to physical science, the Adams of the *Education* finds his best new definition of flux in the kinetic theory of gases. The self-proclaimed child of Enlightenment rationalism does not adjust easily to statistical approximation as a replacement for "clear and distinct ideas," even though the new sciences introduce a much higher degree of precision. Once again he shows how difficult it is to move from what Comte called the metaphysical stage to the final positivist stage. He sees the kinetic theory as "an assertion of ultimate chaos." There is a tone of misgiving, to say the least, in his formulation: "In plain words, Chaos was the law of nature; Order was the dream of man" (451). Whatever the drawbacks of his statement, it does fit his historical argument. "Supersensual chaos" (459), his term for the unknown, is very different from Spencer's "unknowable," which Spencer and his followers did not hesitate to treat as if they knew a great deal about it. Adams recognizes that scientists, with advances in their technical and conceptual apparatus, apprehend phenomena that have hitherto been beyond the reach of unmediated observation (hence, "supersensual") and rational comprehension (hence, "chaos"). The harvest of new phenomena both disrupts the existing integrations of knowledge and makes possible more inclusive integrations. Every new effort at forging a wider unity entails the breakdown of older unities. He quotes "the physicists" in summary: "All that we win is a battle—lost in advance—with the irreversible phenomena in the background of nature" (458). Comte's positivism had not prepared him for twentieth-century science, which he dates from Madame Curie's radium, that "metaphysical bomb" (452), or Roentgen's x-rays, which could also be classed as supersensual. The child of the eighteenth century finds himself in need of "new mental powers" (461) if he is to grasp the new breakthroughs. The history of science proves to be open-ended beyond his ability to keep up.

Another major correction to Comte's grand narrative comes not from the unfolding present, but unexpectedly from the past. Adams's 1895 travels to Coutances and Mont-Saint-Michel opened his imagination to a Middle Ages that as a historian of medieval institutions he had known in the abstract but never really felt. It was different, also, from anything he had known in the nineteenth century. He had learned about art as a purchaser of objects for sale—drawings, houses, a sculptured monument. The cathedrals he saw were collective creations, collective possessions. With only the vaguest descent from the Normans, or for that matter without it, he could freely claim a share in the collective experience. "One could not at first see what this novelty meant," he writes in the *Education*, but it is in effect "a new sense of history" (354, 355). There was no way simply to lump this new discovery with other past cultures in an omnibus religious stage. Digging deeper and deeper into this world of which he was newly conscious, Adams turned himself into the author of *Mont Saint Michel and Chartres*, his great study of medieval architecture, literature, and belief. This vicarious past, more remote than his eighteenth-century background and thus more selective, became a primary value. His inherited "Quincy" habits of mind might account for his equivocal responses to positive science as he encountered it, but the past recaptured in *Chartres* gave him an Archimedes fulcrum that he used to frame a critical view. In *Chartres* he commented ironically on how the centuries express their aspiration in different ways—"a miracle or a dynamo; a dome or a coal-pit; a cathedral or a world's fair."[30] The passing irony of the earlier book becomes an imaginative hypothesis in its sequel.

Adams had attended the Chicago World's Fair of 1893 and seen that electricity made its White City as luminous by night as by day, but his lively consciousness of the dynamo dated from the Paris Exposition of 1900. There he saw the massive machine do its work with no more sign to the human senses than a quiet hum. Adams's friend and physics tutor Samuel Langley—also an astronomer, aviation pioneer, and head of the Smithsonian Institution—tried to explain to him how the dynamo transformed the potential energy of coal into electricity. What Adams perceived was that the process went on beyond the human senses and common-sense experience, like a miracle. The casual phrase from *Chartres* became a clue to bringing together the unrelated and hitherto unrelatable ages of the Dynamo and the Virgin. In the *Education*, statistics of coal production compounding in millions of tons and being converted into compounding millions of steam horsepower seem to have a narrative momentum of their own. The history of inventions is the story of technologies imposing themselves on society willy-nilly. Scientific discoveries that transcend natural observation and common sense come faster and faster. It is as if a hidden force were driving the plot. The dynamo becomes a metaphor for the force that, like a hidden god, shapes the narrative. It represents the age-old human effort to dominate nature as it reaches a crisis of comprehension and control.

The approaching climax of intellectual history is not confined to the supersensual realm of modern machines and modern science. The crisis is also political, and its dangers can be immediately apprehended. The urgency of the case was such that Adams, who had forsworn politics in the 1890s, became a political author again in writing the *Education*. But in resuming the great theme, he did not resume the Jeffersonian faith of his earlier years. It is tempting to say of him in his sixties what he said of his Jeffersonian hero Albert Gallatin in his fifties, that "he had outgrown the convictions that had made his strength."[31] The only mentions of popular democracy in the *Education* refer to failures and not to triumphs. Given Cleveland's solution to the Panic of 1893—adoption of the gold standard and acceptance of J. P. Morgan as financial arbiter of the republic—Adams professes to see no hope in further resistance to capitalism as the exclusive power in American politics. He dismisses Populist protest (which in fact he quietly supported) as archaic, a repeat of political solutions that "had been tried in 1800 and 1828, and had failed even under simple conditions" (344). He can no longer imagine how a democratic society might do the work of statecraft.

Even so, illusionless as he claims to be, the Adams of the *Education* holds to a belief that one has to "make the machine run somehow" even though it can "never be made to run well" (373). Moreover, as the age of statecraft recedes further than ever, the need for statecraft is greater than ever. In a world where power is apparently to have the last word, he sees a crucial difference between Coal Powers and Gun Powers. Herbert Spencer, like Comte before him, played with the same two-way split. Spencer was sure that military societies were evolving into industrial societies, with liberal, middle-class Britain in the vanguard and a universal peaceable kingdom in the offing. Adams, holding to his international awareness of wars and preparations for wars, entertained no such vision of progress. By the time he wrote the *Education* he had learned to deplore imperial violence, but he also accepted the imperial maneuvering of his time as a given. In his view, an "Atlantic Combine" (439) of industrial powers was far preferable to the militarist alternative, and the possibility of Germany's going with Russia in a Gun-Power combine implied a nightmare of "continent against continent in arms" (503; cf. 424). His peace policy was more relevant to power politics than Jefferson's Embargo had been, but his Atlantic system was merely a program: his main object was to offer an assessment of danger. The blindness of President Grant to vacuity of policy in peace time was a passing joke compared to the irresponsibility he now saw in high places, as if general war were unthinkable. A salubrious fear made more sense than the prevailing complacency.

But how could fear be salubrious? How could the vivid sense of approaching climax be something other than a melodramatic frisson? Adams the political historian wrote in the conviction that people are by nature political and can, within limits, give intelligent direction to their collective destiny. Given the irresistible rise, as he depicted it, of new energies, new technology, new science, he dismissed the notion that the present industrial society "educated itself, or aimed at a conscious purpose" (483). He went on, though, to cite Francis Bacon: "Nature, to be commanded, must be obeyed" (484). What he called for was the *reactive*, not simply the active, mind. In expressly writing to the student who could be taught to react, he seemed to make a great concession to William James's thesis that important ideas originate with individuals, but Adams put his emphasis on ideas as they become social and have a political effect. Historic changes that at the moment of his writing had only just come on the horizon—"wireless telegraphy and airships" were their provisional names—"might require the reconstruction of society" (496), and the requirement was not impossible. He insisted that transformations can occur, that the future is not some fixed and necessary end.

The *Education* has a Darwinian plot, even though Adams resorts to pre- and post-Darwinian sciences to make his point. Lacking enough mathematics and physics to explain the wonder, he nonetheless invokes the figure of Newton's comet that could wheel in its parabolic course and avoid being sucked in by the sun's gravitation to a fiery end (496). Along the same line, he argues that the accelerated incursion of new forces between 1200 and 1900 (between the building of Chartres cathedral and Madame Curie's metaphysical bomb) now requires nothing less than "a new social mind." He describes that newness in terms of the modern chemist's "phase rule": "As though thought were common salt in indefinite solution, it must enter a new phase subject to new laws" (498). In its open-endedness, the plot is Darwin's, but the reasoning embraces Clarence King's revision that posits a relation between catastrophic necessity and unforeseeable rapidity of change. Adams, who never wholly accepted Darwin's rule "Natura non facit saltum" (nature doesn't go by leaps), had reasoned his way into abandoning it altogether: "Thus far, since five or ten thousand years, the mind had successfully reacted, and nothing yet proved that it would fail to react—but it would need to jump" (498).

Of course, he did not leave Darwin entirely behind. At the end of the *Education*, there are real extinctions. The last chapter is a kind of epitaph for John Hay, like Gallatin a model of the old man as diplomat, and for himself as well. Life stories come to a close as they must, but as a history the book is addressed to the future, to the ideal reader whom Adams the educator hoped to assist. With *react . . . react* echoing in the last words of the penultimate chapter, the last chapter is titled "*Nunc Age*" (now, act). After incremental learning, a new departure is necessary. The student is sent off on his own, into a world that critically needs a reassertion of intelligent control, where the future is still to be made.

The open-endedness of Adams's plot and the seriousness of his pedagogical argument have for some commentators been overbalanced by his flamboyant debunking and his scary representation of the intellectual and political crisis. Some on both the left and the right have deplored the *Education* as conducive to disillusioned withdrawal or, even worse, to watching the game with heartless detachment. To be sure, the book is unlikely to become a manual for activists. But the people who do read it, who make up its wide and continuing audience, do not tend to be politically or intellectually inactive. The argument that some construe as politically disabling has not had that effect. One thing the negative response tends to overlook is the density of experience in Adams's narrative, the multiplicity of his expressed reactions to a wonderfully various world. In this amazing plenty, the ways of the historian and the natural historian converge. Gillian Beer notes that Darwin's indebtedness to Thomas Malthus's *Essay on Population*, with its thesis of population pressures leading to struggle for subsistence, should not obscure a radical change of premise. Where Malthus stressed the parsimony of nature, Darwin posited the fecundity of nature as reason for competitiveness and natural selection. His is a world of profusion: it is profusion that multiplies variations and starts the process of natural selection. Multiplicity becomes the name, not for bewilderment, but for richness. Profusion may not be logically built into historical narrative as it is into Darwin's argument, but it is necessary. Good histories give us a fat world, to use William James's metaphor, and not the meagerness of a schematic argument. They give us a comprehensiveness that is something more than even the professional reader might have thought would be enough. The *Education* is a *fat* book, in which Adams's sensibility, curiosity, engagement constantly enlarge the reader's world.

NOTES

This essay appeared in somewhat different form in *Raritan* 23 (Winter 2004) and is republished here with kind permission of the editors.

1. Henry Adams, *The Education of Henry Adams*, ed. Ernest Samuels (Boston, 1974), 266. All subsequent citations will be to this edition and will be cited parenthetically in the body of the text. The Samuels edition, which keeps the same pagination as the first published edition of 1918 and intervening reprints, is the first to correct the frequently corrupt text of all posthumous editions to date. The Library of America *Education* (New York, 1983), edited by Ernest and Jayne Samuels, is also a corrected text.
2. HA, *Education*, 12.
3. Charles Darwin, *The Origin of Species* (1859; 6th ed., 1872; Modern Library Giant rprt., New York, n.d.), 64.
4. Darwin, *Origin of Species*, 94.
5. Darwin, *Origin of Species*, 46.
6. Henry Adams, *History of the United States during the Administrations of Thomas Jefferson and James Madison* (New York, 1889–1891), 9:227, 236.
7. HA, *History*, 2:21.
8. HA, *History*, 6:69.
9. Henry Adams to Charles Eliot Norton, Apr. 10, 1868, in *The Letters of Henry Adams*, ed. J. C. Levenson et al. (Cambridge, Mass., 1982–1988), 1:569.
10. Henry Adams, "The Principles of Geology," *North American Review* 107(1868):465–501.
11. Clarence King, *Catastrophism and the Evolution of Environment* (New Haven, 1877).
12. King, *Catastrophism*, 20, 21, 25, 37, 24.
13. HA to John Hay, Feb. 8, 1891; HA to Elizabeth Cameron, Nov. 27, 1890; HA to Clarence King, Mar. 3, 1891, in *Letters*, 3:412, 356–357, 439.
14. HA to Herbert B. Adams, Dec. 12, 1894, in *Letters*, 4:230, 231.
15. Chauncey Wright, "The Philosophy of Herbert Spencer," *NAR* 100(1865):458.
16. Herbert Spencer, *First Principles*, 4th ed. (New York, 1882), 498. These citations refer specifically to Adams's own copy, now in the Henry Adams Library at the Massachusetts Historical Society.
17. Spencer, *First Principles*, 499.
18. Wright, "The Philosophy of Herbert Spencer," 457.
19. Spencer, *First Principles*, 396.

20. William James, *William James: Writings, 1878–1899*, ed. Gerald Myers (New York, 1992), 583.
21. Henry Holt, *Garrulities of an Octogenarian Editor* (Boston, 1923), 301.
22. The multivolume *Letters of Charles Darwin* has not yet reached the date of this letter, but Fiske's publishers happily quoted the letter in advertising the book. The quotation comes from a blurb for *Cosmic Philosophy* in the back matter of Fiske's *The Idea of God* (Boston, 1885).
23. John Fiske, "Agassiz and Darwinism," *Popular Science Monthly* 3(1873):692–705; E. W. Gurney to William James, July 22, 1877, *The Correspondence of William James*, ed. Ignas K. Skrupskelis and Elizabeth M. Berkeley (Charlottesville, Va., 1992), 4:580–581.
24. HA to Henry Cabot Lodge, June 25, 1874, in *Letters*, 2:196.
25. HA to William James, July 27, 1882, in *Letters*, 2:466.
26. James, *Writings*, 642, 643, 630, 639.
27. HA to William James, July 27, 1882, in *Letters*, 2:466.
28. HA, *History*, 9:225.
29. Henry James, *Roderick Hudson* (New York, 1907), 1:vii. James's empasis.
30. Henry Adams, *Novels, Mont Saint Michel, The Education*, ed. Ernest Samuels and Jayne N. Samuels (New York, 1983), 439.
31. Henry Adams, *The Life of Albert Gallatin* (Philadelphia, 1889), 559.

Contributors

RICHARD G. ANDRONE is Professor of English at Albright College in Reading, Pennsylvania.

PAUL A. BOVÉ is Distinguished Professor of English at the University of Pittsburgh and editor of *boundary 2*. His publications include *In the Wake of Theory*, *Mastering Discourse: The Politics of Intellectual Culture*, and *Edward Said and the Work of the Critic*.

LESLIE BUTLER is Assistant Professor of History at Dartmouth College. She is the author of *Cultivating America: Victorian Intellectuals and Transatlantic Liberal Reform*.

WILLIAM MERRILL DECKER directs the graduate programs in English at Oklahoma State University. He is the author of *The Literary Vocation of Henry Adams* and *Epistolary Practices: Letter Writing in America before Telecommunications*.

EARL N. HARBERT is Professor (emeritus) at Northeastern University. He is the author of *The Force So Much Closer Home: Henry Adams and the Adams Family*, and editor of *The History of the United States during the Administrations of Thomas Jefferson and James Madison*.

IAN HIGGINSON is Assistant Director of an Arts and Humanities Research Board project entitled "The Ocean Steamship: A Cultural History of Victorian Maritime Power" in the Center for History and Cultural Studies of Science at the University of Kent. He has published on Edgar Allan Poe, Jack London, and Bret Harte.

JOANNE JACOBSON is Professor of English at Yeshiva University. She is the author of *Authority and Alliance in the Letters of Henry Adams*.

PIERRE LAGAYETTE directs the Center for the Study of the American West and Anglophone Asia Pacific at the University of Paris IV (Sorbonne). His publications include *Les Etats-Unis, Centre et Ouest*, *Les Etats-Unis contemporains*, and *L'Ouest américain, réalités et myths*.

J. C. LEVENSON is Edgar Allan Poe Professor (emeritus) of English at the University of Virginia. He is author of *The Mind and Art of Henry Adams* and an editor of *The Letters of Henry Adams*.

BARRY MAINE is Professor of English at Wake Forest University. His publications include *Dos Passos: The Critical Heritage* and essays on members of John Singer Sargent's literary circle.

JOHN C. ORR chairs the English and Foreign Languages Department at the University of Portland. His publications include articles on Adams and other American literary figures from the turn of the twentieth century.

RICHARD A. SAMUELSON recently completed a post-doctoral fellowship at National University of Ireland, Galway. He has published articles on several members of the Adams family and is writing an intellectual biography of John Adams.

ORMOND SEAVEY is Professor of English at George Washington University. He is the author of *Becoming Benjamin Franklin: The Autobiography and the Life*.

CROSBIE SMITH is Professor of History of Science at the University of Kent at Canterbury where he directs the Center for History and Cultural Studies of Science. He is co-author (with Norton Wise) of *Energy and Empire: A Biographical Study of Lord Kelvin* and author of *The Science of Energy*. The award of a Leverhulme Fellowship (2000–2001) made possible this research on Henry Adams.

CHARLES VANDERSEE was, at the time of his death in 2003, Associate Professor of English at the University of Virginia. He had been an associate editor of *The Letters of Henry Adams*.

CINDY WEINSTEIN is Professor of Literature at the California Institute of Technology. She is the author of *The Literature of Labor and the Labors of Literature: Allegory in Nineteenth-Century American Fiction, Family, Kinship*, and *Sympathy in Nineteenth-Century American Literature*, and editor of *The Cambridge Companion to Harriet Beecher Stowe*.

Index